MY HALF OF THE SKY

a novel by

Jana McBurney-Lin

KOMENAR
publishing

Disclaimer: This novel is a work of fiction. The folk stories retold here are traditional and the places are real, but the events and characters described are products of the author's imagination.

Special thanks to ByLine Magazine for awarding the 2005 Short Story Prize to our author Jana McBurney-Lin and Chapter One of this novel.

Grateful acknowledgement is made to the following:
 Jana McBurney-Lin for our glorious cover photograph,
 Shan McBurney-Lin for our map of China, and
 Robert Alan Kato for the photograph of our author.

Book and Dust Jacket Design by Sioban Bowyer.

Library of Congress Cataloging-in-Publication Data available.

ISBN 0-9772081-1-7

First Edition

10 9 8 7 6 5 4 3 2 1

Manufactured in the U.S.A

Dedication:

To my husband, Hui Hui, and our children,
Shan, Jim, T. George and Tianna

You keep my sky wide, my ocean so blue.

MY HALF
OF THE SKY

Chapter One
The Next Set of Tiles

Some fathers always smile and want to hear about your life. Not mine. He had his reasons—which went deeper than me ripping away his manhood or severing his connection to the earth. Today, though, as I stood in line for the telephone, I imagined a smile on his face. I envisioned him calling out to Mother. I thought about him buying a bottle of *maotai* as a celebration, as if he'd just won an important *mahjong* game.

Two people waited ahead of me to use the public phone at the post office. A woman with short orange hair and a vermilion jacket tap-tapped her high heels on the cement floor. A businessman in a tailored suit lifted his jacket and checked his pager. The man on the phone, a young man with long hair that fell below his ears, was missing his forearm. He used his stump like a hand, scratching at his dirty yellow t-shirt. Had the man been in an accident? Been born that way? Was he a burden on his family?

My birth was a handicap for our family. Sure, our late leader Mao Ze Dong had said: "Women hold up half the sky." But that just wasn't so. A girl leaves the house to marry into another family. She doesn't pass her family name to her children. She doesn't care for her parents forever—giving them money when they can no longer work, leading their casket to the other side of the River of Sleep, visiting their gravesites twice a year with spirit money, good foods and love. A man does all these things. Even an armless man who talked too long on the phone. I looked away.

Summer's lingering light filtered in the long, dusty windows, making it seem as if we had more time than we did. No matter the quality of light, the post office closed in ten minutes. And I had to call Father.

In the corner, a clerk wearing black plastic sleeves over her jacket counted out wrinkled *yuan* notes and put rubber bands around each pile, readying her cash drawer for closing. At the next counter, another clerk hurried an old woman with a curved back through the process of filling out the eight forms necessary to send a package.

A guard with a green army jacket and cloth cap stood at the door, letting customers out and arguing with any who wanted to enter.

Our society, our customs, have a history of almost five thousand years. Longer than Mao Ze Dong's declaration of equality. If a male isn't born into the house, life is no longer eternal. Once, after too many cups of rice wine, Father had lifted his bleary red eyes to me and said, "My contact with the earth will soon die." At least today Father would be proud. Graduation from Hua Xia University neared. Counselor Zhang had just assigned my teaching position. I had a proper job. I only wanted Father's favor.

Hammering noises from across the street filled the small postal building. A tall weathered sign said that the building in progress was an American-style coffee shop. Perhaps to cater to foreigners who came to study at the University. I had never tasted the foreign drink. In fact, I didn't know many coffee drinkers. The sign also read that construction should have finished in December of 1993—six months ago. Everyone was running late.

The man with the missing arm dropped the phone in disgust. The businessman stepped up and grabbed the receiver. When Orange-Haired Auntie moved forward, the scent of her expensive perfume stayed behind. I glanced at my watch. Four minutes until closing.

Was her orange hair a new fashion? How much money did it cost to color hair? I had already received several red packets containing auspicious denominations of money from relatives, congratulating me on my graduation and wishing me good luck in the future. I smoothed my hand over my long dark locks, imagining how rich I'd feel with that color in my hair, as if a hundred *yuan* notes dripped across my shoulders.

Orange hair? What was I thinking? I needed to speak to Father. Perhaps I should run down the block to the phone kiosk. They charged more than the post office, more than I could afford. But this was important.

Father had never been totally in favor of me pursuing my studies. I had pleaded with him every moment he was sober and not contemplating his next game. "A waste of precious money," he'd say. Or, "All that time taken from your youth—and for what? You can find a job here." What would he say now that I was an elementary school teacher? An elementary school teacher with a job. Father would be pleased to hear I hadn't wasted my four years in Xiamen. I would use some of my congratulations money to make this happy phone call.

Hearing the approval in his voice would be worth every *fen*. I turned to leave the post office and find the phone kiosk.

A construction worker stood at the door arguing with the guard. The worker was dust-covered, a bamboo helmet hanging from his arm. He held a packet of food and gestured toward the phone with his plastic spoon. Grains of rice flew through the air. No wonder the American-style coffee shop took so long. All the workers took off early to get snacks and talk on the phone. The guard let the lazy worker in. I jumped back to my place in line. Perhaps my watch was fast.

The worker rushed up and pushed me from behind, nudging me with his bamboo helmet, as if shoving me could make the businessman get off the phone sooner. The businessman talked on. Pacing back and forth as if he were in his own private office.

A successful businessman like him. That's what every family wanted. I was lucky though. Many mothers gave up their girls for adoption. I may have put an end to Father's everlasting life, may have been the reason people called him "eunuch," but Mother had held tight to me.

The successful man finished his call and hung up. Orange-Haired Auntie click-clicked forward and picked up the receiver. The worker behind nudged me again until my nose touched the top of Auntie's head. Stiff colored strands of hair tickled. Expensive perfume became my air. I inhaled deeply. Better to have successful Orange-Haired Auntie go before me than impatient Construction Worker. Mother would think it a good omen.

"The post office is closing," Construction Worker said and pushed again. He put on the bamboo helmet. Such a flimsy helmet meant to protect his skull and brain. He tapped his dust-covered fingers on the chest of his ripped t-shirt. "I need to use the phone."

Orange-Haired Auntie turned to him as if to say, "What a coincidence." She even had double folds on her eyelids. Double folds, like Westerners had, were a sign of beauty. Single folds, like mine, a sign of intelligence. As a child, I had wanted double folds, even though Waipo, Mother's mother, said I was beautiful despite my single folds. Mei Ling, my best friend in university, and I often talked about getting an operation to have our folds fixed. The procedure cost big money. Orange hair, red finger nails, even double folds on her eyes. Yes, this woman could hold up half the sky. Certainly she was a good omen.

"Today's my son's birthday," Construction Worker said through a mouthful of rice. "I need to call home."

How could he reveal his personal desires? Like a child—a spoiled child—to me, a stranger?

"He's five today," the man whispered, his brown eyes probably envisioning the boy eating a boiled egg as a celebration, the yellow insides dribbling down the boy's chin. "I haven't spoken to him since the Lunar New Year."

Why did I have to hear this? So he was a migrant worker, far from his province. Did I have to allow him to make his call first? I had news, too. I had a chance to make Father smile, to be proud. Today, I could hold up half the sky, just like Orange-Haired Auntie.

When Orange-Haired Auntie click-clicked away from the desk, Construction Worker pushed in front of me and reached out for the phone. But I grabbed the receiver first. The man swore in a dialect I didn't understand. Too bad for him.

The warm black receiver smelled of perfume. Well, I wouldn't linger. The homesick father might get to make his call too. I let out a deep breath, waiting for the operator to connect me to Zi Mei. Zi Mei owned the small store on the corner next to our house. She and her dull-witted son sold rice and cigarettes, soy powder and candies. She also owned one of three phones on our side of the village. She connected the thousand or so families in the area to the outside world. For a small fee, of course.

The phone rang and rang, the sound hollow and far away. Was Zi Mei selling a pack of Long March cigarettes or a bag of White Rabbit candies? Chatting?

"Post office is closing," the guard called, taking off his cap and rapping the material against the palm of his hand for emphasis.

Construction Worker swore again. He tossed his empty rice packet on the ground at my feet and stomped out the door. He probably didn't have extra money to use the phone kiosk. Well, neither did I really.

Finally Zi Mei picked up. She sounded out of breath. Her son Don Don did his best to help with the shop. But he had his bad days when he would get lost in the way the afternoon light filtered through the branches of the peach trees. Or the way a spider dangled from the roof of the shop. Perhaps he wasn't even there today. I hoped such was the case.

"It's me," I said. "Li Hui."

"You got a teaching assignment," she said.

Perhaps the confidence in my voice gave it away. Then again, Zi Mei had a way of finding things out. She was always the first in our village to know anything. I imagined her short hair pasted to the sides of her head. Her eyes sparkling.

"I need to talk to Father," I said.

"Don Don," she called out. "Go get Li Hui's father."

I cringed, sitting on the edge of the chair next to the phone. My legs bounced up and down. I hoped Don Don would remember his task today.

"Yes, I know Li Hui is still at college," Zi Mei shouted out so loud, I had to pull the receiver away from my head. "Yes, she's a nice girl. No, you don't need to zip your jacket first."

Oh, gods. At this rate, the post office would close before Don Don returned with Father. Outside the post office I spotted impatient Construction Worker shuffling along the sidewalk toward his work site. He had his hands stuffed deep in his pockets, his head down. Perhaps I should have let him call his son. Then again, maybe his local phone system was no more efficient than ours.

"So, tell me about the job," Zi Mei said.

I sighed. I felt as though I'd held my breath four years to say the words. I explained the details to Zi Mei, feeling important at having an educated job. I could tell she was making mental calculations. Was the job worth the place they were sending me? Her lack of commentary said she wasn't as excited as I. But perhaps she didn't know. Anyway, all I cared was that Father was pleased. Not our local gossip. Even if she was a successful business woman.

"Li Hui's got a job," Zi Mei called out.

Ah, wonderful. Don Don hadn't gotten lost in his own world. Father must be close.

I imagined Father walking unsteadily, tossing his cigarette into the street, and grabbing the phone. By this hour, he'd surely started on his rice wine. Now I'd give him reason to drink another cup.

"What's the news?" He breathed heavily into the phone.

Drilling started up across the street, so loud my insides vibrated. Had disappointed Construction Worker taken up a drill to show his anger? How would Father ever hear me?

"I'll earn three hundred *yuan* per month teaching first grade," I shouted, adding Counselor Zhang's words. "Just what the college trained me to do."

I held the receiver tight to my right ear and plugged the other ear with my fingers to block out the sound of the drill. I wanted to hear Father's words of happiness.

"Where?" Father shouted back, his tone full of hope. "Beijing?"

"Not Beijing," I said, those two small words using up all the breath in my lungs.

Beijing and Shanghai had the most prestigious reputations. These cities had good economies, good food, good schools, good everything. To live in such a place would bring honor on our family for generations to come.

"Well, where?" he shouted, as if we'd been tricked. As if just because I was one of two people in our village to go to university, just because I was in the top ten percent of my class, I could choose the best job.

"Counselor Zhang said I'll be showing Mother China how grateful I am," I said, the receiver growing heavy in my hands. My words sounded as meaningful as flowers on a manure paddy. The drilling across the road ceased. Yet my insides still vibrated. How could I have thought Father would be pleased?

"Where?" Father cleared his throat and spat.

"Xin Jiang," Zi Mei sang out in the background before I had a chance.

"What?"

Father's disbelief exploded like a firecracker in my ear. No smile radiated across the telephone line. No happiness embraced my accomplishment. My omens dissolved in an orange haze of dyed hair and the memory of Construction Worker's nudges.

"But Counselor Zhang said it's my duty as a good citizen to go where I'm needed," I explained, attempting to reason with him.

"No," he whispered into the phone.

"But, Father . . ." If I didn't accept this job, I'd have nothing. Four years and nothing to show for it. Just as he had predicted. "Father, if I don't—"

"No," he repeated. "This is obvious discrimination. It's just because you're from a small village that you're getting such a bad assignment."

"Oh, Father."

The remnants of Orange-Haired Auntie's perfume clogged my throat. Weights hammered against the back of my eyes. I clenched the receiver with both hands.

Father knew the whole economy had slid like rocks from the mountain, especially after those foolish students in Tiananmen Square had irritated the government—and the world—with their silly Statue of Freedom. Why didn't he see that now wasn't the time to be acting like a shopper choosing fruit at the marketplace?

"Seriously, Li Hui," he said. "You'd be better off begging on the streets."

"Post office closing," the guard called again. He pointed his cap at me, indicating that I should end my call.

"Talk to Administrator Zhang," Father said, hanging up before I had a chance to explain further.

I listened to the hum of our severed connection. Certainly Father was right. After struggling for four years, the last thing we wanted was to live in Xin Jiang. Once in that poor province, we'd be stuck there forever. We couldn't just travel around the country and look for a job anywhere we pleased. To live in a different province—that was as difficult as getting a visa to the outside world. I replaced the grimy receiver. Orange-Haired Auntie's perfume now smelled like a gas leak. I needed air.

A cuckoo clock from Counselor Zhang's government-sanctioned trip to Holland chimed eight times. My long legs hit up against his cold metal desk, a desk that took up over half his giant office. He'd managed to bury every inch of the grand surface with papers and books. Counselor Zhang looked through one of those books now. His bushy eyebrows made a long furrowed line across his forehead. His short hair dark hair was parted straight down the side, not a hair out of place. My best friend Mei Ling had warned me against coming.

"You're going against the system," she'd said slapping her palm on the bamboo bed mat for emphasis. "You'll either be kicked out of Counselor Zhang's office or punished. Or both."

I held on tight to the bag containing a bottle of Dutch liquor. I'd used up half my congratulations money to buy the small bottle. This was the right thing. I felt it.

I often felt things. Nerves in my stomach when a shopkeeper planned to cheat me. A squeezing of my heart, as if it were boiled cabbage, each time Mother didn't get to adopt the new baby boy in the village. Especcially after all the effort she went to with her knitting, her gifts, her kind words. Sometimes I felt like a light bulb dangling from the ceiling, the electricity moving through my veins.

This when Father argued with his friends over a card game or cricket fight. At this moment, I felt a burning inside. As if I were buried in Hainan Island's white sand beach, the calendar picture that hung on Counselor Zhang's wall.

Counselor Zhang struck a match on the side of his chair and lit his cigarette. He turned another page in his journal. His eyes seemed focused far away. He must be mulling over my refusal of the posting in Xin Jiang. Finally, he looked up.

"I thought you understood," he said, blowing a plume of smoke across the desk. "You're needed in Xin Jiang."

"My parents." I cleared my throat. "My parents, they feel uncomfortable with me taking a job so far away."

"They are welcome to move with you," Counselor Zhang said, tapping the end of his cigarette against a white ceramic ashtray in the shape of a windmill. "The permit allows for that."

"But the distance—it's so far."

"I see." Counselor Zhang sat back in his chair, the leather squeaking. "You want to have a say."

"No. No say." I wasn't like those rebellious students in Tiananmen. "It's just . . . you understand, I'm the only child."

Counselor Zhang stared out the window overlooking the cafeteria where students stood around talking and laughing and finishing a last mouthful of breakfast. Here was the man responsible for securing my "rice bowl." Mei Ling and I always laughed that his office was right across from the rice. Now I couldn't even muster a smile. Father's directive had drained me of even trying to hold up a part of the sky. After all, who wasn't an only child these days?

"I don't see how we can help you." He took several puffs from his cigarette. The end glowed like the eye of a devil. "If you're going to be so choosy about where you take an assignment."

If only our family had enough face in the community that I could borrow lots of money. Then I wouldn't be dependent on administrative decisions. I could sneak overseas and have success, just like Mei Ling planned.

"Forgive me for causing trouble," I said, handing him the liquor I'd spent hours locating. The paper bag crinkled, a desperate sound. "This is a small present for your efforts."

"Oh," he said, his eyes on the bag. "You don't have to do that."

"I want to," I insisted.

Back and forth we went three times, as was our custom. Finally he pulled the bottle from the bag. Mei Ling would have been surprised at his smile.

"Ah," he said, shaking his head in disbelief. "Jonge Graanjenever, the spirit of the nation. This is wonderful liquor. Thank you."

"It's nothing at all," I said. "I appreciate your help."

Counselor Zhang puffed more on his cigarette. He stared at the bottle nodding his head up and down. Was he recalling a small bar in Holland or thinking of Xin Jiang?

"Miss Huang, do you feel like you're embodying the spirit of the nation?"

People never questioned their assignments. They went where they were told and were happy to do so. But how many of them had a father like mine?

"Like our nation." I cleared my throat again. "I too am planning for the future. Five, ten, twenty years from now. I just want to make sure I can properly care for my aging parents. As I said, I'm the only child."

I'd spent my life waiting for this moment. Studying as I washed cabbage in icy well water for the pigs. Studying as I helped Mother stack potatoes for the winter. Studying. Studying. Studying. I'd spent four years waiting for Counselor Zhang to give me a job assignment. Now I was tossing that out the window like a used tissue.

Counselor Zhang pulled his ledger from beneath a stack of papers. He flipped through pages filled with dates and times. Surely he was thinking of his next appointment. Surely he had finished with me.

Counselor Zhang rubbed a thick hand over his long eyebrows. He fixed a stray hair that had crossed the otherwise perfect part in his head. He mumbled something.

"Excuse me," I said, my voice just above a whisper. I stared at the scorching sun on Hainan Island, certain that I—not the sand—was on fire.

"There's an opening in Yunnan." He looked over at me with serious eyes. "Will you take it or not?"

Electricity started at my toes and traveled up to my heart. Yunnan had a better economy than Xin Jiang. Was closer. While Counselor Zhang offered less salary—two hundred *yuan* per month—the trade-off wasn't bad. The stamp of residency was what we wanted. A permit to live in Yunnan. A new job. This would make Father happy. This must make Father happy.

I sat in the chair in the old post office building, drumming my fingers against the desk in concert with the hammering across the street. I waited for the operator to connect me. A long time had passed since Father had won more than he'd lost the previous night. In fact, fifteen years. Fifteen years since he'd won enough money over his annual Chinese New Year marathon *mahjong* tournament that we could build our own house. People still talked about that win. Especially Father.

Zi Mei didn't answer the phone. Father did. Had he been expecting me to call?

"We won," I said, the words tumbling out. "I start in two weeks. We'll be assigned a house near the school. The pay will certainly get better as the years go by. Besides, this is Yunnan."

I paused to catch my breath. Father had gambled big this time. Well, he'd convinced me to gamble big. And he had won. We had won. I'd gone to Counselor Zhang and done an unheard of thing, rejecting his employment assignment. Yet he'd offered me another position. A better position. I'd done it. I could already hear Father telling his gambling buddies of this win. He'd be telling this success story for years to come.

"Yunnan, ah?" Father said. He chuckled. He was happy. At last.

I sat back in the old chair. Across the street I spotted Construction Worker, the man who hadn't been able to wish his son a happy birthday. He leaned over on his ladder, hammering at two beams above him. His boss shouted from beneath, tapping the ladder with a bamboo cane. Construction Worker reached higher, eager to satisfy. Migrant workers, living illegally in the city, didn't have much choice as to jobs. They took what they could and were treated no better than cattle. Lucky for us, I had been offered an official position. Actually, not one but two. A second when the first one should have been all I could expect. This was good. This was very good.

"Not enough," Father said.

Certainly he was talking to Zi Mei or Don Don, saying he needed more cigarettes than were being pulled from behind the glass case. Yes, he was celebrating the change in the winds of fortune already. My heart felt full. I twirled the telephone cord with my fingers. Outside, the worker held the beams with one hand and hammered with the other. The reach looked painful, the strain unbearable.

"Did you hear me?" Father asked.

"Were you talking to me?" I dropped the cord.

"Who else?" Father said. "See if Counselor Zhang doesn't discover a bigger city that needs you."

How could he say this? Why couldn't he see how the gamble had paid off? But then he'd often used one win as a reason to keep playing. "You never know what's going to happen with the next set of tiles," he'd say.

"Oh, Father."

"This is an important moment." He exhaled loudly into the receiver. "You can't accept second best after all the work you've put into this."

A loud thud reverberated throughout the room. Everyone in the post office moved toward the windows, their voices tense, excited. Outside a cloud of dust turned the air milky white. What had happened? I stood to see outside.

"Oh, my mother!" I whispered spotting a form dangling in the cloud.

Construction Worker had reached ever higher. Too high. His bamboo ladder tipped, then shattered right next to the boss. Construction Worker hung from a rafter. The boss stood up and brushed off dust from his shoulders. He glared up at Construction Worker. He would make Construction Worker feel the burning sting of the cane tonight.

"You just see," Father said, "if Counselor Zhang has an even better opening available. He sounds like a reasonable man. If you ask, you shall receive."

Outside workers and passersby gathered around the dangling man, shouting advice. Inside I wondered how much further I could push Counselor Zhang. So much noise filled my head, it hurt. I shut out the noise. I listened. This was Father, after all. He believed we'd hear funny northern accents and feel the brisk wind of success within a few weeks. All without borrowing money, without leaving the country. He believed we sat in front of the winning house of *mahjong* tiles. Perhaps he was right. It would be worth every *fen* of my congratulations money, if another present perhaps smoked fish from Counselor Zhang's beloved Holland—bought me a ticket to Beijing.

"You can do it," Father said. "Remember. This is our future."

Outside a crack sounded, like that of a branch breaking. Another thud shook the earth. Shouting filled the air. The rafters across the street had given way under Construction Worker's weight. He had fallen, the heavy beams landing on his head.

Counselor Zhang sat across from me. He didn't pretend to look through his book. He didn't flip through his daily appointment ledger. He didn't even answer his ringing phone.

"Please understand," I began again. "Yunnan is a fine place, I'm sure. It's much closer. It's just that Mother and Father are old and would appreciate the conveniences of a bigger city."

"Like Shanghai?" he asked, looking past the gift I had brought, a kilo of smoked salmon from Holland. "Or Beijing?"

I didn't answer. His voice mocked me. I felt him staring at me through his bushy eyebrows. Was he angry? Incredulous?

"Any help you could give," I said, my eyes on the smoked salmon. The gift stood awkwardly on the table, still in the bag. My knees trembled. My palms sweat. "I appreciate—we appreciate—any help you can give."

"I've done all I can," he said, pushing his chair back. The metal casters grated. He stood up, signaling an end to our meeting. "The university can offer you nothing more."

Counselor Zhang's voice sounded like the crack of the rafters above Construction Worker's head. I saw again Construction Worker outside the post office buried under those heavy beams that had fallen. Those bamboo helmets the construction workers wore didn't protect them, except from the sun. That man wouldn't ever get to wish his son a happy birthday.

As Father had directed, I'd approached Counselor Zhang again. I had sought an even better position. No, gambled for a higher spot. Like Construction Worker reaching too high, I had also fallen off my ladder. Father's prediction from way back had come true. My education was now worthless. And most certainly I couldn't prove that the new world order worked, that women held up half the sky.

Chapter Two
The Lost Horse

Whenever something didn't happen the way I wanted or I thought my luck was poor, Mother's mother—Waipo—would rub the wrinkles on her hand, as if smoothing a shirt fresh from the laundry line, and say, "Remember the farmer and his horse?" Waipo had already passed to the other side of the River of Sleep. But I still remembered this story, a story that went back thousands of years to the Qin Dynasty.

A poor farmer lived on the outskirts of a village. Whereas his neighbors had large plots of land and several horses to plow their fields, he had only a small plot of land. He had but one horse.

Still, Poor Farmer was a happy man. He had healthy parents. His wife had borne him a strong son. And at least he had a horse with which to plow the fields.

One morning, when he went out to the pasture, he couldn't find his horse. He looked in the barn. He looked up and down the road. He even walked into his rich neighbor's field. But his horse was gone.

"What poor luck," Rich Neighbor clucked, glancing proudly over to where his own son hitched up one of their many horses.

"You never know," Poor Farmer said, raising his eyebrows and shrugging his shoulders.

A week later, while Poor Farmer and his son were out pulling their plow, they heard a familiar grunting. Their horse had returned. Not only that, the horse had brought home a lovely wild mare.

"What good luck," Rich Neighbor called out.

"You never know," Poor Farmer replied, although he couldn't help but smile.

The next day, Poor Farmer's son took the wild mare out for a ride. He lost control of the untamed animal and fell off and broke his arm.

"What poor luck," Rich Neighbor said, putting his arm around his own unbroken son.

"You never know," Poor Farmer said, his brow furrowed.

Just then, Emperor Qin's men rode into the village. A war had begun. The Emperor needed all able-bodied men to fight. To die in service to the country. The Emperor's men went from house to house picking recruits. Rich Neighbor's son had to join the army despite his father's lavish donations. Poor Farmer's son with his broken arm got to stay home and live.

As Waipo always said, "Good fortune turns to disaster, disaster to good fortune. The cycle has no end, nor can the mystery of it be explained."

I wasn't sure how sweating in the middle of the town park alongside beggars and migrant workers could be compared to losing a horse, but maybe. At least I was home with my parents. Able to watch over them. And just maybe I'd find a client, a job, some money today. I wiped a drop of perspiration trickling down the side of my cheek and shifted my tutor sign to my other hand. Exhaust fumes made my eyes itch. The gray sky hovered like an extra blanket. The park would soon be filled with lunchtime traffic.

Fuqing was a relatively small town, with close to a million people. In the rural section, which was dotted with rice and vegetable fields, even eel farms, the town felt small, like a village. Here though in the center of town, traffic and human congestion was thick like in the big city of Xiamen, with its several million population.

Counselor Zhang had promised I'd never have an official job as a teacher. Why had I pushed him so? Yunnan would have been a fine spot to work and live. And, so far, there hadn't been any opportunities for me at home. At least one out of every three of us in the town had no job. That's what I had noticed these last couple weeks since I'd been home. Not the grain growing in the rice fields or the goats grazing by the side of the road. Not lychee or mangos ripening on the branches. Not the things I'd missed while studying in a big city, like the smell of the air after a rain. No, I had noticed the number of women—and even men—sitting around, talking, knitting, sleeping on carts in the afternoon sun. All of us unemployed.

As always, the park was crowded. Migrant workers lined up shoulder to shoulder, hawking peanuts, cigarettes, balloons, paper cuttings, ceramic statues and fortunes. I stood wedged between two other tutors, both of whom had asked for my help in writing their signs. Behind me a palm reader studied the hand of an old woman. He had taken up the spot that was normally the paper cutter's. Was Madame Paper Cutter sick? Had she been arrested? Had she found a better place to sell her cuttings?

"You're a tutor?" a woman asked.

I turned to see a short woman carrying a purse and plastic shopping bag. She wore a black cotton skirt that draped past her knees. A small child held onto the hem of that skirt as if the cloth were his special blanket.

"Yes," I said, smiling at the boy. "I specialize in working with young children."

"I thought you were going to be a real teacher," the woman said, brushing the stray bangs off her forehead. "Isn't that why you went off to college for all those years?"

"I'm sorry?" I looked at her closely. Did I know this middle-aged woman with simple clothes, dark bags under her eyes, a young son?

"Fifth Cousin," she said, putting out her hands to grasp mine. "Remember?"

"Oh, yes. Yes. Of course." I grabbed both her hands in mine. My, how she'd aged. Lines etched deeply at the corners of her eyes. "And you're interested in a tutor for your beautiful young son?"

"No, no." She chuckled. "He doesn't need a tutor yet. He's only three."

"It's never too early to start," I said. "I studied early childhood education."

"No, no." She waved her hand back and forth, shooing away the idea. "I don't need any of that. I didn't sing to my baby while he was in my womb either. Although I saw a program on TV that the best mothers do that."

"Yes." I nodded. "Studies show that the earlier the contact, the more alert the child."

"What is this?" She pointed to my sign, to my existence in the park along with migrants and other tutors, most of whom had no real education. Her tired eyes shone as if she'd discovered that the white object everyone called a pearl was just another rock. "After all the effort that you went to. All that expense and time."

"Well, these things happen," I said.

Fifth Cousin wasn't a bad sort. Everyone in the village agreed that the university experience had set me off course, had ruined my future. Fifth Cousin wasn't as crass as some. Still, I was glad Madame Paper Cutter wasn't here to listen to this onslaught.

"Unbelievable," she said, shaking her short locks back and forth, her lips in a thin line. "What will you do now?"

"I'm doing it," I said, forcing cheer in my voice. Why hadn't Father and I been satisfied with Yunnan? Why hadn't Counselor Zhang managed to find just one more place for me?

From next to us, the grating of wooden wheels on the cement pavement filled my ears. I looked to the sound. A migrant worker selling water chestnuts approached with his pushcart. He would want to get by. I clutched my sign to my chest and stepped back, away from Fifth Cousin and her little boy. This was as good a chance as any to put an end to this unpleasant conversation.

"Nice to see you again," I called to her, backing up so the migrant could push his way between us.

Fifth Cousin looked at me with dark eyes. She wanted to continue chewing on my failure. How could I be so rude? Then she took the hand of her son and turned. Soon she was a distant head bobbing in the daily crowd, disappearing into her world of errands and responsibilities. Leaving me in the hot sun and crowded park to hold up my sign again for all to see.

If I got just one little job long enough to restock the essentials in the house and to buy Father a bottle of rice wine, maybe people would stop discussing my sad situation. At the very least, Father would stop asking about the "final conversation."

"What time of the day did you visit Counselor Zhang to ask for a better assignment," Father would ask. Or, "Did you bring a gift to compensate for all the trouble he had gone to?" Every day he had a different theory as to what I'd done wrong. Even when I mentioned that Mei Ling, who studied to be an herbal doctor and didn't get a good job assignment either—even when I said that—Father wondered what the both of us had done wrong.

That was one of the differences between Mei Ling's father and mine. Mei Ling's father didn't sit around long enough to analyze where she'd made the mistake. Instead he had borrowed money from all their relatives, so he could send her off with a snakehead on a boat to Japan. She should be leaving for the Land of Rising Opportunities any day now. My eyes prickled like a thousand needles stabbed them. Some people left for five or ten years. Some people never returned. I missed Mei Ling already.

Father once suggested that I best get on a boat somewhere. But this was just talk. The same as when he threatened to take the butcher knife and chop off our neighbor the zealot's manhood. Or when he said he'd give Zi Mei an earful of his anger if she didn't loan him money at a good rate until he won his next game. Father just imagined all of these things over and over again.

"You're a tutor?" A middle-aged man stopped and lit a cigarette. His crisp white shirt was decorated with lunch. A grease spot on the chest, hot sauce on the belly. He certainly ate well.

"Yes," I said, standing up straight. "I teach young children."

His black leather shoes shone like new. He wore a Gucci belt. Real or imitation?

"How young?" the man asked, pointing his cigarette at me, the end of it stopping too close to my cotton shirt.

Did I know him? He didn't have a child in tow. Would this be another commiseration session or did he really want a tutor? I ignored the burning stick in his hand.

"I studied early childhood education. Youngsters. Seven, eight."

The man looked around the park, as though searching for another prospect. He smelled of cigarettes and aftershave. Such luxuries. He would have money to pay for a tutor, any one of us. All of us. He must have an older child.

"Nine, ten, eleven," I added with a smile. "In fact, there's never been a child of any age I couldn't teach. I have my certificate here." I reached in my shoulder bag and pulled out the round tube.

"Save it," the man said waving away the tube. "Anyone can buy a graduation certificate."

He spoke the truth. In fact, several of the tutors nearby surely had paid for such a document to go along with the signs I had made for them.

"I just graduated a couple weeks ago," I said. "From Hua Xia University."

"Alright. Alright." The man took a puff on his cigarette and whistled across the street toward the greasy hamburger restaurant with the lucky golden M. A boy emerged from the crowd of shoppers and made his way toward us. Slowly. He listened to something through headphones as he bit into a hamburger.

"How much do you charge?" the man asked.

"Twenty *yuan* per day," I said.

"Oh, please." The man threw his cigarette on the ground and blew a plume of smoke in my face. "I'll give you ten."

"Maybe you could get one of those other graduates for ten," I said, nodding to the others in the park. "But I'm a good teacher. I won't tutor your son for less than nineteen *yuan*."

"Fifteen," he suggested.

"Eighteen," I said.

"Hey, Baba," the boy called in between bites of food. "Over here."

The boy had stopped in front of one of the other tutors. The so-called tutor had long hair in a ponytail, a silver hoop earring in his ear. The boy handed his headphones to the man. Mr. Ponytail and Earring smiled and nodded his head back and forth to a rhythm.

"Is that a real tutor?" the father asked me.

I was sure that tutor hadn't gone to any university. But then, Mother always said it's not wise to speak bad words about a stranger. You never knew what connections people had. How angry they would get.

"I don't recognize him from my university," I said. "But then . . ."

"Eighteen, then," the father said, tossing his cigarette on the ground next to my feet. "Eighteen *yuan* a day."

"It's a deal," I said.

He shook my hand and gave me his business card with his phone number. He had his own phone. What an expense. Perhaps I could talk him into giving me a bonus.

"Now, about time—"

"Wait right here," the father said and left to retrieve his son. "I'll be right back."

I put the name card in my purse. I rocked back and forth on my feet. I had a job. Finally. Something metal brushed against my bare ankle. I turned. Scissors.

"You're here," I said and nodded to Madame Paper Cutter.

Madame Paper Cutter was a migrant from Sichuan Province. An older woman with a few grey hairs poking out, she wore thick eyeglasses. Her rough and wrinkled fingers guided scissors across the paper like a magician, creating peaches and pomegranates, dancing girls and healthy boys. Each day, she showed me how to make a new paper cutting. Each day I gave her a new list of characters to practice. She had never been to school. But she was eager to learn.

"Looks like I won't be able to do much this afternoon," I said.

She wanted me to help her write a letter to her daughter. She would teach me how to cut a crane. Still, I was excited to start working today, if this man's son had time.

"Every year that man comes with his son," she said, not looking up, but cutting a circle out of a piece of red paper.

"Really?"

Madame Paper Cutter was good at seeing people. The park had been her life for so long—three years, she had told me—that she saw people and things most of us missed. Like when the woman who lived in a box next to the greasy hamburger shop had found a new box. Or when a policeman was coming through. Or, now, when she remembered a certain customer.

"That Little Emperor is lazy," Madame Paper Cutter said, pushing her large glasses up on her nose. "He's not interested in doing anything but listening to that thing on his head."

I looked over to where the son stood arguing with his father. The son obviously wanted to pick his own tutor. Is that why the man changed tutors each year?

"Laziness is an untapped mind, my teacher always said." I could get the boy interested in studying, especially for eighteen *yuan* a day. I'd try telling him some of Waipo's stories. I'd pick up a book on discipline.

"I've warned many a tutor," she said.

Warned? Perhaps she'd just chosen the wrong word. She wasn't used to speaking our dialect. I watched the way her scissors cut triangles and circles. A snip here. A snip there. The air around her smelled of chili and garlic. I was sorry we wouldn't be helping each other today. But, at the same time, I wished the father and boy would hurry back to discuss our tutoring schedule.

"Last year's tutor is over there." Madame Paper Cutter nodded in the direction of a woman standing at the edge of the park.

The woman held a well-written sign with one hand. In the other, she clutched a paperback book up close to her left eye. Her right eye was half-covered with skin. As if she'd been burned. What had happened? Why hadn't she worked out as a tutor for this boy?

"If the son does poorly." Madame Paper Cutter tapped her scissors on her right cheek just below her eye. "That father is unforgiving."

I looked at the tutor's face again. Had the man really burned her? He had come close to me with his cigarette. But, would he put one in my face? No. Certainly not. The woman must have asked for such a punishment.

"Help me write a letter to my daughter," Madame Paper Cutter said, watching me. "She's going to enter summer school next week, as preparation for first grade. I haven't seen her in three years."

"Perhaps tomorrow. I could meet you here early in the morning, depending," I said, putting my sign away in my purse. "Depending on the schedule."

The man had taken his son's headphones away and was shouting. I caught words, in between the honking of taxis and the pounding of machinery. But nothing significant. I would go over there.

"Wait." Madame Paper Cutter grabbed onto my ankle. "She loves to be read to. She loves to study. If you could just spare a minute."

"Tomorrow I will." I knelt down and held her hand. "I promise."

Then off I went to put an end to all the haggling. How ridiculous to even consider hiring uneducated Mr. Ponytail and Earring. Certainly he offered a lower price. But I'd remind that father that this wasn't the place to be saving money.

"Oh, there you are," I said to the father. "I was just on my way to another appointment. By the way, we didn't decide on a schedule."

Mr. Ponytail and Earring gave me a sour look. The father looked down at his son. The boy stared off into the park, his dark eyes small and unblinking.

"This tutor says he will allow my son to listen to music while he studies," the father said. "Will you do that?"

So this wasn't about price? How did one study while listening to music? How could the father even consider such a silly idea?

"I think it depends on the study," I said. "Certainly music can sometimes—"

"I like to listen all the time," the boy said, his chest heaving against his tight striped shirt. Like his father, he ate healthy meals. Too many of them.

"Of course, you love your music," I said. An untapped mind of an adolescent who may have been almost as tall as his father, but not quite. He obviously struggled to find his place, that's all this was. "We can find time to listen to your—"

"See?" The boy cut my words off. He pointed at me with a small, accusing finger. "She won't let me listen. I know she won't."

"She wants you to focus," the father explained, his eyes pleading with the boy. "That's all. This is about you getting into a good school. Why can't you see that?"

"Is it?" the son asked, jutting his smooth young chin out. He nodded to Mr. Ponytail and Earring. Then he turned on his shiny heels and walked away. My father would have caned me within seconds had I been so disrespectful.

"Son, wait," the father called not even glancing in my direction. "Don't you walk away from me like that. Son? Son?"

The overindulgent man ran after his spoiled child. That was one of the problems with having only one son. Parents gave in too easily. But perhaps Mr. Overindulgent would return. I returned to my spot and pulled out my sign to wait. Madame Paper Cutter held up her finished art piece. The lucky red crane.

"That's lovely," I said. My voice was full of disappointment. I tried again. "Really lovely."

"During ancient times, all girls knew how to do this," she said, her voice soft, her cadence slow. "In fact, a girl who couldn't make decent paper cuttings was not considered a worthy bride."

Despite the kindness in her voice, my heart beat hard from frustration. A dull ache surrounded my skull. Would Mr. Overindulgent and his son return?

"Let me show you how." She took out a fresh piece of red paper. She reached out and touched my arm.

Ah, dear Madame Paper Cutter. Who grew excited by the shapes a simple piece of paper could take. Who wouldn't let me wallow in my anger.

"Fine," I said and looked away from the street. I could no longer see Mr. Overindulgent chasing after his son. I threw my shoulder bag down on the ground and flopped next to her. "What's the first step?"

"Patience," she said, looking up at me through her large lenses, like a giant goldfish.

Patience. I wanted that. But I wanted a job more. Any job. I wanted my disaster to turn to good fortune.

Chapter Three
The Lucky Crane

I waited for Mr. Overindulgent and his son to return. Until a cool wind blew. And the sky grew dark. Then a large drop of rain splattered on my arm. Little chance of the man coming back now, so late in the afternoon, such unfavorable weather.

"I know a place to wait out the rain," Madame Paper Cutter said, folding up the letter I'd written for her daughter, sticking it underneath the waistband of her pants. "If you want to wait."

"Thanks, no," I said.

I thought of New Neighbor, the zealot, and his stones. As Father always said, the man was missing a piano string or two. Would he and Father have started arguing already? I helped Madame Paper Cutter gather her cuttings into a plastic bag. I'd much rather stay with her. I'd much rather wait.

Why had New Neighbor chosen to build his house in front of ours, I thought for the hundredth time. He and his wife used to live further down the road. Nice and far away. Then their son had been killed. They claimed that bad spirits flowing from a grave near their old house had pushed the son's truck over a bridge, dropping him like a boulder into the cold waters below. Less superstitious people had suggested the boy had fallen asleep at the wheel. Mother said it wasn't right to pass judgment on what people believed or didn't. Father said he wouldn't if they would just keep to themselves. Which they never did. Especially when it rained.

"I should get home." I handed the bag of cuttings to Madame Paper Cutter. "When it rains, it's best if I'm at home."

Madame Paper Cutter's features relaxed into a smile. She looked in the bag, took out one of her lucky paper cranes, and handed it to me. Perhaps she worried that Mr. Overindulgent and Little Emperor would come back, that I would work for them.

"Tomorrow," she said and squeezed my hand.

On the bus home, I stood in the aisle and gripped my umbrella. Rain poured down against the windows in sheets of white. Why had

I waited so long for Mr. Overindulgent? Why hadn't he returned? The bus turned down the hill toward our side of the village. Rice and vegetable fields filled my vision. At least the crops must be singing with delight at this gift from the clouds.

The small beep of a motorcycle's horn sounded. Our bus honked in reply, the sound echoing throughout the bus. I peered out over the shoulder of the man in front of me. The motorcyclist continued to beep as he zoomed around and in front of our bus. He had no head covering. Not even a bamboo helmet. He held a white plastic bag around his shoulders with one hand, as protection from the rain. No wonder he was in such a hurry.

We passed the eel farm. Workers fumbled with black plastic sheets, covering the eels that had been put out to dry. The rain showered over the pungent odor that normally filled the air. For once I didn't have to hold my breath.

A couple of high school children walked by the side of the road. A girl and boy. The boy held up an umbrella to protect them both. They walked so close their uniforms touched. A first love? At such a young age?

The motorcycle toot-tooted past them, shooting up water. Our bus would certainly do the same. The girl shrank from the side of the road and brushed water from her uniform. The boy, incensed, handed her the umbrella and pulled something from his pocket. A slingshot. He aimed and released.

I felt as if the boy had missed the motorcycle and hit me. A cold numbing sensation spread across my heart. I squeezed my purse. The purse which held Madame Paper Cutter's lucky crane, a symbol of happiness and love.

Father had always warned me to focus on my studies. To not be misled by the foolish meanderings of my heart. I had ignored the stares of many boys, including intelligent Classmate Zhang who sat near me in English class at university. I had focused. I had never felt the protection of a boy's umbrella over my head, his slingshot at the ready. Now it was too late according to Madame Matchmaker.

Madame Matchmaker had been one of the first people to visit upon my return from university. To tell Mother that a match for me would be difficult. Very difficult. Not many bachelors remained in our village. And who wanted a bride with an education? She returned for a visit every few days. She enjoyed chewing on this sorrowful situation, like a cow grinding on a tasty mouthful of grass. Why was I so old and useless? Madame Paper Cutter had said to learn patience. But I thought I needed to learn to act faster. Today, I should have run after Mr. Overindulgent. At least then I would have had a job.

Our bus passed a large plot of land filled with graves. I was almost home. The gravestones looked shiny-silver in the rain. All this rain. Would Father hold back his unkind thoughts of New Neighbor this time? Would Mother remember what Mei Ling's advice about New Neighbor's winding dragon?

I glanced out the back of the bus. The boy had his slingshot aimed at us now. His pants were soaked from the spray our tires splashed. Some things even he couldn't protect the girl from.

A car honked. I looked up again, out the front window. Now the impatient motorcyclist had driven into the lane of oncoming traffic to pass a slow-moving bicyclist in the middle of our lane. The honking car headed straight for Mr. Motorcycle. The car honked and honked for Mr. Motorcycle to return to our lane. Mr. Motorcycle just beeped back. They stubbornly raced toward one another, like two cocks fighting. Would the car slow down? Would Mr. Motorcycle move out of the way? How would this game end? Especially in this weather?

"Patience." I heard Madame Paper Cutter's voice in my head. Sometimes it was hard to be patient. Especially with the rain falling in your face and wetting your trousers. At the last minute, Mr. Motorcycle swerved back toward our lane. But his tires skidded. He lost control and went sliding off into the fields. Oh, gods. I gripped so tight to the seat back my fingers hurt. A chill ran down my spine.

The other cock didn't even slow. Would Mr. Motorcycle be all right? Or would we all soon be standing along the road saying farewell as relatives carried his coffin up the mountain for burial? What would happen to his family? I leaned forward, my nose pressed against the window glass. But the only thing I saw was a white plastic bag sailing away. Then I spotted the pink turrets of Millionaire Huang's castle up ahead. My stop. At last.

"*Xia che,*" I called, squeezing past wet people and umbrellas. "My stop."

I jumped off as soon as the bus pulled to a stop. I ran past Millionaire Huang's six-floor castle. He wasn't outside today. Perhaps he exercised in his great hall.

I passed the high school. Children clustered under a mango tree in the yard despite the rain, drinking soy milk and sneaking cigarettes. Past Uncle's unfinished house. Dark clouds hovered over the empty windows. Past the gravestone maker. My stomach felt tight. Please let me be home before Father and New Neighbor started fighting.

I rushed past Zi Mei's store. Don Don stood out in the road, his face up to the sky, his mouth open.

"Delicious," he said, sticking his tongue out. "Delicious."

"Go inside." I patted him on the shoulder. "Go inside now."

I ran up the stairs next to the store. Water cascaded around my shoes. I heard Father and New Neighbor shouting. I was too late. Father, New Neighbor and Mother all stood out at the edge of our courtyard. Mother held a bucket. She had forgotten Mei Ling's advice.

"You turtle egg," Father shouted above the rain. He was not as tall as New Neighbor, but his voice was deeper, stronger. "You can't do this."

We all had our houses facing south to allow for maximum light and life. Everyone in the village believed in geomancy to a certain degree. Many of us had the eight trigrams symbol from the I Ching above the door, like the Christians placed a cross on a wall. But New Neighbor made us look like nonbelievers. The man was maniacal about *feng shui*. He had painted his front door red to bring in good luck. He complained that the peach tree in our back yard obstructed his "entry of wealth." And, every time it rained, he built a mountain of rocks to block the water rushing down the hill from our house to his. That water, he claimed, carried away his health and prosperity.

The dam he built each time it rained however threatened our health and survival. All that diverted rain water flowed into our courtyard and seeped under our front door. My nose twitched imagining the mildew that would linger for days in this humidity. The rice at the bottom of our bin—what little we had—would become drenched, infested. My mouth tasted sour. My stomach already felt pangs of hunger.

Mother had already imagined the same, for she bent to fill a bucket of rainwater from our courtyard. Then she stood up and stepped forward to toss it over onto the neighbor's property. Oh, Mother. This wasn't the advice Mei Ling had offered.

"Don't throw that water over here," New Neighbor said.

New Neighbor moved close to Mother. He towered over her in his black shorts and stained undershirt. Mother pretended not to hear. She pressed her lips together in a thin line. Her eyes stared at the ground as she continued moving forward.

"I said, don't do that!" New Neighbor growled and pushed Mother in the chest using the flat of his hand. Water from her bucket slopped over onto her flowered shirt making dark patches like bruises on the cloth. New Neighbor had gone too far.

"I'm back," I called running over and standing between them.

New Neighbor stared right through me, as if I didn't exist. That was expected. I was bad luck as my failure to get a university-sponsored job proved, worse than all the rain flowing past his house carrying his good fortune away. Still, I hoped my presence—a child—would have a calming influence on Mother and Father. Perhaps now Mother would remember Mei Ling's advice about the winding dragon.

Father grabbed my umbrella. As protection from the rain or from the neighbor? Soaked Mother leaned down and scooped another bucketful of rainwater. She tossed it past New Neighbor's outstretched arm onto his property. She wasn't going to give up.

"Stop it," the desperate man screeched. "Or else."

He searched the ground. What was he hoping to find? He reached down to the bottom of the rock pile. He picked up a jagged piece of metal. I thought of Mr. Motorcycle and that oncoming car. Of two people so stubborn that only one could win.

"Mother." I latched onto her arms, looking her in the face. "The winding dragon. Did you try the winding dragon?"

She blinked. Cocked her head. Set the bucket down.

"Go inside, Li Hui," Father said, nudging me with the side of the umbrella. He handed the bucket back to Mother. "It's wet out here."

"Li Hui studied *feng shui* while at university," Mother said.

"What a farce." Father laughed. "She doesn't—"

"She took a special course." Mother stepped forward in front of Father, as if to block any words that might come forth from his scowling lips. "Yes, a special course on water flow." She leaned down over the rock pile.

"Don't touch that," New Neighbor hissed.

Cold rain pelted my face. Drops of sweat rolled down my armpits. Would he use that metal piece?

"The water, according to the Professor of *Feng Shui*, would be luckier for you if you created a winding dragon here." Mother made an "S" figure with her finger. "The way it is now, all the water backs up into our house and creates bad *qi* for us. You don't want a neighbor with bad *qi*, do you?"

"That's what the mirror is for," New Neighbor said, pointing to a large mirror on the back of his house. "To deflect your bad *qi*."

His dark eyes were intense. He'd thought of everything. He waved that jagged piece of metal at us as he stepped forward. Mother looked to me.

"Yes," I said. "But the Professor cited several cases in which evil spirits had bypassed the mirror. Especially just one mirror."

The water in our courtyard was ankle deep. Talking wasn't working with this man. Perhaps I should have stayed out of it. Let Father fight him off with the umbrella.

New Neighbor looked toward the mirror. It was a large octagonal-shaped mirror, one of the most expensive. Who was I to question the quality of this precious piece? Doubt moved across his face.

"Because, even with such a good mirror," Mother continued. "Sometimes those spirits are smarter than you think. And, once one of those tricky evil spirits gets in your house . . ."

He stepped back. He bit his bottom lip as he glanced up at the mirror, then down at the rock pile. Was he calculating the risk of following his neighbor's beliefs?

Before he changed his mind, Mother knelt down. She and I positioned the rocks so that, instead of creating a dam that flooded our hall and ruined our food supply, the stones allowed rainwater to curve slowly past the neighbor's house. Not straight and evil. Not fast and life-sucking. Meandering just as "Professor" Mei Ling would have suggested.

New Neighbor watched the slow-moving water. Then he turned and went inside his house, the red door slamming behind him like a clap of thunder. Mother and I both slumped with relief. We could have lost our rice supply. Now our food was safe. Delicious, I thought.

"You should have come earlier," Father said, turning to go inside.

"I'm sorry." I took a deep breath, picked up the bucket, and followed Mother into the house.

We stood in our great hall, staring at the water that had seeped in. Father scooted his wooden chair close to the open door to watch the neighbor and the winding dragon. Mother went upstairs to replace the rain soaked rag in the broken window in the hall.

I took a broom to sweep out the thin layer of water that had accumulated by the door. The broom made a pleasant whisk-whisk sound against the cement floor. My heart felt surrounded by a warmth, as if Mei Ling had been there with me, helping me to deflect this volatile situation. I would send her a letter and tell her how Mother had called her Professor. I would thank Mei Ling for masterminding the first peaceful ending to the rain at our house in a year. I would even include the lucky paper crane that Madame Paper Cutter had given me. Mei Ling would like that.

Father pulled his chair closer to the door. He had removed his soaked shirt and sat bare-chested. He chewed on sunflower seeds, in deep thought. Father had always loved the rain.

"Nice, isn't it?" I asked. Rain pounding on the cement courtyard sounded peaceful. The air felt cool.

"Real nice," Father said. His voice lacked sincerity.

He stood up and went back into the rain, just like he used to do when I was a little girl. Before he started gambling. He would walk in the rain until his clothes were soaked through, saying it was a meditation, a cleansing of the soul. He hadn't done that in a long time.

I leaned on my broom and watched. But Father didn't head for the road, where he could walk and walk without any obstruction. Instead, he went over to the back of the neighbor's house. He leaned down, picked up a rock and threw it at New Neighbor's mirror with the I Ching eight-trigram drawn on its reflective surface. He hit the man's roof. What was he doing?

"Father?"

A ping sounded as this time the rock hit the edge of the mirror. If he wasn't careful, he'd break the man's mirror. Then we'd really have trouble.

"All this time, that stupid turtle egg has been deflecting bad luck on us," he said, picking up a larger stone. "No wonder you didn't get a good teaching position."

"Oh, Father."

I rushed over and put my arm on his. Perhaps he felt guilty about the university gamble. Perhaps he was desperate to find a reason. I didn't want him to feel too badly. I was still grateful for my university experience. For that knowledge. Even if my brain deflected potential suitors as if I had a trigram mirror on my forehead. Father shook my arm off. He took aim.

"But I do have a good job," I lied. "As of today."

"You do?" Father's hand relaxed. He let the stone fall to the ground. "Why didn't you say something?"

I thought of Mr. Overindulgent. His card still heated the bottom of my purse like an egg fresh from the nest. When the rains subsided a bit, I would go down to Zi Mei's and call the number on his business card.

I gathered up the dried pieces of laundry from the top of our rice bin, the stair banister, the table. Mother sat down on a stool, ready to fold. Like Waipo used to do, Mother's hand smoothed the cloth like an iron, taking out the creases over and over. When she finished, the clothes looked as if they had just been taken from the package at the store. Waipo had patience. Mother had patience. Why did my blood always itch?

"Knock knock," a woman's voice called. A familiar voice. Madame Matchmaker? No, not again.

Father snorted once, shifted in his chair and continued to snore. Lucky man. Able to not only ignore the unpleasant encounter but snort at her besides. I covered his bare chest with a dry shirt.

Madame Matchmaker stepped inside. She wasn't a big woman. In fact, she was shorter than all of us. Yet, she took up so much space—both emotional and physical. She wore a bright yellow rain slicker, like a giant caution light in the city.

"Zi Mei heard shouting," Madame Matchmaker said, her eyes glinting with this news. "I just thought I'd stop in." She inclined her head toward our neighbor's house and raised her eyebrows. "And see that everything's all right."

Mother didn't say anything. Mother didn't believe in too much talking, good or bad, as either way you might arouse the gods. They would either be jealous that your life was going too well or angry that you complained about your poor circumstances.

"Some tea," I offered.

"I've had already," Madame Matchmaker said.

She unsnapped her slicker and left it dripping on my freshly swept floor. She squeaked in her wet black pumps over to a stool near sleeping Father. Had her motorcycle broken? Had she walked in the rain to get here? And for what important purpose?

I didn't argue, but hurried outside to the kitchen attached to the front of the house to make a fresh pot of tea anyway. I didn't want to listen to her grinding on my tasty failures. My lack of a husband, my lack of a job, my ridiculous education.

I lit a fire beneath the wok. We were almost out of matches. Four sticks left. I would fry some broad beans, a modest snack. We always had so little.

The rain on the tin roof grated on my nerves. I needed that tutoring job. If I could just start tomorrow. I would go down and call, rain or no rain, as soon as I finished making this treat.

When I returned to the main hall, Father had donned his shirt. He, Madame Matchmaker and Mother sat huddled next to one another. Each of them raced to speak first.

"Three thousand dollars a month." Father whistled. "That's about fifteen thousand *yuan*. A month!"

"And a house," Mother added. She shook her head from side to side in disbelief.

"Don't forget the car which seats four people," Madame Matchmaker said.

I put the beans down on the table. I poured tea for all of us. Father took a loud slurp. What were they talking about? News from a relative overseas? A potential job opportunity?

"It sounds too good," Mother said. She banged her hand on the table for emphasis.

"Nonsense," Father and Madame Matchmaker said together.

Father popped a hot bean in his mouth. He spread his legs wide. Puffed his chest out.

"Then again." He stopped chewing. "Do universities really pay that much money?"

I leaned over Mother. A letter lay in front of them. The calligraphy was uneducated. I spotted the line about the car.

"What is it?" I asked.

"It is a rich country," Madame Matchmaker said, grabbing onto Mother's hand and shaking her clenched fingers.

"Fifteen thousand *yuan* a month." Father's eyes sparkled.

"I've never heard of so much money," Mother said, holding onto his arm.

"*Ba*?" I asked. "Father?"

Was this a job opportunity? Who had sent the information? Was it legitimate?

Madame Matchmaker and Mother looked to Father. He leaned

back in his chair and gazed out at the winding dragon of rocks where the bad buildup of *qi* now curved nicely past the neighbor's house. He pulled a cigarette from his pocket.

"Madame Liang," Father said, reaching over and clapping his hand over mine, "from the other side of the village, is writing about her thirty-two-year-old son, Guo Qiang."

"The name is lovely," Mother said, pointing to the letter. "The characters mean prosperous country."

"So noble," Madame Matchmaker added.

"He's a professor now at the University of Singapore," Father said. "He's in search of a wife."

"I see." I fingered the rim of my tea cup. "What do you know about their family?"

"Mr. Liang has already passed," Mother said. "According to Madame Matchmaker."

"But his death was a fluke," Father added. "They have strong, healthy genes."

"According to Madame Matchmaker's sources," Mother said, handing me the letter, "Guo Qiang is prosperous, intelligent and kind."

Madame Liang wrote that she was old now. The only unfinished business in her life was to close that last open circle, to find a suitable wife for her son. She gave the basic particulars of Guo Qiang, including his blood type and his date and hour of birth, so we could consult the astrologers. She asked Madame Matchmaker to please respond as soon as possible.

Madame Liang's note was short and straight. Maybe her command of characters was limited. Ah, but her son sounded perfect. Educated. Successful. Much older than I—ten years, in fact—but that would just mean maturity. My hands held that letter as if it were a lucky crane that might fly away if we breathed. I had gone to college thinking that was how I would find the way to take care of my parents. But perhaps Madame Matchmaker had the answer.

Chapter Four
Echo of Blue Cotton

Despite my parasol, the sun bored a hole in my brains as I stood next to Madame Paper Cutter with my tutor sign. Unlike the lush green parks in the big city Xiamen, no trees shaded this patch of dirt we used as a park. I beat my lower back with my free hand, the action consuming all my energy. Only a half hour more and I could pack up for the day.

We hadn't had rain for two weeks now, even though this was our rainy season. Temperatures were high, humidity like a heavy cloak. The gods were preparing me well for Singapore, I decided. That's what Mei Ling would have said.

I had already received a letter from Guo Qiang. He had written of the different kinds of people living together in Singapore, his calligraphy strong and intelligent. "Some believe in elephant gods." I couldn't imagine that. "Some go on a month-long fast." Why would anyone starve voluntarily? "Some are as dark as a moonless night." Mother thought that sounded frightening. But I was captivated by the poetry of his description.

I chuckled. Mother had worried that the rains had stopped the moment Madame Matchmaker had sent our introductory letter to Madame Liang. Then Madame Matchmaker had accused Mother of sounding like our overzealous New Neighbor.

"Have you offered a sacrifice to the gods yet?" Madame Matchmaker had asked.

Mother just worried. She and Father had been united by a matchmaker. And, while she wasn't one to question the wisdom of her parents' decision, she wanted to ensure that my match would be more successful.

"You seem awfully cheerful these days," Madame Paper Cutter said. She looked up from her cutting. She was showing me how to cut out a baby boy holding a peach. Another auspicious symbol meaning fertility and long life.

"Do I?" I asked.

"Yes, you do." She held her scissors in the air, waiting.

"Have you ever—" I'd learned over the weeks that despite my initial guess, Madame Paper Cutter was but a year older than I. These days she often felt like a friend more than an elderly park acquaintance. She could read me better than any of the characters I taught her. "How did you know—"

"What?" Madame Paper Cutter tapped the concrete with her scissors. "You're making me nervous. You're not tutoring that Little Emperor, are you?"

"No, no," I said. I'd never gotten through to Mr. Overindulgent and Little Emperor. The man's phone was either busy or it kept ringing. I had noticed though that Mr. Ponytail and Earring hadn't come to the park recently. "I think the man with the earring got that one."

"Good riddance to the both of them," she said. "What is it, then?"

I opened my purse and glanced at the letter from Guo Qiang. I wanted her to know the contents, his humor, his sense of poetry. I couldn't read the letter out loud here in the park though. And, while Madame Paper Cutter's ability to read had improved, she still would struggle with this. I would only embarrass her.

"Li Hui?" Madame Paper Cutter tapped me on the leg with her scissors.

"Tell me. Your husband. How did you know him?" How had I blurted out such a personal question?

"Ah." Madame Paper Cutter took off her glasses and rubbed the bridge of her nose. "He was the skinniest boy in the village. Like a bamboo rod." She looked out over the park, as if she could see him far away. "But our local matchmaker insisted he was a good man." She put her glasses back on. "He was the best thing that ever happened to me."

She looked up at me, smiling and nodding for emphasis. I hugged my purse. Maybe Guo Qiang would capture my heart the same way.

I watched the bus pull into the depot. My bus that would take me home to my side of village. I stood in a long line of tired people. In front of me an old woman organized her plastic bags of produce—snap peas, garlic, cabbage. An old farmer holding his chicken nudged me from behind. I moved forward a bit.

The farmer looked defeated, as if he'd spent all day calling out the virtues of his chicken—tender, young, best price—and no one had bought. I sympathized. I had done the same with my tutor sign in the park for yet another day.

The farmer's chicken thrust its neck out, nudging me forward. Or was it picking at my blouse? I pushed my way up onto the bus and found a seat way at the back, away from the defeated man. I scrunched next to a woman in a thick jacket and her small child. How could she suffer such heavy clothes in this heat? A middle-aged man stood, holding onto the back of the seat in front of me. His hands were so black with grease he must have spent the day fixing motorcycles. I imagined Guo Qiang. Would his fingernails be as ink-stained from reading and writing so much?

Across the way, Madame Barber squeezed her son's fat little cheek. Zi Mei, the small shop owner on our corner, sat next to her. Zi Mei had been the one to tell us—or rather Mother—of that boy's birth. The child had been born on an inauspicious day, according to the lunar calendar. Zi Mei was certain Madame Barber would let Mother adopt the boy. That was the last time Mother followed Zi Mei's advice.

I took Guo Qiang's letter from my purse. He had such humor. After talking about Singapore and his job as a computer science professor, he'd gone on to describe his good colleague. "He married an outsider," he wrote. "An American." He had written how the strange woman collected items from the garbage—even a couch. How she would stand in the heat for hours to take pictures of birds. How once she'd even jumped out of a car to stand in a free parking spot so no one else would take it. I smiled as I put the letter away. His writing put a space around my heart, sheltering me from this crowded bus and my long, hot, unsuccessful day. I was eager to get home. Perhaps another letter awaited.

The bus hit a pothole. My seatmate fell against me, her thick jacket emitting the oniony odor of sweat. That thick jacket. Perhaps she was ill. Perhaps she had just given birth and wore the jacket to keep the wind from getting into her joints. But, no. The child in her lap looked to be at least two years old. She caught me looking at her and stared back defiantly. Her face softened.

"Aren't you?" She snapped her fingers. "Li? Li Hui?"

I looked at her warm round cheeks, her short perspiring forehead, her stringy short hair. Should I know someone who paraded about in a winter jacket in the middle of summer?

"Cheng Min," she said, before I could place her face. "Fifth grade, you sat right in front of me."

"Cheng Min, of course." I grabbed onto her arm. I remembered her name. "I didn't recognize you."

"That's what children will do to you." She laughed. "Push you here, pull you there."

"You have a beautiful little girl though," I said. Ah, a wife who had borne a girl. Another eunuch husband, as the villagers would call him.

"Two of them." She smiled and ran a hand through the girl's long hair. "I have two little girls."

"Two?" While Beijing didn't allow more than one child, the government forgave our traditional rural areas. We were allowed two children. But two girls? "That's so nice." I squeezed her arm again.

"You look the same." She leaned over and took a pear and a knife from her bag. She put the knife's sharp edge to the skin of the pear to peel the treat. "Children haven't taken away your good looks—"

"I don't have any children," I said. I thought of Guo Qiang. Perhaps by next year that would change. "Yet."

"No time for anything but study, right? You still have that long, silky hair." She reached out and touched my hair. "Remember that girl? What was her name? She was appointed our class leader."

"Yes, yes," I said. I could see the nasty little girl in my head. Short, wrinkled uniform. Dull, brittle hair. "I forget her name."

"How could you?" Cheng Min nudged me with the handle of her knife. "She was always out to get you. Remember how she made a new rule that everyone cut their hair like a boy, because she was jealous of your hair? Perhaps she thought it wouldn't grow back."

I laughed. I hadn't thought of that in so long. It was as if Cheng Min held out a rope and pulled me back over the years I'd been gone—to high school, then university. My mind whirled with thoughts of games we had played. Stones, jumping rope, hide and find.

The bus went into another pothole. My old classmate's pear slimed up against my arm. I took out a package of tissues and wiped pear juice from my skin. She handed me a slice, although I put up my hand to protest.

"Remember that time—" she started.

"You son of a whore," a woman shouted from the front of the bus. Her voice was slow like Father's when he had had too much drink. "Stop it."

Everyone stopped talking, stopped making noises. Cheng Min

sat forward, craning her neck high to see up front. But the bus was so crowded we could only hear the woman's angry words. Everyone was grumpy in this weather. Was this another fight caused by too much heat?

"Husband's Second Uncle was robbed on this very route," Cheng Min whispered.

Now I remembered more. Cheng Min could relate thousands and tens of thousands of disasters, all in a whisper.

"Someone sliced a hole into his shirt pocket." She made a slicing motion with her knife. "Just like that."

She took my purse from my lap and wedged it safely between us. If only she knew. The only things of value inside were the letter from Guo Qiang, a book, a pair of scissors, and today's paper cutting. Still, I appreciated her concern.

"Has your family ever been targeted?" Cheng Min asked. Perhaps she imagined Father had been an easy mark for thieves and swindlers with me so far away at school.

"No, no," I assured her. Thieves and swindlers knew Father had no money.

"Have you heard the latest?" Cheng Min whispered more urgently, handing me another slice of pear and not waiting for an answer. "The mob has a special liquid drug. Touch you with it. You're under their control."

"I've heard about that." I nodded.

Father'd told me as soon as I arrived home to be careful and not let anyone touch me. Maybe when he was a child helping Yeye sell vegetables in the market, that was a possibility. But the town had changed during the time he'd stopped making trips here. Every move you made, someone touched you with a bag, a chicken, a pear.

"That drug stuff scares me," Cheng Min said, her eyes wide.

"Is that why you wear the heavy coat?" I asked.

"Stop it," the woman up front called again.

The man with the grease-stained hands in front of us made a long sound in his throat, then spat on the floor. "Stay away," that spit warned. I hoped the thief up front heeded that disgusting warning.

I looked across the aisle. Madame Barber had switched places with Zi Mei so the shop owner was closest to the aisle now. Was Madame Barber fearful for her son's safety? But no. She held her son's bottom out the window to do xi-xi. Still, she turned her head every few seconds to watch the front though, for more signs of an evil dog among us. Some of the boy's *xi-xi* sprayed on her face.

"*Xia che. Xia che.*" The woman up front yelled to the driver to let her off. "My stop."

The bus pulled over. The loud woman may as well have been an opera star who came to the village each year, and for whom we all carried our chairs from home to watch, crowding as close to the stage as the legs of our chairs would allow. People from the other side of the bus pushed against me to see out the window. Two old men in front of me stood up to get a better view.

That woman. I had seen that woman. I'd stood behind her while waiting to board the bus. Now she stood alone by the side of the road. No attacker nearby. No slit in her pocket. No missing purse. But she did have a hole in one of her plastic shopping bags. Fresh snap peas spilled to the ground.

"The poor woman," Cheng Min said. "How did she get such a big hole in her bag?"

The snap pea season had come to an abrupt halt with the lack of rains. She had probably spent a long time choosing them at the market, arguing with the seller until she got the best price.

"What a shame," I said.

Each time the old woman tried to grab the bag with the hole in it, or bent over to pick some of the snap peas up off the ground, the hole grew bigger. More snap peas fell out. Where were her children? Her grandchildren? Did she have no one to help her? I fussed with the leather strap of my purse. I knew now who the "son of a whore" was with his unsold feathery bundle. I was glad I had decided to sit in back, far from his pecking chicken.

The bus shifted into gear. But, before we moved far, a tall man jumped off. He had broad shoulders and muscular arms, which stretched his white t-shirt. He wore dark blue cotton trousers. He grabbed the old lady's bag of peas. I held my breath. She beat him with words, calling him worse things than she had Mr. Chicken Farmer. She tried to beat him with her other bags. But her thin grocery-laden arms could only sway back and forth, like branches in the wind. How could this healthy man take an old woman's food?

"What a cockroach," Cheng Min whispered. She pulled me closer to her, as if he were right near us, ready to attack.

I stared back at the man. How could anyone be so desperate? Wouldn't the old lady's children or neighbors come help her? He ran after our moving bus, still holding the peas, fiddling with the bag.

Was he making the hole bigger? Was he so hungry he couldn't wait to taste the crunchy texture against his tongue? The lonely old woman hobbled after him. She'd never catch him.

Our driver slowed for a pothole in the road. The man caught onto the handle of the bus and pulled himself up. My mouth went dry. He hung onto the handle with one arm. He leaned out toward the road, as if he were in a parade and waving to the masses. Except the bag was in his hand.

"Look," I said. Something flew through the air and landed at the old woman's feet. "The bag of peas. He's thrown the lady her bag of peas."

"Maybe it's coated with that drug," Cheng Min said, putting her nose out the window.

The old woman stared at the bag, as if she thought the same as Cheng Min. Then she picked up the bag. The peas no longer fell from the bottom. He had tied a knot where once there had been a hole. The old woman put her hands together in a gesture of thanks and shook them at the man.

"*Xie xie*," she called as our bus pulled further away. "Thank you."

Mr. Motorcycle Fixer made another long noise in his throat. This time he didn't spit directly beneath him, but in the direction of the man with the blue cotton pants.

"He's got a point," Cheng Min said. "Who does Mr. Helper think he is, sticking his nose in business that isn't his? Making us all wait while he finishes his foolishness?"

Father certainly would have agreed with Cheng Min. Mother would have been more concerned that Mr. Chicken Farmer found offense with the old woman's swearing. That Mr. Chicken Farmer would take revenge on the old lady. And anyone who helped her.

"It was kind," I said, surprised by my defense of the man. Where was my head?

I opened my purse to show Cheng Min my letter from Guo Qiang. Perhaps her marriage had been arranged. Perhaps she knew of the Liang family.

"What are you reading?" Cheng Min pointed to the paperback in my purse.

"It's a book about discipline." It was a Chinese translation of an American discipline handbook. I had bought it at a used book store hoping Mr. Overindulgent would hire me to teach his Emperor.

What a waste.

"I could use that." Cheng Min laughed. "My little girls don't do anything I say. It's always, 'Nainai said I could.' Or, 'Baba said I could.'"

"Sounds difficult," I said. I hoped she wouldn't be chasing after her child in the park someday.

"That's so sweet of you to read up on child-rearing before you even have them," she said without malice. "I'll have to come to you next time I have a problem."

"I haven't read much of it at all," I said.

"Yes, but I remember you," Cheng Min said. "You never had to read the entire sutra to understand."

The woman spoke so kindly of me and without the daggers I'd felt from everyone since my return. She wasn't educated. She didn't appear that rich. But she seemed comfortable, happy with herself. And could be so with me. I moved my head around in a circle to make sense of this, to loosen my muscles. That's when I saw that strange man in blue. He stared out the window at rows and rows of silver eel skin put out to dry, as if they were the most fascinating thing he'd ever seen. The heat had cooked up such a strong odor, the smell made my eyes water. Cheng Min put her hand over her daughter's nose to protect the child.

The man smiled. I knew. Because he stood in the aisle right next to me.

"The eel smell signals it's time to move to the front," Cheng Min said, patting me on the shoulder. "It always takes us a long time to get off. And our stop is coming."

She stood with her daughter. Then, she spotted the strange man standing in the aisle next to me. She leaned and put her mouth right up against my ear.

"How did he get back here?" she whispered. "You want me to stay?"

"No, no." I patted her arm. "I'm fine. Don't worry."

She stood and re-adjusted her bag over her shoulder. She looked at Man In Blue as if she might spot him pulling out a drug with which to attack me. Then she looked back at me. I nodded that I was fine. Really.

"Good seeing you," she said and pushed her way down the aisle.

"Wait," I called, standing up.

She rushed back, her arms tight around her daughter, her purse tucked between them, her legs kicking in front of her. Perhaps she thought I'd changed my mind. Perhaps she thought Man in Blue had attacked already.

"Here." I offered up the discipline book. "You might enjoy reading this."

"Oh," she said, relaxing her hold on her daughter and putting her leg down. "No, no. I never have time to read."

"There are some good parts in there on how to tell your child no," I said, sticking the book in her bag.

"Okay, okay. Thanks. I'll make sure to get it back to you. You're still over by Zi Mei's shop, right?"

"Right." I grabbed onto her hand, ruffled the baby girl's hair. "Come by anytime."

As soon as she disappeared up front, blood rushed through my body. The seat next to me was now vacant. Would the Man In Blue take this empty seat? My heart pounded like the big war drums actors brought to the village when someone sponsored a show. A woman with a large red department store bag pushed past the strange man. Then she wiggled around me to the empty seat next to the window, her jean material skirt brushing against my nose. She settled her bag in between us. The top of the bag felt sharp against my leg.

I moved my head around in circles again, all the time aware of Man In Blue standing next to me. He stared out the window at the eel skins. His dirty blue cotton pants seemed closer to my cheek than necessary. His mud-covered boots jolted next to my feet when the bus stopped for another pothole. There were so many potholes. This man was so strange. What a nuisance.

I took out Guo Qiang's letter. Perhaps studying his strong, confident characters would quiet my fluttering heart. Would I get a new note today? That would be good. In the distance, dynamite exploded at one of the rock quarries. I glanced up. Man In Blue stared right at me. Right into my eyes. How forward. I looked away, out the window.

The bus stopped. I spotted Zi Mei's plump figure shuffling toward the front. Was this my stop? Already? Zi Mei. The woman with the phone. With all the information. She knew who had marriage trouble, who was in debt—Father wasn't the only one—and who planned to follow the snakehead overseas. Certainly, with all the commotion, she had looked around and seen me. And this strange man. And I didn't want to become her next article of conversation. My university failure had finally fallen in conversational priority behind the lack of rain and drooping crops. Now she'd wonder delectable scenarios for the ears of all, if I didn't get off the bus.

I stood. Strange Man In Blue was taller than me—by a head. His hands were thick and calloused. The bus shifted into first gear.

"*Xia che*," I said, but my voice got stuck somewhere deep inside. What was wrong with me?

The bus passed Millionaire Huang's pink castle on the corner. Six stories with a turret. Cheng Min walked past the castle, fanning her baby with my book. She must live near. The driver shifted into second.

"*Xia che*," I tried again. "My stop."

My request came out deep and loud. So deep that I realized it wasn't me.

"*Xia che*," strange Man In Blue called again. He spoke our dialect without an accent. "*Xia che*."

The bus stopped so suddenly I fell into his shoulder, dropping my purse. He held my forearm to balance me while he leaned down to retrieve my purse. He had been kind with the old lady, in a most untraditional fashion. Where did his grace and manners come from?

"*Xie xie*," I said, my voice a whisper. "Thank you."

I held my hand out for him to return my purse. He didn't. This man was a fool after all.

"You—you—" I looked up, not sure what to call him.

He stared at me with his single-lidded dark brown eyes. His face broke into a smile, making dents in his cheeks. He slid the purse on my arm.

"*Xie xie*," I said, swallowing my unkind thoughts.

"No problem," he said.

My cheeks flushed with heat as I hurried down the aisle and off the bus. This strange man didn't walk the line of our culture. Yet he appeared to be just a simple laborer—one who could never support a family like mine. So why did my limbs tingle? My heart beat so?

Chapter Five
The Fly with a Morsel

I felt the eyes of strange Man In Blue watching me, even though the bus had long since disappeared in a cloud of black exhaust. He had crossed the boundaries of etiquette and stared into my eyes. His voice had been so deep, so bold when he had called to the bus driver that it was my stop. I remembered the small dents in his cheeks, his smile so broad it had felt like a hug. "No problem," I repeated as I walked toward the pink castle. I felt my hips sway from side to side.

Perhaps Guo Qiang looked like that man. I stopped and stared down the road. What if that had been Guo Qiang home for a visit? He was headed for the other side of the village. He certainly behaved like an outsider—helping that strange old woman with her peas. Amazing.

Amazing. Aiya. I was the amazing one. Perhaps all those days in the park had melted a few of my piano strings. Guo Qiang was a distinguished professor in Singapore. That kind and unconventional man on the bus looked to be no more than a day laborer. How could I think the two of them were one? I turned away from the road, shaking my head. I wanted to shake off the image of those dark eyes, those high cheekbones, those muscular arms. But the picture was singed in my heart.

I passed the perfect pink castle, perfect except that the only one inside was an old man. Sometimes I'd see him in front of his house practicing *taiqi* or drying soybeans. His wife had passed to the other side of the River of Sleep. His son was overseas making big money. Perhaps I'd be overseas soon as well, doing the same.

I passed the path that led out to Millionaire Huang's swimming pool. He owned three gas stations in town and had a big piece of land with not only a six-story house but a huge swimming pool. The first year he had built the pool, people had laughed. Why waste good land to make a pool? The ocean was only a mile away, with reservoirs and ponds in between. Besides no one knew how to swim anyway. Now his idea was so popular he charged admission—six *yuan* a person. Not everyone had to venture overseas to make big money.

I hurried by the middle school. Sometimes I'd stop to share a cigarette with Second Cousin and his friends who played basketball in their Magic Johnson t-shirts. Not tonight. Other things were more important. A letter might be waiting.

I skipped past the shell of a house Sixth Cousin had built. He'd managed to finish the outside walls, then had run out of money. The windows twinkled in the late afternoon light, laughing at me. My clothes looked worn. My shoes had scuff marks, worn heels. Still Man In Blue had smiled. Why had that strange man, that undistinguished day laborer, made such an impression on me? Why couldn't I rid my thoughts of him?

"No problem."

I'd have to write Mei Ling about him. She would be pleased that I was finding so much joy and adventure at home, despite being unemployed. Then again, perhaps she'd worry. Here I was daydreaming about a stranger on a bus.

I slowed in front of the cemetery engravers. Engraving tools whined as men from Sichuan province sat on the ground and carved into the smooth rock surfaces of cemetery markers. This business Third Uncle had set up after getting out of prison. Father often used Third Uncle as an example. Third Uncle had succeeded despite his excesses. Any day our luck might change, too. That's what Father believed.

A pain shot down my back. My monthly would arrive soon. I stopped to sit on a big piece of rock. Workers would shave smooth and engrave this stone with the name of a person who'd moved to the other side of the River of Sleep. Would one of these workers make a headstone for me one day? Or would I be buried in Singapore?

The neighborhood loudspeaker crackled. Something about electricity bills being due. I didn't catch all of the words, as Community Leader didn't like talking into the microphone. His words sounded as if his mouth were full of rice. Something about a new theater in the planning. A need for contributions. Money. Money. Money.

"Little sister, what are you doing?" One of Third Uncle's employees approached, a cigarette dangling from his mouth. He wore a dusty shirt and pants. His accent was just as dusty.

"I just needed a rest."

I smiled and pulled a thread from the sleeve of my blouse. Had that stupid chicken on the bus pecked the thread loose? Would I have even noticed strange Man In Blue if that chicken hadn't pecked a hole in the old woman's bag? I lifted the hair off the back of my neck to let in a breeze. I beat my lower back with my fist. That wonderful chicken.

"This isn't a park," the employee grumbled, moving closer, tossing his cigarette in front of me. "You can't just sit down where you please."

"Li Hui, is that you?" a woman's voice called. Zi Mei.

What was she doing so far behind me? She had been first off the bus. Zi Mei stopped, her short hair pasted with sweat to the sides of her head. And why had she hurried to catch up?

"Chi bao le mayo?" she asked. "Have you eaten?"

"Yes, yes," I responded to the ritual greeting. "And you?"

"Yes." She cocked her head to one side and looked at me. Her eyes twinkled with more than the light of the setting sun. She leaned on one foot and then the next, like a child who must do *xi-xi*. Or a gossip who has news to tell.

"Young sisters, this isn't a gathering spot." Grumble coughed, waving us away with his arm. We ignored his noise, as though he were just a mosquito whirring by.

"I just got back from town," I said, as if I hadn't noticed her on the bus. She may have had news. But for once I wanted information. "We had an unbelievable ride. This man on the bus jumped off to help an old woman. Then he caught up with the bus and jumped back on."

"I saw that," Zi Mei said.

I leaned forward. The echo in my heart beat louder just thinking about Man In Blue's stretched t-shirt, his bangs falling in his face.

"Young sisters—" Grumble started.

"Fool," Zi Mei said.

Her brow furrowed into a thousand lines. Her dark eyes looked harder than the stone on which I rested. Grumble and I both stiffened. He walked away, like a dog who'd been hit on the nose with a cane.

"Fool held up the entire bus," Zi Mei said. "What nerve."

"Yes," I said without much conviction.

Despite his appearance to the contrary, I realized I'd still held a rice grain of hope that Man In Blue was Guo Qiang visiting from Singapore. What else explained his unconventional behavior? The way he'd jumped off the bus to care for an old woman? The way he had helped me call out for the bus to stop? The way he had stared into my eyes?

"What?" I asked.

"I said, 'Have you ever been in Drink Happiness Tea Shop?' Across from the bus depot?"

"No," I said. "Well, once."

"What do you think?" Zi Mei asked.

Was this her news? Why did I expect her to linger over the incident on the bus? Perhaps because I wanted to.

"Well?" Zi Mei probed.

The manager of that tea shop had been so rude. She'd hardly taken her eyes from Fashion Fortune Magazine long enough to give me a sampling of tea. I'd never gone back.

"Certainly they have lots of tea," I said. "Lots of fashion magazines."

"That's a good family." She cocked her head and stared at me with her twinkling eyes. "They've been through many troubles."

A loud noise erupted nearby. A cloud of dust shot up around me. Grumble had turned on his stone smoother.

"There's a club in town where you can sit and—" he yelled, over the whine of the motor.

"I know there's a club in town," Zi Mei barked. "Because my money helped build it."

Zi Mei had no patience with workers from outside provinces, never mind that many of them had lived here longer than some of us had been alive.

"Don't get excited," Grumble said. "Just move off my boss's stones."

I barely got off the stone before he dropped the whirring blade on top of it.

"Are you sure you're alright?" Zi Mei brushed the back of my pants, looking again for a tear, some evidence that the migrant worker had almost sliced my legs off.

"I'm fine, really," I said.

If I hadn't been so quick to jump up, surely the man would have stopped before he hit me. Surely. Perhaps he had a schedule to keep. Perhaps he was paid by the stone.

"The insolence of that man." Zi Mei looked to where the stone engraver worked, her lips pursed. "After all Third Uncle has done for him. After all we've done for him."

I looked over. I hadn't done anything for the man. I'd talked to him for the first time today.

"I mean we welcome him into our village," she said when I didn't murmur an appropriate noise of support. "We allow him to live and work here. And what does he do? He almost shaves off your legs. Are you sure you're not hurt?" She stopped, grabbed my waist and turned to look at the back of my pants. "What's that? Is that a tear down there?"

I twisted around to look where she pointed with her thin shaking finger. An old mud stain.

"No, no," I said. "I'm fine, really."

"I tell you, I will not let the sun set without talking to Third Uncle," she said. "He will hear about this and do something about it."

"That's too much trouble for you," I said. Whatever news Zi Mei had about Drink Happiness Tea Shop, she had forgotten in her zeal to punish this outsider. "After all, we were putting a stop to the man's work—"

"Nonsense." She waved my words away. "We were resting after a harrowing bus ride where a foolish man had stopped the bus and held us captive."

Was Man In Blue really a fool? My calves itched. I was eager to get home and see what the afternoon mail had brought.

"My legs get so stiff sitting on that bus ride," Zi Mei said. "I'm getting old."

She stopped to rest in front of the fields. Fourth Uncle's cow chewed dry grass a few feet away, chomping and snorting and shifting the weight on her legs, as if she too wanted to be moving.

"No, you're still very capable," I assured Zi Mei, patting her on the arm, looking up the road.

Zi Mei's store was at the end of the block. Our house stood just a hop up the steps from there. Both places seemed so far away. I took a deep breath. Waipo had often said, "When you're impatient, breathe. In. Out. Look around. Enjoy the moment."

Nearby the neighbor on this main road scooped well water from her bucket and bathed withering plants. Her plants were smaller, not as green—even when there was rain. She was one of the few who didn't use a chemical sprayer. The neighborhood kids called her Prehistoric Lady for refusing to adopt the latest farming innovation. But she could walk through her fields in bare feet, without concern of holes burning through her skin from chemicals.

"Her daughter-in-law has happiness," Zi Mei said.

"How nice," I said. How did Zi Mei know this? Why didn't she have more information about Man In Blue?

"Again," Zi Mei whispered. "She already has two daughters." Zi Mei held onto my arm. "Why do people think they can get away with such things? That their lives are more important than the rest of the world?" She squeezed my arm so tight, her short nails dug into my flesh. "So she doesn't have a son. Neither did your father. And look at you. You're so, so—intelligent."

"No, no," I said. Now my scalp itched. I couldn't even find a job.

"So, they call her husband a eunuch. Does that mean she can fill up the world with more bodies until she delivers a boy?"

Whoever this brave woman was, she wasn't the first in our village to try for three. The last I remember was Madame Butcher. She had been so determined to have one more child that, during her third pregnancy, she went from relative to relative, friend to friend, never spending more than one night in one place. Except for one night. That one night Madame Butcher stayed at a friend's place too long. The Birth Control Unit leader found her and took her to the nearby clinic. They removed the baby from her body right there. People say the baby would have been a boy.

"What is that foolish girl thinking?" Zi Mei went on. "Did she tell you?"

"Me?" I asked. I barely knew Prehistoric Lady, much less her daughter-in-law.

"You sat next to her on the bus," Zi Mei said. "Didn't you used to be classmates?"

A chill covered my skin with goose flesh. No wonder Cheng Min had on such a thick jacket. Would her third baby be a boy? Would she deliver him safely? Get to keep him? I needed to pay Cheng Min a visit and warn her that her secret now danced on Zi Mei's tongue.

We continued on. Slowly. So slowly. I took another deep breath.

"Your father used to have that job," Zi Mei nodded toward Prehistoric Lady.

I nodded. What had triggered this memory? Zi Mei jumped from topic to topic, never concentrating on any one too long, like a fly rubbing her legs together over a juicy piece of meat and then flitting off to find another morsel.

"Everyone worked side by side, back then." Zi Mei watched Prehistoric Lady pick off dead leaves, making everything appear green again.

Father's job back then had been called Well Digger. He filled up everyone's buckets with water from the well. That was back in the days of the commune when Chairman Mao Ze Dong gave everyone a job, made everyone equal. Father was still known by that nickname, although these days the joke was that every night Father's cards dug him deeper and deeper into a well.

"Those were good days." Zi Mei sighed.

Mother had never referred to the commune days as good. Everyone was tired. Angry. Hungry.

"People aren't equal," Mother had whispered into her lap, as if fearful of an outsider hearing. "The ones who worked hard were pulled down by the lazy ones. There was never enough food to distribute at the end of the month because someone in the commune had miscalculated the amount of seeds to plant, forgotten to water the seedlings, or pulled up the plants too early."

I looked over at Zi Mei, her eyes marveling at the history she'd re-created, having pulled away all the unpleasant truths, leaving only the lovely green ones. Crickets chirped. The sound of a tractor putt-putted down the road. Sweat drooled down the back of my knees. I thought of a car which could seat four. Plush seats that cushioned my sore back. Windows rolled down to let in the afternoon breeze. I hoped there'd be a letter waiting for me today.

I left Zi Mei at her shop, went up the stairs and walked past New Neighbor's. Since the last encounter with New Neighbor, we hadn't been having any unhappiness. In fact, New Neighbor no longer turned and walked in the opposite direction when he saw me coming. He even nodded and offered customary greetings.

I entered our house. Mother was not in sight. Father sat in his chair, a cigarette hanging from his mouth. What was he doing home? Why wasn't he out playing his nightly game? He glanced up.

"You're back," he said, talking with the cigarette between his lips, as if it were just a toothpick. The ashtray on the table overflowed with butts. The table also held a tea cup and a bowl of apples. But no letter.

"Some tea?" Father offered.

He seemed in a rare good mood. Had he already won a game and stopped playing for the night? That wasn't his style. I hated not to share the moment with him. Not to find out more. However I just wanted to drop off my purse and tutor sign. Then I'd go visit Cheng Min and warn her to start moving from house to house. I wouldn't offer our house. We were too close to Zi Mei to be of any safety.

"No, thanks," I said.

"We have new tea," he said, holding up a canister.

I took the canister. What was this? Had a relative dropped by with this gift? I opened the foil and breathed in the sweet smell of the black buds.

"Smells good."

"The best," Father said, taking a long drag off his cigarette, leaning forward. "That's ten-*yuan*-a-kilo tea from Drink Happiness Tea Shop."

The same tea shop Zi Mei had just mentioned right before the stone engraver had sliced off my legs. Why had she brought up the tea shop in the first place? Had she forgotten to finish her story?

"A gift from your new boss," Father said.

My new boss? I sat down. Was Father speaking metaphorically? People always said that you never married a man. You married your mother-in-law. She was the boss. Was Madame Liang in town? My heart beat fast. Perhaps that man had been Guo Qiang dressed in labor clothes for the day, helping some old friend.

"Yes." Father took a drag from his cigarette. He examined the short burning stub like he did when he was about to make some big statement. He exhaled a cloud of smoke. "Old Man Chen. Remember my *mahjong* partner? He needs your help managing his tea store."

So this wasn't about Guo Qiang. Oh, Father. I fingered the tea canister. The foil that held the leaves felt sharp. The small black buds inside looked as large as water wheels. Hadn't Old Man Chen been one of the ones to boast how well his daughter had done the past four years while I'd wasted time?

"His daughter." Father cleared his throat. "Well, it turns out she's been losing lots of money."

"That's a shame." I put the tea down on the table. What would I do in a tea shop? Besides I still wanted to teach. Even if it were free lessons in the park with just Madame Paper Cutter.

"I told Old Man Chen." Father stood up. "That you'd make the place grow."

He stood firm, placing his hand on my shoulder. He hadn't been drinking. He was serious.

"But, Father—"

"He's agreed to take you on a trial basis." He pushed his cigarette down into the pile of butts, igniting the remains.

"But, Father, I don't know anything about business." Acrid smoke drifted up my nose. "I studied teaching."

"If you can learn to teach." He walked toward the door and then turned. "You can learn to do business."

He rapped his hand on the side of the house and left. I stared at the box of tea. We never had money for such a luxury as this high grade tea. But me? A tea seller? What an idea.

"No problem." Man In Blue's voice came to me again. I felt his presence as if he stood tall before me, sliding my purse on my arm. His dark eyes searched mine. Perhaps Father was right. I was intelligent enough to listen and understand. It would be just like taking a new class. Besides, this was a job.

Chapter Six
A Useless Stick

Drink Happiness Tea Shop stood across the street from the central bus depot in town. Old Man Chen's daughter, Feng Gu, was the proprietress, the same woman I remembered from the one time I'd visited this shop. Feng Gu had a small nose, which stuck up like a wild mushroom. Her nose wrinkled with distaste as she gestured for me to sit across from her in the center of the shop. I sat on the cherrywood stool she indicated. Behind me, in a back room for storage, a few boxes of tea stood stacked against the wall. A simple cot rested in the corner. Above the door hung a black framed ancestral photograph of a young boy. A youthful picture of Old Man Chen's father or grandfather? Had he died at such a young age? Or was this picture from his youth the only one available?

In the front room, next to this cherrywood table, a desk held a worn abacus and a brass weight. An upright fan shook its head back and forth at us. Tea bins lined the wall. No expensive high-tech digital weighing machines, calculators or cash registers like they had in the big city of Xiamen. No air conditioning. Father said the shop was losing money. But she hadn't thrown money away in the most obvious ways.

Feng Gu poured me a cup of tea. Some of the liquid sloshed over the side. She didn't notice.

"Thank you," I said and moved my legs a bit, as the pool of tea dripped off the side of the table. "This is a lovely table."

"My great grandfather carved it," she said. Her voice was high pitched, like an actress in an opera.

A rag hung on the side of a bucket. Would she be offended if I wiped the spill? Would cleaning up after this woman be part of my job? I grabbed the rag.

"He enjoyed carving," Feng Gu said. She pointed over my head with her stubby tea-stained fingers. "He made that, too."

I looked up from where I swiped the spill. Cobwebs dangled from the corner of the ceiling. An old wooden sign hung on the wall. It read: "Life is like Tea. First it's bitter, then it's sweet."

"Nice," I said.

Madame Paper Cutter certainly held such a saying in her heart. What would she have to say about Feng Gu? Madame Paper Cutter. She would wonder where I was this morning. I'd have to go by the park, perhaps at lunchtime, if I had a long enough break, and tell her of my new job. Perhaps I could bring her a sample.

"So, we have two harvests," Feng Gu said. "One in winter and one in summer."

I never knew that. I took a note pad from my purse and wrote that fact down. If I was to learn the business, I better take notes.

"The winter harvest is bitter. We export that crap—" Feng Gu looked at my note pad and stopped herself. "We export those low grade leaves to Japan."

"Japan?" I asked and circled the word. Would Mei Ling drink bitter tea? I'd have to make sure to send her some of these high quality leaves. "I have a friend—"

"Yes, my cousin works there, too," Feng Gu said. "Just sent home some money for the shop."

And still the shop was losing money? Perhaps this cousin was just paying back money he owed. Had Feng Gu sponsored many relatives? Was that where all their profits went? Or was her father as unlucky with the tiles as mine? Then again, at her age, perhaps her husband was the one who tossed the money out faster than she could gather it.

"My cousin was lucky," Feng Gu said, leaning across the table, so close her hot breath on my ear made my neck itch. "It's getting harder and harder to go overseas these days. The man next door who repairs bicycles. You know the one whose hair is balding at the top even though he's not even thirty?"

I nodded. I wasn't sure who he was. But that didn't seem to matter.

"He paid fifty thousand in American money for a fake marriage to a Japanese."

"Whaaa," I said. I knew getting overseas was expensive. Mei Ling had mentioned she'd paid twenty thousand American dollars. Surely Feng Gu exaggerated.

"No, that wasn't the worst part. When he got to the airport." Feng Gu tapped my pad with her short finger. "His fiancée wasn't there to meet him."

"Whaaa," I said again. "That's terrible."

"The Japs—" Feng Gu stopped herself again. "The Japanese immigration sent him back."

"And the fiancée?"

"Who knows?" Feng Gu stroked her shoulder-length hair. "Probably went on a shopping trip with that fifty thousand."

"He didn't get any of his money back?" I asked. "Wasn't there a guarantee?"

"Yes." She laughed, showing a mouthful of crooked teeth stained the color of tea steeped too long. "A guarantee that he will taste acid every time he thinks about that moment at the airport."

I drew circles on my note pad. Perhaps discussing other people's monetary disasters made Feng Gu feel less of a failure. It made me nervous. Mei Ling was scheduled to leave any day now with a snakehead. She had been guaranteed safe passage and a job for her twenty thousand American. Surely she would fare better than Baldy next door.

"He always comes by for a free cup of tea." Feng Gu tapped my hand. "Don't give him the good stuff though. He can't tell the difference between the top of the line and mosquito piss—" She coughed. "Our less expensive grade."

"So, Mr. Bald—" I drew another circle. "The man next door gets the inexpensive stuff?"

"Oh, not just him," Feng Gu said. "You have to be sensitive to each customer."

I looked over at her. I didn't remember her being sensitive to my presence the one time I'd come to buy tea. Perhaps she'd changed.

"Unless a customer really knows his tea, don't bother giving him the good stuff." Feng Gu used her hand to flip her hair back on either side, as if she had long, long tresses. "And then there's Madame Tsui Ping. She would think she was being poisoned if you gave her the good stuff."

"Why is that?" I asked. Was this another exaggeration? Perhaps that was Feng Gu's way.

"Although." Feng Gu tapped her head and smiled. "She had an education. Like you."

Feng Gu spat out those last words as if Madame Tsui Ping and I had done something dirty. Heat rose to my face. What was I doing, trying to be a good student in this rundown tea shop? I put my note pad and pen back in my purse.

"During the Cultural Revolution," Feng Gu continued. "The

woman was accused of being a spy for Evil America."

"Aiya," I said. "Why?"

"She taught English. She had a lot of English books in her house."

"What a shame," I said. Many educated people had been persecuted then. Each story was a sad tale. Especially those of the teachers.

"Yes," Feng Gu said. "She lost her job. They burned her evil books. Now she grows patriotic cabbage. She drinks piss-poor—the less expensive grade tea."

Feng Gu stood up to show me the different grades of tea. I followed. Waves of heat engulfed me as we stood away from the purring of the fan. This was certainly easier than standing in the park with my sign. But Feng Gu had an edge to her. A high-pitched edge. She seemed bitter like the first taste of tea. I missed the friendly chatter with Madame Paper Cutter.

All morning, Feng Gu giggled over my inability to weigh the tea with a brass measure, pointed out my error in sealing the bags too close, and barked at my slowness with the abacus. At the same time, she stroked her hair and told stories about the customers. So, by the time we sat down at the cherrywood table for a mid-morning cup of tea, I felt saturated. My ears hot. Infected.

"Yes, and you need to watch yourself," Feng Gu said, appraising me as I emptied the cold tea in the bucket. "Especially with that long hair of yours."

"Why is that?" Should I have put my hair up? Employees in some of the newer stores did that.

"The owner of Golden Dance Club," Feng Gu said, nodding her head up and down and pursing her lips. "Oh, he's harmless, if you know how to handle him."

What did that mean? Was that why Feng Gu's hair was short? Would I have to cut mine?

"He has a roving eye." Feng Gu leaned forward, her elbows on her knees. Her eyes sparkled as if in admiration. "In fact, he has so many women he doesn't know where to spread his seed next."

Like an overenthusiastic farmer. How did some people have so many possible mates? I had difficulty finding just one. I sprinkled some fresh tea leaves in the pot.

"That's too much," Feng Gu said, pulling on her hair. "You don't need that much. You're wasting leaves."

I took a few leaves out. Counted how many. Feng Gu appeared to be counting with me.

"Now, that's not enough." She wiggled on her stool, obviously wanting to reach across and fix the tea herself.

I counted out a few tea leaves into my hand. I put those back in the pot. I stood to go into the back for hot water. But Feng Gu's lips were tight as if she had just bitten into a sour plum.

"This isn't science class. You just need to feel the right amount." Feng Gu waved her hand toward the teapot. "Put a tad more back."

I stopped counting. I added a tad more. Had I added enough tea leaves?

"I'm going to the outhouse," Feng Gu said, standing up and heading for the back door. Perhaps she couldn't bear to watch me any longer.

After filling the teapot with hot water, I settled back down and pulled out my note pad. I mulled over the information I'd learned about the shop so far. They exported tea to Japan. They had income from relatives overseas. Their tea wasn't so overpriced people wouldn't purchase it. In fact, the tea tasted elegant. But where were all the customers? And what was I doing here? No. No. I didn't want to beat the ungrateful thoughts out of that blanket again.

I put the note pad away and took out my scissors and a fast food advertisement. I needed something mindless and quiet. I needed my cuttings. My fingers glided to the sharp point of the scissors. The sharp point.

Waipo had a story about sharp points. She first told me that story when I complained my high school math teacher ignored my raised hand when I had the answer. She told me that story again when another teacher moved me several rows back, despite my high grades. Of how she used to gather rice husks in big burlap sacks to use as kindling in the kitchen stove.

The light husks when added together in a burlap sack became quite a load. She would carry that load using a brass hook. Everyone used a brass hook—a sturdy, sharp brass hook. One day, she stood at the rice threshers stuffing her burlap sack when a thick pointy stick scraped her bare ankle. She kicked the stick out of the way and continued with her work. What was a stick doing out here anyway?

When her sack was full, she tied the bundle with a piece of rope. She reached down to the ground to grab her brass hook. It wasn't there. She had forgotten her brass hook. She stood there, her burlap sack bulging, at a loss as to how to get the bundle home. Her eyes spotted that pointy stick again. That useless pointy stick. She reached down and picked up the stick. It might just be strong enough to hold the bundle. She poked the sharp end through the sack and carried the bundle home.

She often told me I was like that pokey stick. That it was no matter people didn't expect certain things from me. They would one day find a use for what I could offer. I would eventually find my place in this world.

I cut a round shape. This, the first cut of the baby boy with the peach Madame Paper Cutter had taught me yesterday. Yesterday, the day I rode home on the bus and saw the strange Man In Blue. I still clung to a wisp of hope that this man was more than just one of the thousands of strangers in the village. In my heart, I hoped that Madame Paper Cutter's lessons were really predictions. The day she gave me the lucky crane, I'd been offered the chance of a mate. The day she gave me the peach boy of health and fertility, I'd seen Man In Blue. I made some snips on the pamphlet for toes.

Since the moment I'd walked down the aisle and off the bus, away from Man In Blue, I'd started looking for him. I'd looked for him around every corner. Expecting that, just because he filled my heart, he would fill my vision as well. He had to. I'd felt a connection with this man. With those dark brown smiling eyes.

I held the cutting up to appraise it. Certainly the crooked figure was not of a quality to show Madame Paper Cutter. Still, the act of cutting the little boy calmed my buzzing brain. My ears no longer vibrated from Feng Gu's high-pitched chatter.

"What's that?" Feng Gu returned, shaking water from her hands. "Looks like a ball someone sliced with a razor."

"Oh, it's nothing," I said. I put the cutting down. Poured Feng Gu a cup of tea. "A woman in the park—"

"You didn't pay money for that?" She whistled as she picked up the thimble full of amber liquid. She brought the fragile cup to her rough lips.

"No, no." There was no sense in trying to get out an explanation. "I was just practicing."

"You studied art?" She spat out a mouthful of tea. She stood over me, her mouth open as if she'd been punched. "Father said you studied business."

"No, no. I didn't study art," I said. What had Father told his *mahjong* buddy?

Feng Gu dropped her teacup on the table, her eyes shifting from me to the paper cutting. She didn't believe me.

"Well, whatever you studied, it certainly wasn't the art of tea preparation," she said, changing the subject. "The tea can't be left to steep for more than ten minutes or it doesn't taste any good."

I often drank tea that had steeped much longer. I'd never been bothered. Perhaps my taste buds were not discriminating enough.

"I can tell this has been sitting for—" She touched the side of the pot, put her head back. "At least twelve and a half minutes. Am I right?"

Should I have been timing the tea? All the time I'd instead been talking away my anger with Father, remembering Man In Blue, concentrating on making this "ball with the razor slits."

"It's a good thing." She spat into the bucket next to the table as if to rid her taste buds of the rancid lukewarm tea. "It's a good thing I'm not Old Man Department Store. We'd have lost his business forever."

Her prediction reminded me of Cheng Min, who could relate thousands and tens of thousands of disasters before anything happened. My old classmate hadn't been at home when I'd stopped by last night. Perhaps she'd already heard that Zi Mei now carried her secret, meaning the news would soon be in everyone's ears. Perhaps Cheng Min had already gone into hiding.

I poured the pot of tea out into the bucket. I couldn't imagine any customer with such an unforgiving nature returning to this shop. To Feng Gu and her Fashion Fortune Magazine. Still, I best try to remember. Mr. Department Store was a real connoisseur, as was Mr. Farmer. Mr. Baldy couldn't tell the difference. Neither could that crazy teacher named Tsui Ping. A thought tugged on the outskirts of my brain. Did any of these characters really exist? I hadn't seen a one all morning.

I held the teapot. Should I start over with new leaves? We never did at home. But then we drank lukewarm tea sometimes too. I looked up.

"You can use the leaves six to eight times," she instructed. "Unless they can't tell the difference. Like with Madame Tsui Ping."

I went in back to fill the teapot with hot water. I remembered to glance at my watch. Madame Tsui Ping, the crazy teacher. Did she miss teaching? Did she even remember teaching? The handle of the teapot felt too large. The quiet spaces in my brain filled with noise. My mind buzzed again.

"Are you having trouble filling the teapot," Feng Gu called.

"No, no."

"Don't they drink tea at college?" she called.

I ignored the jibe. This was just a temporary situation. Waipo had called me a sharp stick. I would poke through one day.

"I thought you got lost back there," Feng Gu said.

I sat down, glanced at my watch. The tea had been steeping for three minutes. Only three minutes had passed.

"You'll have to work faster than that," Feng Gu said. "You can't leave a customer out here by himself all that time. He'll help himself to a handful of tea leaves and be gone by the time you come back."

I nodded. Yet another rule that Feng Gu probably didn't adhere to. What made her so uptight?

"You want to take your time?" She stood. "Take your time on this."

She pulled a key chain from her back pocket and moved to the desk. She ran her hands over the dozen or more keys on the ring, picked out one, and unlocked the middle drawer. She removed a leather book. A book. Did she like to read? I had assumed the extent of her interest in literature lay in the pages of Fashion Fortune Magazine. I picked up the pot to pour her a cup of tea.

"Not yet." Feng Gu held up her hand. "Four and a half minutes. Not long enough."

Was she watching the clock? Or did she have an ingrained sense of timing? Would I ever know the exact moment to pour tea? And, by that point, would I be as bitter as she?

She took the teapot from me and gave me the black book. Not a novel. An accounting book. Over the next two steepings of tea, she talked of projected earning ratios and fiscal quarters.

"Business has been bad all year," Feng Gu concluded in a loud voice, as if talking to the ancestor in the back room, as well. She pointed to the figures on the book in front of her. "Father said you could help."

She didn't seem convinced. Neither was I. I nodded my head anyway, as if of course I was capable.

"Yes, although we received another offer of assistance from an—" She sniffed, probably stopping herself from using one of her colorful expressions. "A persistent person who knows our situation well. Father insisted you'd know best." She pushed her accounting book in front of me. "Well? What do you think?"

Feng Gu tapped the book. The figures added up correctly. She was a good mathematician. But was I to create a synopsis of their business from this? Deduce why they were losing money?

"Well?" Feng Gu asked again.

"There's more going out than coming in," I said.

"I knew it," she said, pulling the book from me. "I knew it."

She stood up, holding the book tight against her chest. I smiled. That had been simple.

"Are you sure you didn't study art?" she asked, obviously unimpressed with my summary of the situation.

"I'm sure." Heat rose to my cheeks.

She returned the book to the drawer and picked up a copy of Fashion Fortune Magazine from next to the abacus. She sat in front of me and flicked through the magazine. I felt as ignored as I had the only time I'd come into this shop to buy tea. Oh, Father, how could I work here?

"This kind of problem," I said. "This kind of problem takes time. There is no quick answer."

She turned a page and studied the make-up advice as if reading a sutra. What could I say? All morning not one customer had come in the shop. She had a lot of tea, delicious tea, but no customers. Maybe she'd offended them all, as she had me so long ago. As she attempted to do now. People in new China expected good service. Then again, maybe this was an afternoon place. Maybe customers didn't shop for tea in the morning. I couldn't imagine why not.

"I need to watch the daily business," I said, trying to get her attention away from plucked eyebrows. "See how things work here. Then maybe I can make a good suggestion."

She fingered through the magazine. Then she put her hand in her pocket and extracted a few *yuan* notes. She tossed them over to me.

"Sounds like a waste of more money to me."

"I understand," I said.

I picked up the bills—my morning's pay?—and went in back to collect my purse. Perhaps this was for the better. I wouldn't be able to take Madame Paper Cutter a sample of tea. But at least I'd get to work near her again. I'd get to teach her, if no one else. I'd go there this afternoon. Besides, she might have an idea where Cheng Min could stay safe until the birth of her baby boy. I didn't relish the idea of returning home. I could already hear Father, struggling with a shaky hand to light his cigarette, asking me to explain one more time how I only lasted two hours working at the tea shop.

"I'm not paying for more than two more hours of your time." Feng Gu tapped me on the shoulder with her rolled-up magazine. "If you want to stick around and watch my business, that's fine."

So, I wasn't dismissed. Yet. I turned to her. What if I came up with a solution to this failing business? But it took more than two hours? I couldn't afford to give her free reign of my time and ideas.

"That sounds fine," I said. She walked back toward the front room. "Unless." I cleared my throat. "Unless, I come up with an answer to your problem. Then you must pay all my hours."

"Unless." She snorted. "The art major comes up with an answer."

She had no faith in me other than that I could make a "ball with razor slits." But I had faith. I put my purse back beneath the cot. Took a deep breath. This sharp stick would be of use some day. Surely.

Chapter Seven
A Simple Cutting

My head pounded from a day of drinking tea at Drink Happiness Tea Shop. I drank. Feng Gu talked. The only customer we'd had was Zi Mei. Certainly there to gloat. I was tired and ready to go home. Instead I walked across the bridge. Past the hamburger shop with the lucky M. To the park.

A woman jostled against me with her plastic shopping bags. I passed a migrant worker hawking balloons shaped like cartoon characters—Mickey Mouse, the Monkey King, Hello Kitty. A man shouted on his cell phone. So many people. The tea shop was like a Buddhist monastery in comparison. Why did I feel so empty there?

I spotted Mr. Palm Reader examining the hand of an old woman. Next to them sat Madame Paper Cutter. She pushed her glasses up on her nose, then returned to a piece of paper. She wasn't cutting. She was writing.

"Chi bao le mayo?" I called to her. "Have you eaten?"

"Li Hui," she said, grabbing onto my hand. "Where have you been all day?"

I knelt down and glanced at her characters. They were legible but lacked confidence.

"Don't forget the dash on this one," I said. "I got a job."

"How fortunate." Madame Paper Cutter held onto my hand. "I knew you'd find a job here. Who's the lucky student?"

"Well, I'm not exactly—" I started. "I work in the tea shop across from the bus depot. Drink Happiness."

Madame Paper Cutter let go of my hand. She took up her scissors and a red piece of paper. Would she show me a new cutting? In celebratory red, no less.

"It's not exactly what I hoped for—" I explained. "But the place is losing lots of money. Father says I can help turn it around."

"That's great." Her voice lacked conviction.

"Well, it's a job," I said. Mother would frown at my candid words. But this was Madame Paper Cutter. "My boss isn't the most wonderful human being under the sky. All I did was drink tea and listen to her all day."

She replaced the red paper and took out a yellow piece. She cut a point. A bird's beak?

"I didn't show you how to do this one," Madame Paper Cutter said. With a snip here and snip there, she had cut up a simple outline of a bird in flight.

"That one I think I can do," I said. I took out my scissors and grabbed a fast food pamphlet from the ground. Snip. Snip. "There." I showed her my bird. "That's a simple one."

"Exactly," Madame Paper Cutter said.

"I could have churned out hundreds of these by now," I said. "Instead I've been struggling all afternoon on that baby boy with the peach. Why didn't you show me this one earlier?"

"A true teacher needs a true challenge," she said, looking down at the sidewalk.

I caught her double meaning. But I didn't enjoy any challenges standing in the park with a sign. Then again, I did get to teach Madame Paper Cutter. She always surprised me with her questions. "How can you remember so many strokes?" Or, "How should I hold the pen best?" I had to dig into my brain to discover an answer for her every time.

"Don't worry about me," I said, putting the bird cutting down. "Father's only trying to help. Besides, this is not a long-term kind of thing."

"They never are," she said and looked across the park. Her office. Her home. "I've been here three years already."

What did Madame Paper Cutter expect me to do? We needed cooking oil and matches in our kitchen. Besides I'd never work for bitter Feng Gu for three years.

"Who knows?" I said. "Perhaps I'll be back here tomorrow."

"Tomorrow," she said. She wrote the two characters that made up the word on her paper. Her hand moved so slowly, I had time to focus on each character—first the one for "bright" and then the one for "day." I'd never really thought of the separate meanings that created the word. Would tomorrow bring brightness? Clarity?

"Tomorrow." She circled the characters. Then she pushed her glasses up on her nose and smiled at me. "I'll save your space."

Madame Paper Cutter, despite her youth, was so wise. Her gentle manner gave me comfort. I would be back here tomorrow.

Chapter Eight
Mountain of Debt

There was a tapping on my leg, a shaking of my shoulder. The air smelled of steamed rice. I pulled my eyes open.

"You'll be late," a voice called. Mother leaned in through my mosquito net.

Morning and I wasn't eager to return to the tea shop. To move at all. I'd stayed up late, writing in my journal. I'd written of Cheng Min and how I hadn't recognized her, how she was in danger, how I hadn't been able to talk to her yet. I'd written of Feng Gu's tea shop, the air in the shop smelling desperate. How could I change that? I'd enclosed the simple bird cutting.

I felt sympathy for Feng Gu. How had she ended up being in charge of the family business? Her father was a *mahjong* player, like mine. However, wasn't there a responsible uncle? A brother? I couldn't make customer's flock to the store. Money appear. As Waipo would have said, laughing and shaking her head at Feng Gu's impossible problem, "Even the Emperor can't eat rooster eggs."

"Hurry now," Mother said, patting me on the arm.

"Ma." I nestled my head in my pillow. I still wanted to find out how Cheng Min was doing. I looked forward to the park and Madame Paper Cutter. "The tea shop. That's not really a job."

"Don't talk such nonsense." Mother swatted me with a wet rag. "Don't you dare talk such nonsense."

I sat up. Mother's eyes were red, swollen. What was wrong?

"You need that job." Mother looked at the mosquito netting, picking at non existent loose threads.

My heart raced. My palms sweat. I thought again to last night. Father had stumbled in late, kicking stools on the way to his room. Not the noises of a man who won big. But not an unfamiliar sound in our house.

"How much?" I asked.

Mother's eyes welled with tears which she brushed away with an angry fist. She kept that fist next to her cheek, shaking her head back and forth.

"How much?" I asked Mother again.

"A hundred and fifty *yuan*," she whispered.

Oh, gods. But I didn't really have a job. Feng Gu had offered me two more hours pay. Four *yuan*.

"How many times have I begged him to stop?" She rubbed one hand over the other. Frantic. "We don't have any more winning houses of tiles in our family."

"Yes, we do, Ma," I said, grabbing onto her hands, holding them tightly. She'd never spoken this way. "Yes, we do."

A hundred and fifty *yuan*. I saw the number everywhere. On the pages of the magazine, the tile floor, the tea bins. Even on the back of Feng Gu's cotton shirt as she visited the outhouse. Where would we find such a sum of money? All morning, the tea shop had been quiet. I was wasting my time sitting here. I would never turn this business around. Never earn any money.

A shuffling noise made me look up. An old lady hobbled in on a cane. Wisps of long white hair cascaded over her shoulders. She wore an old flowered dress that fell past her knees, but not far enough to cover sores on her legs. Was this the homeless woman from the hamburger shop? No. That woman didn't have gray hair.

"Can I help you," I asked.

"I don't know you," the woman said.

How abrupt. Was this a relative of Feng Gu's? Perhaps this was how everyone communicated in this shop.

"Feng Gu has stepped out for a moment," I explained. "She'll be back soon."

The woman didn't look in my direction or nod understanding. She wore rubber flip flops. She turned her back on me and shuffled over to the one-*yuan*-per-kilo bin.

"Back soon," she repeated. "Back soon."

She picked up a handful of leaves and inhaled the fragrance. Then she dropped the leaves back in the bin. She repeated this ritual several times. Each time as if she had just arrived. Perhaps she was senile.

"Can I give you a sample?" I asked, moving close to her. "Would you like to buy some tea?"

She backed away. Stuck her cane out toward me. I raised my hands, palms out.

"I don't know you," she said.

"Feng Gu will be back soon," I repeated.

I wanted to pat her on the arm. Reassure her. I returned to my seat at the cherrywood table. I'd fix the old woman a cup of tea.

While the tea steeped, I closed my eyes. Oh, Father. Father. Father. How could he dig our well so deep? I would never earn money here. Not a hundred and fifty *yuan*. Perhaps Zi Mei could offer us a loan. Again. But a hundred and fifty *yuan*?

"Did you say something," the old woman asked.

"No," I said. Perhaps I had mumbled.

"Yes, you did. You said a hundred and fifty *yuan*," the old woman said, her mouth scrunched up. "You think this tea is worth a hundred and fifty *yuan*?"

"No, no." I laughed. What a ridiculous thought. I poured her a cup of tea, indicating with my hand for her to come sit down. "I—I— was thinking out loud, I guess."

"That you would charge me a hundred and fifty *yuan*?" Her words came out so forcefully that spittle flew through the air.

"No. No." Perhaps this woman was more than just a bit old. I stood up and made a show of looking at the bin. "What's that tea? That tea over there is one *yuan*—"

"You don't know what tea and you tell me a hundred and fifty *yuan*," the woman said, leaning heavily on her cane. Her arms trembled.

"I'm sorry," I tried. "I was—ah—joking."

I went over to the one-*yuan*-per-kilo bin she indicated and put a handful of tea in a bag. Then another and another. I'd give this strange old woman a sample to take home. Quickly. Strange old woman. An alarm went off in the back of my head. Something Feng Gu had taught me yesterday. Madame Tsui Ping?

I glanced over my shoulder, relieved to see that the old woman— Madame Tsui Ping?—no longer stood there. So I'd lost a sale. Fortunately Feng Gu hadn't seen her come or go. I could imagine Feng Gu's high-pitched voice, "You were supposed to help me make this business better. Not get rid of the few customers I have."

A tapping sounded on the cement floor, and I turned. On the ground behind the cherrywood table sat the old woman. Her skirt had flown up to her thighs. Her gray hair covered her face. A shiver ran up my spine, as if a gust of air conditioning from the department store had entered my cotton blouse. I dropped the tea bag into the bin and scrambled over to the woman. Perhaps she had tried to sit down and fallen. Why hadn't I heard her fall?

"There's no problem, is there?" I knelt down.

The woman's arthritic legs were gnarled like the trunk of a banyan tree. I couldn't get her up without help from Feng Gu.

"There's no problem?" I repeated.

"Joking means not telling the truth," the old woman shouted. "Why don't you want to tell me the truth? I'm asking you one more time."

Oh, no. Oh, no. Oh, no. Certainly this was Madame Tsui Ping. She sounded as though she had fallen back in time to the Cultural Revolution. Was she recalling an interrogation by the Red Guards?

"I'm sorry, Madame Tsui Ping." I touched her arm.

"I don't know you." She flinched as if I'd held a torch to her jacket. "How do you know me?"

"What's going on?" Feng Gu came out of the back room, shaking water off her hands.

"I'm not sure." I stood up, relieved. "One minute she was standing behind me, then she was on the floor."

"Well, why don't you help her up?" She nudged me out of the way. "No wonder she's shouting."

"She—" I started. "She doesn't seem to want to get up."

"Nonsense." Feng Gu touched the woman's shoulder. "Tsui Ping?"

Tsui Ping didn't flinch this time. She stared straight ahead, rocking back and forth. Beads of sweat rolled down her forehead.

"Tsui Ping? The floor's dirty. You'll get sick down here. It's me. Feng Gu. Your tea seller."

"I don't know any tea seller," Tsui Ping shouted. "I'm not so elite that I drink tea. I only drink hot water."

"I've got some for you." Feng Gu pointed to the table where I proceeded to pour a cup of hot water. Feng Gu put her hand out to help Madame Tsui Ping up. The old woman spat on her.

Two young women stopped at the shop entrance. One of them had a purple mark over her cheek, like a permanent bruise. They both carried bags from the Eternal Happiness shop located around the corner. Customers? I took a few steps toward them.

"Can I help you?" I asked.

"Zi Mei mentioned we should stop by and have a cup of tea." The woman with the mark surveyed the shop, her head moving up and down like a bird. "That the place had new workers."

So Zi Mei really hadn't just come in to gloat yesterday. She had tested us. We had passed.

"Come in." I forced cheer into my voice.

"Looks like you're busy." The woman pointed at Tsui Ping and giggled. How could these women stand and laugh at the old teacher?

"Not to worry," I said, as if we always had Madame Tsui Ping on our floor. "I have some tea ready just for you."

"No thanks," this unpleasant woman said. "We'll come back another time."

But they didn't leave. They stayed by the edge of the door. They watched. Feng Gu knelt down next to Madame Tsui Ping and whispered to her. Madame Tsui Ping continued to rock back and forth, hugging herself.

A man drove his motorcycle up onto the sidewalk and turned off his engine. Something on the back of his bike was steaming. Buns? Meat? Noodles? Perhaps this delivery man didn't want to leave his motorbike to purchase tea. I moved away from the two women.

"Can I help you?" I asked him.

"Who is that?" he shouted over my head to the women. He pointed at Tsui Ping. "What did they do this time?"

This time? What other events had occurred here? I moved back toward Feng Gu to see what progress she was making. We had to do something. Tsui Ping was attracting a crowd.

"She must be getting worse." Feng Gu stood up.

"It's my fault," I whispered. "I was thinking out loud. Madame Tsui Ping—she thought, she thought I was trying to charge her the wrong price."

"How could you tell her the wrong price?" Feng Gu yelled. "She always orders the same one-*yuan*-per-kilo tea. You know that. What price did you tell her?"

"I wasn't—" I whispered. "I wasn't actually charging her. She heard me say a hundred and fifty—"

"What?" Feng Gu's eyes grew large. "A hundred and fifty *yuan*?"

The two women by the door giggled. I looked at them, wishing they would continue on with their shopping. But now there were more people. Even the migrant workers who set up shops on the street had come to watch. Too bad one of them wasn't a helper like Man In Blue.

"What should we do?" I whispered.

"I don't know." She looked outside to the street filled with staring people. She glanced at her watch and shook her head. The sounds of lunchtime traffic filled the air– motorcycles zooming up on the sidewalk, rickshaw driver's frantically ringing their bells, taxis blaring their horns.

"There's too much traffic for an ambulance," she said.

She was right. We were lucky, being in town, as now we had ambulances. Back in our side of the village, we would be left on our own. Still, the ambulances were too big to zoom in and out of heavy traffic. Their sirens were just extra noise. Nobody pulled over for them like they did in the movies.

Feng Gu's brow was furrowed. She pulled on her hair, as though grabbing onto a fortune stick at the temple.

"Maybe in a half an hour or so, we could call for one," I suggested.

"And in the meantime?" Feng Gu's voice was like a whip.

Feng Gu went over to the phone. Perhaps she would try for the ambulance anyway. I went back over to the crazed woman and bent down.

"Madame Tsui Ping," I said.

I didn't know what else to say. Come back to today? We're not Red Guards. We won't hurt you. Her eyes stared off, as though seeing something far away.

"Can I get you a fresh pot of tea?" I pointed to the ten-*yuan*-per-kilo bin. "It's our best tea. Let me make you a pot."

I stood up and headed toward the back room for more hot water. Feng Gu hung up the phone.

"Well?" I asked.

"Father will be here shortly." Feng Gu glared. "Maybe all your dreaming and theorizing would be good for a philosophy class. It's not helpful in selling tea."

Perhaps I was that Emperor who wanted to eat rooster eggs. Had Father found me a job which was not too easy, as Madame Paper Cutter suggested, but way above my abilities? My half of the sky had such dark clouds rolling in, I didn't know where to move.

"Well, what did you do last time this happened?" I asked.

"This," Feng Gu hissed pointing at the form of Tsui Ping on the ground, for that's all she was, a form, mumbling and laughing and mumbling some more. "This has never happened before."

Chapter Nine
The Best Fish Sauce

I went into the back room. Why hadn't I been more attentive? What could I do to make the demons in Madame Tsui Ping's mind go away? The demons that insisted she was a spy whose books, like *Gone with the Wind, Call of the Wild*, and *The Old Man and the Sea* must be filled with secrets from Evil America.

Last week's Fashion Fortune Magazine lay on the card table next to Feng Gu's lunch tin. Perhaps showing Madame Tsui Ping the latest styles would bump her heart out of the past. Then again, maybe she'd think I was joking. How could I have mumbled a hundred and fifty *yuan*?

Maybe Madame Tsui Ping was just hungry. Waipo had often said an empty stomach could make you mad. I looked through my purse. My wallet rested against the tea shop brochure Feng Gu had given me yesterday. Feng Gu had even pointed out the English paragraph on the back, as if to say she wasn't so dumb. I looked in my wallet. Empty. Perhaps I had some small notes in the bottom of my purse. Notes I could use to buy Madame Tsui Ping a pork bun, a treat.

The growing crowd of voices trading theories and gossip filtered all the way into the back. Madame Tsui Ping's cane bashed on the floor as if punctuating their thoughts. Then I heard a loud crash. I rushed out front to see the old woman pull down the last of the tea bins. The crazy old teacher sat surrounded by piles of tea. She'd knocked all the containers down, including the golden ten-*yuan*-per-kilo tea. She used her cane like a giant spoon and stirred the leaves together, as if making soup.

"This is all your fault." Feng Gu glared and pointed her trembling finger at me.

I had a momentary desire to run out the front door. But the crowd of onlookers now blocked the entrance to the shop. I sat down on the cold floor next to Madame Tsui Ping. Grit scraped my thighs. My heart thumped so hard it was difficult to breathe. I had to help this woman somehow.

"You must be hungry, after all your efforts." I dropped my purse in between us. I dug inside. I was sure I had at least one note.

"Would you like a pork bun? The woman across the street makes the best pork buns around."

Madame Tsui Ping joined me, digging in my purse. My dry well. Perhaps she thought this was a game. I didn't mind. She had stopped rocking back and forth, stopped staring so far away.

"I just need *wu mao*," I said. "Fifty cents."

A little boy wearing a dirty shirt and mud-stained pants rushed next to my feet. Madame Tsui Ping's grandchild? He grabbed a handful of tea.

"Shoo," Feng Gu yelled. "Get out!"

Madame Tsui Ping put her hands up, as if fearful Feng Gu would hit her. She began to rock back and forth again. The boy dodged through the crowd.

"You, too," Feng Gu cried. "Go. Just get out."

I looked up expecting to see another dirty little boy, but she was looking directly at me. Shame filled my entire being.

"No bad feelings, you understand," Feng Gu said, as if trying to remember she had the manners of a shop owner. She smiled, revealing all of her jumbled brown teeth. "But I have a business to run. It may not be a great intellectual challenge. But you've gotta pay attention. A hundred and fifty *yuan*. What the hell were you thinking? I mean, I mean no bad feelings. Just leave."

I had made such a mess of this simple job. My eyes prickled. I reached for my purse.

"I found it," Madame Tsui Ping cried, grabbing onto the strap of my purse. She extracted the tea pamphlet. Then she dropped it. "Just joking."

"It's okay," I said, patting her papery skin. "We don't need the *wu mao* right now."

"I found it." She grabbed the pamphlet again. "Just joking."

She held the pamphlet up, bringing the English portion so close to her face the paper almost touched her nose. I stood, brushing grit and stray tea leaves from my pants. Strange how something that happened so long ago continued to haunt the old woman—and now me. Nobody talked about the Cultural Revolution anymore. Father used that period, when the uneducated were given jobs as doctors and engineers, and the educated were sent off to the farms to do hard labor, as a reason why I shouldn't be educated. That, and the fact I was a girl and would scare off any potential mate.

He and Waipo had argued in whispers, as if transported back to

Revolution times, when a wrong word traveling on a breeze to the nearest child's ears meant trouble. A knock on your door at night, a search through your possessions that revealed something anti-establishment, a public shaming that led to death or suicide. Now the Cultural Revolution had cost me this job. Madame Tsui Ping murmured something. How would Feng Gu take care of this woman by herself? Why did I care?

"What did she say?" Feng Gu nudged me.

"I don't know," I said.

Now what would I tell Mother? I'd held her hands that morning and promised her we'd find a way out of Father's latest debt. She was counting on me.

"I thought you were educated." Feng Gu threw her short hair back. "Knew English."

Educated. Yes. Educated. So educated and still unable to hold up my portion of the sky. I bent over Madame Tsui Ping. She had stopped rocking back and forth. Her eyes were focused on the pamphlet.

"We have problem here," she said in English.

"What?" Feng Gu barked.

"A problem," I translated.

"Right here." Madame Tsui Ping tapped the pamphlet.

What was she talking about? Her eyes shone with the light of discovery, of tapping into something she'd forgotten she was good at.

"Good Luck and Prosperity Tea Company harvests tea on its northern tea plantations," Madame Tsui Ping read, her voice more confident with each word, as if reading before a class of children. "Twice a year, in summer and in winter."

The two young women at the front giggled at this dirty woman sitting on the floor, speaking foreign sounds. The rest of the group joined in. Feng Gu pretended to listen to Madame Tsui Ping, but her eyes roamed about at all that tea on the floor. How much money did each bin of tea cost? Would Feng Gu charge me for everything? Was I destined to be a well digger like Father? I hung onto Madame Tsui Ping's every word, waiting for this old English teacher to tell us the problem here. To return to our world. I didn't hear one. Maybe she was traveling into another darkened cave of the past. Was reliving her days when she stood at the front of a room and read the classics.

"Never mind," Feng Gu said, waving a dismissive arm at me.

"Really."

She looked up and over the crowd, searching for her father. Would he know how to deal with the old woman? Or would his efforts to help his daughter be as effective as a boy aiming his slingshot at a bus? Madame Tsui Ping laughed again, so hard her whole body shook.

"The summer harvest is the—" Madame Tsui Ping pointed to the pamphlet. "S-w-e-a-test. Get it? Summer? Sweat?"

I peered over Madame Tsui Ping's shoulder. She was right. That's what the pamphlet said.

English had lots of those confusing spellings. Like "beet" and "beat," and "feet" and "feat," and "meet" and "meat." It would be easy to mix up "sweet" and "sweat." In fact, the writer probably thought she was clever, having spelled the word with an a, showing off her ability to mix the vowels. Madame Tsui Ping wasn't so crazy after all.

"What is it?" Feng Gu stuck her mushroom nose in between us.

I showed the spelling to Feng Gu. Her eyes remained as blank as the stares of the crowd. She didn't get it.

"Madame Tsui Ping is a fine editor," I said, nodding my head with great exaggeration and smiling at the old woman.

"Of course she is," Feng Gu agreed. "I knew that already. Didn't I tell you she was an English teacher? Didn't I tell you a lot of things?"

"You didn't tell me," Madame Tsui Ping said. "Help me up from here. An old teacher shouldn't be left here on the floor like this to hear such things."

Feng Gu's eyes widened. Her mouth parted. This was our chance to get the lady off the floor.

"Well, you heard the teacher," Feng Gu said, grabbing the delivery man at the front of the crowd to help us. The three of us pushed and pulled, trying to get Tsui Ping to her feet, or at least to one of the chairs. She alternated between giggling like a schoolgirl and weeping.

"Tea, anyone?" Madame Tsui Ping smiled, when her bottom finally reached the stool. She looked about the room, as if it were her own great hall.

"No, thanks," the delivery man said. "I have to get back to work."

He hurried over to his motorcycle, fired up the engine, and

backed into the crowd, before Feng Gu could ask for more assistance. The rest of the crowd dispersed, now that there was nothing to look at but piles and piles of tea.

"My, this place is a mess." Madame Tsui Ping shook her head. "No rain for weeks—and now this. A typhoon." She giggled and picked at leaves that had stuck to the sweat on her legs.

"Yes, indeed." Feng Gu looked over at me as if I were the strong wind that had blown all the canisters off the wall. "Can my helper take you to the bus?"

"Oh, no," Madame Tsui Ping said. "I couldn't leave you with this mess."

"Don't worry," Feng Gu said, helping her up and leading her to the door.

"Of course not," she said. She picked a tea leaf from her elbow and held it up. "Did I ever tell you two ladies about the time I helped my father at the market?"

"I look forward to hearing that next time," Feng Gu said, patting Madame Tsui Ping's arm so hard I thought she'd make a bruise. "See you—"

"When summer changed to autumn, the mornings got so dark. I couldn't see, I tell you." Madame Tsui Ping came back into the center of the room, standing on a pile of tea leaves. She looked down at her swollen feet, her flip-flops, her toenails thick and yellow. "I couldn't even see my own two feet, it was so dark."

"That must have been frightening," I said.

Feng Gu glared at me. She gave a slight shake of her head as if to say "Don't encourage her."

"Actually, I didn't mind so much," Madame Tsui Ping said. "We all walk in the dark. We just don't know it. Yes, we all walk in the dark."

Feng Gu rolled her eyes. I refrained from uttering a word.

"One morning, I was so tired—or maybe I wasn't really concentrating. Who knows?" Madame Tsui Ping laughed until she had tears in her eyes. "I walked my bicycle right off the side of the road into a ditch. The entire basket of fish hooked to the back spilled everywhere."

She surveyed the pile of tea, as if staring into a ditch filled with fish. She rubbed her eyes. Shook her head.

"How horrible," I said.

I imagined young Madame Tsui Ping in charge of the day's catch.

What would she say to her father? That his fish was now sewage? Madame Tsui Ping latched onto our arms and pulled us together.

"Everything will be just fine," she whispered fiercely. Spittle formed at the edges of her lips. She gestured to the tea. "Don't worry about this."

"We won't worry," Feng Gu said, patting her on the shoulder and steering her in the direction of the bus depot.

As soon as Madame Tsui Ping was out of sight, Feng Gu sighed so loudly the walls of the shop groaned.

"Well, we survived that," she said.

She had said "we." Maybe, despite Feng Gu's sharp edge, she appreciated not bearing this business alone. I went to the back to retrieve a broom. I looked over at the black-and-white picture of the ancestor. I was no better helper than he. In fact, I was worse.

"What is it?" Feng Gu yelped.

I rushed out front. Madame Tsui Ping was back. She had tears streaming down her cheeks.

"Can my helper take you to the bus depot?" Feng Gu motioned with her arm for me to come help.

"No, no," Madame Tsui Ping said. "It's just I forgot to tell you the most important part of the story. The reason I told you the story in the first place." She chuckled long and hard, more tears running down her face. "Customers all commented on how it was the most unique fish sauce they'd ever tasted."

"This is a disaster." Feng Gu threw down the telephone receiver. She'd been on the phone for many minutes, trying to order more tea for the next morning. "Even Golden Supplies wants double the price, if I need the tea by tomorrow."

I picked up my purse from the floor and draped it over a stool. I had swept all the tea into one neat pile. I was out of line making suggestions to the boss. But then I sensed I didn't have many days left in this shop. As soon as Feng Gu calculated all that I had lost, I would be gone.

"Maybe you should forget it," I said.

"This isn't like some paper you can just decide not to write," she said, shaking her finger at me like a stick, her nose high in the air. "Some test you can decide not to take." Had she been denied an education? Was that what gave her such a sharp edge? "Some class you can decide not to go to. If I don't have tea, I don't have a business." She sighed, banging her hand on the side of the desk. "No business."

Despite her bitter edge, I felt sadness for her. She kept this ship afloat all on her own. Now the ship was sinking.

"Remember what Madame Tsui Ping said?" I suggested. Perhaps she hadn't been listening. Perhaps she didn't think the situation applied to her.

"How could I forget?" Feng Gu said. "In fact, the whole town probably knows about Tsui Ping by now. That's why I can't get a good price on the tea."

I picked up a dustpan full of tea and dumped the contents back into the bin.

"What are you doing?" she asked. "Go on and dump that out in the alley."

"It was the most unique fish sauce the customers had ever tasted," I said. I picked up another dustpan full of tea.

"I can't believe you," she said. "No, I take that back. I can't believe Father. What made him think I'd benefit from having a college graduate helping me? He might as well have sent me the village idiot."

"We can call it the Professor's Medley," I persisted. "After Professor Tsui Ping."

"What's a medley?" She asked. "Some kind of disaster?"

"No, no," I said.

Poor Feng Gu. She did her best, without help from anyone. Her father, despite her calls for help, had chosen to stay and finish whatever his "business" was. Perhaps he took his game of *mahjong* as seriously as Father.

"A medley is a mixture," I said.

"Why would we mix up dirty tea, then tell the customers that's what we've done?" Feng Gu shook her head. "Do you think Tsui Ping told her customers that the fish sauce she sold was fish mixed with ditch water?"

"It's not just mixing." I cleared my throat. "It's a fine mixture, an elegant mixture." I stirred the leaves in the bin with my free hand, pulled out a stray hair.

"That's ridiculous." Feng Gu grabbed the dustpan from me. "You stop by tomorrow. By then, I'll have worked out the bill for all of this."

"Fine," I said. "I'm sorry. I really am."

I went into the back room to collect my lunch tin. My hands, which had reassured Mother just hours before, felt like dull, dead branches. Useless. A fire hazard. I grabbed the tin with trembling fingers. I headed for the back exit.

"What are you doing here?" Feng Gu said.

Feng Gu's voice was sharp, angry. I paused at the door. A man's voice replied. Deep, soft. Had her father finally left his house of tiles? How could she speak to her elders that way?

"You're too late." Her voice was nervous. "You're always late for everything."

Well, almost everything. There was still the matter of what to do with the new employee—me. But I didn't stay for my public shaming. I went out the door.

The thick smell of incense from the Eternal Happiness store filled the alley. A woman walked by, her high heels tapping lightly on the pavement. The sound was like laughter, like the sound of those young ladies in the crowd today giggling at Madame Tsui Ping. The woman carried her small boy in one arm, held a bag of fish in the other. What would be so wrong with mixing the tea? Certainly it was different than selling people sewage sauce. People would rinse the tea once before drinking a pot anyway. Any sweat from Madame Tsui Ping's bottom, any dirt from the floor, would wash away.

But Feng Gu was stubborn. The only good ideas were hers, not those of some foolish college graduate. Father would be so disappointed in me. Here I had studied four years and had lost the one job he'd found me. I had nothing to offer, not even *wu mao*—the fifty cents—in my purse. I felt for the strap. My purse. I'd left the bag on the stool in the front room of the tea shop.

I stood still and closed my eyes. I didn't want to go back in that shop, especially with Feng Gu's father now there. But I felt as if Waipo were near, reminding me of my manners. "Of course you should at least thank Feng Gu's father for offering you the opportunity. Apologize for the disaster. That would be the right thing to do." A gentle breeze like the hand of Waipo urged me back toward the shop.

I hurried through the back room certain that if I stopped to listen I would lose what little nerve I had. I raced out front. A strange tickling started in the lower part of my back and traveled down my knees. A snatch of blue cotton. A white t-shirt. That tall muscular body. Man In Blue was just leaving. What had he been doing here?

Feng Gu sat at the cherrywood table, her eyes no longer focused on the heaps of tea. Her eyes not apparently focused on anything. I approached the table. She jumped.

"You're still here? What are you doing here?"

"I forgot my purse," I explained, picking the leather bag off the stool. "Besides, I thought I heard voices. I thought Madame Tsui Ping might have returned."

She stared into her empty teacup. Was she recalling each gesture, each word Man In Blue had made? Did her heart beat like big war drums?

"So," I said. "I guess I didn't hear any customers."

"No." She grabbed the rag from the side of the bucket and wiped at the table. "No Madame Tsui Ping. No customers buying tea. No business. No business at all."

"Tomorrow," I said, remembering Madame Paper Cutter's handwriting. The two characters that gave such hope.

"Word's out all over about the incident with Madame Tsui Ping." Feng Gu pulled on her hair and shook her head.

"Tomorrow," I whispered to myself, like a prayer to the gods.

Chapter Ten
A Thief Among Us

I walked down the main road toward home. The bus ride home had been one big blur. I kept hearing the swish of Man In Blue's trousers as he left the tea shop. I kept seeing Feng Gu's blank face, her high-pitched voice telling me that, "No, no one had come into the shop."

Prehistoric Lady wasn't out watering her plants. Was she somewhere taking care of Cheng Min? I still hadn't had a chance to talk to my old classmate. I would try once again, as soon as I stopped at home and let Mother and Father know I was home. I looked forward to another visit with my sweet-spirited old friend. I walked up the steps past Zi Mei's.

"You're back," Zi Mei called, coming out.

"I'm back," I said.

"Did you have new customers today?" Her eyes shone like a child who had finished a drawing.

"Yes," I said, remembering the woman with the purple scarred face.

"I sent them to you," she whispered, as if someone were listening. "That's a good tea shop, a good family," she said patting my arm. "You're going to do just fine."

If it was such a good tea shop, why did she have to round up customers? Why did she think I'd be fine there, when Madame Paper Cutter felt I was cheating myself? Just wait until she discovered the latest disaster. I patted Zi Mei's arm back. Tomorrow, I thought.

Father wasn't sitting in his chair. The ashtray was absent of any use. Perhaps he had stayed away all afternoon.

"You're back." Mother came shuffling out of her room. The skin around her eyes was still puffy. She clutched onto my hand.

"Ma," I said. I hated to tell her what I'd done. But then why give her false hope? She deserved more than that. "Ma, there was an incident at work today."

She returned to her room. Perhaps she didn't want to know how dark my sky was. Perhaps she couldn't bear to hear anything other than good news. She returned.

"Ma," I started.

An explosion from the quarry sounded too loud. Too close. Mother clutched my hands.

"Don't worry." She held a thick envelope in her hands, like joss sticks at a temple. She held up the letter. "Maybe you won't need that job for long."

She passed me the letter. The contents bulged so, the lip of the envelope had been taped down. A colorful stamp of a tropical bird indicated that the letter was from Singapore. Guo Qiang. Despite the losses of the day, I felt warm. Full. Was this how Father felt when he thought a win was on the horizon?

I sat under my mosquito net, a pillow propped behind my back. My fingers pried the envelope open, then pulled out the letter. One-two-three-four-five-six pages. Gooseflesh covered my arms.

"That was better than a video game," a child shouted, as he ran by beneath my window. "Kaboom!"

Guo Qiang's characters were strong, firm. He had divided his letter into different parts, like a thesis. Work. Culture. Food. How professor-like. I looked at the Work section first. Guo Qiang's description was so full of big words I felt as though I'd been transported back to my dorm room. One of my roommate's had studied computer science. But even she didn't use all of these words. I skipped to the Culture section. He wrote again of how the government provided housing for everyone, of how they mixed the races together, so not too many people of one race stayed in one place. Had he forgotten that he'd already told me this? Or maybe this bothered him as much as it did Mother.

He wrote again of his colleague's wife, Lee Sa. The other night, he said, while he had been visiting their apartment, playing Chinese chess, loud noises erupted from outside. Some kids played a game called Spetakra, a game which reminded him of ping-pong, only you played not with a paddle, but with your feet. He went into a lengthy explanation of the history of the game, which originated in Malaysia and was played in Singapore, mostly by Malay teenage boys. Lee Sa had been upset by a group of boys playing the game outside their apartment. It was late. Their son couldn't sleep for the noise the teenagers created. Guo Qiang had offered to go down and talk to the boys on his way home.

I put my head against the wall. So he did have a bit of that helpful spirit in him. Just like Man In Blue. What had Man In Blue been doing at the tea shop today? The memory of his voice from the bus made my spine tingle. I looked at the letter again.

When Guo Qiang went down to talk to the teenagers, the man who guarded the apartment building suggested calling the police instead. I stared at the rice paper. The police? We never called the police in on matters. They created only more trouble.

Zi Mei had once told me of her friend's cousin who had come home from America for the Lunar New Year with his wife and child. It had been years since he'd been back to the village. So much had changed. So many things he'd forgotten. The day after the Reunion Dinner on New Year's Eve, he had been helping to return some chairs borrowed from the community center when a bunch of thugs kidnapped him. His wife went to the police station for help. That's what you did in America. The officer informed her that it was the Lunar New Year and nobody was available to investigate this unfortunate incident. To come back in a week. Unless she really needed help. For a thousand *yuan*, he could help her. She turned around and went to the American Embassy. They caught the thugs, and the man and his family returned to America. Even though the words came from Zi Mei's mouth, most of it was probably true. Was Singapore with its big Chinese population, over 80% Guo Qiang had written, more like China? Or America? I returned to my place on the page.

"You know what the police asked?" Guo Qiang wrote. I couldn't imagine. In the rich country of Singapore, how much money would the police ask for to help out? Five thousand *yuan*? Ten thousand? "They asked, 'What is the race of the people playing the game?' They wanted to be sure to send the police officer of the correct race—just so there would be no doubts about fairness. As Mother always says, a common culture shares common understanding." His mother sounded wise. Like Waipo.

"Li Hui?" Mother called from downstairs.

"Yes?" I said. Singapore sounded so strange. Like a storybook. I wanted to read more.

"Li Hui?" Mother called again.

"Coming." I put the six pages of this story back into the envelope and went downstairs.

"There's been an accident," Mother said.

The dynamite. The excited voices. Kaboom.

"Where?" I asked. "The quarry?"

"No," she said, handing me what first aid supplies we had available—the last of Father's rice wine for anesthesia, some rags, some of the blood-stopping medicine *Yunnan Bai Yao*. "Up to Third Uncle's place. An engraving machine exploded."

"What?" I asked. How did an engraving machine explode? Had Zi Mei gotten Mr. Grumble in trouble with Third Uncle? What had the short-tempered employee done?

"Or something." Mother pushed me out the door. She would stay behind to keep the house safe from anyone who might take advantage of all the excitement and drop in on a house or two. She pushed me across the courtyard. "Something exploded."

Dusk blanketed the village. Darkness would envelop us soon. The heat of the day had given way to a light breeze. Were evenings cool in Singapore as well? I ran down the steps next to Zi Mei's. Her son Don Don stood behind the shop door, his face pressed against the window. His eyes wide with fear. Poor man. Had she left him to guard the shop? How much did he understand?

At this time of night, the good clinic would already be closed. Only the ones without real doctors or good medical supplies remained open. Hopefully Third Uncle didn't need real medical attention. Two men headed toward me, their voices loud. But not shouting for help loud. I heard laughter. Perhaps nothing bad had happened.

As they neared, I recognized one of them as Fifth Uncle's adopted son. Fifth Uncle had a temper like a rabid dog, especially after his son had been killed in a factory accident. This new son quickly adopted not only Fifth Uncle's surname, but his temper. In fact, the son was worse. He shot birds out of trees. He hammered frogs to the community ping-pong table. He poured oil on the streets and laughed while people slipped and fell. I couldn't imagine being surrounded by people of different colors and races like in Singapore. We had enough trouble getting along as one race, one people.

"Kaboom." He laughed, pushing his buddy—a man I didn't recognize—toward a cow paddy on the street.

"Enough already," the man said.

"What's going on?" I asked, my voice stern.

Certainly Fifth Uncle's son hadn't blown up one of Third Uncle's engraving tools? Certainly he had some respect for his adopted family.

"What's it to you, little sister?" Cousin came close. "Oh, Li Hui. It's you."

He smelled of cigarettes and beer. He wore chains on his imported American jeans. His hair stood spiked up with gel, making him look like a porcupine.

"I heard something was going on up at Third Uncle's," I said, gripping tight to the bottle of rice wine.

"I don't know anything about that." He eyed the wine. "We weren't invited."

"No, no," I said. "The explosion. Mother said an engraving tool exploded."

"What?" Cousin hooted. "Did you hear that?" He punched his friend in the arm. "An engraving tool exploded."

"Or something," I said. Mother's explanation had sounded funny to me as well. But then, I'd been immersed in the six-page letter, the storybook world of Singapore. I was eager to return and learn more. I still had the Food section to read. With my free hand, I pushed a strand of hair away from my face. "We heard something."

"What you heard, Cousin, came from the prehistoric bat's place."

Prehistoric Lady? But she didn't even use chemicals. What could have caused such an explosion? I looked in the direction of her house, out over the fields, the fields she watered each day with buckets of well water and no chemicals. The dark sky was darker over there. Smoke billowed upwards. Small bits of light—flames?— taunted the night sky. What could have exploded?

"Oh, my mother," I said.

"Yeah," Cousin agreed. He put his hand out and grabbed onto Father's wine bottle. "Don't think anyone's going to need this."

"What do you mean?" I pulled the bottle away from him. A metallic taste singed the back of my throat.

"Well, the prehistoric bat was at the Community Center," he said. "And that eunuch son of hers was in town."

"That's good," I said. Perhaps no one needed help. I swallowed. "So no one got hurt."

"I didn't say that," Cousin sang as he walked away. "Just not the son and his mother."

I gripped the rice wine and ran through the fields. How could this be? I'd just seen Cheng Min on the bus, peeling a pear for her daughter and sharing the fruit with me. Surely she wasn't hurt. I slowed at the edge of the field where by the light of the rising half moon, neighbors wet down the rice field. The smell of smoke and something more pungent choked me. Cheng Min's house stood as always, save for a gaping hole that had widened the front door and strewn a wall calendar, a table, and a pot of rice outside.

I jostled in between the gathering neighbors and relatives, my mind numb. I listened to the voices. Had she left her gas cooker on and fallen asleep? Had her husband angered the wrong people? Had he been stockpiling dynamite to sell to quarries on the black market? I felt metal in my hands. A bucket of water. I put the rice wine down on the ground and used both hands to toss the water over the brown rice paddy. On the dry stalks which beckoned to the sparks floating through the air near Cheng Min's front door.

Where was Cheng Min now? Was she already at the clinic with no good doctors? Had she even been home? And what of her daughters? I tossed my bucket down and reached for another. The full bucket felt light in my hands.

"We're gonna be out of water soon, if you don't be more judicious," a voice reprimanded.

"Yes, don't use so much," another voice added. Zi Mei.

"Where is she?" I asked, holding out my hand. She grasped onto my fingers.

"The hospital," Zi Mei whispered, as though divulging a secret. She had probably repeated this information many times over. "The children were eating dinner when it happened."

"When what happened?" I asked.

"The children were eating dinner when it happened," Zi Mei repeated. "They're, well, the family will have to hire a priest to do a special ceremony and make their spirits whole again."

"Oh, my mother," I said.

Perhaps Zi Mei didn't know what had happened. It didn't matter. I imagined the two little girls, their small bodies blown to bits along with their souls. Poor Cheng Min. I dipped my hand in the water bucket. The water felt cool. Like a miracle.

"I hear the mother was with happiness," the woman next to Zi Mei said.

"Yes," Zi Mei said. "I didn't say anything to anyone, though."

She'd told me. Was I the only one? Was I disappointed she hadn't had a chance to tell this story while it was still good gossip?

"It's a good thing none of the fields got hit," the woman said, passing Zi Mei another bucket of water.

"Or my store," Zi Mei agreed.

"Hit?" I asked. The ground beneath my feet felt fragile. The night air vulnerable.

"Taiwan," Zi Mei said in a conspiratorial tone.

"Taiwan?" I asked.

Taiwan was like an arrogant child, like Adopted Cousin and his spiked hair, his fancy jeans, his chains. Ever since that thief Chiang Kai-shek had escaped there in 1949 with all of China's jewels, as if he'd discovered his own private island, he'd screamed for independence. That would be like me locking myself in my room with all the family's heirlooms—not that we had any—and claiming independence from the household.

Taiwan was so small though. Advertising was their normal method. Erecting large signs on the beach across the sea, welcoming people to wonderful Taiwan. Or dropping leaflets extolling the virtues of an independent country. Surely they wouldn't nudge a sleeping dragon by dropping bombs. That sounded as plausible as the exploding engraving tool.

"There's no logic to it." Zi Mei laughed, as if reading my mind. "But then they've never been logical."

My skin tingled. Surely this was just village nonsense. Besides, why our village?

"Shouldn't we take shelter?" I asked.

"No, no," Zi Mei said. "We don't need to do that. The village loudspeaker would warn us."

I threw one last bucket of water on the field. Most of the fire was out. The lingering sparks would die off soon.

"I'll be back in a moment," I said. I ran off to find Father and Mother and shelter for us all.

Chapter Eleven
Three Hundred Grams of Silver

Dense smoke filled the room of the local Seniors' Club. Men lay on cots, shirtless, fanning themselves with old bamboo squares while they waited their turn to play. Others sat four to a table, staring at cards or *mahjong* tiles. Would these men even pay attention to a warning from a loudspeaker. If such a warning came? I stood on the threshold. Where was Father? I needed to find him.

A man near the door called to me, pointing to the back of the room. I put one scuffed shoe inside. Then another. I felt as if I were rushing into a classroom late. I didn't belong. Should know better than to interrupt.

Was Feng Gu's father here as well? Had he heard the news from the tea shop? Madame Tsui Ping's outburst in the tea shop a few hours ago seemed like dust in the wind compared to the solid brick of an old classmate struggling to survive. Of her two daughters, whom she'd protected from polio and mumps and scrapes and falls, disappearing in less time than it took to step outside and test the firmness of a bunch of peanuts the neighbor had clipped from her fields. Those solid bricks of pain hit me right in the face. Made my nose burn.

I spotted Father playing a game of *mahjong* with three other men. None of them Feng Gu's father. One man mixed the *mahjong* tiles with both hands, the clickity-clacking sound like water rushing over pebbles. The other two sat back and lit fresh cigarettes. They must have just finished their game. What good timing.

"This time be more careful," Father said to the tile mixer.

The man didn't look up. He ignored Father. The air was filled with electricity, like that before lightening strikes.

"Did you hear me?" Father asked. "Last time, you—"

"You better hold your words, Mr. Huang." The man leaned forward over the white plastic tiles, his face swollen with anger.

"Father." I grabbed onto his arm. He smelled of drink, perhaps too much. "We must go. Now."

"Curfew." The tile dealer spat. The other two men laughed, one of them revealing two gold front teeth. "Your keeper has come to take you home."

"I'm not finished playing," Father said.

Father shook off my hand. He didn't appreciate the implication that he was less than in charge of his own destiny. How could I get him to listen? Certainly a night of *mahjong* wasn't as important as a night of safety. At least until we discovered what dragon threatened our peaceful village.

"This is important," I said.

"So is this." Father nodded toward the door, dismissing me. "I'll come later."

"But, Father," I said. "There was an explosion. Rumor has it Taiwan attacked us."

"What?" Mr. Dealer stopped mixing the tiles.

"Didn't you hear the kaboom?" I said, using Cousin's description. "Two people are already dead. According to Zi Mei, Taiwan is attacking."

"Zi Mei would know," the man with the gold teeth said, his voice filled with sarcasm. His white shirt was unbuttoned. A worn but clean undershirt peaked out. He tossed his cigarette to the floor and glanced at the dealer. "Now, deal."

"Aren't you concerned?" I asked.

"Did you hear a plane go by?" the gold-toothed man who disdained news from Zi Mei asked.

I hadn't thought of that. Then again I had been more concerned with the tea shop disaster, with Mother's swollen eyes, with the letter from Singapore.

"I didn't," Mr. Non-Believer continued, flashing his gold tooth in a smile. "How does one drop a bomb without a plane? Didn't they teach you that in college?"

The men laughed. Father included. I would never get him to leave.

"What if it was a gang?" I said.

"You speak some sense," Mr. Non-Believer said, arranging his house of tiles. "But certainly they wouldn't attack a bunch of old turtles playing *mahjong*. Care to stay and be safe with us?"

This community center didn't feel safe to me. Lights blazed, making the building a beacon in our otherwise dark village. My idea of safety was to find First Uncle's underground hide-out. He had built the shelter when Evil America threatened us. Weeds must have grown over it by now. But Father could locate the place. He had helped dig the small spot.

"Father?" I patted his arm.

How could these men sit here as if I'd said nothing more than a summer rain is coming? "Oh, we won't get wet," they'd say. "We're safe here." But this wasn't just a summer rain. Surely Father would come home, if nothing more than to reassure us.

"Go home, Li Hui," he said. "I just need to finish this game."

I hoped Father meant what he said. That he'd be home soon. I hoped Mr. Non-Believer was right. That there was nothing to fear. I returned to the darkness of the night.

New Neighbor's winding dragon of rocks felt soft and useless beneath my feet. Why hadn't the man's luck extended down the road to Cheng Min? I stepped into our courtyard. The night air was still. Cloying. Sweat pasted dirt on my ankles. I would need to wash. Two big branches, where we hung our daily laundry, stood like sentries at the door.

"Li Hui?" Mother called out from behind the closed door. "Is that you?"

"I'm home," I said.

"I was worried." She unbolted the lock, her face relaxing into a smile. "What took so long?"

"The explosion was up at Prehistoric's place," I said, taking her arm and walking in the house. My clothes smelled of smoke. My hands were muddy from the buckets. "Her granddaughters both...."

"What?" Mother's face crumpled. She shook her head. "How?"

"No one knows," I said. I debated repeating Zi Mei's theory. "No one knows."

"And the rest of the family?" she asked.

"Her daughter-in-law is at the hospital," I said.

"Oh, my mother," she said. Tears pooled in her eyes. "That girl had happiness. Zi Mei told me just the other day."

A shiver ran over the back of my neck. Zi Mei's statement rang in my ears. "I didn't say anything to anyone, though," she'd said like the thief who stole three hundred grams of silver.

Once Waipo hadn't come in from the fields at lunchtime. I had eaten my rice. I had looked over at her bowl filled to overflowing. Surely she wouldn't notice if I nibbled off a few grains from the top. I had nibbled a little, then a little more. When she had finally stepped into the courtyard, only a few mouthfuls of rice remained in her bowl.

"I didn't eat the last of your rice," I said.

She smeared dirt across my skin as she grabbed onto my arm. She held me there, her whole body shaking. Not with anger. With laughter.

"You ever hear of the thief who stole three hundred grams of silver?" she asked, pulling me close to her sweat-soaked body. "The police knocked on everyone's door asking if anyone knew about the crime. When they got to one man's door, the first words out of his mouth were, 'I didn't steal three hundred grams of silver and bury it in the backyard.'" She patted my belly, swollen with food. "That's exactly where the police found the stolen money. You sound like that thief."

Zi Mei had sounded like that thief, as well. Who had she told about Cheng Min's third happiness? Why had she felt guilty? What had it to do with the explosion?

"Cheng Min will be fine," I said, patting Mother's arm. I hoped. I saw the image of my old classmate fanning her baby with the discipline book. I wanted to reach out and touch them one more time.

Mother had been so upset about Prehistoric Lady's family that, after I took a quick shower, I went to her room. I should have used the time together to tell her of my terrible mistake at the tea shop. But I couldn't bear to give her anymore bad news. I had pulled out Guo Qiang's letter instead. Mother patted the bamboo mat on top of her bed. The tiles of bamboo were cooler than a sheet. Still, as I sat next to her at the bottom of the bed, my thighs sweat beneath my nightgown.

I knew she wouldn't want to hear about the Culture anymore. All those races living together. That frightened her. I skipped to the work section. Work. Why wasn't Father here helping me with Mother? Why did he always leave her—us—alone to deal with everything? How could he stay back and continue to hope for a winning set of tiles, leaving Mother to worry about how deep our well was? How safe we were?

"He works with computers," I explained.

"Computers?" Mother asked. Her hands twisted and re-twisted a rag. She wiped her palm across her eyes. "What is this?"

"A kind of machine. You can do all sorts of things with them. He programs—"

"Wa—so many pages," she said, fingering the letter. "What an intelligent man."

She wasn't interested in computers. Especially now. I skipped to the Food section.

"Listen here. This is interesting. 'Everyone eats different foods. The Malays have their own style of cuisine. The Indians theirs. There is an array of Chinese food from Cantonese to Fujianese.'"

"So much food." Her eyes teared. Was she thinking of the little girls who would never eat food from this world again? Was she worried about Cheng Min?

"On top of all these choices," I continued. "There is foreign food."

"Foreign food?" Mother asked. "Isn't Indian and Malay food foreign?"

"I think he means foreign as in Western." I read further. "He says, 'Even when the ingredients are the same, I am continually amazed by the variety of consumption methods. A dear friend of Lee Sa's.'" I looked up from his letter. "That's his colleague's American wife. 'A dear friend of Lee Sa's loves fried shrimp, but people in the village would cry out at the way she eats them. She always throws away the heads and tails, only eating the meat inside.'"

"No," Mother said, dropping her rag. "All those nutrients? Someone throws that away? Are you sure you didn't read it wrong?"

I repeated the lines slowly, showing her each character as I read. On this second reading, I noted that he didn't mention a variety of consumption methods. Only this dear friend of Lee Sa's. Perhaps he'd just wanted to tell me this story. Mother tapped the letter as if the thin pages were Guo Qiang, and she was patting his arm.

"That's the most ridiculous thing I've ever heard." She laughed. The sound was not like the hysteria that had erupted from Madame Tsui Ping's lips. Nor the nervous bubbling that came from Zi Mei. Her laughter was like the comforting clinking of a goat's collar. Like home. Safe home. Safe from smoke, hospitals, gangs, and the thief and his silver.

The following morning, Mother followed me outside. The sun had picked its head up off the earth, just barely. The air gave off a coolness that made me shiver. A rooster gave a sorrowful crow.

"Go carefully," she said, not letting go of my arm.

Her fingers touched my skin with warmth. Surely she'd follow me out to the road, would wait with me until the bus arrived to take me to the tea shop. Darkness circled her eyes. Her face looked crumpled. Had she sat up most of the night, weeping for the loss of the babies, as if they were her own? Waiting for Father to return? My skin tingled. Why had the gods pulled two of us away? Those baby girls were so little, so innocent.

We passed Zi Mei's, where a larger-than-usual crowd sat smoking and speculating in hushed voices about Taiwan. All except Don Don. He held a broom against his shoulder as if it were a rifle and marched back and forth in front of the shop like a sentry. I gulped down the cool morning air. Like the neighbors, I preferred the idea of an outsider displaying such violence. We could band together against an outsider.

But I kept hearing Zi Mei's words in my head. "I didn't say anything to anyone." I kept recalling Mr. Non-Believer's voice. "Did you hear a plane?" I kept remembering Madame Butcher and the rough treatment she had received when she tried for a third child. I kept seeing that front door—the face of the house, the face of the family—torn away. Perhaps this had been a message, a warning, which had gone too far.

Mother and I didn't look off to the south where the ruins of Cheng Min's house blotted the earth like mold on a bun. Not looking, we could erase the fire, the charred babies, the uneasiness in our stomachs. We could pretend this was any other normal day.

We'd be at the road where the bus came soon. I'd be back at the shop. Strange how that debacle felt like relief. How big would our new debt be? We passed the stone engravers. Had Prehistoric Lady already put in an order for headstones? One wasn't supposed to have to bury their own grandchildren.

Mother held onto my arm. Sweat formed beneath her fingers. Like tears. Maybe I couldn't hold up my half of the sky and, in fact, my half of the sky was about to fall around me like all that tea in the tea shop. But Mother loved me.

"Go carefully," she said again.

Chapter Twelve
The Professor's Medley

The metal floor clanked as I walked up the aisle of the bus. The cushion wheezed as I sat down next to a woman fixing the handle of her plastic shopping bag. In front of us a group of schoolboys looked at their notes. The man behind me smoked cigarettes, one after another, after another. None of them seemed concerned about Taiwan, about bombs, about houses with their faces torn off. Or even about a tea shop that had lost all its tea. This was just another day.

The bus passed a man on his bicycle, wobbling from the weight of a dead pig tied to the back. Was someone getting married? Perhaps this pig was for a funeral. Or two. Or three. Had Cheng Min survived the night? The woman next to me picked up her bag and shook it back and forth. The knot she'd made in the handle came undone. She turned to the man behind us.

"Let me use your lighter," she said putting out her calloused hand.

Was this her husband? Husband's friend? Or was this woman just very bold? I wished for some of that boldness now. I would need some of that boldness to stop thinking of Cheng Min. I would need some of that boldness when dealing with Feng Gu. We couldn't afford to pay a big tea bill. I still needed a job. Perhaps she'd let me work our debt off. My insides felt as firm as the smoke that surrounded me.

The man passed his lighter to her, and she lit a flame beneath the plastic handles of her bag. Burned the handle pieces together. The smell made my nose twitch. I saw Cheng Min's house again. I shook my head to eradicate the images of the little girl sitting on her mother's lap, of pear juice brushing against my shoulder, of Cheng Min's kind voice telling me I was still pretty, so intelligent. Of the gaping hole that used to be a front door. Why hadn't I pursued Cheng Min until I found her? If I'd been more persistent, she might have avoided the explosion.

The bus honked-honked again. An old woman street sweeper stood in the middle of the road. She either didn't hear us or didn't care as she scraped the road with her broom, brushing the leaves to the side of the road, the garbage into piles. The bus passed onto the other side of the road, around her. The piles reminded me of Tsui Ping and the mess of medleys. Had Feng Gu managed to get a new order of tea to replace the whirlwind that fell to the floor yesterday? How big would our bill be? Was death better than being crazy?

The bus passed a series of graves. Surely Cheng Min's in-laws were already looking for an auspicious location for their grandchildren. Bribing this official and that so they wouldn't have to crowd the little ones into a spot in the government's new plan—graveyards. So they could make a large, round land-consuming memorial.

At least we weren't like Xiamen, where people were asked to burn their dead relatives. Burn them. Then again, Cheng Min's little girls were already burned and the priests were most certainly trying to bring the fractured souls back together. What a nightmare. My eyes blurred so that, instead of the gas station and stores lining the street, I saw burning bits of my old classmate's house. A calendar. A cloth diaper. A pot of rice. I wished a different ending for Cheng Min's babies.

The bus pulled into the town's central depot. How had we arrived so quickly? I needed more time to think of how to deal with Feng Gu.

"Will you look at that?" the man behind me said.

He lit up a fresh cigarette, pulled off his cap, and stared out the window. I followed his gaze. The parking lot was filled with buses and bicycles and people fighting for space. The sounds of hawkers calling out their wares filled the air. "Radios!" "Warm buns!" "Tickets!" And across the street, a crowd gathered outside the tea shop. Had there been another bombing? There was no smoke. No shouting. Had there been an accident?

The woman with her fixed plastic bag scooted past me. Commuters pushed their way through the aisles. But my legs felt glued to the leather seat of the bus. I clung to the metal rail of the seat in front of me.

Waipo had often told me a story about one of our local heroes who had worked as a tutor for the Emperor's son. While the Emperor was a great man, his son was a wild one—like a stallion. He took whatever, whomever he liked. One day, he took the wife of a villager. She was so ashamed, of course, she committed suicide. Her husband complained to the local governor, then followed his wife in death.

The local governor took all that blood seriously. But he was also not one to offend the Emperor. He passed the complaints to the Emperor's tutor. The tutor felt such shame for his student. This was the future leader of the country. He had violated a young woman. He had been the cause of her death and her husband's death.

When the Emperor's son came in for lessons, the tutor stood, pulled his sword, and slashed the boy's golden robe. Then he walked out, left the palace and returned home. He knew what would follow. He asked his wife to make his coffin extra long, drank some poison and climbed inside. A day later the Emperor's soldiers showed up to arrest him.

"He's already passed," the tutor's wife said.

The soldiers insisted on seeing the coffin. They stabbed the head of the coffin, just as the tutor had stabbed at the Emperor's son's clothing. But, as the coffin was extra long, the tutor's body remained intact. He made it into the next world in one piece. No need for priests to bring his body back together.

Waipo had said that people had lined the streets from the capital to our town to show their respects to this great man. She always told me that story to remind me to do what was right, no matter how hard, no matter what the consequences. I stood to get off the bus. Do what was right. Just then, in front of me, a school boy dropped his folder. Papers spilled all over the floor.

"Wait, please wait," he said turning to me and the handful of other remaining commuters.

He dropped to his knees and grabbed at the flurry of sheets. I was happy to wait. I wasn't eager to see Feng Gu. A bunch of boys hopped over the seats rather than wait. The man who had sat smoking behind me walked right past, his shoe leaving a large print on one of the papers.

"Oh, gods, please," the boy said.

He wiped a dirty hand across his brow, leaving a smear on his forehead. I picked up a piece of paper near my foot. "The Characters from The Monkey King." An interesting subject for a report. He snatched the paper from me, as if I might take it. Then he looked back down on the floor and grabbed at the rest of the papers.

I waited, looking out the window. Outside, a crowd of people purchased tickets to the bigger cities. Guanzhou, Xiamen, even Shanghai. The oyster-cake lady ladled out batter for cakes, the radio seller set out his wares on a plastic tarp. The cigarette man held up a handful of tobacco sticks. The noise was dizzying. Another normal day. Just another normal day. My heart thumped in my throat. I would offer to work for the dirt cheap sum of one *yuan* per hour until our debt was paid.

I glanced across the street. The crowd in front of the tea shop had grown larger. Why were people there? Surely Madame Tsui Ping had not returned this morning. Surely she wasn't over there re-enacting a scene from her tortured memory.

"What's happening?" I called to the bus driver. He dug dirt from beneath his long pinky fingernail. He glanced in his rear view mirror, saw the boy blocking the aisle, returned to his nail.

"Hurry up, boy," he called. "This isn't your private study room."

"No." I pointed out the window. "Over there."

The man grunted and flicked another piece of dirt from his nail.

"Drink Happiness Tea Shop," he said.

Zi Mei would have given me all the details by now, as she leaned on one foot than another. Her short hair pasted to her head. Her eyes wide with excitement.

"An accident?" I asked.

There wasn't the circle of onlookers that had accompanied yesterday's nightmare. Still, perhaps there was another problem. I felt small relief that I wasn't the cause.

"No." The driver tapped his long clean, pinky nail on the steering wheel. "No accident."

I sat back down. Breathed in. Out. So nothing to overshadow my disaster. But what were all those people doing? They looked like regular morning shoppers with their plastic baskets and bags. The boy gathered the last few sheets of paper. His white shirt had come out of his pants. His fleshy arms glistened with sweat.

The Monkey King. Waipo had often told me stories of the Monkey King, how he was given the job of traveling to the West to find the golden sutras. All the adventures he went through. I loved the stories. Did this boy? I'd found my English teacher an English translation of the Monkey King. She had had orange hair like stringed carrots, dots all over her face, a big nose and a wide mouth. The following day, she'd brought the book back to me.

"Maybe the translation was bad," she'd said. "I fell asleep on the second page."

She had laughed showing all her gold fillings. She always laughed, mostly at us. The way we would spend many minutes arguing over a few *fen*. The way many people had a cell phone, but lots of people still scooped water from the well. The way people didn't line up, but formed a circle which just got wider and wider.

I breathed in. Out. Looked around. The line at the tea shop was getting wider and wider. I stood up and pushed past the boy who had finally gathered all his papers together.

"It's hard to avoid a line," the driver said. "I hear the Teacher Mix is the good one."

"What?" I asked. My ears vibrated as if I'd stood too close to a gong.

"The Teacher Mix . . . or something like that—"

"You mean Professor's Medley?" I asked.

"If you already knew, why did you ask me so many questions?"

A warmth ran through my chest. Had Feng Gu taken Madame Tsui Ping's advice? Was the tea shop finally getting business?

Chapter Thirteen
The Rooster Guards the Nest

I stood in the back room, peering into the shop. Feng Gu rushed back and forth from the bins to the counter like a frenzied ant who had discovered a pile of crumbs. She filled bag after bag of tea for the circle of people standing shoulder to shoulder. One. Two. Three. Four. Eight. Ten. Twelve. More than twenty people crowded together in the shop. More out on the street. On the side of the bins, in Feng Gu's crude handwriting, were the word's "Professor's Medley."

Had Feng Gu scooped up all the remnants and shuffled the leaves together in there or had she gotten a new order of tea and just given her bins different names? And, with a crowd like this, why hadn't she moved the bins closer to the cash counter? Watching her run back and forth made me dizzy.

"You just can't depend on people these days," a woman said.

She held her ten *yuan* bill out over the shoulders of several people, hoping Feng Gu would pass her a bag before her turn. My fingers itched looking at that bill. Feng Gu needed assistance.

"There's just no loyalty anymore," the woman said.

Loyalty? What were they talking about? Had they all heard about the bombing? Were they discussing Zi Mei's loudspeaker of a mouth? Maybe this was a personal moment shared between just these two.

"That's true." Feng Gu took the woman's outstretched bill. "You give someone a chance to earn money, and she leaves you out in the summer heat to rot."

A chance to earn money? Was Feng Gu talking about me?

"These college people have a head full of theories, but when it comes to practical everyday life, they're at a loss," Feng Gu added, handing the woman a bag of tea, not seeing the irritated faces of those who'd been waiting first.

"You had a college girl here?" a man said, waving his bill like he'd seen the woman do. He inhaled on his cigarette. "The books must suck the common sense out of them."

The doorway felt sharp beneath my fingers. I coughed loudly

and went out to join Feng Gu.

"Li Hui," Feng Gu said. "You're late. Hurry up."

"Yes." I grabbed several empty bags, filled them with tea leaves, and brought them over to where Feng Gu waited at the cash counter.

"Best bring them one at a time," she said in a loud voice. "You don't want any spilling on the floor."

Was she joking? Was this new tea? Perhaps she was just strutting about, performing.

"Maybe we could move the bins closer," I whispered, my lips bumping against her hair. "Then I could help you better."

"Ha! Those things weigh a ton," she said. "You'd never be able to move them."

As she had instructed, I took one bag, returned to the tea bin and filled it. Then I returned to Feng Gu, who waited hands outstretched.

"You're going to have to work faster than that," she said, again so loudly my ears burned.

The crowd rippled with laughter. I looked out and spotted two young men. Two strong young men standing in a tea shop in the middle of the morning. With no job. Feng Gu followed my gaze.

"You two," she called out. "I need you up here."

The burly workers pushed through to the front, past the old man still waving his bill. They held their heads high, the corners of their mouths turned up. Perhaps they thought they were getting special treatment as young men.

"I'll have one kilo of the prof's mix," the taller one said.

"First bring the bin over," Feng Gu said.

She put her hands on her hips, posing like a rooster surveying the yard. The men's smiles vanished. But they were already up front. They moved over to one bin, tossing the sign away to get a better grip. Then they pushed and pulled.

"Closer," Feng Gu crowed. "Here."

Perhaps the books hadn't sucked all the brains from my head.

All morning long Feng Gu and I stood there like a rice-threshing machine. Money in, tea out. Money in, tea out. My fingers were numb, my lower back pulsed. The rhythm eradicated other thoughts. About bombs and explosions. About small babies blown to bits, no longer whole for the next world. About Cheng Min and the Birth

Control Unit. Money in. Tea out.

In the afternoon, as the bins emptied, the line of customers trickled to an end. The shop was quiet again. Not the anxious silence Feng Gu and I had endured the first two days as we waited for one, just one customer to please come. This was peaceful. This was an abundant silence.

"Can I pick you up something to eat?" I asked.

My stomach gurgled. Surely Feng Gu was hungry, too. Would she want a packet of rice and pork? An oyster cake? A hard bun filled with meat and fish cakes? Or a steaming pork bun?

"No, thanks," Feng Gu said, patting the cash drawer. "I'm full."

"This has been quite a morning," I said falling onto a stool at the table. My calves tingled. "Who could have guessed?"

"Guessed what?" Feng Gu said.

She took out a handful of bills from the drawer and stuffed them in her leather purse. Her chubby fingers patted the full purse, a thin-lipped smile on her face. She hadn't pulled on her hair all morning long. Had the shop ever done this well?

"Guessed what?" she repeated.

"The Professor's' Medley. That it would be such a hit?" Perhaps I'd not only be paid for all my hours, but would receive a bonus as well. Father, Mother and I would be able to climb out of the well soon.

"Hmm?" Feng Gu said. She counted another handful of bills and added them to the first pile in her purse. "What do you mean? I knew as soon as I saw that mess you made on the floor that this was the only answer."

My heart froze as if a bucket of cold water had been thrown in my face. I could understand Feng Gu's desire to be more capable than a college girl, but what gall to pretend that Madame Tsui Ping's idea had been hers. Perhaps Feng Gu was just not good at giving others credit. She was so used to being the rooster here, she didn't know how to share the field.

"Well, don't just sit there with your mouth hanging open." She indicated the empty bins on her way out the door. "I need to get this money over to the bank—and, you, you better fill up these bins."

Fill up the bins? With what? We'd used all the tea. Had Feng Gu deliberately given me an assignment at which I'd fail, so she could find more fault with me? A new reason to send me away?

"Is another supply of tea on the way?" I called after her.

"No," Feng Gu shouted back. "Thanks to you, I couldn't get a good price."

What had Father arranged? Did he know all along that I wouldn't be compensated for my time? Was this his subtle way of showing me what a waste of time felt like? How he had felt all those four years I'd been studying? Well, if that was his plan, he'd underestimated me. They both had.

Chapter Fourteen
The Magic Pen

I sat at the cherrywood table staring at the sign on the wall that Feng Gu's grandfather had carved: "Life is like tea. First it tastes bitter, then it is sweet." I wanted to taste sweet. I had studied hard all my life to enter university. I had studied hard through university to get a teaching job. Having failed at that, I stood out in all kinds of weather trying to get a tutoring job. Now that I finally had a job, Feng Gu was about to cheat me. I could feel it.

I got up and went to the cash desk. I pulled on the drawers. Each one I tried was locked. I tried the last drawer at the top left side. Scraps of paper and receipts filled the small drawer. Some of the slips just had amounts written on them, some were legitimate stores, like Eternal Happiness, a few restaurants, Golden Supplies. Golden Supplies. Feng Gu had mentioned that name yesterday. I went through the pile of papers again, pulling out the few that had been written out by Golden Supplies. I looked at the purchase dates. Three months apart. No, this must be some kind of service. But Feng Gu didn't have an air conditioner. No machines. What kind of service could this be? I picked up the phone. A man answered on the first ring.

"*Wei?*" he said. "Hello?"

"Is this Golden Supplies?" I asked.

"Who are you?" the man responded.

"This is the Drink Happiness Tea Shop."

The man hung up. Maybe that wasn't the regular supplier. Or Feng Gu had had her usual effect on people. I looked through the pile of receipts one more time. If only I could take a look at the ledger. Surely she wrote her supplier in the ledger. I looked at the lock on the drawer. A cheap lock. I looked around and out to the street. A rickshaw driver pedaled by. Two highschoolers listened to a tape recording of Madonna. The street was filled with lunchtime traffic. No one watched me. I yanked on the drawer. Nothing happened. I yanked again. The drawer still wouldn't open.

I went in back, hoping to find some other receipts. The empty bins sat in the corner, but there was no identifying mark on them. They were just silver bins. If Feng Gu were here, she'd already be yelling that I was spending too much time in back. That a customer could easily walk in, take a kilo of tea and be gone without my even knowing. At least there was nothing to take, and that lock on the cash drawer was stronger than it looked.

Only Fashion Fortune Magazine occupied space on the small table next to the cot. The cot held just a mattress and pillow. I even checked under the pillow.

"Hello? Feng Gu?" a man called from the front of the shop.

A man's deep voice. Her father? Her husband? The tea supplier? I rushed out front. I stopped.

"It's you," the man said.

A dark lock of hair fell over his single-lidded eyes. His shirt sleeves were rolled up to the top of his arms, showing a patch of muscular white that the sun had not browned. His blue cotton pants hung loosely on his long legs. Strange Man In Blue.

"Can I help you?" I asked, hearing the sound of each word come from my mouth. "Feng Gu stepped out for a moment."

"Who are you?" he asked.

I wanted to know the same. This was the second time in as many days that this man had shown up at our shop. Surely he wasn't a tea drinker. Was this Feng Gu's husband? Certainly no.

"I'm Feng Gu's assistant," I said.

"Assistant?"

His eyes stared right into mine, his eyebrows raised. Not the actions of a married man. Perhaps a relative?

"I'd heard the shop did well this morning," he said. "I didn't know business was so good that she needed help. Unless you're the one."

"The one?" I asked. I knew what he referred to. He had come in yesterday right after we'd cleaned up after Madame Tsui Ping.

"The one who—" He fumbled with keys in his pocket. He stared down at his mud-covered boots. His long eyelashes fluttered. I felt color rush to my cheeks.

"Looks like you turned that disaster around," he said, looking back up at me.

"No, no," I said, although the compliment felt like a pat on the arm. "Madame Tsui Ping had the answer for us. She may have her weak moments—"

"I guess we all do." He smiled, showing the dents in his cheeks.

Those strong, high cheek bones. He spoke the truth. Here I was wobbling like the man too weak to pull the pig on the back of his bike this morning. Those kind dark eyes. On top of that, I needed to find us some tea.

"Who is the tea supplier here?" I asked. "Do you know?"

"Golden Supplies," he said, looking for the first time to the empty bins.

"Are you sure?" I asked. Why had the man from Golden Supplies hung up on me?

"The family's always bought tea from them," he said. His forehead furrowed. "Why?"

"Nothing," I said. Perhaps the man from Golden Supplies had accidentally dropped the phone and not intended to hang up at all.

"You need some help?" he asked, looking again at the empty bins and around the shop as if hoping to spot more. As if ready to offer to fill the bins.

"No," I said. "Thanks."

"No problem," he said, turning to go.

I wished I'd dropped my purse, so I could feel his arm brushing against mine as he returned it. Instead, he was almost out the door.

"Do you want to leave a message for Feng Gu?" I asked. I wanted to know his name. I wanted it to be Guo Qiang, Guo Qiang Liang.

"No, no." He shook his head. His bangs shook back and forth. "It's enough to know that the shop is doing well."

I stared after him. In my heart, I still felt him standing right there, his eyes on me. I heard him saying, "Do you need help?" His brow furrowed. His eyes genuine.

He reminded me of one of the characters from one of Waipo's stories. A man named Ma Lian. Ma Lian was always trying to help others—especially the poor. He wasn't good at much, but he liked to paint. He wasn't rich. But he did have a kind heart.

Ma Lian helped one neighbor dig a well to supply water for the crops. He held onto the shoulders of another while the man cried over the loss of his one and only cow. One night he dreamt that he had been given a special paintbrush. When he awoke, a paintbrush was by his side. The first picture he drew was of a bucket of water, as he remembered his neighbor struggling to pull water from the well. When Ma Lian had finished, droplets of water splashed over the sides of the bucket and wet his hands. The water was real. He drew another picture of a cow. The animal stamped its feet and snorted. His paintbrush was magic.

Ma Lian went about the village drawing pictures of rice fields and chickens and cows and horses. Word spread of the kind man with the magic brush. Word landed on the ears of a greedy rich man. Mr. Greed had an army of men capture Ma Lian. They threw him in prison and took his brush away. Mr. Greed used the brush to paint pictures of friends he wished he had. He drew their faces and waited. Nothing happened. Then he drew mountains of gold. Again nothing happened.

"Ma Lian," Mr. Greed called. "Draw me a mountain of gold, and I will set you free."

"How can I trust you?" Ma Lian asked.

"You have my word," Mr. Greed said.

What did that mean? But Ma Lian wanted to be free again. He wanted to be back in his village. So he picked up the pen and drew waves. Mr. Greed looked at the picture and became angry.

"I said gold," he said. "Not water."

"I'm getting there," Ma Lian said.

He continued drawing the ocean. On the other side of the water, he drew a beautiful mountain of gold. Mr. Greed could almost feel the hard cold coins lining his pockets.

"But how do I get there?" Mr. Greed snapped.

Ma Lian drew him a ship. Immediately, Mr. Greed and his family clambered into the ship and set off. Ma Lian watched them go.

"This will take forever," the old man shouted. "Give me wind."

Ma Lian added a fierce wind. But, with it came huge waves. The boat soon toppled. Everyone aboard drowned.

Then Ma Lian returned home to continue to help his people. No evil men bothered him or his pen any more. He went about his business and brought much wealth and happiness to the village.

I'd seen Man In Blue help the old woman. Then he'd offered to help me. And his heart felt kind. Just like Ma Lian.

"Looks like you turned that disaster into a success." His voice rang in my ears. Too bad he wasn't my boss. Still I'd show Feng Gu that she needed to appreciate me. I'd show Father that I didn't waste time. I rubbed my sweaty palms together, picked up the phone and dialed the number for Golden Supplies again. The phone rang and rang.

"*Wei*! Hello!" a man barked. The same man who had hung up

on me earlier.

"I need another order of tea," I said.

"Who are you?" He and Feng Gu had the same rough manner. No wonder they had worked so long together.

"Drink Happiness," I said.

"Why come to me for tea?" the man said. "You already have a different supplier."

"We always get our tea from you," I said, trying to keep my voice from sounding like a question. Perhaps Man In Blue didn't know the family as well as he professed.

"That's what I thought," the man said. "But yesterday the boss over there was crying you have no tea. Now I hear you have some Professor delivery."

I breathed. My lips curved upwards. This was our supplier. The one who had tried to gouge Feng Gu on the prices yesterday. Ha. What a friend. I looked at the receipt from three months ago. One hundred *yuan* per bin.

"I wanted to give you another chance." I gripped the phone. "Are your prices any lower today?"

"Since you're such a good customer," he said, sucking in a deep breath, as though smoking a cigarette. "I'll give you a deal. A hundred *yuan* per bin."

Even allowing for possible inflation, that didn't sound like a deal.

"Seventy," I countered.

"I'm already giving you my best deal," the man said. "Ninety-five."

"Well, I wanted to give you another chance," I said. "But, if you can't come any lower than that . . ."

"Ninety. Ninety's as low as I can go."

"Eighty-five," I said. "Eighty-five and we'll call it a deal."

"Deal," he said. "I'll have it there by tomorrow morning."

"I need the tea now," I said.

"Tomorrow."

He hung up. I called back, but the line was busy. Busy. Busy. Too bad I didn't have a magic pen like Ma Lian with which to draw bin after bin of Professor's Medley. I looked at the empty bins. Why had I bargained so? Was I a gambler like Father? If I'd agreed on a hundred *yuan*, would the man have delivered today? Feng Gu would not be pleased.

Chapter Fifteen
A New System

Feng Gu breezed in from the back room, as though skipping through the fields. The bank balance must have been good. Perhaps she also imagined an afternoon of good sales. I attacked the cobweb above her grandpa's sign. I'd succeeded in listening to Madame Tsui Ping's idea and thus doing well for the shop. I'd gotten us a good price from the supplier. I'd even seen Man In Blue. While we waited for the tea, we might as well give the shop a good cleaning. Make the place look more welcoming.

"Don't waste your time doing that," Feng Gu said, twirling her now thin purse on her finger. "I told you to fill the bins."

"We don't have anymore," I said. The cobweb floated to the ground.

"That's right." She stopped twirling her purse. "I forgot."

Maybe she hadn't tried to trap me. Perhaps she was so overwhelmed with the morning's business that she hadn't thought about the supplies. After all, I'd only known her a few days. She plodded her way toward the cash drawer. Her fields were now thick and muddy. She pulled on her hair.

"I'll have to order—"

"I just did," I said.

"What?" Feng Gu picked up the phone. "How did you know where to call? You can't just go calling anyplace in town. People take advantage."

Certainly she would know.

"Just as we pull our heads above water," she said shaking the receiver at me. "You pull us down. How much are they robbing us for?"

"Eighty-five."

I leaned on the broom. She needed me. Whether she gave me credit or not. Surely she would soon realize that it would take both of us to hold up the sky here.

"How'd you get that price?" She stopped waving the receiver. "You know you can't just order from any old shop. They may not be selling real tea leaves."

I knew that. We could get fake certificates and I.D.'s, fake brand watches and handbags, fake tapes and CDs. I hadn't heard of fake tea leaves. But certainly somewhere such a product was available.

"Besides, we always order from Golden Supplies," she continued. "Always."

"Yes. The man on the phone mentioned that," I said. "He didn't want to lose our business. And, for some reason." I put my hand to my mouth to cover my smile. "For some reason, he thought we had a new supplier, Professor Deliveries."

Feng Gu laughed so big, her jumbled teeth looked ready to spill out of her mouth. I joined her. Amazing how stories got changed around so quickly.

"Did you correct him?" she asked.

"No."

"I thought you just said you called in an order." She sighed. Her shoulders sagged as if the sky fell on top of them.

"I told him we wanted to give him another chance . . . if his price was right."

The clock in the back room ticked. She tossed her hair back and smiled. Her eyes were so filled with delight, as if she'd just been given a red packet of money on New Year's day.

"You should have let me do it." She dropped the receiver back into its cradle. "I could have gotten him lower."

We both knew better. She was so used to ordering at a certain price, doing it a certain way. The thought surely had never occurred to her. Still I let her comment pass. I had seen this bitter woman smile, a genuine smile of delight. We would be able to come to some kind of understanding.

Feng Gu fussed with the bins, pushing them closer to the counter. She tugged at her hair and looked at her watch. Her eyes followed me as I washed down the walls.

"I still can't believe those two men were able to move this thing," I said, indicating the tea bin. "We'll need some more strong men to move it back." I was thinking of Man In Blue. Hoping it would be him.

"What time did Golden Supplies say they'd bring the tea?" Feng Gu asked.

I wrung out a rag. The walls behind the bins probably hadn't been cleaned since Grandpa had set up shop. The white rag was black as the night.

"The afternoon crowd will be here any minute." Feng Gu picked up her abacus and flicked several beads up. Was she guessing as to the afternoon's profits? "When is the delivery coming?"

"Tomorrow," I said.

"Say again." She looked up from the abacus.

"Tomorrow." I cleared my throat. "Early in the morning."

"Tomorrow?" She stopped flicking the beads of the abacus. She stared up at me. She cocked her head, as if certain she'd misheard me.

"That was the earliest he could make it," I said, running the rag over the wall one more time. "I asked him to come earlier, but he hung up on me. And then I couldn't reach him. I—"

"*Tamade*," Feng Gu swore. She threw the abacus on the counter. "What had you planned to do? We just get a hit and now we're going to have to turn people away."

"Well, I've been thinking—" I said, letting the dirty rag hang from my hand.

Feng Gu glared at me, as if I had sworn. She marched to the back room. I dropped the rag and followed.

"Something similar happened to me when I was in university," I said.

"You're not in university anymore," she said, shaking the tins as if she could conjure up more tea with each shake. "This is real life."

I should have known better than to mention university. She didn't want to hear about any of that. She wasn't going to give me a chance to explain.

"You're right. Still," I rushed through my idea. "This bookstore was out of a popular book. They didn't stop selling it though. They took orders."

"Orders?" She banged on the side of one of the tins.

"Yes. You take the name, address and half the payment and—"

"I know what orders are," Feng Gu said, looking over, her eyes hard and angry. "But you forget one important point. This is not some big city. We don't do things like that."

She returned to the front with one of the tea tins. She dumped the meager contents from the bottom into the bin next to the cash drawer. The particles of tea fluttered out the way dust floats in the wind on a hot summer day. Would she really try to sell that? Should we rename it Professor's Dust?

The rustle of plastic against plastic made us both turn toward the shop entrance. A young woman fixed her shopping bags on her wrist, as though readying to carry another purchase. Our first afternoon customer.

"I want a bag of the new mix. The what's it called?" she asked. "Professor's Medley. That's it. I want a bag of that."

She had a flat nose and high cheekbones. She peered into the empty bin, then looked around the room searching for the tea. Feng Gu reached into the bottom of the bin with a grand sweep of her hand.

"This is really popular," Feng Gu said, picking at the bits.

"Is that what it's supposed to look like?" the woman asked, reaching in the bin and coming up with tea granules on her hand.

"This is the best of it," Feng Gu said. A drop of sweat rolled down her cheek. "Consider yourself lucky."

"I want real leaves," the woman said. "Big leaves. That's . . . that's—"

"It's our last bag," Feng Gu said. "If you don't take it, someone else will."

"I don't want that." The woman turned to go. "I was told you had a great new tea. That's just garbage."

Feng Gu glared at me. Heat poured on me from the tip of my head to my toes as if the gods had touched me with a torch. Just as someone had started the rumor of our Professor's Medley and how wonderful it was, this woman would pull that rumor away. Feng Gu would not continue to write black numbers in her ledger.

Why did Father put me in this tea shop, asking me to succeed at something I'd never done before? To be able to do what I had studied. To be able to do it well. That's all I wanted. My heart pounded.

"Wait," I called. "The Professor's Medley. You wanted the Professor's Medley?"

"That's what I said," the woman said from the door.

I took a piece of paper and a pen from the drawer and nodded at Feng Gu. Feng Gu looked away.

"How many bags?" I asked.

"One." She came back to the cash table. "Just one will do."

"What's your phone number?" I asked.

"What's it to you?" the woman said.

Feng Gu tilted her head at me, as if to say, "See. This isn't like the big city."

"We're taking orders." I went to the drawer and pulled out a handful of receipts to make it seem like we had a lot of orders.

"Now, your number, please," I said.

On the sheet, I wrote her telephone number.

"We'll have that by—let's see . . . " I checked my watch, as though calculating. "Tomorrow morning."

The woman nodded and turned to go. Feng Gu rolled her eyes at me, as if to say, "What nonsense is this? We're no better off than before the lady came in." But I wasn't finished.

"That'll be five *yuan*," I said.

"What?" the woman asked. "I have to pay up front? What kind of game is this?"

"We have to reserve this for you." I twirled the pen in my fingers. "If you make an order and forget to pick it up, then we've kept tea we could have sold to someone else. This way we can keep the tea for you until you come."

She thrust five *yuan* in my hand and walked out.

"Not bad," Feng Gu said taking the five *yuan* from me. "You should have asked her for ten though. The whole amount."

All afternoon, I took orders. Some people refused to give out their phone numbers. Some refused to part with their money. But, at the end of the afternoon, we'd taken in money for seventeen kilos of tea. Oh, sweet tea.

"That tea better come tomorrow, or we're in big trouble." Feng Gu counted and re-counted the slips of paper that made up the orders. "Are you sure—"

"That's what the man promised," I repeated for the third time. Another thought occurred to me. This was as good a time as any. "Speaking of promises, you mentioned the first day I came here that if I—"

"If you turn the business around," she said. She tugged at her hair. "Nothing has changed yet."

Oh, but it had. The last time she ordered tea was three months ago. Now here we were taking orders for a bulk of that order in one day. She obviously was going to continue raising the standard of what turning the business around meant. Or at least try.

"We had one lucky morning of sales," she said.

"And another lucky afternoon of orders," I countered.

"Which will be another disaster if that order of tea doesn't come in tomorrow."

I couldn't stay here working for free. She either had to hire me on or tell me to go. I had to find a way to hold up my half the sky.

"Feng Gu," I said, looking directly at her.

"Alright, alright," she said. "You're hired. Two *yuan* an hour starting today."

"I started two days ago," I said. "I've worked twenty-three hours so far."

"Yes, and you caused our most loyal of customers to have an anxiety attack. We'll probably never see her again."

Would a one-*yuan*-per-kilo customer make that much difference in her ledger? Besides, Madame Tsui Ping would be back. I felt it. If for nothing more but to witness our success .

"I can't afford to bargain with my time," I said.

I stood as if ready to leave. Here I was gambling again. Just like Father. But I held no *mahjong* tiles. Instead I was sure I held the reins of Feng Gu's newfound success.

"Alright. Alright," Feng Gu said. "You're hired, starting two days ago."

Twenty three hours. Forty-six *yuan*. If business continued like this, I could ask for a bonus. Not today though. Today I was happy with what I'd won. Another week, and we'd be able to climb out of the well. To see the sky. The sweet sky.

Chapter Sixteen
The Echo Returns

I stood at the cross walk near Drink Happiness. I checked my watch and looked across the street. At this time, three days ago, Man In Blue had ridden the same bus as I. Yesterday he had come into the shop around this time. I looked around hoping to spot him. But what would I do? A thin crust of sweat covered my body. My hair felt greasy. My black pants and white blouse looked tired and uninteresting. My pumps scuffed and old. What would I say? And why did everything revert somehow back to him?

I wanted to talk with Madame Paper Cutter. So much had happened in the last day. Cheng Min's house getting blown up, her babies killed. Man In Blue visiting the shop. Feng Gu hiring me on as a real employee. Man In Blue visiting the shop. Still, I was so exhausted. Perhaps tomorrow I'd stop by during a lunch break, if we had one.

I pushed my way across the street, in between shoppers and bicyclists and motorcyclists. The lady walking next to me wore black high heel shoes with pink bows on the heels. So elegant. By the end of the month, I might be able to purchase a new pair of shoes. Perhaps. If Father were careful.

As I walked toward the bus, I let my eyes slide over toward the taxis lining the streets. Comfort. Air conditioning. A clean seat. Soft music. Mei Ling always said that you had to distinguish between the good drivers and the crooks. I'd laughed at her. I'd never had to worry. I always rode the bus. Now, someday, I might have money to ride in taxis. Or in my own private car which seated four.

The bus line extended past the lady selling hard buns. She sliced buns and filled them with fish cakes as fast as she could grab customers. I searched her line of customers, then the bus line. I didn't see Man In Blue. Just then, out on the street, two motorcycles slammed into one another. Metal crunched, glass flew. Both men hopped off their bikes shouting at one another. Like dogs growling.

"Move along, little sister," a man behind me shouted, grabbing his bun from the hawker and nudging me with his elbow. "Hurry up."

Was I really so tired I didn't want to visit Madame Paper Cutter? I let the man push past. Or was I really hoping to run into Man In Blue? How shameful of me to ignore a true friend in favor of a stranger. I stepped out of line and headed back toward the street crossing.

A radio seller argued with an elderly woman who insisted she had bought a radio just the previous day, and it was already broken. As I passed the line of taxis, a woman with too many shopping bags stumbled over a pebble on the sidewalk and into me. I bumped against a taxi man in a smart black suit.

"Sorry," I said.

"You want a taxi?" He grabbed onto my arm.

"No need," I said.

The persistent salesman apparently didn't hear me though. He led me toward his taxi. I pulled my arm away and pointed, indicating that I was heading for the crosswalk.

"For you, a special price," he winked. "Ten *yuan*."

"I can ride the bus for fifty *fen*," I said. "Besides, I have other business right now."

I walked away. Surely Madame Paper Cutter would be pleased with all the success I'd helped bring to the shop. I wasn't just a simple bird cutting.

"Ah, but you must be tired." The taxi driver came up alongside me. His chubby fingers wrapped around my arm. "Come. Come. You don't want to do other business when you're tired."

He pulled me back toward his taxi. I tripped in a hole. My shoe came off.

"Aiya!" I looked back over my shoulder. "Oh, my mother. My shoe."

"Don't worry." He pushed me down on the seat of the taxi. He put his hand on my head to hold me inside, as if I were a chicken trying to escape from the cage. Mei Ling would have called this one a crook.

"Stop," I said.

"Wait." A voice joined my protests, grabbing the door. A calloused hand held out my shoe. "Is this yours?"

"Yes, yes," I said, relieved to get the scuffed black thing back, hoping to push my way out of the taxi.

"I thought you said you were riding the bus today," the deep, gentle voice said.

Oh, my. That voice. Certainly it couldn't be. Man In Blue?

"No, she has other business today," Mr. Persistent Taxi Man tried.

The man with the calloused hands opened the door further, pulling me out of the taxi. He wore the same work clothes, the same muddy boots. He had the same sparkle to his eyes. My Ma Lian. My Man In Blue.

"Okay, you have a friend," Mr. Persistent Taxi Man continued. "I'll take you both. For ten *yuan* each. That's fair. Get into the taxi. It's much better than that crowded old bus. How about eight *yuan* each? Five?"

Normally I would have heard the incessant yapping of Mr. Persistent Taxi Man. Normally I would have heard the unhappy customer yelling to the man who sells radios that she expected a replacement for free. Normally I would have heard the motorcycle riders making damage on each other's faces, fighting because they almost had an accident. But the gods put a microscope on one part of my life. Everything around me faded away. That day, the gods ate every sound except for the firm footfall of Man In Blue, the rustle of his t-shirt against his chest, the fluttering of his long lashes as he blinked. We'd found one another again, an amazing occurrence in our town of close to a million. Perhaps he'd been watching for me, too.

He led me back toward the bus, the line having thinned as people had dispersed to watch the motorcyclists fight. As we waited in line, he fished a Butterfly brand cigarette from the package in his shirt pocket. Not a foreign brand. Not an extravagance.

"I'm called Chen Chan Hai."

He traced the cigarette over his large palm, making the characters "wise" and "ocean" that composed his given name Chan Hai. Of course, I'd guessed this wasn't Madame Liang's son. I felt as if metal grates had clanged shut in my heart, the thud vibrating throughout my body.

"I'm the son of Chen Yi Dao and Zhao Pingyu," he continued. "The nephew of Chen Yifei who owns the Fu Lu Shou, Good Luck, Long Life and Prosperity Quarry."

Ah, so he lived on the other side of the village. He worked in the quarry by the brick mine where Mother occasionally went to buy eggs for special occasions, like my birthday. Those chickens laid the largest eggs anybody had ever seen. But why was I thinking of eggs? My face grew hot.

He put the cigarette to his full lips and snapped open his lighter, clicking until the flame stayed. His hand was steady. His eyes watched me.

I'd heard a few things about the quarry from Zi Mei. Chan Hai's uncle had started his quarry with an investment from a relative living overseas. But the rocks that came from the quarry were "mosquito piss poor" as Feng Gu would say. They were white and fetched a low price. Not blue-black rock, which people wanted to have and would pay good money for.

"You look disappointed," he said.

This working class man didn't need the burden that came with a woman who had no brother to take care of her mother and father. Especially a father like mine who enjoyed the cold feeling of the *mahjong* tiles in his hand and the burn of rice wine trickling down his throat. Besides this wasn't Madame Liang's son.

"No, no," I replied. "I just remembered I was supposed to stop at the park and meet a friend. I should go."

He dropped his half-smoked cigarette onto the sidewalk. His boot twisted back and forth over the butt, grinding the embers out slowly. Then he looked up at me with those dark brown eyes.

"Seriously," I said. "Thank you for your help. Nice to meet you."

"Let me walk you there," he said. "I'm not in a hurry to be home."

I was. Standing so near this man, with his strong arms, his high cheekbones, his long eyelashes, felt dangerous. Surely he could not afford a relationship with people like us. And I could not afford to risk the perfect match with the professor in Singapore.

"I don't want to trouble you," I said.

"No problem," he said, smiling.

What harm could a simple walk to the park do? Besides, perhaps Madame Paper Cutter could give me her opinion of the man. My heart felt full. Surely he would make her smile.

"So how long have you worked at Drink Happiness?" Chan Hai gestured across the street.

"Twenty-four hours," I said. "Three days."

"You like it that much?" He laughed. His blue cotton pants

brushed against me as we struggled through the crowd.

"No, no," I said. "It's just. Well, today we were calculating. Feng Gu is good at calculating."

He looked down at me. I didn't realize how tall he was next to me. Or maybe how small I felt with him so near.

We walked toward the bridge. At the foot of the bridge, a young girl in northern Chinese dress sold figurines. A mangy dog barked at everyone who passed. A man struggled to hoist his bike loaded with bricks, over an uneven part in the cement. The poor old man. Chan Hai rushed forward, grabbed the back of the man's bike and lifted. Where did all his kindness come from? His ability to turn thoughts of pity into actions?

He returned to me, not even a little out of breath. He led me to the side of the bridge where we watched the water flowing down the river. The banks of the river were piled high with garbage—old tires and rusted bicycles and tubing and lights and wrappers and beer bottles.

"I love this river," he said. His voice seemed genuine.

"It's so dirty now, though," I said. "Like a public dump."

"You just don't look at the garbage." He stood behind me and put his hands up on the sides of my face, like blinders for a horse. "See?"

His hands against my cheeks felt rough like a wool scarf. His calluses were probably from picking up sharp rocks all day at his uncle's quarry. They made me feel warm inside. Chan Hai dropped his hands and pulled another cigarette from his pocket. He lit the end and took a deep puff. Then he turned to me.

"So, am I to call you Madame Assistant?"

"I'm called Li Hui," I said. "I'm the only child of Huang Binkin and Li Yu Lian."

My heart broke having to disclose the identity of my impoverished parents. My gambling Father. All the heartache he had brought to our family. All the burden he had thrown on the village. But Chan Hai didn't even pause.

"Nice to make your acquaintance, Little Sister Huang."

Perhaps he had not heard of Father, although I found that doubtful. Perhaps, like the river, he refused to look at the unpleasant parts. How generous.

We were still a couple blocks from the park. We passed an

electronics shop, a boys clothing store, a CD shop, and a tire shop which had recently changed owners. Now the small shop was a nursery, selling flowers of all kinds for those people rich enough to tend to such things. Chan Hai pulled me inside. Bells chimed alerting the owner to our presence. A fern brushed against my cheek. The air was warm and difficult to breathe.

"Have you ever been here?" Chan Hai asked.

"No," I said. We didn't plant flowers. We planted things we could eat.

"This is a wonderful place," he said.

He pointed out golden chrysanthemums that were larger than my hand. He took me around to show me tiny purple flowers—violets, he said. In fact, he named almost every flower in the place. I was amazed, especially coming from a man.

"You know a lot about flowers," I said.

"I want a shop like this when I grow up." He laughed at himself. "I'm good with flowers. I especially like mixing them and making new hybrids. They're beautiful and much more resilient." He wiped imaginary dust off his arm. "What about you? What do you want?"

No one talked like this, about dreams. Father would never think to ask. Mother would laugh at such foolishness. But, coming from Chan Hai, I wasn't surprised.

"I studied how to teach elementary school," I said as we stepped back outside and maneuvered our way across the street.

A motorcycle slowed and swerved around us. A taxi honked before stepping on the gas. Chan Hai held tight to my arm, but said nothing even when we had stepped safely to the other side. Why did I shove my education down his throat? He hadn't mentioned his education, so certainly he had, at most, gone only as far as high school. Then again, maybe he hadn't heard me. And, the park was just ahead.

"Father says my job at the tea shop will someday earn us more money than we could get if I was a teach—" I coughed. "Than I could hope for doing anything else. That's the beauty of this new capitalism."

Why couldn't I stop talking? I had said all the wrong things. I didn't dare to look over at him. I kept my head down, watching the sidewalk littered with fast-food cups and papers, a mound of seeds, a hard bun. The trash lady hadn't been by to clean up this street. Lucky for me. I had much to look at.

Chan Hai pushed me away. But then he pulled me back. He pushed me away again, then pulled me back. Pushed me away—

"What?" I looked up at him. His brown eyes smiled at me, like that first day on the bus.

"Stop moving," he said.

What was he talking about? He had pushed me back and forth. What did he mean?

"You sound like a pebble in the ocean," he said stopping me in the middle of the sidewalk. A band of high school children in their dark blue uniforms walked around us like a giant wave. "Rolling this way or that depending on the strength of the tide."

How was I supposed to be? Wasn't that the way everyone was, turning and twisting depending on the latest government plan? Didn't we all have to jump at opportunity, wherever and whenever? Then again, perhaps Chan Hai didn't need to worry about where his next meal would come from, where he would find money to pay the electricity bill, to buy soy sauce and rice vinegar, even matches. Perhaps he had the space in his wallet to think about dreams. That sent a warmth through my chest. Maybe he would be just as good a match as Madame Liang's son.

We arrived in the park. Among the usual crowd of hawkers and shoppers, I spotted Mr. Palm Reader with his sign. Madame Paper Cutter wasn't sitting next to him though. Had she found a different spot? Had she left early?

"Do you see your friend?" Chan Hai asked.

"Actually, no," I said. Sweat trickled down my back. "She looks about forty. Wears glasses that make her eyes look like those of a goldfish in a bowl. She makes paper cuttings."

"An artisan," he said. "That kind of cutting takes real skill."

I looked up to see if he was being sarcastic. His expression showed concern as he searched the park. So he wasn't bothered by her illegal status in the park. He revered her for performing this artwork.

"I don't see her," I said.

I hoped she was alright. I wondered how her daughter was. Although I was bursting to tell her that I'd earned so much money, I wanted her news as well.

"Maybe she's having dinner," Chan Hai said, leading me out of the back of the park. "Are you hungry?"

"No, no," I said.

My stomach was so empty it felt full. Besides, a friendly chat on the way to the park was one thing. Having dinner together was a different matter. I didn't feel comfortable taking control of my heart without some kind of assurance from Madame Paper Cutter or Mei Ling or Mother.

"Have you ever been to Mr. Dumpling's shop?" Chan Hai continued. "He's a neighbor of ours."

"Are we near Mr. Dumpling's?" I asked, following his gaze down a road I rarely traveled.

I thought Mr. Dumpling's shop was further at the edge of town. In fact, that was why Zi Mei had said he didn't get too much business. Perhaps had she exaggerated.

"Can't you smell the pork and garlic?" he asked.

I sniffed the air, expecting to get a whiff of what were the best dumplings around. I'd never eaten in his restaurant, but once Mr. Dumpling had brought a batch of his dumplings to Grandfather's New Year's festival. Zi Mei spent the entire afternoon telling us all about his restaurant, how Mr. Dumpling had put up lots of decoration on the walls to try to attract any foreign visitors passing through town. Foreign visitors liked decorations as much as food, she said, believe it or not. Mr. Dumpling's son had learned that while working in Singapore. The Singapore son had also insisted Mr. Dumpling add a bathroom and put pictures in it, as well as toilet paper. At least Zi Mei had told it that way. After that New Year's festival, many of the neighbors went by just to see if what Zi Mei said was true—that he spent money on his bathroom like it was an important place. I'd never seen it. I sniffed the air again.

"I don't smell anything but car exhaust," I said.

"You're not trying."

"I am." My stomach rumbled as I peered ahead hoping for a glimpse of the restaurant with the decorated bathroom. "Are you sure it's this way?"

"Well, maybe not." He smiled. "But certainly now you're hungry. Shall we get a bite to eat?"

My insides tingled. What a charmer. Surely Madame Paper Cutter, Mei Ling, even Mother would feel the same.

"I'd like that," I said.

Chapter Seventeen
Full of Yes. Full of No.

Chan Hai led me through a bunch of streets I'd never traveled to a thin alley between a motorcycle shop and a helmet shop. These two-story shops stood shoulder to shoulder, allowing little space and light for a small eating area in between. Thick smoke like a dream chamber in a temple filled the air. An energy surrounded us, making my skin tight, my rumbling stomach dance.

"Here we are," he said. His breath felt warm against my ear. His fingers felt strong beneath my elbow. Surely a short dinner together would not be cause for concern.

On one side of the alley an old green refrigerator stood next to a gas burner blackened from use and a red washing hose. On the other side, young men crowded around three Formica tables. They huddled over their soup, slurping as if they hadn't eaten in days, smoking at the same time. Their legs bounced up and down to some internal rhythm. Each man had a striped plastic case stuffed in between his legs. Salesmen at a monthly meeting?

"*Huai le*," Chan Hai swore, looking up and down the alley. "I forgot it's the first Thursday of the month."

"First Thursday?" I asked.

What was important about the first Thursday? Was he in charge of the night shift at the quarry on that day? Did he have a meeting? How could he blurt out his personal issues like that? Make them my burden? I was reminded of the construction worker who wanted to call and wish his son a happy birthday, the construction worker who had fallen from the rafters. Perhaps this dinner wasn't such a good idea. I looked away from his troubled face. Pork bones littered the dusty cement floor. Perhaps the first Thursday was the day before the *yongren* came to clean. Although the chances this place had a *yongren* were as thin as a rice stalk. A cockroach scampered by the wash bin.

"I know another place." His long, slender fingers pulled gently on my elbow.

A man without a suitcase, without that hunger in his eyes, spat a pork bone on the ground, stood up and squeezed past us. An opening in the crowded circles of hungry humanity. Was this an omen?

"It's okay," I said. "Perhaps I'd better get back."

"Little Chen," a man called out to Chan Hai, indicating his familiarity with Chan Hai, as well as his elder status.

The man pointed to the just-vacated spot. A dirty apron hugged his round belly. Sweat poured from his heavy face. The shop owner? Chan Hai nodded, then he looked at me for agreement. Perhaps he thought I was frightened by this dirty restaurant full of starving, chain-smoking men. To be honest, I was more concerned with the knot in my chest which thump-thumped so hard. I was more concerned with the frown I imagined on Mother's face. "A stone quarry worker?" she would ask, knotting her hands together. "What can you be thinking?"

"I know the place looks bad," he said, winking. "But, trust me, this man makes the best pork that will ever touch your tongue."

"I'm sure you speak the truth," I said. Certainly the food would have to be spectacular for him to insist that we stay in such a cramped, grungy, dark place.

Chan Hai nodded again at the owner and led me toward the small space available at the crowded table. The men around us looked familiar, as if I'd seen them around town on the bus, out in front of McDonald's, wandering through the park. What did they sell? Why just men? The owner rushed in back, probably to his living quarters, and returned with another stool.

"There you go," he said.

Chan Hai and I squeezed in between a young man who smelled sweet from sweat and one who had just had his hair cut. Stray hairs decorated the collar of his white shirt. His hand shook when he lifted his spoon to his mouth.

"You're going to love this." Chan Hai moved over to give me more room. "I promise."

I hoped he was right. Surely Mother would disapprove of me sitting in this smoky place surrounded by men. Mei Ling would not agree with my being out with a stranger from the bus. Even Madame Paper Cutter would push her glasses up on her nose and shake her head.

Trembling Customer next to me splashed soup on the table. Scalding drops of liquid hit my bare arm. I scooted onto the side of Chan Hai's stool. Our legs touched. A shiver engulfed me. My skin felt on fire. My heart beat loud and strong.

In between sips of his soup, Chan Hai explained how the owner had started hawking his pork soup out on the street until there was a line so big it blocked traffic. Then the owner had finally borrowed money from his business-savvy cousin. The rich cousin sounded like someone I knew. But my heart was busy singing from the warmth of Chan Hai's deep voice, from the heat of his leg near mine, from the softness of the pork.

The soup, a light combination of salty and sour, was hard to stop drinking. The bits of pork melted in my mouth. If I closed my eyes and ignored the occasional bone hitting my pants leg, the nervous man's elbow knocking into my arm, and the suffocating smoke, I could imagine being in the finest restaurant in the kingdom. Chan Hai was right. This was the finest pork to touch my tongue.

The owner came by to give Chan Hai a second helping. Chan Hai nodded his thanks and passed the man a *yuan* bill. So the soup was a reasonable cost. Had Madame Paper Cutter ever come here? I'd have to tell her about it. What did she eat for dinner? Where did she eat? With whom? At least here she'd get a good meal for very little money.

"How's Fu Lu Shou?" the owner asked.

He reached between us with his dirty rag and wiped a stack of bones from the center of the table into Chan Hai's now empty bowl. The owner's sweat-drenched arms dripped on my cheek. His blood-splattered apron rubbed against my arm.

"Uncle thinks if we dig deeper, we'll be fine," Chan Hai said blowing on the steaming broth of his second bowl of soup.

The owner nodded, his thick jowls wobbling. His thin hair glistened with sweat. His thin eyebrows came together in a straight line. He wiped at more imaginary bones. Cleared his throat.

"Who's the young miss?"

Chan Hai stopped sipping from his bowl. His neck went crimson.

"Daughter of Huang Binkin," he answered. "From your cousin's side of the village."

The owner nodded some more. Looked at me.

"The well digger?" he asked.

"Yes," I said. Did the man know Father as a child helper or a gambler?

"Near Zi Mei's shop?"

He must know Father the gambler. How shameful. The space so near to Chan Hai felt claustrophobic.

"Yes." I smiled. Despite the painful welts swelling inside, I held my head high. Father may have trampled on our reputation, but I wasn't a gambler. I had a job. I was doing my best to hold up my half of the sky. Especially today.

"You have a difficult neighbor, I understand," the owner said.

I nodded. New Neighbor wasn't so bad anymore. He was just frightened. Frightened that his only son had been killed. Frightened that his wife was ill. Frightened that we didn't all believe the same stories he did.

"Is he treating you well?" the owner asked.

I hesitated. What could I say? The neighbor had been quiet as of late. But before I answered, I noticed the owner indicated his head toward Chan Hai. He spoke of Chan Hai, not New Neighbor.

"Oh, yes," I said. "Yes."

"She's full of yes," the owner said, making one final swipe at the table.

"Good soup will do that to you," Chan Hai said, picking up his bowl and nodding his appreciation to the owner.

"Yes," I agreed.

A smile again tugged my lips upward. My face felt hot. Chan Hai nudged me with his knee. The owner laughed. We'd only known each other a short time, and we already had our own joke. This must be right.

"Little Chen needs a good friend." The owner patted Chan Hai on the shoulder before returning to his vat of soup.

A loneliness passed through Chan Hai's eyes like winter wind. Had something bad happened? I wanted our light moment to return.

"Yes," I said. "Don't we all?"

"Don't we all," a man's voice agreed. Not Chan Hai. A man behind him.

What a strange man. This man who had spoken to us. How overbearing and intrusive his behavior. But Chan Hai didn't seem to hear the man's words. He dug his chopsticks into his bowl in search of more meat. The man stood up, cleared his throat and spat on the floor. An unpleasant electricity emanated from his slicked back hair, his large girth. Around us stools scraped against cement as the salesmen stood up and gathered their bags. Trembling Customer next to me knocked his ceramic spoon on the floor. The china shattered. The monthly gathering was over? Perhaps the intrusive man was their leader.

This sales leader put one shiny black leather loafer on the back of Chan Hai's chair. Chan Hai moved forward to accommodate the man's leg in his back as though being jostled on a bus. He still didn't register this strange man's presence. The sales leader looked at me, his eyes roaming like a fly trying to locate a spot to land.

"If you want to go, Ms. Huang," he said. "I could arrange a special deal for you."

Go? Special deal? I looked to Chan Hai. His bowl was up to his face as he drank the last drop of soup. The delicious broth still worked magic on him. But what was I to say? A beggar pushed his way through the crowd of men and slipped into a vacant stool across from me, grabbing up the remains on the table. I tried to focus on this newcomer, a man with scraggly hairs protruding from a sallow face. But the sales leader's eyes felt like two suns on my head.

"I'm fine, thanks," I said, meeting his gaze.

Chan Hai looked over at the sound of my voice. His face was tender, as If I had awakened him from a good dream. From a fine bowl of soup.

"Yes, I can see that," the sales leader said. "Very fine."

Chan Hai twisted around to look at this man who watched me so closely. His eyes turned to stone.

"*Tamade*," Chan Hai swore, standing up and knocking the table over.

Bowls fell to the ground. Soup and shards of china flew through the air like a hailstorm. A chill ran up my spine. Surely a fight was about to take place. How could this be happening?

"Little Chen," the owner shouted and rushed over.

The owner grabbed onto Chan Hai and patted his back, as if to pacify him. The owner held onto Chan Hai's arms, as if to prevent any violence. Did the two men, Mr. Sales Leader and Chan Hai have a bad history? Surely, Chan Hai wasn't so bothered by the leers of this middle-aged man, no matter his obvious wealth. Chan Hai's dark eyes narrowed to points sharper than daggers. He squeezed his hands into fists. Where was the kind man from the bus? What kind of response was this?

Mr. Sales Leader gave Chan Hai's stool a fierce kick and stormed out. Certainly Mr. Sales Leader's manner had been coarse. But that was no reason for Chan Hai to swear at this man, to taunt him, to beg for a fight. Chan Hai was lucky the man just kicked the stool.

The salesmen shuffled out. The owner let go of Chan Hai, continuing to pat him on the back as one would a mentally slow person. I kneeled down to pick up the broken china.

"I've got it. I've got it," the owner said, kicking the shards away with his foot. "Take your friend home."

Yes, I needed to get him—and me—away from this place. I could see Madame Paper Cutter shaking her head at me, her oversized glasses sliding down her nose. She wouldn't approve of this companion's behavior. She would be right.

We walked away from the fine pork soup shop. The crowd of salesmen now stood along the main road waiting to board a van. Cars honked. Signs flashed on and off. The air smelled of vinegar. Were we near another restaurant? A vinegar shop? Or was that vinegar spreading through my own heart?

Some friends—not Mei Ling—had bucked our tradition of thousands of years of match-making and started relationships based on love. They had talked on and on about how they just knew when it was right. The problem with love relationships, as Mei Ling always said, was you didn't know what you were getting into. I, too, had thought Chan Hai and I were so right. Little could I have guessed that he had a temper problem. I'd heard people talk to strangers that way. But there was always a reason—like the stranger's chicken pecked a hole in your bag of peas. There was no explanation for Chan Hai's violent behavior.

"I'm sorry," Chan Hai said, putting his arm around my shoulder as we walked up the street. "I should have known better than to stop there on the first Thursday."

A pit settled in my stomach. His arm felt like a wet towel hanging around my neck. I needed to get away from this man who was not Madame Liang's son. How long would it take to get to the bus depot? I picked my hair up off my neck forcing Chan Hai to move his arm away. This had been a harmless dinner. I wanted to keep it that way.

"Ruins the taste of the dinner," Chan Hai said.

"No, no," I lied. "Nothing could do that."

"I'll have to tell the owner you said so," Chan Hai said.

His voice was quiet. A totally different personality from the man who had shouted obscenities five minutes ago. Was he as embarrassed as I? Or had his temper problem disappeared like a fast-moving dark cloud? He held onto my arm. His shoes scuffled against the pavement, louder than the disco music which thumped in the bar on the corner. How could I have made such a decision, such an error? At least no one had seen us together. As soon as we parted at the bus depot, this dinner could be forgotten. I picked up my pace.

"Are you still hungry?" Chan Hai asked. "Would you like some ice cream? I know a new place around the corner. Just opened today—"

"No, I'm fine," I said.

I wished I'd kept a closer watch on the roads we'd taken to get to the restaurant. I wasn't clear on how far we had walked, so busy had I been listening to the patter of his voice as he talked of his dream to own a nursery.

A drunk old man peed in the gutter. He leaned forward, as though he were standing over the pit in the ground in his outhouse, rather than out here surrounded by curious onlookers. I felt shame for him. I felt shame for myself. My decision to have dinner with Chan Hai was also not a private matter. Not just between the two of us. It affected my family, Madame Matchmaker, Madame Liang's family, the village. I'd ignored all those important relationships, certain I'd felt something special. Certain Chan Hai was my dream man. A hero. But he was just a poor man with a bad temper.

We walked in silence. I felt stiff. Each step required concentrated effort. The hush between us felt more and more uncomfortable, like a sunflower seed caught in my throat.

"How about a drink?" Chan Hai tried again, as we passed the bar on the corner.

"No, really. I've—"

"Had enough?" Chan Hai finished.

"No, no."

I didn't want to offend him. I didn't want to be on the receiving end of his temper. He let go of my arm and reached into his pocket.

"You're suddenly full of no," he said, stopping under a light and looking down at me.

I couldn't meet his gaze. Those dark brown eyes which looked through me. I would be home soon, no worse for the wear, and could forget I'd made such a ridiculous mistake.

"If you ever want to reach me—"

He took out his Butterfly cigarette package, tore a piece of paper from the top and wrote something. The darkness of the night strangled me. The horns and music sounded too loud. I hugged my arms to my chest. I didn't want that paper or anything to remind me of my foolish heart.

He put the pen back in his pocket, and we kept walking. He folded and unfolded the bit of paper in his hand.

"The lady with the best chickens around has a phone," he said, his deep voice trembling as though a breeze had blown through him. "I'm only a few minutes away."

He held out the paper. His long rough fingers remained steady. The small piece of paper which held the memory of a horrible error pointed at me like the blade of a knife.

I stopped and looked around. Up ahead two golden arches lit up the night. The greasy American *hambaobao* restaurant with the lucky golden M. The small park where I'd spent many a day standing and waiting to be hired as a tutor. All of those familiar landmarks had been right next to me. I glanced back at the small side street from which we had emerged.

"We were so close," I said.

"What?" He too stopped. He came back to where I stood, standing so close the button of his pants brushed against my side. "Did you actually speak more than one word?"

"I—I had no idea we were so close to here," I said. There I was, talking to this man again, as if he were a friend. "I get turned around easily."

"Not just you," Chan Hai said. "It's amazing how all of us can be so close to something and still not see it."

His voice seemed distant. As if that winter wind had entered his heart. A squeezing sensation surrounded my heart. I reached out and took Chan Hai's number.

Chapter Eighteen
The Snakehead

We stood there a moment, the two of us, in the darkness. Across the street, gas lanterns dotted the park like fireflies. Was Madame Paper Cutter there? Could she see me with this strange man? The sound of a metal grate closing filled the air. A cart squeaked past, a man calling out, "Adult videos for sale." A red neon Tsingtao beer sign flashed on and off.

"The night is a different place," I said.

"That it is," Chan Hai agreed.

He stepped closer. He lifted my chin. Just then a man rushed between the two of us. I gripped onto my purse. Father would never stop talking if I was the victim of a purse snatcher. Not that there was any money in my purse yet. Still, the scissors Madame Paper Cutter had given me were there. I wouldn't want to lose those.

"Watch where you're going," Chan Hai said.

The man didn't even turn. He kept going. He carried a striped suitcase. Was he late for the monthly sales meeting?

"Hey," Chan Hai called. "Hey," Chan Hai called again and ran after the man.

I looked away. Sure, the man had been rude. Probably was a horrible salesman. But how did Chan Hai plan to correct that?

Across the street came the sound of cardboard being dragged across the cement. The homeless woman unrolled her bedding for the night in front of the greasy hamburger shop. First, Mr. Overindulgent with his spoiled Little Emperor had picked me out. Now Chan Hai. Did I attract violence? Shame covered me like a blanket. If I didn't trust Mother and Madame Matchmaker to find the right man for me, I'd probably end up like that lady in front of the hamburger shop. Every day scraping for a few *fen*. Every night cold and lonely.

A scuffling sound made me turn. The red flashing neon Tsingtao Beer ad blinked on and off, illuminating the rude salesman who now stood in front of Chan Hai, shuffling from one foot to another, like a scarecrow in the wind. His striped suitcase sat by his side.

"Old Chen?" the rude salesman squawked like a frightened

chicken.

Old? Just as in the soup shop, this man called Chan Hai with a title of familiarity. Perhaps the poor man had had a fight with Chan Hai before.

"I knew that was you," Chan Hai replied.

The red light blinked off. The darkness of the town returned. Shadows loomed from shop buildings and the movie theater.

"This isn't what I lent you money for," Chan Hai shouted, his voice wound up like a string on an instrument which had been pulled too tightly.

Money? Perhaps Chan Hai had chased the rude man over more than a shove. A taxi honked, swerving to miss a man pulling a cart of plastic jugs. Two young men passed me, the smell of alcohol emanating like perfume. They turned and looked in my direction. The night air felt cold against my neck. I rubbed my arms and folded them across my chest. Surely Chan Hai would be finished talking soon. I could walk to the bus depot on my own, but a strong male companion on a dark night felt much safer. I walked toward Chan Hai and his friend, stopping several feet away beneath a "No Honking" sign. The neon ad blinked on.

"What are you saying, Little Wu Lu?" Chan Hai shook the man's shoulders. "You showed me an acceptance letter."

"Old Chen, there's no such thing for people like us."

Little Wu Lu pulled away. His thin face glowed red in the light, darkening at a large crescent-shaped burn mark on his left cheek. Had he ever been a tutor for Mr. Overindulgent, the man who had pushed his cigarette at me in the park? Perhaps this scar was just a birthmark.

Little Wu Lu fumbled in his pockets and pulled out a packet of cigarettes, offered one to Chan Hai. Chan Hai wasn't so angry that he refused the gesture. What was all this about money and acceptance letters? Had Little Wu Lu come to Chan Hai for support for schooling? But Little Wu Lu looked older than a college student. His thin face told of many years. His thick, strong arms revealed many hard jobs. The light blinked off. The flame from the man's match trembled as he lit both cigarettes. Did Chan Hai make the man nervous?

"And I thought you even sent a down payment," Chan Hai said.
"What? Was all of this a—"

"No. I didn't bullshit you," Little Wu Lu said. "I had all those things. Acceptance letter, place to live, notice of payment. I'd even picked out my classes."

So this Little Wu Lu had planned on going to school. The light blinked on, casting a pink glow on the scar. Chan Hai had given him money. Chan Hai must be in a better financial position than us.

"And?" Chan Hai said.

"I couldn't get a visa." Little Wu Lu puffed hard on his cigarette, as though drawing breath.

"Maybe you didn't try—"

"Five times." Little Wu Lu held up one hand. His eyes were tired. "Five times I went to that *cao tamade* American Embassy."

Ah, so Little Wu Lu had attempted the impossible. The American Embassy.

"And?" Chan Hai asked.

"Each time they told me I hadn't provided enough evidence to show my economic ties to China. To show that I would return home after my studies. I have my ancestors here, my parents, my son , my wife. None of that was enough." He pointed his cigarette at Chan Hai as if it were an extra finger. "I didn't know what else to give them. Cut my heart out and leave it at the desk? You tell me—how do you prove ties to your country? How?"

"This isn't the answer, Little Wu Lu," Chan Hai said, his voice still tight. "Don't do it."

The light went off. The two men stood in the darkness, the glow from their cigarettes jumping up and down, up and down. Do what? I thought of all the nervous men with their striped suitcases. Of the well-dressed man with the leering eyes. Of the van they all boarded. My skin burned, as if Fourth Auntie had just touched me with her new chemical sprayer.

The intrusive, arrogant man at the soup shop had looked like any other harried businessman. But he wasn't. He was like the predatory fish for which he had been named. A fish which ate whatever crossed its path. A snakehead. How could I have been so naive to assume that Chan Hai was bad tempered?

Some people would have said Chan Hai behaved like an old mother. We southern Chinese believed in risks. We were the cowboys of China. We had the most entrepreneurs, the most daredevils. We weren't afraid to lose—not even fifty thousand on a fake marriage. We weren't afraid to follow snakeheads over the waters, in the belief that, no matter the poor survival statistics, we'd arrive safely. Only old mothers, fearful for the safety of the future generations, would do the same as Chan Hai. I pinched the bridge of my nose. Mei Ling had put her life in the hands of a snakehead. Why did I assume she would be successful? Why hadn't I thought to question her decision?

Obviously Chan Hai's heart was strong. Stronger than reputations and expectations. I took several steps and stood in a good place next to him. The light flicked on. Our shoes touched.

"I don't have a choice," the man said, finally looking at me rather than Chan Hai. He took one last pull on his cigarette, as though inhaling strength. "My wife's been ill for over a year. The doctors don't know what's wrong. But whatever they suggest." He rubbed his thumb over his fingers. Big money.

"Where are you—uh, they—going?" I asked.

"Singapore." Little Wu Lu flicked his cigarette on the ground and picked up his suitcase.

"Do you know what happens to illegals who get caught there?" Chan Hai's laugh sent a chill down my spine. He shook Little Wu Lu by the shoulders. "Do you?"

"Old Chen—"

"They're caned until their manhood is gone, that's what."

"I've already got my son." Little Wu Lu pushed Chan Hai away.

"Besides, it's too damn hot there for anything but cockroaches to survive," Chan Hai persisted, his voice filled with power like a wave crashing against the rocks.

"The temple priest said now was a good time," Little Wu Lu answered.

Chan Hai stared at Little Wu Lu, flicking the ashes of his cigarette. Those piercing eyes demanded Little Wu Lu pay attention. Face the truth.

"If the government would just make jobs for us, Old Chen, we wouldn't have to go to a foreign country."

Little Wu Lu had a point. I had a college degree and still didn't have a job. Mei Ling had a degree, and she still had to go overseas to find work. Not everyone was as fortunate as Chan Hai to have an uncle with a rock quarry. The light flicked off.

"Let me talk to my uncle," Chan Hai said.

"Thanks for the offer. But even that salary isn't going to get me far."

"And digging a hole of debt will?"

A van careened to a stop at the corner. Old-fashioned music blared from the television screen inside. Was this the same van from outside the restaurant? The driver honked.

"Hurry up and let's go," well-dressed Snakehead from the restaurant called, leaning over the driver and shouting out the window.

I wrapped my arms tight across my chest. I leaned closer to Chan Hai. Even with the Tsingtao light off, I felt Snakehead leering.

"I've got to go," Little Wu Lu said, shaking my hand goodbye, although we had only just met. His palms were cold and sticky. "Take care of my family," he said, hugging Chan Hai.

"No," Chan Hai whispered.

Little Wu Lu and I looked at him. How could he say such a thing when Little Wu Lu was getting ready to leave for three, five, maybe ten years? Maybe forever? Why didn't he give his friend support?

"Come on, Old Chen." Little Wu Lu patted Chan Hai on the arm. "I'll repay your money as soon as I get a job."

"Remember?" Chan Hai 's voice went up. "Remember how you used to follow us around all the time when we were kids?"

The van did a u-turn and pulled up next to us under the "No Honking" sign. The car lights shone on us. The driver leaned on the horn.

"Take care," Little Wu Lu said, patting Chan Hai on the arm.

"Every summer we'd catch crickets," Chan Hai said, holding onto Little Wu Lu's arm. "You always caught the most. Until that one summer—"

"Don't think bad things." Little Wu Lu glanced down in my direction.

The driver of the van pulled up onto the sidewalk inches away from us. Faces of the men from the soup shop pressed up against the van window, watching, waiting. Exhaust from the tail pipe heated the air around us.

"That summer, you caught a whole bunch of crickets, insisted on saving them, so you could hear them sing all summer in your room." Chan Hai pulled on Little Wu Lu's arm. "Remember?"

"I'll write." Little Wu Lu pulled away from Chan Hai. He patted Chan Hai's arm as you do when you're trying to leave a grandfather who won't stop reminiscing.

"Only, in your excitement, you neglected to put enough air holes in the box. Your grasshoppers died. One by one."

"You remember everything." Little Wu Lu laughed.

The driver blasted the horn again. Snakehead got out and

opened the back door. The rollers of the door screeched with age and misuse.

"Get in," Snakehead said.

Chan Hai followed Little Wu Lu to the van. A look of fear passed over Chan Hai's face. Why didn't he rejoice at his friend's opportunity? Not many people could afford to take such a trip. Sure, it was dangerous. Chan Hai already pictured Little Wu Lu suffocating in a container like a grasshopper. But everyone accepted that danger, like they accepted the smell of the eel farms and the coal fires. It was part of the air we breathed. Why did Chan Hai act like this was different? Why was my heart heavy as if I could feel Chan Hai's pain?

Snakehead stood flicking his cell phone open and closed. Open and closed. But Chan Hai took his time situating Little Wu Lu's suitcase under the seat, positioning and repositioning the plastic bag, which probably held nothing more than a change of clothing, cigarettes, dried fish, buns, apples. Snakehead banged the side of the van with his fist.

"We don't have all night."

He got back in the passenger side and shut the door, staring at the moves of a young woman in a tight-fitting *qipao* as she sang a country tune from Cultural Revolution times on the television hanging between him and the driver. Then he turned and looked at me.

"We're going whether you shut that door or not."

Chan Hai pulled the handle. But, just before he shut the van door, he pointed to a red envelope sticking part way out of Little Wu Lu's pants pocket. The corners were well worn, as if Little Wu Lu had held the envelope a long time, fretting over his decision.

"What about the man's money?" Chan Hai asked.

"Oh, yeah." Little Wu Lu's short fingers fumbled with the bulging packet.

Snakehead smiled his appreciation in the rear view mirror, putting his fat fingers back to take the packet. But Chan Hai was fast. He intercepted that thick envelope filled with money, slammed the door, and took off across the street and through the park. Hawkers shouted as the van crashed through their makeshift stalls after Chan Hai. The tires of the van spat out broken clay models of Jesus and Kuanyin—the Goddess of Mercy—onto the grass. At least Madame Paper Cutter wasn't in danger. At least I hoped she hadn't returned to the park and wouldn't be there to see all of this.

Pressure pounded behind my eyes. My insides felt like all that broken chaos on the grass. Certainly it was kind of Chan Hai to show his concern for his old friend. I hadn't done as much with Mei Ling, so excited was I for her to grasp after a life with better opportunities. But surely he'd gone too far. I walked back and forth in front of the park, back and forth. Would he be alright? Would he come back?

"Everywhere we go, little sister, you're waiting," a tall man said.

The two men who smelled like alcohol. They stood one on either side of me. One of them was tall, not quite as tall as Chan Hai. The other was my height. They puffed on cigarettes.

"What are you waiting for?" the tall one asked.

I took a step away. Father's warnings filled my head. Beware of people getting too close. They might drug you with their touch. They might kidnap you. Take all your money. My ears felt hot. My stomach tight. What was I waiting for?

"A friend," I said.

"A friend, huh?" The taller one, mischief in his voice, tossed his cigarette to the ground. "I could be a friend."

He had spiked hair like a teenager. Like an animal. His face looked worn. He didn't need a friend. Surely at home he had a wife and child.

"No, thanks." I moved further into the park. "My friend—he's up there."

I wished Madame Paper Cutter to be there. Perhaps we could sit together a while. Go to the bus depot together. Where did she live? Why couldn't she be here right now?

"Well, your friend's about to be part of the trouble," the short one said, pointing at the appearance of red-and-blue flashing lights in the park.

I stopped. A policeman had driven his motorcycle on the grass. He parked and got off, leaving the engine running, the lights flashing. He withdrew a flashlight from the container on the back of the bike. Switched on the narrow light. With the beam, he surveyed bits of broken clay next to the stone engraved slogan, "With Your Heart and Soul Serve the People." The slogan was spoken so often, we didn't really think about the words anymore. They had lost all meaning. And, while this stone engraving was meant as a reminder to us all to be pure, it seemed as meaningful as the flashing Tsingtao beer ad under the policeman's lights. Surely the officer would use his heart and soul to serve the people. His people. His family.

The officer looked at the popped plastic balloons on the grass. From where I stood, they looked like leaves from some strange tree. He examined where the fence around the stone carving had been crushed in. He gave an exaggerated shake of his head. Who would he blame for this? Who would pay? And would the money he took ever repair the broken fence?

"Your friend's certainly taking an awfully long time," Spikey said. "You sure he's coming for you? Cause it's dangerous for a woman like you to be out here all alone."

Spikey or the policeman in the park, which would be safer? I looked back at the park. The officer shone his flashlight on the inhabitants of the park. Picking out his victims. My underarms prickled.

"I'm certain he's coming." I put my watch close to my face. "Any minute now."

I rushed up the walkway away from the leering Spikey. I didn't see Madame Paper Cutter. Perhaps she had gotten away, although maybe she hadn't been here at all to witness this destruction. What would she say when I told her the man who made my heart tremble so had caused such a disaster? Would she have any words of advice? I spotted Mr. Palm Reader. He gathered his charts and stools, ready to flee before suffocating from the foul smell of the law. He bent to pick up the extra stool he reserved for customers. I sat down.

"Please," I said. "Remember me? Can I just sit here a minute?"

"Now's not a good time, Little Sister," Mr. Palm Reader said, looking over his shoulder. His eyes twitched.

"Just for a minute," I asked.

"No. Really," Mr. Palm Reader said. His eyes grew large as he spotted something behind me. "I was just on my way home."

"You're not supposed to be here," the policeman said. His flashlight darted back and forth from me to Mr. Palm Reader.

"I was just leaving," Mr. Palm Reader said. He shooed me off his stool, picked up his gas lantern and cardboard sign which showed the different areas of the palm and their significance in telling the future.

"Quite a mess here," the policeman said.

The policeman sounded friendly, almost jubilant. Mr. Palm Reader fumbled with his stool, his eyes cast toward the ground. He shuffled his feet back and forth as if that could speed up the process.

"Let me help you," the policeman offered.

His words seemed so full of heart, but his stiff bearing suggested otherwise. The policeman stood no taller than Mr. Palm Reader, but his authoritative manner dwarfed the jobless migrant. Surely he was about to step on this man.

"I'm fine," Mr. Palm Reader said. His hands now shook like an old man who hadn't taken enough fish oil. "Don't worry."

"It's fortunate that you had nothing to break," the officer said taking Mr. Palm Reader's stool and folding it.

"Yes." Mr. Palm Reader sounded wary.

"You still have all your goods, all your money." The officer shone his light in my eyes. "You even have a customer at this late hour."

Mr. Palm Reader exchanged a crumpled bill for the stool the officer held. The officer bent over and looked at the ten *yuan* note in the light of Mr. Palm Reader's gas lamp to check that it wasn't a forgery. Ten *yuan*. That was twenty bowls of fine pork soup, five hours of working at the tea shop. How long had it taken Mr. Palm Reader to earn this amount? I had held Mr. Palm Reader up. I had caused him to lose this money. I wished I could offer to pay for him.

"And what about you, Little Sister?" The flashlight shone in my eyes again. "What are you doing out here all alone at this time of night?"

"I—I—" My heart beat like an engraver's pick against my chest. "I'm waiting for a friend."

"A friend?" The officer chuckled long and slow. "Does your friend have a name or will any friend do?"

"Of course my friend has a name," I said. How offensive. I resented his implication. So much so, I didn't think before speaking. "In fact, I was heading over to meet him just now."

"Oh, really." The officer stepped forward, his palm already twitching at the thought of more money to be had. "And where would you be meeting?"

"We're supposed to meet next to some slogan," I said. "I haven't been here in such a long time, I forget. Isn't there a slogan around here that reads, 'With your heart and soul serve the people?'"

"Yes," the officer said, shining his flashlight toward the stone engraving. "But there's no one next to that slogan now."

"You're so right about that," I said, looking to where the officer had padded his pocket with Mr. Palm Reader's money.

The officer stepped back a bit. Cleared his throat. Put his hand in his pocket as though to cover this stolen money. This act which didn't serve the people.

"You best just go on home," the officer said.

"Yes, sir," I said. "Thank you for your concern."

He nodded his dismissal. Then he surveyed the crowd for others who hadn't lost their fortunes to the fiasco. Others who could offer him a little "oil and water."

Small fingers touched my leg. Then my arm. Then my neck. I swatted at the fingers that crawled all over me, as the hawkers lamps receded further up the road and I was left in darkness. I listened to the high whine of those fingers, those mosquitoes. I couldn't wait any longer for Chan Hai to return. I walked out of the park and back to the road. The homeless woman in front of the greasy hamburger shop had already fallen into a deep slumber. I too would soon be home and in bed.

A van careened around the corner. The right tires rolled up onto the sidewalk ahead of me. The van sputtered and whined as the driver attempted to shift gears. Either he was in a hurry beyond all reason, or he was one of many who drove without a license. The van screeched to a halt. Then backed up right next to me. The sound of a Cultural Revolution song blared.

"I knew you wouldn't go far," a voice called out the window.

No. This couldn't be. Snakehead? Again?

My heart beat fast. Why would he want to find me? Perhaps he had caught Chan Hai and wanted to show me his ability to slay this dragon.

Snakehead got out of the van and opened the back door. Smoke billowed out as the men inside sat knee-to-knee puffing away. Snakehead pulled Little Wu Lu out and threw his suitcase on the ground.

"Nice trick," Snakehead said.

"Please, Mr. Huang," Little Wu Lu said. "I didn't know my friend was going to run off with your money. Please believe me. I'll have my wife get it to you."

Chan Hai would be pleased his friend didn't get on the boat. Still, why had Snakehead come find me before sending Little Wu Lu back home?

"Call me when you get the money." Snakehead shuffled change in his pockets. "Then I'll arrange for your transport next month."

"But I'm ready to go now." The scar on his cheek quivered.

He had probably spent lots of time and money trying to get a visa to further his studies in America. When that hadn't worked, he'd spent more time gathering money to go to Singapore. The temple priest had told him now was an auspicious time. He thought he was on his way, on his way to building a better future for his family. Chan Hai, no matter how good his intentions, had stolen that. I was powerless to do anything but watch.

"Now, Miss Huang, it looks as if there's an extra space." Snakehead stepped right next to me. His breath smelled of liquor and cigarettes. His gold bracelets brushed against the front of my blouse. My mouth tasted sour. "This is the chance of a lifetime."

"Thanks, no." I stepped close to Chan Hai's good old friend for protection.

"I'll pay you double," Little Wu Lu, his limbs shaking, promised the snakehead.

I held my breath. Chan Hai wouldn't have wanted his friend to beg like this. Snakehead waved his arm in the air, as if Little Wu Lu were a whiny mosquito.

"A clever girl like you could earn so much money." His eyes darted up and down my body. "Easily enough to buy your parents a new house five stories high."

"I have a job," I said.

"I can find you a job that would allow you to live in luxury." Snakehead laughed. "Not eating in dives or walking the streets alone late at night."

The van driver honked. The sound, familiar during the day, seemed out of place. Like a warning.

"Boss, the boat leaves in forty-five minutes," the driver called.

I looked back at the park. The policeman had put his flashlight away and mounted his bike. He must have oiled his pockets for the night. The blue-and-red lights flashed our way.

"Mr. Huang." Little Wu Lu bowed his head. He held his hands together as though praying to the gods. "Please."

"Come on, Young Miss, it's decision time," Snakehead said, patting my arm. "You heard the driver."

I grabbed onto Wu Lu as if he were a rock in the middle of this tumultuous sea.

"Take both of us," Little Wu Lu said, grabbing onto my arm. "She'll come if I go, won't you?"

"No," I shouted, struggling to break free.

Little Wu Lu's face was thin and haggard. But his arms felt as taut as the rope used to pull water from the well. He pulled me up into the van with him.

"Sounds like a bargain to me." Snakehead laughed, rubbing his hands together, then slamming the door.

"Help," I cried, as the policeman's flashing lights neared.

Had Little Wu Lu and Snakehead agreed on this performance beforehand? Perhaps Chan Hai was even part of the set-up. Chan Hai, who had followed me from the taxi stand, who had insisted on taking me to that cruddy little restaurant. Had he been planning to kidnap me all along? How much of a cut was he getting from this?

"Help," I called again so loudly my body vibrated with the effort.

Little Wu Lu slapped his palm over my mouth. His fingers smelled of tobacco and sweat. His grip was so strong I thought he'd break my jaw. The motorcycle slowed. The policeman tapped on the driver's window. Would he help me with his heart and soul?

The driver rolled the window down. Snakehead leaned over, his greasy hair flinging against the back of the seat.

"Did you have dinner yet?" Snakehead asked of the policeman.

"Old Huang," the policeman said. "It's just you."

I bit hard onto Little Wu Lu's fingers. He pulled his hand back.

"No," I called out to the policeman. "Help."

The light shone into the back of the van. At last. He would help me.

"I thought I told you to go home," the officer said.

"I—"

"Well, I see you've found many friends," the officer said, chuckling that long, slow chuckle. He switched his flashlight off.

"No," I cried before Little Wu Lu slapped his hand over my mouth again.

The officer rapped his knuckles on the side of the car. Before the traffic light had even changed to green, he was gone. I wasn't surprised. Just disappointed. The same way I had been when Counselor Zhang dismissed me from my office. The same as when Mr. Overindulgent picked another tutor over me. The same as when Feng Gu attempted to cheat me. The same as when Chan Hai helped these men to kidnap me. My heart burned, as if a lit match had been dropped down my throat. But what these people didn't realize is I wouldn't give up.

Chapter Nineteen
The Temple Bell

There once was a foolish man whose only desire was to steal the clapper from the temple bell. That silver clapper, when melted down, would buy him clothes and food for the rest of his days. Each day he passed that beautiful temple. Each day he schemed of how he might get that clapper. One night, he snuck into the temple grounds. He tiptoed past a sleeping guard to the ornate temple bell. Here he was about to achieve his dream. Just as he reached inside to untie the clapper, the guard snorted in his sleep. The foolish man's hands shook the clapper up against the side of the bell. The bell rang out for the entire village to hear. Rather than run, the foolish man stood where he was and covered his ears.

Whenever I pretended not to see a problem, or thought I could succeed doing the impossible, Waipo would turn to me and say, "You cover your ears while you steal the bell clapper." Is that what I had done tonight? Despite my reservations about Chan Hai's background, about his not being Madame Liang's son, about what Mother and Mei Ling and Madame Paper Cutter would think of him, I had covered my ears and insisted on following the man with the dimples. Despite my concern over his bad temper, I had covered my ears and stayed behind, putting my feet next to his.

Now, here I was stuck in between the legs of Little Wu Lu. His arms locked around me. The other men in the van had their heads turned toward the windows, staring at the Good And Plentiful Department Store up on the left, not wanting to be involved. Soon I'd be in a container, fighting off seasickness, with my nose to the small vents, hopping like a cricket, hoping for some fresh air, any air. I could cover my ears no longer.

The van driver switched into a lane of oncoming traffic. He sped down the road, heading away from the bus depot. Far away from home. My home. Was Mother standing outside Zi Mei's closed shop, looking up the street, waiting for signs of my return? Did Father even realize I was gone? Or was he playing one last game of *mahjong*? When would he notice my absence? Or would he?

I squirmed this way and that to loosen Wu Lu's hold. My purse banged against my thighs. My purse. No money in there to bribe my way free. Nothing but my identification and Madame Paper Cutter's scissors. What would Madame Paper Cutter say now? What would she cut for me to show her thoughts?

"How can you do this?" I said. "This isn't right."

Little Wu Lu held me with one arm, as though I were a chicken under his arm. He fumbled in his pocket for his Butterfly cigarettes. He tried to light a match using one hand, but the small paper sticks only made a sulfury smoke. I dug my hands in my purse, suddenly cold. As if I was trapped in the center of a fierce wind. Shivering.

On the right, a spiral loomed in the night sky. The romantic Wei Min Hotel. A grand building with glass windows in the ceiling so dining couples and wedding parties could view the night sky, sometimes even a full moon. According to Zi Mei. Was she offering Mother solace? Would news of my disappearance now be the first item from her lips rather than the "Taiwanese" bombing at Cheng Min's?

If I went to Singapore this way, I'd never know if Cheng Min survived. If she got to have her third child. I'd never meet Madame Liang and her son. I'd never get the satisfaction of watching the tea shop flourish, of being paid for my hand in making it a success. A rush of icy wind from a sudden crack in my heart made water overflow from my eyes.

"This isn' t right." My voice shook.

"You'll be fine," Little Wu Lu said. His voice was cold. Surely his face, that scarred face, looked like the cold stone of a mountain.

"Oh, stop all the chatter," Snakehead called from the front.

He turned up the volume on the television. More Cultural Revolution songs.

"We're going to be late," the driver called over the upbeat sound of an old marching tune.

"Well, hurry up then," Snakehead called back.

The driver maneuvered in and out of oncoming traffic, passing the slow cars in our lane. Little Wu Lu let go of me for a moment to light his cigarette. If only the van driver would stop. If only I could escape.

Up ahead, an old man on his bike wobbled out of the entrance to the Wei Min Hotel. The back of his bike was piled high with old cardboard boxes, which although flattened and folded, still stacked higher than his head. He couldn't see us coming.

"*Tamade*," the van driver swore.

Traffic came zooming at us from the opposite direction, so there was nothing the van driver could do but slow down. He sped up. He honked his horn like an angry chicken, hoping the old man would pull off the road. Instead, the frightened old man jerked his bike further into the road.

"*Tamade*," the van driver swore again, slamming on the brakes so hard that we all lurched forward.

Little Wu Lu's cigarette flew out of his mouth onto the floor. The van was stopped. This was my chance. The driver honked and honked, begging the old man to move. Little Wu Lu reached down to grab his cigarette. I squiggled out of his grasp and grabbed the van door.

"What are you doing?" Little Wu Lu tightened his hold on me.

We both watched the glowing coal of the cigarette smoldering on the rubber mat by our feet. The acrid smell of burning rubber bit my nose. He put his foot out to stamp the cigarette out. I kicked the burning piece of tobacco out of his reach.

"I've got it," Snakehead said, leaning back, picking up the cigarette and returning it to Little Wu Lu.

"Go ahead," I said to all of them. "Kidnap me. We can all die together."

"Don't talk like that," Little Wu Lu said.

I sensed his scar twitching. He was superstitious. Like my neighbor.

"You die," I said. "What good are you to your wife?"

I didn't really think he would die. But I also knew I didn't want whatever lay ahead on this boat, in this hot country where only cockroaches would survive.

"Shut up." Little Wu Lu squeezed me so hard one of my ribs made a cracking sound.

"Both of you shut up," Snakehead said, snapping off the television. "You'll have time to squabble when we get to the boat—IF WE EVER GET THERE!"

The van waited for the old man's bike to wobble back to the side of the road. So slow. So slow.

"Hit the old turtle," Snakehead said. "Just move."

What a horrible person. If he had no qualms about hitting an old man to get to the boat on time, to get his money for transporting this human cargo, certainly he would not care about my life or death. I had to get out of this van. I clutched the metal scissors in my purse. This was my only chance.

"Let go of me," I said, extracting the scissors and stabbing out at little Wu Lu.

"You!" he cried out as warm blood shot from his leg, splattering my arm. "You bitch."

He reached for the scissors. I stabbed his hand. At the same time, I put my other hand up to open the door.

"Where do you think you're going, Little Sister?"

Snakehead looked back, a gleam in his eye. He put his arm back to block my path. I thrust the blades at him. He pulled his injured arm away. The other men sat silent, not interested in fighting to have me on board the van. The boat. Up until now, I had meant nothing to them good or bad. But now, with the van late and the boat about to leave, they weren't eager to risk wounds or tardiness to keep me as part of the crew.

Little Wu Lu, the only one save Snakehead with an interest in my presence, put his bloody hand up to grab me once again. I jerked the scissors toward him. But he grabbed my wrist, pushing hard on a pressure point. My scissors, my only protection, dropped to the floor with a thud. Just then, a thick arm came between us. A man from the back. He blocked Little Wu Lu from grasping onto my other arm. He pulled open the door. Little Wu Lu grabbed at my pants, his pudgy fingers like an iron yoke. There was nothing I could do.

"Let her go," a voice bellowed. The snakehead.

Little Wu Lu hesitated. Would he still get to go to Singapore, even without me? Would he still be able to realize his dream?

"I'll find her later," Snakehead assured.

With that pronouncement from the leader of the group, Little Wu Lu kicked me out of the open door. I flew through the air, landing on the grass so hard, my lungs felt as though they were being thrust out of my body. I didn't even wait to find my breath. I stood up and ran to the entrance of the hotel.

Taxis queued to take home the long line of diners. I didn't have time to wait in a line. What if that crazy van driver pulled around and Little Wu Lu stepped out to grab me? What did Snakehead's "later" mean? A couple stepped out to board the next taxi. I jumped in ahead of them.

Chapter Twenty
The Moon is Dark, the Wind is High

The ripped vinyl of the seat poked my thigh. The taxi pulled to a stop. So soon.

"We're here." The taxi driver turned on his overhead light.

I looked out at Zi Mei's darkened shop. The phone booth on the side stood like an old friend. I imagined the smell of the plastic receiver, could feel the chipped area in the mouthpiece. I was home. Almost.

Had Snakehead Huang followed me, even if it meant missing the boat? I reached for my scissors. All I felt were sticky fingers. Blood. I wished the taxi could spoon me into the house, like soup from a bowl. But our house was surrounded by other houses. No road led to the front door.

"My older sister used to work with chickens, too," the taxi driver said.

The taxi driver's nonstop chatter I'd appreciated all the way home. Like a soft-playing radio in the background. But, perhaps he was a little off, just as the rest of my world had become.

"A tough job." He nodded at my hands, my pants.

"Yes," I said. I looked at the blood caked black on my fingers, my ripped pants. "Very tough."

My insides quaked. I could still feel the warm blood spurting from Little Wu Lu's leg. I hadn't hurt him too bad, I was sure. Just enough to make him let me go. I could see the irritated looks on the faces of the other passengers when the door flung open. They hadn't wanted to bother with me in the first place. And then there was Snakehead. Excitement filled his eyes, as if he had found a challenge. Had he come looking for me? I took a deep breath.

I looked out into the darkness. All was quiet. Too quiet. Where was Zi Mei who often stayed after closing to chat with a neighbor? Where were the young men who often lit up the darkness with their cigarettes, with their laughter?

"Forty *yuan*," the driver said.

The taxi driver. He stared at me. He wanted money.

"Forty," I said. I didn't have forty, didn't have twenty, didn't have ten. What a ridiculous sum. "Forty?"

"Yes, you have to pay the parking fee for the hotel as well," he explained taking out a receipt pad which had twenty *yuan* written on it. Where had he bought those?

"I didn't park at the hotel," I said.

"But I did." He handed me the phony receipt. "And I waited for you. So you must pay."

I studied the receipt. The top read "Blue Water Swimming Pool." The driver counted on me not reading.

"This isn't for the hotel," I said, pointing to the words.

"Yes, it is." The driver's eyes blinked rapidly.

"You're playing with me," I said. I crumpled the receipt and dropped it on the floor.

"Fine, fine," the driver said. "Then thirty *yuan*."

"It's twenty," I said.

"But it's so late," the driver said. "I'm tired."

"That's not my problem." I pushed out of the taxi.

"Miss?"

"I don't have all that money here," I said. "Wait here a minute, please."

"I'm waiting." The taxi driver sighed, took out a comb from the tray next to his seat and ran the prongs through his greasy hair.

I took a deep breath and ran up the steps next to Zi Mei's. Perhaps, on the unluckiest night of my life, Father would have had some luck. I crossed the neighbor's backyard, squeezed through the small opening behind our shower room and ran up to the front door. The heavy wooden doors were closed. My mouth went dry. My breathing was like that of a dying fish. The doors were closed. Would Snakehead pop out from the corner of the house? If I could just get inside.

I banged on the wood so hard, the heel of my hand grew numb. The door opened a crack. Father hadn't yet thrown the bolt. I was home. A tingling sensation ran through my body. The sweet smell of Father's rice wine filled the great hall like cheap perfume. I laughed out loud. I had made it. I looked over to where Father sat slumped in his chair. Had he been waiting for me?

"I'm home," I whispered.

I looked around for signs of money. An extra bottle of rice wine sat on the table. A celebration perhaps? Good Father. Always there in a crisis.

"*Ba*, I need some money," I said. I nudged his shoulder with my elbow. "*Ba*? *Ba*? Can I borrow eighteen *yuan*?"

"I told you I don't have any money right now." He pulled away from me with a jerk. "I'll pay you–oh. Li Hui, you're home."

So he had no money either. Would the taxi man agree to come back for his money tomorrow? I could get an advance on my first week's salary from Feng Gu.

"Did you say you need money?"

Father stood up, wiping his eyes, holding onto the back of the chair for balance. The light bulb dangling from the ceiling glared at me. The room felt too small. I hid my bloodied hands behind my back.

"Just—well—only a—"

"You work hard all day and ask your retired father for money?" He shifted his feet, cleared his throat.

"No, never mind," I said. "Go back to sleep. It's late."

"What are you doing all day that you need money?" He ran his hand over his bleary eyes again. "Are you sure you're going to work? Or are you out shopping? Playing in the town until—" He twisted his watch to look at the time and stumbled.

"No, no, Father." I leaned against his shoulder. As a small girl, this snuffed his anger like a pot of water on a burning stick.

"Your mother is negotiating day and night with Madame Matchmaker to find you a good husband. It's hard enough to find a man willing to take someone so old and with a university degree. But who's going to want a wife that plays all night, spends all her money?"

Father's body was so rigid with anger, I stepped back. I'd seen this before. Would he strike me?

"It's not what you think, Father. I worked hard at the tea shop all day. And, I—I never spend money frivolously."

"Miss? Miss?" The taxi man called from the courtyard. "Do you have my twenty *yuan* yet? It's late. I want to go home."

"Who's that?" Father whispered, his grip boring holes into my shoulder.

"I was just so tired," I explained. "I took a taxi home."

"Miss, please. My shift ended half an hour ago. Please pay me so I can go home."

"But twenty *yuan*?" Father asked. "Where were you coming

from? The moon?"

"The Wei Min Hote–"

I stopped, but it was too late. He released me, as if he'd touched something foul. He went over to the door, pushed in the heavy wooden bolt, and went off to his downstairs room without a word. It was worse than being slapped. The gods had put me on an alien planet where I was as tiny as dust. And as hated.

"Miss, please," the taxi driver called again, shouting from the courtyard, so all the neighbors in the surrounding houses could hear.

What could I do? The only thing I had of value was –nothing. If I could just talk to him, I could promise to pay him tomorrow. I looked at the heavy wooden bolted door. Father would be furious if I opened those heavy wooden doors. I grabbed a piece of paper and pen. I would write the man a note of promise and toss it out the hole in the upstairs hall window.

"You seem like an honest woman," the driver called. "I trusted you."

"There aren't any honest women here," Father shouted from his room. Each word felt like a stab. "Now quit your caterwauling and let us sleep."

"But I need my money," the driver called. "Do you know where the young miss who works with chickens lives?"

"With what?" Father laughed so loud the walls vibrated.

"Chickens," the taxi man repeated.

"You mean those dumb, squawking birds?"

"Yes, those."

"You tell them to shut up and move, and they just don't get it?"

The taxi man was silent. I closed my eyes in shame. Father's verbal abuse of this man had no honor.

"They just don't get it," Father said. "Until you have to break their scrawny necks."

A rock hit the door. The thud vibrated in my chest, as if my heart had diminished in size to that of a soy bean. That of a small bell clapper. I wanted to cover my ears.

Chapter Twenty-One
A Large Cane

The morning sun had risen enough that a grayness beckoned from my bedroom window. I could toss and turn in my bed no longer. My mind overflowed with questions. Why was my heart so weak that I had followed an obvious kidnapper like Chan Hai? Had Little Wu Lu's wound stopped bleeding? Had Snakehead and his van full of men arrived at the boat on time and gone away to Singapore, far away from me? Would Cheng Min survive the injuries from the bomb that had exploded in her house, ripping away the front door and her two small girls? Did Cheng Min's third child rest safely in her womb? Or had that been ripped away also? These thousands and tens of thousands of questions I wanted to ask Mei Ling or Madame Paper Cutter or Waipo. I'd even try asking the gods.

I dressed in an old black skirt of Cousin's. My pants had been ripped in three places. Bloody hand prints covered the backside where Little Wu Lu had grabbed at me and grabbed again. I would have to soak them for many long days. Even then, those pants would look as if I plucked chickens for a living.

I tiptoed downstairs. The house was dark and quiet. Not even Mother had awakened. I unbolted our door. The wooden cross bar sounded loud, louder than Father shutting it last night. He had been so cross with me then. He reminded me of Feng Gu, the way he didn't listen, the way he assumed the worst from me.

I stepped across the neighbor's winding dragon, stopping where a stone had been knocked out of place. Perhaps Father worried over his debt. I hadn't had a chance to mention my new full-time status at the tea shop. Our successes. I repositioned the stone. We could use all the help we could get.

Madame Zi Mei's shop still had the shutters closed. I took in a deep breath of the cool morning air. At least I wouldn't be the topic tripping off Zi Mei's tongue today. I wasn't a missing girl.

A bicyclist passed carrying dripping red meat on the back of his bike. A meat seller on his way to the fresh market? That dripping red meat reminded me of blood, warm blood spurting out onto my hands, my pants, in Snakehead's van. The image, like a bad piece of meat, burped into my head each time I thought I'd rid myself of the nightmare.

I walked up the road, past Cheng Min's house. Newspapers covered the hole where the blast had taken off the front door. According to Zi Mei, Cheng Min had gone to the hospital with burns so bad her skin had melted to the bone. She must be in agony. The doctors would want her burns to "breathe." But would those burns stay free from infection in our crowded hospital? I imagined one of her neighboring patients lighting a cigarette or churning up the air with a fan or too much chatter. She would surely scream out. Certainly her mother-in-law would take good care of her, protecting her from the humanity around her, and cleaning the wounds when the doctors were too busy. But I would also need to visit her, perhaps offer to stay with her a night or two. Dear Cheng Min.

I passed the stone engravers. The migrants were not out. Their blades lay silent. Just a few days ago Zi Mei had been clucking away about the migrant worker's disrespect toward me. Was I sure I wasn't hurt, she'd asked. Today my ribs ached from Little Wu Lu squeezing me. My backside was bruised from being kicked out of the van and landing on the hard ground. I felt tired and old. All of these actions were done by our own people. Not migrant laborers.

I passed the pink castle. Even at this early hour, the old man practiced *taiqi*, his body swaying forwards and backwards as he tossed an imaginary ball. His motions were as graceful as wheat blowing in the wind. No troubled thoughts interrupted this meditation, making ramrod stiff, jerky movements. Just a fluid dance across his courtyard. How did one find such calmness in a world all crazy like mine?

I hurried on to the side of the road to wait for the bus. Surely the buses had started operating already. I felt as if I were one of the only ones awake, yet the world had been moving for quite some time now.

The park held little evidence of last night's disaster. The street sweeper had removed the popped balloons. The jobless migrants had moved back to their spots. Only the break in the fence near the stone engraving revealed that something had happened. Blood raced through my body. The hairs raised on the back of my neck. My toes stiffened in my black pumps. I looked back to the street, as if expecting a van to come careening around the corner. A few cars drove by and a truck loaded with pigs. Only honest, hard workers. I let out a deep breath and turned back to the park.

I hadn't taken but a few steps toward my old spot when I saw Madame Paper Cutter. As if I'd been lost and just spotted a familiar landmark, I raced toward her. My insides tingled with relief and anticipation. She wore a knit cap on her head as she hunched over her paper. She was already busy making a paper cutting. Did she no longer practice writing characters or were cuttings her kind of morning meditation, her *taiqi*?

"Madame Paper Cutter," I called.

She didn't look up. Perhaps the cap made hearing difficult. I went closer and put my hand on her arm.

"Ah, Li Hui." Madame Paper Cutter's voice felt like the first sunshine after a bitter winter.

Her eyes had dark circles beneath them. Her thin arms were covered in sweat. Her body emitted a strong sour odor. Like vinegar. Something wasn't right.

"Madame Paper Cutter?" I tilted my head.

"It's nice to see you," she said. "How is your job?"

Now I heard the raspy sound from her throat. When had she taken ill? What could I do for her?

"Better than expected," I said. "In fact, next time I'll bring you a sample of our new tea. You look like you could use a nice cup of tea."

"Oh, this is nothing," she said, letting her scissors drop to the ground as if they were too heavy to hold. "Just a cold."

So that's where the vinegar smell came from. Whenever we started to get the sniffles, Waipo had always boiled a pot of vinegar and made us sit and breathe it. She insisted the odor was enough to keep anything away, even germs. I'd smelled vinegar the night before. Had the smell been from my own disappointed heart or had Madame Paper Cutter been near?

"So." Madame Paper Cutter rubbed her palm over her wrist as if massaging away an ache. She coughed, her chest wheezing at the effort. "What brings you out to the park so early?"

"I—uh—I—" Now that I was here, where did I start? Surely with Madame Paper Cutter feeling unwell, all my questions would feel like hailstones. "I just haven't seen you in many days."

"Yes," she said and held her eyes on her cutting. Madame Paper

Cutter picked up her scissors and a piece of red paper. She began to cut. Not the simple bird cutting. Not a circle which would start off the boy holding the peach. Perhaps this would be a new one. "My neighbor mentioned he saw you last night."

She indicated her head toward Mr. Palm Reader. Heat rose to my face. Had he mentioned that I'd held him up? That I'd caused him to pay a bribe? Did she fear I would bring her trouble as well?

"I came to see you," I said. "But you weren't here."

Madame Paper Cutter stopped cutting and looked up at me. Her eyes grew large like those of a giant goldfish in a pond. Her mouth pursed into a small circle. Obviously Mr. Palm Reader had given her an earful, none of which had to do with me searching for her.

"Well, at first," I stammered. "But then I ended up having dinner with—well with this person I thought was a good person. He helped an old lady the other day with her peas. He rescued me from a rough taxi driver."

Why was I building Chan Hai up so? Did I not want Madame Paper Cutter to see me as a complete fool? Or did I still harbor some feeling in my heart for strange Man In Blue?

"I wanted you to meet him first," I said, meeting her gaze. "If only you had, perhaps you could have told me to ignore my irregular heart beat."

"Tell me more," Madame Paper Cutter said. She pushed her glasses up on her nose and continued cutting.

I told her of our dinner, of the snakehead standing up and me thinking this man was just a sales leader, of Chan Hai's violent response. She listened, shaking her head in disbelief. I told her of running into Little Wu Lu, of Snakehead offering to take me to Singapore, of their attempt to kidnap me.

"Can you believe this friend of Chan Hai kidnapped me?" I said. "I'm sure the three of them planned the whole thing."

"Desperate people will do desperate things." Madame Paper Cutter's eyebrows furrowed. She coughed long and hard. I worried that she suffered more than just a cold.

"Yes," I agreed, thinking of my own desperate actions. "When I was trapped in that van, all I could think to do was stab the man— with the scissors you gave me."

She grabbed onto my hand and squeezed. Her bony fingers were strong and hot with fever. She squeezed again. Would she tell me what a horrible person I was? Would she want me to stay away from her in case Little Wu Lu took revenge on me and any of my friends? I held my breath.

"I'm glad you're safe," she said.

"I still feel a fool," I said, my eyes prickling. "How could I have not known what kind of man this Chan Hai was? What kind of restaurant it was? Ha. I even thought to tell you of it—as the pork soup was so delicious yet reasonable."

"Ah, perhaps I know of the place," Madame Paper Cutter said, returning to her cutting. Already a long, thin shape was evident on one side—a knife? A sword? This woman was so clever, so skilled. "He used to sell his soup in the streets?"

"Yes," I said.

"The owner has a variety of customers, but he's not a bad sort." She nodded. "You cane yourself with too large a stick."

"But I didn't even recognize the man in the shop as a snakehead," I whispered. "I didn't even realize I ate dinner with my future kidnapper."

"You should know these things," she agreed. "But not like you know how to breathe. You have to learn just as you learned to teach school." She tapped the point of her scissors on my wrist. "Sometimes the hard way."

I wiped the wetness from my eyes. How long would it take me to learn what everyone else seemed to know?

Chapter Twenty-Two
Samples

I lingered with Madame Paper Cutter until the park filled and the morning sun had risen. Then I walked to the tea shop. Shiny tins stacked one on top of the other lined the wall of the back room. Our new order? Already?

"Good thing you're here," Feng Gu called at the sound of my feet scraping across the cement floor. "We need to get those orders ready."

Perhaps my world had turned circles overnight. But Feng Gu was stuck in the same spot. Irritated with me. This was the earliest I'd ever been to the shop, and she still managed to make that seem like the wrong thing. I picked up one of the tins. The tall container was light, but the aroma surrounding the lid smelled elegant, like virgin wood. Fresh tea leaves. Perhaps a busy morning at the shop would soothe my spirits.

Outside the sky was a dull gray, as it was everyday. Certainly no rain forthcoming. Just more heat and humidity. Like Singapore. What would Guo Qiang be doing? Would he be typing out a new program on his computer?

An old man passed by along the sidewalk. He held a bucket full of cigarettes in one arm. He waved his other arm to get attention.

"Cigarettes for sale," he called.

A vision of Little Wu Lu's cigarette smoldering on the van mat invaded. The sound of his tearing flesh. The feel of warm blood on my hand. I gripped the tea tin tightly and dumped the entire contents into the empty bin by the cherrywood table.

"What are you doing?" Feng Gu asked, looking up from her ledger. "The Professor's Medley is a mixture of teas. Not just one type."

Of course. I knew that. In fact it had been my idea. Mine and Madame Tsui Ping. I tried to focus.

I took out several handfuls of tea, returning the sweet-smelling leaves to the tin. Away from the whirring fan, air moved so slowly, heat seeped through each pore. Sweat dripped down the back of my neck. So hot. Singapore could be no hotter. What else had Guo Qiang mentioned in his letter? Oh, his colleague's strange American wife. She collected garbage, and wasted time and money on pictures of irrelevant items, like birds. Why was she in Singapore? Wasn't America a better place to find a job?

The sound of someone tossing a bucket of slop out the front of their store reached my ears. Motorcycles and taxis zoomed by. A policeman clanged his bell as he rode by on his bicycle. If only our police were effective like those in America or Singapore. If only the policeman had stopped Snakehead last night and set me free, then I wouldn't have had to use Madame Paper Cutter's scissors on Little Wu Lu. He could have been on his way to Singapore. Maybe.

I lifted my hair off my shoulders as if to allow an exit for bad memories clogging my brain. Filling the tea bins hadn't worked. Forcing myself to think of Singapore hadn't helped much either.

The gritty sound of work boots made my hands stop. My blood froze. What would I do if I ever saw that cruel Man In Blue again? I looked up with defiance. A middle-aged man and his wife stepped into the shop. She fiddled with the plastic shopping bag on her wrist. Not Chan Hai, thank the gods.

"I'm here to pick up the tea my wife paid for yesterday," the man said to Feng Gu.

He pinched his lips together and narrowed his eyes. He squared his shoulders as if ready to do battle. Feng Gu continued calculating on her abacus. She wasn't to be interrupted, even by this impatient, obviously worried man. Perhaps, he thought his wife had been cheated.

"Your name, please?" I asked.

"I've been coming here forever," he said. "My grandfather bought tea here."

"Forgive me," I said. "I'm new."

"Zhao San Jie," he said. "That's her name."

I reached over to the table and went through the pile of receipts. I remembered the woman. She was one of the first people to place an order.

"Ah, yes. Here you are," I said, extracting the paper with her name on it and making a check mark next to it. "That will be five *yuan*—the balance leftover from yesterday."

I handed the nervous man his bag of tea and accepted the *yuan* bill. He smiled with relief. He patted his wife's arm, as if to say, "See?

I knew you'd be cheated if I didn't come."

"Would you like a cup of morning tea," I asked.

"No, no time for that," the man said, glancing at his watch.

"Well, thank you for your order," I said. "This was a new idea, and you helped turn it into a great new system."

The man beamed. He stood tall as he took his wife's elbow and led her out the door. Next time she probably would pick up the order on her own. That would be good.

All morning customers streamed in to pick up their orders. Most every one of them brought back-up artillery like a husband or friend, certain they had been cheated. Every one of them smiled with relief when they held the plastic bag of tea in their hands. When there was a break in customers, I joined Feng Gu at the tea table. She took a rubber band from around her paper packet of meat and rice. Was it lunchtime already? I still felt disoriented from last night. I opened the lunch tin I'd brought from home. Rice and pickles and one piece of pork. Mother's pork certainly wasn't as soft as the meat I'd had last night. But the chewy dish would taste safe and full of love.

"Are you ill?" Feng Gu asked.

"No, no," I said.

Why did she think such a thing? Perhaps an illness circulated the town. The same illness Madame Paper Cutter suffered. She looked across the table at my hands, as if she might spot sores growing. She looked at my chest as though waiting for a cough. Did my face look flushed with fever?

"I'm fine," I assured her. Had I misjudged Feng Gu just as I'd misjudged Chan Hai. Maybe she really did care.

"You don't act fine," she said tossing her short hair back. "You dumped all of one tin into what should have been a mixture. You took forever to fill twenty small bags. And now you poke at that piece of pork as if looking for an answer from it. It's almost noon. Yet, you seem . . . I don't know. Not yet awake."

Awake. Awake. Awake. The words flashed on and off like that Tsingtao beer ad. There I'd stood my toes touching Chan Hai's while he "convinced" Little Wu Lu of the dangers of going to Singapore. What would Feng Gu say if she knew? My cheeks flushed with heat.

"Didn't you get enough sleep?" Feng Gu brushed water off the table top.

"Sleep?" I said.

"You can't expect to stay up all night and be able to concentrate on your job," she said. "As I've said before, this job requires focus. If you're not focused—"

"I'm fine," I repeated.

"Well, if you're fine, then I'm Professor Medley." She yanked on her hair. "Where are all our customers? All the people who were fighting over each other to get a bag of tea yesterday."

No. I hadn't misjudged Feng Gu. Her concern was not for me.

"Did you hear me?" Feng Gu asked. "You know the problem here?"

I waited for her to tell me while I adjusted the "Professor Medley" sign on the bin next to the table. Feng Gu's handwritten sign made me cringe. Worse than an elementary school student's. I'm sure that wasn't the problem she had in mind.

"The problem with this order system is we don't earn as much money."

I looked at her out of the corner of my eyes. Was she teasing me or testing me? Did she still think I was an art major? Surely with her mathematical mind, she knew that we earned the same amount whether it was paid in two installments or one.

"Well," she continued. "When these people come in, they only pay us half the amount."

"But they already paid us half yesterday," I said.

"Yes, but yesterday was yesterday," she said, tapping her fingers on the table. "I can't log that in as a profit for today."

I looked at her furrowed brow. Her upturned mouth. I didn't have an answer for that logic.

"Besides, did you notice how fast they left here?" Feng Gu continued. "No sitting around and tasting different grades of tea, no opportunity to decide to buy just one more bag while they're here."

I didn't notice Feng Gu tripping over her toes to offer anyone a seat. Besides, we now only had one type of tea, the Professor's Medley. Where was she coming up with all these thoughts?

"In the forty-two years our shop has been in business," Feng Gu said. "We've never taken orders from customers. Never."

"Just think," I stirred my rice around with my chopsticks. "You've—we've started a new trend."

"That's scaring customers away," she said, picking up the abacus next to her and rattling the beads up and down.

"I don't think so," I said. "New ideas take time. Perhaps we just need more customers. Maybe we need a way to reach more people."

"We have Zi Mei broadcasting for us," Feng Gu said. "What more could we want?"

I nodded. Even Zi Mei had limitations. Surely Zi Mei didn't talk to Madame Paper Cutter or any of those people in the park. Madame Paper Cutter would love this tea. She would enjoy resting her bones on the smooth cherrywood stool. Perhaps we could even practice characters here, so she wouldn't feel she was wasting time. Being frivolous.

"Well?" Feng Gu asked.

"What if we gave out samples?" I suggested.

"We already do that." Feng Gu snorted. "Anyone who walks in here is free to taste our tea."

"Yes, but what of people who don't walk in here?" I said. "For whom this is an unknown location. Like all the people working in the park."

Feng Gu looked over at me. Her mushroom nose wrinkled as though suddenly dried up by the sun. That was the wrong example.

"We don't want riffraff coming in here," she said, her mouth turning down as if she had tasted something sour.

"Of course, you're right," I said. Still, I remembered the ten *yuan* bill Mr. Palm Reader extracted last night. That was more money than I had. Despite their poor appearance, the migrants in the park made good money. "Well, we could have a calligraphy salon. Or ask Madame Tsui Ping to do an English salon. People could drink tea and learn—"

"No, no," Feng Gu said. She wrapped her hair in a small bun and held it to her head. "The two activities don't go together. You would take all the focus away from the appreciation of the tea."

"People don't have time to appreciate anymore," I said.

In olden times, people had sat around the tea set, pouring hot water into the small pot and talking while the tea steeped. They had talked and talked, pouring thimble-sized cup after cup of tea. Refilling the pot when the water became too cool. They had spent hours enjoying the tea, enjoying each other. It was a great tradition for people who didn't have much to do in the afternoons. Couldn't have gone anywhere if they wanted to. But these days with buses and taxis and cell phones and fast food restaurants, who had hours to sit around and watch tea steep? Either the tradition needed to change or just be forgotten.

"They want to order in advance," I began. "They want their tea ready when—"

"No," Feng Gu said, her high voice sharp. She scrunched her eyes closed. She covered her ears. Her elbows touched, pointing at me and shaking back and forth. "No more ideas."

What had made me talk so much, as if I had a say? Was I so relieved to still be here that I couldn't keep my tongue still? Surely I'd stepped too far from my place. This wasn't my business. Still, if the business didn't succeed, I wouldn't have a job.

"Besides," Feng Gu said. "Father thinks it's not a good idea."

Ah, so this was the problem. All that logic had sounded a bit strange even for Feng Gu. All those warnings. Were all fathers such a burden on their daughters, their only daughters? How could he gamble so much with the tiles, but be afraid to think up new ideas? Didn't he realize that a stable business meant more money with which to play?

"Well." I leaned across the table. My heart pumped. My blood raced. "If the shop doesn't earn as much money from orders as it did last summer, you needn't pay me this month's salary."

"Last summer wasn't a good season for us," she said.

"Okay, the last two summers combined then," I said.

Feng Gu smiled, revealing all her brown, jumbled teeth. She picked up her abacus, as though ready to calculate the amounts, already.

"Father can hardly dispute that."

"But," I added. "If we do better, then I will get a bonus of—four hundred *yuan*."

"Four hundred?" Feng Gu said.

She ran her hands through her hair, scratched the back of her head. I expected her to argue. I was ready to negotiate. That's why I'd started so high.

"Three hundred," she said.

Perhaps she knew of Father's debt.

"Fine," I said.

I shoveled rice down my throat without tasting a morsel. I swallowed a pit in my throat. The pit enlarged around my heart, burning. Had I gambled away what little money was about to drop into our pockets? Feng Gu picked at her pants, plucking at a thread. She coughed. A long exaggerated cough.

"And the samples?" she said. "Why don't you cut some small

bags up?"

Now that she had nothing to lose, was she touched by a spirit of adventure? More likely, if I was going to fail, she wanted to see me do it in a big way.

"If we're not busy, you can pass them out to people on the street." She smoothed her pants over her knees. "Not in the park though. That place is dangerous, especially at night."

She spoke the truth. I felt Little Wu Lu's arms locked around me. I smelled Snakehead's alcohol breath. I rubbed my arms. Madame Paper Cutter said not to beat myself with too large a cane. But, even if I accepted the mistake, when would I forget?

Chapter Twenty-Three
The God of Integrity

Children ran about. Vendors called out their wares—water chestnuts, peanuts, CDs, cell phone covers. Bicyclists and motorcycles zoomed down the sidewalk taking the short cut to avoid being stuck with the rest of the afternoon traffic. Feng Gu had said to stay away from the park. But she was concerned about safety. I would be fine.

First I stopped in front of Mr. Palm Reader. When I offered him four samples, he looked around. Then he grabbed the plastic bags with his leathery palms and tucked them beneath his shirt. His face remained solemn, but a light of joy shone in his eyes. A notch that had tightened around my chest last night loosened a bit. I didn't feel so indebted. If I could find the taxi man, I would have given him at least four bags as well.

Madame Paper Cutter sat, arranging several of her cuttings on the cardboard piece in front of her. She looked frail in her knit cap, beads of sweat lining her forehead.

"You're back," she said, swallowing a cough. "No work today?"

"I got off early to distribute samples." I took a small bag of tea from my purse. "This is from our tea shop."

"I have enough tea," she said, pushing the sample away.

We went back and forth three times. Then she wrapped her fingers around the small bag. She would accept the gift.

"Thank you," she said. "This will make me feel better, I'm sure."

"You'll have to come by the shop and try some from our expert tea maker," I said. "Besides, I thought we could work on characters at the same time."

"Your mind is always working," Madame Paper Cutter said. "Certainly you were meant to teach. You do see who's back, don't you?"

She nodded in the direction of the small band of tutors. Most of the faces were the same. Women, a couple of men. And there, in the middle of the group, Mr. Ponytail and Earring. Had he succeeded with the boy already? So fast? Perhaps there was something to listening to music while one worked. I looked back to Madame Paper Cutter. She tapped the end of her ear with her scissors. I looked back to the man. A long red line zigzagged across his ear where once his earring had been.

"What did I tell you?" she said.

I had been so ready to follow the impatient Mr. Overindulgent. I would have taken that gamble. I hoped I would learn some street sense before I ended up like Mr. Ponytail and Ripped Ear. I swallowed the pit in my throat.

"My daughter asked me for a cutting of Guan Gong," Madame Paper Cutter said, handing me an intricate cutting of a warrior holding a sword on high. "You take this one."

So that was what she had been working on this morning. How wonderful that she and her daughter wrote back and forth to one another now. How generous of her to insist on giving me this cutting in return for the tea.

"Ah, Guan Gong," I said. "That's right. His birthday is what? Only a few weeks away."

I had been so wrapped up in finding employment, keeping employment and following this echo in my heart that I hadn't watched the calendar. As a child, I remembered counting the days between one big festival—the Lunar New Year—and another—the Autumn Moon Festival. Guan Gong's birthday was between the two big festivals on the 13th day of the fifth moon.

Guan Gong had been such a loyal person that he had turned his back on the temptations of the Emperor's riches in order to find and help his good friend. On his birthday, we all went to the temple to burn incense and fake money in honor of this man who lived thousands of years ago. For a day, we thought about loyalty and integrity and right actions. And we felt the presence of something larger than our own problems.

"I always tell my daughter to be loyal to her friends," Madame Paper Cutter said. "Like Guan Gong."

Most people said that. Waipo and mother had often told me the same thing. But had I been loyal to them? No. I had gone out with a man that wasn't Madame Liang's son. I didn't deserve such a fine cutting.

"But I also tell her—" Madame Paper Cutter smiled, as if remembering her daughter's innocent face and soft skin. She curled her bony hot fingers around my hand. "I tell her to be loyal to her heart—wherever it leads."

Her words of encouragement felt like a gift I didn't deserve.
My heart had fallen for a man who tricked me with words of
"Now you're hungry. Come eat with me." My heart would have
challenged Mr. Overindulgent and attempted to teach his Little
Emperor of a son. My heart felt unreliable. Surely not worthy of
following. But surely I would learn. I would learn. Madame Paper
Cutter believed in me, even if I did not.

Chapter Twenty-Four
The Peach Tree

I ran up the stairs next to Zi Mei's store. Thank the gods she was so busy inside she didn't come out to offer a greeting. Having seen my school friend in the hospital, surely I would have been tempted to tell Zi Mei of Cheng Min's black sores, of the skin that curled up dry and burnt, like a fish that had been on the fire too long. Of how her mother sat by the side of her hospital bed, blaming Cheng Min for being careless with her condition. Letting people see that she was again pregnant. Again, yes. That's why this happened, she had said.

How much of a reward had Zi Mei received for spreading the news of Cheng Min's third happiness? Certainly her reporting on the Professor's Medley had helped our shop. So her mouth could be used for good. But why didn't she have a filter on the noises that she emitted? Didn't she feel in the slightest bit guilty when she looked out from her shop and saw the blackened frame on Cheng Min's house?

I approached New Neighbor's house. Cheng Min's mother had thanked me for bringing the sample of tea, but said Cheng Min couldn't bear anything warm. Warmth made her wounds burn, her eyes water, her heart sad. My whole being felt so heavy. New Neighbor came rushing out of his house, as though late for an appointment.

"Hello," I said. "Have you eaten?"

"How can anyone eat in this weather?" New Neighbor followed me across his cement courtyard. "We can't survive without any rains. The gods don't like it. They ruin the crops. Now they've started picking on my wife. She has nose bleeds every day."

Nose bleeds? Mei Ling would say the woman was too "heaty" and needed to add some cool vegetables and fruits to her diet. Cheng Min's mother would blame the woman for breathing the wrong way. New Neighbor managed to twist everything into a religious happening.

"That's terrible," I said.

New Neighbor headed off in the direction of the local temple. A pig squealed. A woman's voice crackled over the neighborhood loudspeaker, again mentioning the theater project, the need for donations. She read out the list of contributors so far. Our name was not mentioned. Would it ever be?

Fatigue gripped my shoulders. It had been a long day. A long two days. No, three. I would rest early tonight. I walked into the courtyard, ready to be welcomed by the safe confines of our home. The sound of voices, whisperings, came from the Great Hall. Father and Mother sat close to one another at the table near the door. What was he doing home? Gods, please don't drag us further in debt. Then again Mother sat near him, something she avoided unless we had company. The shadowy form of a third person leaned across toward Father. Who else was there? The voice was that of a woman. I knew that voice. Madame Matchmaker.

People said she was the best in town at finding matches that lasted. She'd been responsible for lots of the marriages in our village. A lot of love. More than any small gift she might receive for her help, she reveled in the reputation she'd built for herself. Did she have news from Singapore? I skipped into the house.

"Nice to see you," I said.

I shook hands with her, taking her puffy hand in both of mine. Today, rather than her bright yellow rain slicker, she wore a billowy white blouse. She looked like a pillow for an elephant. I pretended to be yawning as I smiled instead.

"Have you lost weight?" she asked. She withdrew her hand from mine and pulled on my skirt which sank to my hips.

"No, no," I assured her, hiking the skirt back up. "This is Cousin's old skirt. It's just been so hot—"

"That's for sure," she said. "The fields are like firewood waiting for a match. In all my seventy-two years, I've never seen it so dry."

Coming from Madame Matchmaker, that was quite a statement. She'd been a part of the village forever. Through wars and political changes and all kinds of weather. Mother pulled a stool up close and patted the seat. She nodded for me to join them. She poured me a cup of tea. Surely they had news for me.

"I just stopped by to visit Cheng Min," I said.

"Who's Cheng Min?" Father asked. His eyebrows rose in suspicion. A look of anger flashed across his face. That same look which had filled his face last night.

"You know," Mother said. She tapped the table. "The girl who— Prehistoric's daughter-in-law."

Madame Matchmaker shook her head and made a tsk-tsk sound.

Would she agree with Cheng Min's mother that Cheng Min had brought this all on herself by being careless? What if something like that happened to us? Would Mother sit by my side as Cheng Min's mother did? Would Father even realize something had happened?

"A lot of things are happening these days." Father cleared his throat. He stared at his lit cigarette, then sucked on it hard. He was getting ready to make a pronouncement.

"Must be the weather," Madame Matchmaker said, ignoring Father's pensive posture.

"The price of rice went up another five *fen* today," Mother added.

"A lot of things happening these days," Father said again, as if cueing the women. How long had the three of them been talking?

"Yes," Madame Matchmaker said, looking at me. Her look was one of warmth and understanding though. "In my seventy-two years, I've seen many things."

Madame Matchmaker stared out the back window into our garden. Mother fussed with the lid of the teapot. Her left eye twitched. Father cleared his throat again and spat on the floor. He looked up at me, his eyes hard as black pebbles surrounding a lucky bamboo plant. Surely this wasn't a meeting about my taxi ride home last night. Was he still angry about that?

"I've come to believe that life mirrors what we see around us," Madame Matchmaker said.

I looked around. At the rickety table with tea stains and cigarette burns. A bowl filled with watermelon seeds. The blank white walls which left powdery dust on your back if you got too close. At the rice bin in the corner that was never full. A spider crawled up the wall.

"For example." Madame Matchmaker smiled, her chin creasing into several folds. "Take the peach tree in the yard, there, that you and your cousins used to climb."

Her words felt like a warm arm around my shoulder, massaging slowly and gently about things not important. I sat back on the edge of a wooden stool. Licked my thumb and rubbed the side of my scuffed shoe. Leave it to Madame Matchmaker to find the most beautiful sight.

"You start out shinnying your way up the wide trunk," she said. "Then you must choose to follow one branch or another."

I popped a watermelon seed in my mouth and sat back. For the first time in what felt like many moons, I wasn't worried about money or snakeheads or injuries or even the piercing ache in my heart left by a man I'd been so sure was a good soul. I enjoyed this reminiscing. I could almost feel the scrapes on my legs, the imprint of bark on my palms, the sweat on the back of my neck. I could hear laughter in the air.

"By the time you get to the top of the tree." Madame Matchmaker shifted on her stool. "You have chosen many of your branches—and you have either reached a juicy golden peach or come up empty-handed."

"You speak the truth." Mother nodded. Sweat beaded on her upper lip. "You speak the truth."

"Yes." Madame Matchmaker turned her gaze from the window to me. Her smile remained as if frozen on her face. Her eyes no longer held warmth. "I've been searching through this village for a man interested in taking a wife with so many years as you."

I sat forward again. Had Madame Liang formed a decision? Had Mother and Father arranged my match already? What of Guo Qiang?

"But," she said. All eyes turned to me. "I hear you're making any arrangements impossible by playing on branches that will bear no fruit."

Father and Mother stared at me. What was she talking about? What had she heard? Father wasn't the kind to drop rocks on his own feet. He wouldn't have told her of my late-night return from the Wei Min Hotel, would he? Madame Matchmaker brushed dust from the side of the table, then looked over again. My heart still trembled from the events of last night. I wished for another hug of reassurance that I had done the right thing. But this woman was not Madame Paper Cutter. And I was no longer a child running around the trunk of a tree.

"I'm so bad with directions." I laughed. "Y—y—yesterday, after I stopped off in the park to visit a friend, I had trouble finding my way back home. I think I've been away at university too long. Everything now seems turned around."

Father ground his teeth together. Mother's stool scraped against the cement. Madame Matchmaker tapped the side of her tea cup. It wasn't the truth, but it wasn't a lie either.

"And that." Madame Matchmaker crossed her arms over that great billowing white expanse of cloth. "Is how you ended up eating dinner with Chen Chan Hai in the Fat and Happy Pork Soup Shop?"

Had she heard that our heads had been close, that our knees had been touching? And from where did she hear it? Had Father been out all afternoon, visiting the Senior Center, the park, the marketplace, trying to pick up whatever information he could? The air felt heavy. My chest tight.

"Chen's uncle owns a worthless quarry," Father said, tapping his bony finger on the table. "The stones are no good, but he keeps digging as though hoping to find gold. Meanwhile the entire family is going to starve. No wonder he has such a bad temper."

"Yes," Mother agreed. "Zi Mei mentioned that your 'friend' broke one of her cousin's bowls."

So Zi Mei had spread the word. She would. Chan Hai had mentioned Mr. Fat and Happy had borrowed money from a cousin who owned a shop. Zi Mei, of course. Why hadn't I paid closer attention?

"That he shouted obscenities," Father added. "And started a fight with Chairman Huang."

"Chairman Huang?" I asked. I shook my head. Zi Mei never passed on a story without adding her own spices to it. As if the truth wasn't bad enough. "That man was no chairman. He was just a—just a—snakehead."

"I know Chen Chan Hai has the sense of a donkey's ass," Father said. "I expected a bit more from you."

He hit the table for emphasis. The sound reverberated in my heart. What was he saying? That this snakehead was actually a town official? But surely Chan Hai knew that. Chan Hai had been a part of the snakehead's kidnapping scheme.

"It's not good to fart in an official's face," Father added, blowing a plume of smoke across the table. "It might end up exploding in your own."

"But the fight was just a show," I said.

What good actors they all were. Chan Hai upending the table with such vehemence. The snakehead looking bored. Little Wu Lu appearing so desperate and frightened. A show at the community theater could not be much better. How many times had the three of them done this? Had any of their other victims escaped? Madame Matchmaker stared at me, her eyes wide. Father laughed. The sound made my skin itch. What didn't I understand?

"They all work together," I said.

"When the sun rises in the west," Father said.

"What?" I asked. Goose flesh covered my arms.

"The ducks and the dogs don't share the same eating dish," Madame Matchmaker said.

So Chan Hai wasn't friends with Chairman Huang? It hadn't been a set-up? Chan Hai had really stood up to that predatory man to protect his friend? My heart beat strong for the first time all day. Then again perhaps Father and Madame Matchmaker didn't know. Still I wanted to believe that my instincts hadn't pointed me in such a wrong way. "When the sun rises in the west" rang through my head like a beautiful piece of music.

"I said." Father tapped me on the knee. "What was this fight about?"

"What?" I rubbed my arms. "Oh? The fight? Uh—they wanted—Chairman Huang wanted me to go on the next boat to Singapore."

I hoped that man hadn't really been a chairman. His shiny leather shoes, his fine dress, his gold rings, his fancy cellular phone all bespoke great wealth. But surely that wealth came from his snakehead business. If Chan Hai wasn't the snakehead's partner and the snakehead was a chairman, Chan Hai would have serious trouble come his way. So might we.

"The next boat to Singapore?" Father looked around for his rice wine. "For how much?"

Why was Father so curious? He sounded the same way he had when I'd called from University about the teaching job Administrator Zhang had offered. A cinch wrapped around my chest.

"Free," I said.

"Aiya." Madame Matchmaker shook her head back and forth, as if trying to shake off dust from there as well. "Your daughter would be . . . would be . . . would be enslaved."

"Now don't jump to conclusions." Father waved his right arm in the air, shushing her. "There are lots of jobs available for an intelligent woman, even an old one like Li Hui. Not just, just that."

I stared at the bowl of watermelon seeds, one of which had fallen on the table. Madame Matchmaker stuffed her hands in the pockets of her billowy white pillowcase blouse. Mother poured Father a cup of rice wine. I saw Snakehead's glazed eyes flashing up and down my body. Their words made me feel dirty, as if I had swallowed all the dust Madame Matchmaker tried to brush away.

"Anyway," Madame Matchmaker said. "That kind of restaurant is no place for a woman. Especially one being courted by a successful professor in Singapore."

"He's an excellent card player," Father said.

Guo Qiang had never mentioned playing cards. He seemed too intellectual to waste time on cards. What else did Father know about this professor?

"How did you leave it with him?" Father took a sip of wine.

Father still spoke of the snakehead, I realized with a shock. Why was he only concerned about this snakehead? Did he worry that we would be in danger? The snakehead knew my name. If he'd listened long enough to the dinner conversation between Chan Hai and I, he knew where we lived as well. I remembered his final words, as I struggled to get free from the van: "I'll get her later."

"Well?" Father persisted.

I thought of the scissors, the blood, the angry shouts. Of having to fight my way out of the deathtrap. Of leaving Little Wu Lu bleeding with wounds in his legs.

"Well," I said.

Had I done the wrong thing? I felt as empty and useless as the day I had called from university to report that I had a real job . . . a real job that Father said wasn't good enough. Father hadn't cared about my goals then. He didn't care about my safety now. He just wanted me to hold up a golden sky over his head. My insides shriveled. I wanted a giant pillow to rest my head on.

"Now, now," Madame Matchmaker said. "Let's not think of it anymore."

She pulled a packet of new stationery from her pocket. The white paper was thick, in contrast to the regular flimsy rice paper. Spring flowers decorated the edges and reminded me of Chan Hai. Of his dream to own a nursery. If he had a nursery, perhaps he could sell stationery such as this as well. I still had his phone number.

"I thought you might need more writing materials." She offered the pretty papers to me.

I pulled on the waist of my skirt. How kind of her to bring me paper with which to write letters to Singapore. My head said that it was wise not to waste the golden opportunity of attracting a rich man from Singapore. My heart thought writing another note to a man whose letters left me feeling uneducated and inadequate a waste of this lovely stationery. Madame Paper Cutter's words of wisdom to "follow your heart" had sounded so logical, so easy. But my heart wasn't like a lone watermelon seed on the table. Many other factors tugged me this way or that. My love for Mother. The wisdom of many generations. The expectations that this college girl would become a success. My heart couldn't just beat for Chan Hai.

I looked out the window at our peach tree. All the peaches seemed far from my reach. I had two ways to get one. I could follow my head and step on the safe, sturdy branch, although it was high and difficult to reach. That peach promised to be juicy and golden. That peach would fill our bellies for many generations to come. Or I could follow my heart and risk my balance on the flimsy branch just above me. That branch beckoned for me, even if the peach was small and may leave us all hungry.

"Time is of the essence," Madame Matchmaker said, pushing the packet of stationary toward me.

Surely she meant that she didn't want me to be seen out at the Fat and Happy Pork Soup Shop again. Here they were all so concerned for what lay ahead for me. Of the success of this matchmaking. Madame Matchmaker staked her reputation on the match. Father saw the security of their future in riches from Singapore. Mother, dear Mother, believed in whatever Father thought was best.

"Time is of the essence," Madame Matchmaker repeated.

I nodded and picked up the gift. It wouldn't hurt to send Guo Qiang another letter. To stand on my branch and think about the situation a while. Perhaps if I stood awhile my heart and head would become as one.

Chapter Twenty-Five
The Blind Men and the Elephant

Feng Gu sat close to the fan, her back to a young woman in the deep blue cloth with intricate batik pattern of the Miao ethnic minority. The summer heat smothered us. The lack of rains created a dry dust which coated every surface.

Feng Gu took a blue and white ceramic spoon from the table, wiped it clean on her thigh, and dug into her packet of pork and rice. Certainly she was hungry and tired. We had had our busiest morning yet, with some people preferring to order tea for the next day. Still, the way she ignored this customer seemed like the old Feng Gu. She just needed a copy of Fashion Fortune Magazine in her hands to complete the picture.

The young woman before me counted out her ten *yuan* in small, wrinkled and torn notes. She gave off an earthy smell. Her body had certainly felt no water for a long time. I recognized her from the park.

"Thank you," I said, taking the wad of bills from her small, grimy hands. "Come again."

She scurried away, as if she had done something wrong. Had Feng Gu made her uncomfortable? Had the woman felt guilty spending money on such a frivolous item? How did someone like that, obviously far from home and without a network of family, find a husband? At least I had Madame Matchmaker and Father and Mother watching over me. Then again, with all of them watching so closely, I didn't have a chance to follow my own heart. My own heart which no longer felt such excitement at the complicated words of the computer professor. I watched the young woman leave, feeling a wisp of envy at her freedom.

I pulled up the waist of my cousin's old skirt and went into the back room to retrieve my tin of rice and pickles. Like a dutiful daughter, I'd written a long note to Guo Qiang, detailing some of the events that had occurred as of late. Just some. I told him of the bombing of Cheng Min's home. I told him of the continued lack of rains. I told him of New Neighbor's theories. Was Singapore experiencing the same dry weather? The words I'd written to Guo Qiang between the flowered borders of the stationery seemed guarded, unlike the first letter in which I'd mentioned my dreams as though whispering a secret. Still, one could hardly find fault with my efforts. I'd been chatty and amiable, as I'd been with the young woman who had just bought tea. How could Guo Qiang expect more when we'd never met?

I'd reread the letter several times, trying to keep my eyes from trailing to the pink flowers along the rim of the paper. As soon as Chan Hai got his uncle's quarry making a profit, he planned to start a nursery. We were the same in that way. As soon as I pulled our family from debt enough that I could move on, I'd look for a teaching job again. How had I misjudged him so? Thinking him mentally deficient at one point, a kidnapper the next?

I was reminded of one of my favorite children's stories—the five blind men and the elephant. Waipo had sworn she told me the story once every moon, and still I asked to hear it again. Of how an animal trainer had brought an elephant to a special village where five blind men lived. The five of them approached the snorting, smelly beast. They'd never heard of such a thing as an elephant.

"Oh, I know what this is," First Blind Man said, feeling the elephant's massive side. "It's a wall."

"No, you fool," Second Blind Man said. He held onto the Elephant's tail. "This is a rope."

"What can the two of you be saying?" Third Blind Man said, holding onto the elephant's trunk. "No rope is this size. This must be a hose."

"Come now." Fourth Blind Man reached high and felt one of the Elephant's ears. "This is a fan. One of the strongest I've ever felt. Made of genuine animal skin, to be sure."

The Fifth Blind Man was unfortunate enough to be standing beneath the elephant. In exactly the wrong place at the wrong time.

"Oh, no," he said. "All of you are mistaken. This is a shower. A nice, warm shower."

I had laughed each time Waipo told that part. I could imagine the silly man putting his face up to enjoy this warm shower of elephant urine. Waipo reminded me that often we acted like these silly old men, seeing people only from one side, not grasping the full elephant. I had unfairly judged Chan Hai. I had judged him by each incident, choosing my opinion based only on that moment in time.

The realization made my mind feel tortured, but my heart light.

I returned to the front of the store and sat down across from Feng Gu. I hadn't had a chance to sit all morning. A red bag from Hundred Happiness Department store was stuffed under the table. The sharp corners of the bag felt like feathers against my numb shins. I hadn't noticed the bag there before.

Feng Gu shoveled a spoonful of rice to her mouth. She always ate as if each mouthful was her last. Had she had to fight for food as a child? Did she still have to? Again I wondered if she had a husband. She didn't wear a ring. Nowadays people followed that Western custom. Still, she was certainly older than I, past marriageable age. Then again, if she were married, her husband would run the shop. Unless he was more of a success with his own business. Surely I'd have heard. Perhaps he was like her father, like mine, with his hands on cool *mahjong* tiles and his nose in the air hoping for a shift in the winds of luck. Or perhaps she hadn't married. Feng Gu. Despite all the information she volunteered about others, she never mentioned her personal circumstances.

I took a small bite of pickle. Oh, but the sour yellow radish tasted so delicious. I was hungry. I sighed, enjoying the way the fan stirred the air.

"Feels good to sit," I said.

"I wanted to talk to you about that," Feng Gu said, a few grains of rice falling from her open mouth.

"Yes?" I asked.

Was she going to ask me to skip lunch and deliver more samples, so pleased by the influx of new customers? Did she want me to think up more ideas? I took a large spoonful of rice.

"Father is happy with the Professor's Medley and the orders," she said.

"And the orders?" I asked. Yesterday he'd been opposed to the idea.

"Yes, I told him of your offer to forego your salary when the month's sales—"

"If the month's sales aren't as high as combined tea sales." I reminded. "If."

"Which will be 'when.'" She tossed her short hair from side to side. "Anyway. He thinks that's a great idea."

But her face didn't look great. Her mouth was set in a tight line. Her forehead wrinkled. She studied her last few mouthfuls of rice.

She pushed around a piece of pork that had more fat than meat. But of course Feng Gu hated admitting anything I did was right. Had she been hoping her father would say differently? Perhaps her father had ridiculed her for not thinking of these shop innovations herself.

"And it's enough," she said.

"Enough?" I asked.

That was it? No bonus? And what about our new advertising through samples? What about a calligraphy or an English salon?

"Father is happy," she said. She stared at her feet. "The business is doing okay. Now we can stop working so hard."

There were those people who only did as much work as was required and that was enough. In fact, in our town there were too many people like that. Feng Gu was one of them. Or she had been. But we'd started to enjoy the challenge of coming up with more business ideas. It made the job feel like more than a simple bird cutting. Why did she want to put a halter around my neck and stop me? Stop us?

"Besides, did you smell that last woman?" Feng Gu wrinkled her mushroom nose. "I had to keep my nose to the fan just so I could breathe. People like that'll downgrade the status of our shop."

I took another bite of rice. The way that young woman had spent her hard-earned savings on our tea was heartwarming. What a compliment to the shop. Why didn't Feng Gu appreciate her customers? Whether the money was dirty or clean made no difference in its value.

"Besides, I don't feel safe with those migrants coming in here," she said in a matter-of-fact voice.

I glanced sideways at her. She twirled her fingers through her short hair. She sat with her back ramrod straight. Her chest in the air. How silly. Why did we put up such barriers, barriers which only created fear? I thought of Little Wu Lu and the snakehead and even that overindulgent father who needed a tutor. They were all from our village. They were all dangerous.

"Those people from the park," I said, scooping up another spoonful of rice. "They're Chinese. Just like you and me."

"Ha!" Feng Gu tossed her head back and laughed. She shifted on her perch, running her right hand over her left sleeve, smoothing out the material. "Not like me. I don't like them in here. It gives me a bad feeling."

"Fine," I said.

This was Feng Gu's business. I would do as she wished. Besides, while Madame Paper Cutter predicted otherwise, for me this job was just temporary. I would find someplace where my ideas were welcomed. Needed.

"And you certainly don't need to dress like you came from the park," Feng Gu added, indicating my over-sized skirt.

My, but she was in a bad mood. Perhaps her monthly was visiting. Perhaps being an avid reader of Fashion Fortune Magazine, she was offended by my shabby dress. But she hadn't mentioned my skirt yesterday. Her jaw worked up and down. My spoon clanked against the sides of my tin. She shifted in her seat and pulled an envelope from her waistband.

"Your pay," she said, tossing the envelope at me.

Ah, so this was it. Of course she despised parting with any money. But certainly having to pay the "art major" to turn her shop around filled her mouth with a sour bile. I counted out the bills. Eighty *yuan*. That would go halfway to pulling Father from his well of debt. Halfway. We were halfway there. Perhaps I would only need to work here for the summer. Maybe I could find a job when the schools started session in the fall.

"Now, tell me about your friend." Feng Gu ran her hand through her hair. She tugged on the ends, as if trying to pull the roots out.

"My friend?" I asked.

Who was she asking about? Had Madame Paper Cutter come in when I'd been off to the outhouse? I hoped Feng Gu hadn't been rude. Or had she heard about Cheng Min and the explosion?

"Your boyfriend," she said, exaggerating the first half of the word. She put the fatty pork in her mouth and raised her eyebrows.

My boyfriend? How had she heard of Guo Qiang? No wonder she wanted me to slow down. She didn't want too many innovations spinning around if I planned to up and leave for Singapore in the near future. Perhaps she was insulted I hadn't told her of this possibility. Still, in my heart, the word "boyfriend" was too heavy to describe our relationship. All we'd done so far was exchange letters.

"My friend?" I put my spoon down. I thought of all his talk of computers and how he'd succeeded in a foreign land so different from ours. "I don't know yet. He seems intelligent."

Feng Gu snorted. She crossed her arms. She shook her head at me.

"I mean, it's hard to tell," I said, rubbing my fingers along the rim of the rice tin. "I don't know much of him—"

"I do." Feng Gu spat out the gristle toward the garbage can and missed. She glanced sideways at me. She nodded her head. "I do."

What a cryptic look. What did she mean? Certainly computer engineering sounded important and interesting. The country of Singapore sounded promising, with no worries about kidnappings and bombings and debts which couldn't be paid. But, what more did Feng Gu know? All I'd been told of was how wonderful and successful Madame Liang's son was. Perhaps she knew him before he went off to Singapore and became a respected professor with a house and a car which seated four.

"He's one bad egg," she said, drumming her knuckles on the cherrywood table. "He's black."

"Black?" I stopped rubbing my lunch tin and looked over at her.

Black. Waipo used to tell me of relatives who were black— unable to go to school, always in trouble with officials, against the Party. But that was yesterday. Today people were allowed to have opinions—to a certain degree—and those who got in trouble paid their way out. No one was black anymore. Besides, Madame Liang's son had made it to university. Perhaps that was why he talked so much about his education. Going on for pages and pages. Using words I had to look up in the dictionary.

"He never made it to Red Guard," she continued. She sucked down the remains of her rice as fast as she could move her spoon to her mouth.

People of Feng Gu's generation still revered the Red Guards, brushing aside the nastiness that had turned normal people like the English teacher, Madame Tsui Ping, into crazy cabbage growers. People like Feng Gu forgot about the tattling on parents who didn't do anything wrong, the torturing, the killing, only remembering the crisp feel of the khaki hats on their heads, the patriotic duty which filled their chests. Had Feng Gu been a Red Guard? Who had she tattled on? Did she still have her khaki hat framed on a wall somewhere?

"No, he never made it," she said, lifting the brown packet and letting the last of the rice drop into her open mouth. "Even though he had top grades and was among the brightest students."

I nodded. So he'd had to leave the country for his intelligence to be recognized. Just as Mei Ling had done.

"At least he's successful now," I offered.

"Successful?" She snorted again, sounding a bit like Fourth

Uncle's horse. She eyed me, as if gauging how much she should say. I assumed her tongue was as loose as Zi Mei's. But perhaps she had a filter.

Boots scuffled across the floor. Another husband coming for his wife's order? We had five more customers who needed to collect their tea this afternoon. I set my tin down, stood up and headed for the drawer with the receipts. I grabbed the pile of receipts stuffed into the small wooden drawer. Wang? Zhang? Chen?

My eyes followed the floor to the dusty outline of work boots. Blue cotton pants. Those long legs. No. I looked around, expecting to see Snakehead, to feel the arms of Little Wu Lu locked around my shoulders. Then I remembered Father's words: "When the sun rises from the west."

Chan Hai stood in the center of the shop. He held two flat round oyster cakes, one in each strong hand. The paper wrappings were dark with spots of grease. The smell of the cakes kissed my nose. My calves tingled. My heart knocked against my chest. What was he doing here?

"Looks like I'm late," he said, glancing at the crumpled up brown wrapping that had held Feng Gu's lunch.

"You're always late." Feng Gu looked over at me and frowned.

Her words were crisp and raw like vegetables you feed the family pigs, not soft and palatable for guests. Was her heart still cold from dealing with the woman from the park, from imagining all the dangerous migrant workers that would soon inundate our shop? Or had she had a bad experience with Chan Hai as well? One that made her heart shiver?

"But surely even a full stomach could find room for the best oyster cakes in the village?" Chan Hai put one of the cakes on the table in front of her.

Oyster cakes were our town specialty—crispy fried outside with oysters and shredded cabbage and pork inside. Everyone knew how to make the treat. Only a few knew how to make them well. To buy one of the better cakes, one had to wait in a crowd, the delicious smell of the oysters tickling your mouth, making your stomach groan, as you counted and recounted the heads in front of you for what seemed like a generation. Had he waited in line for us?

"Here," he said, handing the other cake to me.

He looked at my skirt, then directly into my eyes. His eyes, big pools of brown, were wide and full of sorrow. Was he sorry for deserting me in the park late at night? Was he sorry that his friend tried to kidnap me and stuff me in an airless container to Singapore? Did he even know?

"I just ate," I managed. "I'm too full."

He looked over at my half-finished tin. He didn't push the cake at me, begging me to accept, as was our custom. Instead, he set the oyster cake on the top of my mound of rice.

"Well, then, perhaps you'd like to take a break," he said to me. "Walk off that huge meal."

"We're too busy for breaks," Feng Gu said for me. My stomach tightened. Her tone was harsh. What was it about him that bothered her so? Did she think him as big a fool as Father did? "In fact, we were just having a business meeting when you interrupted."

"Well, good then," he said, standing between the two of us. "Perhaps I could join."

"Why would we need information from you?" Feng Gu laughed. "I certainly don't think a quarry worker can give advice on tea sales. Do you, Li Hui?"

What could I say? His kind brown eyes massaged at my temples, smoothing away my anger and fears from the other night. The air felt so sweet with him standing here. His long limbs, his deep dimples, his unruly hair. I wanted to hear his voice tell me of what happened the other night, of what he knew—if anything—about Little Wu Lu, of nurseries, even of tea sales. Feng Gu's eyes were on me. No longer curious. Annoyed. I had said too much with my silence.

"I'm going to the outhouse." Feng Gu's eyes were as wide as a Westerner. "Goodbye." She turned and looked toward Chan Hai's boots. "When I get back I hope I don't have to repeat that."

She waddled out the back. My insides prickled. She had been more civil to the migrant worker from the park.

"I don't want to get you in trouble with the boss." Chan Hai came closer.

"Not to worry," I said. "She sometimes gets in a mood."

"I know," he said. He smiled, making dimples on his cheeks. He brushed the lock of hair from his eyes. "I know."

How did he know? Had they once been schoolmates? Lovers?

"You and Feng Gu were, uh—"

"Our families are old friends." He touched my arm.

His touch lingered like the impression of birds feet on wet cement. A family friend. Another connection. Everywhere I turned there was some connection. That was one thing I'd forgotten about while in university. In Xiamen, I could walk the city streets and no one knew me. Here I felt as if I were in a small box. Each time I burped, the entire village heard.

Surely Feng Gu strutted about angry that she hadn't been the center of the conversation, angry that I hadn't supported her, angry that Chan Hai was in her shop at all. I imagined her clucking every detail, every detail which would soon reach Father's ears. He would be so upset he'd not even notice the money I slipped into his fingers, relieving some of his debt. I needed Chan Hai to leave.

"You still here?" Chan Hai asked wiggling his thick fingers in front of my eyes. "How about a cup of tea?"

"Tea?" I asked. I could hardly refuse a customer. "Yes, tea."

Chan Hai sat on the stool Feng Gu had just vacated. He stretched his long legs beneath the table and his feet hit against the red bag that had been stuffed under there.

"Here, I'll take that," I said, reaching down, my arm brushing against the blue cotton of his pants. I felt his eyes watching me. "This must be something of Feng Gu's. I'll just put—"

"That's for you," Chan Hai said leaning down, his face inches from mine. He reached out with his long arm, the muscle in his fore arm poking out as he did so. He grabbed the bag.

"What?" I stood up. My cheeks felt flushed. My heart beat hard. How could he know this bag was for me? The crushed bag had been sitting here before he came.

"I brought it in late yesterday." he said. "You weren't here." His mouth was set in a frown. "I take it Feng Gu forgot to tell you."

"Well, the shop's been busy," I said.

He raised his eyebrows. He didn't believe my words. Perhaps he wondered why I defended her. Surely she'd had time to mention this gift. But she hadn't said a thing. Well, she had said lots of things, about not expanding the business, about not inviting riffraff in, about my boyfriend being "black." My mind backed up over that conversation. How she had snorted when I said my boyfriend was intelligent and successful. Snorted. Surely she wouldn't have snorted about a successful professor in Singapore. Oh, gods. Had she assumed my boyfriend was Chan Hai?

"Well, I'm glad I got to give this to you in person."

He held the wrinkled red bag out with both of his thick hands. His eyes enveloped me with warmth. I backed up toward the cash table. My head pounded. Why was I attracted to this man whose uncle owned a worthless quarry, who fought with an official—a good card player, at that—who was "black" on top everything else? Why was I attracted to this man who made the people close to me turn their noses in the air?

"You shouldn't have done this," I said. "You're too kind."

"You make it easy to be so," he said. He stood up and closed the distance between us. He put my hands around the sides of the bag.

"Father heard about our dinner in the Fat and Happy Pork Soup Shop," I said, unable to meet his gaze.

"I always thought Mr. Fat and Happy's pork soup was worth any trouble to taste." His calloused fingers brushed against my arm, back and forth, back and forth. "But last night I wish I'd taken you anywhere else—even to that greasy *hambaobao* place. Were you—are you—I hope you didn't have too much trouble getting home."

"No trouble," I said.

The smell of Snakehead's whiskey breath, the feel of Little Wu Lu's unrelenting grasp, the sight of the door to my home came rushing to me. I grasped onto the bag. How much did he know?

"I shouldn't have left you," he said. His eyes burned into mine. "I won't leave you."

"My father." I had to be honest. I had to tell him that Father, Mother and Madame Matchmaker all hoped I would marry a successful, rich professor in Singapore. That as much as my heart pounded at the sight of his blue cotton pants, his muscular arms, his deep brown eyes, ours would be a rocky path. "My father's a difficult man."

I stole a glance in the bag. A shiny new pair of scissors lay on top of black cloth—the black cloth of pants. How did he know that I'd lost my scissors? That my pants had been ruined? Had he spoken with Little Wu Lu?

"How is your father difficult?" he asked. "Other than he has you worrying about whether your wish to teach is—"

"You saw Little Wu Lu?" I asked. "Is —well—how is he?"

"Gone," he said. His blue cotton pants brushed against my skirt. "Tell me about your father."

"Gone?"

I swallowed hard. But certainly I hadn't stabbed Little Wu Lu that hard? Certainly I hadn't killed him? My knees trembled beneath my weight. I sucked hard, but air wouldn't fill the hole that had opened in my chest. I leaned back on the table, knocking a cup of tea over. The warmth soaked into my skirt like blood. Little Wu Lu's blood.

"You care." He put his fingers inside the waistband of my skirt and pulled me up. "I love that."

"No. Please." I pulled away. "Tell me. What happened to Little Wu Lu?"

"He's not gone to this world."

Chan Hai chuckled. He brushed my cheek with the back of his fingers. I breathed. Thank the gods. Feng Gu's footsteps on the gravel out back sounded.

"When I went to visit him at the clinic this morning, he had disappeared," Chan Hai whispered. "I don't know where the little bastard is."

"You better go," I said. "Afternoon is a busy time."

"I'll come again," Chan Hai said. At the exit, he turned and smiled. "I'll come again."

His words made my insides expand. This man who hadn't planned to kidnap me and had fought against the ruthless snakehead had used money he certainly didn't have to buy me a new pair of pants. What an expense. How thoughtful. How personal. I wanted to accept this gift. But was the relationship he offered with these pants mine to take? Father would have said no. But Father wasn't always right. In fact, in important matters—like accepting perfectly solid jobs from the university, dealing peacefully with our neighbor, learning when to stop gambling and come home—he was wrong. Always.

Still, I would need to convince Father of Chan Hai's goodness somehow. Why was everything so complicated? Would that I were just a child worrying about how to get a peach down from a branch and thinking that the whole sky belonged to me.

I took the pants from the wrinkled red shopping bag. I let my fingers run over the soft black cotton. The pants were my size. Better than anything I would have chosen. And brand new. Like a new year's gift to a family member. Chan Hai wasn't rich, but he wasn't evil. And he obviously cared about me. Maybe I still hadn't seen the "whole elephant." But the parts I knew now enchanted me. Waipo had always told me, "When you know something in your heart, you can fight against thousands and tens of thousands of enemies." I put the cloth of the pants next to my cheek. Oh, but the air tasted sweet.

Chapter Twenty-Six
No Flowers

The morning smells of bubbling rice porridge greeted me. Mother hummed as she sat on her haunches, beating father's shirt on the ground with a scrub brush. A large soap bubble popped on the ground. A rooster crowed. The smells, sights, sounds all seemed sharper today. And the new pants which Chan Hai had given me felt soft against my thighs.

"See you later." I nodded as I walked past Mother on my way to the main road.

"Ay!" She gestured with her soapy brush toward the black pants. Her eyes quizzical "Where did you get those?"

I knew she would ask. I wanted to tell her the truth. In fact, I wanted to shout the news to the world. I was more cautious.

"Feng Gu was upset yesterday at my sloppy dress," I said and continued across the courtyard.

"And?" Mother called. I turned back. She shifted her weight on her haunches. "Even with the salary you brought home, we still have such a large debt. Your father has a plan, but—"

"No, I didn't have to spend my money," I said. "Feng Gu gave these to me."

Well, she was supposed to, I thought. Chan Hai had asked her to.

"How nice." Mother went back to beating the shirt. "How nice. That job's really good for you, isn't it? Your father did good."

She talked more to herself than me, as if she was the one who needed convincing. Needed deceiving. My insides trembled. Wasn't I being as deceitful?

"Ma?" The muscles in my calves tightened. Sweat beaded my face. I looked up to the blue sky and took a deep breath. "Remember Chan Hai?"

"Was he a classmate of yours?" Mother asked.

Suds lathered beneath her brush. Had she forgotten his name already? Or was she pretending? She turned Father's shirt over and scrubbed the other side.

"No. Remember?" Heat rose and tickled the back of my neck. "I had dinner with—we ate dinner at Zi Mei's cousin's place."

"What about him?" She stopped scrubbing.

She wouldn't care how the sun shone brighter, the air smelled sweeter whenever he stood near. Or how his thick fingers wrapped inside the waistband of my skirt felt so right. She would only care about his prospects as a provider.

"He's good with flowers," I said. Sweat ran down the inside of my arm.

"Flowers?" Mother sprinkled more soap on Father's shirt, as if it was dirtier than she'd anticipated.

"He's very talented," I said. "He can take anything and make it grow. In fact, he told me that he's never bought a single flower. He can take snippets from friends and plants along the roadside and his garden—"

"Do you need something to grow?" Mother asked. She stopped brushing and stared up at me. The sun on her face made her features harsh. Her left eye twitched.

"I was thinking—well, you know." I nodded toward the neighbor. "Perhaps a garden along the path would be nice."

Mother swung the shirt against the cement. Thwack. Thwack. Thwack.

"Ma?" I said.

"Your father has a plan. He has everything under control." She wiped sweat from her brow with the back of her arm. "When we get the money, we'll build a winding cement walk."

Get the money? What money? She mentioned Father had a plan. I wanted to believe as she did that Father was in control. But often his plans were just hot air. Any money we had ran down the drain faster than water from the wash bucket.

"You don't need to bother that man who plays with flowers." Mother thwacked the shirt. "You have more important events in your future."

I looked at Mother. She concentrated on cleaning Father's shirt. Did she still love him? Had she ever? Madame Paper Cutter told me to follow my heart. Waipo would have said the same. How would I make Father and Mother see the good in Chan Hai?

Chapter Twenty-Seven
Chairman Huang Strikes Back

I arrived at the tea shop. Feng Gu sat at the cherrywood table calculating the morning's income on her abacus. Instead of sitting down across from her and resting until the next customer arrived, I looked around for something to do. Despite Mother's refusal to accept Chan Hai, I had more energy than I'd ever had. I swept the floor. I filled several sample bags. I called in a new order. What else? I wanted to sit down and write a letter to Guo Qiang telling him the truth about Father, telling him that our family would only drag him down, hoping to push him away from us forever. But perhaps such a letter was premature.

I went into the back room to get my scissors and the red paper bag which had held the pants Chan Hai had given me. The bag was wrinkled, but I could still make something from it. I sat across from Feng Gu so I'd see customers before they came in. I didn't want to miss anyone. Especially Chan Hai who had promised to return. If I spotted him first and met him outside, perhaps Feng Gu would not be so agitated. She had been in such a dark mood yesterday, only opening her mouth to criticize. I was relieved when she had disappeared into the back room to pray to her ancestor, even if that left me alone with all the customers for over a half hour.

I cut out a string of small red paper berries. Outside, boots scraped on the cement. I looked up. Was Chan Hai back? An old man walked by with a load of bricks on his back. His back was curved. Did Chan Hai do that kind of work? Would his strong back also curve from the weight eventually?

"What's that for?" Feng Gu asked, looking up from her abacus and nodding toward the cutting in my hand.

"I don't know," I said. The paper berries lay in my hand. "A decoration."

She looked around, from left to right, as though in search of a spot that would need a string of berries for a decoration. Cobwebs no longer draped the corners. A film of dust no longer blanketed the tile floor. The shop was cleaner and brighter than it had ever been.

"A decoration for where?" Her voice sounded incredulous.

"Not here," I said. I looked at the string of berries, one berry after another. They weren't the same size, each one markedly different from the next. But at least they would lend a splash of color to my hair, which seemed dull and lifeless. "It's a head covering I saw in a magazine somewhere."

"Not in Fashion Fortune Magazine," Feng Gu said. She pursed her lips and wrinkled her mushroom nose as if she smelled something foul.

A man's deep laugh sounded near the door. Chan Hai? Had he brought a friend? Was this one a good person? My toes pressed against my pumps, ready to stand. Two young men walked past, holding a letter between them, laughing at this line and that. If Mei Ling were near, I could imagine doing the same thing with Guo Qiang's letters, pointing out the long words, the didactic sentences, the preachy tone. Perhaps he and his buddies laughed as happily at mine.

"Another strong morning of sales," Feng Gu said, shaking her abacus up and down.

"That's great," I said.

If we managed to keep sales up, I'd be sure to get a bonus. I might even have money to buy a real decoration for my hair. Perhaps a new pair of pumps to go with my nice pants. Here I was frying my eggs before the hen even laid them. Surely Father did the same. The only difference was that he made it to the frying pan before I did.

"Who would have thought an art major could help our bustling tea shop?" Feng Gu shook her head and lifted her shoulders.

"Feng Gu," I said. Why did she insist on foisting that image on me? Everything I did and said was colored by her ill-conceived image. "I didn't study art."

"Sure," Feng Gu said. She reached across and flicked the berries on the string.

"I studied education." I looked up at her.

"Aha," she said, slapping her thigh. "I knew it. So that's why you always want to have this class or that—"

"Childhood education," I said.

"Oh." She sat back. Her mouth open. She pulled on her hair. "Well, let me tell you, before you even suggest it, the last thing we need in here is a bunch of riotous kids breaking cups and spilling tea."

Kids in here? What an idea. I imagined mothers bringing in their small children. Singing songs. Drawing. Writing characters. Mothers could drink tea while children had milk and cookies. I smiled at the dream. No, Feng Gu would never allow such a thing. She always smelled cow dung on the path before she'd even taken one step, one breath. She had to be dragged from her same safe spot to move even one step forward.

"I need to go get some fresh air." I stood. I hoped Chan Hai didn't show while I was gone, but I couldn't sit around any longer. "Can I get you something to eat?"

"Fresh air?" Feng Gu shook her abacus. "There's no fresh air out there. Just a hot sun."

"Not by the river," I said. I stretched and looked outside. I froze. There, standing by the door was Chan Hai. I hadn't heard him coming. He stayed where he was. Perhaps he felt as sensitive about rushing into Feng Gu's space as I. "The river always has a breeze."

"That filthy place?" Feng Gu said. "Do you think that's where Chan Hai got those oyster cakes?"

I smiled. Despite her cold refusal of the oyster cakes, as soon as Chan Hai had gone, she swallowed up that treat in a few bites. Then she had looked over at mine with obvious longing.

"I've never seen an oyster cake woman there," I said. Chan Hai had a smudge of dirt on his cheek. He held up two barbecued strips of beef and raised his eyebrows. I pulled my gaze from him. "But I think there's a place to get barbecued beef. Would you like that?"

"Funny. I was thinking the same thing," she said. "I can smell them already."

"I'll be right back," I said and breezed out the door.

Chan Hai and I walked down the road and up onto the bridge. Around us people and bicycles competed for space. But my heart felt little of the agitation that usually accompanied a walk in the town. The heat of his arm so close to my shoulder made me stand tall. The rustling of his pants made my heart sing. The sweet strip he handed me tasted tender and salty. We stopped at the far end of the bridge and leaned over the railing to watch the water flow. I felt Chan Hai's eyes on me. His eyebrows furrowed.

"Is today something special?" he asked.

"Special?" I repeated.

Today felt special. Special because I had told Mother about Chan Hai and told Feng Gu who I was, what I'd really studied. Speaking the truth felt good. Special because I continued to enjoy the way Chan Hai made my heart beat. Special because I realized if he continued to make my heart pound out this beautiful music, I'd need to break off the match that was being woven for our family. Chan Hai nodded at the decoration on my head.

"This?" I put my hand to my hair. Did he like the berries? "Special? No. I just thought they would be fun."

"Don't hide your hair," he said.

Was I? This morning I'd felt proud of how honest I had been. But was I still hiding? Would I always be? A group of teenage boys laughing and shouting pushed their way across the bridge. Chan Hai jumped behind me, as if to protect me from the onslaught of bodies. As they passed, his body pressed against the back of mine.

"Your hair's more beautiful than any decoration which could cover it." He reached up and pulled the berries away, whispering in my ear. "Like silk woven by the gods."

Heat rose to my face. My heart felt full. He always made me feel so important. Had he done this to others? Why wasn't he already married? Then again perhaps all the eligible women his age thought like Feng Gu—that he was black. A cool breeze from the river kissed my face. The gentle lapping of the water soothed my soul. And Chan Hai stood behind me full of kind words, full of love, full of grace. Nothing had ever felt finer.

"I'm no longer a quarry worker," Chan Hai said.

"That's great." I turned around. His skin smelled of soap. His Adam's apple bulged when he swallowed. The black mark on his face looked like a bit of charcoal dust. Had he earned enough money to start his nursery? If so, why did he look so serious? "Isn't it?"

"No." He looked into my eyes, seeking reassurance. "The quarry's been closed."

"Closed?" Had there been a terrible accident? An explosion which had sent hailstorms of rocks down, burying the workers alive?

"Closed for a health inspection," he said.

"Is that bad?"

Then again what did rocks have to do with health? Had they found something harmful in the rocks? Feng Gu's words—"he's black"—went through my head. I pushed them aside. He rubbed his fingers together, signaling money, lots of money. Ah, so a health inspection was not really an inspection at all. The words were code for a shutdown until the right amount of money changed hands.

"Yes." He sighed, hitting the railing of the bridge with his fist. "The Honorable Chairman Huang has a long reach."

Snakehead Huang? I knew the snakehead held great power. Father had said as much. I remembered Father saying what a fool Chan Hai was for fighting with Chairman—Snakehead—Huang. "It's not good to fart in an official's face," he'd said. "It may end up exploding in your own." Yes, that was happening now. I looked up into Chan Hai's smooth face. Behind his smile, his eyes looked unsettled. How could so much trouble have erupted from that one short evening? Perhaps he jumped to conclusions.

"Chairman Huang?" I asked. "Are you sure?"

Then again I remembered the policeman who had stopped next to Snakehead's van. Rather than respond to my pleas for help, he had inquired about Snakehead Huang's health. Had Snakehead talked the police into closing the quarry?

"I'm sure." Chan Hai's eyes held mine.

"Do you know anyone?" I asked. Perhaps he had a friend . . . or, better, a relative. Someone with more power than Snakehead.

"Maybe."

He stared over my head into the water a long time. Was he seeing the garbage—the floating tires, the cans, the wrappers? Or was the river still lovely and peaceful?

"Maybe," he repeated with more enthusiasm. "My uncle has a friend who has a friend who is a distant cousin of Huang."

So, not more power. Just someone who might be able to change Snakehead's mind. Might be. After lots and lots of talking and oiling. Like Feng Gu with her ledger and abacus calculating profits, I counted and multiplied the friends, the various bribes along the way. This would be a long, complicated process. The figures in my head made me dizzy.

"Don't worry too much," I said to him, rubbing the black mark off his face.

But, while the smudge disappeared from beneath my fingers, I knew rubbing the dirt from Chan Hai would be even more difficult now. Father would not be impressed by someone who had not only crossed a good card player but had no job. Father would not be impressed at all.

Chapter Twenty-Eight
Queen Dairy

As the summer wore on and the tiny brown balls in the tree in the backyard turned to round fleshy peaches, my concern for Chan Hai turned to panic. Whenever he showed up at the shop at lunchtime, I knew he was still without a job. I knew my chances of him winning the heart of Father were worse than ever. If sales at the shop continued, I'd get a big bonus. But it probably wouldn't be big enough to smudge away the dirt Father would see on Chan Hai. In fact, if Mother had her facts right, Father was already spending my bonus before the *yuan* even touched my fingers. Once again.

"Only serious players are invited," Mother had said one night tapping her big wooden ladle on the side of the wok. Well, Father certainly was serious. But that seriousness had never done our family much good.

"Who's he playing?" I had asked.

"It's secret." She had shaken her head at me, not looking up from the wok. "Your father won't even tell me. Although he promised he'd get me a real gas burner when he wins. Maybe even a real toilet."

Her eyes had sparkled at the thought of a house filled with modern conveniences as Mei Ling's house certainly would be. I hadn't heard directly from Mei Ling, but her mother had sent a note. Mei Ling had arrived safely in Japan and already sent money home. They had just bought a big-screen television.

More than a gas burner, a toilet or a television, I just wanted Chan Hai. I had tried to cut off my feelings toward this man who would never win the hearts of my parents. But each time Chan Hai showed up at the shop felt like a cool breeze in this summer, which kept getting hotter and hotter. With no rain.

My overzealous neighbor poured well water down the winding dragon each night, as if that would bring health and good fortune his way. Perhaps even some rain. If I'd been superstitious, I would have thought the heat a prediction that the gods were up to something. I didn't worry though. I was too happy. I sensed Father would never be able to approve of Chan Hai. But for the time being, he was our best friend. Mother was so consumed about Father's big game, his potential winnings, the items she would purchase, she didn't notice when I returned home later than usual from work. She never knew Chan Hai came by each day to escort me home. That we would start out heading for the bridge or the bus depot and end up talking so much that we continued walking.

Each time he showed me a different place—like the start of the stone wall that used to enclose our village in olden times. Or the one place in town that hauled in wood from the mountain tops. Or the nursery, where Chan Hai explained how the fragrant jasmine plants were infused into tea at nighttime. Or how the butterfly orchid, which resembled a butterfly in flight, only bloomed for three months.

At first, I worried that Chan Hai didn't know where we were going, and we'd both end up lost. But, after a couple of times, I let him do the navigating. Why insist on having a say when I didn't know what I was saying? He may have been "black" and without an impressive education, but he knew things. Not just the names of plants. He knew himself, and he seemed to know me. He was a kind person. My heart felt squeezed at the thought of him having to beg from friend to friend for assistance in getting his uncle's quarry re-opened, a quarry where he didn't want to work in the first place. If only I could help.

One morning, I arrived at the shop as vendors wet the streets with water. The sight of all that water made me feel cool inside. But the result was like lifting the top off a steamer. Steam rose from the streets, making the air so thick it was difficult to breathe. Feng Gu stood in the back room talking to her ancestor. Her forehead glistened with drops of sweat as she held out three sticks of burning incense and bowed to the black-framed photograph of the boy. She bowed again and again. She murmured a wish to him and placed the incense in the round brass holder in front of the photo. Her thin hair stuck to her head.

"We don't have power," she said. She put a lock of her short hair behind her ear. "Today's going to be miserable."

I tore a piece of cardboard from one of the supply boxes to use as a fan. Since I had met Chan Hai, I couldn't think of a miserable day. I couldn't imagine one.

The day did go by slowly though. Without a breeze from the electric fan to offer relief, the air in the tea shop felt like the center of a wok, hot and sizzling. My hair stuck to the back of my neck. My clothes felt like a second skin. Not one customer came, not even

Madame Paper Cutter who enjoyed stopping in every once in a while to sit and have a cup of tea. Not even the ones who had orders to pick up.

At lunchtime, Feng Gu and I sat in silence, that familiar tense silence I'd experienced the first day I had come to the shop. You would have thought I'd taken away the power. You would have thought I kept the customers away. I who had the most to lose if sales didn't stay strong. Even after all this time together, she still considered me the intrusive art major. The enemy.

"Perhaps we need to start something new," I said. "If we had a regular Tuesday morning class, people would be sure to show."

"We don't need new ideas," she said, her face bulging with anger. "Something's just got to be done about the old ones."

She stood, her half eaten packet of rice left on the table. She stormed out the back. The heat had overwhelmed her. I had visions of her stopping in an air conditioned department store. The power outages never affected the entire town. Or maybe she'd gone to sit in the pool at the high school. The thought of her squat figure sinking beneath the water while hundreds of school boys swam laps made me smile. I pulled my blouse in and out to manufacture a breeze. I thought cool thoughts, of winter winds, of well water, of next month's Autumn moon.

Father hated the autumn moon—the biggest, roundest moon of the year—the time of year when families gathered to celebrate their unity and harmony. All that "nonsense" reminded Father of how disappointing his own family was. All that disappointment sent him early to the *mahjong* tiles. I feared this year would be the worst yet. While Father planned on me marrying Professor Liang, while he counted on it, I had been mentally composing the letter to drive the long-winded intellectual away.

I'd held off on the letter as I wanted to sit and talk with Father, adult to adult, about my true feelings, my true intentions. But he was always gone when I arrived home. He was always asleep when I woke. I rolled the legs on my pants up higher. From the back room came a scraping sound on the floor like a vendor's wheels scratching against the doorway. Perhaps a rickshaw driver had taken a shortcut to avoid the noon traffic, forcing his way down the narrow passage.

High heels tap-tapped in the back room. Feng Gu had returned. That was fast. Too fast for a swim or even a good cool-down in the nearby department store. She must have discovered when the power would turn on again. Or maybe she had brought ice for us to put on our wrists.

"Here we go," Feng Gu said coming into the front with a flourish.

She puffed up her chest and held up a piece of white chalk. What was this? I'd heard that eating chalk was good for your teeth, but I didn't know it was good at relieving the heat from your body. She kneeled down in front of the entrance and drew a line across the floor. The chalk scraped against the cement. That sound I had just heard. She must have drawn a mark in the back as well. She continued with the line around the room. She reminded me of overzealous New Neighbor. Surely she didn't think evil spirits had inhabited our shop.

I rolled the legs up further on my black pants. Surely people just stayed away from us because of the heat. What would potential customers think if they saw the white line? Especially superstitious potential customers? Feng Gu had found yet another way to offend people. This time I cared. I needed sales to be better than last year so I would get my salary, I would get my bonus.

"Feng Gu," I said. "Perhaps—perhaps you might want to wait for the electricity to come back on."

"What?" she said. "You think I can't see to draw a proper line?"

"No, no," I said. "Your line is fine. It's just—well, maybe our slow morning has something to do with the lack of cool air, the fan not working."

"You know nothing." She shook her head and wiped sweat from her forehead. "You live in a fairy tale."

Why did she say such a thing? What magic solution would Mei Ling have recommended for this irrational behavior? Another winding dragon? I heard the familiar scrape of boots coming down the sidewalk toward us. I looked up the street. Chan Hai held two ice cream cones. Oh, gods. He would only agitate her more. In fact, while I often shared stories of what a kind person Chan Hai was, how un-black he had become, Feng Gu's entire being darkened at the sight of the man. She often retreated into the back to talk with her ancestor whenever Chan Hai stopped by the shop.

Ice cream melted down both sides of the cones. I could hardly nod at him to please keep walking, that we would meet later. I could hardly expect him to eat those ice creams by himself. Ice creams he had bought with precious notes that each day were in shorter and shorter supply.

"Nobody will come here unless I do this," she shouted, leaning down to finish off the line. "I know."

"I will." Chan Hai walked up beside us.

"No, no, no." Feng Gu jumped to her feet, waving the chalk at him. "I especially don't need you here."

Had the heat affected her judgment? Certainly she didn't think Chan Hai was behind the flow of business, slow or fast? My, but she was on a rampage this morning. Chan Hai didn't appear offended though. He merely smiled.

"I brought you some ice cream," he said. He handed me a cone and offered the second to Feng Gu.

"Children eat ice cream," Feng Gu said. She folded her hands across her chest. "It's bad for your *qi*."

"It's from the Queen Dairy," he said, mentioning a foreign shop which had just opened. "They have ice cream and iced drinks."

"Interesting," Feng Gu said, ushering him away from the shop, as though shooing away a feral cat. "I'll have to stop there sometime."

"You will," he said. "It's THE meeting spot."

"You're making that up," Feng Gu said, but she stopped shooing.

"I just saw many of your customers there," Chan Hai said, lifting his eyes from the white line to Feng Gu. "The man who owns the department store, his brother, and Madame Tsui Ping. In fact, when I left, she was offering to help the Queen with her English advertisements."

"She's supposed to be helping us." Feng Gu's high voice whined, grating against my ears. "She still needs to fix our pamphlet. Besides, how could she put something cold like that in her old body?"

"She's not the only one. Everyone's doing it. And they seem just as healthy when they walk out—in fact, healthier. They're not so hot anymore."

I had tasted cold tea. Not only here, but at home. Cheng Min had insisted on only cold drinks while at the hospital. And, even though she was home again, the new skin on her face and arms pink like a rabbit's nose, any hot liquid still made her insides burn. Common wisdom said cold liquids were bad for your body. But common wisdom told us a boy was a must in the family. Look what that had done to Cheng Min and her family. Look what it had done to ours. Perhaps common wisdom was sometimes wrong.

I lifted up my cone and licked the sides. I let my tongue sink into the softness of the top. The ice cream cone was like a breath of fresh air. Better than frozen red bean bars which people sometimes hawked along the streets.

"See," Chan Hai said, winking at me. "She looks healthier."

"What would we do?" Feng Gu laughed. "Have ice in our tea?"

"What a good idea," I said. "What a good idea."

"Have you forgotten everything I've taught you?" Feng Gu ran her fingers through her hair as she fell into her lecture mode. "The tea has to be a certain temperature. A certain temperature or it's not the finest liquid to touch your tongue."

I smiled at her. That sounded like something Chan Hai would have said. Perhaps she wasn't as irritated with him as I had imagined.

"Besides," Feng Gu added, looking at Chan Hai. "Surely you can't be suggesting we put people in harm's way for our own benefit."

Chan Hai chuckled. Not deep and warm, but an empty, false noise I hadn't heard before. An uncomfortable look flashed across his eyes. I was missing something here. Some happening. Some shared history.

"The Queen's customers don't get sick," he said.

He held the cone out to her again. She waved her arm back and forth. She didn't want it. He picked her hand up and placed her stubby fingers around the cone.

"It's against tradition," Feng Gu said. But while she protested the idea, she held the cone up high, letting the drops of melting ice cream fall in her mouth, like a dog waiting for water from a leaky faucet. "Besides, we don't want anyone to get sick."

She was concerned about using ice from the provisioner, ice from unboiled water, ice which would roll around in a dirty truck for a long time on the trip to the shop.

"Obviously Queen Dairy's customers have found clean ice," I said.

"Still—" Feng Gu shook her head. Her expression hardened on her face. Her eyes gleamed like small marbles.

"It may not be traditional," Chan Hai said, stepping closer to the white chalk line, standing so close I could feel the heat from his body. "But tradition isn't always good. Besides," he added, looking around the tea shop, "it can't get much quieter in here."

"Certainly it couldn't hurt to try ice in the drinks," I said.

My words sounded as if I stepped across that white line to stand next to Chan Hai. No matter that he was "black," that Mother didn't approve of him, that Father surely wouldn't. I felt good standing next to him. By his side was where I belonged.

Chapter Twenty-Nine
Water Bug

Chan Hai sat next to me as the bus bounced down the road. His knee pressed against mine. The back of our hands touched. Since the chalk incident that day, I sensed something different in him. The bus came to a stop across from the pink castle and I stood to make my way down the aisle. He put his arm on mine. He was so gentle. Always.

"It's so hot," I said. "Rain would feel nice."

"I know a place that's cool," he said, not letting go of my arm. "Let me show you."

In my mind, I knew I shouldn't follow. I could see Father taking a big dragon puff of his cigarette, blowing the plume in my face and shaking his head. In my heart, I knew I would. Waipo's twinkling eyes, her wrinkled hands pushed me back down into my seat.

I stared at the metal floor as the bus moved along toward his side of the village. I had never come this far. Funny, I'd traveled all the way to Xiamen for university, but hadn't even explored the far reaches of my own village. His hand stayed on my arm.

We got off the bus near a mountainside. On the one side of the road stood a small hut. On the other, bricks lay stacked in the sunshine. A brick factory?

"My uncle's quarry," Chan Hai said, pointing toward the hut and the mountain beyond.

We walked up the dirt road, past the empty hut, past trucks that held no drivers, past a loading area filled with rocks but no workers. I wanted to ask Chan Hai if he'd made any progress in re-opening the quarry. But his silence was so deep, I knew that he hadn't.

We walked further and further back up into the mountain. Short trees surrounded us. This was new growth. I could tell from the size of the trunks, the height of the trees. I could tell because Chan Hai had taught me so.

Oh, but this was not a cool place. My feet felt like lead. No matter how often I sighed, I couldn't expel all the heat from my body.

"I'm melting." I laughed. I wished sometimes that I could.

Melt and disappear into the life I wanted for myself. A life without obligations and responsibilities.

"Then we're just in time," Chan Hai said, as we turned down a small path, a path that was engraved through an opening in some bushes. "Here we go—the reservoir."

The reservoir was a small, muddy pond surrounded by a canopy of trees. Two men splashed water on themselves at one end, washing soap from their bodies. Perhaps the water was cleaner than it looked. Across from the reservoir lay a huge round gravestone. What a peaceful resting place for a grave. Birds flitted from branch to branch. A frog jumped over my shoe. Chan Hai removed a lime and a small knife from his pocket. He sliced the lime in half and came close to me.

"I love this place," he said, squeezing half the juice from the lime into my palm. I rubbed this mosquito repellent on my arms, my face, my neck. Good of him to come prepared.

"You know," he said, dabbing a bit of the juice on the back of his neck, the only place, he said, mosquitoes ever bit him. "When we were little, the water used to be so clean you could see to the bottom."

"Then again," I said. "Maybe when you are little, you just don't see all the dirt."

"No, no," he said, tossing the remains of the lime on the ground and looking up at the gravestone. "I could see to the bottom. I remember."

Most children were never allowed near water. I certainly hadn't been. Why was he different?

"Your parents let you swim here?" I asked.

"Of course not. This was my secret place." He sat down on a rock and removed his shoes and socks. "Now it's ours."

"Well, ours and the rest of the bathers," I said indicating the men still washing up.

"They'll be gone soon," he said. "Come, put your feet in the water. It's nice and cool."

I took off my pumps, rolled up my pants legs and waded into the water. The cool mud on the bottom of the reservoir oozed through my toes. My feet, my legs felt refreshed. But my hair still hung limp and sweaty on my neck. I felt cut in half. Part of me refreshed, part of me still burning from the heat. I wanted to sink into the coolness, to enjoy it with my whole being, to be of one feeling.

"Feels good, doesn't it?" Chan Hai said, looking over at the bathers splashing around in the water. He scooped water into his hands and poured it onto his arms. Then he stretched and made whirlwind motions with his arms. "How about a swim?"

"No, thanks." I backed up and looked at my watch. "I shouldn't stay too long."

"A quick dip will revive your spirits," Chan Hai said.

He peeled off his t-shirt and walked up the bank to a nearby tree. I heard him unzipping his trousers. Oh, but taking off all those sweaty clothes must feel good. He walked past me. I spotted his bare legs, his threadbare boxers, his golden back as he sank below the water. How nice.

"Sure you don't want to join me?" He stood waist deep in the murky water and turned to face me. He held out his hand. The thick patch of hair under his arm was dark and fuzzy.

I'd always been warned to stay away from the water. That swimming was difficult, too difficult for girls. What would Father say if he saw me standing here so close to the water, so close to Chan Hai?

"I don't know how to swim," I said.

"Ah, so now you speak the truth."

Chan Hai moved closer. Water dripped off his brown nipples. The taut muscles in his stomach moved out and in as he breathed. I pulled my eyes away and looked down, heat rushing to my face. Water bugs flitted across the surface of the brown water. Dragonflies hovered.

I wished I could speak the truth to Chan Hai. Speak the truth to Father and Mother, Madame Matchmaker and Guo Qiang. The truth that I shouldn't be here with Chan Hai, that I should be at home waiting with Mother for the mailman bringing intelligent words from the Tropics. That was something I didn't even want to contemplate. The truth that I cared about this jobless man standing in front of me more than I cared about a house and a car which sat four. All my truths were pushed down inside and surrounded by expectations and customs and rules.

"Have you no fears?" I asked.

"From the time I was a kid," he said, taking hold of my hand with both of his. "I was always interested in flowers. I could name every one on the hillside and tell you when it bloomed. My parents laughed. My uncles thought it a preference that should be squashed as soon as possible. My friend, Little Wu Lu—"

"Little Wu Lu?" I asked. The man who had grabbed me and held me so tightly in the van? That Little Wu Lu?

"Fearless Little Wu Lu gave me a beautiful chrysanthemum. I wanted that chrysanthemum to grow so badly, I put dirt all around it, all the way up to the petals." He kissed the tips of each of my fingers. "I watered that golden flower everyday. I smothered that poor flower to death."

"You must have felt terrible," I said. I imagined the small Chan Hai trying to coax the flower back to life, begging and praying and even feeding the plant half his own dinner.

"'You killed it with all your fears,' Little Wu Lu told me." Chan Hai looked down in my eyes. "He was right."

I looked out onto the water. My chest felt tight. Perhaps Little Wu Lu had no fears. But he had turned into such a terrible person, helping Snakehead to kidnap me. Then again, Madame Paper Cutter had called Little Wu Lu desperate.

"Now, how about a swim?" Chan Hai asked.

He must have thought my biggest fear was the murky water. But Father wasn't just a fear. He was unforgiving. He was family. He was my responsibility forever.

"Go on," I said. "I'll just enjoy here for a minute."

"Suit yourself."

His brown eyes didn't register even the slightest disappointment. He dove into the water and swam across to the other side. His arms made more splashing than two ducks in a fight. But, while elegant he was not, he certainly crossed the reservoir quickly. Toward the other side, he slowed, and I worried that he had tired. Was it deep over there? What would I do if he couldn't go further? I went up onto the banks to get a clearer view of him. He definitely looked as if he could swim no further. I looked around, hoping to see the bathers near. But they had gone. We were all alone.

"Power bills are due," the village loudspeaker blared.

I jumped. I thought here in this small forest of trees around the reservoir, we were in our own private world, so far away. But here we were, still within reach of the village loudspeaker, the community, Madame Matchmaker, Mother, Father. Still, if Chan Hai needed help, who would hear me call?

Chan Hai touched the other side. My heart tingled with relief and that emotion took me by surprise. I'd never felt an inner tug like that from a man outside my family. I'd never worried too much about any man other than Father. Chan Hai stared up at the gravestone for a moment, resting. What a long way to swim. The base of my spine tingled. Why didn't he hurry back?

"The Butterfly Lovers," the woman on the loudspeaker continued. I didn't jump this time. "That will be our first production if we can build the theater in time. Our projected date is the Autumn Moon Festival. So, bring your generous donations in . . . along with your electricity dues."

Music from the famous production filtered through the speakers. Ah, the Butterfly Lovers. That was one of my favorites. If we had more money, I'd have liked to donate twenty *yuan* to the project. Waipo and I had watched the show many times in the courtyard on the old neighbor's television.

The sound of splashing water made me look over. Chan Hai's long arms stroked confidently across. I walked into the water as far as I could, unconcerned about my pants getting wet. As he neared, I put my arms out just in case. His arm splashed water on my blouse. I reached out and put my hand on his arm, on his puffing chest.

"You swim so well," I said. "You must be tired."

"I never felt better," he said looking down at my hand on his chest. He took my hand and kissed the back of it. Then he looked into my eyes. "Never."

"Hmmmm, yes," I said. Water dripped from his hand. Each drop like a swath of cool silk stroking my skin. "That feels lovely."

"I told you," Chan Hai said. "Just follow me."

He leaned down, picked me up and carried me into the water. That deep voice beckoning me never failed. I would follow him anywhere anytime. If only Father could be as charmed.

I stood chest-deep in the cool water. With one hand, I clung to Chan Hai's strong shoulder. With the other, I held onto a rotting bamboo stick.

"You're a natural," Chan Hai coached, prying my fingers from his shoulder and putting them around the stick, my "kickboard."

"Tell me how again," I said.

Chan Hai's wet hair glistened. His soft brown eyes narrowed in concentration. He lifted his free arm out of the water and pointed his long index finger across the water. Those strong sure hands.

"If he can do it," Chan Hai said. "You can."

I let go of the pole, of Chan Hai. Had someone come? What

would they think of this? Who would find out?

"Who?" I said. "Where?"

"See." Chan Hai took a few steps and scooped up a handful of water. Brown water. Brown water with something moving across the surface. "Just like the water bug. Legs out and back. Out and back."

He put the bug back in the water. We watched as it flitted so easily across the surface of the water. So fast. So confident.

"But that tiny bug doesn't have all my weight," I said. I held onto Chan Hai's shoulder again. His skin felt smooth and firm. "Every time I take my feet off the ground, I sink to the bottom."

"Kick harder." He grabbed the bamboo pole and put it back in my hands.

"And water gets in my eyes," I added.

"Water gets in your eyes?" He looked up at the graying sky. "How do you wash your hair?"

"I use Flying Horse Shampoo," I explained, now seeing the problem. "Second Cousin insists it makes your hair fuller. Perhaps my hair is too full?"

Chan Hai smiled and pried one of my hands from the bamboo pole. Was he going to suggest we try swimming on another day when my hair was lighter?

"I mean, when you wash your hair, don't you get water in your eyes?" He kissed my palm. "Now try again. When water gets in your face, pretend you're just taking a shower."

I laughed long and hard at myself. Chan Hai, dear Chan Hai, joined me. I had been told so often how dangerous it was to swim, I'd frightened myself before even trying. I even fooled myself into thinking a shampoo could weigh down my body. And this from a college graduate. I laughed until tears rolled down my cheeks.

"There's water in your eyes again," he pointed out.

"Why do you make everything seem so easy?" I asked.

"Why make everything so difficult?" He grinned at me, showing his dimples.

Exactly. Why did I make it so difficult? I loved this man. I wanted him. Why did I get so concerned about Father and finances and the future when this was a simple matter?

With all Chan Hai's coaching, I'd managed finally to kick a few meters. More than that, the short dip made me feel alive and refreshed. My whole being. Then I glanced at my watch. We had stayed for longer than a short dip. It was close to seven. Father would have already left for his nightly game. Mother would be washing up the bowls from dinner. Unless she dreamed of gas ranges and toilets, she would wonder where I was. Chan Hai and I sloshed our way onto the bank.

"That was great," Chan Hai said. "Such fun."

He leaned over toward me and brushed the droplets of water from my arms. He took the ends of my blouse in his fist and squeezed out the water. His touch sent a tingle through my spine. I hated to leave, to put an end to our day.

"There you go," he said. "Good as new."

I bent down and squeezed out the water dripping from the ends of my pants. My clothes would still be damp when I got home, but perhaps not too damp. I headed for the path from which we had come.

"Not that way," Chan Hai said.

"I should be going back," I said.

"We are," he said. "But you don't have to walk up and back, up and back, always following the same trench. I know a different path. Follow me."

"Follow me. Follow me. Follow me," I teased. "You always say that. You sound like a bird."

We walked around the back of the reservoir and past the grave to a small dirt road which was lined with orchards and huts. I glanced at my watch again. The sky seemed awfully dark. Were those clouds? A man cycled past us, a dead chicken tied to the metal rack on the back. Surely he was on his way home.

"What's the problem?" Chan Hai asked.

"No problem," I said.

"There's something," he said circling me. "Something's on your mind—always."

"No," I said, feeling the gods pouring a bucket of mud on my head at the lie.

How could I not tell him of my parents expectations? Of all these matters swarming in my head like gnats? Then again, how could I? Why should I? My heart beat only for him.

A gaggle of geese crossed our path, which had turned into grass. In fact, the path seemed to dead end. Perhaps Chan Hai had made a mistake this time. How could this lead home? Chan Hai pulled me further along. The grass which grew taller and taller, tickled my ankles, then my elbows.

"That place has been there forever," Chan Hai said, pointing to an old temple in front of us.

Perhaps he just wanted to show me another historical site. Then we would turn around on that well-worn path and find our way back. Tall grass grew around the entrance to the temple. The door fell from the hinges. This place had been neglected for some time. He led me to the back of the temple where a mound of sand lay piled high, as though dumped here for later construction.

"No one takes care of the place," he said. "No one even comes near it. Some story about ghosts."

"Well, this place is kind of out of the way," I said. "Even for ghosts."

"You're always so practical," he said.

He stood behind me. The overgrown grasses surrounded us. His soft breath warmed the top of my head. In the distance, birds chattered. Their small voices chirped that the food was over there, not here. My spine tingled.

"This path must be the long way," I said. I didn't glance at my watch. But I could tell by the way the sun dropped in the sky that this day would soon end. "How much longer does it take?"

"How much longer do you want it to take?" he asked.

He picked up a lock of my hair and twirled it in his strong hand. I felt the gesture down between my legs. The gods had drawn me a white line. Chan Hai stood on one side, Guo Qiang on the other. Up until now, I had been standing in the middle, watching from one side to the other, as if following a table tennis match. Now Chan Hai held out his hand for me to join him. To be with him.

"Hmm?" he asked.

He lifted my hair and kissed the nape of my neck. The birds shouted at me again that the food was over there, not here. Over there. Noisy birds. Yes, the food for Mother and Father was in Singapore. But my food, the food for my heart, was right here.

"How long shall we take?" he whispered in my ear.

"Until the ghosts chase us away," I said.

I turned to face him and kissed him full on the mouth. Off in the distance, a streak of lightening laced the night sky. Would we have rain? After over a month of none?

"Look," I said, indicating the sky.

"I see."

He lifted my chin and looked into my eyes. A drop of rain splashed on my arm. Then another.

"Feel that?" I said, raising my arm.

"Hmmm." He kissed my forehead, my eyelids, my nose. "I feel."

"This is amazing." I put my head back as soft, cool drops of rain fell from the sky. "It's wonderful."

"Yes," he agreed pulling me down with him onto the soft pile of sand. "Yes, it is."

Rain not only watered our crops, but fed our souls. The soft droplets signified new life and love. Perhaps this break in the hot weather was a nod of acceptance from the gods. And, my, but it felt good.

I stood in the shower room and peeled off my damp blouse and pants. The rain on the tin roof sounded angry. A draft seeped in under the tin door. I wasn't eager to wash away the smell and the feel of Chan Hai. But I couldn't let Mother see me like this. Too much sand on my skin and in my hair. Too delicious a scent.

I dropped my clothes in the middle of the cement washbasin in front of me. Waipo had always said I was beautiful. Men often stared after me. However, until tonight when Chan Hai insisted on exploring my mountains and valley, I'd never really felt beautiful. I stared at myself under the orange glare of the ceiling bulb. I could still feel his large hands exploring my small breasts, my flat stomach, the insides of my thighs. That area now felt sore.

I climbed up onto the washbasin. Normally I wouldn't take such a precaution. Dirt and water from the shower drained out under the door into our courtyard and the communal drain. However, Mother would wonder if she found granules of sand left behind on the cement floor, stuck under the door, in the courtyard. I brushed sand lightly from my skin down the small hole in the sink.

I felt like a monkey hunched on top of the basin, surrounded by four gray cement walls. I sat down on my damp pile of clothing. Part of my thigh touched the cold basin and my skin turned to chicken flesh, my nipples hardened. The insides of my knees were red and raw. The smell of Chan Hai intoxicating. I closed my eyes, inhaled, and thought of the village dragon.

Waipo had told me how there was once a dragon in our village. He came out of his cave once a year, always during the New Year period when everyone gathered for a big meal to celebrate. He was hungry and angry. He was big and strong and ugly. He forced his way through the village gates, through courtyards, into our homes. Each year he picked up a young virgin in his thick, hairy hands, like a guest picking up a toothpick. Then he disappeared.

All the villagers were terrified of this dragon. They didn't want him lumbering through the village, crushing houses in his wake.

They didn't want him taking away their marriageable daughters. Something had to be done. So they went to the temple priest for help. The priest suggested the people build the village walls higher. So, all year, when the villagers should have been tending to their fields, they instead lay stones. By New Year the wall reached higher than the highest mountain.

I brushed sand from the back of my calves. Back and forth. Back and forth until I felt smooth skin.

The dragon hopped over that wall as though skipping across a stalk of rice. He lumbered through the village, crushing the houses in his wake. Angered by the extra effort he had to endure, he picked up two young virgins this time.

The temple priest suggested they build a fire. So, the next year, when the villagers should have been tending to their fields, they instead chopped down wood from the surrounding mountains. On New Year's morning, they built a fire so strong, the flames licked the rising sun.

I turned the water faucet on. I splashed water over my body, taking sharp intakes of breath with each splash. So cold. I couldn't wait to wash off my body so I could then get under the warm shower.

The dragon looked at those flames, his eyes turning red and orange and green. He opened his mouth and yawned, emitting a stench more foul than our outhouse. Then he walked through that fire and through the village, crushing houses in his wake. This time, he picked up three young virgins.

The temple priest suggested they build their own dragon. So, the next year, when the villagers should have been tending to their fields, they instead spent each day designing and building an effigy of a dragon outside the village walls. His eyes were made of thousands of grains of dyed red rice, the last grains left in the village. His scales were woven rice stalks. His claws were brambles from the blackberry bush, prickly and sharp. He was so fierce-looking, young children dared not go too close.

I rinsed off the last of the sand and hopped down from the basin. I picked up my blouse and shook as much of the sand from it as I could. Then I ran the cloth under the water.

On New Year's morning, the villagers heard the dragon stomping up to the village gates. They waited, hiding beneath their beds, their paltry New Year's meals lined up on the table. Would the dragon crush the effigy? Would he open his mouth and blanket the village in stench? A low rumbling sounded, like thunder rolling across the sky. Rolling. Rolling. Rolling. Was this dragon laughing at them? The rolling laughter continued until evening. Then he stomped into the village, crushing houses in his wake. He picked up four young virgins.

The villagers were miserable. They had spent the last three years fending off the dragon, so they had very little food. Their village was in shambles. Each time they tried to stop the dragon, he took more of their marriageable daughters. What could they do?

The temple priest decided that the only solution was to pick a virgin and leave her outside the village gates. The choice was not easy. However he discovered one of the local fishermen had nine daughters, the eldest of whom had crossed eyes and a cleft palette. Nobody would marry such a girl. Besides, the fisherman's second-born daughter had a fine match arranged to become the fifth wife of the butcher. But Second Daughter could not marry until Eldest Daughter did. That was custom. Surely the priest would be doing this family a favor by ridding them of the ugly girl.

So, on New Year's eve, the temple priest took the deformed girl and led her to the village gates. The cold air bit her nose. The stars above laughed at her. The flame from the priest's lantern threw giant shadows. Boom. Boom. Boom. She could already hear the dragon lumbering toward the village. Or was that the beating of her heart?

"Everyone is afraid of something," Eldest Daughter said, grasping onto the priest's free arm with both hands. Her legs felt wobbly, as if they had turned into one of her father's fishing nets. Her feet refused to move, as if that net had gotten caught on a rock. "There must be some way we can all scare the dragon away."

"This dragon is afraid of nothing." The temple priest shook the ugly daughter's hand from his arm, stepped behind her and pushed her back with the palm of his hand. "He can scale the highest wall we've ever built. He can walk through fire. He even laughs at other dragons." The temple priest pointed the lantern toward the dry old effigy of the dragon they had built the previous year. The rice eyes had been eaten away by crows and desperate families.

"There must be something," Eldest Daughter pleaded as they reached the village gates.

She reached into the pocket of her pants. Her fingers felt around and touched the wedding firecrackers Second Sister had given her. Second Sister would marry tomorrow. Eldest Daughter didn't want to miss that happy day. All the food, the laughter, the firecrackers. She didn't want to miss her happy life. She turned and grabbed onto the priest's arm again.

"Please," she said.

"I'm sorry." The priest patted the ugly girl's hand and gave her his lantern. Then he peeled her fingers from his arm, pushed her outside and slammed the heavy wooden village gate.

Boom. Boom. Boom. The dragon came closer. What could she do? She shivered in her thin cotton pants. She looked at the old effigy and thought, why not? She upturned the lantern onto the dry stalks. A blaze filled the sky. The flames licked higher than the top of the village wall. Surely the villagers had never built such a huge fire.

She stood close to the warmth of the flames, filling her pockets with stones and twigs as she waited. The dragon lumbered down the main street. A gleam filled his yellow eyes. Then they turned red and orange and green. He was not frightened by the blaze. He made that low rumbling sound she remembered from last year. Laughter so strong the earth shook. He lumbered forward and bent down to scoop the poor girl up in his menacing paw.

Eldest Daughter backed away from his claws, throwing a handful of rocks from her pocket at him. He rumbled even more. The earth shook from his laughter. She reached for more rocks, feeling one of the small pieces of round cardboard, that lucky firecracker, in her hand as well. She didn't care. She'd never get to celebrate with Second Sister anyway. She threw the handful of rocks and the lucky firecracker at the beast.

Kaboom! The noise from the small celebratory cracker echoed across the mountains. The dragon drew back, pulling his hairy paw to his chest. His scales turned bright yellow. What did this mean? She dug in her pockets and pulled out another. She threw the firecracker directly into the fire.

Kaboom! The dragon jumped back on his haunches. The ground rocked beneath her. The dragon was afraid. She threw another. Kaboom! And another. The dragon, surprised and frightened, turned and ran off. He ran back to his cave never to return. Not that year. Not ever again. Still, just to be safe, every year, the villagers set off firecrackers from morning until night to keep that dragon away.

Why I thought of that New Year's story Waipo had told me, I didn't know. As I grabbed the plastic spigot and the gas flame in the water heater on the wall roared to life, I not only thought of that New

Year dragon, I thought of all my dragons. Of Father. Of Mother. Of their comfort during old age. Of Singapore. I held the spigot over my head. Warm water cascaded over my hair and into my eyes. How nice.

"How do you wash your hair?" I could still see Chan Hai asking me, as he tried to teach me to swim like that water bug. He had been so loving, so gentle. My heart felt so large, I thought I'd burst. Like I was a New Year's firecracker. Pa-pa-pa-pop. A new year's firecracker exploding above the house and around the village, chasing away the dragons and signaling a new beginning, a fresh start, a bright future.

Bang. Bang. Bang. The tin shower door rattled as someone pounded from the outside. Father? What was he doing home? Bang. Bang. Bang. Such urgency and determination. He'd break the door down. Surely he was angered by my late arrival home. Or perhaps one of the bathers in the reservoir had been a friend. Or that man on the bicycle?

My mouth went dry. I had waited for this moment with Father, a chance to tell him how I felt about Chan Hai, to ask for his permission to pursue this love. But now that Father was outside the door, my brain filled with cotton. What would I say?

"Li Hui?" Mother called.

"Yes?" I smiled, submerging my head under the warm water. What a relief. Not Father. "Yes. I'm home."

"Where have you been?" she called. Her voice sounded shrill. I had worried her.

"We didn't have power today at the shop," I called, taking my head from beneath the spray of water. "I was just so hot."

"Where have you been?" she cried out.

Perhaps she had been waiting for me, counting the minutes. To fold the laundry? Wash the dishes? I turned off the shower. My damp clothes hung from the basin in front of me. I grabbed a small ragged towel. The cloth only reached to the top of my stomach. But my clothes lay soaked on the cement sink. I crossed my arms over my naked breasts. The tin door creaked as I opened it.

Mother held a blue wash bucket over her head to protect her from the rain. Her eyes looked dark. Her brows furrowed. Her lips pursed.

"Isn't this rain wonderful?" I said. I pulled her into the dry safety of the small shower room, right next to the basin. "I just got soaked. At first, the cold drops felt wonderful. But, when I was damp through to my skin, I felt cold. That's why I stopped in here first to take a hot shower. I needed a hot shower."

I bit my lip. I talked too much. The rain on the roof beat loudly.

"Where have you been?" she asked. Her face glowed under the harsh light. "I've been waiting for you."

She looked behind me, as if she might see some evidence that would explain how I'd spent the last four hours. Thank the gods my clothes lay clean and without sand on the washbasin.

"I went for a walk," I said. "To a temple."

"To the temple?" she asked. Tense anger receded from her face. She patted my arm. Smiled. "Of course."

Mother's trusting smile loomed over me. I felt as small as one of the grains of sand I'd pushed down the sink hole. I couldn't pretend any longer.

"Mother," I said. "I've been doing some thinking. About the future—"

"Save your thinking for your professor," she said. From her waist, she extracted a thick envelope. "Came today."

Oh, no, not another letter. Not another long lecture on computer systems. I not only felt childish and ignorant, I felt cruel. No better than Little Wu Lu. It was time to stop this. I'd made my decision.

"Mother," I started. I put my head down. Drops of water from my wet hair fell across my forehead.

"I'm sorry I interrupted you," she said.

"No, no," I said. "I wanted to talk with you."

"You did?" Her voice had a schoolgirl quality, as if I'd just offered to share a secret.

"About Guo Qiang," I said. "Mother—"

"You know I watch you, and I'm full of envy." She looked at the thick letter in her hand as if it were a wad of hundred *yuan* notes. "You have your whole life ahead of you and a successful, kind professor who wants you to be his wife—"

"But, Mother—"

"The world is yours," she said. She looked up and smiled. A sad smile. "Take it."

I stared at Mother. She never spoke to me like this. She only spoke of chores to be done and money to be paid. What was this?

"When I—when I first married your father, I felt like the whole world was mine, too," she continued. She held the envelope with both hands and rubbed her wrinkled thumb over the stamp. Over and over. "It was the best match I could have hoped for."

Heat rushed to my cheeks. I grabbed my damp blouse from the sink and pulled it on. Waipo had told me some of my parent's history. But Mother had said nothing.

"Mother, I just don't think Guo Qiang—"

"I can remember . . . " Her lips trembled. She rubbed the stamp on the envelope as if it gave her power. "It wasn't until I could no longer have happiness that your father slipped away . . . started gambling."

Ah, so that's why Father had started gambling. Because I was born, instead of his son. How hard Mother had tried to find Father a son. Perhaps he hoped for some security in his winnings, security that he didn't feel at home. A blur of knitted blue hats and boots filled my head. The times she had tried to adopt a neighbor's newborn. How much a failure she must feel. Certainly a hundred times worse than I felt when I returned from University without a job in Beijing. How could Father treat us so?

"Oh, Mother," I said.

My heart hurt. I reached out and grabbed onto her hand, stopping her frantic rubbing of the stamp. Those hands which had swaddled me when I was a baby, so Father wouldn't know I was a girl, wouldn't insist on my removal. Those hands which had worked extra hard, stacking potatoes and washing cabbage, so that I could study. Those hands which poured rice wine for Father to keep him happy.

"But you," Mother continued. "You're dependable."

Her head was down. A few gray hairs stuck out on top of her head. When had she gotten those?

"I know that." She put her hands up to my cheek. Her fingers, long and thin, trembled. "I know you'll do the right thing for our family."

I felt divided, as if I stood only part way in the reservoir. My toes dug into the cool mud. My neck itched from the heat. I wanted Chan Hai with all my being. But Mother and Father were family. My whole family. My heart shrunk beneath the weight of this responsibility. If only Mei Ling were near. My feelings went up and down and up and down as if I were climbing seven steps up, then eight steps down. She would understand. She would know what to do. Maybe find a way out for me. But was there any option that would give me Chan Hai and financial security for my parents?

"I'll do my best," I said, taking the letter, helping mother retrieve her bucket and sending her out into the darkness. I closed the shower door and threw that heavy missive on top of my damp black pants. The pants which Chan Hai had given me. The pants which Chan Hai had slid off my legs at the back of the temple. The pants I'd be happy in for the rest of my life.

If only I could live two lives. Buddhists believed in more than one life, but one after the other. I wished for two lives simultaneously. I wanted to be the filial daughter and marry the successful, stable professor in Singapore. Then too I wanted to wake up each morning to the deep voice of Chan Hai, the feel of his hands on my hips, the taste of his lips on mine.

I turned the water back on, jumping when the gas heater sputtered to life. I increased the heat and stepped beneath the water spigot, letting the boiling water scald my skin. Like the little girl who needed to find something to scare the dragon, I needed to find a way to make the professor go away.

Chapter Thirty-One
The Moon Goddess

Cars which seated four splashed mud in the air as they zoomed through the streets. Leaves on the ground glistened like diamonds from the rain. The park vendors and shoppers and loiterers all looked like ants scurrying about their early morning rituals.

I paused at the edge of the park and gulped in the cool morning air. My heart felt as if I'd scrubbed it on a washing stone. With the letter I held I'd scraped away layers of tradition, of parental support. My heart beat naked. Raw. Blood pumped tentatively through my veins as if not sure what to do with all this new space. The letter in my hands felt like a firecracker ready to explode.

I had stayed up all night. I had read Guo Qiang's ten-page letter many times. But I hadn't looked up one computer science term. Not one. Instead I had thought about the temple. About Chan Hai's deep voice asking, "How long do you want it to take?" About his thick fingers running through my hair. Touching my body. His touch still lingered like the sweet smell of jasmine blossoms.

I had used that beautiful stationery with flowers along the borders that Madame Matchmaker had given me. That beautiful stationery that I already envisioned on a stand next to the cash register in Chan Hai's nursery. I had composed and recomposed my firecracker of a letter to Guo Qiang. I had nagged him with questions about the complicated words he used. "What's resolution? Parallel processing? Algorithm?" I had bored him with details of the tea shop, writing down how many sample bags I had made and sold in the past week. Then I had fanned these flames with the real problem—Father.

I told of how we had first built our house with gambling winnings. How Father had gambled away the money reserved for a house blessing and that was why the rest of our family—uncles and grandfather—lived in the old house. How our neighbor thought we were bad luck. How Father just loved his *mahjong* tiles. How Mother thought his nightly trip to the gambling table was a way to assuage his pain over not having a son. I had come to believe his habit was more of a sickness, same as his drinking too much rice wine.

I hoped I hadn't been too disloyal to my parents. I hoped my intentions didn't appear too obvious. I hoped Chan Hai and I could survive together. My heart beat hard. I felt as though I stood in the middle of our courtyard with the largest firecracker ever made. Would it scare more than the dragon of a professor away? Would it burn down my house? Destroy my family? I so wanted to hand over this letter as fast as possible to the woman with the blank eyes and the ink-smudged sleeve covers at the post office. But I needed reassurance that I should light the fuse.

Madame Paper Cutter squatted on a piece of mud-splattered cardboard. Next to her Mr. Palm Reader tested his stool to find firmer ground. Another man spread out plastic sacks to put his hand-sewn dolls on. Chan Hai and I had rejoiced in the rain. But Madame Paper Cutter and the rest of the park dwellers cursed the wet drops that had fallen all night long, turning their firm sales floor into a muddy mess. I hurried over.

"Madame Paper Cutter," I called.

"Why, Li Hui," she said, pushing her glasses up on her nose as she glanced up. Her pants bagged around her waist. She still hadn't regained the weight she had lost when she had that bad cold months ago. "I'm glad it's you."

I squatted down next to Madame Paper Cutter and patted her arm. Her skin was already damp with sweat. How did she survive out here all day long? I couldn't. And surely the heat in Singapore would be worse.

Her eyes darted to the cardboard beneath her. A soggy pile of yellow cuttings lay in one corner. The rain had ruined all her cuttings. But how? Madame Paper Cutter was always so protective of her work.

"Angry customer," she said, nodding at the mish-mash. She licked her lips. Her eyes behind the lenses looked wider than even a goldfish.

"A customer ruined your work?" I asked.

The pile of cuttings would be easy to toss in the street with the rest of the garbage. But how much time had Madame Paper Cutter spent hunched over, planning and creating and cutting? I fingered the letter in my hands. Compared to this destruction, my midnight struggle to find the right words, the right solution to my problem, seemed silly. Gods. My hand itched to reach out and help.

"The turtle said the cuttings from the department store were cheaper," Madame Paper Cutter said. Despite her words, her voice held no anger. No disgust. No feeling at all. She looked up to the gray sky. "More well made. And waterproof."

"So he ruined your work?" My voice rose.

"He was a she." Madame Paper Cutter shook her head. "A young she."

She looked from the litter in the gutter to the mess before her. She shook her head again. I'd never seen her hands so still. Her eyes so cloudy. How could people treat others so? Did such cruelty make them feel better? The way Snakehead had closed Chan Hai's rock quarry?

"Of course department store cuttings are cheaper," I said, using my finger nail to pry away the top cutting. "And waterproof. And every piece is exactly the same."

Perhaps power over others was the only way to gain control in this life. I could see the Professor in Singapore wielding power with his big words, his degrees, his knowledge. Chan Hai wasn't like that. He was compassionate and sympathetic and caring. He believed in pushing people up, not down.

"But," I added. "Those cheap waterproof things are factory-made cuttings. This—" I pointed to the yellow pile. "This is art."

Madame Paper Cutter looked up. She rolled her shoulders. She smiled for the first time.

"The foolish woman had already paid me," she said, nudging my fingers aside with the point of her scissors.

She used the point of her scissors, that sharp knife point, to detach the top layer. I took a deep breath. At least Madame Paper Cutter wasn't out too much money or too much of her time. Speaking of which, I needed to get to the tea shop, or Feng Gu would make noise. Today we'd be starting our new ice-in-the-tea idea. Surely Feng Gu would be nervous.

"If I can dry these out, I can sell them again." Madame Paper Cutter leaned down to follow the point of her blade, her head almost touching the muddy ground. "That rude lady gave me a bonus."

Madame Paper Cutter was always so accepting. I hoped I'd learn to be so. No matter the situation.

"You're so smart," I said.

"Maybe." She tapped the body of the scissors on the palm of her left hand. "I can even ride home for the holidays."

The Autumn Moon Festival wasn't really considered the holidays. But, if you'd been away from your family for three years, this was certainly one of those times when you'd think of them, want to be together. Perhaps after being so sick, she needed some time with her family. How would I spent the night of the full moon? Would I have a tense dinner with Mother and Father or a romantic stroll with Chan Hai? I knew which one I wanted.

"You look very—fresh." She returned to the task of prying the layers of damp paper apart. Swirls and curls. A long flowing robe? The Moon Goddess. "Did you find a new job?"

Madame Paper Cutter had been to our shop once. Once was enough with Feng Gu sniffing around her like a dog. She should have seen Feng Gu with the ice cream yesterday. That would have made her laugh.

"No." I swallowed. I didn't have time to talk now. Although I so wanted to hear Madame Paper Cutter's advice.

"Yes, you look good," she said. "What are you planning for the moon—"

"I found a friend," I said. The words tumbled out, so loud. "He is not the man my parents wish for me to marry. In fact, he hasn't mentioned anything about the subject. Although he will. I'm sure he will. Still, I fear my parents will not approve. In fact, I'm sure they won't. I know they won't. They won't."

I looked at the letter I'd written to Guo Qiang. The letter I still wasn't certain I should mail. Especially now. Why had I even voiced the subject?

"Ahh." Madame Paper Cutter looked up at me, pushing her large glasses back up on her nose. "This isn't retaliation for your father messing up your job after university, is it?"

I'd never thought of that. I still felt an ache of disappointment in my throat each time I thought of Administrator Zhang telling me to go home and find a job on my own. But Chan Hai was not part of that.

"The sun shines brighter," I said. "The air smells fresher when my friend is near."

Madame Paper Cutter nodded. She moved the scissors back and forth as she targeted another section of the pile. What did she think?

"And this friend, he has a—"

"No, no job," I said. "That's the problem. My parents wish for me to marry someone else who is very successful."

"Oh, Li Hui."

She sat back on her haunches. She took her glasses off and rubbed her eyes. My stomach tightened. Did she think me another foolish young person? Why had I thought she would pat my hand and tell me to mail the letter? Remind me to follow my heart. Perhaps she only meant for me to follow my heart to a certain degree, as long as my parents weren't affected. I folded the letter in my hands.

"You know the story of the Moon Goddess?" she asked, peeling a goddess from the pile and laying it on the corner of her cardboard.

I stared at her. Everyone knew that story. Of how once ten suns crowded the sky and burned up the earth. How the Emperor commissioned the help of the most famous archer in all the land to take away nine of those suns. And, in return for the archer's success, the man was gifted the pill of eternal life.

"Tell me the ending to that story," Madame Paper Cutter said.

"While cleaning up one day, the archer's wife discovered her husband's pill of eternal life and ate it," I said, shrugging my shoulders. "The archer became so angry at his selfish wife, he shot her up to the sky."

"That's one version," Madame Paper Cutter said.

"There's another?" I glanced at my watch. Feng Gu would have raised the metal grating in front of the shop. I adjusted my purse strap on my shoulder.

"The one I learned is that, as soon as the wife ate the pill, she started to float to the sky. She cried out for the archer. She wanted to come back to him. He wanted her back. He could have shot her down easily. But, if he shot her, he feared he'd kill her. So, he let her go, let her float up to the moon."

"That's a nicer version." I stood to go. "I like that one better."

I glanced across the street to the book shop, the herbal medicine shop, the post office. I tapped the envelope on my hand. I could wait a while. I'd come back and talk to Madame Paper Cutter later. Get her advice then.

"My point is." Madame Paper Cutter pulled away another perfect Moon Goddess from the pile and stood up, her eyes holding onto mine. "Each generation carries a different version of tradition."

"But you and I are from the same generation," I said.

"Not really," Madame Paper Cutter said. "We may only be a few years apart, but you live in the hardest of times. I have an elder brother to help my parents. Your generation has no such luxury. Yet we haven't changed the stories to fit the new picture we live in."

What was she telling me? I felt as if I were sitting in English class in University, not in the middle of a muddy park with an uneducated paper artist. Her words didn't make sense. I really had to move on.

"Li Hui—"

"I haven't decided what to do yet," I said.

"Oh, but you have," Madame Paper Cutter said. "I see decision all over your face."

She opened my hand and placed the Moon Goddess on my palm. Was the woman we marveled at each fall a selfish lady only interested in her own needs or a kind-hearted soul filled with love? Was it possible to take care of one's needs and one's desires at the same time? I only hoped I had the strength of character to find out. I headed across the street for the post office.

Chapter Thirty-Two
Tea on The Cold Rocks

I walked away from the musty post office, my hands empty of the letter. My stomach burst as though I'd just eaten twelve courses in the imperial palace. My limbs moved as though leaves in the September wind. I felt like the Moon Goddess after she'd eaten the pill of eternal life. I felt lighter than air.

Up ahead two young boys wearing high school uniforms dragged their feet as though chains bound their ankles. They surrounded an old man carrying a small box. They jolted him from both sides. The box flew from his hands. Plink, plink, plink. The sound of metal dropping to the ground was like rain on the roof. The boys laughed and ran off.

I felt no shame for these boys. There were people like this. No irritation that the old man now knelt down on his hands and knees in front of me. I had time. No fear that this might be a ploy to get passersby to slow long enough that the three of them could rob me. I would be alright. Others walked around the old man, gawking and pointing. I stopped.

"Let me help you," I said.

"No, no." The old man put out a dirty hand. Perhaps he feared I'd take advantage of him. "I'm fine."

"Here's one," I said. I bent down, picked up a screw and held the ridged metal out to him.

"Really, thank you," the old man said. He smiled, his dark brown eyes disappearing in a thousand wrinkles. "Surely you have someplace to be."

Yes, I had someplace to be. Right here. In my own village. With Chan Hai. I picked up another screw and dropped it in his box.

Smoke from incense filled the back room of the tea shop. Feng Gu had lit over a dozen sticks, rather than the usual three, in front of her ancestor's photograph. Was today a special memorial day? Or did she want her ancestor to be awake and at attention on the day we started something that had never been done before—putting ice in our tea? I hung up my purse and walked into the front room. Feng Gu sat at the table beside the whirring fan. The monthly ledger lay open in front of her. The abacus rested in her lap.

"I wondered if you were going to come today," she said looking up from the ledger.

Her eyes were swollen with dark bags. She stared at me as if I were an unusual statue. My scalp itched.

"I thought perhaps you had second thoughts," she said.

Second thoughts? I thought of the postal worker rolling a stamp of the Moon Goddess across a damp sponge. The stamp sliding crooked across the top of my envelope. My envelope to Singapore flopping into the cloth bin. No, I had no second thoughts. But surely Feng Gu spoke not of that.

A metal wash bin sat next to her leg, the inside filled to the top with blocks of ice. The sheen on top of the ice reflected the ceiling. The light bulb hanging from the center of the ceiling looked like a moon. A full moon. A round moon. One of harmony and love.

"Sorry I'm late," I said, sitting across from Feng Gu. The wooden stool felt strong beneath me. "I see you got ice."

"Yes." She pulled on her hair. Her dark eyes still focused on me. "Some friend of Chan Hai's delivered it this morning."

"That's nice," I said.

I looked outside over her shoulder as if I might spot Chan Hai coming to check on us. I longed to hear his deep voice which felt like an arm around my waist. We would laugh about water in my eyes, make plans for his nursery, dream of our future together. I longed to see Chan Hai's gentle brown eyes. To feel him close to me. Instead I saw a woman at the curb negotiating for a motorcycle ride. She shook her head and went looking for another taxi. The man who dropped his nails, Feng Gu who waited for me to arrive, the woman who needed a taxi. Everyone else seemed to be having a hard morning. I floated above it all.

I felt Feng Gu's eyes on me and looked back. She searched my face as though trying to find a missing grain of rice. She never had looked at me this way before. Could she see how happy I was?

"Wasn't nice at all," Feng Gu said. She fingered the pages of her ledger. "What a creepy character."

Little Wu Lu was the only friend of Chan Hai's I'd call a creepy character. Just as Zi Mei had no filter on what came out of her mouth, Little Wu Lu had no filter on his actions. No fence between right and wrong.

"Did he have a dumpling-shaped scar on his face," I asked.

Feng Gu placed her palm down on her ledger and stared over at me as though I had just dropped a box of screws. What was she searching for? Did I look so different this morning? Did I act so different?

"No." Feng Gu discovered her voice again. "No scar. He was short with a bald spot at the top of his head. He breathed stale tobacco breath down my neck as I unlocked the gate. Before I even pulled up the gate all the way, he leaned forward and dumped the bin there on the floor."

Again I looked outside. My eyes searched across the street toward the bus depot teeming with bodies, like bees surrounding a granule of sugar. Had Chan Hai been here, and I'd missed him?

"I've spent all morning trying to move the damned thing to the right position here."

Feng Gu rubbed her back. I smoothed my old skirt. All morning? Half the stores on the block still had their gates shut.

"Do you think this is the right position?"

She pointed to the bin. The round tin container sat wedged between the end of the table and the tea bin. A sign taped to the side in her crude writing read: "Hot House Special." What a silly name.

"It's fine," I said. "Looks great."

For all Feng Gu's forced nonchalance, she worried. Whether the tea would arrive on time or not. Whether the bins were in the right place. Whether the tea was hot enough. Should we even try cold? She had probably stayed up all night weighing the pros and cons of this ice-in-the-tea idea.

"You know." She pulled on her hair and stared at the ledger. "I'm not so sure we should do this."

She was a good daughter. She wanted to do the best for the shop, for her father. Heat rose to my cheeks. I, too, would do the best for Father. Chan Hai and I would give him a healthy son. We would care for Father and Mother until we, ourselves, moved on to the River of Sleep. I unhooked the pick hanging on the side of the ice bin and chipped at the big blocks. We had to start somewhere.

"You heard," I said. "How popular Queen Dairy's drinks are, though."

"But." Her eyes widened. "I just want to warn you. You have the most to lose."

"Me?" I asked. I didn't stop chipping. Feng Gu always needed to put the responsibility on me. "Why me?"

"Well, remember you said that if sales didn't surpass those of the last two years, I wouldn't have to pay your salary . . . "

Feng Gu had never stopped paying my salary. Every week like a rooster awakening to crow, she handed over a packet. Last week I bought Father two bottles of rice wine. Two. The summer had been the best I could remember with plenty of rice and soy sauce and matches.

"Feng Gu, that was for the summer time," I said, forcing my lips downward to avoid cracking a smile. Children were back in school. The rice now stood shoulder high, even the few stalks in the Prehistoric Lady's garden. The last of the season's peaches had ripened. "Summer is over."

"Not that you'd notice," Feng Gu said, fanning herself with her hand. "It's still hot."

"Yes, but it's September," I said and stopped chipping. "Even in Singapore, where the weather feels like summer all year round, they don't call September summer."

"How do you know?" she asked, her mushroom nose in the air.

"I have," I said. "I had a friend there once."

There I'd said it. I'd put an end to that friendship. That wasn't so hard. I could repeat this for Mother and Father.

"Well, if this ice stuff turns people away," Feng Gu said, brushing imaginary dust from her pants. "I will hold you responsible, summer or not."

"Fine," I said.

If she needed someone to take responsibility before she breathed, I would be that person. I was sure Chan Hai wouldn't lead us in the wrong direction. I had risked my future and my family's security on that belief. A simple tea idea was nothing in comparison.

"Are you sure?" she asked. "What about your father?"

"What about him?" I said.

Feng Gu had a closer relationship with her father. Most people did. Had he heard something while playing *mahjong* with Father?

"Well, it's just—" Her face reddened.

"What?" I'd never heard Feng Gu trip over her words.

"Is he—" She picked at the knee of her pants. "Father hasn't seen him at the gambling center these past few days."

Was that why she had stared at me so? Because Father hadn't

been at the gambling center? And, with my father, he would have to be close to death to stay away from his game.

"He's fine," I assured her. Mother had mentioned some important game. Obviously that game didn't include any of his regular partners.

"Are you sure?" Feng Gu asked. "We could wait a few days."

"I'm sure," I said. Poor Feng Gu was so worried about this new ice idea she was even willing to make Father ill.

"Besides." She pulled on her hair. "The weather is bound to cool down. Especially after last night's rain. Cold tea on a cold day would just be foolish. We'd be an item to laugh about for months."

"Feng Gu." I continued tapping the ice. "We'll be just fine. We have the ice here. Let's just see what happens."

Toward the end of the day many customers had visited the shop. But none of them had wished to try our "Hot House Special," as Feng Gu called the drink. What a silly name. Doubt filled my veins. The chipped ice in the bucket had turned to a pool of water with but a few pieces of ice floating on top. Water had seeped out the crack in the bottom of the bin, first like a trickle, now like a river. Surely Feng Gu had dragged that poor old tin container across the floor one too many times.

"What a mess." Feng Gu pointed to the leak on the floor.

I grabbed a rag from beneath the table and threw it on the floor. The water soaked the center of the dirty orange cloth. My insides felt empty, as if I too could lay on that floor and water would soak into the center of my body. I wasn't so much concerned about people not wanting to try the "Hot House Special." I was concerned with where Chan Hai was. The man had not been by all day. He didn't always come to the shop. But last night had been so special. In the rain together. I could still taste his thick, hungry lips. Surely he would have time to come see me.

"Well, that was a waste," Feng Gu said with a sigh, picking up a copy of Fashion Fortune Magazine.

Was it? I thought of the letter to Singapore. Had I been too hasty? I rubbed the back of my neck, then pushed the wet rag further into the puddle on the floor. Perhaps Chan Hai had been successful in getting help to re-open the quarry. They were so close to finding the blue-black rock that was in such demand, Chan Hai had said. If the quarry started making a good profit, he could borrow money to open a nursery.

I balled up the wet rag and took the dripping mass outside the front of the store to wring out the water. Water dripped down my arms and off my elbows. Were Chan Hai's words meant to be considered with care? Or were they excess air that trickled all over—a waste? As soon as I leaned outside, fingers touched my arm. Not thick calloused ones. But bony gnarled ones. Ah, the crazy old English teacher.

"Madame Tsui Ping," I said, patting her hand. Her papery skin smelled of the reservoir. Did she swim, too?

"Looks like you had another accident here," she said, following me back into the shop. She wore a large plain blue dress. Her cane tapped across the cement floor. She studied the river still flowing from the ice bin. "Yes, an accident. An accident."

Feng Gu glanced up from Fashion Fortune Magazine. She hesitated as if gauging Madame Tsui Ping's state of mind. She rested the magazine on her knees.

"Come try," I said. I poured her a cup of tea and plopped one of the remaining ice chips in it. "It's our Hot House Special."

"Your what?" Madame Tsui Ping whooped. She banged her cane on the cement. She leaned down and peered at Feng Gu's crude sign.

"A foolish idea," Feng Gu said, picking the magazine back up and flipping through page after page. "I agree. Li Hui here insisted that people would want ice in their tea. Imagine."

Madame Tsui Ping laughed so hard she had to sit down. She bent forward on her cane for support, her long white hair falling in her face. She rocked back and forth. Back and forth. People lined up to drink ice in their cola over at that new Queen Dairy. Ice in tea wasn't that different. That strange. Certainly not cane-stomping funny. Then again this was Madame Tsui Ping.

"She's always trying to change things around." Feng Gu joined Madame Tsui Ping in laughter. "Make her own mark."

Madame Tsui Ping heaved a sigh and leaned back. She wiped at her eyes with the back of her thin arm. Did this crazy old woman see me as a fool as well?

"I mean we've had hot tea for thousands of years," Feng Gu said tossing the fashion magazine on the table. "Why would people suddenly want cold tea? That's just craziness."

Madame Tsui Ping stared outside. Her brow furrowed as she looked off into the distance. Had Feng Gu made the wrong choice of words? Tsui Ping rapped the top of her cane with her thick fingers.

"But that's what happens when you have a college graduate working for you," Feng Gu continued. "Always have to fend off their silly ideas."

"There's nothing wrong with the idea," Madame Tsui Ping said.

She shook her head, looked up to the ceiling and took a deep breath. Then she closed her eyes. Feng Gu gave the crazy old woman a sideways glance. She scooted her chair closer to the tea bins to protect against any sudden moves. I put my hand on Madame Tsui Ping's arm. I would escort her to the bus station.

"Perhaps your only problem is that ridiculous name." Madame Tsui Ping's shoulders shook. She opened her eyes. "It sounds like a cheap restaurant dish—or a whorehouse."

"What?" Feng Gu looked up.

"Yes, surely that's it."

Madame Tsui Ping stood and paced back and forth in front of the tea bins. Feng Gu and I followed. I handed Madame Tsui Ping her cane as if to remind her we were there. But Madame Tsui Ping's eyes looked vibrant, aware. Her arm, when she reached down to the ice bin, was steady. She tore Feng Gu's sign from the side of the bin. She sat back down, leaned the cane against the table, and pulled a pencil from her pocket. Of course, as a teacher, she must have always carried a pencil. That part of her she had not forgotten. She wrote out characters in a large slow hand.

"There," she said holding up the sign.

"Tea," Feng Gu started, looking at the characters.

"On the Cold Rocks," I finished for her.

"No, no, no," she said. "You have to say it like the character in—what was the name of that book?" She looked to the ceiling, tapped her cane. "Anyway, one of the Western cowboys who was tall with dark hair and blue eyes—foreigners think that's handsome. He always said, 'I'll take a bourbon on the cold rocks.'"

I smiled at her gravelly voice. She loved her books. Did she still have any left in her library or had they all been burned by the Red Guards?

"Or on the big rocks." She looked at Feng Gu. "Something like that. You try."

Feng Gu shrugged her shoulders. She looked over at me and jerked her head as if to say, "Take this woman away." Madame Tsui Ping had offended her. She didn't want to play any dumb literature game.

"Come on." Madame Tsui Ping rapped her cane on the floor. "Try."

"I'll take tea on the icy cold rocks," Feng Gu said.

"Just on the cold rocks," Madame Tsui Ping corrected. "And you sound like that lady on the village loudspeaker. I take tea on the cold rocks . . . and don't forget to pay your electricity bill. Come on. You want that handsome cowboy to notice you. Li Hui, you try."

I felt as if we were students in her class being called on to recite lines from an important poem. Sometimes she was so lucid and sane. Other times flailing in the waters, seeing things that none of the rest us did. Again I wished to see inside the woman's head.

"Li Hui?"

Madame Tsui Ping leaned forward. I imagined calloused fingers on my arm, full lips on my hair, smooth golden arms around my waist.

"Tea—" I said. "Give me tea on cold rocks."

"You're good." Madame Tsui Ping applauded, her cane crashing to the floor. "Surely you'll find your cowboy."

My lips twitched. Heat filled my cheeks. I hoped she was right.

"Yes, just change the name, and you'll be fine." Madame Tsui Ping stood up. "People just want something good."

I clasped onto Madame Tsui Ping's weathered hands. Ah, just change the name, and we'd be fine. Perhaps this same theory would work with Mother and Father. I felt an urge to hug this old English teacher. I just needed to convince Mother and Father that I could take so much better care of them if I were nearby, in the village with my small business owner Chan Hai. Then perhaps they would buy this new tea.

Chapter Thirty-Three
Father Throws an Egg

Feng Gu pulled the shop's gate down at the end of the day. A day that had started with us offering the unpopular Hot House Special and ended with the popular Tea on the Cold Rocks. The sound of metal sliding against metal grated on my insides. I clutched my purse, my fingernails pinching the old black vinyl.

"Well, then." Feng Gu tugged on the gate to test the lock.

In the last hours of the day, Feng Gu had hidden behind her Fashion Fortune Magazine, only appearing to bark at me for adding too many tea leaves or not enough. To growl that I was too slow in wiping up a spill. To howl over the youth or the smell or the disrespect of all the customers who flooded in to try Tea on the Cold Rocks. She reminded me of a wounded dog howling at being left in the rain by the oh-so-educated Madame Tsui Ping. A knot had formed at the back of my neck.

"Yes," I said. "See you tomorrow."

She gave a curt nod, tugging on the gate again. She would let me go ahead. She always did.

"No matter the name," I said, pausing a meter away. My lips froze at the end of that thought like two ice chips. Surely Feng Gu would latch onto my words and set to barking. Surely her mind couldn't get over the fact that we had had dozens of customers interested in trying the Tea on the Cold Rocks and none interested in the Hot House Special. "No matter. It's still the Hot House Special. Still a good idea."

Feng Gu straightened her shoulders. She shook out her short hair. Shook out all that rain.

"Tomorrow should be a busy day," she barked. She snapped the keys to the ring on the side of her pants. Then she looked up at me, the hint of a smile in her eyes.

"I won't be late," I promised.

I went up the street and across the bridge. I would stop at the local department store and pick up another bottle of rice wine for

Father. He already had two bottles, but one more would not make him unhappy. One more might loosen his heart enough that we could talk, that we could say the words normally untouched.

I passed a woman selling inflatable rings for the swimming pool. They would be fun in the reservoir. The reservoir. Where had Chan Hai been all day? It wasn't like him not to visit sometime during the day for a walk up on the bridge or a snack. Perhaps he'd too been busy thinking of the future, trying to get the quarry opened.

A pink station wagon pulled right in front of me up onto the sidewalk. I walked around the garish vehicle. The back door had a picture of the wall of water at the Wei Min Hotel. Two lovers stood in front of the cascading water holding hands. Hanging above them were the bright red characters for "double happiness." A wedding limousine. What would it feel like to emerge from that grand vehicle, which was longer than two cars and more decorated than a new shop? What was the inside like? I glanced back waiting for a happy couple to emerge.

The dream vehicle held no lovers. Just the driver. He was dressed in a black suit which looked too large for him, as the back of his coat hung down past the back of his knees. How ridiculous. Chan Hai and I would never waste money on such a frivolous expense.

Across from the liquor shop, I stopped at a telephone kiosk. A woman sat behind the low kiosk with her hair drawn back into a pony tail like a little girl sat. She put out her hand for payment without even looking up. I handed her a *yuan* note, reached for the receiver and dialed the number I'd memorized but never called. The line rang and rang.

"*Wei*," a woman shouted. "Hello."

"I'm looking for Chan Hai," I said.

Chan Hai lived just around the corner from the shop. His family would get a phone soon, as soon as the quarry started making good money. That surely wouldn't take too long.

"Haven't seen him today," she said. "Look over there," she called to someone else.

"Well—" I gripped the black receiver. "Is there any news?"

"Who is this?" the woman asked.

"I'm—" I swallowed. "I'm a friend."

"Well, then you should know if there's any news."

She hung up. I replaced the receiver. The woman with the pony tail put her hand out again for more money, as if expecting me to make another call. A man on a bicycle whizzed by, the tire grazing the toe of my shoe. I shook myself. Chan Hai's neighbor was so short with me. Perhaps so busy. But I shouldn't worry. Mei Ling always said, "Only bad news travels fast." Surely all was fine. Perhaps Chan Hai would even have good news for me.

I looked down at the long thin paper bag hooked onto my wrist. A bottle of rice wine, the top shaped like a vine, poked out of the top. A celebratory vintage I would give Father when he returned home tonight. We would talk then of the future.

I stepped over New Neighbor's winding dragon and into our courtyard. The day's laundry, three shirts and a pair of Father's pants, hung draped on the tree limbs next to our front door. Although the clothes stood stiff and dry, Mother hadn't brought them down yet to fold. That was strange. A basket of soybeans from our garden was upended next to a short stool. The round beans lay in the corner of the courtyard like stars in the sky. Perhaps Mother had gone to the outhouse.

I peeked into the kitchen. Our metal rice pot sat on the square wooden table, the insides already scraped clean. Two bowls had been used, one for Father, one for Mother. A cockroach scampered across the table. These must be leftover from lunch. Mother never left dirty dishes around. Where was she? Why had she left the house like this? Perhaps she'd been inside Zi Mei's shop talking. Perhaps she had some good news. But it wasn't like her to leave the house unattended.

"Mother?" I called. I stepped in the house and set the wine on the table next to the half-filled teapot. "Mother?"

From my right, I heard the creak of her wooden bed. What was she doing in bed at this time of day? Had she felt ill? She was getting older. She even had a few gray hairs. She'd need more and more naps as the years wore on. This was one more reason I needed to be near home. In the same village. I could hardly help her if I was six hours away by plane in Singapore.

"Mother?"

I moved to her bedroom door. I turned the metal knob. If she wasn't too ill, she would have come out to the hall when she heard me making noise. Poor Mother. Had she eaten something bad?

The bulb hanging from the ceiling in the middle of her room had not been turned on. The window facing the winding dragon was shut tight. The room was dark and musty. Mother's small figure lay on the bed in the corner of the room beneath a light cover.

"Mother?" I went over and touched her cheek.

"Oh, Li Hui. You're back," she said, but she didn't move to sit up. She didn't open her eyes. Her skin felt damp not feverish. From tears.

"Can I get you something?" I asked. "Are you feeling unwell?"

"I'm fine." Mother grabbed onto my wrist and held my fingers close to her cheek. "You're a good daughter. A good, good daughter."

Heat rushed to my neck. Why did she say this? To remind me that I hadn't been a good child at all? Had she found out that I'd been in the temple last night with Chan Hai? Did she know I'd sent a terrible letter to Singapore? No. How could she?

"Where's Father?" I asked. I almost preferred Father's banging around to Mother's tears and cryptic statements.

"You know your father." She sighed a deep sigh and pulled the coverlet up over her shoulder, as if suddenly cold. She smiled, but tears fell down her cheeks. "He's got an important game. One that's going to change our luck forever."

Our luck? Her words echoed in my heart making goose flesh on my skin. Forever?

"Feng Gu mentioned that Father hasn't been at the Senior Center," I said, shaking the strange feeling away. "Does he have new playing partners?"

She glanced up at me, her dark eyes pooling. Then she pulled the coverlet higher. She gave a deep sigh.

"He was invited to play with Chairman Huang," she mumbled into the covers.

I sat down on the bed. There were lots of Huangs. Our whole village was full of them, as we had initially been formed by the Huang family. In fact, there used to be a rule that you couldn't marry within the village for fear you'd be marrying a close relative. We also had lots of Chairmans. But I also remembered Father's eyes gleaming when I told him of my escape from the hungry clutches of Snakehead Chairman Huang. "He's a good card player," Father had said. I grabbed onto Mother's coverlet.

"Chairman Huang?" I asked.

"Yes," she said, her small brown eyes blazing at me. Her chin trembled. "The same Chairman you met while playing where you shouldn't have been."

How could this have occurred? I remembered Father marveling at Chairman Huang's ability to play cards, more so than he worried at the Chairman's offer to take me to Singapore for free. Had Chairman Huang sought out Father? Or had it been the other way around? What was Father betting with? Next month's salary from the tea shop?

"Don't throw an egg at a rock," Waipo would often say. The egg will lose. Lose. Lose. My mouth felt dry. My heart beat at the base of my throat. What was wrong with his old pals at the Senior Center?

"How is he doing?" I asked.

Even as the words emerged from my mouth, cluttering the small room with their loudness, I knew she wouldn't answer. What if the gods heard her response? Oh, Father. How deep of a well were you digging? A slow trickle started down my neck as if ice water from the bin at the tea shop dripped down my spine.

I sat on the side of my bed staring out my window at the peach tree in the garden. I was tempted to lay down and fall into a depressed slumber, as Mother had. How could I climb the right branch to claim the juiciest peach if Father was always chopping down the branches on which I stood. I had done well at school and had been given a great job, better than I had expected. Then Father had chopped that branch. Now I had a good job that kept our family in oil and matches, even rice wine. Chop. Chop. Chop. Father was at it again.

Outside I heard Father's unsteady footsteps scraping across the cement in the courtyard. I straightened my coverlet and went downstairs. By the time I reached the bottom step, he was already inside and struggling to drag the wooden crossbar over the door. His shirt tail hung out on one side.

Now that I was down here next to him, I didn't know where to start talking. How much to say. Besides, how much would he remember in the morning? With each step I took, the smell of rice wine grew stronger. As if Father had taken a bath in it.

"Let me help," I said moving toward the door.

Father looked back, surprised to hear a voice. His cheeks were flushed. His eyes glassy.

"I've got it," he said, pushing at the piece of wood. He kept pushing and pushing, but the angle was wrong. The wooden piece wouldn't fit into the metal square.

"How was your night?" I asked, putting my hand on the wood,

trying to straighten it.

"Wonderful," he said. "Every night is wonderful. Isn't that what your Waipo would have said?"

He laughed a shallow laugh. His eyes darted about like a fly afraid to land. Surely he had lost.

"Your friends miss you at the Senior Center," I said.

"Ha," Father snorted. "Those old ladies play for matches. I can't be bothered with that stuff."

Matches? The last time he lost there I remember it cost me two week's salary. My underarms tickled.

"Matches are good," I said. "They may be small, but the fire they light can cook the rice. Feed the family."

"Go on to bed," Father said, waving me away. His hand trembled.

"Father," I said. "I have a friend. He is a good man."

"I know that." Father gripped my arm with his tobacco-stained fingers. Spittle flew from his lips.

"I'm not talking about Professor Liang," I said.

Father still held onto my arm. He stared as if a sutra were written underneath the flesh. Then he threw his head back and laughed.

"The professor," he said. "Of course. That's it."

"Actually, I want to stop this business with the professor—"

"You are brilliant," Father said patting me on the arm. "No wonder you made it to college."

He threw his head back and laughed again. Then he stumbled away to his room, slamming the door behind him. What had I said? What had he heard?

"Father?" I called.

But he didn't return. I was left to slide the wooden crossbar across the front door, to protect the house, the family.

Chapter Thirty-Four
The Fisherman and His Knife

The thick bundle of incense Feng Gu burned for her ancestor in the back room made the tea shop air thick. Difficult to swallow. While her filial respect should have warmed my heart, I felt hollow, devoid of emotion as I responded to the commands of our morning customers. Like one of Professor Liang's computers.

Zi Mei had come by with her son. He kept exclaiming how cold the tea was, the tea was too cold. Madame Tsui Ping had brought in a new sign written in India ink. Mr. Department Store, although he'd sniffed at what he called the "diluted quality" of the tea, drank four cups. Even Mr. Bicycle Repair had come by just to take a look before settling on his "old" favorite, the Professor's Medley.

Feng Gu had just left for the outhouse, bouncing with each step. The shop was doing well. Why did my body feel so fragile, as if my skin were made of eggshells? Why did I keep seeing Mother's swollen face, hearing Father's voice? "Those old ladies?" Father had laughed, his bloodshot eyes widening. "They play for matches." He was playing with big money. And losing. And why did he say I was such a genius for bringing up Professor Liang in Singapore? I wished to be at home. I needed to be at home. Surely Mother had pulled her sad head from the pillow by now.

Mother hadn't been awake when I went downstairs this morning. The warm smell of her rice porridge hadn't filled the air with love. The tree limbs, those sharp branches, stood outside the front door had been decorated with the stiff cloth of yesterday's laundry. Soybeans had been left scattered like a broken necklace in our courtyard. It was as if Mother had just disappeared.

The stool across from me scraped against the cement floor. Mr. Farmer, the man who owned the Golden Dance Club and had many young girlfriends, sat down. His gray pants were neatly pressed. His blue shirt, unbuttoned at the top, revealed the starched white ribbing of his undershirt.

"Haven't seen you for a while," I said, pouring him a cup of Tea on the Cold Rocks.

"Yes." He sat down. Then he looked up at me and smiled so broadly his eyes wrinkled. "It's been too long, too long."

This was our ritual greeting. Mr. Farmer only came by every few weeks to stock up on tea for his club. Sometimes he sent one of his employees, much to Feng Gu's chagrin. She often spoke about him, about his young girlfriends. Did she feel slighted that he didn't include her in that circle of debauchery? She would be disappointed to have missed him again.

"I hear you have another new hit," he said, nodding toward Madame Tsui Ping's sign.

"Is that what people are saying?" I asked.

This was great news. Business would only get better. I would ask Feng Gu for my bonus today. That would bring a smile to Mother's face, some life back into our house.

"That's what they say." His gold chain-link bracelet clinked against the table, as he reached for the Tea on the Cold Rocks. He swirled his cup around as if the amber liquid were fine rice wine. He tossed the tea back in one gulp and held out his cup for a refill. "Yes, that's what they say."

He wiped his lips with the back of his hand, then he looked across at me. His eyes penetrated through that hollow space in my chest. I grabbed the ice pick. I had a sinking feeling. That wasn't all that they said. That's what his eyes told me. I suddenly had a vision of him sitting in his Golden Dance Club with important customers, lawyers, policemen and chairmen. Perhaps Chairman Huang poured him a glass of Chivas Gold while regaling him with details of Father's latest folly. My gods. Was there no end to our shame?

"Yes, that's what they say." He coughed and patted his legs.

"And?" I asked. I dropped a shaving of ice in his tea. "What else?"

"And?" Mr. Farmer shook his head. He took another gulp from his cup. How big of a rock had Father hit with his egg?

"Li Hui," Feng Gu barked, shaking water from her hands as she came in from the back room. "I told you not to—" Feng Gu stopped, the order on her lips arrested. She curled a lock of hair behind her ear. "Oh. Hello."

"Little sister." Mr. Farmer raised his cup toward her. Was that relief on his face? Relief that he didn't have to share what comments he must have heard? I picked up the ice pick. "This is so satisfying."

Feng Gu turned red starting from the neck up. She stood in the center of the room, a smile so broad all of her jumbled teeth would have fallen out if not nailed to her gums. She put her arms behind her back, then over her chest. Then she smoothed out her pants.

"Now, don't stab the ice, Li Hui" Feng Gu said in a voice I'd never heard before. Soft and gentle, as though she were teaching a toddler.

I dropped the pick. I hadn't realized I'd been stabbing the ice. Hitting with such force. As if I could stab away Father's stupidity with my pick. I didn't want to stop.

"I wish my workers were half as diligent," Mr. Farmer said, winking at me.

"The sooner you chop that block, the sooner the ice melts," Feng Gu said, her words quick and fierce, as if she hoped to engage him in a debate over the issue. Her mouth twisted upwards, quivering.

Why hadn't Feng Gu stayed at the outhouse a moment longer? Mr. Farmer had been so close to telling me about my foolish father. A waft of incense made me choke on those disrespectful thoughts. Father just wanted us to be a winning family. Especially with the annual Moon Festival coming. Surely he couldn't bear to sit next to his brothers, all four of whom had successful sons overseas—selling shoes in Italy, doing construction in Japan, working as a waiter in Australia, setting up a laundry business in England—when here I was without a teaching job, earning sesame seeds. Not holding up even a corner of the sky.

"Li Hui," Feng Gu said, putting her hand on my shoulder as if I were a slow child. "I said, 'Stop chipping the ice.' Don't you remember what happened yesterday?"

Yesterday. Of course I remembered. Mother had wept the Yellow River for Father who was playing with more than just "matches." And losing. On top of that, I hadn't seen or heard from Chan Hai.

"Well?" Feng Gu waited for an answer, one hand on her hip. Then she indicated the bin with an exaggerated roll of her head. "The slivers of ice melted before the lunchtime crowd."

"You're right," I said, furrowing my brow and nodding. "How could I have forgotten?"

I felt a tapping on my toe. Mr. Farmer's foot. His brown eyes twinkled. Was he being sympathetic or recalling Father's hilarious loss?

"Think. Remember. Act," Feng Gu said, sticking her small chest out and rubbing her palms up and down over her thighs. "That's what my father always says."

Think. Remember. Act. Did her father really say such a thing? Surely her father wouldn't be playing *mahjong* with my father if this were the case. Surely Feng Gu wouldn't get all nervous each time a new idea wafted beneath her nose, if she thought, remembered and acted. Why did people make up these grand-sounding rules that they didn't follow? Then again perhaps they did follow the rules, but their memories were the problem. Her father only remembered the money touching his palm, not the time it took Father to pay him. Just as Father exaggerated each small win he made and diminished his monumental losses. And Feng Gu only remembered disasters that accompanied each new idea. Surely with this Tea on the Cold Rocks she would only remember the way Madame Tsui Ping criticized her grand name Hothouse Special and the way the ice melted all over the floor each afternoon.

Feng Gu went around me to the ice bin. She leaned down picking up slivers of ice from the bottom of the bin and putting them back on the larger blocks. Each time she leaned down, her bottom shot out in front of Mr. Farmer. How ridiculous. I hadn't thrown myself at Chan Hai this way, had I?

"That won't do anything." Mr. Farmer lifted his thick wrist from the table and pointed to the bin, the heavy gold chain dangling. "Unless you have glue."

"Glue?" She looked over, her brow furrowed like an eager student. "Glue?"

"Just joking." He smiled, drinking down the last of his tea. "Your provisioner is going to bring a new block in the afternoon, isn't he? I have mine deliver to the club three times a night."

"I'm sure we could have him deliver twenty-four times a day." Feng Gu laughed. She lifted her right hand and rubbed her thumb over her fingers. "If we wish to spend our money that way."

Poor Feng Gu. If only she could hear herself talk. So self-important. No, I didn't act that way with Chan Hai. Then again, I couldn't.

"Li Hui, the gentleman needs a fresh cup of tea," Feng Gu said, pointing to his empty cup.

"No," Mr. Farmer said, patting his stomach. Coughing. "No, I don't. Thanks."

"But you've only just arrived," she said.

"I've been here a nice long while," Mr. Farmer said. He tapped my toe again, then stood. "I need to make a move."

Perhaps he wanted to tell me something in private. A warning? A piece of advice? I felt a chill, as if my feet sat alongside those blocks of ice.

"Oh, just one more cup," Feng Gu said, filling his cup with tea. Her hand shook as she poured. Her insistence seemed like just village custom. But I knew she really wanted him to stay.

"No, really," he said. "I'm fine."

"But surely you haven't had the chance to enjoy the aroma," she said, putting her hand on his arm. "To feel the quiet of the moment. To—to—"

"I have some business to take care of," he said, glancing at his thin, gold watch.

His mind had already left the slow pace of our shop. He stood abruptly, bumping into Feng Gu. The pot of tea in her hand jolted and a spray of tea shot out onto his nicely pressed blue shirt. A big oblong-shaped stain soaked the right side.

"Oh, dear," she said. "I'm sorry."

I held out a rag to Mr. Farmer which Feng Gu intercepted. She took the orange cloth and blotted at his heart, her cheeks turning as red as a chili pepper.

"I'm fine," Mr. Farmer said, grabbing at the rag. He tossed it on the table.

"Let me at least wash the stain out for you," Feng Gu offered. "It will only take a moment. You can wait in our back room."

How could she suggest such a thing? As it was, Mr. Farmer seemed agitated. Late for something. She didn't really expect him to sit in the incense-filled back room next to the portrait of her ancestor for a few hours? She was like a child who latched onto her mother's leg on the first day of school.

"I have another shirt at the club," Mr. Farmer said, taking steps away from Feng Gu. "This isn't the first time I've had drinks spilled on me. Just the first time it's been nonalcoholic."

"Oh, but this will only take a moment," she said.

What did Feng Gu think the man would do? Walk into a business meeting with a big wet splotch across his chest? I wished she'd let go. Certainly he was a good businessman with a kind smile. But he was at least old enough to be her father. And why would you wait in line behind a bevy of other women to look at that smile? I hurried to the front of the shop before she could beg more. Mr. Farmer sidled up next to me.

"Thanks." His breath smelled of tobacco and garlic. "See you next time."

I nodded, hoping he'd say more. Something. But he walked past me. I watched after him, waiting for him to give me a sign. He didn't even turn around. A truck pulled from our curb and a motorcycle taxi took its place. Perhaps I'd just imagined Mr. Farmer had a message about Father for me. Maybe he'd just stopped by to try the tea. I let out a deep breath.

A woman rushed through traffic to speak with the motorcycle driver. He shook his head at her and waved her away. Obviously she didn't have enough money to pay the driver for a ride. Why didn't the men who gambled with Father do the same? Wave him away? Although Mr. Farmer had said nothing, my legs felt shaky.

Dark clouds blanketed the sky. The air felt stifling. The ice bin in front of me had already turned to a pool of water. Feng Gu sat in the back room filing her nails. Across from me, the young woman from the park who wore black and yellow Naxi ethnic minority dress stood up.

"Well, lunch time is over," she said. "I need to get back to work."

How could lunchtime be over? Chan Hai hadn't stopped by with an oyster cake or beef strips. Not even an ice cream cone. I tried not to keep track of the days this way—had I met with Chan Hai or not? But there was an elastic band inside my heart. Each day—no, each hour I didn't see those dark brown eyes and feel his tall, strong presence, the rubber band stretched further and further. The band would break any moment.

"Thanks," the woman said, smoothing out her black skirt with the bright yellow and green diamonds across the bottom. She made a slight incline with her head.

"Come again," I said. My throat felt thick.

"Yeah, come again," Feng Gu called from the back, waving a newly manicured hand. While she wouldn't chat with them at the tea table, she had gotten better with our migrant workers from the park.

As the woman stepped onto the sidewalk, a man brushed past her and into the shop. He wore a wrinkled brown shirt smudged with dirt. A rope tied around his waist held up his too large mud-splattered pants. His flip flops slapped across our floor.

"You the college graduate?" the man asked, scratching his head and furrowing his brow.

It was no secret that Feng Gu had a college graduate working at her shop. But no one had ever come specifically looking for me, the graduate. My heart fluttered for a moment. Perhaps one of the local schools needed a new teacher. Then I got up to take the tea pot from the melted pool of water. I returned to my senses. The man's hands were darkened with dirt and grease. His oily hair flew about in uncombed directions. Most jobs were given through connections, like Father and Old Chen, his *mahjong* buddy. But certainly no one sent the school groundskeeper looking for employees.

"There you go." I pushed his Tea on the Cold Rocks across the table. "Our shop's latest tea."

"I don't want your warm buffalo piss." The man looked around the shop.

Feng Gu must have heard. She stood up so quickly, her stool fell to the floor with a crash. She came to the front and stood near me.

"This is Tea on the Cold Rocks," she said.

"Except you don't have any rocks left," the man said. "Just as Hua Gong predicted."

"Who?" I asked.

"Mr. Farmer," Feng Gu whispered. She checked her nails and pulled on her hair. Her eyes brightened.

"He told me to stop by and make sure you got a delivery," the man said. "You want it or not?"

I looked to Feng Gu. She gazed at the bucket of water and glanced at her watch. I could see her thoughts spinning. In but a few hours the day would be done. Besides, if the dark clouds let loose, who would want cold tea? Still, if she refused this delivery, a delivery dear Mr. Farmer had suggested, he would be embarrassed. He wouldn't even consider adding her to his circle of women friends.

"I've got other deliveries to make." The man scratched his oily scalp again.

"Yeah, we'll take it," she said, picking up her abacus, ready to bargain.

The man stood there, shuffling from foot to foot. Had Chan Hai's friend been this dirty? This creepy?

"I'm not paying you until you bring the ice," Feng Gu said. She was no fool.

"I'm not bringing the ice," the man said playing with the rope around his pants. "Until you give me an empty bin."

What a snob. His hands weren't so clean he couldn't empty the bin himself. I carried the bin to the front of the shop. I dumped the water out onto the sidewalk, including the slivers of ice that moments ago had seemed like gold. Compared to the new ice that the provisioner would chip from his big block for us, these melting slivers were as precious as the empty cigarette pack in the gutter. As important as my salary was compared to Father's new debt.

"You're a quick study," he said.

As soon as the last of the water dripped out, the man grabbed the bin from me. He hurried down the street. I could hear the chipping of a pick against ice. He must have a big block in the truck.

The click-click sounds of Feng Gu's abacus punctuated the air of the shop. Her small hands flicked the beads of her abacus up and down. Up and down. Ten beads per row. Ten pages of a long letter from Singapore. Professor Liang was brilliant and successful, no doubt about that. Mother would never have had to worry about Father's debts again. Oh, why had I mailed away that letter to Guo Qiang?

Madame Paper Cutter had said I had decision written all over my face. But all day—yet another in which Chan Hai did not appear at the shop—I'd felt a wavering of that decision. Feng Gu had a satisfied glow on her face at the end of a successful day of selling Tea on the Cold Rocks. But a pit sat in the bottom of my stomach as if I'd swallowed a peach.

I passed the bicycle repair shop. Mr. Baldy pulled an inner tube from a box for a customer and ran his hands across the rubber to demonstrate the fine manufacturing, the lack of faults. He was the one who had been turned back at the airport in Japan when his "bride" hadn't shown up. How was Mei Ling doing? What would she have said of my letter to Guo Qiang? Surely she'd say one of my seven emotions was in excess. My *qi* was out of balance. I needed a cooling herbal drink to bring my mind back to reason. Tea on the Cold Rocks wasn't enough.

I hurried toward the park. My brain buzzed as though filled with a thousand bees. What made me think Chan Hai cared for me or could care for me? What made me think Father would ever agree to our union?

I crossed the street to the park. Madame Paper Cutter sat

hunched over a piece of paper. Her fingers gripped the pen as her hand moved across a page of paper. Why had I listened to her words? Her concerns were small. Would she get a good price for her cuttings? Could she resell them? How did you write a certain character? Nothing high tech, like the latest license plate registration system Guo Qiang had developed and hoped to market to Singapore's Ministry of Transportation. Nothing that would change the way people lived. Nothing that would provide support to a gambling father. A father who gambled with more than "matches." Madame Paper Cutter's clothes looked disheveled, worn. She looked ridiculous, not wise in her goldfish glasses. Why had I come? I stopped and turned to leave.

"Li Hui?" her voice called out. "Is that you?"

I saw the post office in front of me, the herbal shop, the bookseller. I could keep going, as if her voice were a breeze in the wind. The ground had dried since yesterday, although from the looks of the dark sky that wouldn't last. Dirt crunched beneath my black pumps. Hairs tickled on the back of my neck.

"Li Hui?" Madame Paper Cutter ran up next to me and grasped onto my arm. "I thought that was you. I hope you're not in a hurry."

"Actually." I pushed her hands away and continued on.

"I've got the best news." She followed, jumping up and down next to me. "I sold all those moon goddess cuttings. I'm going home for the Moon Festival."

"Great," I said.

My voice didn't sound great. How long would she be gone? Just for the Moon Festival? I could already see myself stuck waiting on drunk Father, wishing someone would shoot me up to the moon.

"You were the one who helped me straighten the cuttings out," she said. "I was ready to just ball the whole thing up and throw it in the road. But you came by just in time. You stopped me."

I had stopped her? I had actually thought throwing the pile of cuttings away would be much easier as well. How could she credit me with her own patience?

"Thank you," she said. Her mouth turned into a broad grin while her eyes filled. "I haven't been home in so long. Three years and three months. I probably won't recognize my daughter."

"No problem," I said.

Her eyes sparkled like a small child. Her cheeks glowed pink.

How could I not rejoice in her enthusiasm for a moment?

"And what about you?" she asked, taking my arm and leading me back to her spot. "How's your friend? Did you mail the letter?"

"I haven't heard from my friend," I said. "And my father—my father is in a big game with Chairman Huang, the snakehead who tried to kidnap me to Singapore."

Madame Paper Cutter looked into my eyes. She took her hand and brushed a hair from my face. She clutched my fingers.

"Oh, dear," she said.

"I should have thought before mailing that letter," I said. "Such words of finality."

"Oh, dear," she repeated, not letting go of me.

"Do you think the post office would still have the letter?"

She drew a design on my arm with her forefinger. Was she recalculating the profit she'd made? Tracing her route home? Thinking of a new design? Obviously she hadn't heard me.

"Do you—"

"Have you," she interrupted. "Have you ever heard the story of the fisherman from the state of Zhou who lost his knife?"

Of course I knew the story. Waipo had told me this one many times too. But how would this child's story answer the question of the postal worker's efficiency in getting out mail? Of what I should do to calm the winds that blew through my heart? Of what I could do to save Father and Mother?

"Actually, I was wondering about the post—"

"A fisherman from the state of Zhou was crossing a river in his boat," she said, ignoring my concerns.

She sat down on her piece of cardboard and picked up her scissors, a piece of black paper. I looked across the street to the post office. I should just go and find out. Offer to dig through their mail bin, even their mail trucks.

"Halfway across the river, the fisherman's knife fell into the water," she said snipping off the end of the paper. A boat.

She looked up at me. I had always heard that the fisherman dropped a sword—not a knife—but I didn't want to interrupt. I smiled, hoping to encourage her to finish her story. What if the postal workers were sorting the overseas mail right now?

"The fisherman," she said, pushing her glasses up on her nose. "Brilliant man that he was, immediately took some fish blood from the bottom of the boat and smeared a mark on the side of the boat, saying, 'This is the spot where my knife dropped in the water.'"

I nodded with exaggerated motions. I'd heard this story thousands and tens of thousands of times. Waipo reminded me of it whenever I was too rigid. Whenever I set a goal and went after it without taking into consideration possible changes in the surrounding conditions. But how did that help me now? I looked toward the street. An old lady bargained with a taxi driver for a ride. Would she get to sit in the plush air-conditioned taxi which took her to her destination or would she end up walking, her calves aching, her lungs burning?

"When the fisherman reached shore," Madame Paper Cutter continued, her fingers grasping the simple boat cutting. "He jumped in the water and looked for his knife at the place where he had marked the boat."

"Yes, I remember that one," I said, my eyes scanning the park. I longed to see Chan Hai's gentle brown eyes. I longed to feel him close to me, to soothe my confused heart. "My grandmother told me often."

"Just because you mark your boat." She looked up at me over her big round glasses. "Doesn't mean you'll find your knife in the same spot it was a hundred years ago, fifty years ago, yesterday."

"So, I guess that's your way of saying, no, you don't think the post office still has my letter?" I laughed, despite myself. She was so long-winded she should have been a priest or a politician.

"Well, that too," Madame Paper Cutter said. "But, just as the boat moves forward in the water," she said, her arm moving the boat up and down until the paper crashed into my hand. "We move forward in time. Keep moving."

Moving. Moving. So, stop rowing back to that fateful day in Counselor Zhang's office when the smoked salmon from Holland hadn't measured up to Father's strong wishes for a job in Beijing. Stop rowing back to Father's debt which chained me to the tea shop. Stop rowing back to re-examine a decision my heart had already made. I grabbed onto the boat. Madame Paper Cutter always gave me something to think on. Even if she was just a simple paper cutter. I squeezed her shoulder. She would be going home to her family soon. I would find peace with mine. I just had to keep moving forward.

Chapter Thirty-Five
Silence Before Thunder

I stood in front of the phone kiosk near the park, beating my lips with the back of my hand. The woman behind the kiosk stared at a flower plant in front of her. Was it an orchid, Chan Hai's favorite? She picked a few dead petals off. Patted the live ones. A boy on a bike rode past, his flat back tire making a thwap-thwap sound. My left leg jiggled up and down. What would I say?

Across the street, clear bottles lined the window of the liquor store. Those bottles no longer looked like a magic potion which would bring my father into agreement with his only daughter. His loving daughter. They seemed an evil drug which sent him further and further down the road of demise. Dragging us with him.

I hated to burden any man with the responsibility of Father. Not that Chan Hai had made such an offer. I had not heard nor seen him since our night together in the temple two days ago. I still felt his rough hands so gentle on my face, my breasts, my thighs. But my heart was no longer full. With Father's foolishness and Chan Hai's absence, my heart felt like that boy's tire, the joy seeping out, the only sound an empty thwap-thwap-thwap against my rib cage.

"Are you gonna make a call or not?" the woman at the kiosk asked, patting her hand over her braided hair. "This is not a rest area."

I stared at the orchid. I wanted to feel alive and loved like one of the purple petals. I wanted to feel settled. I handed her a bill and picked up the black receiver.

The phone rang and rang. I thought of Feng Gu attacking Mr. Farmer with the orange rag. I wasn't doing that, though. I was just curious as to how Chan Hai was doing. Had the quarry been re-opened? Had he been to the reservoir the past couple of days? Did he want to go today? No, I didn't need to ask all of those questions. I just wanted to hear his voice.

"*Wei*? Hello?" Chan Hai's neighbor wheezed into the phone. Perhaps she'd run in from outside.

"I'm sorry to bother you," I said, a tremor in my voice. "I'm looking for Chan Hai."

"Today?" she squeaked.

What a strange question. Yes, today. And now.

"You're that lady that called yesterday," she barked. "Aren't you?"

"Yes," I said. Had Chan Hai given her news to relay? "That's me."

"Well," she sighed. "Don't you think he's probably with Old Man Chen today?"

There were as many Chens in the village as there were Huangs. Zi Mei was a Chen. My old math teacher was a Chen. Madame Matchmaker was a Chen. Was Old Man Chen an inspector of some sort? Would he give Chan Hai a new license to operate the quarry?

"Old Man Chen?" I asked.

"Don't tell me you don't know Old Man Chen? His daughter Feng Gu?" The woman's voice squeaked again. "What kind of good friend are you?"

She hung up. I pulled the receiver away from my ear. The woman at the telephone kiosk held her thick braid with one hand and made a circular motion with her other. Move along or make another call. I felt as if I'd been slapped. What was Chan Hai doing with Feng Gu? Certainly this neighbor lady spoke of another Chen. Feng Gu had never let anything but dirt pour from her lips when the subject of Chan Hai came up. Surely if she had planned to meet him, her mood would have been black all day. Did I want to make another call? But I had no one else to call.

I walked across the winding dragon, looking down to make sure all the rocks were in place. Why had our luck turned so? Father was off playing with our future. Mother was more depressed than I'd ever seen her. Chan Hai was now with Feng Gu. No, surely not.

I heard Mother before I saw her. Scrape, scrape, scrape. I looked across to the courtyard. Gone were the soybeans. The laundry no longer stood stiff at attention on the branches. The front door looked a shade lighter, as though the wood had been scrubbed. The courtyard had never appeared so clean. Who was here?

"I'm back," I called.

Thud. Scrub. Scrub. Scrub.

Perhaps Fifth Uncle's wife had come down from the big house to care for Mother. She wasn't fearful of our bad luck. After losing her own son, then attempting to reign in her angry adopted son, what more did she have to fear? Still, she was always full of criticism. I didn't relish the verbal beating that lay in store for all of us. I stepped inside. The small square pinewood dining table had been pushed close to the wall. Stools stood nearby stacked one on top of the other. Father's cherrywood chair had even been dragged into a corner of the room.

Scrub. Scrub. Scrub. I looked to the sound. Mother squatted on her haunches in the corner next to the front door, an oblong scrub brush in her hand. A plastic blue bowl of dark soapy water sat in front of her.

"Mother?"

She glanced up, her eyes dark and puffy. She gave me a brief nod before returning her attention to the smudge of dirt in the corner. A drop of sweat ran down her cheek. I looked around. The walls had been brushed down. The old calendar had been taken away. The metal doorknob to her bedroom shone. Mother only cleaned like this once a year, before the New Year. That's when the Kitchen God came for a visit. That's what Mother believed. The Kitchen God would inspect the cleanliness of the house and report back to the other gods. The following year would be filled with rewards or punishments, depending on her report. But the Lunar New Year was still four months away. Why did Mother feel an urge to wash down the entire house now? This was almost as frightening as her burrowing up in her room.

I went and kneeled next to her. Her thin polyester blouse stuck to her back. Her arms were slick with sweat. Her cheeks were rosy from effort.

"Can I help you?" I offered.

"I'm fine," she said.

"Let me do that," I said, taking hold of the wooden handle of the brush. She pulled it back.

"You get some rest," she barked, waving me away. The bristles of the brush spat water on my legs. "I'm fine."

I stood. Perhaps she needed time alone. Perhaps the rhythm of the brush soothed her soul. I walked across the cement floor to the staircase. Even the linoleum on the steps shone. Perhaps all this scouring cleansed her life as well. Helped her to move forward. I needed something to soothe my soul, to make me feel as clean.

I sat on my bed beneath the mosquito net. A gentle breeze blew in through the window, warning that rain would soon follow. A few remaining leaves from the peach tree outside my window danced back and forth. Downstairs, I heard Mother. Scrub. Scrub. Scrub. I picked up a piece of stationery—that beautiful stationery Madame Matchmaker had given me. I took up my scissors. I would try the bird. Or the piece of paper with slits, as Feng Gu had called my efforts three months ago. Just like Mother, I needed something to take my mind off my empty heart.

Feng Gu. I could still hear the neighbor lady squeaking that Chan Hai was off with Feng Gu. But I just couldn't envision that. She had laughed at him, criticized him. She'd even gone out and bought chalk to draw a line around the shop to keep out his bad spirit. Still, where was Chan Hai?

I curved the wing of the bird. If only I could be free like the bird. If only I could fly somewhere that would release the heavy feeling in my heart. Madame Paper Cutter's words were so wise. "Just as the boat moves forward in the water, we must move forward." Still, I wasn't sure how to do so. A tap-tapping on my bedroom door jolted me. I sliced too far, clipping the side of the bird's wing. Had Chan Hai come to visit? Had Mother let him in? I put the scissors down and went to open my bedroom door.

Mother stood alone and dabbed her puffy eyes with a dirty rag. Her hair hung in damp ringlets. Her forehead and cheeks were flushed red. Was she done? Did she need my help? Did she want to talk?

"You're making paper cuttings," she said walking by me into the room.

"Just playing around. Relaxing." I picked up the injured bird cutting and used it as a fan to send a bit of a breeze toward Mother. "Do you need me to do something?"

"You don't need to spend your time playing that way," Mother said, her voice so bitter I felt a rip at the back of my throat. She fingered the mosquito net over my bed. "The professor won't be needing any more paper cuttings."

"What?" I asked.

Mother walked over to the window and looked out at the peach tree. A breeze blew the fragile branches back and forth. Mother's shoulders trembled.

Had Madame Liang's son received my letter already? I

remembered when it had taken weeks to get mail to a foreign country. It had only been two days. I guessed those workers at the post office weren't as slow as they appeared. Perhaps Madame Liang had already called Madame Matchmaker. That must be why Mother's eyes watered so. Especially now that Father gambled with Chairman Huang.

I knew her concerns. She needed financial security. She needed a daughter with a husband. She needed a grandson. I wished I could tell her that, while I had ruined the match with the successful professor from Singapore, I was engaged to marry a handsome, wise, thoughtful man who had great plans for a flower business. But, while I hoped that I'd live out my days with Chan Hai and bear him a son, I didn't know if he wished the same.

"Mother," I started. "I know you and Father wanted me to marry the professor, but—"

"Let's not talk," she said, waving the rag in front of her as if to block the incoming words, as if fearful my words would hang in the air like dust from a coal fire, making our throats close, our eyes tear. Blackening the walls of our souls forever. She caught a stray tear rolling down her cheek with the rag. "I just wanted you to know that Madame Matchmaker will be here Friday night."

Surely Madame Matchmaker was livid. This was a black mark on her reputation. She would never help us again.

"You're expected, as well," Mother said. Her glassy eyes burned a hole in me.

"Of course." I walked closer and put my arm out to her. "Mother—"

She turned and walked out. Her footsteps retreated down the hall, then down the steps. Each thud reverberated in my heart. How could I have done this to Mother? The woman who saved me at birth? Who stood by my side every moment of my life? I fingered the sliced wing of the bird and sat back down on the bed. I would not let her down. I would take care of her. Even if this bird couldn't fly far. Even if I wasn't sending money from Singapore.

Chapter Thirty-Six
The Injured Wing

I opened my eyes. The sky was still dark. So dark. I sat up in bed and cocked my head to listen. Scrape, scrape, scrape. Was Father home? My hand still clutched the paper bird cutting with the injured wing. I had fallen asleep that way, waiting for Father. The words I had planned to say still jumbled in my head. Surely he would understand my putting an end to the relationship with the professor. Singapore was so far away. The future of the world existed in China, and Chan Hai would ride that future with his nursery. Besides, hadn't Father always been the one to insist we choose the best option, never minding common sense? Wasn't following my heart the best option?

A bird gave a shrill cry. A rooster crowed. I released the paper cutting with a deep sigh. The scrape, scrape, scrape must be Mother washing clothes. Morning had arrived. I pulled on a pink blouse and the black pants Chan Hai had given me. Outside my window, the sun was visible only as a small pinprick in the black sky. In the garden, the stark pointy branches of the peach tree appeared menacing. Did the peach tree know I'd tossed the professor away, as well?

The smell of rice porridge carried across the morning breeze. Poor Mother. We didn't always have a peaceful relationship. That was part of the cycle of being together. Some days were good. Some not. How could I assure her that I was the same respectful daughter she had sent off to college four years ago? That I wouldn't neglect my duties to her or Father, no matter what happened between Chan Hai and I?

I rubbed my palms against the nice soft pants and headed downstairs. When I got to the bottom step, I paused and gripped onto the wooden railing. The cement floor shone as bright as the year Father and the neighbors had first poured it. The chairs and table were gone. Even Father's chair was gone. Oh, Mother. Poor Mother.

I was reminded of Madame Tsui Ping. She had been beaten so many times by the Red Guards that something inside her had snapped.

She had forgotten who she was. She raised cabbage like any good farmer. Had Father and I beaten Mother one too many times? With his gambling away of money? My gambling away of good jobs and good marriage prospects? I went out back, half expecting to see her down on her hands and knees in the garden planting cabbage.

Stools surrounded the square pinewood dining table in the middle of the garden. Father's chair leaned by the side of the door. Had she dragged the heavy cherrywood chair out here all by herself? Mother stood over the table, humming to herself. Scrape. Scrape. Scrape. She moved back and forth, sanding away a burn mark Father had left with one of his cigarettes.

"Mother?" I called.

"The porridge is ready in the kitchen," she sang out, not even breaking her rhythm.

I stepped around the stools. Each one was white with soap suds. I continued on to the outhouse. As I opened the corrugated iron door, the smell of lemon filled my nostrils. I stepped up and inside. The floor had been washed down. A few lemon seeds lay scattered around the rim of the hole, where she must have squeezed a lemon. I'd never seen anyone do this before. Was this a new cleaning tip? Was Mother alright?

"Can I help you wash these stools down?" I said returning to Mother. "Bring them inside? I hear a typhoon is on the way."

She wore the same polyester shirt as yesterday. Her hands were chafed red. Had she been up cleaning all night?

"The porridge is ready in the kitchen," she repeated.

"Mother, I have a bonus coming."

I don't know why I said that. I wasn't a hundred percent sure Feng Gu would give me a bonus, especially now that she was spending more money on ice. But, perhaps this offer of money would take some of the pressure off of Mother's brain. Perhaps she would stop trying to purge all the dirt and unhappiness from around her. She stopped scraping a moment. Took a deep breath. Then she found a new stain.

"The porridge is ready in the kitchen," she said.

My temples pounded. I couldn't have eaten rice porridge if I tried. I grabbed a bucket and filled it with water from the outdoor spigot.

"I'll rinse these down."

I couldn't think. I felt as if Mother had sanded a hole in my head. The time had passed for me to leave for work. But I couldn't leave Mother like this. Surely, if I stayed long enough, she would be alright. I doused each stool with water from the bucket.

"Looks good," I said, indicating with one hand the powdery tan color of the dining table.

She had sanded the entire surface. She stood back to look. Then she got down on her hands and knees, repositioned the flimsy sandpaper around her hand and sanded the bottom of the table. She had never done this, even for the Kitchen God's wife. The bucket handle slipped from my grasp, the remains of the rinse water splashing out on my pant leg. Maybe she wouldn't be alright. I needed to get her some help.

I grabbed my purse and broken umbrella and ran down the steps toward the street. I sucked in air as fast as I could, but none reached my lungs. Perhaps Fifth Auntie would come watch over her. I didn't know what to do. Had my simple letter caused all this grief?

Zi Mei's son Don Don walked back and forth in front of their shop. He had the usual empty smile on his face. He carried an umbrella over his head, stopping every few moments to peek out and look at the dark sky. He turned at the sound of my footfall on the steps. His hair was cropped in a bowl cut over his protruding forehead. His eyelashes were thin and light.

"Umbrellas and raincoats for sale," he called. "Don't forget your umbrellas and raincoats."

Oh gods. Where would Fifth Auntie be at this time of the morning? Back from the market? On her way?

"Looks like you need a raincoat already." Don Don indicated where I'd spilled the bucket of water on my pants. He looked up at the sky as if it had started raining. Stuck out his tongue to make sure.

"No. I'm fine." I gave Don Don a big smile. I could already hear Feng Gu's shrill voice telling all who would listen how late I was, how unreliable these college people are. She wouldn't even consider that something had happened at home. "Have you seen Fifth Auntie go by?"

"No," Don Don said, his thick brow furrowing as he looked up the road. "Did she need a raincoat? Was I supposed to give her a raincoat?"

"No, no," I said. Perhaps today the gods were teasing anyone who was mentally on edge. Mother. Don Don. "Don't worry. I think Fifth Auntie's fine."

"But what about you?" He pulled me over to the bench in front of the store where a stack of raincoats lay. He pulled the top one out of its plastic covering. Shook out the wrinkles. "Here," he said, holding up a yellow jacket that would easily have fit both Fifth Auntie and me at the same time. "I think this is your size. Yes, your size."

"I—I—thank you," I said, shaking my extended palm back and forth. "I don't need one."

"You'll get wet." His droopy eyelids blinked several times. "Big storm is coming. Big storm."

"I heard." I nodded. "I heard."

"Why, Li Hui," Zi Mei said coming out of the shop, holding three lemons. "I thought I heard your voice. What are you doing here?"

"I was." I gestured toward the yellow rain jacket in Don Don's hands. "Don Don was showing me—"

"Is my son pestering you?" She grabbed the raincoat from Don Don with her free hand and dropped the huge plastic garment on the bench. "I'm sorry."

"No, no," I said. "He's such a—a—an enthusiastic salesman."

"Aren't you late for work" she asked, a strange twinkle in her eye. "Or have you quit the tea shop already?"

I looked at the lemons in her hand and thought of our outhouse. She already knew about Mother. Did that fill her with happiness? Or was any gossip enough to make her eyes sparkle?

"I haven't quit," I said. Although I would have to if Mother didn't improve. "I was just looking for Fifth Auntie."

"Why didn't you tell me to give Fifth Auntie a raincoat?" Don Don said looking at Zi Mei with a look of betrayal, fingering the big yellow blob of plastic on the bench. "You didn't tell me. Did you—"

"Not to worry," Zi Mei said, shaking her head as if to rid her brain of Don Don's noise. She patted the lemons in her hand. "I was just going to take these up to your mother. She said she needed more. Don Don and I can help her."

"You're too busy." I patted her arm. Zi Mei wasn't family. This wasn't her problem.

"I have a new helper coming in half an hour," she said, her voice crisp and efficient, having lost its usual gossipy lilt.

I looked up and down the road hoping to spot Fifth Auntie. I was late for work and here was Zi Mei, a woman used to dealing with mental issues, offering to help Mother. So she wasn't family. She would look after Mother.

"I don't want to burden you," I said, my voice apologetic. Actually I needed her.

"Don't worry." She thrust her hands out, shooing me away. "Go on now. You'll be late for work."

I nodded and attempted to smile. But my face was so stiff, I knew if I moved my lips upward, my eyes might crack open. Tears would fall. I nodded again and turned to go.

Chapter Thirty-Seven
Thorns

The bus swung into the depot. The dark sky promised an afternoon of heavy rain. A typhoon, Don Don had said. Perhaps I should have bought a rain jacket from him. A new umbrella. Although a few drops of water from the sky were the least of my concerns. Had Mother stopped cleansing and settled down to a friendly cup of tea with Zi Mei? What was Father up to? Where was Chan Hai?

The gears of the bus whined as the driver downshifted. The brakes squealed to a halt. My feet which had been so firmly planted in the aisle skidded from beneath me. I grabbed onto the back of a seat, my hips banging against the metal edge. People pushing and jostling toward the front sounded loud around me. The old woman sitting in the seat I had bumped against stood and pushed by me as if I were just a bundle of wheat standing in a field. Outside hawkers called out for people to buy meat-filled buns and fruit on a stick. For passengers to buy tickets to Xiamen and Shanghai. For shoppers to ride this motorcycle taxi not that one. The same sounds as always. Yet different. As if the noises were all part of an opera I sat on the sidelines watching.

Move forward. Move forward. I kept repeating Madame Paper Cutter's words in my head. But my thoughts kept tiptoeing back. What if I hadn't sent the letter? What if I had instead wrote of how eager I was to meet the Professor? Mother wouldn't be on her hands and knees sanding the table for the benefit of spiders who crawled up underneath there. Then again, was it all my fault? If Father had stayed and played with his old cronies, rather than Chairman Huang, perhaps she wouldn't be so worried. How much money had Father lost?

"Are you going to get off the bus, lady," the driver spoke into his rear view mirror. "Or what?"

The leather seats were bare. The long metal aisle empty. I stood on the bus all alone. Move forward. Move forward. I couldn't sand away my mistakes. Those were there forever. But, perhaps I could make good on my promises for the future. I would talk to Feng Gu about my bonus. I let go of the seat back and hurried off the bus.

Feng Gu sat at the cherrywood table, her abacus resting in her lap. The light scent of incense wafted from the back room. Today she hadn't lit as many sticks for her ancestor. She wore a new fitted blouse, black with pink cherry blossoms. Was that silk? Sewn by a local tailor? How much did such a costume cost?

The ice bin no longer sat next to her legs. I looked around. I didn't see the holder anywhere. Had the hole in the bottom become so large that Feng Gu had thrown the bin away? Had she decided this Tea on the Cold Rocks wasn't profitable if we had to order ice twice a day? Or was she like Don Don, already preparing for the storm? People wouldn't want Tea on Cold Rocks when their limbs were numb from the cold rain.

Out on the street, motorcycles putt-putted by. Taxis honked. Shop owners threw garbage in the street. Move forward. Move forward.

"Well, well, well," Feng Gu said, her lips pursed as though she sucked on a sour plum. Her mushroom nose stuck high in the air. She wouldn't believe a story about Mother. Nor would she care.

"Sorry," I said, stepping forward to the table. "Sorry, I'm late."

"You're not the only one," she said, shaking her head and nodding toward the bare floor. "The ice provisioner should have been here centuries ago. If he doesn't hurry, we'll have our plain old Hot Tea on No Rocks. I should have known better than to trust some friend of Chan Hai's. That man doesn't know the difference between a friend and . . ."

"Feng Gu." I sat down across from her and folded my hands around the softness of my umbrella. "I need my bonus."

"Now?" Feng Gu shook her abacus up and down, up and down. "Now?"

I nodded. She stared at me. Waiting. As if I might give her a different answer. My cheeks felt hot.

"Because, actually." Feng Gu made a quick calculation, the beads of the abacus creating a rat-at-tat-tat. "Now is not the best time."

"I know." Now was a terrible time. What with all this money going out for ice. And while customers had streamed in yesterday, who was to say when that would stop? Our tea was good but we weren't as fashionable as Queen Dairy. Still, thoughts of Mother sanding the underside of the table filled my being. I leaned forward.

"I know, Feng Gu. But—"

"We thought of a new idea," she said holding on tight to the sides of the wooden abacus.

"We" meaning who? She and her father? She and Mr. Farmer? She and Chan Hai? In the back of my head, I heard Chan Hai's neighbor saying, "He's off meeting with Feng Gu." My mouth felt dry.

"We?" I asked.

"Well, to be honest, it was Mr. Farmer's idea." She ran her chubby forefinger over a dent in one of the abacus beads. "A refrigerator."

"Oh," I sat back, let out a deep breath.

Thank the gods. She and Mr. Farmer were putting their heads together. Not she and her old family friend, Chan Hai. I felt such relief that this was her big announcement. As if I'd been carrying two full buckets of water from the well and she had come along to carry one for me.

"You don't sound excited." She looked up at me, twisting a lock of her short hair in her fingers. "I was sure you'd be clearing space for the machine before I even finished telling you."

"No, no," I said, pulling my mouth into a smile.

No wonder now wasn't a good time. How much did refrigerators cost? Only rich people had those—rich people with money to spare. "And for what purpose?" Father always said. "To make you think your meat is fresher than when it came off the cow?" Did Feng Gu have money to spare? Obviously not enough that she could pay out a bonus at the same time. I needed my money now though. Now, before Mother slid further down the well of insanity.

"That's . . . well," I said. "What an idea."

"Mr. Farmer says it will be expensive at first," Feng Gu said, flicking some beads on her abacus. "In fact, I was just trying to figure how we could manage. And now here you come asking for a bonus."

"I'm sorry," I said. "But maybe—especially now—we could get by on the ice."

I turned and pointed out the front of the shop. People hurried by, rushing to beat the weather. Dark clouds formed like giant mud puddles in the sky.

"So, your father lost that much, huh?" she said.

My eyes blinked. My smile faltered. I wanted to ask what she knew. I swallowed and gripped onto my umbrella.

"Remember. The afternoon customers are never happy," she

said putting the abacus aside. "The ice doesn't last long enough."

I should have been pleased for Feng Gu. She always wanted to be a part of Mr. Farmer's circle. She had always been so afraid to do anything new. Here she had Mr. Farmer, and she was reaching out, ready to try. But I felt frozen. Needles pricked at my heart.

"And the ice won't melt in the refrigerator?" I said, hating myself for making such a false suggestion in the hopes Feng Gu changed her mind. Damn Father. Why did he do this to all of us?

"Mr. Farmer said we won't need ice with a refrigerator." She flicked her short locks back with both hands.

"I just hate to see us move too fast on this cold tea thing," I said, rubbing my hands together as though trying to stay warm. "I mean, look at the weather. A typhoon is coming. It will be winter soon."

"Nonsense." Feng Gu stood and paced around the room. "Besides, Mr. Farmer thinks we can earn back our investment easily."

"Feng Gu—"

I needed to be honest with her. Perhaps she would help me, if not as an employer, as a friend. The scuffling of boots made us both look back toward the entrance to the shop. Chan Hai, his long bangs hanging in his face, came shuffling in. He held our full ice bin in his arms. His white cotton t-shirt was caught on the side of the bin. The taut muscles of his stomach showed. I ran my fingers through my hair. I felt warm all over. I wished I were that ice bin he held so tightly to his chest.

"Ice delivery," he said, stepping inside. He gave me a slight nod, his brown eyes unreadable.

"It's about time." Feng Gu frowned, crossing her arms over her chest and scrunching up the beautiful cherry blossoms on her shirt. She tapped the toe of her shoe on the cement floor.

"My friend came into town on a different route this morning," he said holding the bin with one hand and pointing down the road to where the ice provisioner's truck was parked halfway on the sidewalk. Dark underarm hair peeked out from beneath the sleeve of his shirt as he gestured. Those soft straight hairs. I had tickled them. I had tasted them. "He's a nice old guy, but not always awake." He looked up at Feng Gu, his eyes naked and searching. "Guess he had a late night last night, too."

A late night last night, too? A strange sensation ran up the back of my neck. Beads of sweat tickled my scalp. What was he talking about? Obviously Feng Gu had busier nights than I imagined. She had spoken at length to Mr. Farmer. At least long enough to hear of Father's losses, long enough to brainstorm over the refrigerator idea. Had she gone to his club? And she had met up with Chan Hai. Where did she get such energy? I often felt so exhausted at the end of the day, I just wanted to be home in bed. Especially these days. Especially right now.

"Is that what you call a new ice bin?" She ignored his puppy gaze and pointed to where a trickle of water already flowed from the bin.

"This was the best I could find," he said, holding up the bin and turning the dented container from side to side. His biceps rippled from the effort. He set the bin down on the floor, his damp t-shirt sticking to the front of his chest. "Besides it's better than your other one."

"That's not saying anything."

Feng Gu snorted and shook her head. But she didn't ask him to leave. Instead, she came over to the cherrywood table and scooped up her ledger and abacus, making room for him to have tea. She stood at the check-out counter, leaning over the abacus, her short hair creating a wall around her face. One hand moved down the side of the ledger as the other flicked beads up and down. Was she calculating the cost of a refrigerator plus my bonus? Or was she thinking of last night? And what exactly had happened last night?

Chan Hai sat down at the cherrywood table and stretched out his long legs. I poured him a cup of tea. Here I had waited so long for him to show some sign that I meant as much to him as he did to me. But why now, when I was in the middle of talking to Feng Gu about my bonus? When I was so worried about Mother. When there was some extra something going on here. I took up the ice pick and chipped away a sliver. I added the chunk to his cup and held out the refreshment to him. My arms tingled.

"Ah," he said, taking the cup from my hand with both of his. He looked across at me and winked. "Just what I needed."

Just what he needed? What he needed was a bribe for Chairman Huang large enough to open the quarry so his uncle could continue the search for the blue-black rock which fetched a good price on the market and which would enable Chan Hai's family to buy a phone, enable Chan Hai to start his own business. How could he just sit here and smile and sip tea? I felt out of breath thinking of all the things he needed.

A motorcycle beeped. Beads clicked against the side of the

abacus. Chan Hai's blue cotton trousers rustled as he crossed his legs at his ankles. He set his cup down. I reached out to give him a refill. His thick calloused fingers rubbed the inside of my wrist.

"And you are—" His voice was hoarse.

"I'm fine," I said.

Moments ago all I longed for was the feel of his fingers against my skin. But now he had me thinking of things I needed. I pushed the refill toward him and stood. Feng Gu looked up from her ledger. Would she be able to give me my bonus? Would that money be enough for Father? For Mother?

"Well, then." Chan Hai pulled his long legs out from under the table. He left his full cup untouched. "I better start my day. You never know when the quarry might just re-open."

"How can you joke about it?" I barked, gripping onto the side of the cherrywood table.

Why was he so carefree? He had already greased the palms of many a friend and relative. Wasn't he going to do something other than hoping and paying? Like. Like. Like Father with his *mahjong* tiles.

He stood and walked toward the front exit, as if I hadn't spoken. He stopped at the white chalk mark Feng Gu had drawn to keep him and other evil spirits at bay. He used the tip of his worn brown boot to rub away part of the line. Some things were easy to change.

"What else do you expect me to do?" he said, looking out at the street, the dark sky.

His voice was like the point of a sharp knife, pricking at my heart. The clicking of the abacus ceased. I felt Feng Gu staring at us. What shame to be airing our problems in public like this. Why didn't he just keep walking? My insides burned.

"This kind of weather makes people so antsy," Feng Gu said. She curled a lock of hair behind her ear. "Have another cup of Tea on the Cold Rocks."

"Yes," I spat. "Have more tea and enjoy not having to work at all in this heat."

"Little sister." Chan Hai turned and gave me a look that I'd seen but once before—when he spotted Snakehead Huang at Mr. Fat and Happy's Pork Soup Shop. "Your words are lined with thorns."

He turned and walked out. I stared out after him, expecting him to return. Surely, as the keeper of my heart, he knew that I hadn't meant to draw blood with my words. I was just in a mood today. So much had happened. Then again, perhaps he couldn't understand everything. I took several steps toward the door. I would go after him.

"You mentioned you needed your bonus," Feng Gu said, grabbing onto my arm, her fingers like a vice. "Chan Hai isn't badgering you for money, is he?"

I stared down at her fingers. Was that why he had met Old Man Chen last night? Had he asked Old Man Chen for a loan? Why did I feel so off-balance, as if the bus had just swung into the depot?

"I knew it. I knew it." She pulled me down on the stool. Patted my shoulder hard. Like a command. "Why he crossed Chairman Huang in the first place, I still don't understand." She shook her head, wrinkling her mushroom nose in distaste. "That Chairman Huang is ruthless."

I remembered that night I had escaped from the Chairman's van. The Chairman telling the driver, "Don't worry. I'll get her later." Well, he had me now. Father played *mahjong* with the ruthless man and lost—a big amount. As a result, Mother was going insane. And now Chan Hai was angry with me. My whole life revolved around the Chairman in one way or another.

I looked up toward the door. The memory of Chan Hai's eyes, cold and angry made my heart cold. I rubbed my hands together. My neck ached. My temples throbbed.

Chapter Thirty-Eight
The Blue Tarp

Customers streamed in all morning looking for Tea on the Cold Rocks. Customers who would have taken my mind away from debts and cleanliness and thorns, if Feng Gu hadn't been there. Her high-pitched chatter reminded me of the first day I'd been at the tea shop, about this man who lost money and that man who borrowed. She had it stuck in her head that I needed the bonus to help Chan Hai, despite my assurances to the contrary. I felt suffocated.

A lady walked in wearing baggy black pants held up by a man's belt on her thin frame, a shirt which could have fit her daughter. She had short wiry hair, which she smoothed down with her fingertips, fingertips covered with gray-colored clay. A sour smell wafted in with her. A migrant statue vendor from the park. Feng Gu pointed her mushroom nose in the air and scooted into the back room with her magazine. I sighed. Thanks to this woman I'd get a break from Feng Gu. At last.

I poured the woman a cup of Tea on the Cold Rocks. I had seen her situated beyond the Palm Reader. I never knew she made the statues, though. I thought she just sold them.

"Ah," she said. "Tastes good."

"You must be thirsty," I said.

I poured her a refill. From the back, I heard Feng Gu tapping her feet on the floor. The sound of her whipping through pages of Fashion Fortune Magazine slapped the air. She hated when I gave the park people refills. Engaged them in conversation.

"I've seen you around," the woman said. "You buy one of my statues?"

"No, not yet," I said.

Feng Gu giggled. I was certain she wasn't making commentary on some silly fashion, but on the thought of me spending money on a statue of the Goddess Kuanyin or Jesus. Like I'd do that.

"I sometimes visit Madame Paper Cutter," I added, hoping the woman from the park didn't notice Feng Gu's foolish laughter.

"Ah, that's right," she said. Her Mandarin was clipped, basic.

"She good woman."

"Would you lend her three month's worth of your salary?" Feng Gu called from the back room.

Oh, Feng Gu. I never planned on lending Chan Hai money. I couldn't if I wanted to. Besides, even if I could and did, it was not her business.

"No," the woman said, turning on her stool. She looked toward the back. All we could see were Feng Gu's slacks rolled up to the knee, her skin fleshy and porcelain white. "No, I wouldn't."

"See." We heard the sound of Feng Gu tossing the magazine on the table, the scrape of her stool as she stood. Her figure appeared in the doorway, her hands on her hips. "See? And that's for a—a—a hardworking woman. Chan Hai isn't that."

I'm sure Feng Gu's mouth burned from calling a park woman hardworking. She was so full of bigotry. Why wouldn't she let this subject go? She was like a dog who'd discovered a tasty bone.

"If she not planning to leave so soon, though, I would," the woman said, looking right at Feng Gu. "She good woman. She giving me her spot until she return. If she return."

"If?" I asked. Madame Paper Cutter had said she was going home for the Moon Festival. Surely she planned to come back.

"Her mother-in-law is tired of taking care of Madame Paper Cutter's daughter," the woman said. She drained the last of her tea. "Don't envy her going home to that witch."

Madame Paper Cutter had told me of how her matched marriage was the best thing that could have happened to her, of how her daughter was so intelligent, of how she looked forward to being home after such a long absence. Maybe this woman spoke of someone else. Surely, if Madame Paper Cutter had a horrible mother-in-law I would have heard of that, too.

"You see?" Feng Gu nodded up and down, her eyes wide. "Whatever this woman's excuse is, she wouldn't go throwing money into the wind."

Feng Gu sidled her way into the front room and over to the check-out counter. As if some invisible circle surrounded the woman from the park. I focused on the dragon carving of the table. My cheeks burned.

"I'm going out to order that refrigerator now," Feng Gu said, counting out bills from the cash drawer. "I want you to be thinking while I'm gone." She held up a wad of bills in her hand and shook them at me. "About what? Not about whether Feng Gu will be able to give me a bonus after spending so much money on the refrigerator. Not how I would throw away that money as fast as possible if I got it—so that someday my future will be back in the park, scraping and smelling like this lady. No, I want you to be thinking about a name. We're gonna need a new name for our tea. It won't be Ice Tea on the Cold Rocks anymore, will it? And I don't want Madame Tsui Ping laughing at us again."

I gulped. The woman from the park raised her eyebrows as she comprehended the words hitting her ears. She pulled a bill from the inside of her belt and threw the money on the table like an apple core. Then she stood, her lips smiling but her eyes filled with pain. What had gotten into Feng Gu? I had an urge to pat Feng Gu on the shoulder and lead her out the door. She chattered so much and her words were always lined with thorns.

Some moments, like now, it amazed me that people from the park, from anywhere, came to our shop. Feng Gu could be so rude. My heart hurt. I thought of the little girl who lit firecrackers to scare off the cruel dragon. Feng Gu lit firecrackers even when there wasn't a cruel dragon. She scared everyone away. I couldn't bear to watch this innocent woman be bombarded with Feng Gu's insensitive words. I picked up the tattered bill from the table. As the woman walked past me, I grabbed onto her gritty arm and stuffed her hard-earned money back in her hand.

By noon, our ice supply had turned to water. The remains formed a pool on the floor. I sat at the cherrywood table with a pen and pad. As much as I tried to think up names, all that came to me were things like "debt free" or "sandpaper" or "thorns." I lifted the hair off the back of my shoulders, trying to let a breeze cool my neck. Ah, cool summer breeze.

Feng Gu peered over my shoulder. I could sense her squinting, attempting to read what was written. Then she tossed a rag on top of my pad of paper. The orange cloth covered my ideas.

"Keep thinking," she said.

Instead, I picked up the rag and knelt down near the water spill. I couldn't keep thinking. I felt like a block of ice. If I started thinking, I'd melt into water. I wiped the mess on the floor and took the rag out front. The water dropped like tears onto the sidewalk.

"I need some fresh air to think," I said, dropping the rag on the floor. Not waiting for a response from Feng Gu. Just wanting to be outside and away from her.

The park was filled with afternoon shoppers. An old man bought a balloon for his grandson from the balloon vendor. Mr. Palm Reader studied a young woman's hand. She wore a red skirt and matching jacket. Perhaps an executive from the nearby hotel. Why did she need her palm read? I looked further to Madame Paper Cutter's spot. The piece of cardboard that normally held her cuttings had been replaced by a blue tarp. The blue tarp held statues of Mickey Mouse, Jesus, the Goddess of Mercy. My heart beat in my chest. Where was Madame Paper Cutter? She couldn't have gone already? I looked around the park. Looked for big glasses and wiry limbs, a woman carrying scissors and doing as much to cut up worn ideas and fashion beautiful new ones as she did to make paper cuttings.

I stepped closer. A water chestnut vendor rolled his cart past, the wheels running over the blue tarp and knocking over a statue. A god of some sort. Mr. Palm Reader pointed out a line on the crude hand chart to his customer. The sights and sounds made me dizzy. I kneeled down in front of the statue, hoping the world would stop moving, hoping to feel some of the air that Madame Paper Cutter had breathed. I thought of all the stories Madame Paper Cutter had shared with me as she slowly, deliberately sliced up piece after piece of paper. About the God of Loyalty. Of the Moon Goddess. Of the Old Fisherman and his knife. I thought of all the events we had shared. Of the ruthless father who looked for a tutor. Madame Paper Cutter and her cold which wouldn't go away. The rude customers.

Why had she left without saying goodbye? I thought she was a friend. Still, just this afternoon I had learned things Madame Paper Cutter hadn't shared with me. Perhaps I hadn't really known her at all. Then again, maybe I didn't really know anyone. My eyes stung. Even myself.

Chapter Thirty-Nine
Voices

I walked fast down our road trying to shake off the cloak of sleep that still enveloped me. I had fallen asleep on my stool during the afternoon, when we had run out of ice and customers had slowed to a trickle. I had fallen asleep again on the bus ride home, being jolted awake each time the mechanical teeth of the bus ground into a different gear.

Our refrigerator wasn't due until tomorrow morning, because Mr. Housewares' delivery man had hurt his back—worthless worker that he was—and Mr. Housewares hadn't found a replacement. That was Feng Gu's story that she had repeated over and over. I could still hear her high-pitched tones scraping at the back of my head.

I was awake now and walking. I felt as though the dark sky above was inside of me, making my mind dark and foggy. What with Father gambling and Mother having lost her senses and Chan Hai so angry his eyes burned holes in my heart. And even Madame Paper Cutter disappearing without a word. I picked up my pace. Would Mother still be cleaning? Had Zi Mei and her son stayed with Mother all day? I patted my purse. I'd remembered to bring home a bag of tea as thanks for Zi Mei.

"Li Hui," a soft voice called.

I looked up from my scuffed black pumps, from the dirt path. An old neighbor across from Zi Mei's boarded his windows with plastic in preparation for the typhoon. He focused on hammering a nail. A motorcycle carrying a plastic bin filled with buns zoomed by the cross street, the vendor not bothering to call out his goods. Don Don stood out in the middle of the road with his rain slicker still on, his umbrella still up. Perhaps I'd imagined the voice.

"Li Hui," the voice called again.

I looked out over the fields. My old classmate Cheng Min moved toward me. She was as thin as a rice stalk in her long pants and long-sleeve shirt. Gone was all the fat she had held while pregnant with her third child. Gone was all the fat she'd ever had. She looked like an old chicken. And her clothing didn't hide the patches of skin which had been grafted over her neck and cheek.

"Hello," I said. I cleared my throat. "Hello."

I grasped onto her hands and held on. I knew she had left the hospital days ago. Zi Mei had said that Cheng Min and her husband were having lots of trouble. He wanted to take a second wife. She wanted them to adopt a son instead. I hadn't had the time to visit. Or the nerve. Her hands felt cold and frail.

"Hello," I repeated.

She looked down behind her. Then off toward the house. She let go of my hands and fingered her blouse.

"I still hear them calling to me," she said. "I still smell them."

Zi Mei had said that Cheng Min had insisted her girls be buried in a large circular plot rather than taken to the crematorium. Even though the girls were already burned in the explosion. Even though the government didn't want us to take up more land with big graves.

"What are you doing out in the fields?" I asked.

Helping her mother-in-law tie a tarp over their as-yet-to-be-fixed thatched roof. Fastening plastic to the window panes. Bringing potted plants inside the house. Those were the things I could imagine her doing before a typhoon. Certainly the fields didn't need tending.

"My eldest was always so sensitive to sound," she continued.

"Don't think too much," I said, the words sounding cold and empty. Sounding as if I wanted to rush on home to see about Mother. As if I wanted to rush on with my own life.

"My eldest, she could hear the crabs Father-In-Law caught opening and closing their mouths in the bucket of water by the door. She could hear Mother-In-Law's knitting needles clicking in the next room." Cheng Min's bottom lip quivered. "When the rains came, she would hide her head under a pillow to protect her ears. She always said it sounded like a funeral. Like cymbals crashing. Did the gods in the sky have funerals, she wondered?" Tears slid down her face like water leaking from our ice bin in the tea shop. She rubbed her eyes with the back of her hand. "So now I wonder if this typhoon is a big funeral for both my darlings."

We looked up at the dark clouds, dancing slowly across the sky. Pressure formed behind my eyes. My throat burned. My heart ached. She twisted the bottom of her blouse in her fingers. She wiped her eyes again with her hands. She leaned over and held one side of her nose as she blew her sadness on the ground.

I spotted a book sticking from the back of her pants, one edge slightly burned. The book about disciplining children I'd lent her. Why was she carrying that around? Was she still reading the book? Did she imagine various scenarios with her daughters? A chill filled my veins.

"You should rest," I said, patting her arm as she straightened. "Get inside before the rains come."

The book fell from her backside to the ground. I looked up the road, away from her, as if she had dropped her pants to pee in the gutter.

"That's right," she said, leaning over to retrieve the paperback. "I knew there was a reason I wanted to talk to you—other than just to see your kind face. Your book. I don't need it anymore. Sorry about the edges."

"No matter," I said. She always spoke with such kindness about me. Her words naked and full of heart. My face felt warm. I took the book from her. "Thanks."

"I guess I should be thanking you," she said.

I raised my eyebrows. What for? I had not helped her save her children nor even taken time to visit her much while she was in the hospital.

"I was reading the chapter you recommended on saying no the night—that night. That night." Her eyes turned glassy. "Second daughter wanted one more song before bed. Just one more. I said no. Just like the book said. No, she couldn't ask Nainai for a song. Nainai was talking to the neighbor outside. No, she couldn't ask Yeye. He was testing the hardness of the peanut plants in the garden. Just no, I said, going outside to still my beating heart. As soon as I stepped out into the courtyard, the house exploded. That no saved my life." Thunder sounded in the distance. "Although some days I'd rather be having a funeral in the sky with the gods . . . and my girls."

I grasped onto her hand, then hugged her tight. Her tears wet the front of my blouse. Her small frame crumpled into my arms. Why did things happen the way they did? Why did Cheng Min and Fifth Auntie who loved their children so much have them taken away? Mother would have said the gods were jealous of all that love being bestowed on one living being. Waipo would have talked about the farmer and his horse. Yet none of these stories had to do with the people I knew. None of these stories felt right.

Chapter Forty
Lucky Li Hui

I continued walking toward home. The old neighbor across from Zi Mei's still fiddled with the plastic covering on his window. Don Don still paced up and down along the road in front of Zi Mei's shop, eager to sell raincoats. Not much time had elapsed in my brief discussion with Cheng Min. Yet I felt years older. My insides felt raw, as if they had been scraped along the ocean floor.

Through the window of the shop, I spotted Zi Mei's short figure moving behind the glass case filled with candies. Had she been able to calm Mother down? Talk some sense into her? Was Mother feeling better? I wanted to rush in and ask Zi Mei a dozen questions. At the same time, I hesitated. I felt as if she had seen me in my underwear this morning. My cheeks flushed at the thought of looking the woman in the face. At least she was alone and not surrounded by a group of customers eating up every word she handed out.

"Don Don," I called out a greeting. This was just a normal day, like every other, I told myself.

"Ah, Li Hui. Is Lucky Li Hui." Don Don nodded his big head up and down and pointed at me with a chubby finger. "Lucky Li Hui. Lucky Li Hui."

What was he talking about? Was I lucky I didn't have to spend the day watching Mother? Had she been that bad? Or that I didn't get caught in the rain? Or, praise the heavens, had Father finally won something? No. More likely Don Don just enjoyed the sound of the words. I took the sample of tea from my purse. I reached for the shop's metal door knob, my heart beating faster.

"What is this?" Don Don lumbered over and pointed, his chubby finger touching the side of the bag. His eyes wide.

"A gift for you and your mother," I said, holding out the tea sample.

He pulled the sealed plastic bag from my hands and held it up, shaking the contents, watching the tea leaves rustle back and forth inside the plastic. His full lips turned upwards into a smile.

"Tea," he said. "Mother likes tea. Mother!" Don Don shouted

as if he'd been robbed. He pushed inside the shop in front of me. "Mother! Lucky Li Hui brought thank you tea!"

I cringed at the loudness of his voice. I followed his big bulk inside the small store. Cigarette smoke filled the air. Zi Mei was not alone.

Zi Mei's shop was not big—in fact not much bigger than our shower room. She had organized well, though. The walls were lined with sacks of rice and soy and cigarettes and milk powder. She wasted not an inch of space. And in front of the sacks of rice sat the cronies Father played with, smoking and spitting. Normally men didn't congregate at a woman's shop. Had they stopped off to get more cigarettes and been ensnared by Zi Mei's gossip? Or did they have news to give Zi Mei? I felt naked.

"Why, Li Hui," Zi Mei said coming out from behind the glass case. "We were just talking about you."

I could only imagine. Did these men know what Father was up to? Probably more than I. My ears burned at the thought.

"I—I—I." I wanted to ask about Mother. Now was not the time. "I just wanted to drop this off. Thank you."

Zi Mei attempted to protest the gift. However, when she reached over to grab the tea out of Don Don's hands to return the sample to me, he pulled the bag away. He threw the bag up in the air out of his mother's reach. He caught the bag on the other side of her head. He did this again and again.

"Thank you," I said again, patting her arm. I wanted to leave and check on Mother.

"It was no problem," Zi Mei said. "Besides, it's about time this happened. Your family deserves this."

The men giggled as if they'd heard a dirty joke. Zi Mei's short hair frizzed in this weather. Her eyes smiled. Surely I'd heard wrong. Zi Mei may not have a filter on her mouth. But she wasn't ruthless. How could she be so cruel as to suggest I deserved to have a mother with a nervous breakdown? I pulled my lips into such a big smile that my cheeks hurt. My heart hurt. I turned to leave.

"You need a raincoat?" Don Don said. "How about a raincoat? A typhoon is coming. Big typhoon."

My black pumps crunching over a few grains of spilled rice as I exited the shop sounded like thunder. My skin prickled as though raindrops slapped me. Inside, a typhoon already raged.

Zi Mei's comment made my face sting. How could she say such a thing? Perhaps she had noticed that Don Don was getting no better. Surely she must worry about who would take care of her when she no longer could bend below the glass case to pick out a handful of White Rabbit candies for the neighborhood children, could no longer see whether a customer handed her one *yuan* or five, could no longer hear if a man wanted one stick of tobacco or a whole pack. She had been such a big supporter of the one-child policy, had tattled on anyone who disobeyed. Especially since she had her son. Especially since she was sure he would grow out of his illness. Yet, surely she must be having second thoughts. Perhaps she was turning bitter.

I went around the side of New Neighbor's house, stepping over the winding dragon. The smell of ammonia made my nose burn, my eyes water. What was he up to now? Had he heard of Mother's fragile state of mind and taken this as a sign from the gods? A sign that he must protect himself even more? The closer I got to our courtyard, though, the more my eyes watered. The smell came from our courtyard.

The clothes had been taken in from the branches. The ground had been swept clean. Bright and sterile. On the sides of the door, Mother had hung fresh couplets—characters promising good health and good fortune to our family. "The Earth is ready," read one side. "The garden will be fruitful," read the other. Normally we put up couplets for New Year's, hoping that the words would shine on our lives in the coming year. This wasn't the New Year. Not even close. Certainly I didn't deserve this. No one did.

"Mother?" I called. "Mother?"

Scuffling noises sounded from her bedroom. An angry voice. Father. How could he be angry at this lovely house? We had never had such a clean dwelling. Then again, perhaps he too was afraid of Mother's condition and showing anger was all he could do. I knocked. No reply. I opened their door.

Mother sat on the edge of the bed surrounded by clean clothing she had taken down from the branches. Her eyes had dark circles beneath them, as if she had just been awakened. She sat rigid.

"I ask for a boy," Father bellowed, his big lips snarled into hatred inches from mother's face. "You give me a girl. I ask for a boy, you give me nothing. I can't even ask for a shirt free of wrinkles."

His white suit shirt indeed had many wrinkles on the left arm and the front, as if he'd slept in it. Or more likely Mother had accidentally fallen asleep on it.

"Look at this." He stood over her, pointing to the front of his shirt. "Look!"

He was building himself into a frenzy. He would lose control at any moment, as often happened when he felt scared or guilty about something. Was this about Mother? Was he concerned about Mother? Or was this about money?

"You have no respect for me," he shouted at her.

He tore off his shirt, the buttons flying off and hitting the floor. Anger filled my being. Poor Mother would soon be down on her hands and knees locating the buttons. She would stay up late sewing them back on. I would soon be handing over my salary to be dumped into his well of debt. Who had no respect? I bit my lip, swallowing my ungrateful thoughts. This was Father after all.

"Father." I moved toward him and patted his back, as a child pets a stray kitten. My skin felt repulsed with each touch. My heart beat hard. "Father."

"To hell with you both," he shouted and walked out the door naked in his undershirt.

The room felt cold. Mother looked exhausted. Shaken. She closed her eyes for a long moment.

"Mother." I sat down across from her, the pile of clothes between us. "Are you alright?"

"I shouldn't have fallen asleep," she said, her eyes still closed tight. "I shouldn't have fallen asleep."

Why did she always blame herself? Shut her eyes. Surely she didn't believe that his anger was caused by a wrinkled shirt. That if she'd been a more alert housewife, anger wouldn't be bouncing off the walls as if lightening had hit the house.

"How much?" I asked.

"What?" Mother opened her eyes in alarm and concentrated on the pile of clothing. She picked up a pair of Father's pants, running a trembling hand across the fabric, smoothing away the wrinkles. She picked an imaginary string from the pants. She folded and refolded the cuffs.

"Mother," I said stifling her hands.

"Twenty," she mumbled, her left eye twitching.

I patted her hand. Twenty *yuan*. That was affordable. So Father's anger must have been caused by his concern for Mother.

"Twenty thousand *yuan*," she said.

I gripped her hand. I felt as if the gods had sucked in a big breath, leaving no air left in the room. I couldn't breathe. Twenty thousand *yuan*. That would take me over two years of working at the shop to earn.

"Don't worry," she said, extracting her hand from my grip. Her eyes were dark, guarded. "Everything will be fine."

"But how?" I asked. Even she couldn't shut her eyes that tight, could she? "How?"

"I don't know." Her left eye twitched again. She handed me a blouse to fold. "Father has it all worked out."

"Oh," I said. "That's good."

But relief didn't flood my soul like a lucky Li Hui. Instead the blouse felt foreign in my hands. The woman across from me a stranger.

Chapter Forty-One
Progress

Feng Gu paced back and forth in front of the cherrywood table. She patted the top of her head with the palm of her hand, as though beating on a drum. She looked up each time a truck's engine sounded. You would have thought her father had lost twenty thousand *yuan*.

I looked down at my pad of paper which still had but a few name ideas. That was my job this morning. To think of a name for our refrigerated tea. I tore off the top sheet and picked up my scissors. Perhaps I would get a name idea from making a cutting. More likely the cutting would calm my head, which was so shaken I couldn't think.

Father shouting about disrespect, the spittle from his mouth, the buttons from his shirt flying everywhere. Mother, her eye twitching, telling me all would be alright. That Father would somehow pay up twenty thousand *yuan*. Zi Mei saying, "You deserve this." Perhaps she had known about the money. No wonder all Father's cronies had gathered in her shop. Perhaps she—they—had known that someday this would happen. And they all had laughed so.

"It's after nine," Feng Gu said and looked over from her post at the door. "Mr. Housewares promised delivery of the refrigerator before nine."

I opened my mouth to make a soothing noise. Just yesterday Chan Hai had stood in that same spot, his eyes filled with anger. When I had gone to see Madame Paper Cutter in the hopes of some advice, she was gone already, having left without a sound. Cheng Min was certainly a friend. Her concern so genuine I often felt embarrassed. But her pain was already so deep, I wouldn't push her further down with my small issues. Would Chan Hai ever return? Which kind of friend was he? The kind who didn't care as much as I? Or the kind whose care was so deep I had to stretch on tippy toe just so that my fingertips reached. I had no words for Feng Gu. I rubbed my fingers over my temples.

"It's nine thirty," Feng Gu announced, pulling on her short locks. "Where is that refrigerator?"

"Maybe the typhoon has slowed them up," I said nodding toward the dark sky.

Feng Gu turned to look out the entrance way. She looked at the sky and then down the street for signs of a truck. A wrinkle ran down the back of her pant leg. From pacing too much? The wrinkle reminded me of Mother's trembling hands, her quivering mouth. The cold sensation that I didn't know this woman who had raised me.

"What typhoon?" Feng Gu asked.

"What typhoon?" I repeated. I could think of many.

Feng Gu turned on her pumps to look at me. She crossed her arms over her chest, her brow furrowed. She needed some noise from me.

"Yes, it is strange," I said, my words echoing in my ears. "The sky keeps filling with more and more dark clouds, but it has yet to rain."

"Weather's been strange all summer," Feng Gu said, uncrossing her arms. "In fact, ever since you arrived. First there was all that heat. And now these clouds that look like they're going to explode on us at any minute. Have you angered the gods?"

Had I done such a thing? I thought of all that heat. All the heat that had started the summer. With the Professor interested in a match. With Chan Hai walking me home each day. Now there was nothing but dark clouds. Had I made a wrong move? Surely others had said no to their traditional marriage arrangements. Surely they hadn't angered any gods. Then again, perhaps others didn't need an arrangement as badly as I.

"I said." Feng Gu crossed over to where I sat, her hands on her hips. "Have you thought of a name yet?"

"Uh." I looked at the cut-up piece of paper in my hand. Debt-free. Sandpaper. Firecrackers. "Uh, how about Summer Breeze?"

She stared at me as if the words from my lips were a prelude to something more. Then she wrinkled her nose. Like she smelled garbage.

"That's it?" she asked, her voice so high the notes hit the ceiling. "How's anyone supposed to know we're even talking about tea? And not a weather report?"

"Well," I said, wishing my brain could function. Wishing I had something more for Feng Gu. For Father. For Mother. "Perhaps they'll be so curious, they'll be enticed into trying it."

"I doubt it." Feng Gu pulled on her hair. "We'll call it Refrigerated Tea on the Cold Rocks. That way Madame Tsui Ping will be happy."

"Sounds wonderful," I said. I liked Summer Breeze better.

"Now all we need is the refrigerator," Feng Gu said, glancing at her watch. "I'm going to see what happened to Mr. Housewares."

"Feng Gu," I said as she headed for the back room, the exit into the alley. "About my bonus—"

"I know. I know," Feng Gu said, shooing my question away. "You'll get it. I'll have three hundred *yuan* for you by the end of the day."

"Thank you," I said, clasping my hands together in thanks. "Thank you."

Three hundred *yuan*. That was so much money. So generous. But compared to what Father needed, such a sum was merely a grain of rice. Not even enough to pay Zi Mei for loaning us the money owed Chairman Huang.

I continued with my cutting. The Moon Goddess. Had Madame Paper Cutter already reached home? What would she say of my predicament? Would someone ever love me as much as the archer had loved the Moon Goddess? My scissors snagged the tip of her gown. I sighed. My neck felt stiff. I put my head back to massage out the kinks. That's when I heard the sound of scuffling shoes across the back floor. Could that be Feng Gu back already from Mr. Housewares? Dragging her feet with irritation? I hoped not. I twisted my head back to look. A snippet of blue fabric filled my vision. Blue trousers. Dirty Boots. Chan Hai.

"Let me guess." He came right up behind me, so close I felt the light sensation of his trouser leg against my back. He bent over, his long hair brushing against my cheek. He stared at the cutting in my hands.

"What are you doing here?" I turned toward him. The shop felt small as if his broad shoulders touched both walls and his long legs filled the whole room. He didn't back away.

"The Moon Goddess," he said, his pants rubbing against my cheek. He pointed to where I'd ruined her gown. "Sort of."

How had he spotted that small error? How could he see my faults, always? I wanted to grab him around his thighs, tickle his sides, see the dents in his cheeks appear. But despite our proximity, there was a distance between us. I crumpled the cutting in my hand.

"Why did you do that?" Chan Hai asked, his voice quiet and deep. His eyes focused on my balled-up fist.

"What brings you here?" I asked, an edge to my voice. I looked around for the ledger, for something to make myself appear like a busy and important tea shop seller. The tea table was empty. I rubbed away an imaginary spot with my thumb. "We won't have any Refrigerated Tea on the Cold Rocks until later this afternoon."

"Refrigerated Tea on the Cold Rocks?" He sat down in the stool next to me. "That's certainly a mouthful."

"Well," I said. His dark pants were just inches from my skirt. The distance felt a lifetime away. "We won't have it until this afternoon."

"That's why I'm here actually." He rubbed his hand through his hair, smiled so quick no dents appeared. "Refrigerator delivery."

"You?" I said. Several short hairs poked out from his chin and upper lip, as though he'd lost his razor.

"A man's got to have a job," he said, standing as quickly as he'd sat. "Mr. Housewares doesn't pay as much as the quarry. But then a closed quarry doesn't pay anything at all."

He went through the back room toward the alley. I followed. Out back his truck was squeezed so tightly in the alley, the side mirror kissed the cement wall of Eternal Happiness. He pulled down a large box as though it were a pillow, the muscles in his arms bulging under the weight. Those muscles that had held me—on the bus, in the water, at the temple—and the long dark hair which had tickled my breasts, the insides of my legs.

"Where do you want it?" He looked up at me.

"Huh?" I looked away, embarrassed by my thoughts. "I don't know."

He set the box down, took a knife from his pants pocket, bent over and sliced open the sides. Slice. Slice. Slice. I leaned against the door jam, my heart ripping apart.

"Feng Gu would probably want it out front, close to the counter," he said, lifting the shiny green refrigerator over his shoulder as though lifting a small chest of drawers and waiting for me to move out of his way. "I even brought her an extension—"

"No, she wouldn't," I said. My voice loud, too loud. "I think she'd prefer it in the back room, so it doesn't look like—look like—well, there's a monster in the shop."

He looked down at me a second longer than necessary, as if I were that noisy bird from our first date together, as though waiting for me to speak my mind. I wasn't that girl anymore. Still, I had too much on my mind. And all my thoughts were jumbled together like a sparrow's nest.

"Fine," he said, his voice hard.

He set the refrigerator down next to the table in the back and returned to the truck. After plugging the refrigerator into the wall, I went out to thank him for his efforts. To talk to him. Without thorns. He was already gone.

"Chan Hai?" I called. The alley was empty. "Chan Hai," I whispered. Why was I always one step behind the rest of the world?

Feng Gu bounced down the alley to where I stood hoping the truck and Chan Hai would return. She seemed bubbly, like a fizzy drink. Perhaps she was finally nervous about this refrigerator idea. I hoped not. I didn't have the energy to calm her fears.

"Li Hui?' she called. "What's the matter? Did Chan Hai not come?"

"He was here," I assured her. "He was here."

She led the way into the back room, stopping when she spotted the green refrigerator between the table and the cot. Her lip curled upwards. Her nose wrinkled. Had she not expected this color?

"What's it doing back here?" she clucked, shaking her head. Her stubby finger pointed at the cube. "Doesn't it work?"

"Of course it works." A bitter taste filled my mouth. I hadn't even bothered to ask how it worked.

"There's no cold air." She leaned over and patted the machine on the side, opening the door. "Where's the cold air?"

"The bulb lights up," I said.

"I don't want a box that lights up." She closed the door, stood to her full height and turned to me. "I paid for a refrigerator."

She stared at me, waiting for me to say I'd asked Chan Hai to demonstrate how the machine worked, that this was a fine machine. Well, I hadn't. I'd been too worried about all the cold air circulating through my body to worry about getting some from a machine.

"Perhaps we have to turn on a switch or something." I tore off the manual taped to the side of the door. If this refrigerator didn't work, would Chan Hai exchange the machine or pretend he knew me no better than the homeless woman outside McDonald's? Would Mr. Housewares give Feng Gu a deal on a second machine? How much had I made her waste on this error?

"Chan Hai didn't show you?" Feng Gu opened and closed the

door, watching the light go on and off.

"He was." My lips quivered. "In such a big hurry." I flipped through the fat manual.

"What does it say?" She closed the door again and looked over.

"Nothing, so far."

Why hadn't I remembered something as simple as to ask how the machine worked? Just like Feng Gu said, as soon as the shop started succeeding, I pulled it down again. Just like Father. As soon as we were out of debt, he pulled us down again.

She took the book from me and scanned the instructions. Her eyes grew large, like a carp that had just bumped its nose on the edge of a pond. She held the book out with trembling hands. She pointed to the middle of the page. I followed her shaking fat finger to the character inside a big box—Death.

"That?" I read her the warning. "Don't place appliance on an unstable cart as it may fall, causing serious injury or death to any child or adult in the vicinity."

Feng Gu hopped away from the refrigerator, landing on my toes. She clutched onto my arm. Her brows furrowed in concern.

"It's not on an unstable cart," I pointed out, moving my feet from beneath hers. "Besides, it's not THAT big."

"What's that next box say?" She passed me the book, her mouth pinched together.

"Same thing," I lied. Why did this company write so much unnecessary information, frightening people for no reason? If they could just tell us how to use the thing, that's really all we needed to know. "Here we go," I said. "Plug in and wait for the desired temperature before placing perishables inside." I patted the side of this new weapon. Breathed a sigh of relief. "We just have to wait. This works fine."

"I'm going back to Mr. Housewares." She let go of my arm. She backed toward the exit, her eyes never leaving the green metal cube.

"But, it says here—" I paged through the manual looking for a more definite prediction.

"I don't care what that book says," she said, glancing up at me. "All I know is I already spent too much money. Then Chan Hai hides it in the back room where nobody can see it. What kind of sense is that?"

A spasm made me cough. I held my mouth down in a frown, my cheeks aching from the effort. Typical Feng Gu. Always so concerned about how things looked. At least she was no different than yesterday. As soon as her pumps hit the gravel in the alley, I laughed. I laughed so hard tears rolled down my cheeks.

While she was gone, I sat at the tea table. Would Feng Gu bring Chan Hai back, or would Mr. Housewares send someone else? My legs bounced up and down. Would I have a chance to talk to Chan Hai about more than desired temperatures? I glanced out onto the street. A bicycle whizzed by skidding to a stop next door. Several older women walked by arm in arm, each talking over the other. A hawker called out for hungry customers to hurry. He had but a few steamed buns left. We would soon have thirsty customers—and no cold tea to offer.

I stared at the forty-three-page instruction manual. Don't do this, the manual instructed. I saw Chan Hai's long eyelashes. Beware of that the manual warned. I heard Chan Hai's deep voice saying, "Why did you do that?" I felt his calloused hands on the inside of my wrist, as though he were holding the manual with me. I sighed, closed my eyes, opened them and began reading again. And again.

One line said we would have to wait four to six hours for the refrigerator to reach the maximum coldness. Feng Gu would be disappointed. Perhaps we should order ice from the provisioner. I flipped back to the beginning, yet again, hoping I had missed an important point. Perhaps you could speed up the process. Ah, here was something. About a temperature dial. I stood up to see what level of coldness our refrigerator was at.

The sound of a man clearing his throat made me turn toward the front. A man shuffled through the entrance. He looked older than me. His hair hung in uneven clumps. His hands were stuffed deep in his stained pants. He spat on the floor. I looked to the back of the room. Could I just run back there and look at the dial inside the refrigerator for a second? Feng Gu had told me not to leave customers out here. But wouldn't she be pleased if I discovered that the box she paid so dearly for actually got cold? Probably not. Especially with customers like this out front.

The man also looked toward the back room. Jingled metal in his pocket. Keys? Nails? Perhaps word had already spread about our new purchase. Had he come for a glimpse? Had he come instead of Chan Hai to move the refrigerator?

"What do you want?" I asked. I wanted Chan Hai to come back.

"What do you think, College Girl?" He sat down and rapped his knuckles on the table. The smell of sweat wafted toward me. "I come to a tea shop, and you ask what I want?"

Chan Hai might still be on his way. This man was just a customer. A customer who didn't appear a tea connoisseur, who probably just needed some liquid to wet his lips. I poured some leftovers from the teapot.

"There you go," I said.

I pushed his Tea on the Cold Rocks across the table. The light liquid, which wasn't cold at all, sloshed at the brim and a drop splashed out. I reached for a rag to clean up the spill.

"College Girl, don't try to fool me." He pushed the cup back. His hand trembled. His eyes blinked in rapid succession. "I want a strong cup of tea. Not some leftover buffalo piss."

"Of course." I tossed the liquid in a bucket. Feng Gu had never mentioned a rude man like this. "I just thought you might want to try our Tea on the—the Lukewarm Rocks."

"I don't need fancy stuff, College Girl," he said glancing around. "Just a cup of tea."

I put some fresh leaves in the teapot. College Girl, he called me. How did he know? Certainly no one could tell I was a college girl anymore. Memories of classes and grades were like the lion's tail at New Year's. I chased and chased, but could never catch more than a color or a smell. Like the dark green of the blanket under which I'd huddle in the winter time. The way the sky opened up in the early morning, after Mei Ling and I'd spent the night discussing how we would change the future of China. The musty smell of my textbooks.

College Girl. That girl seemed like a character in one of Madame Tsui Ping's books. Not me. I was the girl who handled tea. Half-kilo bag. Kilo bag. Professor's Medley. Tea on Cold Rocks. Now Refrigerated Tea on Cold Rocks. My learning consisted of small circles, like bees about a flower. About Mr. Farmer's latest girlfriend, or Mr. Department Store's cholesterol problem, or the stench of the park people. I hadn't sniffed this flower before me, though. Who was he? His eyes darted from my hands to the pot. Was I taking too long? Why did he make me nervous?

I went in back and filled the teapot with hot water. When I returned to the front room, he hurried back to his stool, tripping and falling against the table. Perhaps he was shy about looking around.

Perhaps he was used to dealing with Feng Gu.

"Feng Gu will be back soon," I soothed.

"Who?" he asked. Jingle-jingle.

We both sat back down. We stared at the pot of tea. He twitched his shoulders up and down. He stubbed out his cigarette.

"Don't you think it's ready yet?" he asked.

I didn't think so, but I poured him a cup. I wished for this brash man to leave. I never felt that way about anyone, even the park people. What made me react so?

The liquid in his cup appeared as light as water, but he did not comment. He took another glance toward the back room. Of course. He did come to see the refrigerator. I got up and opened the door to the back wider, so he could get a better view.

"I'll take a half-kilo," he said, staring at the short green box that should soon give us cold tea.

He stood up. My nerves relaxed. My lips curled into a genuine smile. Here was this rough-looking man who sat around waiting and waiting for just a glimpse of our refrigerator. He probably didn't even need the half-kilo of tea. I couldn't wait to tell—who? Who would I tell? Madame Paper Cutter was gone. Chan Hai was gone. There was no one I really wanted to tell.

"Half-kilo of the Professor's Medley?" I asked.

"Yes."

He paced up and back in front of the check-out counter, shaking the metal in his pocket. Jingle-jingle. I pinched a handful of leaves from the tea bin and dropped them into a half-kilo bag. Even Feng Gu would get a smile out of this customer. Too bad she couldn't see him. What was keeping her? I moved to the check-out counter. Stood next to the man. He stood taller than I by a few hairs. I picked up the metal rod, balancing a weight on one end, the bag of tea on the other.

"Just right," I said.

The man pushed the weight off the rod, grabbing the small metal piece with his grease-stained fingers. His unclipped nails appeared jagged and menacing. His hand trembled.

"Why do you keep trying to cheat me, College Girl?" he said holding up the weight in front of my eyes. "That's no kilo."

I stepped back. A feeling jolted my spine, as if his words were a hammer. Something was wrong here.

"I thought you said half-kilo," I said.

"Sure you did." Jingle-jingle.

I picked up the bag of tea and returned to the bin. Maybe my mind had been so busy thinking of refrigerator warnings and Chan Hai, I hadn't paid attention. I could almost feel Chan Hai's eyes on me, staring at me, shaking his head at all the noise in my head. I stuffed the man's tea bag so full of leaves, there was no need to measure. This bag held more than a kilo.

"That will be ten *yuan*." I moved behind the check-out counter and plugged in the electric sealer.

"That's a ridiculous price." The man made a high-pitched chuckle. "I'll give you two."

I made a sour face. How long had it been since he'd been in this shop? If he ever had.

"It's ten *yuan* per kilo," I said.

"I know." The man twitched his broad shoulders up and down. His eyes blinked again and again. "You like to cheat, College Girl."

His constant harping on me as a college girl now irritated. I wanted him to leave.

"Eight then," I said.

He put twenty *yuan* on the counter. I turned to seal his bag. I placed the opening of the bag between the lips of the sealer and pressed down.

"College Girl," he said. "Hurry up."

I opened the sealer before the light turned green and thrust him the bag. If he couldn't wait patiently for me to finish packaging his tea, I wouldn't bother trying. I reached on the counter to grab his twenty. My hand slapped against bare wood. Where was the twenty I'd seen him put down?

I looked on the floor. Under the counter. Perhaps I'd already put the bill away in the drawer. I opened the cash drawer. But the top note in the drawer was a hundred *yuan*. The man leaned over and peered inside. Heat spread through my body. The back of my neck itched. The beads on the abacus appeared like boulders rolling down the hill to crush me. I couldn't have lost his money. The man looked at me, shaking the metal in his pocket, as though trying to spur on an old mare. I wished Feng Gu were here.

"What did you do with your twenty?" I lifted the abacus. No bill there.

"What are you talking about?" He looked to the back room, again. "What twenty?"

I breathed. The beads retreated to their normal size. He hadn't paid me yet.

"College Girl" he said. "I gave you a hundred *yuan* note. No twenty. Where's my change?"

I opened the drawer, again. That hundred *yuan* note on top wasn't his. His own mother probably didn't have a hundred *yuan* note. Besides, I hadn't touched the drawer until just now. I was sure of it.

"Hurry up, College Girl. I've got work to do," he said. "One hundred minus seven is ninety—"

"We agreed on eight," I said. Surely he was lying about this. What would Feng Gu do? Of all her talking, she'd never told me what to do in such a situation. "The tea is eight *yuan*. No lower."

"Fine," he said. Jingle-jingle. "Give me my change—or let me have my money back and I'll find a more efficient store. You make me wait so long, even your special Professor's Medley will taste bitter."

I counted out the notes. I tried to focus. If only Feng Gu would come back. She would know how to deal with this man.

"Gods, you're slow," the man said.

He leaned over the counter, his eyes full of anger. Hate. I counted and recounted the bills. All the while, he yapped in the background like a dog at the end of his chain. About how dumb I was. About how everyone said how great college was, how only 1% of Chinese were smart enough to attend. But here was a college girl who couldn't even remember a simple order of tea. First gave only a half-kilo when he had ordered a kilo. Then couldn't even add. His talk made my spine tingle, my fingers tremble. A bead of perspiration ran down my neck. Feng Gu must come back. Now. I needed her.

"That's it. Ninety-two *yuan*," he said, thrusting his greasy hand out.

"Let me just double check." I counted the bills again from the beginning, stalling.

"There's no need," he said. "I counted with you."

"I just want to be sure," I insisted.

"How many times are you going to count the stuff, College Girl?" He stuffed his hands in his pockets. Jingle-jingle.

"It's just—I want to be sure," I said. "You wouldn't want me to make a mistake."

"You mean another mistake," the man said.

He reached across the counter with both hands, hands that now had metal chains interlocking his thick fingers. He grabbed both my wrists. The metal chains hurt.

"Let go," I said. "You're hurting me."

"Give me the money," he said putting pressure on the insides of my wrists. My fingers automatically opened. He scraped the bills out of my hand and stuffed the wad in his pocket. "Ha, College Girl."

I looked in back, hoping Feng Gu would come through the door. Tell me this was all a game. That this customer was just a bit strange. The silly green refrigerator stared at me, warning me to do something. I reached for the metal rod on the counter to bat the man away. He slammed his chains against my arm. I pulled my hand back. My skin burned. I dropped the rod. He turned and ran out.

Chapter Forty-Two
A Rat in the Water Bucket

The man jumped over the small white fence that separated the sidewalk from the street. He dodged between cars and trucks and bicycles as he ran down the side of the road. How would I ever catch him? I stopped just outside the doorway. I couldn't leave the shop. Not with our new refrigerator sitting in back. Not with the cash drawer open like that.

"Stop him," I shouted. No one listened. I might as well have been standing on the shore shouting at the ocean. "Stop him!"

"What is it?" Feng Gu said, coming in from the back room, Chan Hai in tow.

"Our money," I said. I jumped up and down and pointed to where the man dodged in front of a taxi, hitting the hood of the car with his hand. The taxi blared at him. I wished the taxi would stop honking and just hit him. "Gone—over there."

Chan Hai didn't wait for the explanation, but brushed past me like the wind. Feng Gu came up next to me. We watched as Chan Hai darted in the center of traffic in pursuit of the man. Horns blared, drivers shouted and gestured. Chan Hai seemed oblivious to everything except the thief.

If only I'd stalled the man a few more seconds, Chan Hai and Feng Gu would have arrived. The man probably would have disappeared. And our money would still all be here. What would happen to my bonus now?

The thief got sideswiped by a motorcyclist and tripped forward. Chan Hai was right behind. He put his hand out to grab the man's shirt. And missed. The man jumped back onto the sidewalk and dodged between shoppers and commuters and hawkers.

"It just happened so fast," I explained as we watched from the front of the shop. "He was so noisy and demanding. I got confused. 'Hey, don't give me this buffalo piss. Hey, don't give me just a half-kilo. Hey, College Girl, that hundred *yuan*'s mine—'"

"What?" Feng Gu looked at me. She cocked her head to the side and held onto a lock of her hair.

"He insisted he'd given me a hundred *yuan* bill." My underarms tingled. "And there was one right there—"

"No." She dropped her hand from her head, waving her palm back and forth at me. "What did he call you?"

"College Girl."

My face felt hot. Feng Gu had always disdained my education and she was right. If I wasn't inspiring customers to pour our tea leaves all over the floor, I was handing them money from the cash drawer. I might as well have been an art major. Or no major at all.

The man ran up toward the bridge. He passed the woman who sold inflatables for the pool, kicking up her rings as he went. A ring bounced and rolled back, hitting Chan Hai.

"That's gotta be College Boy," Feng Gu said, nodding and pulling me further up the street, now unconcerned about leaving the shop unattended.

"Who?"

Of course Feng Gu knew him. Perhaps this was a game, and the man would finally zigzag back to the shop, hand me the money back, show me for the fool that I was. I was already a happy fool.

"Imagine," she said, shaking her head back and forth. "That thief came to our little shop."

Maybe he wouldn't return. Frustration filled my veins. If he didn't return our money, I'd surely get no bonus.

"They call him College Boy," Feng Gu leaned over and explained, her words hitting my ear like dynamite at the quarry. "Because he always wanted to go to college. His test scores weren't good enough— by a fraction. He only steals from graduates, eager to show them he's smarter."

"He proved that alright."

My chest burned. College Boy headed across the bridge. Where would he go? How long could he keep running? How long could Chan Hai?

"Normally he targets big stores, though," she said. "Banks. He robbed a bank in Xiamen for four thousand *yuan*."

"Oh, My Mother." Four thousand? Had the clerk been fired? Had she been required to reimburse the bank?

"Imagine. He came to our little shop." She linked her arm in mine.

"Yeah," I said. "Imagine."

Chan Hai's pace slowed when he reached the bridge. He stopped.

But rather than slump over forward with exhaustion, he stared out into the traffic. What was he looking at?

"Maybe with our medleys and Tea on the Cold Rocks," Feng Gu said, no longer watching Chan Hai, but glancing around at all the vehicles and pedestrians as though they had come to see her. "We've gained a big reputation."

Her eyes sparkled. Maybe she could afford this loss. Maybe she wouldn't add the amount to our family's ever-increasing pile of debt.

"Look." Feng Gu pointed up on the bridge. "He's got a partner."

A man waited on a motorcycle at the far end of the bridge behind a long cart of garbage. He took a last drag from a cigarette, tossed the burning ember on the ground and started his engine. Chan Hai still stood in the same spot and stared.

"He looks familiar," Feng Gu said. She tucked a lock of hair behind her ear, squinting her eyes up into the dark sky, as though trying to remember.

"How do you know all this stuff?" I asked.

Why wouldn't Chan Hai run anymore? Just a few more paces and College Boy would be on the back of that motorcycle, he'd be off spending all that *yuan* he'd stolen from us.

"I've just been around." She smirked, crossing her arms across her chest, pulling me along. "I think that's a friend of Chan Hai's— dammit."

I looked toward the man on the motorcycle. No. I shook my head as though to clear the image of the man sitting there with a red crescent-shaped burn mark on his cheek. Little Wu Lu. Air wouldn't fill my lungs.

"Look," Feng Gu said, gripping my arm so tight, her nails pinched my skin. "Chan Hai's back on him."

Chan Hai had started running again, this time as though to save his life. College Boy dodged in between a motorcycle taxi and the woman carrying the long cart of garbage. Little Wu Lu maneuvered in on his motorcycle as close as he could, but those rods sticking out from the back of the garbage cart were like giant hands holding him back.

I thought of crickets and Snakehead Huang and slashing my way to freedom. Was this a return favor? For me or Chan Hai? Was this how you returned the loyalty and love of a friend? My stomach twisted in knots. Had I returned the loyalty and love of Chan Hai any better? Here he'd been trying his best, and all I could tell him was it wasn't good enough.

College Boy jumped over the cart. The back of his shirt caught on one of the metal rods. He tore himself free. He got caught again. This time by Chan Hai. College Boy twisted and turned, trying to break free from Chan Hai's grip. Chan Hai wouldn't let go.

College Boy turned and punched Chan Hai in the face. In the stomach. In the face again. Chan Hai kicked College Boy in the stomach. The man didn't even flinch. He was tough.

"Come on, Chan Hai," Feng Gu whispered like a prayer.

College Boy grabbed a handful of metal from the garbage cart and threw it in Chan Hai's face. He fought dirty. My eyes burned. The money no longer seemed important. No matter how much.

College Boy pulled a short metal rod from the cart. My insides screamed. The old garbage lady went to the back of her cart and pointed and shouted. What were they doing back there, she seemed to say. Couldn't they see she had worked hard to collect all this garbage? She wasn't interested in picking it up again. College Boy ignored the old woman. He pulled out that rod and swung it as though thwacking soybeans from their branches. Chan Hai coiled over from the blow. The old lady retreated to the front of her cart. Then College Boy kicked Chan Hai in the face. Hard.

Chan Hai grabbed onto the garbage cart with one hand, so he wouldn't fall down. With his other hand, he held fast to the thief's collar. College Boy kicked Chan Hai in the chest. Again and again. My chest thumped hard, higher and higher toward my throat. Why didn't Chan Hai just let go if he couldn't fight? And why didn't he fight? My body trembled.

College Boy kicked Chan Hai's manhood. How could Little Wu Lu watch his friend be beaten this way? Chan Hai fell to his knees, but he still wouldn't let go of College Boy. College Boy pulled his leg back to kick Chan Hai again. I couldn't look. I couldn't watch this gentle man, who helped old ladies with peas and saved friends from certain death, being pounded like a fish at the market, pounded until there was no movement left in his body.

A huge thwack sounded. The rice in my stomach surged to the base of my throat. I buried my head in Feng Gu's shoulder.

"Oh, my mother." She shook me away.

The thwacking sounded again. I looked up to see the garbage

woman beating College Boy with her broom. She beat the thief harder and harder, beating him as though he were the reason for all her unhappiness—a job sweeping garbage, a salary which would not buy enough food, a day which contained something she didn't expect.

When she beat one more time, Chan Hai grabbed the broom. Just held the bamboo stick and waited for the old woman to calm down. Then, he reached down and pulled the wad of *yuan* from the pockets of the lifeless fish. He stood up and stared at Little Wu Lu.

Little Wu Lu didn't bother to look over. He was no longer the man who had given Chan Hai a plant. No longer a friend with helpful advice. He gunned his engine and roared off down the road. My eyes stung. How could Little Wu Lu be so heartless? He was like a rat who you save from drowning in the water pail. Rather than thankful, that vermin turns around and nibbles a hole in your cloth bag.

Chan Hai held out a few bills to the old woman She backed away, shaking her head. She returned to the front of her cart. Chan Hai followed after her, grabbing her arm and putting the money in her hand. She pulled her hand away. She shouted at him. Chan Hai returned to the back of the cart, picked up College Boy and dumped his unconscious body on top of the pile of metal rods. The garbage woman smiled and put the bill in the waist of her pants in return for the extra load of garbage. Chan Hai called after her. Whatever he said, she didn't respond. She was already watching the long road ahead.

Chan Hai came up to us, his chest heaving up and down. His shirt was torn, his pants ripped. My heart had quit thumping so loud, but my arms still trembled. I wanted to reach out and hold onto the standing, breathing Chan Hai.

"Here," he said, handing over the wad of bills to Feng Gu. He didn't even look my way.

"Many thanks," Feng Gu said, handing back a few notes as a reward.

"What for you want to give me that?" He spoke in a high voice, sounding like an old woman. Was that what the garbage woman had said? He pocketed the reward with a smile.

"Some tea?" Feng Gu offered.

"I've had already," he said. "I've got to get back to work. I think I was supposed to move a refrigerator."

"Never mind about that," Feng Gu said.

She pulled him into the shop and sat him down on one of the stools in front of the cherrywood table, as if he were a good friend. Not a black soul who we needed to guard ourselves against by drawing lines of white chalk. I felt warm inside.

"You could have wrestled that metal bar from the bastard, easily," she said, her voice loud with excitement, her hands flying through the air. I smiled. Waipo would have said Feng Gu was ever the strategist after the battle had been decided. Waipo would have been happy Chan Hai survived this battle. Certainly. "You need to learn to use your strength." Feng Gu waved her finger at Chan Hai. "That puny thing beat you to a—oh, gods, you need to get to a clinic."

What was she talking about? I rushed toward him. His right cheek, where College Boy must have kicked him, had a big gash. Blood dripped faster than a leaky faucet.

"You should visit the clinic," I heard myself repeat. Not that the clinic was the best place. Often they were out of medicines. Even dressings were hard to come by.

"No need. No need," Chan Hai said, brushing his hand over the slice and smearing blood all over his fingers. "It's nothing. I don't feel a thing."

"Let me take a better look." Feng Gu lifted his chin up as if she were a doctor. She stood up. "We need some *Yunnan Bai Yao*," she said, talking of the blood-stopping white herbal powder.

She would leave Chan Hai and I alone. I would get a chance to reach out and touch his warm, calloused hands. How could I have thought anything bad about Feng Gu? She was like an older sister. Only eager to help. I smiled my thanks, moving in closer, ready to take up her seat when she stood.

"Get the big size," she said handing me a ten-*yuan* note.

I ran outside, across the river, past the park, down the same street as the *hambaobao* shop. Chan Hai would be fine, never mind that huge gash. Then again, what if his skin popped further and he began gushing blood? When had Little Wu Lu started working for this thief? Would he come back? Had he rubbed my face deep enough in dirt? Certainly, I'd been stupid, counting out all that money for that thief while he jingled his metal chains and called me College Girl. Some things you didn't learn at college.

"I've been around," I could hear Feng Gu's voice, smirking.

Chan Hai would be alright. If his face bled harder, Feng Gu knew to take him to the clinic. I ran faster, although my calves felt full of wet corn powder, until I reached the big glass door to the pharmacy. I flung the door open so wide, the pane rattled. Mr. Medicine Shop wasn't in sight. A helper stacked boxes of tiger paste underneath the counter. He didn't look up at the bell which announced my entrance.

"*Yunnan.*" I took a breath. "*Bai Yao.*" A rice-pounding mallet beat the sides of my head, over and over again. Sweat rolled down the insides of my arms. "Yunnan Bai Yao," I repeated.

Mr. Helper disappeared in the back where his colleague stood behind a large glass partition, cutting up sea horse parts for male problems. I tapped the counter, waiting, waiting. Would Chan Hai have the sense to lie down on the tea shop floor, rather than insisting on sitting on a stool or worse, deciding he must move the refrigerator? Then again, the floor would be cold. And dirty. I looked around. This black-and-white tile floor was always spotless—although I did see a piece of paper near the door the sweeper had missed. A box on the window blew cold air.

What took Mr. Helper so long? Even when Mei Ling used to take me through the store and point out all the herbs she studied—chrysanthemums for toothaches or red flowers for unwanted pregnancies—even with her there, pointing and talking and theorizing, we breezed in and out before the smell of menthol touched my nose. The back of my neck, now cold and dry, itched. I clasped my hands together. Mr. Helper came back with a box of tiger patches. He piled them inside the glass case. Had he forgotten I was there?

"*Yunnan Bai Yao?*" I asked again.

"Finished." Mr. Helper arranged the boxes.

"Finished?" They had sold out? This was the only pharmacy in town.

"Come back next week." Mr. Helper took out another handful of patches.

"I need it today," I said. "Now."

He glanced up at me, his eyes roving about, as though trying to find my bleeding place. He stopped at my private area and then looked up, a question in his eyes. Was my "monthly" bleeding too strong? Would I not need the liquid herb rather than a powder? Could he tell just from looking that this month my monthly was late? I wish Mr. Medicine Shop were here to help me, instead.

"It's not for me." My face felt hot. "It's for a friend with a bad cut . . . on his face."

"You better take your friend to the clinic." He turned away.

But Chan Hai needed help now, not an hour from now, after we had taken a taxi to the clinic and pushed our way through a line with thousands and tens of thousands of other sick people all of whom might have used up all the clinic's blood-stopping powder.

"Don't you have something?" I asked.

Waipo had always insisted that *Yunnan Bai Yao* worked best. But Mei Ling had taught me that it was a brand name. Like aspirin or tiger paste. Surely the shop had the Emperor herb, the chief ingredient, for stopping blood.

Mr. Helper looked at me, at my eyes which must have shone too brightly. He knew that my friend would not make it to the clinic. He went in back and returned with a small brown bottle.

"This is mine," he said. "But, since you need it so badly, I'll sell it to you."

I felt warm inside, despite the cold air blowing at me from the window box. This was the first kind stranger I'd met all day.

"How much?" I asked.

"*Yunnan Bai Yao* is always two *yuan*," he said.

I waited for him to say how, since he'd already used half the bottle, he would give it to me for much less. That's what Mr. Medicine Shop would have said. He didn't say any such thing. He didn't carry the same heart that Mr. Medicine Shop did. How could Mr. Medicine Shop leave this helper in charge?

"Fine." I handed him the ten *yuan* bill and waited while he went yet again to the back, this time for change.

I shook the small brown vile up and down. Would there be enough? Why hadn't the man just given me the bottle? Two *yuan*. I could already hear Feng Gu clucking unhappily—saying how I had spent her money so foolishly. I glanced toward the back. What took the man so long just to count out eight *yuan*? Like a wild goose making a twelve centimeter long poo. I opened the bottle to calculate just how much was inside. Was this really *Yunnan Bai Yao*? The powder looked white rather than light brown. Perhaps the man had filled an empty bottle with sugar crystals.

I picked up the piece of paper off the floor and put it on the counter. I poured a bit of the powder on the paper. It did look a bit brownish. I sniffed. Ah, I got a whiff of that familiar burnt smell. I was just about to return the powder to the bottle, when I heard the click-click of Mr. Helper's shoes on the tile.

"I don't have the correct change," Mr. Helper said, as he returned to arranging boxes underneath the counter.

He wore a look of sorry, but I knew he was lying. Maybe the man in the park who sold water chestnuts didn't have change. Maybe the migrants who sold peanuts or plastic animals didn't have change. But not this fancy, air-conditioned shop. What had happened to our friendly village that people no longer cared? Were only after themselves? Would rob a house which was already on fire? I looked at the small pile of powder which would stop Chan Hai's face from bleeding. I thought of that ten *yuan*—a day's salary for some.

"Give me my money back," I said. "I don't need it anymore. After all this time, I'm sure my friend has already gone to the clinic."

Mr. Helper grabbed the medicine vile and threw my ten *yuan* on the counter. He turned and stalked off, like a boy who had lost a game of marbles. I should have felt dirty for what I did, but I felt like I'd just gotten back a test paper with every question answered correctly. I felt like I had a grasp on life after college. I could hear Feng Gu's chuckling voice, saying "I've been around." And I chuckled, too.

Outside, I stopped next to a bush in the park and ran my hand along the waist of my skirt. I didn't have to search long to find the paper. I opened it and checked to make sure the Yunnan Bai Yao powder was still inside before I started the long run back to the tea shop.

Chapter Forty-Three
Making Rain

The tea shop was empty. No Chan Hai lay on the floor or even sat on a stool. No Feng Gu held onto his cheek, turning it this way and that. The door to the back room was closed, as it was each day when Feng Gu closed up shop. Yet the shop was still open. Perhaps Feng Gu had rushed Chan Hai to the clinic so quickly, she didn't have time to pull down the metal grate out front. She hadn't even had time to ask Mr. Bicycle Repair to watch our place. Then again, perhaps she knew I'd be back soon. I bent and steadied myself on the table. Would the clinic be able to help Chan Hai? I couldn't get enough air in my chest.

My knees crumpled beneath me and I sat down. I rested my head on the cool wood of the other tea stool, a tea stool that not long ago had held Chan Hai. A laughing, smiling Chan Hai. Why had that ruthless Medicine Shop Worker made me wait so long? Surely Chan Hai must have felt I didn't care enough to hurry. I had to tell him that wasn't so. I'd close up shop and go visit the nearest clinic.

I sat up and took a deep breath. My cheeks flared from heat. The world rotated around me. I put my head back down. The smooth hard wood felt good against my cheek. The hardness stopped my thoughts from spinning so fast.

"Little Sister?" an old man's voice called.

I flinched. Here I was alone in the tea shop again. I sat up and turned on my stool.

"Am I glad to see you," Mr. Farmer said. He rushed up and sat down right next to me. He had his pants rolled up to his knee. His long brown socks were rolled down to his black tie shoes. Sweat circled his armpits. More than a nightclub owner, today he really looked like a farmer. "I've been waiting outside for over five characters for someone to show up."

"Five characters?" I repeated, staring at my watch.

Five notches on the dial. Twenty-five minutes. Feng Gu had been gone a long time. She and Chan Hai must have left shortly after I went to the Medicine Shop.

"Do you have any Tea on the Cold Rocks?" he asked.

"Not yet," I said, standing, hoping he would leave too. I wanted to find Chan Hai.

"Well, then." Mr. Farmer cleared his throat. "Just give me whatever's in the pot."

I poured him a small cup of tea. The brackish liquid had been sitting all morning, ever since I'd prepared a special pot for College Boy. Feng Gu would have been appalled that I served this, especially to her dear Mr. Farmer. Mr. Farmer took two loud slurps. If he noticed too much flavor, he didn't say so. Then he put his hand out for another cup.

"I'm just so hot I feel like I'll burst," he said. He raised his eyebrows. "Those clouds out there are like a beautiful young maiden. Smiling, flirting, but offering no relief."

A surge of heat filled my cheeks. My skin prickled. Perhaps Feng Gu would have enjoyed this sexual humor. I felt shame.

"Can I sell you a kilo?" I moved to the tea bin and started filling a bag.

"No, thanks." Mr. Farmer settled back in his stool and took a pack of cigarettes from his shirt pocket. He put the pack on the table. He planned to rest a while. "I just needed some refreshment."

I shifted from foot to foot. Now that my head had stopped spinning, I couldn't wait to leave the tea shop. I couldn't wait to see Chan Hai's scraggly face. To make sure he was alright.

"Have you tried the drinks at Queen Dairy?" I suggested.

"Queen who?" He took out a handkerchief and mopped his face. "Oh, that nonsense. I wouldn't go there if Buddha offered to meet me. I hate when people use foreign words to try to make their product seem more interesting. Doesn't fool me."

"I hear it's a very popular place," I tried. Chan Hai had said so. He had said so the day he brought us ice cream cones, his long legs straddling the white chalk mark on the shop floor. His face smooth and full of love. "I hear that everyone should go there at least once."

"You mark my words." Mr. Farmer leaned forward and beckoned toward me with his finger, as though sharing a secret with some of his cronies in the club, in between a hand of cards. "They'll be sorry."

I smoothed out my skirt. I held my breath, not wanting to spur him on in this topic. He was talking about the same disaster Madame Tsui Ping lived in fear of—of the day when everything foreign would be considered bad again. There were always doomsayers, although

I'd never expected Mr. Farmer to be one of them. But, I didn't want to ask him any leading questions, to propel the conversation forward. I wanted him to focus on his tea, on draining his cup and leaving.

"Yes." Mr. Farmer twirled the contents of his cup around. "Sorry. That's what they'll be."

I stood there nodding and smiling like a scarecrow in the wind. I felt a stab of guilt that I wasn't being more entertaining to this man my boss favored so. But my calves tingled to be going.

Eventually he set his cup down and put his cigarettes back into his pocket. I would show him out and close the gate behind us. I'd be off to the clinic in no time. I moved toward the entrance.

"You ever hear of Admiral Zheng-He and his treasure fleet of ships?" he asked, tapping the table with his manicured forefinger. He wanted a refill. I sighed and returned to the table. I poured the dark liquid from the teapot, my mouth tasting sour just thinking of how bitter it was. I should have been ashamed of my treatment of Mr. Farmer. But why couldn't he just leave? Didn't he need to open his club? Weren't there *mahjong* tiles to sort? Karaoke songs to choose? Girlfriends to visit? Twice today the gods had made me wait—first at the medicine shop, now here. Why did they test me so? A vision of Madame Paper Cutter came to me. She smiled as she handed me a lucky paper crane. "Patience," she whispered.

"I assumed," he continued. "Someone intelligent like yourself would have heard of the Admiral."

I nodded my head to indicate that, yes, I had heard of the great man. But Mr. Farmer didn't notice. He already moved along like a bicycle down a hill, the breeze blowing his hair back as he repeated a story he enjoyed telling, about Admiral Zheng-He. The Admiral had been sent out by the Emperor in the early 1400s to find new land. He found lots of places, rounding the Cape of Good Hope, exploring the Antarctic and the Arctic, North and South America, even Australia. I took a deep breath and held onto my skirt. Mr. Farmer would be done with this story soon. I focused on the soft patter of his voice.

"Then a new Emperor came to power," Mr. Farmer said. "And he was so jealous of all of his father's accomplishments, he called a halt to all exploration. He shut down the borders. Burned everything that had to do with the outside world."

"Strange," I said. I looked toward the front exit.

"We fight so hard these days to gain permission to work and visit North and South America," he said. "Just think. Those lands could have been ours."

He and Feng Gu were alike that way, strategizing after the battle had already been fought. Oh, Feng Gu. Where was she? Was Chan Hai still bleeding?

"Sometimes I think we Chinese are all a bunch of turtles," Mr. Farmer said. "We poke our heads out and find new lands or discover new inventions. Then, at the slightest noise or shadow, we pull our heads in. We surround ourselves with a hard shell. No ideas get in. We wallow in stinky old ideas while the rest of the world moves on."

I sat down across from him. All of his talk had slowed my anxious heart. For a moment. And, in that moment, I could see past all the unhappy feelings between Chan Hai and me, past the impossibility of our future, past the obligations to my parents and ancestors. None of that nonsense mattered. We wouldn't wallow in stinky old ideas. We would poke our heads out and discover the new together.

I wanted so badly to hold onto Chan Hai, to talk to him. I rubbed my neck with the palm of my hand. I had a strange sensation that he was near, the same feeling I'd had so many weeks ago on the bus that first day we met. Was this a bad sign? I stood up again.

Mr. Farmer continued to lecture on how it was important to exercise care in latching onto the tides of the present—in case the tide changed. But I kept thinking about the past. About a particular day in university. The day I'd been sitting at my metal desk in Education Class. My professor pulled his nub of chalk from the board and stepped aside for us to see his notes. As I put my head down to copy his words onto my paper, I felt the presence of Waipo near.

"You'll do just fine," she whispered in my ear. "Yes, you will."

I knew then, before the principal sent a note to my dorm room, that Waipo was gone to this world. I knew that no matter where she was she would always watch after me. I knew she had stopped by in spirit to say goodbye.

In the tea shop, I didn't hear Chan Hai saying anything. I just felt him. Had the gods brought Mr. Farmer to me so that I would have to listen to his long story, would have to slow down, and would eventually feel the presence of Chan Hai one last time? The hairs on the back of my neck stood up. My limbs trembled. No, no.

"More tea, Little Sister?"

Mr. Farmer pointed to the pot, moving his cup forward on the table with his thick fingers. I poured the last of the tea. The dregs. Then Feng Gu's high-pitched giggle came from the back room, from behind the closed door. I took a deep breath. She was back. All was okay. She wouldn't have left Chan Hai at the clinic alone. But what could be so funny? Was she trying to fool the gods like Mother used to do whenever she came back from visiting a new mother, from not getting a baby boy? Only the small muscle next to Mother's left eye twitched, only her shaking hand when she spooned rice porridge in our bowls revealed that she didn't get what she had wished for. The jealous gods never knew.

I turned my head to the back door, waiting for Feng Gu to come out. Surely she must have heard us out here. Surely she would come out and tell me how Chan Hai was. Unless he was in such bad shape she didn't want to share the news in front of a customer. Even her dear Mr. Farmer.

"Little Sister." Mr. Farmer tapped the table. "Where are you?"

I jumped. Mr. Farmer's tea pooled over the top of his cup onto his hand. I stopped pouring.

"I'm sorry." Fortunately the tea was not hot at all. "I'm sorry," I said again.

"Not to worry." He wiped his hand off with his handkerchief and winked. "Actually, I was thinking the same thing. Nothing like listening to the sound of fresh rain."

I looked outside. The sky was still dark, but there was no rain. I swallowed. What was this dirty old man talking about now? Did he always have sex on his mind? I dropped the teapot on the table and went over to the checkout counter to work the beads on the abacus. I didn't get a rag to clean up the tea spill on the table, hoping that the liquid would drip on him, make him get up and leave. But he used his handkerchief to stop the stream of liquid. He took another sip of tea and stared at the back door, nodding his head with a knowing raise of his eyebrows.

"Rain," he said, licking his lips.

I heard Feng Gu whisper in between tiny laughs. Surely Mr. Farmer was imagining. Surely she was talking to her ancestor. Then again her laughter sounded . . . sounded bubbly. I flicked the beads. Flick. Flick. Flick. Well, at least Chan Hai must be fine if Feng Gu was in the back room making rain. But with whom? I cleared my throat.

"More tea?" I asked.

"To be honest," Mr. Farmer said, removing his cigarettes from his pocket again. "It's not very good. Too bitter." He lit a cigarette and blew a plume of smoke toward the closed door. "But the added entertainment—unbeatable."

My face grew hot, as though Mr. Farmer and I had our heads pressed to the floorboards over our parents' room. Feng Gu's behavior was all so sudden. So strange.

"Did you hear about the fight this afternoon?" I asked in a loud voice. We didn't need to eavesdrop on her intimate moment.

"Everyone knows about that," Mr. Farmer whispered. He waved his arm to shush me.

"I was shocked," I continued, moving the electronic bag sealer around on the check-out counter, as though trying locate the perfect position. Screech. Screech. Screech. "I never imagined big thieves coming to this part of town. Is nothing sacred?"

"It's a shame." Mr. Farmer didn't take his eyes off the door. But he pointed to the ceiling with his cigarette. "And they all went for what? Twenty-four *yuan*?"

"Ninety-two," I said, resting my palms on the sealer. Perhaps I had misread his gesture.

"Still," he shook his head. "Today's better than before the Communists took over. Back then, we had bodies stacked on the roadside like stalks of rice. Dead from hunger. Fighting."

"Wait a minute," I said. Chan Hai had been beaten up. So had College Boy. "Nobody died."

"Sure." He flicked an ash on the ground. "One man's on his way to the village dump. The other guy—a big, strong man who you would think would be a great fighter just stood around and let himself be beaten. He had so many injuries he bled to death. You didn't hear?"

Chan Hai. I saw him again being punched and kicked and beaten. Surely he'd been in shock at the sight of his good friend, now a thief, Little Wu Lu. Chan Hai hadn't just let himself be beaten. He must have been stunned into inaction. I thought of how I'd felt Chan Hai in the room. Just as I had Waipo. The sealer felt large beneath my hands, like the cool slab of a gravestone.

"Feng Gu," I called, rushing to the door to the back room.

I beat against the solid wood. I couldn't wait for her to stop talking with her ancestor or doing whatever she was doing. I couldn't wait for Mr. Farmer to leave. I couldn't wait any longer. I heard the creak of the day bed, the rustle of clothing, more giggling. I turned the knob, pushed hard and fell into the back room.

She sat on the day bed holding a pair of trousers and a shirt. Next to her sat Chan Hai, his legs bare, his golden chest naked. He wore but a ragged pair of briefs. His face was swollen. The blood had stopped dripping, leaving a red gash under his eye like a giant teardrop.

"Feng Gu?" I said.

My voice croaked in the back of my throat. I wished to be a turtle. I didn't want to know. I didn't want to see. Instead I wanted to pull my head inside and hide.

"I just needed some hot water," I said, grabbing the hot water pot from the table and closing the door behind me.

Chapter Forty-Four
The Sky is Blue, the Ocean is Wide

I fell back onto the stool. Mr. Farmer grabbed the hot pot from me. He pushed down on the lid, filling the teapot with steaming water.

"Drink," he said, pouring me a cup.

The tea burned my throat, but no more so than the fire that settled in my chest. How could that man in his underwear be the same one I knew? The same arms that had held onto mine in the duck pond? The same lips that had whispered to me of his heart? His dreams? How could Chan Hai have picked me and played with me like a stick he'd found on the ground, throwing me away into the gutter when he got tired? All those times I'd stared at his face, his long eyelashes, his high cheekbones with their dimples, thinking I could stare at him forever and never be tired. He was like a Buddhist Sutra to me. But I'd been nothing more than a ten-*fen* comic book to him. He had been so good, so convincing. Sharing his dreams for the future, teaching me to swim, wanting me so close. All of that seemed far away, as if an ancestor had dropped a hatchet between Chan Hai and me. The cut wasn't clean though. I felt a piece of me missing.

"What?" I took another gulp of tea.

"I said—why did you do like that? Poor Feng Gu. Victims need soothing, too." He pushed his stool back, sighed, lit another cigarette. "You know about the Japanese war, right?"

Mr. Farmer talked, his words falling down around me, only some of them penetrating my buzzing brain. My heart thumped in my stomach like a ball rolling in an empty barrel. Feng Gu had always expressed such hate for Chan Hai. How had that changed? Why? Mr. Farmer talked of the time Japan came to our village and forced everyone into the small temple by the seaside. Was that the same temple Chan Hai and I had made love behind?

The temple was tiny, Mr. Farmer said, but the Japs beat the villagers with wooden planks until everyone squeezed inside. His father had been just a young man then, had been busy carving a stool. That was the family business. So his father had been practicing, carving a stool with a phoenix dragon on it. Not an easy thing to do. His father was one of the last ones to gather. An angry Japanese soldier whacked his father into the temple, whacking him so badly, he could never use his hand again. A young woman had stayed up all night nursing his father's wounds. Mr. Farmer winked at me. He was born ten months later.

He paused so I could say something, nod. Indicate that I was listening. My lips parted, but no words came out. I couldn't drag my spirit away from the back room where Chan Hai sat in his tattered underwear. I had trusted him, trusted him so much that I had already decided our future was together. How could he do this?

Mr. Farmer's brow furrowed in concern, as if he didn't know how to handle this woman so shocked at her boss's behavior. His eyes were no longer filled with mirth. He leaned over to refill my tea cup.

"I've had enough," I said, waving him away. The burning liquid didn't put out the fire in my chest. The feeling only spread—to my eyes. "Enough," I repeated.

"The sky is blue, and the ocean is wide," he said, lifting his arms above his head.

Why didn't I feel his optimism? Why did I feel like the end of his cigarette, smoke circling up through my insides, making it difficult to breathe, making my nose tingle, my eyes burn? The daybed squeaked. Footsteps sounded. Mr. Farmer glanced toward the door to the back room.

"I guess I'd better make a move." He stood.

Me, too. I'd never left early before, practically begging Feng Gu to keep me until the last minute every day. Besides I still had the shop's ten *yuan*.

"Tell me about that temple," I said, suddenly feeling closer to this philandering history lover than the man I'd given my heart to. "Which temple was it? Did your grandfather ever teach you to carve? How did you get into the nightclub business?" I stabbed at the air with questions, hoping he'd latch onto one and pick out a different memory.

"I need to make a move," he repeated, letting all my questions float to the ground.

He picked up his wet handkerchief from the table, stuffed the cloth in his pocket and hurried toward the front exit. I followed. I couldn't sit here and pretend my world had not shifted. That the sky was blue, the ocean wide. I followed him outside as though he were an important customer, walking him toward the bus depot.

"Thank you," I called after him. "Come again."

The further I walked from the shop, the harder it was to turn around. Returning to the tea shop seemed like too much effort, like retrieving a lost hat from the fields after a big rain. The mud would suck at my feet, pull me down.

Someone brushed up against me. Always someone brushed up against me in this town. So many people. With bags and boxes and carts. How would people move in twenty years? In fifty? Too bad the Emperor had closed China. We could have used that space in the Americas.

The bus depot across the street looked inviting. I didn't have my purse, but I had the ten *yuan*. I stood and stared at the people boarding the buses. I would join them. Someone else ran past me, bumping my shoulder, sending a shiver down my spine. I knew before I even looked who it was. He stopped right in front of me.

"You must have had a big customer," Chan Hai said, indicating the money I held in my hand. He was fully dressed now.

My natural reaction was to tell the truth. That, no, I didn't have a big customer. This was the tea shop's ten *yuan*. But, why should I bother being honest about all the trouble I had gone through buying the *Yunnan Bai Yao* to stop his face from bleeding, when he was so busy, so busy, so busy. My chest burned again.

"Mr. Farmer," I said, staring at the bill in my hand. "Bought a kilo of the Golden Medley."

The words came like dead wood from my lips. Like the dead wood the Japs had used to beat the villagers. Full of sweat and blood but no feeling.

"You're such a good salesgirl," Chan Hai said. "That's what Feng Gu wanted me to tell you. And to give you this."

He handed me a thick envelope. My bonus money? Where was she? Too ashamed to show her face? And since when did she trust Chan Hai to do anything? Especially pass along such a large amount of money. Then again maybe this was their plan. To give Chan Hai and me time alone, so he could brush my anger away like crumbs from the table. I could almost see Feng Gu telling him what to say. Surely she didn't want to risk losing me. For, despite her insistence that every new idea was hers, that I was just a foolish intellectual, she knew I was helping the shop. I looked up at him, at those dark brown eyes. He did not look away. But silence had its cup on us, as if we were two bugs trapped under a jar.

"Feng Gu's good," Chan Hai finally said.

He looked with great exaggeration at the back of his pants, lifting up the sleeve of his t-shirt. Small stitches made with great care closed the tears in his clothing. I looked away. A big lump, like the seed of a plum, blocked my throat. I felt shame that he tried to fill the air with such excuses, excuses which swirled around like exhaust from an old tractor, settling on me and making me feel dirty. Besides, if Feng Gu was so good, why had she needed Chan Hai to take his clothes off? Why had she needed half an hour to sew a tiny hole? Why had she found the chore so hilarious?

"Feng Gu's an old . . ." He cleared his throat. "An old friend."

I walked past him, up the street and into the tea shop. I headed straight for the back room. Feng Gu stood by the refrigerator.

"You have to feel this." She opened the door and stuck her head in the refrigerator. "It's cold in here now."

"It certainly is." I tossed the ten *yuan* and the *Yunnan Bai Yao* in the bottom of the cold box and grabbed my purse. "I have to get home. I don't feel well."

"Yes, you rest up," she said, giving me a lopsided grin. "Tomorrow is going to be busy. I just know it."

I ran down the alley, my face as hot as a burning coal. A drop of saltwater rolled down my cheek. I brushed the liquid away, knowing that if I didn't, my face would rain for days. Surely I was overreacting. But I heard Chan Hai's neighbor's voice in the back of my head, saying, "Oh, he's off with Feng Gu." I heard Feng Gu's bubbly giggling. I saw him naked. Perhaps, as usual, I was the last to figure this elephant out. Perhaps everyone I passed—the shoe-heel fixer, key maker, tobacco seller—knew of Feng Gu and Chan Hai playing in the back room of the tea shop, knew of my shame.

I ran across the bridge, down the street, to the park. What would Madame Paper Cutter say now? I longed to touch her warm hands. She would know what to do. And I could help her gather her cuttings before the rains started. I stopped at the edge of the park. As if a spirit had punched me in the stomach. Her spot was now occupied by a blue tarp and lots of little clay statues. Yes, she was home with her sweet daughter. How could I have forgotten?

I walked by, nodding at Mr. Palm Reader. He didn't have a customer. In fact, what few shoppers wandered through the park, did so at a quick pace, as if the sky would burst open at any moment.

I had been so wrong. I had been certain Feng Gu had cared for the lecherous Mr. Farmer, not black Chan Hai. The water chestnut seller stood to the side of the park, peeling chestnuts. A motorcycle zoomed over the sidewalk, zigzagging through a group of businessmen and an a woman with a big shopping bag. I looked back up the road, certain if I stared long enough I would see Chan Hai waiting to give me more shame.

"Little Sister," a voice called. Mr. Palm Reader.

He beckoned to me from where he sat on his stool. What would my palms say? Would Mr. Palm Reader only see darkness and disaster? I clenched my fists together.

"No need," I said, shaking my head.

He left his stool and came toward me. Did my hands call out to him? Could he see straight through me? I turned to hurry away.

"Wait," he called, coming up to me and tapping me on the arm with a piece of paper. "Here. Madame Paper Cutter left this for you. I meant to give it to you yesterday, but I was busy with a customer."

I took the paper from his smooth soiled fingers. A dirt-smudged envelope. Had she written me a letter?

"Thank you," I said.

I stopped next to the water-chestnut seller to get out of the flow of people traffic. I extracted a thin cutting. A thin cutting of a phoenix, the magical bird of the Emperor. The details were so intricate. This must have taken her hours and hours to make. I looked inside the envelope. Nothing else. No letter, no home address, no phone where she could be reached. I turned the bird over. Nothing written on either side or in the corners. I turned the cutting back over. It was then I noticed the wings. She had cut a tiny Chinese character all along the sides of the wings. "Fly."

Fly. Dear Madame Paper Cutter. How had I ever doubted her? Why had I expected her to not care for me? Perhaps I was no better than Feng Gu. Feng Gu who mouthed off to everyone, seeing dragons wherever she turned. I wasn't as noisy, but my heart was no less frightened. I returned the cutting to the envelope. Just that one person, that one word of encouragement, lifted the weights from my heart. Fly. I wasn't sure what that meant for me now. For the moment, I didn't care. For the moment, the sky was wide, the ocean was blue. I pressed the envelope to my chest as I walked toward the bus depot.

Chapter Forty-Five
A Sweet Breeze

The bus lumbered down the road. Heat strangled my arms and legs. Drops of perspiration rolled down the sides of my cheek, the back of my neck. Normally Chan Hai and I would be so busy talking that the bus ride seemed to take less than a character to get from the town to the village. But today, despite the Phoenix in my purse, I was aware of every turn in the road, every stop. I felt the bus go over the main road to our section of the village, smelled the stink of death and knew we neared the eel factory. The smell seeped into my pores and strangled me. I couldn't bear to stay on the bus a moment longer. Even if the bus was faster. Even if Mother did expect me home early to meet with Madame Matchmaker. Perhaps the angry woman would be draped in white, the color of death.

"*Xia che*," I cried out with what was surely my only remaining breath. "My stop."

The bus pulled over to the side of the road and dumped me out. I walked along the road, breathing. A car whizzed by. A group of middle-school boys waded around me, breaking arms with one another only long enough to pass. I felt the presence of someone. Perhaps, this time Waipo was there.

I glanced at my watch. Madame Matchmaker wouldn't be at our house yet. Instead of turning at the pink castle, I kept walking, toward the other side of the village to the spot where we had buried Waipo. Along the way, I stopped at the provisioner and bought some incense, then I followed a dirt path behind the provisioner which led to several vegetable paddies. The grasses had been stamped down by many feet. Mine had not trod here for weeks. My shoes quickly filled with dry dirt, but I didn't have the energy or care to stop and shake them out. I didn't have the concern to avoid letting my shoe catch on a rock.

"Argh." I tripped and stumbled to the ground. The incense tumbled with me, flying out of my hand. Again I felt Waipo near. I gathered the sticks of incense. Fortunately none had broken. Then I stood. Pains shot down my right leg, burning my toes.

"Why didn't I see that stupid rock?" I cried out.

I took off my cruddy old shoes and threw them into a heap of corn stalks by the side of the paddy. A breeze blew. Waipo's voice filled my soul.

"Well, dear little gem," her soft voice whispered. "You didn't see the restaurant full of villagers preparing to go overseas illegally. You didn't see the snakehead. You didn't see College Boy. You didn't see Chan Hai. There are a lot of things you don't see. That you may never."

"Why not?" I called out to her.

She didn't respond. Perhaps I'd offended her. Perhaps only the ancestors could see everything. And I would just have to wait.

I limped over to her grave which stood round and alone at the edge of this field of vegetables. Mother rarely came here. Her time was to be spent with Father's family. That's where she belonged. But Mother's elder brother took good care of the grave, keeping the weeds from growing, keeping Waipo well-fed and loved. The beauty here was so simple, my eyes tingled.

Out to the left, mountain after mountain was dotted with fields and the occasional round sparkle of a grave. Out to the right, somewhere way out there, the sea, that space that went on and on forever, with no walls. Mei Ling was out there somewhere, having success in Japan maybe. Earning lots of money maybe. Did she feel so alone? Did her heart burn? Was her family worried about her marriage or were they too busy buying telephones and bigger televisions?

I rubbed my eyes. A farmer coaxed a bull across the field. A group of young children ran along the dirt islands between the fields, trying not to lose their balance. Everything looked so normal. Why did this normal life suddenly look so strange? So painful to see? I lit the three sticks of incense, waved them up and down, called to Waipo. Then I knelt down and put the incense in the small holder at the front of the grave. I rested my head on her cool stone. At least here, next to her, my world felt safe. Full of love.

I'm not sure how long I stayed there. But, when I sat up, I felt calm, as if Waipo were nearby, running her soft, wrinkled hands through my hair.

"Don't be too sad," she whispered.

"I should be home." I patted her stone. Mother held enough sorrow in her heart. The last thing she needed was to be chastised alone by Madame Matchmaker.

"Take your time." A small breeze caressed my cheek. Waipo had always caressed my cheek that way. I lay my head back down on her cool stone and let her soothe the heat from my face, the sadness from my heart.

"Oh, Waipo," I said. "What is this?"

"It is what it is," Waipo whispered.

Another breeze blew, this time so hard, the hair raised off my neck sending a chill down my back. I heard a scuffling in the dirt right behind me. But my head was so heavy, I couldn't look up at the passing villager.

"Waipo," I said, sure she was as close to me as if she were sitting there, her hair tied in a knot on top of her head, her hands picking out wasted soybean shells or scrubbing the dirt from the knees in my pants or picking the dead leaves from a bundle of vegetables. "I still love him."

The air went still. A drop of sweat trickled down my chest. Perhaps she was disgusted by my selfish heart. The back of my neck went stiff.

"Waipo." I heard a deep voice behind me. "I still love her too."

Chapter Forty-Six
Elder Brother

Had he followed me home? How long had he been standing behind me? I felt his dark brown eyes staring at me. Waiting for me to look up at him like that first time we saw each other on the bus. How much had he heard? Why did he have to strip my heart naked and beat it over and over like a butcher pounding a fresh piece of meat? I stared at my dirty feet.

"Why do you follow me like a spy?" I asked in a low voice.

"Everyone says I must keep a watch on you." He made a shallow-sounding laugh. "Or I'll lose you to a bucket of gold."

Zi Mei again? Her gossip was not only harmful, it was old. Like a parable which hadn't been changed to fit the times.

"What difference does it make?" I stood with one hand resting on the cool gravestone for support. My ankle felt sore. My heart ached. "You still have Feng Gu to 'sew your pants'."

"You don't understand." He stepped so close, I felt the cloth of his t-shirt against my nose. I could almost taste the sweat dripping down his neck.

"I'm not blind," I said. "And I may have a college degree, but that doesn't make me totally stupid."

"I know," he said, putting his thick fingers under my chin, turning my face up to look at him. The cut at the corner of his eye puffed out black and crusty. His eyes looked cold, angry. "I should have told you earlier."

Oh gods. All this time I thought he'd come to the shop each day to see me. That he'd brought an extra ice cream or oyster cake for Feng Gu out of shyness. So as not to appear too intimate with me. Oh, what a fool I'd been.

I turned to go. But he reached out and held onto my shoulder, put his arm around my neck like a thick necklace. I wish I could say that I was so full of anger I swept that damp golden weight off of me and marched away with my head high. That I didn't want this cheater anywhere near me. That's what Mei Ling would have said to do. She was wise to men and their ways. But his touch was like a drug. When his lips brushed the top of my head, all I felt was a warmth inside that made tears come to my eyes.

"The reservoir is nearby," he said, his breath caressing the tip of my ear.

"And?" I asked inserting a shrillness to my voice.

I forced myself to take his arm off my neck. I stepped far away. Surely he didn't think we could just go on like this, the three of us.

"I need . . . " Chan Hai paused so long I looked back. He folded his hands together in front of him. His eyes locked onto mine. "I need you to come there with me."

"You must be joking," I said. "It's going to rain. Besides Mother expects me home. She's not doing well. She's—" I clamped my mouth shut. This was no longer his business.

"Please," he said. "Please follow me."

A bitter taste coated my mouth, as if I had swallowed a piece of metal. I had followed him. I had followed him more than he ever knew.

"Maybe some other time," I said. "I hurt my ankle back—"

"I know," he said. He stepped close, bent down and thrust me over his shoulder.

"Chan Hai," I shouted. "Put me down."

An old woman and her daughter passed us, carrying handfuls of leafy vegetables freshly picked from the field. The daughter pointed to me. The old woman put a hand over that finger and plastered a smile on her face as she hurried the child on past us.

"I need to get home," I said.

He continued walking. He walked through the fields, balancing on the narrow dirt pathways like a man from the circus. Up ahead was the quarry, the closed, silent quarry. Further up the mountain, the reservoir.

"I didn't say yes," I called to him. "I didn't say I'd follow you."

"I know." He stopped and craned his neck to look at me. "But often your mouth makes noises that your heart doesn't mean."

He was right. His wisdom silenced me. As if the gods spoke through him.

At the edge of the reservoir, the water mirrored the dark sky. The large grave across the way now held remnants of a feast— chicken bones and paper wrappings. An empty wine bottle. Fresh chrysanthemums filled a cup in the center. Bundles of incense stood upright. I wished to be back talking with Waipo.

"Everyday I think of this place." Chan Hai set me down gently. "Especially on a hot day like today."

I winced from the weight on my ankle. For what purpose did we have to come all the way here? Not even the bathers were out today. I hopped to a nearby rock.

"It's not so hot," I said, wiping away a drop of perspiration that slid down my cheek.

"Well, I didn't get to ride in the palanquin," he said.

He pulled off his t-shirt. I looked up, confused. He made circling motions with his arms, as if to rid kinks in his shoulders. His "palanquin." He winked at me, bringing his lips into a small smile. How could he make jokes?

"You flatter yourself." I leaned down and rubbed my ankle.

"Never."

"You must have been sure I'd come here," I said.

"I've never doubted you for a minute." His words brought heat to my cheeks. I had doubted him. Then again I had had reason to.

He removed a pocketknife and a small lime from his pants. Then he knelt down to rub my legs with the stinging juice. I put my palm up to stop him. I didn't need the mosquito repellent. I wouldn't be staying that long.

"When I was a child," he said, indicating the reservoir with his arm. "There was lots more water. We got a lot more rain back then. It was so deep in the middle, you couldn't touch the bottom."

I nodded, and Chan Hai kept talking, talking as if he were explaining village life to someone else, talking as if he couldn't stop. And I kept wondering why. Why were we here? What was the point?

"I used to come here with my cousins and friends," he said. "Especially my best friend, Feng Gu's *gege*."

"Feng Gu's older brother?" I repeated.

Despite a slight breeze, my skirt clung to the sweat around my waist. My skin itched. Heat radiated off Chan Hai's body in quick pulses.

"Father always told me not to come here," he said, pacing up and down in front of me. "Threatened to beat me with the cane if I disobeyed."

What nonsense. Not his father caning him for swimming—every child got that punishment. But Feng Gu didn't have a *gege*. I would have known if she did. In fact, I would have worked side by side with him everyday, if she did, as he would be in charge of the tea shop. Not Feng Gu. Or maybe he would be overseas earning lots of money, which Feng Gu would talk about over and over again until my ears vibrated.

"We came everyday in the summer anyway," he said. "We would swim and cool off. Then we'd sit out on the rocks until our bodies and underwear dried and we could get dressed and go back home. As if we had been doing nothing more than playing stones."

I reached down and grabbed a handful of small stones. This was all very interesting. Or it would have been if I didn't know him so well. If I hadn't seen him with Feng Gu. I swallowed the salty taste in my mouth.

"Feng Gu liked swimming," Chan Hai said.

He brought me all the way here to tell me this? That he and Feng Gu had a long history? That I was never so important to him. Maybe he just called Feng Gu Elder Brother for being so brave. Obviously she was able to swim, whereas I'd done so poorly.

I imagined Feng Gu at the far end of the reservoir, holding onto a stick of bamboo and teaching herself to stay above the water. Not complaining about the liquid dripping in her eyes. I imagined Chan Hai, as he got older, interested in this girl splashing around in her underwear. Maybe he'd offered to help her swim, as he had done with me, his strong arms covering hers as he showed her to stroke outwards, outwards, like a water bug.

I tightened my grip around the rocks. Sharp edges sliced indentations into my palm. Chan Hai was just like any other man, Mei Ling would certainly say. So proud he had to push my face into his dirt so I would know how insignificant I was. I swallowed the lump of salt in my throat and stood on shaky legs. I stared across the water at the gravestone. The cold, round cement stone felt lodged in my chest.

"So," I asked. "That's it?"

"One day," he said. He shook his head. He looked out into the water. He shifted on his feet. "It was so hot—hotter than anything I can ever remember. Each time Gege and I got out of the reservoir, sweat poured down our backs."

There was that Elder Brother again. When had he started calling Feng Gu Elder Brother? When had he started playing with her? I shifted the rocks from one hand to the other. I was tempted to throw them in his face, hoping at least one would cut him as deep as he was cutting up my heart.

"Eventually," he said. "I could tell from the sun that it was almost dinner time—and I pointed this out to Gege. 'We really need to go home,' I told him. All our friends—all the other kids—had left."

Chan Hai paced back and forth in front of me. His balled fists stuffed in his pockets. His eyes on the ground.

"With the sun gone," he said. "I worried there would be no way to dry off my under shorts. Gege still didn't want to leave, though. It was one of those nights when the heat vibrated in the air long after the sun had disappeared. I hoped that this vibration would be strong enough to dry my underpants, but I had the bad feeling that it would just make them damper. I told Gege to come on, we were going to be in big trouble already."

Chan Hai stopped. He rubbed his temples with his fingers. He opened his mouth to speak. Then closed his trembling lips.

"Ha," he whispered. "Gege said, 'If we're going to be in trouble, we might as well make the most of it.'"

That sounded exactly like Feng Gu. Had she swam naked or in her underwear? Perhaps she'd wanted to stay until all the others left so they could do some other kind of swimming. Was he going to tell me every dirty detail?

"I acted as though I were leaving," Chan Hai continued. "And I went out to the road. Gege was not a very good swimmer, so I was sure I wouldn't be waiting alone long." Chan Hai laughed that shallow strange laugh again. "I was wrong. But, just as I tired of waiting and was about to return to the reservoir and show big anger, our brigade leader came by on his tractor. 'Hey, little friend,' he called. 'What are you doing out here so late?'

"I was pleased he couldn't tell from my damp hair and wet pants what I'd been doing. I lied and told him I was just walking home. He offered me a ride. I was stuck. How could I refuse when it was already so late? So, I took his offer. At the time, I thought how lucky I was that I got a ride back home and stubborn Gege would have to walk. I even had an excuse to tell my parents—how I was helping the brigade leader. They would hear us putt-putting our way up the road. They would be so impressed. And, riding on that tractor, I was flying faster than even the quickest mosquitoes."

Despite myself, I felt sorry for Feng Gu. How could Chan Hai leave her behind in that deep, dark water, even if he did think her so brave that he called her Elder Brother?

"That night, Feng Gu came to me," Chan Hai said, his voice as nervous as a small boy caught stealing sugar cane from the back of a truck. "She came to me when I was shutting the front door for the night."

I imagined her having walked all the way back from the reservoir, her long hair still damp, making her white blouse see-through at important spots. I imagined her slipping into the door before he shut it for the night, slipping upstairs with him before his parents saw. Anger burned in my stomach.

"You eye of a fart," I said. I shouldn't have listened to all this detail. My throat tasted sour. A tingling burned up to the top of my nose. "You—y—you bastard."

I threw the fistful of rocks at his face. My aim was not accurate or strong, but he stepped forward into the line of fire, compensating for my error and strength. I leaned down and picked up another handful. Again, with his help, all my rocks hit him full in face. Why was he allowing me to do this? I felt a loud knocking on the door to my conscience. A squeezing sensation around my chest. But I picked up another handful of rocks.

"Is Gege here?" Chan Hai continued like an explosion. He knelt in front of me, his dark eyes glassy. "'Tell him to come home,' she said. 'It's way too late to be out playing.'"

I was confused now. I thought Feng Gu was Gege. Just as he had taken to calling me Water Bug.

"Not one sunrise happens without me thinking of him," Chan Hai said. He turned on his knees and nodding across the reservoir to the gravestone.

Oh no. Oh no. Oh no. So, the picture of the young boy at the tea shop wasn't Feng Gu's grandfather. Or uncle. But her elder brother. No wonder Feng Gu had warned me away from Chan Hai. She must hate him to the core. Her elder brother was not only gone, but now she was the only one to take care of the shop, her parents, her ancestors. I grabbed Chan Hai's shoulders and pulled him up on the rock next to me. His body was as limp as old celery. I held him tight, kissing each mark on his face, letting the handful of rocks trickle down his bare back.

"What if I hadn't taken that ride from the brigade leader?" he said. "What if I'd taken Father's threat of a caning more seriously? What if I'd stayed to help my friend swim until he was finished?"

Perhaps this accident was why Father had warned me away from Chan Hai as well. And Madame Matchmaker. I ran my hand through his hair, trying to massage away his guilt and sorrow.

"What if," I whispered. "Feng Gu's *gege* hadn't been so stubborn?"

Chan Hai let go of a big rush of air, as if it had been trapped somewhere deep inside for a long time. How long had he been caught like this? Frozen by his guilt and his black reputation.

"What if," I continued. "Gege had been concerned about you getting in trouble? About you getting a beating?"

I rubbed the back of his neck. His muscles were so tied in knots, they felt like the metal balls sold at the market to increase coordination and blood circulation in old people. He let go of another rush of air and with it came a flood of tears. He kept wiping away the tears with the back of his hand. But no matter how fast he wiped, the tears continued. Certainly he was embarrassed for showing such big emotion. So I wasn't surprised when he stood up, away from me. He unzipped his trousers and let them fall to the ground. He took a few steps into the water and dove in.

As I sat there, waiting for him to emerge, the village loudspeaker crackled with music. Who would make the announcement this time? Did they still need donations for the theater? When would they be showing the opera of "The Butterfly Lovers?" How did one walk through a day that a child or close friend no longer filled? Dear Chan Hai. Poor Cheng Min. Even Mother. How many times had she opened her heart and knit a blanket to include a new baby boy and then been told no?

Mother. I needed to be home with her and the angry Madame Matchmaker. But, compared to Chan Hai's sadness, that concern felt as important as a stray hair in my face.

How deep was Chan Hai's responsibility? Had he promised to care for Feng Gu's parents like a filial elder son? Had he promised to have his first-born son take Feng Gu's family name? To marry her? I couldn't wait for him to come out of the water. I waded knee-deep in the reservoir. The thick mud below oozed between my toes. Something rubbed against my leg.

"Chan Hai?" I called, holding my skirt with one hand and feeling around in the water with the other.

He emerged in front of me, rubbing his face as if awakening from a nightmare. In the dusk, he looked old and tired. I couldn't bear to barrage him with even one of my questions. Not now.

"I should have explained everything to you earlier." He rubbed the water off his body as he waded out. He picked up his shirt, as though suddenly embarrassed by his nakedness.

"It's a big story to tell." I pulled my feet out of the mud and up onto shore.

Had he told me the whole story, or was I to guess the rest? Maybe he and Feng Gu had already been promised to one another, just as Mother had wanted to promise me to the computer science professor. I watched him struggle to get the t-shirt over his damp skin. His chest was smooth and strong. A drop of water rolled down off his nipple, like one more tear. I wanted to reach out and brush it away. Instead I sat back on the rock and let my feet dangle in the cool water.

"Wednesday was the fifteenth anniversary of . . . " He looked up at the gravestone.

"I see."

That explained the incense, flowers and feast leftovers on the gravestone. Surely they had held a big feast to celebrate the anniversary. No wonder he and Feng Gu were together. Now everything started to make sense, like the way grains of rice start out floating all over the place and then boil up to form a thick, cohesive pot of porridge. Still, one uncooked grain of rice stuck out of that smooth porridge. Each time I thought of Chan Hai naked in the back of the tea shop, my throat constricted. I might as well have broadcast my thoughts over the village loudspeaker. Chan Hai sat down next to me on the rock, rubbed his foot against mine.

"Feng Gu wanted to talk to me today," he said.

I raised my eyebrows. Now wasn't the time to push him. But I always talked better with my clothes on, I thought.

"She said she always thought of me as the . . ." He rubbed one big hand over the other, as though washing away dirt. "An enemy. Until this afternoon. She spotted Little Wu Lu on the bridge and just assumed I would help him, since he was my good childhood friend. She never expected me to save the shop."

I nodded and pulled on my ear. That grain of rice still poked its rough head up. But I couldn't bear to do more than pretend this was a fine explanation for sitting naked next to Feng Gu.

"She said it's time to make peace," he said, wiping his eyes again. "She said she wants to have me as—" His strong shoulders glistened with water from the reservoir. He sat up straight. I held my breath. "She said she wants to have me as the big brother she no longer has."

I let my breath out. That wasn't too big a responsibility. There was still room for me. Maybe.

"By sewing your pants?" I asked. "I would have—"

"And helping me find the right connection to re-open the quarry."

I nodded. I pushed that uncooked grain of rice into the mixture. I believed him. We sat watching the dark water. Our feet swishing in and out. But there was something still lodged between us, like a cold stone.

"Now you know everything," he said.

He let the sentence hang there. I pulled my feet up onto the rocks and wrapped my arms around my knees. I rocked back and forth. I thought of Father's twenty-thousand *yuan* debt. To me, this shame seemed worse than a death fifteen years ago.

"I also have no elder brother," I said. I knew he knew that. "Mother tried so hard to adopt." Crickets sounded. Water dripped from Chan Hai's hair onto the rock. Drip. Drip. Drip. I sighed. "My parents . . . my father is a big responsibility."

"So." He rubbed his thighs. "You are promised to a man whose pockets are lined with gold?"

"No," I said looking him straight in the eye. "That's old gossip."

His face broke into a smile, showing the dents in his cheeks. He wiped away more tears from his face. He put his wet hand over mine.

"But my family," I said. "We are always scraping here and there—"

"Life." Chan Hai squeezed my hand, stopping my words. "Life with me will not be easy. But it would be nice to wake up every morning and see you."

I could hear Father already. "Ha! A refrigerator salesman? He'll never be able to take care of us. Don't you care anything about your parents?" I could already feel Chan Hai's pain as he struggled to do so anyway.

"I couldn't allow you to do that," I said. "My father—you don't know my father."

"You don't know all the things I can do." He put his hand on my knee. "Besides, I'm sure the quarry will re-open soon. I have a good feeling."

A lump formed at the base of my throat. This time, one as sweet as honey. I had a good feeling too.

"We should go," he said, kissing the back of my hand, the tip of my knee.

"Yes," I said. "It's probably getting late."

The dark sky was not a good indication of the time. I'd left the tea shop before closing. Still, I was sure I'd spent all that extra time visiting with Waipo and talking with Chan Hai. Mother—perhaps even Madame Matchmaker—would be waiting. Would they take this marriage proposal as good news? We could let Madame Matchmaker claim credit. Her name would not be tarnished. Much.

I'd experienced so many different emotions today while the clouds gathered together in the sky. Fear, anger, jealousy, hate, sadness, relief, forgiveness. The heavens still threatened a big storm. However, all those forces which had pounded on my heart and head had disappeared into the distant past. In their place was exhaustion. How would I ever walk all the way home? Surely Chan Hai must feel the same.

"You must be tired." I ran my forefinger around the cut at the corner of his eye.

"No." Chan Hai stood and put out his hand to help me up. "Not tired."

"Hungry?" I asked.

"Very."

His eyes burned into mine. He kissed my palm, the inside of my wrist. When I stood, he leaned down and kissed my forehead, my nose, my neck.

"Let's go," he said, kissing me so deep and long I knew that the home to where we headed required no walking at all.

Chapter Forty-Seven
Six Bowls

My body felt attached to Chan Hai's. His heartbeat sounded deep and strong as we lay together on the ground, our clothes piled beneath us. The water in the reservoir shimmered with light. I knew that light was from the moon which shone around the clouds like a lamp behind a black curtain. I imagined the shimmering beauty a sign from Feng Gu's *gege* that Chan Hai's darkness had been lifted. I ran my fingers over Chan Hai's arm.

"I'm starving." He lifted his head up and kissed me on the forehead.

"I could make you some dinner," I suggested. I peeled myself off him and swatted in the dark at a mosquito.

"Soon," he said. "You'll be tired of making me rice. I have a big appetite."

He pulled me back to him and kissed me long and slow. But, this time, the hunger in his tummy was stronger than the other hunger. He sat up and gave my nose a soft tap. Then he stood and walked into the reservoir. I saw a faint outline of him splashing himself clean.

"Come in," he called from the water, his voice low and husky.

"I'm okay," I said.

I felt around the rock for my bra and panties. My body felt thick with sweat and dirt. I would take a shower at home.

"Trust me." Chan Hai put his hand out, beckoning.

Trust me. So many weeks I had not dared to let go of control over my feelings, not dared to allow someone else to know better, not dared to trust. Finally I was free. I was flying. Madame Paper Cutter would surely be happy for me. I pushed myself up and into the water, knowing that even if I stumbled he'd catch me before I fell.

He rubbed water over my shoulders, my arms, my breasts. His touch was so gentle. Yet full of efficiency. I looked up in the direction of the gravestone. I knew how Feng Gu's *gege* must have felt. I too wanted to stay just a little longer. I didn't want to leave our little piece of heaven, never mind that the world had continued to turn, that Mother and Madame Matchmaker expected me home.

"There you go." Chan Hai carried me up to the bank and set me down on the ground. "Good as new."

He brushed the droplets of water from my body. My heart pounded. One minute this man was part of me, couldn't stay out of me. The next he was leaving. I didn't want to separate from him.

"I can heat you some dinner at my house." I pulled on my skirt.

"Thanks for the offer," he said, zipping his cotton trousers. "But your parents . . . it's late. They'll think we've been , well . . . "

"But we have." I leaned against him, wanting to be as one again. I wanted him to hold me close, to quell the fire that re-kindled between my legs.

We had talked until my mouth felt like rubber, but there was still so much to discuss. Wedding plans and the future. Would he want to continue on at the quarry even if Feng Gu helped get the place re-opened? Would he ever get to work at a nursery? Would I ever get to teach? Frogs croaked. Crickets sang. A bat whooshed overhead. I turned my head toward the grave of Feng Gu's *gege*. The moonlight on the reservoir rippled, as though the water—was that Gege?—chuckled. I understood. None of my questions, these details mattered. For Chan Hai and I inhabited this world now as one.

We stumbled through the tall grasses, the fields and along the streets. Sometimes our path was lit, when the moon would jump out from behind the clouds or a street lamp shone. But sometimes the path before us was so dark all we could do was hope that the silverish strip we followed continued to be the road. That this path we crept along didn't lead us to one of the roadside ditches, which dropped down a long way and was full of human waste and the occasional dead animal. I held on tight to Chan Hai in the darkness, listening to the soft approval of the crickets. His arm felt like a part of me.

A clap of thunder sounded. A drop of rain fell. Then another. Chan Hai didn't change his pace. But I thought about the typhoon. Those dark clouds which had been hovering over us for days were finally going to let loose. He would get caught in the middle of the downpour, if he took me all the way to my door. Besides, he'd had a long day, moving refrigerators, fighting his childhood friend, revealing a secret he'd buried for so long. His head must be numb. His stomach must be as empty as a drum. When we reached the pink castle, I stopped. I knew the rest of the way home so well, I could walk it blind.

"You better get on home now," I said. "I'll be fine from here."

"You sure," he asked. The rain fell in steady drops now.

"I'm sure," I said. A pair of headlights appeared through the drizzle, the vehicle heading toward his side of the village. "Besides, here comes your bus."

He dug into the pocket of his pants. Was he searching for a *yuan* note to pay the bus driver? We would struggle for a long time, he and I, even with my regular job and my bonus *yuan*. Father would keep us struggling. I felt a surge of pain.

He took his hand out of his pocket and held it up to flag the bus down. Then he turned and slipped a necklace over my head. Dear Chan Hai and his gifts. Pork buns, ice cream, pants. Now this.

"No, no," I said. "I have no need for this."

"I want you to have it," he said. "I saw a woman selling this in the park and thought of you."

I felt the object on the end of the string. Small, plastic, pointy ends. A bird? An angel? I couldn't wait to get home to the mirror in the kitchen and see.

"No, really," I said, refusing out of custom. "I have no need."

"It's for you," he insisted.

The bus swerved to a stop, the wheels spraying us with water. Chan Hai held my arm with one hand. He ran his hand through my hair with the other.

"See you tomorrow, Water Bug" he said, giving my arm a squeeze.

He jumped up onto the bus. The ticket taker waited for me to follow. I shook my head. She pulled the doors closed with a squeak. I watched Chan Hai clunk up the stairs, wiping water from his face. Then the bus pulled away and all was dark. He was gone.

Tomorrow. I would see him again tomorrow. But that was years away. I pulled the necklace from around my neck. The points poked my fingers. As I passed the pink castle where light shone from an upstairs room, I looked down in my hand. A bird. A beautiful yellow glass bird. I thought of the time in the reservoir when I'd made fun of Chan Hai, saying, always saying, "Follow me." "You sound like a bird," I'd told him. Was that why he had chosen this? I smiled at his sense of humor. I was ready to follow this bird. I held onto the necklace and started counting the seconds until tomorrow.

I passed the middle school. Sixth Cousin's shell of a house stood nearby. The one he had started but had been unable to finish. That house no longer seemed like an embarrassment, shouting poverty and stupidity. The naked windows now seemed a promise, a promise of something better to come.

I passed Third Uncle's stone engraving shop. The tools had long since stopped whirring. But, from the wall behind the shop, I heard the click-clack sound of *mahjong* tiles being mixed. Too bad Father wasn't behind one of these friendly walls playing. "It is what it is," Waipo would say. Who knew? Maybe tonight he would be as lucky as I was. Not only was my purse filled with a large bonus but my heart overflowed with thoughts of Chan Hai.

I passed Prehistoric's field and looked over toward the tarp-covered house. A small light shone from behind one of the black plastic sheets covering a side window. Kind of like the moon. I wanted to cross over and knock on the door and tell Cheng Min my news. I had a man I loved. He wanted to marry me. But I had been away from home too long. Surely Madame Matchmaker had gone home already. Mother would not be pleased. I needed her to be in a good mood when I told her about Chan Hai. I needed her to help me convince Father that this was a good match.

I walked as fast as possible on my bare feet. Bumps formed where mosquitoes had feasted on my naked skin. My body smelled of more than water from the reservoir. I was emerging from my drop of heaven. I'd better sneak in the shower outside before entering the house.

Rock music blared near our corner. The strains of that Mongolian singer Dao Lang singing of how he could wait, he could wait forever for his love. Perhaps Zi Mei's son played a radio to block out the sound of the rain. Surely she kept her busy. She'd never notice me or my new necklace.

Then, where the light from the shop shone on the road, I spotted a large van, the kind people hired to travel long distances, to the next town or the airport. The kind Snakeheads favored. The music didn't seem Chairman Huang's style. Sill, my breath caught in my throat. What now? Perhaps Chairman Huang wasn't interested in waiting long for payment and was here to shake Father up. What could I do? What could I promise? That we—I already included Chan Hai—that we would have the money in a year? Less, if the quarry re-opened?

I went up to the van, an old black vehicle with a dent in the front. I had my hand in my purse, all ready to turn over the envelope containing my bonus. Bills which had seemed like such a fortune.

But which now felt like slivers of ice next to the giant block in the provisioner's truck. I didn't see Father in the van. Nor the Chairman. The driver had his head back against the seat. Had he been struck? Had he and Father already fought? Perhaps the loud music which emanated from the van had been used to drown out the sounds of the struggle. I pushed my nose against the window. Steam fogged up the glass. I wiped it away. A clap of thunder sounded. The driver turned his head to the left, his jaw working up and down as though he were chewing a spoonful of pork dumplings. Then he sighed and opened his mouth. He was sleeping, perhaps dreaming of a meal to come.

Maybe this was a relative of Zi Mei's, and she'd already talked him into a deep slumber. Then again, perhaps Chairman Huang was in our house—and had been there a long time. My head felt light, as if I'd taken a long drink of Father's rice wine. The last person in the world I wanted to see was Chairman Huang. I hurried up the steps next to Zi Mei's shop. The door to her shop opened. A trickle of sweat ran down my cheek.

"Your visitor is here," Zi Mei called out.

Our visitor? Who was our visitor? Damn that Zi Mei and her mouth. Why did she always know so much? Like her life depended on it.

I was tempted to stop and find out who this could be. The thought of Chairman Huang's shiny black shoes clapping across our great hall filled me with horror. I could see him sitting in Father's spot, resting his slick-backed hair against the back of the chair as he examined Mother's breasts with his shifty eyes. Damn Zi Mei. If only she would be loyal to someone. I couldn't afford to stop and let her see me looking as if I'd rolled on the ground with Chan Hai all evening. Surely she would see me, know everything and tell everyone.

"Goodnight," I called as my bare foot padded onto the top step.

I crossed New Neighbor's front stoop. A slow trickle of water filtered down across the rocks. Ah, the winding dragon still worked. I hoped this meant good luck for both of us. I ran across the courtyard. The sound of rain pelted on the tin roof of the kitchen and shower. The smell of garlic and spring onions emanated from the kitchen. Perhaps our visitor was just Madame Matchmaker, and that van had nothing to do with us at all.

I listened again. When I heard no shouting or scuffling, I slipped into the shower. I couldn't allow Madame Matchmaker to see me looking like this. I was now soaked to the core, like a rat who had been dumped in a drowning bucket. The tin door to the shower squeaked as I pulled it closed.

"Li Hui," Mother's voice called. "Is that you?" She poked her head in the shower room before I had a chance to hook the lock. "Come," she grabbed my arm. "There's no time for that."

I looked back to the shower spigot, the hot water heater. What was the rush?

"You have a visitor," Mother said, pulling me into the kitchen.

Noodles boiled in the wok on the stove. Her cheeks glistened red from the heat. Was she still in her strange mood or had she felt so guilty at tarnishing Madame Matchmaker's reputation that she had splurged on cooking this fine dish?

"I'm sorry," I said. "I'm sorry I kept Madame Matchmaker so long. I didn't realize she would wait for me."

"Here," she said, grabbing on the side of the washtub for a dry rag. She pointed for me to sit down on the stool next to the wall. "Dry off your hair. Your face. Your arms. Your feet. What happened?"

"I went to visit Waipo," I said.

My words sounded false, ridiculous. The real reason for my late return had nothing to do with Waipo. I sensed Mother would not want to hear that. Not now.

"My old shoes broke," I said, rubbing away mud from my legs. "When I climbed the mountain."

I didn't want to tell her I threw my only shoes away, especially when her mind automatically calculated every *fen* we spent. She looked at me, waiting for an end.

"My shoes got stuck in Mr. Pig Farmer's yard, in the manure," I said, hoping to brush her fears away. "I'll go back for them tomorrow."

"Unh," she grunted. She picked up a bucket and went outside to the sink to get some water.

Tomorrow. Tomorrow would be a busy and wonderful day. Perhaps Chan Hai would help me retrieve my shoes. All the stories I'd kept inside—about our first meeting on the bus, our first dinner together, how he taught me to swim and to think and to love—bubbled to the surface. Maybe Mother would want to hear these stories.

"Mother," I said, fingering the string around my neck.

"Aiya!" Mother exclaimed.

She set the bucket of water down. She bent over next to me, her head right near my waist. She would ask what the smell on my body was. The salty, sticky seed filled the air around me. The liquid drained down my thighs.

"What happened?" she asked.

"Mr. Pig Farmer sprayed his pigs with some new fertilizer to make them grow faster," I improvised. "That's what that is."

"Aiya," she said again, pointing at my ankle. "The fertilizer puffed up your foot like that? How can?"

"No, no," I said. Mother was only worried after my safety. That I wasn't hurt.

"You know better than to take the short way." She dumped the bucket of water on my feet. "You look worse than an old lady with arthritis."

My ankle had puffed up like a blowfish. But my heart was so full. That silly lump at the end of my leg felt far away, a distant ache. She grabbed the rag from me and dried my legs with rough, hurried movements. Pains shot across my foot.

"How can you make a proper wife, if you look like this?" she asked.

"Mother?"

Had I heard her correctly? Thunder sounded across the sky. A gust of wind rattled the tin roof. The visitor. I thought it had been just I who felt a draft enter my heart the moment Chan Hai left. He must have felt the same. Perhaps he'd jumped off at the next stop and raced me to the house. Why didn't that sound right?

"He's a good man to wait for you," Mother said.

Chan Hai couldn't have been waiting long. If it was Chan Hai. I felt for the necklace.

"Look." I pulled at the string around my neck, holding up the yellow bird like an amulet.

She grabbed my cheeks in her firm hand. She turned my face away so she could inspect my neck. Her eyes furrowed in anger.

"That's the biggest mosquito bite I've ever seen," she said, dropping her grasp. "You look like a homeless beggar. Who would ever want you?"

She raked her hands over my hair, yanking out pebbles and grass. She took the comb from a nail on the wall and pulled the teeth through my tangled locks. My scalp ached.

"Feng Gu is going to help Chan Hai get the quarry re-opened," I continued.

"You have such lovely hair." She concentrated on a knot.

"That's what Chan Hai said." My words sounded insistent, loud. As if I were begging for candy at the market.

"When I was young," she said and continued combing. "I had love in my heart too."

I put my hand back over my shoulder and grabbed onto Mother's arm. I'd worried that she wouldn't approve of Chan Hai, would think he was too common, unable to sustain the weight of Father's debts. But, if she thought he was worthy, that was half the battle. I waited for her to say more, but she just squeezed my hand. Then she arranged my hair on my shoulders.

"There," she said. "That'll just have to do."

Perhaps our visitor was Chan Hai. I bit my lip. Just a few hours ago, my world had been so dark, as if I were trapped inside a rain cloud. Now the man who held my heart was in the Great Hall, and I would soon be a happily married woman. I remembered Waipo and her story of the farmer and his horse—how she always said, "You never know what something means."

Mother got up and took the wok off the fire. The air felt warm and delicious. She'd made long life noodles. Normally the flour noodles took her hours to make. Maybe these were store-bought. Or maybe she'd had a sign from the gods.

"Smells delicious," I said. My stomach rumbled.

"Grab six bowls," she said.

"Six?" I asked. My heart thumped against my chest. "Six?"

"Hurry." Mother shooed my question away with both hands. "Your husband-to-be is surely starving by now."

Yes, he had mentioned that. But six bowls? The ground trembled beneath my feet. My foot throbbed.

"Come, let's eat." Mother's voice was as hollow as a bamboo reed.

Perhaps she felt as giddy as I. But then, why didn't she see the beautiful necklace Chan Hai had given me? Why didn't she ask more about him? Why did we have so many bowls? I followed her toward our front door. Rain splattered in my face. A great wind pulled at the string on my neck. I stumbled on nothing at all and fell into the Great Hall.

"Ah." A man's voice, high pitched and nasal. "So Li Hui has finally arrived."

It wasn't Father. And it wasn't Chan Hai.

Chapter Forty-Eight,
The Ancestors Decide

Four people waited for us in the Great Hall. Father sat forward on a stool huddling over the last of his cigarette. Madame Matchmaker spilled over her stool in a green diamond-studded dress, as though she'd been pulled off the stage in a nightclub to show up here. In Father's chair sat a woman with short hair, curled in the fashion of the village and called a perm. She wore—not cotton pants rolled up to the knees like Mother and every farmer in the town—but a cotton dress. Simple, but well cut. Expensive. The man on her right had brown leather shoes, tailored pants which he didn't roll up, and an expensive silk shirt with many designs. His arms were light, the color of rice flour.

Who were these people? My throat constricted. Mother had said my husband-to-be, but I'd never met this man. That woman must be his mother. I thought of the long-distance van outside. The airport. Singapore. Was this Guo Qiang? Surely not. Hadn't Mother said that arrangement was over? Or had she?

"You don't need to send anymore cuttings to Singapore," she'd said when she came up to my room the other day and found me making a cutting of a bird. I had been so worried then about where Chan Hai was and why he was with Feng Gu. "Madame Matchmaker will be here on Friday. You need to be here too." That was all she'd said, though. In fact, when I tried to talk to her of Chan Hai, she waved her rag in my face, stopping the words.

The six bowls in my hands grew heavier and heavier. Madame Matchmaker and the woman chatted, but there was too much noise in my head—the sound of Mother sandpapering the table, of Father laughing, of Zi Mei saying, "Your family deserves this." I couldn't hear anything more. I couldn't add to the conversation. I could only nod when Mother introduced me.

I sensed Waipo's eyes following me, urging me to smile, not think. I put one bare foot in front of the other, as though balancing on a thin beam of wood all the way to that empty stool next to Mother. I sat down, lifting a metal spoon from the table to scoop the steaming noodles into bowls. Six bowls.

"Li Hui, Madame Liang just asked you a question," Mother said, tapping on my arm.

"Where have you been so long past sunset?" this Madame Liang asked.

A shiver ran down my spine, as if I still stood naked in the cold waters of the reservoir, the night breeze caressing my skin. "Trust me," I heard Chan Hai's deep voice calling. I thought nothing would ever be more frightening than plunging into dark water, feeling liquid surround me, taunt me, threaten to take away my breath forever. I was wrong.

"I—"

"Foolish girl," Mother said, her voice traveling high. "She's probably shy to say. She walked all the way to my mother's grave."

"It's not even time to pay respects," Father said taking a deep puff of his cigarette and blowing out the smoke. Madame Liang put her head back as far as possible to avoid the onslaught. Guo Qiang batted at the air as though he could push Father's smoke away.

"But then," he added. "She's always been one to act on impulse. Just like a girl."

He and Mother and Madame Matchmaker laughed. Act on impulse? Who always acted on impulse? Who was the one who went out each night and gambled, sure that tonight's game was the one? I forced my lips into a smile.

"Fortunately my mother is still where we put her," Mother said. "Two *li* past our house."

I knew what she was doing. Attempting to make me seem unusually filial—walking so far on a hot day, coming home in the driving rain. Especially when some young people didn't even bother to pay respects anymore. She was proud of me. And she was proud that she had managed to keep Waipo's grave where it was.

"You're certainly very lucky," Madame Liang spoke, stomping all over Mother's pride like a buffalo on flowers. "These days, the government doesn't like graves all over the place. They've moved the larger ones, like my husband's, to a central location."

Surely Mother would tell this rude woman how we had paid lots of money for that good spot on the mountain, how we wouldn't want to move Waipo's new home. And didn't Madame Liang worry that her husband's ghost was wandering around, lost? But Mother kept her words inside.

I stood up and walked to Madame Liang, handing her the first bowl of noodles. As I set the bowl in front of her, she grabbed onto my arm. Her slender fingers gripped my flesh with such force. She inspected three mosquito bites and sniffed the air.

"How often do you visit your Waipo's grave," Madame Liang asked in a voice filled with disbelief. Or maybe she wasn't happy that I gave so much attention to Mother's mother.

I looked to Mother. But she still chewed on Madame Liang's insult. Her mouth wouldn't open.

"I—" I said. "Whenever I have something special to say."

"And today you had special things to talk about?" Madame Liang asked, as if she were already my mother-in-law and could root around in my head for whatever she pleased.

"Of course," Madame Matchmaker said, leaning forward and fingering one of the diamond jewels on her dress. "Today is very special."

"I asked Li Hui," Madame Liang said. She sat rigid in Father's chair, her head held high, her black eyes like stones from a cold river bed. "Well?"

I returned to my stool and stirred the pot of noodles. There had been so many things—the robbery, the ordeal at the medicine shop, and definitely the scene in the back of the tea shop. They all led back to Chan Hai. Chan Hai. I wanted to turn and run back to the safety of his big strong arms, his deep voice. I wanted it to be tomorrow.

"You shake, little sister," Madame Liang said. "What's wrong?"

"She's hungry," Madame Matchmaker said. "And cold. It's a long walk to that grave. Surely she was rained on the whole way home. Aiya."

"No," Father said. "She's just a stupid, young girl. She doesn't know how to act around a man, especially someone as sophisticated as your son."

My face burned. I hoped all their noises would be enough for Madame Liang. I scooped a spoonful of noodles into another bowl. Silence filled the air like steam from a hot wok.

"We had a big robbery at the tea shop today," I finally said.

"No," Madame Matchmaker and Mother chorused.

"Did they use that new drug on you," Father asked. "Is that why you shake?"

"How big a robbery?" Guo Qiang asked in his nasal voice.

"A famous thief named College Boy," I said. "He tried to make off with ninety-two."

Mother and Madame Matchmaker both took in deep breaths of the smoke-filled air. Then Madame Liang chuckled, and the two of them joined in. Guo Qiang smiled. If you earned fifteen thousand *yuan* a month, perhaps ninety-two didn't feel like much.

"Is that all," Father said in a big voice. Then worry crossed his face like a dark cloud. "You didn't let him, though, did you?"

"Fortunately," I said. "Chan Hai was near."

"Not that fool?" Father barked. He looked in the corner of the room for his rice wine. Mother had cleaned that away, too.

"Who is Chan Hai?" Madame Liang asked, her voice like a needle piercing the air.

"Chan Hai captured the thief and got our money back," I said.

Just saying Chan Hai's name over and over made me feel happy. Safe. I was reminded of the time I had ridden the bus home in the rain and a motorcyclist sprayed water on a young couple. The incensed boy had pulled out his slingshot to protect his girlfriend. I hoped repeating Chan Hai's name like a mantra would be more effective than the boy's slingshot. I wished him to be here by my side. Steam from the pot of noodles covered my hands as I stirred and stirred. Madame Matchmaker's stool creaked.

"That's the trouble with China." Guo Qiang scraped his stool back across the cement. "There's no law and order. No law and order."

"Chan Hai helped the tea shop?" Mother said. Perhaps she knew of his troubled history.

"I didn't think the donkey's ass was capable," Father said. Then to our guests, he explained, "This man gets in fights with officials, knocks over tables in fine dining establishments. He's just a fool."

"Perhaps that's just his game," Guo Qiang said. "Acting the idiot."

"What?" I stared at him until Mother pulled on my skirt.

"Your father mentioned you're impulsive." Guo Qiang smiled, his thick cheeks like two *mantou* buns. "Perhaps the whole thing was a farce. And you fell for it."

I wasn't following his logic. But I didn't like the way my story was being hashed up like rice in the threshing machine. I ladled more noodles into his bowl.

"Seriously," Guo Qiang said, leaning forward with a slight tilt of his upper body. "That's what I've noticed since my return. There are dozens of new scams. That man you thought was such a hero may have planned the entire robbery."

"No," I said. This time not a sliver of doubt about Chan Hai poked at my heart. No matter how eloquent and studied the good professor sounded. "Never."

"You gave him a reward," Guo Qiang said. "Right?"

"But—"

"Right?" Guo Qiang tapped the table with his pudgy forefinger.

"Not a lot," I said. "Besides, he was beaten like a fish at the market."

Mother shook her head. Madame Matchmaker made a tsk-tsk sound. Father snorted.

"Some people don't mind a beating." Guo Qiang nodded with certainty. "If it means their tummies will be full later."

"You speak the truth," Father said, smiling and shaking his head. "It's amazing what some people will do to keep their stomachs happy."

I stared at Father as he inhaled deeply on his cigarette. He concentrated on the glowing ember in his hand. How could he say such words as if he were far above such an evil crowd?

"That's an interesting observation," I said. I needed to be polite to this man, respectful to Father. They both made it so difficult. "But I know Chan Hai very well and—"

"Yes," Father interrupted. "We all do. And, knowing this horse's ass, he took that reward and split it with—what did you call him? College Boy? Before the two of them went off to do another job somewhere else."

Father took another drag from his cigarette, stubbing the remains in the ashtray. He seemed so eager to impress this Guo Qiang, to agree with whatever the man said. He'd be so disappointed when I told him I was not interested in this match. That I preferred to marry the horse's ass.

"That's China," Guo Qiang said.

"No," I said.

Father coughed across the table at me, as if his smoke could stop my words. Mother's eyes widened. Madame Matchmaker laughed.

"Why, you're wrong," Guo Qiang said. "It's come to my attention over years of observation that—"

"No," I said.

I wished this arrogant man and his rude mother would leave. I slopped another spoonful of noodles in his bowl. Maybe if he ate, he would go. I added one more spoonful and picked up the full bowl.

My fingers burned as if I'd set them in a fire. Too much soup. I'd added too much soup. I rushed toward Guo Qiang.

"Here," I cried.

Chan Hai would have been up off his feet. He would have lifted the burning bowl from my hands and set it down. This man didn't move. I couldn't hold on any longer. I dropped the bowl of long life noodles right at his feet. The china shattered, the soup sprayed everywhere. Surely Mother would see this was not a good omen.

Guo Qiang took a white silk cloth from the pocket of his tailored pants. He brushed off several drops of soup which had sprayed onto his cuff. He pulled one long noodle off his shiny brown shoe and threw it on the floor. Then he tucked the cloth back in his pocket and folded his arms.

"Clumsy child,' Father said.

Father laughed, and Madame Matchmaker and Mother joined. But they sounded artificial, like professional laughers in a Chinese Opera. Madame Liang stared into her untouched bowl of noodles, as if the patterns were telling her some secret. I wished that secret told her to leave. Now, before anything more happened.

"It's my fault," Mother said grabbing the soup ladle and filling a new bowl. She passed the filled bowl over to Guo Qiang. "The soup's especially hot."

He held onto the sides of the bowl with both hands, lifting the soup to his nose and inhaling the aroma, holding the dish up as if to admire such fine, chipped porcelain. As if his hands were made of wood. Wood so thick and strong, he'd never drop this hot soup. Especially in front of an honored guest.

I went and grabbed a rag from my parents' room. Madame Liang's eyes stayed on me, as though she were inspecting a piece of pork from Madame Butcher, eager to spot places where there was excess fat. I knelt down in front of this man, cleaning up the mess of noodles.

"I feel shame," Mother said, dishing out a bowl of noodles for Father and then one for Madame Matchmaker. The two of them slurped noisily as if in a race to see who'd finish first. "You will have the burden of teaching my girl manners again."

"You say what?" Madame Liang asked over the noise.

"My daughter has her head so full of English and studying, she forgets her manners," Mother called out, as if she were shouting for a half-kilo of vegetables over the heads of other shoppers at the wet market.

Guo Qiang leaned over. He rubbed his palms together. His eyes sparkled.

"How much English can you speak?" He switched to the foreign tongue.

My head still reeled from the conversation about College Boy and Chan Hai. Why hadn't I watched how much soup I had added to the bowl? I was so close to being able to say what I felt—that I knew Chan Hai would never do a thing like that. Chan Hai was my friend, my lover, my fiancé.

"I—"

"Everyone can take the English class," Guo Qiang continued, thrusting out one of his doughy hands. "But how much can you articulate yourself?"

"I—"

"How well can you express your thinking?" He tapped his head with one pudgy finger.

"I—" Oh, but this man was irritating.

"How many turn-of-phrases do you know?" He raised his eyebrows. "Real world is not like the English class. Is very different."

Father, Mother and Madame Matchmaker, who hadn't understood anything he'd said, stared at me, begging me to answer. Guo Qiang finally stopped talking, stopped demonstrating his extensive vocabulary. My lips were glued shut.

"Waaa—you speak so well." Madame Matchmaker shook her hand out at Guo Qiang, the extra folds of skin under her arms flailing back and forth. "I have trouble enough remembering my own dialect, much less all those monotonous, hard sounds."

She put her empty bowl down. She waited a beat for me to jump into the conversation. Then she shook her hand out at Guo Qiang again, putting on a big smile.

"Li Hui has always tried to teach me though," she continued. "Even as a child she would say hello to me in English. It was so cute."

"What's cute in the village," Guo Qiang said. "Doesn't necessarily translate into cute in the city."

"You speak the truth," I said, dropping the wet rag to the floor. I touched a small spot on the end of my black skirt. A dirt spot from the reservoir. Then I looked up at this man's shiny brown shoes, his finely tailored pants, his thick leather belt, his silk shirt, his thick face. I stared into his eyes. "I'm sure I wouldn't fit in."

"Don't be ridiculous," Mother said, waving at the air as if erasing all those words. "She's just so shy."

"Shy to be in front of such honorable company," Father added.

"Still," Guo Qiang whined, as if talking to his mother, convincing her that this was not a good cut of meat. "In order to get a job in Singapore, she must know English."

"She'll get a good job," Father said. "She may be shy but she's a hard worker."

Madame Liang took a small slurp of noodles. She set her bowl down. Then she rose to her feet.

"Well," she said. "We better make a move."

Guo Qiang stood up. He brushed off the front of his pants. He moved to take his mother's arm.

"So soon?" Mother asked.

Guo Qiang smiled and nodded, as he steered his mother toward the front door. I resisted the urge to throw my soggy rag up in the air. While Madame Liang had taken a polite taste of her noodles, she was leaving. They were leaving. I jumped up from the floor, not joining in this attempt to extend their stay.

"Have some more noodles," Father said. "Surely you have much tastier noodles at your house. But these will fill your stomach."

I felt shame for not being a good daughter, not making a good performance, not winning the prize husband for our family. But, if I were to search deep in my heart for the honest truth, as Chan Hai always insisted, I had to say that my shame only tingled on my skin, not penetrating deeper. Relief coursed through my bloodstream. Tomorrow I'd be back safe in the arms of Chan Hai.

Rain thundered across the courtyard, spitting ferocious drops at us as we stood at the front door. Madame Liang paced back and forth, berating her son for leaving their umbrellas in the van. Where was that van driver anyway? Didn't he have the sense to come and bring them their umbrellas? This was the poor service one could expect in China.

Madame Matchmaker went out with her large umbrella in search of the errant van driver. Father shook out our one umbrella leaning against the front of the house. Half the umbrella folded up at an odd angle where the material no longer tied to the spokes. His large fingers fumbled with the small plastic vinyl beads at the end of the material, as he attempted to fix the umbrella. Mother looked about for a piece of cardboard or a bucket. We would find sufficient covering and escort these guests to their waiting van.

I stood by the door, a polite distance from Guo Qiang. He took a pen and notebook from his shirt pocket. He made a notation. Had this visit interrupted some of his important computer research? I'd tried to save him the trip. Why had he come anyway?

Outside lightening flashed as if the gods had a Polaroid camera and had just taken a picture of the moment. Water falling from the top of the door looked like the water wall at the Wei Min Hotel. Couples often had their pictures taken in front of that wall after their wedding dinner. There had even been such a picture on the pink wedding limousine. Would Chan Hai and I have our wedding at the Wei Min Hotel? Would we have such a picture?

"It's good to see you smile," Madame Liang said, pausing next to me. She nudged her son. "She has a beautiful smile, don't you think?"

He looked up from his notebook, his brow furrowed in irritation. Then he nodded and returned to his writing. I wished Mother would hurry and find something for us to use as an umbrella. Or Madame Matchmaker would return with an umbrella-laden van driver. Or Father would finish fixing the broken spokes and just lead these people out to their car. Obviously Guo Qiang had work to do. And there was nothing more to discuss.

"This rain is something, isn't it?" I said.

"Not really," Guo Qiang said, making a notation on the corner of his pad. "China has typhoons every year. It's part of the weather pattern."

"Yes," I said. "But the weather patterns have been strange this year. Even my boss says so."

"Your boss, the meteorologist?" he said, his pen poised in the air, his eyes a challenge. "Or the tea salesman?"

Feng Gu wasn't just a "tea salesman." She had other abilities. She was brilliant with numbers, making her a great accountant. She was courageous to take over the management of the tea shop for the family. And she had a forgiving heart, not only allowing me to make mistake after mistake, but turning around to help Chan Hai, the man she must have hated most. Did one have to have a degree to make an intelligent comment? I pointed in the direction of Zi Mei's shop. She was the most successful business woman in our village.

"Even Zi Mei's son has been selling umbrellas and coats for days now," I added, my voice rising.

"Yes," Guo Qiang said, twisting his silver pen shut. "We saw that idiot in front of the store. He tried to sell me a rain slicker meant for a child."

"He's a kind person," I said.

"He's a grown man," Guo Qiang said. He returned his expensive pen to his chest pocket. He checked his thin gold watch. "In Singapore, they have special schools and homes. Idiots aren't just left to wander around in the rain."

His words stung. Everyone knew that Don Don was missing a few piano strings. But no one would actually verbalize such a thing. Zi Mei kept him at home. We all pretended nothing was wrong. Oh, but this man was so annoying. So without compassion.

"Sounds as if you really enjoy Singapore," I said, crossing my arms over my chest. "I'm sure you'll be glad to get—"

"Here we go," Mother called. She held last year's calendar, a gift from the Bank of China. She'd kept it on her wall to cover a dent Father had made in one of his moments of anger. "Sorry to keep you waiting. Here we go."

Guo Qiang swallowed. Madame Liang sniffed at the air, her lips pinched together. They probably weren't used to making do.

"Shall we?" Mother said.

Her voice seemed awfully cheery, despite this awkward moment. The promising match had failed. Was Mother attempting to fool the gods with her performance? Then again perhaps she too had been unimpressed by these rich guests, especially after all Madame Liang's talk about Waipo's grave.

Father pulled the last vinyl bead over the metal spokes. He wiped his hand across his brow and handed the fixed umbrella to Madame Liang. Mother held up our old calendar to Guo Qiang as a second covering. Instead, Guo Qiang took his mother's elbow and led her out into the downpour.

"Don't trouble yourselves to come out in this weather," Madame Liang shouted above the roar of the storm.

"It's no trouble," Mother called back. "No trouble at all."

The two of them went back and forth three times. I slipped into a pair of Father's flip-flops. Father took charge of the calendar. The three of us huddled underneath this makeshift umbrella, as we sloshed across the courtyard and down the steps. Mother and I had to hurry to keep pace with Father. He seemed as eager to see these people go as I. I could already see him taking a large sip of rice wine and sighing, "Well, that was a disaster." And I could nod with him, thankfully.

Madame Liang and Guo Qiang walked to the van, where Madame Matchmaker stood tapping on the driver's window. Guo Qiang pulled on the back door. The door didn't open.

"They're ready to go," Father said stepping in front of Madame Matchmaker and banging on the window with his fist. The driver jerked in his sleep. He snorted and let his head fall back again. Madame Liang reached around Father and rapped once using her jade bracelet. The driver snorted and sat up. He fumbled out of his side of the car and opened the back door. Madame Liang scooted into the van. Guo Qiang followed. What a relief. They were leaving. I nodded as everyone made appreciative comments about hospitality and trouble taken. I was already thinking of the hot shower and tomorrow.

Madame Matchmaker stood back, engulfed in her large, modern umbrella which kept out the rain even in the fiercest winds. Father, Mother and I stood huddled underneath the old calendar. The poster was wet and soggy now. If Father didn't hold the sides with care, the cardboard would disintegrate in his hands. Mother reached out and patted Madame Liang on the hand before pulling the van door closed.

The van driver started the engine. I rocked back and forth in my father's flip-flops, enjoying the feel of the rain thumping on my shoulders. I could hardly contain my excitement.

Guo Qiang pulled back the window. An old squeaky window which caught half way. Surely they didn't have squeaky windows in Singapore. I stifled a smile as I watched his doughy fingers struggle with the latch. Surely he'd opened the window to continue with the ritual of parting. I was only too happy to say goodbye.

Instead Madame Liang switched on an overhead light and extracted a wad of bills from her purse. The wad, tied with a rubber band, was so thick I couldn't imagine how much money she had there. Thousands. Tens of thousands. She was brave to travel around with so much money on her person. Perhaps they didn't worry about robbery in Singapore.

I glanced at the van driver. He yawned and rubbed the back

of his neck. I hoped he was a good person and wouldn't give these people more reason to criticize our country. I hoped they'd make it to their destination safely. I looked to Father. He should warn them. His eyes were as large as two moons. His mouth had parted. Surely drool was forming. Oh, Father. How would poor Chan Hai deal with Father?

But Father was on the alert. He leaned forward. I was sure it was to give Madame Liang a word of warning. She nodded, handed him the entire wad of money and tapped the driver on the shoulder to signal they were ready. I blinked. Why did Madame Liang give Father such a vast sum of money? Thousands and thousands of *yuan*? Cold raindrops pelted my head like pieces of ice.

I remembered the other night when Father had come home late. So drunk. Unable to even close the front door. I had mentioned the professor, wanting to tell Father that I was not interested in such a union. He had cut me off, laughing. A faraway look in his eyes. He had said something about how intelligent I was to think of the professor. No wonder I was a college graduate.

A gust of wind slapped me in the face. Surely, he hadn't called on the professor to relieve his debt? And what had he promised in return? I opened my mouth to say something. But my lungs had been punctured. I couldn't breathe.

Chapter Forty-Nine
The Sky Crumbles

My head pounded, as if our ancestors rolled around in there, laughing until their sides ached. Chicken flesh covered my arms. First I had thought Chan Hai had come to ask for permission to marry me. Then I had assumed the meeting with that horrible family had been thrown away as a disaster. But now Father had taken all that money. Madame Matchmaker had left, a satisfied smile on her face, the diamonds on her green dress sparkling in the rain. Obviously, while I had been out expressing my love for Chan Hai, Madame Liang and Father and Madame Matchmaker had been making arrangements. What arrangements? I put my hands to my temples as rain continued to pelt down on me.

"Li Hui," Father said, pushing the soggy old calendar into my hands as if it were more than just mush. "You and your mother take this for cover."

I took the piece of cardboard from him and held the covering over Mother and myself. The firm dates were now damp and soggy against my fingertips. Father took our old umbrella and held it over his head. He rolled his shoulders and felt around in his pocket for his cigarettes. Then a gust of rain pelted him in the face. He shut his eyes and let his hand fall to his side. He'd smoke later.

"Father?" I called, as he stepped out to the road.

"I have business," he called, waving us away with his free hand.

Business? Was his business paying Chairman Huang that wad of bills? And what of me? I heard Counselor Zhang's voice in my head, taunting, "You want to have a say, don't you?" I heard Madame Paper Cutter saying, "It's important to be loyal. But it's important to follow your heart too." I saw thin, frail, burned Cheng Min that day she returned my discipline book, saying, "No. No saved my life."

"Father," I shouted, wanting to rush to him and ask what this was all about and yet not able to move as I held our makeshift umbrella for Mother. "Father. A typhoon is coming."

"Don't you think I know that?" he yelled. "Oh, that's right. On your way back to the house, you two check on that sneaky neighbor.

Make sure he hasn't started building a dam at the bottom of our property again."

Then he continued on down the road. How could Father not come home with us and explain what was happening here? How could he talk only of something so trivial? As if everyday visitors came from foreign lands and handed him thousands of *yuan*.

"Come," Mother said, grasping onto my arm and leading me up the steps. "Let's go home."

"I'm in love," I said. Cold water cascaded around my bare feet, small and uncovered in Father's flip-flops.

"Did you say something?" she called, holding onto the stair railing and pulling me forward.

"I'm in love," I shouted above the roar of the rain.

Lightening flashed across the sky. A clap of thunder sounded. The metal windows of Zi Mei's shop rattled—from the wind or the weight of her big ears pressed firmly to them, I was not sure.

"That's wonderful." Mother clasped my fingers in hers. "So fast."

"With Chan Hai," I said.

She let go of my hand and shook her head. Shake. Shake. Shake. Not letting my words inside her world.

"That Professor Liang's a good man," she said, pulling me along, her voice all cheery. "A stable man. He will take good care of all of us. Did you see how Madame Liang just handed your father twenty thousand *yuan* as if it were a wad of old tissues? I've never seen so much money in all my life. Except one time on the movie screen. When we went to the community center to see a movie. You couldn't have been much higher than a stalk of cabbage. And now look at you." She looked around and whispered in case the gods were listening, "You've brought luck on our family."

"Mother." I stopped walking. "Chan Hai wants to marry me."

Shake. Shake. Shake.

"Mother, please," I said. "Please listen."

"You will grow to love the professor someday." She yanked on my arm.

"But I already love Chan Hai," I said.

Shake. Shake. Shake.

"Chan Hai and I will find the money for Father," I said. "Can't you talk to Father? Please? Mother, please?"

"Stop your begging," Mother said, her head snapping up, her

eyes smoldering. "You're worse than a child."

My ears stung. Was I acting like a child? Worse than? My face grew hot with shame.

"You should be happy," she said, pointing a finger at me. "And grateful at this wonderful marriage. The Liangs are a fine family. They will bring good fortune on all of us for generations to come. And Professor Liang is very distinguished. Did you hear him? Talking about weather patterns and the advanced systems in Singapore. Waaah. So intelligent. And he even speaks English. You should feel lucky."

Lucky? I remembered his doughy skin and his obnoxious attitude. I remembered him criticizing China at every turn, even accusing Chan Hai of being a thief. I remembered him pulling one of Mother's fine-crafted noodles off his high-priced brown leather shoes as if removing a goose turd. No, not lucky. Lucky would be the Liangs returning to wonderful Singapore and having nothing more to do with us.

"You're right," I said. I continued walking. "Professor Liang is a great man. They seem like a wonderful family. But Chan Hai wants to marry me—"

"That was never an option," she said, her voice clipped, cold. "Didn't we warn you to stay away from that turtle's egg?"

Stay away? But he was like a magnet, like one of those heavy red and black magnets our elementary school science teacher kept locked in her tall glass case. I was just a sliver of metal. I could never stay away.

"Besides," she said, her voice shrill. She put up her hands and ticked off items one at a time. "He has no job, no future. And he killed his best friend." She shook her hands at me. "Did he tell you that? Huh?"

Mother thought of one horrible thing about Chan Hai after another. It reminded me of New Neighbor and his rock piles. Only she was building a wall between herself and me.

"His best friend drowned, Mother," I said. "Please, Mother."

"Besides," she said crossing her arms across her chest, her voice colder than the winds from Siberia. "The generous and distinguished Chairman Huang gave our family an option. Your father chose the one that protected you and our family to the greatest advantage."

What did that mean? Snakehead Chairman Huang? I felt a howl deep inside. If I opened my mouth I feared that noise would come out, pelting Mother in the face so hard I would do permanent damage. I couldn't do that. Not to Mother.

"And here," she said, her voice quivering as she hop-stepped into the safety of our house. "Your dear father has gone off in the driving rain just to save you, his precious daughter."

To save me? What had been Father's option? To pay up right away or hand over his daughter? To marry the Professor or to go with the Chairman? Chairman Huang had once said that he'd get me. He finally had. I stood out in our courtyard.

Happy and thankful? When Father had first suggested I turn down my job offer at the university and I was given a new one, I had been happy and thankful. Then he had wanted me to push further. Never mind that I didn't get that or any job from university. Then I had been happy and thankful to get a job at the tea shop. I was doing well there. Now I had a heart bursting with love. And Chan Hai wanted to marry me. I was happy and thankful. Now this.

Every time I found my patch of sky, Father came along to destroy it. All I wanted was a small patch. A small patch with Chan Hai. The cardboard calendar I held above me—like my sky—crumbled in my fingers. Rain hit down hard on my head like plastic beads.

Chapter Fifty
The Moon Festival

I stood in front of a pool of water in the lobby of the Wei Min Hotel, staring at the Wall of Water. Around me relatives and friends gathered in groups, chatting and laughing. The smell of fine foods—roast duck, fried frog legs, turtle soup—filled the air. How fast the water rushed down the sides of the smooth granite wall, splashing into the small pool. How quickly things had happened.

Only a week had passed and here I was standing in my new gold pumps. A traditional red *qipao* dress sewn by the finest local tailor hugged my chest and thighs, the long skirt flowing down to the shiny marble floor. My hair had been curled into an elaborate twist, fashioned with a long jade pin. I looked more elegant than ever. A lovely bride waiting to enter the finest wedding dinner. Only my perfect groom was not in attendance.

The sound of the water splashing in the pool reminded me of the steady patter of rain on my bedroom window. That sound had been constant all week. The roads had turned to mud. The peach tree in the back yard had lost all its leaves and shook angrily in the wind. The inside of our house smelled wet and moldy. I had sat many hours, watching the rain trickle down my bedroom windowpane like tears, while I stared out toward the road that led to Chan Hai.

If only I had followed my instincts that night Chan Hai had asked me to marry him. I hadn't wanted to leave him then. I hadn't wanted to go home. What if instead I had run barefoot all the way to his side of the village? I had run that scene in my head all week long, a thousand and ten thousand different ways. As I stood there listening to the water, I did so again.

Through that Wall of Water, I could almost see him standing by the edge of the road. Waiting. He smiled so the dents in his cheeks showed. As I approached, he opened both his arms. I ran to him, burying my face into his chest. I told him I couldn't bear to be away from him, I couldn't bear to go home, that something felt wrong.

"Shhh," he said and put his thick fingers up to my lips. "Shhhh. It's okay."

I took a deep breath. How did he know things would work out? In fact, why had he been waiting for me?

"How did you know I was coming?" I gulped.

"I knew," he said, his lips brushing my forehead, my cheek, my lips. "I just knew."

Then, he pulled me to him, his hand tight on my arm. His fingers thin and bony. His nails long.

"Our room is ready," Mother-In-Law said, her hand tight around my arm, pulling me from my reverie in front of the Wall of Water. I stared at that water rushing down, not eager to leave the images in my head. Chan Hai's face. But he no longer beckoned. Instead he covered his eyes with his large hand. His thick lips were turned down. The small hairs on his chin which he hadn't had a chance to shave off quivered. As if he knew. As if he could feel my sorrow. I reached out and touched the wall of water as I passed. My wall of tears.

I sat between my new mother and my new husband. An army of waitresses surrounded our twelve tables, passing out small dishes. Cold cuts. Squid. Peanuts. The efficient staff helped guests unfold napkins, fill water glasses, and serve food.

Red lanterns shaped like winter melons hung from the ceiling. Along one wall red banners with shiny gold foil proclaimed, "Double Happiness." Along another was a giant circular paper cutting with a dragon and a phoenix. In the center of our table sat a figurine, a boy in traditional dress carrying a girl on his back. They were both smiling and happy. I thought of Chan Hai carrying me to the reservoir.

"A toast." Mother-In-Law nudged me. "They're offering a toast."

A toast? But we had just barely sat down. I needed to pay attention. I picked up my glass, pulled my face into a smile and listened as someone at a back table called out for us to have a fat, happy boy. Lots of laughter ensued. Glasses clinked.

The waitress behind Guo Qiang refilled his cup with rice wine. She wore a long red *qipao* dress with slits along the sides all the way up to her thighs. Her long black hair was tied up with a red and gold butterfly hairpin. A red and gold butterfly. I stared at that butterfly. Waipo's voice filled my head. I let my mind wander. Waipo rocked back and forth, as if she held me in her arms, repeating her favorite love story, the one that would be performed at our new community center, if ever enough funds were raised. The Butterfly Lovers.

Long ago there lived a curious and intelligent young woman named Zhu Yin Tai. She was the daughter of the Emperor. Girls weren't meant to study anything but sewing and flower arrangement and music. However, she so wanted to study characters and history and math and government that she cut off all her silky long hair, disguised herself in men's robes, and ran off to study at the university. Her father thought she had been kidnapped. So he sent out large contingencies to find her. She was of marriageable age now. He had found her a husband. It was time for her to come home before anything unfortunate befell her.

At the university, Zhu Yin Tai felt she had finally found her real home. She loved this endless world of knowledge. She became best friends with a fellow student, Liang San Bo, a young man from a distant province. They studied until late together. They took meals together. They shared their hopes and dreams. After graduation, she invited him home to meet her family.

"You're going to need a wife now," Zhu Yin Tai said. "And I have a sister who I think you'd like."

Liang San Bo followed her home. On the way, she revealed her true identity. He proposed marriage. Oh, yes. Oh, yes. Oh, yes. Zhu Yin Tai hoped her father would accept. But Zhu Yin Tai's father was not impressed with this classmate. The poor villager had nothing to offer but his degree. Besides her father had already arranged for her to marry a wealthy man of the court.

Liang San Bo was distraught at losing Zhu Yin Tai. She was everything to him. She was his life. And if he couldn't have her, then he didn't need to walk around on the earth pretending he was alive. So he killed himself, asking that he please be buried on the roadside near Zhu Yin Tai's palace.

The following day, the grand wedding of the court official and Zhu Yin Tai took place. As the procession went down the road and passed Liang's grave, the sky darkened. Lightening struck. The ground shook, and his grave opened up. Zhu Yin Tai jumped out of her palanquin and into that open grave. The earth closed around her.

The wedding guests stopped their carriages, got out and surrounded the grave, shouting Zhu Yin Tai's name. Even her husband, the court official deigned to step down to see what fuss his young bride had created. He leaned over the loose dirt.

"Where is my foolish wife?" the official asked. "This is

nonsense."

"Look," a small girl who held up the robes of one of the court ladies shouted.

"Where?" the official said. "I don't see anything."

"There," the girl said, dropping half of the robe and pointing to a giant butterfly. Then two.

"I meant my wife," the official spat. "I'm looking for my wife."

But the crowd of wedding guests gave a sigh of wonder as the two beautiful butterflies arose from the ground. They were the largest butterflies anyone had ever seen. Their colors celebratory red and gold. And they fluttered through the air as though dancing. As though dancing, happy and free. Free at last to be with one another.

"Did you want something," Mother-In-Law asked.

I realized my hand had reached up toward the waitress, toward her red and gold butterfly hair pin. Oh Waipo. Chan Hai. Why am I here and you all so far away?

"No," I said. "Thank you. I'm fine."

I tapped my new gold sandals on the carpet. This was the moment every girl waited for. I looked up at the skylight which Zi Mei had told me about many times. Rain tip-tapped on the skylight. Lightly now. Peeking outside of a dark cloud, the full moon shone through like one more giant table. The Moon Goddess was up there suffering eternal life. Alone. Could she see our banquet? What would she have said of Father's decision? Was true love not meant for this world?

I stared at the gold-rimmed plate before me, the red-and-gold chopsticks lying across the porcelain rest. I felt a lot like Zhu Yin Tai. I didn't want to marry the rich man my father had found for me either. If there was a way Chan Hai and I could be together in a different world, I would jump into that world. No questions asked.

The waitress with the butterfly hairpin read off the menu to Guo Qiang. Peking Duck, Sweet and Sour Bass, Salted shrimp. All foods I'd only heard of. Before she finished her list, a man cut in front of her. He wore a shirt creased in squares, as if it had just been removed from its cellophane package. His pants were pinned at the bottom. His loafers cracked and worn.

"Congratulations," the man said.

He nodded to Guo Qiang and passed him a red envelope. Guo Qiang put his hands together in thanks for the wedding money. But the man didn't retreat to his seat, didn't allow the waitress to come back and finish discussing the order.

"When are you going to Singapore?" Creased Shirt asked.

"Tomorrow morning," Guo Qiang said. "We have an early flight."

My stomach fluttered. So fast?

"I brought you a little something to take with you," Creased Shirt said, pointing to two boxes in the corner. Their mud-splattered sides had been tied together with dirty string. A gift for our house? Bundles of tea or dried mushrooms or dried fish?

"Thank you," Guo Qiang mumbled. I nodded in appreciation.

"They're down jackets," Creased Shirt said, smiling and revealing a mouth full of crooked, tobacco-stained teeth. "I got them at a great price."

I'm sure he had. The summer had already lasted longer than anyone had expected. We wouldn't need them in tropical Singapore. But certainly family here could use the warm jackets. Again I nodded our thanks.

"I'll sell them to you dirt cheap, too," Creased Shirt continued. "I understand you can take up to two carry-ons per person. I was thinking each one of you could take one box. They look heavy, but they're—"

"Thank you," Guo Qiang interrupted. "Thank you. But I think those would be difficult to sell."

"Oh, no," Creased Shirt said. "I have a friend in Canada who is making hundreds a day off of these things. Every single day."

"That's great." Guo Qiang nodded, as if hundreds a day meant a lot to him. "But it never gets cold in Singapore."

"Oh, come on, now." Creased Shirt nudged Guo Qiang. His eyes sparkling as he probably envisioned Guo Qiang not only returning the red packet filled with congratulatory money, but adding hundreds of *yuan* to the pile. "I know you'll be busy with your pretty young wife. But this is a great—"

"Singapore," Guo Qiang said, his smile wide but his eyes small pebbles. "Is situated only 128 kilometers from the equator."

"The what?" Creased Shirt said. He cocked his head to the side and stuck his mud-stained forefinger in his ear. He jiggled around and around. "Don't start talking educated now. Using big words."

"It just means it never gets cold," Guo Qiang said.

"Not even in winter time?" Creased Shirt took a step back and looked at Guo Qiang, as though waiting for the punch line to a joke.

"No such thing," Guo Qiang said.

"What a load of horse manure," Creased Shirt said. His mouth dropped open as if he'd been punched. He stared across the room at those boxes he would have to haul back to wherever he got them. "Just because you've been there, you think you can tell anybody whatever you want about the place."

The poor man. Surely his request was not only inappropriate but impossible. Still he was just trying to make his life better. We all were.

"Well, if you don't want to sell them," Creased Shirt indicated the boxes. "Who's going to?"

Guo Qiang looked up at the ceiling for an instant. Then he shook his head. He fingered the red packet in his hands, as if trying to remind this strange relative that we weren't at the morning market but at a wedding dinner.

"I think they're getting ready to serve the fish," Guo Qiang said.

Creased Shirt grabbed a carton of cigarettes from our table. I leaned over to ask Guo Qiang who the man was, but the waitress stepped forward again to discuss the menu. I watched Creased Shirt sulk toward the exit. He put his hand against the wall and tore the circular paper cutting of the dragon and phoenix up the middle. Madame Paper Cutter would have called the man desperate. Pain stabbed at my eyes.

Chapter Fifty-One
Chaos

My head rested against Chan Hai's firm golden chest, our naked bodies doused in sweat. His left arm cradled me loosely, while he ran his other hand through my damp hair and whispered sweet words over the top of my head. My heart felt full.

"Li Hui," he whispered. "Wake up."

That voice wasn't his. I opened my eyes. Mother-In-Law's black skirt swished in front of my nose. Five days of marriage and I still escaped to Chan Hai at any opportunity.

"We have a date for tea," she said, turning and swishing out of the room, her sandals clacking on the white floor. Guo Qiang said it was called tile. That, no, it wasn't special. Everyone had this kind of floor. No one had cement here.

I turned onto my back, my head resting on the red rice-filled pillow with the characters "Double Happiness" on them. I hadn't meant to fall asleep. I'd just come in the bedroom to put away some clothes in the long gray closet that lined our wall. My clothes only took up a hand's width of space in such a big area. In fact, Mother and Father's clothes could easily fit in here, as well.

Mother would love this luxury. She would also enjoy the matching gray table with a mirror on my side of the bed. I had taped Madame Paper Cutter's phoenix to the top of the mirror. But you could still see your image clearly. I could imagine Mother sitting there, leaning close to the mirror as she searched for and removed any white hairs on her head.

I could imagine Father staring at that gray table as well. For a different reason. Since we'd arrived three days ago, we'd paid visits to and received visits from so many friends and relatives, I had difficulty remembering all the faces. They had all offered us presents of money and wine. Father's eyes would spin at the sight of all that money. His mouth would water over the fine wines. And, I smiled, he would appreciate our white walls, white walls which didn't rub off on his shirt when he stumbled against them.

The sun still shone bright through the windows on my side of the bed, although surely the afternoon was gone. I sat up, pulling off the light cover which also said "Double Happiness." Double Happiness. I didn't feel happiness. Or sadness. Or anything at all. Just numb and tired. I fell back over and closed my eyes. Chan Hai smiled down at me, the dents in his cheeks deepening. I reached up and kissed his long eyelashes.

"Li Hui?" Mother-In-Law rapped her knuckles on the bedroom door.

I reached out to touch the whiskers on Chan Hai's chin, but he had already melted away. I sighed and yawned and sighed again. Then I rolled out of bed. Both my ankles were swollen now, and not from my fall in the fields two weeks ago. Guo Qiang said it was the airplane ride. That if I'd listened to him and walked up and down the aisles instead of staying huddled in my seat, eyes closed, afraid that the slightest movement would send the plane crashing to the ground, I would have nothing to complain about now.

I went into the room next to Guo Qiang's side of the bed. The indoor shower room. The floor also had tiles, the shower walls smaller tiles. Singaporeans seemed to like tiles. I splashed cold water on my face and neck. Father and Mother would get a laugh out of this room which housed not only a shower and sink inside the house, but a toilet as well. Imagine. A toilet. In the shower room. All that filth in the one place you go to get clean. What silliness. At least it was a flush toilet. Mother-In-Law had explained not to be afraid to push the lever. That the toilet was supposed to make that loud noise when flushed. As if I were a country dolt.

"Li Hui." Mother-In-Law's voice through the door was impatient. "Be quick."

I looked in the mirror over the sink. Yes, there was a mirror over the sink as well. I wore the black pants Chan Hai had given me and a white blouse he had taken off me. Both were wrinkled. Mother-In-Law said I should know better than to wear pants all the time, like a farmer's child. We were in the city now. But that's all I wanted to wear. Perhaps she wouldn't notice, if we were in such a hurry. No, she'd notice. But perhaps she'd forgive. I ran a brush through my tangled hair. Touched the yellow bird around my neck. Then I went out to join them.

Guo Qiang sat on the couch reading the newspaper. He held the English-language paper up high over his finely tailored blue slacks. From behind the paper, I spotted a multi-colored shirt with large blue and green squares—like computer terminals. Not the shirt he wore to work this morning. Had he slipped in and out of our bedroom to change without a word? Had he heard me dreaming of Chan Hai? Mother-In-Law sat next to him, examining the side of her black purse.

"She's ready," Mother-In-Law said, glancing up. Her face turned to a grimace. She didn't like my "farmer" pants.

Guo Qiang read a moment longer, then folded the paper with a loud thwack. He stood and opened the door for us, pointing to the bin which held our parasols and umbrellas, so we wouldn't forget. Not like a loving husband who made my life double happiness. But like his computer that he loved to talk on and on about. A computer performing a function. He performed his husband operations well. Most of them. He drove and opened doors and presided over the dinner table and was generous with money. But one function he hadn't performed yet. Drink had overcome him on the four nights we'd been married. I was only too grateful for that.

"Where are we going?" I asked

"You don't remember?" Guo Qiang asked.

He pulled the door closed behind us, pushing the metal knob back and forth to ensure the lock had caught. He looked over at Mother-In-Law, his eyes bulging out of his thick round face. He tightened his thin lips into a line. His thick eyebrows scrunched together. Not again.

"Oh, that's right," I said as if I'd remembered.

I hated that look. I would rather pretend something I knew than see that look. Besides, I would figure it out soon enough.

He took Mother-In-Law's arm and led her down the steps. We lived on the second floor of a twelve-story building. This big building was not special either. We were surrounded by apartment buildings, all stacked together like golden rows of corn. Guo Qiang said some parts of the island had houses, where people like the Prime Minister, rich Singaporeans and foreigners lived. But I'd only seen these tall buildings.

At the bottom of the stairs, Guo Qiang paused. Was he checking for his car keys? Would we ride in the car which seated four, as we had the other day when we had visited all the relatives who had gathered over at Second Uncle's place? Second Uncle had come over after WWII as a rickshaw driver. He was now an old man, with thick white hair and a mouth full of gold fillings, but he still worked. He had laughed that these days, his cargo was heavier than ever—the tourists at the Raffles Hotel.

We still needed to pay Fourth Auntie a visit, Guo Qiang had said. She hadn't been at the gathering the previous day, as she couldn't get out of her apartment or move around much at all. She had bound lotus feet. Walking, standing, even breathing seemed painful. She had been in the country over thirty years, Guo Qiang said, but probably knew about as much about her surroundings as I. Guo Qiang was good at explaining things. In fact, he often talked on longer than the cloth used to bind lotus feet as Waipo would have said, and my mind drifted away. Where had my mind been when he had mentioned this date for tea?

He didn't pull keys from his pocket in preparation for the run to the parking lot. He took the parasol from me, opened the frilly white protector and went out into the sun. Mother-In-Law opened a second parasol, grasped onto my arm and led me out behind him. Well, we must not be going too far. The wet market perhaps? But then Guo Qiang had said the market closed at two in the afternoon. Besides it was best to arrive early in the morning when the meat and fish were still fresh. Maybe the hawker center next to the market, which sold prepared food and drinks? We walked and walked. Mother-In-Law's sweaty arm kept pushing against mine. Even with the protection of the parasol overhead, the sun pored through me, sucking the breath from my body. My only desire was to return home to the softness of my bed.

We passed the marketplace where the scent of old pork mixed with fresh-cut flowers. The ground was so clean. In the village, the ground would be covered in blood and fish heads and vegetable skins. You would know where you were. Here I felt lost. We passed several stores—a framer, a haircut shop, an electronics shop, a clinic.

"Look here," Guo Qiang said.

Guo Qiang waited for Mother-In-Law and I to catch up. He pointed all around. For as far as I could see, we were surrounded by high-rise apartments. Bamboo poles decorated with the day's laundry hung from each window, the clothes flapping in the breeze. Those poles reminded me of home. Sure, Mother hung our laundry on tree branches. But most people had bamboo poles. Was he pointing out the similarity? Trying to make me feel more at home?

"What does this place look like to you?" he asked.

"Home," I said, more of a question than an answer.

"No," he said dropping his hand with a sigh. "A city. This same spot where you see high-rise apartments and playgrounds and shops was only ten years ago covered with coconut trees and grass so high you couldn't walk. Tigers and monkeys and boar prowled about. The only houses were Kampungs on stilts."

"Ah," I said.

Another lesson. We didn't have normal conversations. He was always explaining things to me as if to a child. Testing me like a student.

"This is now the island's industrial area. Some 70% of Singapore's manufacturing is situated here," he said. "Do you remember what area you're in?"

His voice was a challenge, the same as when he'd grilled me on my English ability. Why was he so irritated with me? So I couldn't remember where we were going. My brain had been in a fog ever since Mother had said, "You should be happy and thankful with the choice your father made."

"Well?" Guo Qiang asked. His thin lips had formed a smirk. His thick cheeks were tilted high.

"Jurong," I said. "Jurong West."

"It's also known as The Jungle," he said, trampling over my words. "In fact, taxi drivers still refer to it that way. They don't want to go out to The Jungle."

"Is that why you bought a car?" I asked.

I imagined him stuck in the center of the city having to walk back home in this raging heat, because taxi drivers refused to make the half hour drive out to some area that was long ago a jungle. When would their minds change to fit reality?

"No," he said. "The island has a wonderful mass rapid transit."

"The MRT," I said before he could quiz me.

"You can get anywhere by train and bus," he said. "If you have the time."

"So?" I pressed.

"I like," he said, his eyes darting to Mother-In-Law. He fingered his shirt as if one of the computer-looking squares would spit out an answer. "I like to drive."

His doughy face colored. He looked down at the cement walkway. Perhaps he'd bought the car for Mother-In-Law, paying the 300% tax on vehicles, buying the special car license, shelling out money for the special permit needed to drive into the center of the city. I knew cars were a major expense. Guo Qiang had explained that to me already. Perhaps he was embarrassed to say so in front of her. At least the air between us was quiet for a moment.

Buses chugged by on the road, neighbors called to one another from their windows, flip-flops slapped across the walkway. We ducked under the deck of a blue apartment building. Guo Qiang handed his parasol to Mother-In-Law.

"These blue buildings are owned by the two universities on the island," he said having overcome whatever had given him pause. "Nanyang Technological University and Singapore University."

A guard sat out in front of the bank of elevators. Our apartment building didn't have a guard, even a sleepy old one who leaned back in his chair, his eyes half closed.

"This is housing for the foreign workers," Guo Qiang said.

Off to the right, a dark man, half naked, stood surrounded by shelves of candy, newspapers, a glass case holding canned drinks. There was even a large pink phone situated nearby. This enterprising foreigner had managed to set up a shop. I thought of Madame Paper Cutter. Perhaps she too would have her own art shop someday.

"I see," I said.

The man wore a giant white cloth, wrapped around him like a woman's skirt and held up by his big belly. No farmer pants for him. The hair that covered his naked chest looked like a field of burnt grass. I nodded toward the dark man and lifted my eyebrows.

"Not foreign meaning that gentleman there." Guo Qiang snorted. "He is Singaporean. Indians comprise 7% of the population. Although small in number, Indian culture is pervasive throughout the country."

I nodded. So he wasn't a migrant worker. More like the Zi Mei of the neighborhood. What was Zi Mei saying now? I hoped that her ears had heard all the words I'd said to Mother, of my love for Chan Hai, of how I didn't want to marry this professor. I hoped her words had carried over to the other side of the village. I couldn't bear to think of Chan Hai feeling abandoned. Again. First by Feng Gu's *gege* who drowned on him. Then Little Wu Lu who had lost all sense of loyalty in his quest to survive. Now me. Oh, dear Chan Hai. I bit my lip. My eyes burned. I turned my attention back to Guo Qiang who was still talking.

"The name Singapore, for example," he said, "is from the Sanskrit Singha Pura, meaning Lion City. As the first-time explorers spotted the island, they saw a lion."

Guo Qiang went up to the elevators and punched a button. A light turned on, but nothing happened. What a relief. The idea of riding in a tiny box up to another floor made my armpits tickle. We didn't have these new conveniences in the village even in the more recent buildings which had six stories and all the modern fixtures.

"I'll be just a minute," he said, walking over to the Indian.

I hoped he'd take longer. The sound of the gears grinding behind the elevator doors made my heart thump too fast. I looked over to Mother-In-Law. Her small black eyes stared straight ahead at the closed elevator doors. Her lips were pursed together and pulled downward. She always looked as though she were pulling a heavy rickshaw through a crowd. Now her load looked heavier—like she pulled one of Second Uncle's tourists from Raffles. Did she disapprove of Guo Qiang talking to the dark man? Or did she fear stepping on board that small moving box as well?

The dark man handed over a bag of shrimp crackers, and Guo Qiang handed him a bill. The man said something. Guo Qiang shook his head and pointed to me. His eyes looked white against his dark skin, like white beams of light searching me up and down. Then he smiled at Guo Qiang and shook his hand. The sound of a bell emanated from behind the elevator doors. Guo Qiang came running over as the doors banged opened. He jumped inside.

"Hurry up," he said, holding the door open with one arm. His eyes scanned the panel of buttons inside. "This is an old one. Doesn't like to wait."

My skin prickled. My mouth felt dry. I was back on the plane with my eyes closed, fearful of scratching the itch on the tip of my nose for fear of unbalancing the plane. But this ride was shorter than the airplane ride. And I had survived that.

"They have a staircase," I pointed out. "The exercise will do me good. You were saying that just the other day. That I needed exercise."

"That was on the plane," Guo Qiang said.

Guo Qiang let the jaws to the box almost close, before putting his arm up again. The doors snapped back open. Snapped at me. I swallowed. My palms sweat. My knees trembled.

"We'll meet you up there." Mother-In-Law patted my arm turning me toward the staircase. "I used to walk many *li* up the mountain to fetch firewood for our cook stove."

Guo Qiang shook his head at us. He beat the buttons inside the elevator. Just as the doors closed, he called out, "Colleague lives on the seventh floor."

Ahh. Of course. Colleague. Colleague who was married to an American. Lee Sa. Or Li Zhi as Mother-in Law always called her, unable to remember the correct pronunciation. Guo Qiang said she might be able to help me find a job. How could I have forgotten? I bit my lip. When would my mind change to fit reality? When would the fog lift from my heart?

The staircase was hotter than being out in the sun, if that was possible. However it was quiet in the stairwell. No lessons or quizzes. Our shoes echoed on the cement. A bird sang nearby. And, at the top of each floor, there was an open-air space. A small breeze from outside blew toward us like a kiss of congratulations that we had climbed another floor.

Mother-In-Law was kind to accompany me on this long journey. She may have walked many *li* to fetch firewood when she was younger. But certainly, if a car had come by offering to take her to the mountain top, she would have been a fool to refuse. That's what Guo Qiang's shaking head said to me. That we were fools. Fools he had little patience for.

"Quit dragging," Mother-In-Law called from the middle of the stairwell. I hurried to catch up.

"Was I dragging?" I asked. "I'm sorry."

The heat melted my thoughts. I just wanted to stay in one of the open air spaces and feel the breeze, listen to the birds. I forced myself to focus on this mission. On chaos. That's what Teacher Sarah—in university—had called it. From the day she arrived, she talked about chaos. That it not only made the world turn faster but made the difference between a good English speaker and a bad one. She laughed with her mouth wide open, and we could see all her gold fillings. Mei Ling, who sat next to me, whispered, "Show off."

But we soon realized that was just Teacher Sarah's way. That she liked to laugh—especially when we spoke new words—and she'd never been taught how to do so properly. Teacher Sarah always said we put the accent on the wrong syllable, making the words sound like a foreign language. Classmate Zhang had raised his hand.

"But English IS a foreign language, isn't it?" he had asked.

Teacher Sarah had liked Classmate Zhang. She said he wasn't a bump on a log. And he obviously liked her too. Once I heard him complimenting her beautiful gold fillings.

"No, no, no," Teacher Sarah had written on the board, underlining each no. "Foreign means 'strange and unnatural.' And English is only strange and unnatural if you don't take it into your hearts."

I hadn't always followed what she meant. But I still remembered the pronunciation drill she had us say at the start of each class:

There is CHAos, not chaOS.

In the LANguage, not lanGUAGE.

So, it's WELcome, not well COME

But goodBYE, not GOOD buy

I repeated this to myself as I followed Mother-In-Law. The drill gave a rhythm to my climbing, kept me from thinking too much about the heat, about Guo Qiang and that moving box I had been too frightened to enter, and about other things as well.

Mei Ling and I used to practice Teacher Sarah's poem together while we washed out our clothes each morning. Was Mei Ling this hot in Japan? Chan Hai had said Singapore was so hot only cockroaches survived. How had he known? Then again, he'd always been so wise. Wise like the ocean—that was what his name meant. And he was. I still remembered us standing in the reservoir and him asking with sincerity, "How do you wash your hair?"

"What's funny?" Mother-In-Law turned around on the steps.

We weren't yet at the top of a floor being kissed by a breeze. A drop of sweat rolled down my forehead. The saltwater stung my eyes. My throat tickled. What could I say? That my lover and I laughed all night long at the thought of my shampoo making me too heavy to swim?

"Well?" She took a step down toward me. "Aren't you going to share your humor with your Mother-In-Law? I've never heard you laugh."

"I guess I'm just nervous." My fingers toyed with my yellow bird necklace.

"Well, don't be." She started back up the steps. "You'll just end up embarrassing all of us."

"You're right," I said.

Teacher Sarah had done many introduction lessons with us— from talking on the phone to gossiping at a cocktail party. She had always told us not to worry too much about talking after we said, "Nice to meet you." She had said people were usually happy to do all the talking. Guo Qiang was a perfect example. Often I didn't have to prompt him at all. I rubbed the bird around my neck again. How I longed to be listening to the deep voice of Chan Hai talking about anything.

Mother-In-Law paused on the staircase again. She fidgeted with the strap of her purse and looked up the flight of steps. Perhaps this trip up the stairs was more difficult than walking several *li* to get firewood.

"Are you tired," I asked. "You want to rest?"

"It's interesting," she whispered. "How fate puts people together."

Why had she stopped? Had she read my thoughts? Could she see to all the spots Chan Hai had caressed and Guo Qiang had yet to discover?

"Like friends," Mother-In-Law suggested. "And marriage partners."

Was she telling me that a friend is a friend, but marriage is a commitment that affects every generation to come? Perhaps, she knew about Chan Hai. My cheeks filled with heat.

"You're right." I cleared my throat.

"Some people don't have any concern about future generations," she said. "They only think about the moment in front of them. Like a child with a new toy."

I nodded. She saw right through me and yet accepted me. A true dear mother. I wanted to tell her how difficult it was to leave one's childish heart behind and try to build a responsible relationship. I needed her to guide me.

"Some people," she said, whispering so fiercely, I felt spittle on my ear. "Some people, don't even consider that they are diluting their own culture, their own bloodline."

I coughed and swallowed my foolish thoughts. She spoke not of me, but of Colleague. Colleague, his foreign polluted wife, and their diluted son.

"Is that you?" Guo Qiang called from the top of the steps.

"We're coming," Mother-In-Law said.

She continued climbing. But rather than have me follow her, she stayed by my side. She clutched onto my arm.

"It's sad. So sad," she said, her hot breath on my cheek. "Young people these days just don't give a thought to their responsibility in the circle of life. Don't give a thought to the children."

Guo Qiang had mentioned how cute this boy was. How intelligent.

How talkative. But Mother-In-Law obviously didn't feel the same. She probably only thought of how thoughtless to create a child that wasn't 100% Chinese. How he would never be accepted as a Chinese. Would be scoffed at by the ancestors. She was old-fashioned that way.

"And." Mother-In-Law pulled on my arm to slow me. "And, while Guo Qiang always laughs at stories about Li Zhi, that woman is a little...." She pointed to her head to indicate a mental issue.

"Really?" I asked.

Was this true or just Mother-In-Law talking? Guo Qiang thought Lee Sa was great. He was happy to share memories of her. Besides, why would his colleague marry a crazy woman? Still Mother-In-Law's palms were sweaty, her face serious. Her feet plodded slower and slower the closer we got to the top of the staircase. The closer we got to this crazy Lee Sa.

"Really?" I asked again.

"Really," she said. But she didn't offer an example so I could judge for myself. "It was just a tragic accident."

Guo Qiang had never mentioned an accident. Maybe Lee Sa hurt herself like that man in Xiamen who had fallen from the construction site, that big board collapsing from his weight and falling on top of him, breaking all the connections in his head.

"Li Zhi's parents must have made Colleague's parents feel obligated."

Mother-In-Law made a ball shape over her stomach. Aha. Poor Colleague had put happiness inside a crazy woman, and now was stuck. An arranged marriage of a different style.

"The sun is going to set soon," Guo Qiang's voice chided from above.

I gripped the handrail, pulling myself and Mother-In-Law up the stairs. In the five days I'd been here, I'd felt so isolated. Guo Qiang, when he wasn't at work lecturing to his students, lectured to me. Mother-In-Law ordered me around. Even the stall owners at the wet market were too busy to do more than bark quantities and prices. Here I'd had a chance to make a real friend on this island. I sighed. A crazy woman.

Chapter Fifty-Two
Crazy Lee Sa

Guo Qiang helped Mother-In-Law up the last few steps, handing her a handkerchief to wipe the sweat from her forehead. I joined them, my calves aching, my cheeks burning, sweat trickling down my back. A swim in the reservoir would be nice now.

The stairway was situated at the end of a long hallway. Apartments lined the right side. A chest-high cement wall on the left opened to the outside. Over the side of the short wall, cheers erupted. I peeked over.

We stood so high off the ground, higher than my required math class at university which was on the fifth floor. Higher than the pink castle which I'd never been inside. If I dropped over the side, there'd be a crash louder than the one where the construction worker fell from his ladder outside the post office near my university. A big accident it would be. I held tight to the wall. The base of my spine tingled.

Down on the ground, some dark-skinned boys stood on either side of a net. The ones on the far side appeared to be waiting, their bodies hovering close to the net. The ones closest to me surrounded one boy. When I leaned forward, I noticed he was kicking at something. A ball?

"That's a Malay game," Guo Qiang said from behind me. His voice urgent, as if he could nudge me forward. "It's called Spetakra. It was created—"

"They seem to enjoy it," I interrupted, diverting him from the long, dusty educational path he intended to drag me down. A path I had a vague sense he'd taken me on before. He'd written to me something about this. About Lee Sa being so upset the game was played too late that she had called the police. I remembered being amazed anyone would involve the police. What a crazy thing to do. Now I understood. This was a different place with different rules.

"How they can run around in the sun with their dark skin is just a wonder," Mother-In-Law said. "I always thought dark colors attracted the sun." She looked at my black pants. "You must be miserable."

I smoothed my hand over my thighs. Hot maybe. Not miserable.

The pants, like the bird around my neck, made my heart feel light. As if Chan Hai weren't so far away. Gone.

"Dark or light has nothing to do with it," Guo Qiang instructed. "The skin becomes more sensitized from living here. To you, the sun is hot. To them, we are heading into the winter monsoon. The temperature has dropped a few degrees. It's cool."

My brain pulsed with heat. The air was so thick, my nose hurt when I inhaled. How could anyone think this was cool? How long would it take before my skin became sensitized to my surroundings? And, even if my skin became accustomed, would my heart ever?

"I don't think I'll live that long," Mother-In-Law said.

I felt the same.

"Of course you will," Guo Qiang chided. "You would probably be able to notice slight differences already if Li Hui wasn't taking you on marathon walks up the steps. Li Hui, you're going to have to learn to ride that elevator. Mother is being too kind to you."

I nodded. My throat ached. Here this old woman had guided me up the steps so I wouldn't have to ride the moving box. She cared about me. Why did my heart feel like a piece of wood?

Guo Qiang led us down the hallway past several apartments. Just as in our building, these apartments had long windows which allowed us to view inside as though passing a store or watching a giant TV. In the village, we would never have windows like this. Our house had small windows that didn't allow for too much peering in or out. Some of the newer houses with large windows had large walls around them. Singaporeans and foreigners must not mind being watched.

Guo Qiang walked straight past each window. Certainly he'd seen inside before and had already programmed the contents in his brain. But I hadn't. Obviously neither had Mother-In-Law. We peered inside where a Chinese woman bent down to the floor with an old rag. Her young son stood a few feet away, his head down, his eyes on the floor.

"I thought I told you I'd get you some juice when you finished practicing your Mandarin studies," she scolded in clipped Mandarin tones. She wiped at a spill on the floor. "I don't know why you can't listen. No wonder you have trouble with your grades. You probably don't listen to your teacher either."

Perhaps this woman needed a tutor for her son. I hadn't yet seen a park where tutors stood with their signs. I looked to Guo Qiang on the verge of asking him. But I hated to get him going again. Whether he knew the answer to my question or not, I'd have to listen to every fact he'd ever learned about parks in Singapore. Their history, dimensions, cultural heritage. Besides, I didn't want to appear as if we didn't need to visit his colleague's crazy wife for help. Surely Guo Qiang knew Mother-In-Law's opinion of the woman even if her fingers weren't digging into his skin. I wouldn't add to that pressure.

In the next apartment, pictures of funny-looking creatures decorated the wall. A naked woman with many hands. A man with an elephant nose. On a short wooden table stood a golden joss holder with several sticks burning. Through the open window, the smell of incense was strong. As if I'd just walked into the back room of the tea shop while Feng Gu lit incense for her elder brother. I hoped Feng Gu would take care of Chan Hai, as she had promised. Help him get the quarry re-opened, support him in starting a nursery, even sew his pants and give him a son if that's what he so desired.

A man who looked like the one we'd just seen downstairs selling shrimp crackers came into the room. He had the same kind of towel-type outfit wrapped around his big belly. How had the man gotten upstairs so fast? Maybe he'd taken the elevator as well. As we got closer, I noticed he had a red dot on his forehead. His face looked heavier. Perhaps he wasn't the same man as the salesman downstairs. I looked up to see if Mother-In-Law had experienced the same confusion. She grabbed onto me with both her hands. But she looked ahead down the hall. Guo Qiang had stopped in front of the door at the end of the hall. This must be Colleague and Lee Sa's apartment.

Plants decorated the small area outside the crazy foreign wife's door. The greenery amidst all this concrete looked like a patch of fuzz missed while shaving. No matter how silly, I could hear Chan Hai's deep voice pointing out the palms and the orchids, telling me of the different varieties and the life cycles. Just looking at them and hearing his voice calmed me.

Hidden among the flowers and plants stood a couch where you could sit and pretend to be in a jungle. Or watch the neighbors' laundry hanging off bamboo poles at the apartment building across the way. Perhaps this was the piece of furniture Guo Qiang had written me about, the one Lee Sa had picked up from the garbage. Mother-In-Law scurried past that couch as if this were the case. As if the cushions were inhabited by ghosts and one of them might jump up and grab her.

"Remember," Mother-In-Law ran up alongside Guo Qiang and whispered. "We'll just stay long enough to have Li Zhi test Li Hui's English. Offer advice. We don't want to bother Colleague too long." Her lips pursed together. Her eyebrow furrowed. "It's not just hot," she continued. "It's almost dinner time. And you have your work to think about. You don't want to spend so much time—"

Guo Qiang turned and stared at her. His eyes had a strange glaze which made them shine like the coated-pork Mother always made for the New Year. Was this a difficult trip for him to make? Perhaps he felt sorrow for his colleague who had not only stepped out of his common boundaries, but was stuck with a crazy person. Mother-In-Law's nervous chatter didn't help. His look said as much. Guo Qiang raised his fist to knock on the blue door. But, before he had a chance, the door opened.

"Come in," a man said in hushed Mandarin. Colleague. "Come in."

I realized with a start that made me want to laugh out loud that I had expected him to speak in English. As if by being married to a foreigner, he wasn't really Chinese anymore.

"Please," Colleague said, ushering us into the cool breeze of his living room.

A box on the wall whirred up and down, just like in the herbal pharmacy or department store at home. I expected to see rows of tiger patches or ladies dresses. Instead the place looked like the park after a police raid. A newspaper covered the floor next to a short oblong table. Small socks, several pair, were strewn about the room. Toys scattered everywhere. My new sandals stuck to the floor as I navigated my way behind Mother-In-Law to the couch. The mess made my eyes itch.

I didn't see or hear the crazy foreign wife. Maybe she had been busy in the kitchen all morning and not had a chance to see the disaster in the rest of the house. Obviously Colleague's parents didn't live here. They would never allow guests to see such a mess. Perhaps Colleague was not the eldest son. Or perhaps the parents were still distressed over his marriage.

Colleague picked up a child's t-shirt, an orange and black tiger-striped cloth, and a few blocks from the couch so we could sit. He was taller than Guo Qiang and had high cheekbones, like a Mongolian. On his left cheek, right next to his eye, was a scar like half a fish scale. It wasn't large, but it stood out because the rest of his skin was golden brown. My nose tingled looking at that scar, as if a sudden draft of chili peppers had wafted from the cooling box on the wall. Chan Hai probably had a scar like that now from his fight with College Boy.

"Some small treats for you," Guo Qiang said to Colleague, sitting down between Mother-In-Law and myself. He cleared space on the table, pushing aside a toy car and some candy wrappers, and set the bag of shrimp crackers down.

"Oh, you didn't have to bring gifts," Colleague said, picking up the shrimp crackers and putting them in Guo Qiang's lap. "You take them back home."

Colleague and Guo Qiang fought over the crackers for many minutes, Guo Qiang offering and Colleague refusing, three times. In their enthusiasm, the cracker bag broke open. Several of the pink chips fell to the floor. I retrieved them along with a half a cookie and couple of noodles.

"Well, we'll just have to share them," Guo Qiang said. "And fast."

I smiled and nodded. I knew this one. Guo Qiang had mentioned to me several times that, with 98% humidity in the air, food didn't keep long.

Colleague disappeared into the kitchen, probably to find a bowl and tell the foreign wife we were here. Mother-In-Law shifted in her seat, pulling out two wooden toy blocks from beneath her. She shook her head and looked at Guo Qiang, as if to say, "What a sad situation your fellow countryman is in." Guo Qiang ignored her and picked up the paper from the floor. Mother and I stared at the walls. He started reading the front page. Outside the boys playing the game from Malaysia cheered. The air conditioner on the wall blew air up and down. Hadn't he already read this paper?

I didn't hear any voices in the kitchen. Cupboards opened and closed, opened and closed. Didn't they speak to one another? If the kitchen looked anything like the living room, Crazy Lee Sa would never find the bowls or the tea.

I scanned the mess around us trying to find a clean place to rest my eyes. That's when I spotted a picture of a small boy in a sandbox. A black-and-white photo. Like the one of Feng Gu's dead brother or Guo Qiang's dead father. The precious photo lay next to my chair in a nest of tissue paper. Blood rushed through my body and beat at my temples.

But maybe this wasn't an ancestral photo. Even in the village, more and more people spent money on making pictures. They weren't worried that the camera would take away part of their spirit or too much of their money. Still, this picture was black-and-white and in a black frame. I looked around the room, craning my neck to see if I could find more such pictures. But there was just this one in that black frame. Why hadn't Guo Qiang said anything? Why hadn't Mother-In-Law mentioned this event during our talk in the stairwell? Maybe she assumed Guo Qiang had already told me. That our nights were filled with thunderous conversation and rain-making. Chili peppers bit my nose again.

I could see now why this foreign wife was crazy and the house in such disarray. Poor Cheng Min who had lost all her children said she heard voices. The children still calling to her. Certainly her house would look no better if Prehistoric Lady wasn't there to help her. I looked at Guo Qiang, waiting for him to glance up from his paper, see me looking at the ancestral photo on the ground and whisper the date the boy had died. But, while he sat next to me, he didn't sense anything I was feeling or wondering. Not like Chan Hai had. I nudged his foot. He moved over to make more room for me, as if we were passengers crowded on a bus. I cleared my throat.

"Look," I said, nodding my head toward the nest of papers. The ancestral photo. "There."

"Isn't that neat?" he said, glancing at the floor before returning to the paper.

"Neat?" I repeated. Was he being sarcastic? Would his friend stay in this bad marriage now that there was no son?

"Yeah." Guo Qiang folded the paper with a flourish. This was twice today I'd interrupted his reading. Once when we came here and now. "Don't you remember?"

But he'd never told me anything about this boy's death. How had it happened? Had he fallen off the wall to the play area seven long stories below? Choked on a fish bone? Been blown to bits?

"The things people think of," he said, reaching down under the chair next to the photograph and picking up something. "I remember we used to play with stones." He turned to me. "Did you—no, you're probably from the metal era. And, now," he rolled a purple plastic jack around in the palm of his hand and threw it on the table. "Now, they have plastic."

Was he purposely ignoring my question? How could he just sit there, playing with a dead boy's jacks? I pinched my nose to keep the tears inside, tears which had nothing to do with this stranger's son. Which had nothing to do with any dead person. But with the dead feeling inside of me.

Colleague's shoes flip-flopped as he entered the living room, putting an end to discussion and speculation. He held a tray laden with teacups, a flowered teapot, a bowl of shrimp crackers.

"Lee Sa'll be out in a minute, I'm sure," he said, setting down the tray and looking at me. "It's dusty in here, isn't it? It's always so dusty from all the factories nearby. It makes my eyes water, too." He spoke so normally. He even smiled, making his fish scale scar wink at me. "Reminds me of the village," he added.

"No." Guo Qiang sat forward. "This is a different kind of dust. In the village, it's dirt from the ground and coal fires. Here it's smoke from factories."

The two of them launched into a debate about the difference in the dusts. Guo Qiang had heard of unpublished studies—because, of course, the government would not want the public to know what they were breathing. Colleague countered that dirt was dirt. Mother-In-Law stared in her teacup, as if expecting a ball of sludge to appear on the bottom. I thought of my shoes filling with dirt as I ran toward Waipo's grave to talk to her about my love for Chan Hai. "It is what it is," Waipo had said.

Perhaps this was our mission. We all had big goals which we ran after as though chasing a feather in a typhoon. Father to win another marathon *mahjong* tournament. Mother to live peaceably with Father. Me to get a good job, marry my lover, hold up my half of the sky. Perhaps our mission wasn't the goals but the attitude we maintained when life handed us something else instead. Surely that was what Guo Qiang was doing here, discussing dirt with such passion. Helping Colleague to move forward, to avoid discussing other, unpleasant issues. Colleague followed the idiotic conversation, even though his life was crumbling. What strong men they were.

The crazy, foreign wife was a different matter. She didn't come out, as Colleague had promised. Perhaps seeing an old friend was too hard. As the afternoon stretched out and the tea in our cups grew cold, I wished Guo Qiang would put an end to this visit. He wanted to introduce me to this foreign English expert, but this obviously wasn't a good time.

Mother-In-Law rearranged her purse in her lap and scooted to the edge of the couch. She was probably thinking of all the chores still waiting for us at the apartment, especially after all this talk of dirt. Eventually, even Guo Qiang ran out of conversation and dropped into silence like a motorcycle which had putt-putted to the end of the corner and run out of gas. I looked once more to the photo on the floor.

"Another jack?" Guo Qiang asked.

"I find those things everywhere." Colleague laughed, reaching down under the chair to pick it up. His hand touched the photo instead. "Oh, what's this? Lee Sa mentioned we'd gotten a package."

We stared at the photo. Here was this topic we'd skirted around all afternoon staring us in the face. Mother-In-Law made a tsk-tsk sound, holding on tight to Guo Qiang's arm. Guo Qiang gazed at the picture, as if he wanted to reach out and touch the boy, who he'd said was so cute and talkative. What could we say? Anything would sound trite. The poor man.

"Don't be too sad," I finally said.

"No." Colleague looked up at me. His face broke into a smile. "No. This is—"

"A bad omen," Mother-In-Law said. "How could someone with intelligence put a living boy in an ancestral frame like that?"

So he wasn't dead? Air flowed through my lungs once again. What a relief. But then where was everybody and why did this house look like chaos?

"Some people just have no common sense," Mother continued, as though stomping on a spark in a dry field. She probably worried the ancestors would be offended by this picture. Take action. "Some people think their way is the only way and never think about others."

I patted her arm. She probably didn't want Colleague to feel too worried about this photo, that it held any deep meaning, that he would need to do anything more than pay a visit to the temple and make an offering. But her comments made my skin feel hot.

"How could anyone be so selfish?" she asked. "So foolish?"

"Well, it's definitely..." Colleague gave us a quick smile, his cheeks quivering. He tucked the picture under his arm like a newspaper. "It's definitely . . . "

"A beautiful photograph." Guo Qiang spoke for first time, standing up to take a better look.

Mother-In-Law drew in a sharp breath, as if she'd been kicked.

She rushed over next to Guo Qiang as if her physical proximity would pull him away from his horrible thoughts.

"No, no, no," she said. "It's wrong. Just wrong. No, no, no."

"Mother," Guo Qiang said. "Black-and-whites are an art."

"Well," Colleague said, pulling out the picture and smiling at the boy in the picture. "This is a nice shot of him. Very artistic. You're right."

How could anyone consider a funeral photo art? How did Guo Qiang not see this as a bad omen, a death pronouncement, a temptation to the gods to take the child away? He obviously hadn't remembered to carry with him all of his culture and upbringing.

"But that frame." Mother-In-Law shuddered.

"You're right," Colleague said. "It should be red."

We stood there, in a tight circle around this photo, as though it were a magnet holding us there. The creak of the bedroom door sounded. Bare footsteps slapped across the floor. I turned to see a large woman enter the room. She wore only short pants which stopped at the top of her thick thighs. Underwear? A tight cloth wrapped across her breasts the size of pomello fruits. I was reminded of the underclothing Waipo wore, before China had bras. The ancient Chinese undergarment held onto this woman's breasts so tightly, we could see every bulge, even the large bumps in the middle. How did Colleague deal with such large appendages? Yes, he was a brave man.

"Have they left?" the almost-naked woman asked in English. Then she spotted us. "Oh. Hi."

The English noises from her mouth were like cymbals breaking the actors into movement in a Chinese opera. We all sat back in our spots. But the crazy foreign wife didn't move. She looked back toward the bedroom door, as though deciding whether or not to run back inside. Perhaps she didn't like strangers. Or more likely she was embarrassed.

"Come join us," Colleague said, not bothered by her nakedness. Maybe he was used to forgiving this kind of behavior.

"I was just trying to get Kevin to sleep," she said. Her deep blue eyes were like that of pictures of the devil. She had short hair, like women used to have in the days of Mao's Cultural Revolution, a long face like a horse, and a small bump for a nose. "He wants some milk. If I don't hurry back, he'll be out here in a flash."

We all listened for a boy to grumble for his milk. Colleague's eyes fastened on her face. He held up his hand, beckoning to her.

"I don't hear anything," Guo Qiang declared. "Besides, it's too hot to sleep,"

"Lee Sa's always so concerned about nap time and bath time and bedtime." Colleague patted the arm of his chair for her. "Everything is time, time, time. I tell her, when I was a kid we didn't have all those times. We let things happen naturally, and we survived without being too sleep deprived."

"Oh, please." Lee Sa came forward. "Don't get started on that. You also didn't have electricity or any toys to speak of—"

"Not true." Colleague held up a finger. "We may not have had electricity until—when did we get that?"

"1968," Guo Qiang said.

"But we had lots of toys," Colleague said. "In fact, a lot of the toys, the games, are the same. They've just become high tech."

"Or plasticized." Guo Qiang picked up the jack and threw it on the table.

"Hey, where'd you find that?" Lee Sa leaned down, her big breasts threatening to fall out of her top. "Kevin was looking all over for that so we could play."

"It was over there on the floor," Guo Qiang said.

"You're kidding." Lee Sa looked to the floor, as if she might find another. "Hey, what happened to my picture?"

"Right here." Colleague pulled the ancestral-looking photo from beneath his arm.

"Nice, don't you think?" Lee Sa asked.

Lee Sa took the picture from him. Then she held up the square as if showing a picture book to a first grade class. Her back and arms and neck, which were naked, had many sun spots. She looked like an old woman who had spent her days in the field. Maybe she never carried an umbrella. Maybe they didn't have money for umbrellas, after spending all their cash on high tech toys, plastic jacks, and wooden blocks for the boy who wasn't dead. Or maybe she was just too dizzy in her head to remember such things.

"Well?" she asked. "Doesn't anyone have a comment?"

Nobody responded, not even Guo Qiang who had said such wonderful things about this art just a few minutes earlier. Mother-In-Law refused to even look at the ghostly picture again. Colleague poured more tea.

"Is art," I said.

Lee Sa's arms had fine hair, like new grass. I felt her staring at me with those big blue eyes. My skin prickled.

"Yes," she said. "That's Zhu Dee for you."

"Zhu Dee?" I repeated. What was this? Who was this?

"She can take any moment," Lee Sa looked down at Guo Qiang. "Well, almost any moment. And turn it into art."

A cheer erupted from outside where the boys played their Malaysian game. The air conditioner creaked up and down. Mother-In-Law stared at her black purse, her lips set together in a tight grimace. There was something here I wasn't hearing.

"Lee Sa," Guo Qiang said in a big voice. "This is my wife, Li Hui."

"Yes." She gave me a big smile. "I assumed that's who this was. Nice to meet you, Lee—what was it?"

"It's pronounced 'way,'" Colleague helped. He must always have to translate the names, the holidays, the culture. How tiresome. "Just think of that Frank Sinatra song, 'I did it my way.'"

"Oh. Leeway," she said, nodding her horsy face up and down. "Like space to let me get by. Freedom to move. Leeway. What a great name."

"Thank you," I pushed out. Crazy Lee Sa talked so fast. I was pleased to have been able to jump into the conversation at what I hoped was the right time.

"Leeway," she repeated, her tongue rolling around in her mouth. She sat down on the edge of Colleague's chair, her shorts riding up her legs, showing every part of her thick thighs. "I can't say I've heard a lot about you. In fact, this is all—" She put her arms out. "Such a surprise."

"Li Zhi." Mother-In-Law cleared her throat and moved forward on her seat. She stared down at her purse and cleared her throat again. We waited, watching for the English words to squeeze from her lips like the last bit of toothpaste from a tube. "Li Hui has eagerness to meet you."

"Yes, Mother's right," Guo Qiang repeated. "She's been eager to meet you."

"That's so sweet." Lee Sa's blue eyes twinkled.

Mother-In-Law nudged Guo Qiang so hard, he bumped against me. Was she irritated that he had corrected her English? Did she want him to say goodbye now?

"Will you tutor my wife in English?" he asked.

I put my sandal over his loafer and pressed down. I thought we were here just for an interview—a little advice—maybe just to make acquaintances. Why would Guo Qiang ask this crazy woman to teach me English? Unless this was his way of offering help to Colleague. It would have been nice in all his talk of water retention and humidity and taxi drivers and industrial zones if he had mentioned this to me.

"Any help—" Guo Qiang turned his palms toward the ceiling and held them up. "Any help you can give her—"

"Oh, Guo Qiang," she said, waving her hands in the air. "You know me. I'm no English teacher."

The way she flailed her arms about reminded me of Madame Tsui Ping dumping tea all over the tea shop. I leaned forward and put my hand on my tea cup. Although even if she knocked my tea on this floor, it wouldn't be noticed.

"But," Guo Qiang insisted. "Aren't you teaching that moving to Singapore—"

She threw her head back and laughed, showing several gold fillings at the back of her mouth. Would she start rocking and crying, as Madame Tsui Ping had done? I nudged Guo Qiang with my elbow. We should say goodbye.

"You mean 'Settling in Singapore?'" she asked.

"Yes." Guo Qiang threw the jack again. "That."

This woman had a job? Perhaps she was like Don Don, being watched over and told what to do and how to do it. Or maybe "Settling in Singapore" was what they called their mental institutions. Hadn't Guo Qiang said Singapore had special places for people like this?

"I'm awfully busy," she said.

"But." Colleague gave her a look. "You teach those newcomers to Singapore only twice a week. The rest of the time, you're free as a bird. As a Leeway."

"That's not the way the word's used." Lee Sa glared at Colleague.

"See, there you go." Colleague patted her thigh, as if the two of them were alone. "You're a natural teacher."

What was this all about? They didn't really expect this woman to teach me? I felt a shiver run up my spine, as if I stood in the reservoir. Here these people surrounded me with their clothes on. They stared at me in my nakedness. They knew what they were talking about. I did not.

"I've seen how you teach Kevin," Guo Qiang added. "You're

good."

"Yes," Lee Sa said, examining me with her devil eyes. "Well, he's four."

"But that boy speaks like an adult," Guo Qiang said. Then he nodded in my direction. "She studied English for eight years and can barely say a word."

"Barely a word?" Lee Sa stood up and put her hands on her hips. "I studied French in school for umpteen years, and I can't say more than *bonjour*."

Colleague shifted in his seat. Surely he felt shame that Lee Sa bragged about her French ability, when we weren't even talking about French. Her naked thighs were nothing compared to this embarrassment. He stared in his tea cup, perhaps waiting for her ranting to end. The poor man.

"You see." Lee Sa pointed her finger at Guo Qiang. "It's not how much you study, but how often you have a chance to use the language. How often did she have a chance to use English in a small village in China?" She looked over at me. "I take it you're from a small village in China—"

"You right," I said. "Same small village as Guo Qiang. We have million people."

"Some people would call that huge." She laughed again. She liked to show her gold fillings. "But, the point is, you probably never spoke English, right?"

"Not speak a lot," I said. I thought of the few times I'd had to use my English training in the village. With Madame Tsui Ping down on the floor of the tea shop, surrounded by mountains of tea. Then again when Guo Qiang demonstrated his vast knowledge of vocabulary.

"You see?" Lee Sa put her hands up to the ceiling, as though imploring the gods. "How can you expect so much?"

I smiled to myself. She really thought Guo Qiang meant I couldn't speak English. Did foreigners not refer to their spouses with great humility? Or was this just part of her mental condition?

"Well?" Lee Sa insisted, thrusting her hands toward Guo Qiang.

"Exactly," he said, not even flinching. "You're exactly right. So, will you give my wife a chance to use her English?"

Lee Sa sat back down so hard that the sofa leg scraped the tile floor. My ears hurt. My temples pounded. Why was Guo Qiang so insistent?

"I'm not sure I can." She nodded toward the closed bedroom

door and rubbed her hairy arms. "That rascal takes up most of my time."

"I know you're a busy housewife," Guo Qiang said.

Lee Sa's blue eyes widened. She put one of her hands on her hips again. She opened her big mouth to speak.

"So." Guo Qiang stopped her. "I'll make it worth your while. How much can I pay you?"

"Fifty dollars an hour," she said as if she'd been thinking about it.

More than Don Don even. Back in the village, an English tutor only charged the equivalent of one dollar per hour. Surely she was missing at least a few piano strings. How could anyone expect to earn, basically, one dollar per minute? What nonsense.

Colleague rubbed his temples with his fingers. Poor, poor man. Although Mother-In-Law didn't understand much, she ground her teeth. Guo Qiang patted his knees and stood up.

"Sounds fine to me," he said, reaching in his pocket for his wallet. "She'll come once a week, starting tomorrow."

Why did Guo Qiang agree to this nonsense? Why was this so important? I was standing in the reservoir again. The water kept rushing over my eyes. I couldn't see.

Chapter Fifty-Three
Frames

Mother-In-Law and I marched down the hallway in front of Guo Qiang as though chased by ghosts. This time we didn't look in the windows to see what the dark, naked man was doing in his living room or whether the Chinese boy had finished his Mandarin studies. We were eager to return to the safety and sanity of our home.

When we arrived at the staircase, Guo Qiang joined us on the walk down. Perhaps he sensed our discomfort with the arrangement he'd made. Perhaps he would explain why he had offered to pay Lee Sa the equivalent of my weekly salary at the tea shop for an hour's worth of English. Did Colleague need money? Was this Guo Qiang's way of helping them out?

"Unbelievable," Mother-In-Law spat out, as soon as her black tie shoe hit the first step.

I thought the same. Best to let Mother-In-Law say it though. Guo Qiang's face was impassive, as if he registered not a word.

"How his parents allowed for such a union," Mother-In-Law huffed. "It's beyond comprehension. She let us sit in that pig pen until my backbone felt brittle. Gave us nothing to eat. Made that poor excuse for a man provide what little refreshment we got. And then, then, if that wasn't enough, that picture. How could she display that picture of her son as though selling the last piece of meat at the market? Surely the gods will take the boy. Surely. And, with a fool for a mother, perhaps he's better off."

Mother-In-Law paused on her step and looked back at Guo Qiang. But he didn't say a word. I had no desire to, either. In fact, I'd forgotten what my original question was, the staircase was so stuffy with her opinions. Even the waft of air when we reached the next landing seemed an unwelcome intrusion.

"The elevator's on this floor," he said, moving into the hallway.

What an excuse. Surely he'd had a change of heart. He'd had enough of Mother-In-Law's noise. So had I. But I knew I'd never make it inside that moving box. Not today.

"It stops on the sixth and eleventh floors," Guo Qiang continued.

"To save electricity. The Housing Board did a study—"

"I see," I said.

I didn't relish a trip down with Mother-In-Law. Her brow was furrowed. Her eyes narrowed. She was certainly working on another crop of stories to tell.

"Well?" Guo Qiang asked. "Is anyone coming?"

"Mother-In-Law is," I said. "You heard her say her spine was sore. Best not to aggravate it by walking too much. That's what my best friend in university who studied to be a doctor would have said."

"A Western doctor?" Mother-In-Law asked. "Because, while China keeps looking to follow the West, I don't believe in anything those—"

"An herbal doctor," I assured her.

She allowed me to guide her toward Guo Qiang. Then I turned and went down the steps. The stairwell was quiet and welcoming, like an old friend. But all of my friends were so far away.

While Colleague was Guo Qiang's good friend, I wasn't eager to be close to Lee Sa. She was so loud and hairy and rude. Perhaps Colleague and Guo Qiang were used to her strange behaviors, but I didn't see how I'd ever become accustomed to sitting with her in her underwear and feeling those devil blue eyes scrutinize me as if I were the crazy one. I hopped down the steps, two at a time. While I enjoyed the respite from Mother-In-Law's noise, I was eager to get down to the bottom. What exactly did Guo Qiang expect of me with regards to Crazy Lee Sa?

Mother-In-Law and Guo Qiang stood at the bottom of the steps waiting. Guo Qiang glanced at his watch. Mother-In-Law rearranged her purse strap on her shoulder. The guard slouched in his chair, his head falling down on his chest, mouth open. Fast asleep.

"I was starting to wonder if you got lost," Mother-In-Law said.

Her shoulders were rigid. Her mouth set in a thin line. Her eyes narrowed. The ride in the elevator hadn't done anything to improve her mood.

"I'm sorry you had to wait," I said, feeling perspiration drip from my forehead. I wished Guo Qiang would offer me his soft handkerchief. I took a stiff piece of tissue paper from my purse and dabbed at my face.

We passed the naked man who was standing behind his shop

counter. Now that we didn't need shrimp crackers, he didn't even acknowledge us. Guo Qiang opened his parasol and walked out onto the sidewalk. I walked up next to him, with Mother-In-Law on my right. She leaned over about to start up again on Lee Sa, I was sure.

"So," I said, before Mother-In-Law had a chance. "Lee Sa already has a job. She must be awfully busy."

A group of children ran past us, shouting in English and pointing ahead. Some of the children had Chinese features. Some of them darker, their faces puffy like a plum which has been left too long to ripen. So many different-looking people here.

"She works with foreigners twice a week. Helping them get used to Singapore." Guo Qiang's eyes followed the children. "Not foreigners like them. Or us. Westerners."

"Perhaps she's too busy," I said. "I hate to take up more of her time."

"Oh, no," Guo Qiang said, chuckling. "The Singapore Settling thing is hardly a challenge. Unless you consider trying not to laugh a challenge. You should hear some of the stories she tells."

"Yes," I said. "Well, I just—"

"She gives tours through the supermarket," he said. "So the housewives can find supplies similar to what they get at home." He rolled his eyes. "Tours. Can you imagine?"

"No," I said. Why would women need to have their hands held through a market? It sounded like a school field trip. "Still, I hate to bother her—"

"She does the same with the wet market," he said. "Gives tours. Although she says most foreigners don't want to go there. They don't like the smells, the noise. They're embarrassed to bargain. They think the place is dirty."

The woman Guo Qiang described sounded not only sane but intelligent. Someone who knew the culture enough to show others how to adapt. The person I had met didn't seem this way. Not to me. Not to Mother-In-Law. Was this an old Lee Sa he remembered from way back when? Would he ever get around to mentioning why he threw all that money at her? Did he really expect me to take an English lesson from her?

A woman and young girl hurried around us. The young girl wore a blue dress that puffed out at the sides. She looked lovely except for a long blue bow at the back that dragged. The woman—her mother?— chased after the young girl who wouldn't stop, attempting to tie the bow. That's how I felt. As though I were chasing after Guo Qiang, trying to tie up this one issue that dragged.

"Just last week," Guo Qiang went on. "She said she had a woman who was in a panic, as if she'd lost the family jewels, because she couldn't find someone to clean her swimming pool."

Well, maybe this Lee Sa was just a good story teller and had Guo Qiang fooled. I hadn't seen any swimming pools around here. Nothing like Millionaire Huang's small round community pool. Nothing even like the reservoir.

A Chinese child toddled past. She held onto her mother with one hand, gripping tightly to a red balloon with the other. The letter M was emblazoned across the balloon. The child pulled the string and watched the red balloon bounce up and down. Two dark-looking teenage boys came up behind the mother and child. They sucked on straws from plastic cups as they walked. They passed the child, knocking the balloon from her hands.

"I told you to hold on tight," the mother scolded as the red balloon floated up into the sky, growing smaller and smaller.

"And another time," Guo Qiang went on. "A woman came in complaining about her 'maid from hell.' That's how she described the woman. From hell."

What I really wanted to hear about was why Guo Qiang brushed off money from his being like raindrops from his skin. I felt like the main idea of our conversation was floating away like that balloon in the sky. If I didn't grab on, the point of this conversation would disappear.

"What is this about?" I asked, navigating my way through a line of people which had formed at the market. My voice sounded loud. Rude. But I wanted to understand what had happened back there at Colleague's apartment.

"Oh, that's right," Guo Qiang said. He nodded as though finally understanding my frustration. Then his hand swept toward the crowd. "Some new fast food restaurant has its grand opening this evening. The first hundred customers get a free drink and balloon."

"And that Li Zhi didn't even bring her own son," Mother-In-Law said. "Instead she made him take a nap. I tell you—"

With Mother-In-Law returning to the conversation, the balloon disappeared. I followed them back to the apartment, wondering how people got so excited about the opening of a restaurant. About free drinks and balloons. How Mother-In-Law could chew so long on the topic of Lee Sa. And when would I understand where I fit?

We sat at our round glass dining table. So clean and lovely. So round and harmonious. The table was filled with dishes. Salted shrimp, fried greens, egg drop soup and steamed rice. Surely this fine meal in this harmonious setting would restore our balance. Bring peace.

Guo Qiang had emerged from his study with great reluctance to join us, surely fearful that Mother-In-Law was not finished with her unhappiness. All evening she had followed me around the house, polluting the air around me. Did I remember to dust the corners of the window sills? Or did I want to end up living in a cow's barn like Li Zhi's? Did I plan on making a soup as well? Guo Qiang had been starved all afternoon. My head pounded from her incessant beating. And each time she mispronounced Lee Sa's name and said "Li Zhi"—which is the same as the word 'pear' in Mandarin—I thought of fruit. Of peaches. Of Madame Matchmaker warning me about the peach tree. How I would climb out on a limb and not find any ripe peaches.

I looked across the table at Guo Qiang's thick cheeks. His skin was pink with heat. His eyes focused on his bowl of rice. My peach was certainly large and round and pink. Just the kind of peach Mother and Father wished for our family. But the skin was so tough, I couldn't taste the insides.

"Too salty," Mother-In-Law said picking up a shrimp from a dish in the middle. "But delicious just the same."

Guo Qiang picked up a pink shrimp in his red wooden chopsticks—a wedding present. He stared at the antennae. He wrinkled his nose.

"I can't eat this," he said, setting the shellfish back down.

"It's not that salty," Mother-In-Law said. How kind of her.

"It's just, once you become sensitized," he explained, "it's like being reprogrammed."

I took in a large breath and held it to prevent a huge sigh from escaping. Well, he had been working in his office for the last few hours. Surely computer talk was on his mind. But what did that have to do with eating shrimp?

"Don't talk gibberish." Mother-In-Law yawned. "Eat your food before it gets cold."

"Zhu Dee always took the shell off," Guo Qiang said.

Mother-In-Law's head whipped around as if she'd been slapped by the strong hand of a ghost. One that had followed us home from Lee Sa's couch. There was that name again. The name that had been mentioned in connection with Kevin's photograph. What had Lee Sa said? "Zhu Dee can take any moment—well almost any—and turn it to art."

"Zhu Dee loved shrimp," he said looking out the window as if he might see this person. "Said it was so cheap here—"

"Which it's not," Mother-In-Law said.

"It all depends on where you're coming from," Guo Qiang said. "Remember, output depends on input."

Guo Qiang and Mother-In-Law went back and forth in what seemed like an old argument. He leaned forward as though giving some impassioned plea. But Mother-In-Law just shook her head back and forth, as though she already knew what he would say. I felt naked in the reservoir again. "The only one without clothes. The only one without understanding.

"Who is this Zhu Dee?" I asked.

"Zhu Dee?" Guo Qiang asked, savoring the name.

"Can you imagine?" Mother-In-Law answered for him. "Someone who loved shrimp yet always peeled off the outside, all the calcium, the vitamins, the nutrients?"

"Really?" I wondered. He had written something about this, but I didn't recall the mention of Zhu Dee.

Mother-In-Law spoke of the past. Had this person died of a nutrient deficiency? Who was this person to Guo Qiang?

"Yes." Guo Qiang laughed. "Zhu Dee always took the shell off the shrimp with a face like this." He scrunched up his nose, turned his mouth down.

"Like something dirty," I said.

"Yes, yes."

He laughed and laughed until he had tears in his eyes. I'd never seen him enjoy himself so. His professorial eyes softened. He looked a bit handsome.

"How silly," Mother-In-Law said, and we joined in his laughter. The shell was the best part.

"And now." Guo Qiang stopped laughing. He wiped his eyes with the back of one doughy hand. "That's the only way I can eat it."

"Oh, that's foolishness," Mother-In-Law said. "These are delicious. Enough talk now."

But I peeled some shrimp for Guo Qiang, anyway, feeling a bit as if I were feeding an old man with weak teeth or a young child. Which of these was this Zhu Dee? Certainly a child. A child to whom I was grateful for bringing laughter to our table and releasing the tension of the day.

"You take your time eating," Guo Qiang said, popping one last shrimp in his mouth.

He pushed his chair back and stood up. He glanced back toward his study. Perhaps he had some work to finish. He was a hard worker. I focused on eating my rice. The sound of his shoes heading toward the front door made me look up.

"Where are you going?" Mother-In-Law asked. "It's already late. It'll be dark soon."

He nodded, but kept walking, as if he were listening to the village loudspeaker. That's what Mother-In-Law sounded like. A disconnected voice talking about life in the village. Here, it stayed light until after 9 p.m. And, after that, the street lights illuminated the sky without the accompanying heat. How could she say it would be dark soon? Guo Qiang obviously agreed. He opened the gate.

"I'll be back," he said looking over at me.

Maybe this was his way of making time for us to talk. To get up while Mother-In-Law was busy eating and take me out on a walk. Perhaps he too had been thinking about our new relationship, comparing it to the sad situation we'd witnessed at Colleague's house. Perhaps he would explain about Lee Sa. About this English lesson. I dropped my chopsticks and hurried to join him, pulling the strap of my sandals up around my ankles as I hopped across the floor. The air outside was fresh, like a whisper of hope. I latched onto his arm. It felt soft and fleshy.

"You go finish dinner," Guo Qiang repeated, shaking my arm off. "I'll be back in a while."

I watched him disappear down the hallway, heard the click-clacking of his shoes on the steps. Perhaps he didn't see any reason to further thrash the subject of Lee Sa. The same way I hadn't met with Chan Hai to discuss and fret over what was unchangeable. Or perhaps after a day of Mother-In-Law, there was nothing more to say anyway. Maybe he just needed to be alone with his thoughts. I leaned over the wall. He headed in the direction of the market.

Several children rode by him on their bikes, a serious-looking little boy on his blue bike, a smaller girl on her red bike which had four wheels, not just two. But these bikers didn't ride toward the market or on any other errand, for that matter. They just rode around and around the little playground which had a metal slide and a cement tower. Did Kevin ride a bike like this, around and around with no purpose? To think I'd imagined the boy dead—having fallen over a wall such as the one I leaned up against now. Heat rushed to my cheeks as I giggled at my stupidity.

"You let him go?" Mother-In-Law called from the front door. I jumped at her voice. "Why is that so funny?"

"He told me to come back and finish dinner," I said.

I looked over to where Mother-In-Law stood at the door. Her eyes were large with worry. Her mouth was turned down, making deep wrinkles on her chin.

"The temple priest warned me of this." Mother-In-Law shook her head.

"What?" I stepped inside.

I closed the gate and put the lock on it. But I left the front door open, so we could feel the breeze. So I could hear the bike wheels zooming around and around the playground. What a joyous sound.

Mother-In-Law pulled out my seat at the table and filled my bowl with shrimp. She must have sensed that I was still hungry, so busy had I been peeling shrimp for Guo Qiang. But actually my stomach felt full, numb. It had for days. Numb with anxiety, bewilderment, and sadness.

"Singapore is a beautiful country," Mother-In-Law said, running her hand over her permed hair. "Don't you think?"

"Yes." What a relief that Mother-In-Law had finally dropped the subject of Lee Sa. Perhaps she'd exhausted herself on the topic. "Yes."

"There are so many lovely flowers," she said, sitting back in her chair and resting her hands over her stomach.

"That's true." I crunched on the antennae of the shrimp. Chan Hai would be happy to see all these flowers. I wished I could show him.

"Flowers," she said. "Flowers so beautiful need lots of water."

I smiled. This talk of flowers came out of nowhere, seemed headed nowhere. Like those children on their bikes going around and around without purpose. Chan Hai would say that flowers needed water, but not too much. I remembered him telling me of how he'd fretted over the flower Little Wu Lu had given him, watered the small plant so much that it had died. That his fears had killed that flower. I glanced up. Mother-In-Law gazed across the table at me. Waiting. She didn't want to ride her bike alone.

"Flowers. Yes," I said and nodded. "Well, Singapore's the perfect place for them, right? According to Guo Qiang it rains somewhere on this tiny island everyday. Two hundred and twenty-nine centimeters a year. He said sometimes the rains looks like a shower. The rain can be falling on your head and you run a few steps. Then, like magic, the faucet in the sky has turned off, and you are out in the sunshine. But you must know that. Have you ever experienced—"

"Flowers that don't get water." She leaned forward and tapped my bowl with her manicured fingernail. She looked over at me with those beady black eyes. "Just shrivel up and die. They never produce more beautiful flowers."

I should have known better than to think the noises from Mother-In-Law's mouth were ever without purpose. I dropped my chopsticks back into the dish. My cheeks filled with heat.

"Sometimes a flower needs to dress up." She reached over and ran her stubby fingers—the same stubby fingers as her son had—over the pants Chan Hai had given me. "Let the farmer know she needs watering."

"You speak the truth."

I picked up my dish and took it to the kitchen. Mother-In-Law followed, her skirt swishing, her curls bouncing, like a spider who had captured her prey.

"Don't worry," she whispered, handing me her dish and looking around with the same superstitious eyes that Mother had. "There's good news. The Temple Priest said that, although difficult, you will give me a grandson."

She retreated into the other room. I turned the faucet over the sink on. Each time the water came rushing out right there in the sink, I felt amazed. Here we had water right where we needed it, whenever we wanted. No trips to the sink in the backyard or, when the faucet wasn't working, the village well. The water felt cool on my fingers. I put my arms under as well. I was reminded of the cool silky feeling of the reservoir, of Chan Hai's solid arms holding—

"Daughter," Mother-In-Law called from the kitchen door.

Not only was I thinking thoughts I shouldn't have been, but surely I'd let too much water run. I put a dish over the hole in the sink to stop the liquid gold from disappearing down the drain. She stepped forward and raised her arm from behind her back.

"I don't want you to have too difficult a time," she said.

She held up a large black and gold shopping bag. I would have been less surprised if she had hit me. For my wasteful behavior. My disloyal heart.

"I don't need anything," I said, pushing the bag away with my wet fingers.

"This is nothing anyway," Mother-In-Law said, setting the bag on the counter.

"No, no," I said, putting my hand out to grab the bag and return it to her. She thrust a dirty dish at me instead, then retreated to her room.

I don't remember washing the rest of the dishes. I took the gift to the bedroom, shut the door and looked inside the elegant bag. Nesting in a mountain of white tissue paper lay a frilly white dress with a giant pink ribbon at the back and huge, deep pockets like an apron in front. I guess this was Mother-In-Law's way of letting the farmer know I needed watering. But the farmer wasn't home. And I felt so tired. A soft knock sounded on my door. Mother-In-Law.

"Let's see how you look," she called.

Perhaps Guo Qiang would be coming back soon. I didn't want to disappoint Mother-In-Law. I put that lovely white dress on and opened the door. She twisted me around, this way and that. Then she turned me around and tied the ribbon tight in the back. I was reminded of the little girl in her blue dress that afternoon and of the child whose balloon had disappeared in the clouds. With Guo Qiang staying on his side of the bed, I could fool myself that I was visiting a country and staying with a cousin who had no space but right beside him. I could imagine that Chan Hai would show up one day and take me home. With this dress on, I felt all that was shiny and possible was about to disappear—like that red balloon in the sky.

"What a lovely flower you are," she said. "I'm feeling very tired tonight. I'll retire early."

Then she turned on her heel and went off to her room. Perhaps this was her way of saying that she would grant us privacy. I remembered Waipo telling of how the only thing that had separated her marriage bed from her in-laws' was a dishcloth. In comparison, this huge apartment with two bedrooms, a living room, a dining room and kitchen was like a palace. I combed my hair into a pile on top of my head and went out into the living room. I straightened the piles of magazines and books on the table. Wiped off the dust.

I sat down and tried to read the newspaper, The Straits Times. What a funny paper. Each time I finished a sentence, I felt as empty as when I started. The words plunked in my brain, each one making sense, but the combination of words a mystery. How one man had "offended the modesty" of a woman on the train station. How did one offend another's modesty? The offender had been fined one thousand dollars. A thousand. The fines here were all that high—for spitting, not flushing the toilet in the public restroom, for littering. In the airport, I'd seen a foreigner wearing a white t-shirt which said "Singapore is a fine country" with all the fines you had to pay listed below. Father wouldn't last long here, the way he spat and threw his cigarettes. He'd rack up fines without even turning over his *mahjong* tiles.

Another article talked about how the Government had launched the annual Clean and Green campaign. What was a Clean and Green Campaign? Green didn't sound clean to me, but like a moldy bun. Or like Feng Gu's refrigerator. How was she doing? Did Madame Tsui Ping like the name of our new tea? I struggled through one more article, my lids feeling heavy, about how a politician was investigated for corruption. What an idea to investigate for corruption. I put the paper down. Perhaps I needed those English lessons more than I thought. Although certainly not from someone so rude and crazy as Lee Sa.

I smoothed my dress over the flat stomach the Temple Priest said would soon hold a son. I missed the smell of Mother's cooking in the giant wok, the sight of the big peach tree in the backyard, even the sound of Ba's *mahjong* tiles. Surely I would come to love these brown high-rises and the antiseptic market place and the funny newspaper. Surely by the time I had my son. A son who would eat lots of shrimp with the shells on and be intelligent like his professor daddy. A son who would be allowed to ride around and around on his big blue bike for no purpose other than to hear the sound of the wheels on the gravel and to feel the wind in his ears. He would be handsome with dents in his cheeks.

No. Guo Qiang didn't have dents in his cheeks. Chan Hai did. Dear Chan Hai. Was he still working for Mr. Housewares, hauling refrigerators? Bombing up the mountains in search of rocks? Or sprinkling water on the leaves of his beloved plants? I lay my head back to wonder awhile.

A faint sound like an echo rustled from the trees. I was alone in the reservoir, and the water, which was darker than I remembered, kept getting deeper and deeper. Water splashed against my neck. Chan Hai would come soon. Something rubbed against my leg. Was that just water grass or a snake? I pushed my way back toward shore. But, with each step I took, the water became higher and higher. A droplet splashed on my chin. I felt that sensation around my leg again, this time tighter and tighter. Pulling me down, down, down.

"I'm back." The echo sounded louder in my ear.

"Darling," I cried. I put my hands out so Chan Hai could pull me out of this dark, snake-infested water. "Forgive me."

"Never mind," a high-pitched nasal voice said, returning me to the hot, stuffy reality of Singapore. "It's late. You couldn't help but fall asleep."

I opened my eyes. Guo Qiang stood above me, his face and neck blotchy red. His short spiky hair dripped water. His multi-colored batik shirt fell out of his pants. The smell of alcohol filled the space between us. He held a plastic bag which banged against my leg. The snake in my dream.

Shopping again? These people didn't seem worried that there would be no food at the end of the month or that Zi Mei would complain her money wasn't repaid fast enough. They spent money as though a dog shaking off water. I looked closer at the white plastic bag. Lucky Dragon Stationery Store. Something red poked out of the top. What could he have purchased at a stationery store except paper for me to make more cuttings with?

Guo Qiang must have remembered me mentioning my happiness in making cuttings. He must have noted Madame Paper Cutter's phoenix I'd taped on the mirror. Certainly he had gone out and bought me red paper to work with. Heat filled my cheeks. How could I have filled my night with thoughts of anyone but my honorable husband? I cringed as my lover's calloused fingers let go of me.

"I'm going to bed." Guo Qiang's words slurred.

I straightened my dress. The pins from my hair had fallen to the floor. I quickly bent to retrieve them, to do the best I could to tie up my hair. Chan Hai had loved to play with my hair, to hold the locks, to kiss them. I shook thoughts of my lover away and stood up.

When I walked into the bedroom, Guo Qiang was already in bed, lying on his stomach, with the bag of red paper next to him. My stomach felt tight. The air was still. I should remove my dress and go lay next to him. But I had the desire to find my scissors and work on paper cuttings. To do anything really, but step into that space.

"Did you have a nice walk?" I asked.

I stared at his sweat-soaked back, hoping he'd want to talk. If we talked long enough, we'd get so tired, we'd fall asleep. I hoped the Priest was right. That this grandson would take time to make. He moaned. Obviously he was sad for his friend. There was nothing he could do.

"Don't be too sad," I said.

Whenever Mother returned home with empty arms from the house of the latest new mother, she felt depressed like this for days. I went to the closet and took out the red silk robe I'd received as a wedding present. I had yet to wear these. My pink cotton pajamas with the bottoms frayed from so many years of use had seemed so much a comfort. Guo Qiang moaned again. Or was it?

Through the door, I heard the creaking of hinges as yet another moan filled the air. Mother-In-Law's door. Her small feet swished across the tile floor in the hall. I looked over to Guo Qiang. He still had his head down. If he'd noticed his mother spying on us, he pretended not to. I should not let on that I knew either. Dear Mother-In-Law. She just needed assurance that I took her advice to heart, that I behaved like a good wife. That I worked toward fulfilling the Priest's prophecy.

"You've had a long day," I said in a loud voice, pulling off my white dress and tying the silk robe around me. The material engulfed me in a strangling heat. Like Mother-In-Law's hot breath on my neck.

Guo Qiang still said nothing. Was he angry that Mother-In-Law stood outside our door? Still thinking of Colleague? Thinking of another statistic? I got in on my side of the bed, holding the silk belt tight around my waist.

"Yes, a long day," I repeated. "First there was the visit to Colleague's home."

I stopped. Cool air filled my chest. I leaned back against the headboard, flipping the robe wide open to allow the night air to cool my skin. Guo Qiang was sound asleep. I pulled the Double Happiness bedcover over him. Poor man. He must be so sad. In the hallway, Mother-In-Law stifled a cough. I stood up and crossed to the door. I tore off the red robe, my skin already coated with a film of sweat.

"You said you'd rather I wear these," I said in a loud voice, as if

Guo Qiang were still awake with me, making romantic suggestions, as if I weren't so alone. I put on my cool, undemanding cotton pajamas. "How's this? You like it? Oh, dear Guo Qiang, stop. Let me finish buttoning."

I waited a moment. Mother-In-Law's feet didn't swish back down the hall. I could feel her right outside. How long would she stay there?

"Everyday in this house is like Chinese New Year," I said getting into bed next to Guo Qiang. "You and your dear Mother always shower me with food and presents. You're too kind."

I pried the stationery bag from his hand. His stubby fingers were wrinkled, as if he'd stayed in the shower too long. Did this 98% humidity give him raisin-like fingers? A polite person would have waited for Guo Qiang to give me his present. But curiosity superseded my good manners. Besides, I'd waited all night for him to come home. Certainly he wouldn't have brought the bag to bed, if he hadn't planned to hand me the gift right away. If I had rushed in behind him faster, not fussing with my hair in the living room, he would have given me the bag, maybe even said something before passing out.

I peeked inside the bag. Not red paper for cutting birds or baby boys or dragons. A red frame. I forced a giggle. If I were given five lifetimes, I never would have guessed my new husband would spend all evening making such a purchase.

"Why, this is lovely," I said, pushing past a strange feeling in my throat. I wished Mother-In-Law would return to her room, so I could sink into silence. So I could think. "The perfect idea. You think of everything."

I put the bag in the corner of the room near the door. Was she still out there? I switched out the light.

"What?" I asked. "Your back feels sore? Why don't you let me rub it."

I got back on my side of the bed and turned away from him, facing the light breeze which came from our window. Despite the knowledge that I was a filial daughter and that this marriage would bring honor and success on our family for generations to come, even a precious grandson if the priest's prediction was right, I felt as mature as that little Chinese toddler whose balloon had been knocked away. I wanted my red balloon back. I wanted the person laying next to me to be Chan Hai.

I closed my eyes, hoping my dreams would transport me into Chan Hai's arms. Guo Qiang sighed deeply and snored. I jiggled the bed.

"You like that," I said, hoping my voice covered the putt-putt of his breathing which sounded like the village brigade's tractor coming down the lane. Which would be mistaken for nothing but deep sleep. "Let me rub lower."

At last, I heard the swish of Mother-In-Law padding back to her room, the moaning of her bedroom door closing. I relaxed and closed my eyes. But my senses were wide awake, like the time Father almost traded blows with the neighbor over a game of *mahjong*. This time, however, I felt as if I was the one who'd been slapped.

Outside the window, cars roared down the road. Where were people going in such a hurry at this time of night? I shifted positions and dragged my mind back toward the reservoir. But the cool water was filled with snakes. Snakes that sometimes slimed around my legs, their scales pricking at my thighs. Snakes that sometimes felt like plastic bags from the Lucky Dragon Stationery store, the edges poking at me. All of them pulling me deeper into darkness. I couldn't breathe.

I opened my eyes. Where had Guo Qiang been all night? What was so important about a picture of a boy that he called it art? Why was this art so special that he'd spent an entire evening in the first week of our marriage shopping for just the right color frame for that picture? A bright red frame, which poked at me like a thorn from where it sat in the corner in that Lucky Dragon Stationery Store bag.

Chapter Fifty-Four
English Lesson

I threw back my white bed sheet, now as damp as if I'd dragged the cotton cloth with me into my dreams of the reservoir. Perspiration. The air next to me was still. No talking. No snoring. I knew without looking that Guo Qiang was gone.

The tapping of bamboo against the kitchen window told me that Mother-In-Law was hanging laundry. Why hadn't she awakened me? Surely Guo Qiang had already left for work. Mother-In-Law had made breakfast. She'd finished the day's laundry. Even the sun shone through my window hot on my bottom, beckoning me to move. Why had she left me undisturbed? Was she irritated with me? Did she know there was no hope of a grandson yet? Or, perhaps she thought her new dress had brought the farmer running, and I needed the morning to rest.

I swung my legs over onto the floor. The warm tiles beneath my feet made my skin itch. A cool shower would feel nice. Still, I should go out and see what Mother-In-Law had planned. We had done most of the required family visitations to announce our marriage. We'd even visited his good friend. Today nothing was planned. Oh, but the day yawned in front of me, long and tired. I had no job here. Guo Qiang talked too much and drank too much. And Mother-In-Law bit too hard, leaving acid-filled bites. Perhaps I could just lay back down for a moment. Then again, I'd already slept too long.

I pulled on my black pants, straightened the bed, and went out to the kitchen. Mother-In-Law folded a shirt inside-out so the sun wouldn't sap any of the colors, slipped it on the end of the bamboo pole and slid the laundry pole outside. She stuck the pole in a hole right beneath the window. Another convenience. Apartments not only had holes already indented for laundry poles, but special hooks to hang the Singapore flag, something Guo Qiang had said every apartment was required to do for National Day on August 9th. No ratty flags either. If your flag was dirty, you had to purchase a new one from the Neighborhood Committee when they made the rounds to inspect the flag displays. I went over to where she stood in front of a plastic blue wash bin and bent down to pick up Guo Qiang's pants.

"Eat first," she said, taking the pants from me and inclining her head toward the pot of rice porridge on the stove. Her eyes flickered over my black pants. For once she didn't bite.

I went over and stirred the porridge in the pot. A new pot, shiny silver. A thin film, like glue, covered the top of the now cold porridge. Zi Mei always said cold rice porridge made the best glue. She used the goopy mixture to affix stamps to letters.

"Why don't you heat that up," Mother-In-Law said. "It's been sitting cold for hours."

Yes, here she came. Bite, bite, bite. She didn't really expect me to turn the stove on, as she had shown me yesterday, just to heat up the porridge? In our house, we would never light up another stack of kindling to heat our breakfast. What a waste. Then again, perhaps she wanted to see if I'd been listening to her, if I'd remembered how to use the click-click-click stove.

"I prefer cold porridge," I said.

My skin was already covered in a thin film of perspiration. The tendrils of hair on my neck were soaked. The last thing I wanted to do was generate more heat.

"Well, now you need to consider more than just what you prefer," Mother-In-Law said.

"You're right," I said.

Surely she spoke of herself and Guo Qiang. Yet they had already eaten. I took a bowl from the dish rack on the side of the sink and spooned a small amount of the cold porridge in my bowl.

"Nothing too cold," Mother-In-Law said coming over next to me. She took the bowl, dumped the contents back into the pot, turned the stove on. "Nothing too hot. Or spicy. Or acidic. That foolish Li Zhi ate pineapple everyday until the day she gave birth. Her poor son is still sensitive. Coughing all the time."

Mother-In-Law had obviously fallen for last night's performance. I didn't know whether to sigh with relief or frustration. She would stop hounding me about my dress and my ability to attract her son. But she'd already started on my prenatal behavior. Exhaustion shuddered through my body.

"And another thing," Mother-In-Law said. "Be careful what you look at. There are so many ugly people here. Don't go staring. Especially when they do their funny rituals, like poking needles through their jaws or hanging pomello fruit from their chests. You can't watch that. Li Zhi did that too. No one told her that she needed to look at only beautiful things in order to have a beautiful child. And just look at that monkey of a son she has."

Mother-In-Law turned the stove off and handed me a steaming bowl of porridge. The smell wafting up made my stomach flip-flop like a fish on the bottom of a boat. Salt filled the back of my throat. Riding in that airplane and breathing everyone else's air, that's all Guo Qiang had been afraid of. At the time, I thought he'd been making fun of me. But perhaps he was right. Perhaps someone on the plane had been sick, and I was coming down with that sickness.

"What are you waiting for?" Mother-In-Law said, opening a cabinet below the sink and pulling out a mountain of plastic bags.

Yes, what was I waiting for? Sweat broke out around my temple. The rice bowl felt heavy, my stomach already full. How strange.

Mother-In-Law sat on the kitchen floor, took one of the plastic bags from the top of the pile and folded it into a neat square. I pushed the rice around and around with my ceramic spoon. Perhaps the heat was making me feel bad. So much heat and so much change. I set the bowl down.

"My stomach's not awake yet," I said. "I think I stayed up too late last night."

"Of course you did," Mother-In-Law said, flapping a plastic bag up and down as though shaking wrinkles from a sheet.

"Let me do that," I offered. It would be good to concentrate on a task. "Unless there's something else you'd rather I do."

"Oh, that reminds me," she said, shaking the sack at me. "Guo Qiang wanted you to call him."

"Call him?" I asked. That seemed like an awful expense when the university was but a few blocks away. Perhaps I should just walk over there.

"Yes," Mother-In-Law insisted. "Use the phone in the living room."

Perhaps Guo Qiang would give me some direction with the day. I put a plastic cover over the bowl of rice to keep the flies away. I already felt the strange sensation in my stomach receding.

Zi Mei's phone in the village had a heavy receiver and lots of buttons on the base, buttons so old their numbers had worn off. You had to punch down the number 9 with all your might to make it work. Guo Qiang's phone, which stood upright in a holder on the table next to the couch, felt no heavier than one of Kevin's blocks. And all the numbers on this light piece of plastic were on the receiver. I pushed Guo Qiang's number and leaned down close to the little stand. I didn't hear any ringing.

"Hello?" I called into the receiver.

Maybe I hadn't pushed the buttons hard enough. I put the phone back on the base, pulled it off, and tried again. Still nothing. I leaned closer to the base. Mother-In-Law came into the room with a bucket of soapy water. Would she mop so early in the morning? Perhaps she wanted to clean the windows.

"What did he say?" she asked.

"Nothing," I said.

"How dear," she said, sloshing her rag around in the soapy water. Her face broke into a smile. She thought I was being shy.

"The phone," I said. "I, I. How do you?"

"Oh." She dropped the rag back in the bucket, came over and studied the receiver. How silly that it took two adults to figure out how to make a simple phone call. What did Singaporeans have against old-fashioned, easy-to-operate phones? And why did Mother-In-Law insist I call rather than walk over?

"You push the number," she said.

"I did that."

"And then you push the button on the left that says . . ." She held the receiver as far from her face as possible. "What's it say? I don't have my glasses."

I looked at the three buttons she pointed to, seeing them for the first time. Talk. Redial. End.

"Talk?" I asked.

She nodded, the curls on her head bouncing. I pushed the button and heard a melodic beeping. Had I pushed the wrong button? Then a ringing sounded. Mother-In-Law and I stared at the receiver.

"Liang, Computer Science Department," a voice said, sounding as clear as if he stood right in front of us.

Mother-In-Law jumped. Then she smiled. We'd figured out how to play with this toy.

"Hello?" Guo Qiang said.

"It's me," I said.

"Yes?" He sounded confused. Had Mother-In-Law gotten the message wrong?

"Mother-In-Law said you wanted me to call?" I said. She stood nearby nodding as she wrung her rag of excess water.

"Right," he said. In the background, I heard heavy hammering, as though someone were pounding rice into sticky dough. Another phone rang. "I just wanted to make sure you don't forget to bring the red frame."

"Bring the red frame?" I asked. Where was I going with it?

"You know," he said. "The one I brought home last night."

I remembered the red frame. Vividly. But he had told me nothing last night. Was he planning to give the frame to Colleague today? Did he want me to bring the frame to his work? And where was his work place exactly? What else did he think he'd said or done?

"That's all," he said.

"Wait," I said. "That's all?"

"It's in a stationery bag," he said. "In the corner of the bedroom near the closet."

"I know where it is," I said. "I remember. But where am I—"

"You better hurry," Guo Qiang said. "I told Lee Sa you'd be there at 11:00."

"Lee Sa?" I asked.

But he had already clicked off. I had just assumed, since we'd had no further discussion, that Guo Qiang had given Colleague all that money as charity. And when had they decided on the time? My temples pounded. I glanced at my watch. I was late already.

Chapter Fifty-Five
Counting to Five

Mother-In-Law clung to my hand, matching me step for step in silence. I had insisted that I remembered how to get to Colleague's house. But she had left her bucket of soapy water anyway. She was a good mother-in-law to show such concern, to escort me on my errands.

We raced through the marketplace on our way to Lee Sa's. Women dragged metal carts filled with plastic bags behind them. Men clutched leather briefcases under their arms. Mothers pushed babies in little carts with four wheels which took up the entire space on the sidewalk. Watching all those people made my brain buzz. Or perhaps it was the sun which beat down on the top of my head despite my parasol. Then again—Chan Hai's brown eyes stared down at me demanding I search for the real reason—perhaps I was worried about this Lee Sa foreigner. I clutched the plastic bag from Lucky Dragon Stationery tightly. I had survived Madame Tsui Ping. I would be fine.

We walked over to the blue apartment building. The dark man who ran the little shop wore the same towel as yesterday. He filled a glass jar with star anise, the smell carrying over despite the lack of breeze.

"That is not okay," a woman shouted in English, her voice carrying across to us from the play yard where the boys had played their Malaysian game yesterday. "Do you hear me? Not okay."

Mother pulled on my hand, and we stopped. I looked over to the dark man. He was not as salesman-like as yesterday. He didn't look up at us and smile with his bright white teeth. He didn't prick his ears at the yelling nearby. He concentrated on his spice jars. The Chinese guard who had been fast asleep yesterday stood near the elevator. He tore off a piece of paper which had been taped above the buttons.

"Can you hear the words I'm saying to you?" a woman shouted. Her English was perfect. In fact, she sounded like Lee Sa.

The guard grimaced, as if all that noise hurt his head. He crumpled the paper into a ball and went out from beneath the building to throw the garbage in a big round green canister. A sticker on the canister said, "Keep Singapore Green." The Clean and Green Campaign? Did throwing trash in these special bins contribute to the campaign? Perhaps one had to throw a certain number of papers in that bin each day, like in China when we had the "Kill 10 Flies a Day" Campaign.

The guard stayed out under the sun longer than necessary to throw away that piece of paper. Surely he was watching whatever horrible event made this woman yell. I urged Mother-In-Law forward so we could see as well. Whatever caused this woman to make such a scene?

I followed the guard's gaze to the small playground next to where the Malays had played their foot game. The playground was like the one outside our apartment block where the two children had ridden there bikes around and around. There was a metal slide, a cement tower, a cement bench. And, yes, it was Lee Sa. She stood dressed in the same underwear as yesterday, shouting at a slide.

"Do you hear me?" she said. "Do you hear me?"

What was she doing down here? Colleague would be filled with shame if he knew Lee Sa stood out here half naked, shouting at a slide. His fish scale scar would wrinkle. His eyes would shine with sorrow. The poor man. Perhaps this whole English Lesson arrangement was Guo Qiang's way of keeping watch on Lee Sa for Colleague.

"It's almost lunch," Mother-In-Law said, pulling on my hand and nodding her head back in the direction of our apartment. "Obviously this is not a good time."

Certainly, home—even a home with no job and no friends—looked good. Besides, the queasy feeling in my stomach had evaporated. I was hungry now. Perhaps Lee Sa was hungry too. And, like Father, she turned into a nasty mood when her stomach wasn't filled. Maybe she just needed to get upstairs and eat something. She definitely needed to be brought upstairs.

I let go of Mother-In-Law's hand. There were no children riding around and around in circles or taking turns on the slide. Surely the children had escaped inside from the pounding rays of the sun. Or perhaps Lee Sa had frightened them all away. I stepped over next to the guard and jutted my chin out in Lee Sa's direction. Maybe he would give me some advice on how to deal with the lady. Surely he'd seen this before. But he only nodded a greeting. Then he turned and retreated back under the apartment block. He stood next to Mother-In-Law, watching from a safe distance.

"I'm giving you until the count of five to get out here," Lee Sa said, this time to the cement bench.

"Hello?" I called. At least these playground toys were made of metal and cement. She couldn't do much damage.

"One."

"Teacher Lee Sa?" I called again.

I held on tight to the sturdy plastic handle of my parasol. She turned around. Frowned. Did she know me?

"Oh, Freedom. Space." She snapped her fingers. "Leeway!"

"Yes," I said. "Hello."

"I've got a crisis." She waved her arms up and down.

"Oh?" I wasn't surprised by her bluntness. Madame Tsui Ping didn't hesitate to speak her thoughts, the filter of politeness having eroded.

"Sorry, we late." Perhaps we had caused her sudden outburst. Maybe she had come looking for us.

"We?" She raised her eyebrows.

"Mother-In-Law come, too." I pointed to where Mother-In-Law conferred with the guard.

"Great," she said. But her voice didn't sound great. "I'm counting," she called again.

What strange world did she visit? America had had no red guards. They never had people invading and force-feeding strange beliefs. What horrible event had caused this? And in this heat. My scalp itched.

"We go inside," I suggested. "Talk of crisis."

"Sounds fine to me. Only someone has decided to hide." She nodded her head toward the slide. I looked as well. The slide shone so brightly, the metal appeared on fire. What did she see?

"Is too hot outside," I said. I touched her arm, which was wet and fuzzy. "We go inside?"

"Good idea," Lee Sa said, repeating in a loud voice. "We're going upstairs."

I cringed. Her voice seemed to bounce off of all the apartment blocks surrounding us. Certainly the women, even on the tenth floor, could hear us as they leaned out to check the dryness of their laundry on the bamboo poles.

"Hey," a small voice called.

I jumped. I expected a man to ride up on his motorbike with steaming buns on the back, young shoppers to surround us. Just like that day Madame Tsui Ping had lost her senses. Instead, a little boy peered out from beneath the cement bench. A little boy who looked just like he had in that black frame. Kevin.

"Wait for me" the little boy said.

I stared at the boy with his horse face, his tall nose, his brown hair. So Lee Sa hadn't been talking to the slide. Why had I assumed she would be alone? Probably because, in the village, she would have been. Kevin would stay with his grandmother while Lee Sa worked.

"Your son," I said.

"My son," Lee Sa said, reaching out to grab his arm. He scooted back under the bench.

"He looks like you," I said.

"Everyone here says that." Lee Sa sighed. She had her hand up in the air now, counting. "And everyone in my family says he looks like Chao Ran."

"Who?" I asked.

"Colleague," she translated. "Nobody wants to claim the boy. And, when he behaves like this, I know why. Kevin." She yelled so loud, I looked up to see who would glance out their window. "I'm on five."

I smiled. We used the same method back home, counting out the seconds. Usually that threat worked.

"Your mother on five," I told him, thinking maybe he hadn't heard.

He wasn't impressed. He scooted further beneath the bench. Certainly he wouldn't want to come out after being shouted at in public by his nutty mother.

"Is so hot here," I tried.

"Not here," he said. "You're hot 'cause you're in the sun."

He spoke English so well, as easy as breathing. I put the stationery bag down, sat on the ground, put my arm out.

"Clever boy," I said.

"Too clever," Lee Sa shouted, the volume of her words beating us all into the ground. "He always thinks he knows better."

"You come out now," I said. "Like clever boy. Mother wish you to come out, too."

"No," he said. "Mom wants my juice."

I looked at Lee Sa. Had she really taken the little boy's juice? Like a small child. I remembered digging for enough *yuan* notes to buy Madame Tsui Ping a pork bun. At least now I had money to buy juice, if that's all Lee Sa needed to calm down.

"He—he stole the juice from the Indian man's shop." Lee Sa wiped sweat from her brow and nodded in the direction of the dark man's shop. Her cheeks puffed up. Her eyes filled.

"This not good," I said. No wonder the man had not been full of smile this morning.

"You're right about that," Lee Sa said. "Not good in many ways. He's not supposed to have orange juice—at least that's what his father, the doctor, says."

"Your husband is doctor, too?" I asked. This Lee Sa seemed stranger than Madame Tsui Ping. And so much louder.

"Oh, yes," Lee Sa said, her hands on her hips. "He's always prescribing this or that. No orange juice, no air conditioning, no chocolate, more bed covers. He has a doctorate from the University of Old Wives Tales."

The University of Old Wives Tales? What a strange name for a university. Perhaps this was some American University. Maybe that's where Lee Sa and Colleague had met.

"He has a bad cough," Lee Sa said. "Chao Ran thinks it's from the orange juice."

I could see that. All that acid in his system. Just like the pineapple that Mother-In-Law said Lee Sa ate all during her pregnancy. I just smiled.

"I'm on five." She returned her attention to the bench, shaking her open hand to show all five fingers.

I leaned under the bench and whispered, "I have present."

"What is it?" he asked.

"You come." I held up the stationery bag, wishing it held a red car or another ball for his jacks set. "Come see."

He crawled a bit forward. Then he looked over at the Indian shop and back at me. Maybe this was a trick.

"Who are you?" he asked.

"I am wife of Guo Qiang Liang, your father's colleague."

"Who?" He scrunched his eyebrows.

"Guo—"

"Blue Dolphin," Lee Sa translated. "He calls Guo Qiang Blue Dolphin."

"Oh, Blue Dolphin." Kevin scooted further forward and peered up at me. "I know Blue Dolphin. So, YOU'RE the new wife."

"Kevin." Lee Sa grabbed onto his arm and yanked him from

beneath the bench.

My shoulder hurt watching. I stood, brushing the sand from my dress. I held the parasol over the boy.

"He talks so well. So natural." I handed her the stationery bag. "Actually, Guo Qiang buy for both of you."

"Thanks."

She whisked that bag away, not refusing three times, not twice, not even once. Like a street beggar. I sensed Mother-In-Law watching with disapproval.

"What is it?" Kevin pulled on Lee Sa's underwear.

Lee Sa pulled the red frame from the bag, frowning. Perhaps, food would have been better. Kevin grabbed the frame from her and pulled the packaging off. He threw the packaging up in the air and watched the cellophane float to the ground. Then he slid the red frame through the dirty sand like a toy car. Yes, something else would have been more appropriate.

"Guo Qiang think for to hold your art photo—"

"Yes, I figured that out." She flashed a strange, small smile. "But some moments are better left unframed, unsaved. That's what Chao Ran says."

She crossed her arms over her ample bosom, shifting her weight to one leg. Her devil blue eyes looked bright as she stared at me. Perhaps she was coming to the end of her episode.

"We go inside?" I suggested.

"What?" She shook herself like dog who had just come in from the rain, took a deep breath, and pinched the top of her nose. "Yeah."

Her eyes glistened. She reached down and grabbed one side of the frame. What did she mean, some moments are better left unframed? Perhaps this was Colleague's diplomatic way of telling her to get rid of the photo. She picked up the frame.

"Mom, stop," Kevin said. "I'm racing the butterfly." He pointed on the slide to where a yellow butterfly rested.

"You won. Now come on," she said. Then she grabbed the cellophane wrapping from the ground, looked back and me. "Clean and Green."

"What?" I asked.

"You haven't heard of the Clean and Green Campaign?"

"Yes," I said. "I read in newspaper." I also saw the guard filling the bin with his allotment of garbage.

"Most people would think picking up garbage is common sense."

Lee Sa tossed the clear wrap into the garbage can.

"Really?" I asked.

We didn't. We threw garbage on the ground. The street cleaners swept it away. That was their job. That and saving people's lives with their brooms. If people threw their own garbage away, old women wouldn't have jobs and nobody would have been there to thwack College Boy. Chan Hai would have had more than just a scar at the corner of his eye. My heart squeezed.

"—has to turn common sense into a campaign. Or a law." Lee Sa laughed, shaking her head. "No Spitting. No urinating in the elevator. No using the toilet without flushing."

She led us under the blue building toward the bank of elevators. Mother-In-Law joined us. She clasped onto my arm.

"Did you tell her we need to go?" she whispered in Mandarin. "We will arrange to have this English lesson at a . . . a more suitable time."

"I think she's okay now," I said.

I didn't want to have to come back. Besides I was sure we'd already been together with Lee Sa almost an hour, the allotted lesson time. I glanced at my watch. We'd only spent ten minutes with Lee Sa.

"What?" Lee Sa cried.

"I said everything okay now," I said.

"No, everything is not okay," she said waving her arms up and down at the elevator doors. She looked over toward the guard. She walked over and tapped her fingers on the desk. "Where is my sign?"

I remembered seeing the guard take down a piece of paper from the wall. Crumple it up. Throw it in the Clean and Green basket. Was this the sign Lee Sa referred to?

"Best not to leave things unattended," the guard said, pulling out the drawer of his metal desk and staring at the empty insides. Then he slammed the drawer closed and studied the dirt underneath his long thumbnail. "Things get taken."

"You expected me to stand by the sign?" Lee Sa laughed. But her eyes flashed anger. "Besides, who's the guard here? I thought you were paid to watch over this building."

Her words were harsh. Loud again. The Indian man at the store busied himself with his spices. The Chinese guard flicked more dirt from his fingernail.

"Who's your manager?" she asked. "This kind of service is lousy."

"I thought you said she's fine now," Mother-In-Law whispered.

My cheeks felt hot. The guard didn't look as though he understood Lee Sa's delicate mental condition. She was taking us up a mountain from which there would be no easy way down.

"Teacher Lee Sa," I said, hoping to remind her that we were supposed to have an English lesson. "What is this sign? I help you make new."

"What difference would it make?" Lee Sa said. "Besides Kevin spent all morning working on that. Coloring a witch and a ghost and a goblin."

Did Lee Sa normally go around hanging her son's artwork next to the elevators? I didn't understand all the things he had colored, but surely his sign was worse than anything Feng Gu could have done at the tea shop. No wonder the guard took it down.

"It was so cute," she continued, her eyes glassy. "I can't believe it's gone."

"I'm sorry," I said. And here I thought she had overcome her episode.

"This stinks," she said, shaking her head. "This just stinks."

I didn't smell anything aside from the sour smell of perspiration, but was relieved that she had stopped shouting about a child's drawing. Especially her own child's. The sky shone blue now. Toward late afternoon, a yellowish cast would fill the horizon.

"Guo Qiang say factory makes stink," I said. "And dust, too."

She stared at me, her lips curling into a smirk. Then she punched the elevator button. Punch. Punch. Punch. She took a deep breath.

"Thank you," she said, her voice normal now, even quiet. She fluffed her short locks.

I didn't know what to say. Was she okay now? Was this goodbye? Could we go home now?

"Chao Ran always tells me to remember the elephant," she said.

"Elephant?"

Perhaps I had heard wrong. Perhaps we couldn't leave her. Lee Sa spoke calmly now. But the words out of her mouth made no sense.

"Don't you know that story?" Lee Sa asked, pulling Kevin into the elevator as soon as the doors opened. "About the blind men and the elephant? Chao Ran said everyone knew it."

"Yes," I said.

I felt a strange ripple. Like yesterday when I'd expected Colleague to speak English. I also hadn't expected Lee Sa to know about our culture. But she obviously knew one of our stories, about the five blind men who each felt a different part of the elephant and each concluded that the beast was something it was not.

"Well, Chao Ran always tells me not to act like one of the blind men," Lee Sa said. She stepped inside the elevator and held the doors open with her hairy arm. "Your comment about the factory stinking reminded me of that. Just because I know what I'm talking about doesn't mean other people do. Just because I think I'm doing people a favor by putting up a Halloween sign doesn't mean they will think that. Although, Jesus, I can't believe someone took it. The nerve." She banged the doors open again with her fist. "You coming or not? I thought we had a lesson."

A lesson? So we were supposed to have this lesson? Oh, gods. How much time had I wasted of this lesson already? How many dollars?

"I want to ride," I said, gripping tight to Mother-In-Law's hand. I glanced at her stone face. Surely she wouldn't appreciate me speaking the truth to Lee Sa. But making up a story would take so much more time. "But I have—I have fear."

"I know," Lee Sa said. "These elevators look about to fall apart. But the only ones you need fear are the ones at the shopping mall."

"You get on one of those," Kevin added, shaking his little brown head, his eyes serious. "You may never get off."

"Kevin, please," Lee Sa said, messing his hair and laughing. "That's not helpful."

"One time when we were downtown," Kevin said, obviously encouraged by the sight of Lee Sa's gold fillings. "We rode three extra floors until we finally pushed our way out through the incoming crowd. Zhu Dee said Singapore should make a campaign for elevator Eddy get."

"Etiquette," Lee Sa said correcting him.

There was the name Zhu Dee again. Did Zhu Dee hate elevators, too? Who was this person? Why did I keep hearing the name?

"Shall we go, guys?" Lee Sa said, brushing a droplet of sweat from her brow. "This box is hot."

I looked at the elevator, the greenish-blue walls scratched and worn. May never get off. Never get off. Kevin had said that. I wanted to step forward, but I moved back.

"We." Mother-In-Law tugged on my hand and frowned. "We walk."

She led me toward the stairwell. Heat filled my insides. How shameful.

"In public, of all places," Mother-In-Law exploded as soon as we started up the steps. She shook her curls from side to side. Her shoulders hunched with disappointment. The laces on her black tie shoes flapped with disgust. "And in front of the guard."

"I'm sorry," I said. "Next time—"

"Shaking her bosoms for all the world to see." Mother-In-Law imitated Lee Sa. "Oh, that woman, that woman is just too much. I'm sorry we can't offer you better."

I took a deep breath. I hadn't made Mother-In-Law angry. She didn't care about not riding the elevator. She didn't care that I had wasted so much of Guo Qiang's lesson money already. I felt a bit like I did the first day at the tea shop. I wasn't quite sure what I was doing here, but I had passed the first hurdle.

Chapter Fifty-Six
Sitting In the Middle of the Mess

The trip up the steps went by quickly. Mother-In-Law talked and talked. Lee Sa seemed to have the same effect on Mother-In-Law as Chan Hai had always had on Feng Gu. And, like Feng Gu, once Mother-In-Law got started, she couldn't stop. How could Lee Sa parade about the neighborhood naked like that? Even that dark man at the store who wore but a cloth around his waist was so shamed for her he couldn't look our way. How could she make her son play out in the hot sun like that? Let him kneel in that dirty sand where stray cats and drunks passed urine? Shout at the top of her lungs, tearing away every scrap of face the poor boy had? She wasn't just missing a few piano strings. She didn't have any.

Mother-In-Law was right there. Her behavior was definitely not normal. Still she wasn't like Madame Tsui Ping. Madame Tsui Ping went into trances, heard voices. Lee Sa's eyes never lost contact with me. In fact, her blue eyes always pierced through me like a needle. When we reached the seventh floor, I paused, pretending to catch my breath. Surely if Lee Sa knew the story of the Elephant and the Blind Men, she might also understand some of the dirt spewing forth from Mother-In-Law's pursed lips. But she didn't need to be so understanding. I just needed Mother-In-Law to stop talking before we reached Lee Sa's door.

"We're here," I said, lifting the hair off my back to allow a breeze to brush against my neck.

"Let's not stay too long," Mother-In-Law said, just as she had yesterday. "You only need spend another half hour here. Then we can go home. I feel tired today."

"Of course," I said.

"They're here," Kevin shouted from down the hall. "They're here."

"I was starting to think you'd given up," Lee Sa said, opening her gate while licking black goop off her fingers.

She must have been hungry and that had caused her temper to boil over downstairs. At least today she had obviously prepared a snack for us. Mother-In-Law wouldn't starve. I glanced over and smiled at Mother-In-Law. She widened her eyes toward the ceiling as if to say, "The woman eats before her guests. Unbelievable."

"Come on in," Kevin said, putting his small hand out as if to help us up the step into the apartment. A little gentleman. Just as cute as Guo Qiang had said.

If possible, the house looked messier than the day before. Newspapers were unfolded all over the floor along with toys and clothes, as though a typhoon had ripped through this apartment and set everything down where it didn't belong. The air felt cool, though, like an autumn day in the village, thanks to the cooling box on the wall. Mother-In-Law and I stood in the middle of the mess.

"Sorry about all this—" Lee Sa made big round motions with her arms, as though imitating the propellers of a wartime airplane going round and round. "Chao Ran gets upset with me. But, as soon as I clean one spot, someone whose name is Kevin dirties it."

Kevin pointed to himself and smiled. Lee Sa reached out to spank his bottom, and he scooted out of the room.

"It's just a waste of my time to clean—"

She stopped talking. She must have seen the blank look on my face, probably thought I wasn't understanding. I wasn't. I followed the meaning of her words. But, like the Straits Times articles I had read last night, I didn't understand the whole picture. Where did she learn that cleaning house was a one-time job? Like what? I couldn't even think of any one-time jobs, except for filling in the cement at the graveyard. Everything was a cycle, repeating, repeating.

"What can I get you to drink?" Lee Sa asked in a slow, loud voice.

Lee Sa brought her hand up to her mouth as though drinking a glass of something. I looked to Mother-In-Law. She shook her head, frowning. Was she just being polite or fearful of drinking something of Lee Sa's making?

"No," I answered for both of us. My throat felt as dry as rice husks.

"I'd think you'd be dying of thirst." Lee Sa put her hand up in front of her face, fanning herself. "Normally we don't leave the house for anything without a water bottle."

In the room where Kevin had disappeared, water sounded. Lee Sa's attention shifted in that direction so that, while her mouth continued to move, her eyes focused on the doorway that must have led to the kitchen.

"Well," she said. "Well, we only planned to go downstairs for a second. Even in that second Kevin got thirsty enough to grab himself some juice."

A crashing sound made her jump. Had he dropped a plate? Fallen?

"It didn't break," Kevin called out.

"Come on with me for a sec."

Lee Sa grabbed my arm. I hesitated. I hated to leave Mother-In-Law out here. Then again, perhaps Lee Sa needed help with Kevin. Mother-In-Law nodded for me to go on. As I hurried with Lee Sa into the dining room toward the kitchen, Mother-In-Law tiptoed over the newspapers, as if a snake might crawl out from beneath them. She patted the couch to get rid of any lurking ghosts, to locate small blocks, then sat down with an audible sigh.

As soon as I entered the kitchen, heat surrounded me. A giant gray refrigerator stood as high as the ceiling. I'd never seen anything so big. Wouldn't Feng Gu be impressed? Childish drawings were taped up along the wall next to the refrigerator. Three stick figures, a sun, a flower. Kevin's drawings. Had Lee Sa tried to put one of these drawings down at the elevator? No wonder the guard had turned it into Clean and Green fodder.

A Formica countertop ran the length of the opposite wall with painted gray cupboards above and below. In the middle of the counter stood a white stove with four burners. Beneath the burners was a strange glass window. At the far end of the counter were two sinks where a serious-looking Kevin stood on a stool. Water gushed out from the faucet with such force, droplets splashed in his face. He picked up a bowl from the left sink.

"It didn't break," he said, holding up a white bowl with a pink orchid in the center. "See?"

"High five," Lee Sa said with a smile.

She put one hand up as though waving hello. Perhaps this was a form of praise, like "Thanks to the gods." Kevin put his hand up to this Five God, as well. His body shuddered with a cough.

"There he goes," Lee Sa said to me. "Damn."

She raced toward the sink, but did not grab the lovely bowl nor turn off all that water nor scold him for playing in the kitchen. Instead, she patted him on the back with one hand. When his chest stopped racking, she cupped her hands under the flow of water and splashed some on his cheeks. Then she doused her forehead and patted some on her ample chest. Her nipples poked out of her thin bra. I looked away.

"The Housing Development Board only allots two air conditioning units per apartment," she said, her face dripping. "Can you believe it? And never one in the hottest room in the house, the kitchen. If anything, that makes Kevin cough."

She gestured her wet hand toward me. Did I want some water? I shook my head. I thought of Mother thirsty and uncomfortable in the next room. I peeked at my watch.

Lee Sa must have sensed my concern for she opened one of the cupboards and took down a large mug. The mug looked like the plate, with a large pink orchid on the side. These orchids reminded me of Chan Hai. His favorite was the butterfly orchid, a flower which he had showed me on our first date. He had told me the purple blossoms only lasted for three months, although the beautiful images lingered forever. A chill ran down my spine. Our relationship had not lasted much longer, although my love still lingered.

Lee Sa didn't fill the mug with hot water from the hotpot. Nor did she sprinkle tea leaves in the bottom. Instead she reached for a pot on the counter filled with black liquid that reminded me of the color of the village roads after a rain. Mother-In-Law would never drink that.

"I knew you were thirsty," Lee Sa said following my gaze. She grabbed another two mugs. "All you have to do is speak up."

"No," I said speaking in a loud voice. "Really, I—"

"You all drank the last of the tea yesterday," she said filling the cup with the dark liquid. "But this is a fresh pot of coffee."

Coffee. I never thought I'd have a friend, an acquaintance, a teacher who drank coffee.

"Milk?" She opened the refrigerator.

Her refrigerator was filled with cartons and packages. A head of brown lettuce. Had this poor woman been tricked into buying spoiled food? A package wrapped in cellophane caught my eye. I'd never seen anything like it—a tan piece of something pushed against the cellophane window. I stepped closer. The label read "Boneless Chicken Thigh." That small piece of meat looked nothing like a chicken. It had obviously been trapped under that cellophane for a long time, as there wasn't even any blood visible. Certainly she'd accidentally bought food meant for pigs. Ugh. The price, four dollars.

Where did she shop? The salespeople cheated her right and left. I coughed.

"You've got the cough now, too?" Lee Sa asked. "Did you drink orange juice this morning?"

"No," I said. "I must have something in throat."

"Well, do you want milk or no?" she asked, pointing to the container in the refrigerator. Was she offering two drinks at the same time? Did foreigners really drink so much liquid?

"No," I said.

She took the container and poured some of the white liquid into her coffee, like a child mixing mud with flour. I couldn't imagine what this would taste like. Would it be like milk in Chinese tea? My stomach flip-flopped again. Too bad Feng Gu was so far away. I could see her laughing at this story, revealing her tea-stained jumble of teeth. I could hear her telling the story to anyone who stopped in the store, telling it so often that she became the one who had witnessed this strange concoction. Did she already have a new helper? Did Chan Hai still come in?

"Earth to Leeway." Lee Sa waved a wet hand in front of my face. "Earth to Leeway."

"What?"

"Why don't you give this to your Mother-In-Law?"

She handed me one of the mugs. Without waiting for me to refuse, she took the other two mugs with her into the dining room. I stared in the cup relieved to see that it held none of the mud-colored liquid. Lee Sa seemed to understand many of our customs—like the story of the elephant, the habit of drinking boiled water. Yet, she also had no concept of keeping her voice down, showing a clean house, offering refreshments, such as hard-boiled eggs or fresh fruit or meat buns, or refusing a gift three times. Perhaps she wasn't as crazy as Mother-In-Law suggested. Just dim-witted.

Chapter Fifty-Seven
Jumping In

We both sat at the dining room table. Not a clean, harmonious table like ours. But one littered with mail and dirty plates and small books. Sweat lined the insides of my arms. Now what would we do? Especially in just these few short minutes?

"I've been living here eight years." Lee Sa took a long drink of her coffee, as though it were sweet nectar. "And still I'm surprised each day by some strange Singaporean. How could they have taken my sign down? What are they afraid of? Dirtying the walls?"

"Eight years?" I asked before her voice rose too high. Before she rushed down the poster path too far. "Eight years is long time."

"Some days," she said. "Like today, it feels like forever. That guard down there is so useless. Half the time he's asleep. The other half he's cleaning his nails. When we first moved here, I bought an ironing board and leaned it up against the elevator while I bought a snack from the Indian shop. When I turned, the board was gone. You know what the guard said? 'Best not to leave your things unattended.' Ugh."

"You born where?" I asked.

Her eyes looked angry. Her pink cheeks ready to chew some more. She was like a dog returning to a tasty bone.

"Illinois," she said.

"Where?" I asked. Perhaps she wasn't really American after all.

"Chicago," she said, pointing her thumb and finger like a gun. "Al Capone. Middle of America."

"Yes, I understand," I said. "How did you come here?"

"By plane." She laughed as if this was funny. She took another sip of coffee. "My father gave me a thousand dollars to get out and see the world. I've never looked back."

"Your father pay you to leave home?" I asked.

Perhaps her father could not find her a mate. Perhaps men were afraid of her devil eyes like a devil, her boobs so large they'd smother. How sad.

Lee Sa went on and on. And, while I focused on every sound, I could only catch a few pieces here and there. About how she'd visited many places in Asia. How she worked and then traveled. Her words were like hailstones. Why would she spend so much effort earning money and then waste it looking at a different place? Why not send it home? Maybe I'd misunderstood. She said Singapore always had the cheapest flights to other places. Singapore and Hong Kong. Once, while on her way through Singapore, she met Chao Ran. She said they'd been together eight years. Eight years? I thought only six. The same age as Kevin. Was Lee Sa making up her world, had I misunderstood or had Mother-In-Law gotten the story wrong? My brain felt numb. Lee Sa made a big sigh.

"You need more?" She pointed to my full cup of coffee.

"No," I said.

I took a big sip of coffee, as I'd seen Lee Sa do. The bitter liquid grabbed the back of my throat. This was nothing like our tea. Not even tea that had sat for days in the pot. I choked.

"Are you alright?" Lee Sa patted my back.

"It has strong taste." I coughed some more, as if choking on one of Mother's herbal concoctions. "Teacher Lee Sa—"

I hoped that, by using the respectful title, I would take the focus off of me and she would do something like a lesson. A buzzer sounded from the kitchen. Was our time up? It felt as if Lee Sa had been talking for hours, but we hadn't had any lesson, and there went Guo Qiang's money disappearing like smoke in the air. I glanced over toward Mother-In-Law. Her head rested against the soft back of the couch. I wanted to join her.

"It's ready." Kevin came running. "It's ready."

"Excuse me," Lee Sa said.

She got up and followed the boy into the kitchen. I sat for a minute, expecting them to come back. My heart beat fast, too fast. Was it because of all that money gone so easily? Nerves about speaking English? Or, a reaction to this American drink? But then, the coffee hadn't bothered Lee Sa. I clasped my hands together and brought them up to my chest—as if that would slow my heart down. Perhaps we should leave and arrange for another lesson time. I hurried into the kitchen, grabbed onto Lee Sa's arm.

"What is it?" Lee Sa asked. The two of them stood in front of the stove. Kevin pulled on the strange window beneath.

"My—my heart," I said, saying what was on my mind. "It pound fast."

She smiled. She had hairs on her upper lip, as well as on her arms. Like peach fuzz.

"You're worse than Kevin," she said, helping him to pull open the window. "He gets so excited when we make these. He doesn't even care about missing the rest of his Fantasia video."

A blast of warm air slapped us. A strange smell assaulted my nose. Why did she have a heater in her kitchen? Perhaps she had had a friend back in America who insisted heaters would be a good thing, just like that relative at our wedding with his winter coats. Thank the gods Guo Qiang hadn't bought one of these. Kevin coughed again.

"Damn that cough," she said focusing on the heater.

Inside, a coil burned red beneath a rack. On the rack sat a square pan. So this wasn't a heater. But a modern cooking pit. Had Lee Sa, despite her earlier rudeness, actually made a special food for us, using this hot box at noontime when the sun baked the earth? Mother-In-Law would have to be impressed by this.

The boy moved ahead of Lee Sa toward the hot air. He coughed again.

"Darn you," she shouted. "Go away."

But Kevin didn't move away. He just smiled and repeated, "Yeah, go away, cough." Then he reached out to the rack above that red hot iron. Surely the pan was hot.

"What do we need to remember?" Lee Sa asked her eyes traveling to the top of the stove where two large green mittens lay.

He didn't hear her. His eyes were round. He bit his tongue in concentration. He put his hands out. Lee Sa smiled and shook her head as though watching a funny program on television. She reached up to hand him the big mittens. But he didn't stop. I grabbed Kevin just before his little fingers grasped the edge of the pan.

"New Wife," Kevin said. "Put me down."

"Leeway," Lee Sa said. "Her name is Leeway."

"Not careful, he get burn," I said, passing him to his crazy mother. My heart banged in my chest. Bang. Bang.

"And what happens if he gets burned?" she asked. She set him back down in front of that hot oven and handed him the two big gloves.

"Burn is painful," I said.

She would let him get burned to learn a lesson? Her craziness was worse than Madame Tsui Ping's. How had she managed to raise the boy so far, on her own? Why wasn't his body covered in burns and scrapes and—well, why was he even around? The gods must have been guarding him well. I realized Lee Sa was saying a long sentence.

"What?" I asked.

"I said." She had her hands on her hips. "If something is painful, aren't you more careful next time?'"

Yes, that was true. I had been so certain Chan Hai was a kidnapper. I had hesitated at first to go too near. What if I had acted faster? Perhaps we'd be together.

"He just small child." I watched him struggle to put the hot pan on top of the stove. My fingers itched to help.

"Correction," she said. "He's already a child. He's not a baby. And I don't want him wallowing in babyhood forever. He can be independent and make his own choices."

"There we go," Kevin said.

He smiled a great big smile and brushed the mitts together. I patted his soft brown hair. It wasn't pokey like Chinese boys' hair.

"Good job," Lee Sa said, taking the mitts from him. The treat was dark on top, like blood which had cooked too long. Perhaps she'd made a meat pie. Mother-In-Law would be astounded. "Now they just need to cool."

"Oh, Mom," he whined. "Why do we always have to wait?"

I thought the same. I hadn't eaten all morning. The sweet smell made my mouth fill with saliva. Lee Sa lifted Kevin up. He reached to the back of the stove, turning a dial on a clock. Then he pulled free of her hold and bounded off toward the room where the music came from. Perhaps he was studying composers and Lee Sa just pretended he had to wait until he finished his studies for this meat pie.

"Kevin happy to eat," I said. Was this her specialty? With all her lovely utensils, a flame always ready, a refrigerator and dozens of dishes of every size, surely she cooked many wonderful dishes. What meat had she used? "What is ingredient?"

"A little of this," she said putting out one hand, then the other. "And a little of that."

What a humble cook. Almost like a Chinese housewife who could never remember what she added to this dish or that. Is that what had attracted Colleague to her? Lee Sa reached up to the cupboard and pulled down a box. She had many similar boxes on the shelf.

"The ingredients are here on back," she said reading the back of the box. "Sugar, chocolate, flour. I don't want to look too closely at the contents." She put the box back on the shelf and closed the door. "But, hey, it's fat-free."

What was fat free? What did the box have to do with the meat pie? Surely she didn't mean this food came from a box.

"You tell joke," I said.

"No, no joke," she said. "Just add water."

I was reminded of Madame Tsui Ping selling her "fish sauce," the morning's catch mixed with the mud into which the fish had fallen. How did Lee Sa know that the ingredients listed on the back were really what was inside? Without seeing? Without tasting? She seemed so concerned about choice, but didn't she want to choose what she put in her body?

"You put food in your mouth," I said. "And you not know all ingredients?"

"You sound like Chao Ran." She frowned, her chin doubling, her eyes ferocious. She raised her voice. "'You treat your body like a garbage can. Just put everything inside. No wonder son is always coughing.' That's what Chao Ran always says."

I could see his point. This was common sense, wasn't it? My face felt hot.

"But," she said, thrusting her arms out in front of her. "Who on this earth knows everything that goes into their mouth?"

Our family did. We had simple meals. Rice and vegetables, sometimes meat, sometimes fish. No surprises. But I would not say this out loud. She nodded as though my silence was affirmation of her point.

"Besides, just wait until you try them," she cooed leading me back to the dining room.

Sweat beaded on my forehead. Perhaps from the heat of that box or the small boy who almost got burned. Or maybe my heart which still beat too fast. Or Lee Sa and her array of emotions.

"Now," she said. "Where were we?"

"We start lesson now?" I asked.

"Start?" she said and took a long sip of coffee. She peered over the top of her cup at me with her piercing blue eyes.

"Guo Qiang say you great teacher," I said. "You have book. Or exercise paper for me?"

I hoped I hadn't offended her. That she wasn't going to go on another shouting spree. Fortunately Mother-In-Law still rested, so she didn't hear me talking so straight to the teacher. Perhaps if Lee

Sa had been normal in the head, I wouldn't have had to speak so bluntly.

"I have my mouth," she said, pointing to her thick lips. "I talk. You listen and jump in when you can. That's the best way to learn."

I pictured myself listening and jumping. Jumping in where? I would rather have a piece of paper and pencil. Surely Mother-In-Law would want to see evidence of my progress.

"Jump in?" I asked.

"Just talk," Lee Sa said. "But you reminded me of something." She snapped her fingers. "Before I forget."

She pulled a piece of blank paper from the mess on the table. She hunted under a stack of books. Then looked to the floor where she found a pen. She concentrated as she wrote down words. Then she handed me the paper.

"There," she said. "That's simple, don't you think? More official looking. Perhaps you can take that down when you leave."

"Join us for Halloween Trick or Treating," the sign read. "6-8 p.m., October 31st."

My scalp tingled. I didn't understand half of the words that she called simple. Certainly I had offended her with my demands. Now she was exacting revenge by testing me with a string of difficult words. Well, I would not fail.

"What is Halloween Trick or Treating?" I asked.

"One of our great American customs," Lee Sa said, taking the paper from me and holding it out to look this way and that as if it were a great piece of art. "Chao Ran compares it to your Hungry Ghost Festival. But we don't go burning lots of incense and paper houses. The kids get dressed up to scare away the evil ghosts and are rewarded with lots of candy."

"And Singapore celebrate this, too?" I asked.

Singapore seemed to celebrate everything. Guo Qiang said that the Malays had just finished celebrating Hari Raya. The Chinese had celebrated the Moon Festival. And now here was another festival, an American one at that.

"Well, no." Lee Sa tossed the paper on the table and took another sip of her coffee. "That's why I'm starting this campaign so early. To get everyone excited. By next month, Halloween should be a familiar word."

"This must be an important festival," I said.

"A year doesn't feel complete without Halloween," she said, her gaze shifting away. "I can remember every year spending so much time planning my costume. One year I was a ballerina. Another year a princess. Are you understanding?"

"I think so," I said. This just talking was more difficult than listening to her stories. The wheels in my brain spun so fast, my cheeks felt hot. And still I wasn't sure if I was following her. A princess and ballerina were not considered scary in Chinese culture. "Do Americans think princess scary?"

"You're right," she said, laughing so the gold in the back of her mouth flashed at me. "I guess the holiday has kind of lost a lot of its original meaning. But then that's true of all our holidays. If it weren't for Chao Ran asking, 'Why do you do need a tree? Why do you waste so much paper wrapping a present that will be unwrapped the next day? Why do people declare their love only on one day of the year? Or kiss the bride in front of all those honored guests?' I wouldn't bother finding out myself. I'd just keep passing on the traditions, no questions asked."

I nodded. I understood her words, but had no idea what she spoke of. What tree? What presents? She spoke of love and a bride. Perhaps these were all wedding customs. I dared not ask. Like a goat who had lost her way, I didn't know which path would lead back home. Where to jump in. I did understand one point though. One thing we had in common. Our culture kept passing on traditions as well. Even if we didn't always understand why.

I shifted in my seat. The leg of my chair scraped against the tile floor. Sweat had dried on the back of my neck, making my skin itch. I glanced at my watch. Our hour of this strange English lesson had passed. It was time for me to go. I didn't want her charging us extra. In the background, the buzzer in the kitchen sounded again. However Lee Sa was so intent on talking about holidays that she'd forgotten about the special treat. My stomach grumbled. Kevin ran through the room and into the kitchen. Drawers opened and closed. Metal on metal scraped.

"Your talk is iter—inte—" I said, making a show of looking at my watch. I scooted forward on my chair. Arranged books on the table top.

"Interesting?" she provided.

"You live in Singapore eight years." I held my wrist up higher. "In three hours, I live in Singapore six days."

"Oh, my God." Lee Sa jumped out of her chair.

I should have mentioned the time earlier. Did she have another appointment? Then I spotted the object of her concern. Kevin walked past me black sludge dripping from his mouth. I'd seen night buckets with those drippings. A spurt of acid formed at the back of my throat. I swallowed and clenched my teeth.

"Oh, my God," she repeated.

Perhaps she wasn't totally incompetent as a mother. How would she cleanse his mouth? Vinegar? Or something from a box? But, instead of rushing to Kevin, and stopping him from eating that waste, she came next to me and wrapped her hairy arms around me.

"You poor thing," she said. "You miss home so much you're counting the hours."

Didn't she see her precious son putting that—that—that in his mouth? The words were trapped in my brain, swirling. I pulled away from her damp, fuzzy grasp and pointed.

"Of course." She laughed. She rested her arm on my shoulder. "You're right. What you need is a brownie."

She went into the kitchen and returned with a large plate full of the thick, black pieces of sludge. This was not a meat pie. I felt embarrassed that I'd mistaken her fine cooking for manure. Then again, Mother-In-Law said she was crazy. Doubt pricked at the back of my head.

"I think our time finished," I said, getting up. "I should go."

"Oh, don't worry about time." Lee Sa picked up the largest piece of slop. "Hmmmm. These are so good. Go ahead. Help yourself."

"I full." I patted my stomach, as if my insides were overflowing rather than gurgling from emptiness.

"If you don't hurry," she said. "The aunts will beat you to it."

"The aunts?" Did she have relatives here? To help her raise this boy?

"Haven't you noticed?" she asked. "At Christmas, I made a pumpkin pie and made the mistake of following the directions on the package, of leaving it out on the counter to cool. Next thing I knew, the surface was black. Moving black. Ants."

"What shame," I said. Why didn't she use a plastic cover to keep the bugs away, like we did at home in the village? Like Mother-In-Law did here? My full bowl of porridge sat under a plastic cover back in the apartment. My stomach gurgled again. "Is hard to take off the ants?"

"Don't be ridiculous." She waved her hand at me and shook her head. "I threw the whole thing out."

"You throw away?" I imagined throwing a whole pie away. All that food. All that money.

"Ugh." She crinkled her nose in disgust. Pursed her lips. "Can you imagine eating pie that had ants crawling all over it? Of course we tossed it."

"Shame." Ants weren't that big of a problem. Not like cockroaches or rats. We had had both in our kitchen in the village.

"Don't be shy." She motioned toward the plate of sludge. "They say chocolate is better than love."

"Better than love?" Was this another American story? Did her father give her all those boxes when he sent her away from America? Could anything make my heart forget my love?

"Go on," she said, taking another brownie for herself. "It will make you forget about home for awhile. At least you won't be counting the hours."

I looked at the plate of black goop. A small piece dribbled off the far side of the plate. I imagined the droppings in night buckets. I saw chickens pecking at the refuse in the outhouse in our backyard. My underarms tickled. My throat closed.

"It's funny how protective people are of their mouths," she said. "They will go bungee jumping off high buildings and jumping over rivers on motorcycles or even—" She looked at me. "Marry young strangers. But ask them to try a food they've never tasted and all that courage just vanishes."

Lee Sa laughed so loudly the walls shook. I reached across the plate for that small piece of brownie. I wouldn't have her laughing at me. The sweet soft cake caressed my tongue.

"Is sweet," I said.

Sweeter than the sesame or chestnut cakes we made for the New Year which used spoonfuls of sugar. Sweeter than red bean ice treats. Sweeter than the ice cream Chan Hai bought for me. Warmth spread through my body. Like a hug.

"Good, isn't it?" Lee Sa asked.

"Good," I said.

"So, tell me about your love," she said. So bold. Her eyes flashed at me as she had done earlier at the guard downstairs. "Where did you meet Guo Qiang?"

Papers rustled. I looked toward the living room. Mother-In-Law stood in the center of the mess again, her purse over her shoulder.

"You're finished with your English lesson," she said in Mandarin.

"Yes," I said in English. "Finish almost."

"We're having brownies," Lee Sa said. "And thinking of love. Would you like some?"

"It's time for us to go now," she said, still speaking in Mandarin. Her eyes were small like the points of a dagger. Perhaps she was so tired, she couldn't think of any English words. Couldn't be bothered to squeeze them out of her mouth. Perhaps she was thirsty and hungry. "Guo Qiang will be home soon for lunch."

Lee Sa didn't offer the brownies again, although she seemed to understand Mother-In-Law's refusal. Lee Sa had been kind to make us this special love treat. Was this her way of contributing to the marriage? Of speeding up the love and the grandson-making process?

"Thank you for iter—intra—"

"Interesting?" Lee Sa smiled.

"Interesting lesson and delicious brownie," I said, standing and moving over to Mother-In-Law. "You must come to our house. I make you our special hometown treat. Pork dumplings."

"I'd like that," Lee Sa said. "Just tell me when and we'll be there."

When? I hadn't really thought of an exact time. I needed to consult with Guo Qiang and Mother-In-Law first.

"Maybe tomorrow or next day," I said. "I will ask—"

"Tomorrow works best," Lee Sa said. "We'd love that. Thank you."

She didn't say she'd ask Colleague first. She made the decision for both of them right there.

"Tomorrow then," I said.

"Here," she said, reaching across the table to a pile of cards. "Here's my card if you need to call me to make a change."

I pocketed her information. Mother-In-Law dug her fingernails into my skin, pulling me out the door as if running from a disaster. She must be famished. I was, too. As we walked away from Lee Sa and her messy house and her brownies, I found myself looking forward to tomorrow. Guo Qiang would have time with his friend. I would have more talking time with Lee Sa. A bonus lesson. And the faster I learned, the faster I could stop draining our family of money and start contributing.

Chapter Fifty-Eight
A Bucket of Criticism

I opened the windows to let a breeze flow through the living room. We didn't have an air conditioner like Lee Sa. I moved the fan to face the dining table and noticed a light flashing on the phone. Perhaps there was something wrong with the phone. I would have to show Guo Qiang.

I was eager for him to return home, eager to share my experience with him. Mother-In-Law hadn't seemed in the slightest bit interested, issuing forth small grunts at my recital of the stories I'd heard. Perhaps she was exhausted from sitting in that mess all morning, worrying that ghosts might be in the couch.

I went in the kitchen where Mother-In-Law stood next to the ingredients for lunch. A small piece of pork and some greens. A stir fry. First, I put a cup of rice in the cooker, rinsed the grains three times, turned on the cook button. Mother-In-Law moved wordlessly nearby, handing me a cutting board, a knife. Surely, this morning had been a long one for her. I didn't speak, fearing I might use up what little energy she had left. Even I felt exhausted. Oh, I had had English lessons in university. But, in university, I was one of hundreds, and Not-Bump-On-Log Wong always rescued us when we didn't understand. This was my first one-on-one experience. As I chopped the pork, English words and phrases danced in my head. Bungee jumping. Tossed it. A great American custom. Halloween. Did Guo Qiang know all these words? These customs?

I moved to the sink to wash the vegetables. All my years of studying with Wide-Mouth Teacher Sarah had helped. Here I was, in a foreign country, able to talk to an English-speaking person for an entire sixty minutes. Dear Mother-In-Law stood nearby, watching. I felt safe and warm, and again I wondered where Lee Sa's mother-in-law was, why she wasn't around to help with the housecleaning, the cooking of food that didn't come from a box, the raising of Kevin. Gods, Lee Sa could use some help there, the way she almost let that poor child get burned. Then again, perhaps Lee Sa's mother-in-law was ill or already in the next world.

"You're going to choke him to death," Mother-In-Law said. She held up one piece of meat I hadn't chopped as small as the others. "Guo Qiang isn't a pig."

"Aiya. I missed a piece." I left the water running on the vegetables, went to the chopping board, and cut that one big piece of meat into smaller portions.

"If you cut it too small," she said, pointing to the pieces I had just chopped. "The meat will disappear when you fry it. It will be a big waste."

"You're right." I stopped cutting and returned to the vegetables.

"You like waste, don't you?" she said. "I remember your mother saying that she felt shame I'd have to teach you manners. She didn't mention the waste. How you let the water run in the sink as if it were free, as if it were never-ending."

I turned off the water. I knew better. My skin itched.

"You don't eat your breakfast." She pointed to the leftover bowl of rice on the table. "And yet you make new rice for lunch."

"This new rice is only for you and Guo Qiang," I said, turning the stove on underneath the pan. Click-click-click.

"You sit with Li Zhi, laughing and eating like you're at a party," she said, her breath acidic. "Instead of studying the English which we pay big money for." Bite, bite, bite.

Lee Sa was the one who wanted to talk and eat. I had asked for a real lesson. But my reasons sounded defensive. I wouldn't say them aloud. I poured a bit of oil in the pan, then turned to the cutting board and chopped the green vegetables, not too big, not too small.

"And then—" She put her face right in front of mine. "And then on top of all that you go and invite her to come to our house and eat our food."

"I just meant to be polite," I said, moving away from her, scraping the vegetables from the cutting board into the frying pan. The oil sizzled. Steam from the pan and not just Mother-In-Law filled the air. "I just assumed Lee Sa would talk to Colleague first."

"Didn't I tell you she was loony?" Mother-In-Law pointed to a piece of vegetable that wasn't fully chopped. "Didn't I warn you? Just wait until your husband hears that you've invited that ill-behaved half-child to mess up our house and that nutty foreigner to haunt the neighbors with her loud laughter." She shook her head and looked to the ceiling. "Aiya. What to do with a wife like you?"

"You're right," I said.

I had just assumed that Guo Qiang would have invited them many times. They had mentioned the other foreigner, Zhu Dee, who had peeled his shrimp. I figured that had taken place here. Maybe we could take them out to eat instead. And here I thought I was saving him money.

I looked over toward the phone. I remembered how to dial, how to push the "talk" button. But the red light still flashed. Besides, Mother-In-Law, whose morning cheer had evaporated like rain on the sidewalk, would accuse me of wasting more money—and interrupting Guo Qiang. He would be home soon enough. We could talk then.

The house soon smelled of fried pork. I glanced at my watch. Five past one. Guo Qiang should have been back by now. My stomach ached thinking about his return. My famished insides couldn't wait to feel the warmth of rice and meat. On the other hand, I didn't relish hearing Guo Qiang's rebukes over my poor behavior.

A noise sounded at the gate. Mother-In-Law and I rushed to greet Guo Qiang. Mother-In-Law's face was pinched. I knew she carried a bucket of criticisms about me that she would hand to Guo Qiang as soon as he stepped inside. I only hoped he didn't think my faults as terrible as she.

We looked out into the hallway. From nearby the sizzle of frying food sounded, the clink of bowls, the warmth of laughter. Some people spoke in the familiar tones of Mandarin, but other sounds were strange. We had a dark family like the Indian who owned the shop near Lee Sa next to us on one side. On the other side was another dark family, but they wore flowery clothes like Guo Qiang enjoyed. From Malaysia. A small dark child walked down the hall in what looked like yellow pajamas. He trailed a stick behind him, letting it scrape against the doors and walls and gates.

"Children these days have no sense," Mother-In-Law said loud enough for the boy to hear. "Shoo," she called out, as if he were a feral dog.

When he ran off, I went outside to inspect the wall. Surely he meant us no harm. He just enjoyed the feeling of the stick against the bumpy wall, the scraping sound like music. The wall showed no damage, no scratches. I got a cloth and rubbed over the area anyway to make Mother-In-Law feel better. She wasn't just concerned about the cement being scraped, but about the boy's stick dropping off unwanted spirits who would make their home with us.

"You're going to rub the paint off," Mother-In-Law said, poking her nose out between the grill. "If you're not careful."

I went inside and put the cloth away. I re-arranged the dishes on the table. I could almost taste the salted pork melting in my mouth.

"Don't stand around the table like a dog waiting for a scrap," Mother-In-Law said, shooing at me with her hand as she had done to the strange child outside. "Guo Qiang will be here soon. Unless, that is, he already heard about you inviting crazy Li Zhi to our house, and he's too irritated with your foolishness to come home."

"You know how Guo Qiang sometimes forgets about the time," I said.

"Better than forgetting his wits," she countered.

My, but Mother-In-Law was angry. Surely her anger was all a misunderstanding. I had had a good lesson with Lee Sa. I had learned many new words and ideas. Yes, I'd invited her to dinner. But we could remedy that. Perhaps Mother-In-Law was as famished as I.

"Mother, you should eat first." I opened the rice cooker and stirred the rice around. The smell kissed my nose. My empty stomach gurgled. "Come eat." I filled a bowl for her. "You need to keep strong and healthy."

"No, no." She sat down on the couch and folded and refolded the newspaper. "I'll wait for Guo Qiang."

"Eat, Mother," I insisted, piling a bowl high with rice and pork. "Eat."

"I'm not hungry," she said, although she allowed me to guide her to the dining table.

Her lips formed a tight line. Surely she envisioned that as soon as she lifted her chopsticks to her mouth, Guo Qiang would step inside the door. How would it look if she was putting food in her mouth first? Then, again, maybe like me, she also worried.

I opened the gate and peered outside. Humidity bathed my face. Where was Guo Qiang? Had he run into trouble? Was it enough to assign people apartments to avoid racial uprisings? Had there been a fight at work? Had he gotten hurt? My heart pounded. Where would I go look? I knew the direction of the university, across the street from Lee Sa's blue building, but I'd never been there. I breathed, willing Guo Qiang's form to fill the dirty cement hallway even should he be as irritated with me as dear Mother-In-Law. But he didn't appear. And soon noises of lunch stopped in the apartments nearby. The sun moved from its top position in the sky.

"You'll have a grandson soon." Last night's conversation with Mother-In-Law popped into my head. "But it will be troublesome." That's what she had said the Temple Priest had predicted. Would Guo Qiang be hurt for many months and unable to make a child? Would he be killed and Mother-In-Law forced to adopt another son to marry me? I stepped outside and leaned over the wall to watch the children chase one another around the playground on their bikes. Around and around they went. So silly. The same as my thoughts.

"Where are you going?" Mother-In-Law barked.

"I'm just waiting out here for Guo Qiang," I said.

"You wait in here," she said. "It's too hot out there."

I returned inside. Mother-In-Law looked one last time at the doorway. Then she gave a great sigh, sat down, and picked up her chopsticks to eat. Each time her chopsticks hit the rim of her bowl, my stomach hurt. I went to look out the kitchen window, to see if our laundry was dry, to see if I might spot Guo Qiang. Moments later Mother-In-Law came up behind me, grasping onto my arm.

"My stomach is full," she said, handing me her half-eaten bowl of rice.

Then she turned and went off to her room. Perhaps she'd left half there on purpose, to tempt me. But I wasn't about to show my weakness by drooling over her leftovers. I could wait for an angry Guo Qiang.

I put a cover over Mother-In-Law's half-eaten bowl of rice and pork, hunger gnawing at my insides. A grain of rice poked up from the tip of her chopsticks. I took those chopsticks into the kitchen and let that grain of rice fall into my hands. I brought my hand to my mouth. The soft grain rolled around in my mouth. How delicious.

Mother-In-Law's bedroom door moaned. I quickly rinsed her chopsticks and took a rag from beneath the sink. I dusted and mopped and straightened, even taking a toothbrush and cleaning the lines between the tiles. My stomach felt like one of those lines, the hunger scratch, scratch, scratching like a toothbrush. But any minute I expected Guo Qiang to come through the gate. Or Mother-In-Law to march out of her room. I wouldn't be caught shoveling food down my throat like a beggar.

I pulled in the laundry off the bamboo poles, making a pile of clothing on the couch. I sat down next to the pile and picked up one of Guo Qiang's batik shirts. The warm cloth smelled like sunshine. Concentrating on the folds of the shirt took my mind off the trouble I'd created, foolish scenarios about Guo Qiang, the faint ache which pounded at the sides of my head. I thought of Mother. How we used to fold clothes together. I imagined her hand across the cloth, still hot from the sun, her palm smoothing out all the wrinkles. What would she think of Lee Sa? Of Guo Qiang? Of this hot place? I got lost in my thoughts. Had it rained yet back in the village? Was Father still on good terms with New Neighbor? Had Father spent some of the money Mother-In-Law had given him making a concrete gully? Just like he told Mother he planned to do someday? I put another shirt in my lap. The early evening breeze blew through the window. The gate clattered. I looked up.

"You're back." I felt a rush of relief, the same as when our airplane had finally set down on the earth.

Guo Qiang's arms and legs looked the same as they had yesterday. His clothing was unstained except for a ring of sweat around his collar. His face showed no cuts or bruises, but his expression was as lifeless as stone.

"You're back," I repeated. How silly Mother-In-Law and I had been to worry.

He walked right by me as if I were invisible, going into the bedroom and shutting the door. He'd never walked by me without a word. Usually he had something to say. To teach. The chink of his buckle sounded as his pants fell to the floor. Perhaps he was eager to change into something cooler. I went into the bedroom. He was already in the shower. Surely he'd been too hot to speak.

I took his pants and shirt from the floor. I cradled the shirt on one arm to take to the laundry bucket as I hung the pants on a hanger. Just as I shut the closet, the shower turned off. Guo Qiang threw open the bathroom door, a towel wrapped around his middle.

"I had my first English lesson today," I said. "What an interesting experience."

He stepped in front of me, throwing the closet door open so hard the hinges shuddered. He rifled through his clothes like rodents going through the garbage, letting shirts fall from the hangers as he picked the one multi-colored shirt he wanted to wear to cover his naked white chest.

"Lee Sa made us her hometown specialty," I said, trying again. "A brownie."

He buttoned the last button. Even that sounded loud. Then he threw down the towel and pulled on a pair of shorts. Had he had a rough day at work despite the lack of obvious bruises? Had he heard of my useless English lesson? My dinner invitation? Talking had never been his problem. What was this?

"Dinner's ready," I said. "You must be hungry."

"No, actually," he spat, brushing past me. "I'm not hungry at all. I had a big lunch, remember?"

The door to his office slammed shut. His desk chair rolled across the floor, slamming into the wall. Books thunk-thunked on his desk. He sounded like a tiger thrashing about. I dared not follow. I went to the kitchen and took the stir fry from beneath the plastic cover. Even if Guo Qiang wasn't hungry, Mother-In-Law soon would be. My stomach was so empty I didn't feel it anymore. But I knew I would eat much tonight. I went to the stove and started the magic flame. Click-click-click.

Did I remember? What should I remember? When did Guo Qiang tell me about some big lunch he planned to attend? For all the talking he did, I felt as if I understood very little about this family. Just a grain of rice's worth. What made Mother-In-Law so nervous around Lee Sa? What made Guo Qiang drink so these past few nights? Why did he think he told me things—about the red frame, about a big lunch? I turned off the flame and went back to his project room. I leaned my ear against the cool wood. The thrashing had stopped.

"Guo Qiang?"

I opened the door. He sat at the computer, staring at English words on the screen. His fingers tapped across the keyboard.

"You're such an intelligent man," I said, stepping further into the office. "Here you are a great professor in a foreign country. You think so fast, think so many things. I'm a lucky wife."

"Oh, please." His fingers continued to click-click the keys. "You don't need to fill the air with such sweet words. This place is already hot and sticky enough."

"Surely that is not my intent," I said. "Actually I have a problem. A question that's troubling me."

Guo Qiang's fingers paused as he looked up at me. The professor ready to solve a problem even in his anger. I moved closer.

"Is it possible that sometimes you think too fast?" I asked. "Maybe you think you're going to tell me something and just because you've thought it, just because it's registered in your brain, you move onto the next task."

"What are you talking about?" Guo Qiang shook his head and returned to his keyboard.

"I believe you're a thoughtful husband," I said. He peered at his screen as though trying to shut me out. "Who wouldn't want his wife to be rude to Lee Sa by being late for her very first English lesson. Surely last night you thought you told me what time I was to be there. Yet, that thought never materialized into words."

Guo Qiang glanced over at me. He tilted his head to the side. Furrowed his eyebrows.

"Neither did your thought about that red frame—"

"You said." Guo Qiang rolled back from his keyboard. "You said you remembered me telling you."

"That was because Mother-In-Law stood right near the phone. I didn't want her to think . . . well, I just didn't think it was necessary to discuss every detail over the phone, to waste money."

"The phone's not expensive," he snorted.

"And you never told me about a lunch either."

He turned in his chair and faced me. His eyes were dark pits. Worse than the devil.

"I called you," he said, holding up his fingers. "Twice. First, I tried to get you at Lee Sa's, but she said you'd just left. Then I called you here. No one was home, so I left a message."

Guo Qiang had left a message? I'd been at home all day cleaning the house as if the Wife of the Kitchen God were going to make an inspection and report her findings. I hadn't seen any message anywhere. Yet why would he lie about such a thing?

"What did your message say?" I asked.

Perhaps my voice betrayed my thoughts. Guo Qiang glared at me, got up from his chair and advanced so quickly, I ducked. He rushed past and headed for the front door. When he passed the broken phone, where the light still blinked, he stopped as though seeing a traffic signal on the road. He put his hand over his face and shook his head.

Another problem. Despite its fancy exterior, this phone wasn't as sturdy as Zi Mei's. Surely I'd broken it this morning by pushing the buttons too hard. He must think me a big nuisance. He pushed a button on the phone. The machine made a whirring sound, then a click. How strange.

"Can you meet me at the university canteen at noon?" the telephone said in a voice that sounded like Guo Qiang. "My boss is eager to meet you and has invited us both to lunch. The canteen is . . ."

Guo Qiang's voice went on and on explaining how to get there, that they would be waiting at the first table. I stared at the machine. This machine that talked, like a radio or television, only with the voice of Guo Qiang coming out, the voice of a proud husband who wanted to introduce his wife to the boss.

"Didn't you see the message light blinking," he asked, shaking his head at me. "When you came home from your English lesson?"

"Yes," I said. "I saw it."

"And?" Guo Qiang stared at me as if I were an animal that had taken away his dinner.

"It's just . . ."

"You were too busy," he said going over to the couch and dumping the folded pile of clothes on the floor. "Even with Mother around to help you, you're too—"

"We never had these," I said. Surely he hadn't either. Not in the village.

He looked at me as though examining Don Don while he sold rain jackets that were too big. Where was Mother-In-Law? She obviously didn't know how to use the machine either and would have come to my defense.

"I don't know how to use it," I said.

"It's just common sense."

Guo Qiang picked up the pile of clothes from the floor and threw them back on the couch. Then he left, clanging the gate shut behind him. I sensed he was going for a long drink, again.

I should have felt happy that he had so much faith in me. That he thought I was so intelligent I would automatically know how to use all the items in his—in our—house. That he was sympathetic enough that he picked the clothes back up off the floor. I kept those happy thoughts in my heart as I returned to the kitchen to warm dinner for Mother-In-Law.

"Was that Guo Qiang I heard?" Mother-In-Law said, coming in as I filled the steamer with water to heat up the rice.

"Yes, yes," I said, looking up and forcing my lips into a smile. She had a sheen of sweat on her brow. "He's fine. He had a long day."

"He sounded angry," she said bobbing her head up and down. "I told you he'd be angry with your foolishness. I hope you were smart enough to apologize."

"Yes," I said. Although we hadn't even had a chance to discuss my foolishness with Lee Sa. I put the steamer on the stove. "Many times."

"Where is he now?"

She looked around the kitchen as if he might pop out of the laundry area. I turned the dial on the stove. Instead of the usual click-click-click, I heard, "Where is he now? Where is he now? Where is he now?" Where did he go each night?

"He's gone," I said, fussing over the positioning of the steamer. "Gone out for a walk."

"That's nonsense," she said, looking to the front gate, frowning. "It's dinner time."

"He said he had a big lunch."

"See?" Mother-In-Law crossed her arms over her chest as she marched around the kitchen. "I knew it. He wastes lots of money because of you. Spent money at the school canteen for lunch rather than coming home. Now he's probably out wasting more money on food and drink. Aiya."

I stared at the water on the stove. The surface was smooth. Then a bubble emerged, rippling, popping the water. Guo Qiang had called me a country bumpkin. No, he hadn't said the words. But his face and demeanor had as much said so. Why hadn't Mother-In-Law noticed the blinking red light? Did she want to show me I was a worthless intellectual? Educated but unable to take care of her house? Did she want to send a ripple through our smooth auspicious union? But surely not. Surely she wanted only happiness and a grandson from us.

"Mother-In-Law," I said. "How long have you lived here?"

"Don't change the subject," she said, turning up the heat on the stove. "I'm trying to teach you proper behavior and you're mind is wandering off into different pastures, like a cow searching for tastier grass. Besides Guo Qiang has been here for a long time, over eight years."

"And you?" I pressed.

"What does this have to do with your foolish behavior at Li Zhi's house?" she asked, putting a lid over the boiling water. "Of your wasteful tendencies?"

"Is this your first time to Singapore, too?" I gritted my teeth.

"Oh, my mother." She re-arranged the boiling pot on the flame, so it was centered exactly. "No, silly daughter. I came here long before you. In fact, I wanted to come here as soon as Guo Qiang was settled. But, at that time, your late father-in-law was ill. We couldn't travel. Then, when he died, I didn't have the energy, not for many years. I still don't. But I sensed that Guo Qiang's heart was too lonely. I knew I had to come and help him focus on getting a proper wife. And now I need to spend lots of energy helping you."

"I'm sorry to be such trouble," I said.

I did a mental calculation. If she had come when I had started corresponding with Guo Qiang, she couldn't have stayed here for more than four months. Perhaps she also had no idea what this answering machine was. How many other things didn't she know? The water boiled up spitting out the sides of the lid.

"You put too much water in there," she chastised. "Waste. Waste. Waste. You need to stop daydreaming all the time and focus on your tasks."

"Yes," I said, turning off the flame. "You're right."

"And you don't need to keep telling me that. I know I'm right.

That's why I'm the Mother and you're just the Daughter."

That was true. In China. In China she held the wisdom of the ages. She was my esteemed elder, my boss. Yet should I continue to follow her, Guo Qiang would be disgusted. Our auspicious marriage would boil over spitting out hot water in all directions. He wanted a modern wife. To understand all he did. To adapt to new surroundings like a chameleon. I grimaced. The one person who could help me adapt irked Mother-In-Law like a scab that wouldn't heal. While I had been wrong to invite Lee Sa to our house, I found myself counting the hours until tomorrow night.

Chapter Sixty
Waiting For the End of the Storm

When I awoke, faint light still shrouded the bedroom. Birds chirped, calling out to one another in long shrill tones. Morning finally. Guo Qiang had come home in such a state last night, face red and perspiring, that any words seemed a wasted effort. But I needed him to understand. I would never intentionally wrong him. I just wasn't as sophisticated as he.

He had obviously adjusted well to this country. But had he forgotten what life was like in the village? How could he? Eight years wasn't such a long time. Always, always, from the time I was a little girl, we had passed messages through Zi Mei. She spread the word. Surely Guo Qiang had had a Zi Mei on his side of the village. I reached across the bed for him. Surely he hadn't adapted so much to this new common sense that he didn't remember his village. My hand felt the softness of the quilt. Too soft. I peered hard at his side of the bed. All he'd left were wrinkles on the sheet.

I padded out into the kitchen. Mother-In-Law came from the stove to the doorway. I expected her to stand so close to me her hot breath would make beads of perspiration on my neck, her small dark eyes would shrink me to the size of a dust particle.

"He already left," Mother-In-Law informed me, each word slow, an effort. She was still in her nightgown. "Without breakfast."

I expected her to chastise me for not waking up earlier than Guo Qiang, not having a breakfast waiting for him. But she handed me the steamer to start the porridge and teetered out of the kitchen, as if unsure of her footing. Surely she was disappointed that, the day after she had dressed up her daughter-in-law like a flower, I had gone and dumped night soil on everything. The door to her bedroom moaned closed. I poured a cup of rice into the steamer, my lips curling at the thought of food. My stomach felt queasy again this morning. Perhaps all this heat and rich food was hard on my body. If only I could talk to Mei Ling and get an herbal recipe for this strange feeling. Then again, perhaps this feeling generated from this new family.

Mother-In-Law said Guo Qiang's heart had been lonely. Yet,

while he talked incessantly as if a gag had just been removed from his lips, I didn't sense him reaching out to me. In fact, his eyes when not bleary from drink looked glassy and sad. Still lonely. Mother-In-Law, despite her pride in Guo Qiang's career and position, didn't seem happy with this country. Or Guo Qiang's choice of good friends. The whole situation felt off, as if I'd eaten fish that was just a bit old. Salty bile filled my throat.

Now this. My stupidity had caused Guo Qiang to lose face with his boss and Mother-In-Law to wilt at the prospect of that wretched foreigner contaminating our house. I had brought little good to this home. I closed my eyes, my hands holding onto the sink for leverage. Outside, the neighbor's air-cooling machine hummed. A television blared. A car horn tooted. Such strange sounds. Where was the cock crowing, the shout of the bun seller, the ring of bicycle bells, the deep reassuring voice of Chan Hai saying, "I want to wake up to your face every morning."

Beads of sweat dripped from my temples. Pressure hardened in my stomach. I spat bile into the sink. I turned on the cold water and rinsed my face and the back of my neck as Lee Sa had done. Rinsed away the thoughts I shouldn't be having. Wasn't this heaven? This beautiful clean-and-green city with big, tall buildings made of concrete, with cars that zoomed about, with a husband who held a good job and took care of my parents.

The Temple Priest had blessed our auspicious union. Mother and Father could relax into their old age. Dear Mother-In-Law, although gruff, seemed pleased she had closed the open circle in her life. Guo Qiang and I would grow to love one another some day. That was how life worked, Mother had told me. Happiness came from respect, understanding, and friendship, she had said. Love came later. Certainly Mother-In-Law would be kinder when her grandson was on the way.

A breeze blew in the kitchen window. Soft. Cool. I thought of Waipo. Whenever I had gotten upset with tears streaking down my face at some terrible wrong that a friend had done, she had always reminded me, "People must fight to become friends." Whenever I had shouted that I would never ever talk to that Fifth Cousin again or some such nonsense, she would smile and rub my forearm. "Anger is just a feeling unless you let it get out of control. It's not a broken leg or a slit throat. All it needs is soothing, soothing so that the feeling doesn't settle into your bones and become a disease."

I wouldn't let the feeling get out of control. I reached up in the cabinet for the bag of flour. Certainly Guo Qiang's boss would enjoy some homemade pork-filled buns. And that would give me a reason to visit Guo Qiang, to tell him of my blunder in inviting Lee Sa for dinner.

I walked up the long staircase toward the top of the hill where the university stood, scolding myself for waiting so long. The sun, now high in the sky, sucked at every pore in my body despite my parasol. Even Mother-In-Law had not insisted on accompanying me. Only fools missing a few piano strings would wander out in this hot sun.

The staircase seemed to go on forever, up and up and up. I held onto two plastic bags of buns, one which contained three buns for Guo Qiang, the other which contained eight for his boss. Eight, an auspicious number, meaning ever-increasing harmony. Surely Guo Qiang's boss would appreciate the effort, the taste, the number. Then again, a chill trickled down my back. What if he wasn't Chinese? Would Guo Qiang laugh at me? Show even more disgust? I hurried up the steps, taking them two at a time, eager to find out.

At the top of the steps, immense white brick buildings filled the otherwise grassy area. Which one was the Computer Science building? Sweat slithered down the back of my neck. A Chinese woman passed carrying a thin briefcase. I would ask her. I smiled at her, and she looked right through me. Obviously, she was in a hurry already thinking about the lecture for her next class.

I leaned against a memorial statue of the university's founder to catch my breath. The stone felt too warm against my legs and I immediately stood up. In the distance, I spotted a sign which pointed to the Administration Building. I could ask directions there. Another campus visitor passed by with her child. She wore a black dress which covered her from head to foot and spoke to her child in a language I'd never heard. And I thought I was hot.

"Hey, there!" a woman shouted in Mandarin. Strange Mandarin. Not strange like the clipped tones of Singaporean Mandarin, but strange like she'd come from some foreign province and hadn't yet mastered the language.

I looked over. The glare of the sun blinded my vision. Maybe I wasn't supposed to be here. I hurried toward the administration building, trying not to think about Third Uncle on Father's side who had been arrested and put in jail for six months for trespassing on government property without permission. Surely Mother-In-Law would have warned me about such a concern. If Mother-In-Law knew.

Feet rustling through the grass behind me sounded. I hurried purposefully like that Chinese woman with her briefcase on her way to teach a class, hiding the buns in front of me. Fingers yanked at my hair.

Now what had I done? I'd come up here to make friends with Guo Qiang, thinking we'd done our fighting. I could already hear his voice saying, "You have to get permission to visit the university. That's just common sense." Aiya.

"Gotcha," a woman's voice said in English.

I turned. There stood Lee Sa holding the hair-pulling Kevin. My skin tingled with relief. How long had they been out here? Their hair was wet with perspiration. Their cheeks bright red. Lee Sa, as I'd assumed the first day I saw the dots on her skin, didn't have a parasol. She wore only underwear again. Kevin she had dressed in tiny underpants, as well.

"Kevin said that was you." Lee Sa set him down with a big sigh. "I thought the little guy was pulling my chain. He likes me to run."

I nodded. Pulling my chain? Her words hit my ears like rain on the tin kitchen roof back home.

"You're the last person I expected to see," she said, fanning her tight bra and blowing at the deep valley between her bosoms. "Guo Qiang said you were too busy today."

"You saw Guo Qiang?" I asked, looking about.

The black-veiled woman entered a building. A Caucasian man with a big nose and long face carried his bike up the last few steps of the staircase. A lizard scampered across the grass. Everything here looked foreign. I didn't see Guo Qiang.

"Just a few minutes ago," Lee Sa said. She blew some more into her bra. "We went for lunch and a swim. It's so hot today."

"You went swimming?" I asked.

Why was Guo Qiang swimming with someone else's wife in the middle of a workday? Certainly she only imagined such an activity. Where would there be room for a reservoir here? A cool dark reservoir, surrounded by shady trees and the sounds of crickets. Then again, her hair was wet.

"You should come sometime," she said already stepping away, moving toward the stairs that would take her down to her building and out of this hot sun. "Guo Qiang said you were busy with housework.

But then, how much housework can a person have?" She laughed. "Besides, the boys are really good."

"Boys?" I looked down at Kevin who ran around Lee Sa's legs as she backed away. Perhaps he'd been swimming with his friend, Zhu Dee.

"Not Kevin" she said, grabbing onto his shoulders to stop him. "Chao Ran and Guo Qiang."

"I can swim, too, Mom." Kevin looked stung. "I swim."

"Yes, you can, can't you?" Lee Sa patted his head. "Today he swam the width of the pool all by himself."

Kevin smiled a big smile, turning his head this way and that, not even attempting humility. He wasn't very Chinese after all.

"I did it three times," he said holding up his small fingers. "And each time, I only—"

I watched him jump up and down as he relived his success in the pool, relieved for his interruption. Each time I had a conversation with Lee Sa, I felt as if I were walking in the dark, trying to find a light. When Kevin talked, I could stop and adjust my vision, try to assess where we were in the exchange.

So Chao Ran and Guo Qiang were swimming. That would explain Guo Qiang's wet hair, his prune-like fingers the past few nights. I didn't even know he liked to swim. That was an activity we could share. Perhaps Lee Sa knew where his building was.

"—unless you can sew, too?" Lee Sa slapped her thigh so loud that my head snapped to attention. "But of course you sew."

I glanced at her clothing. That same tight bra, the white underwear that slid up her thighs. The threads on the side of her underwear looked ready to burst. But I didn't see any rips. Kevin's small blue underpants hugged his tiny bottom. His orange t-shirt with the words Singapore Bird Park looked in need of a good wash. But I didn't see any need for sewing. Perhaps I'd misunderstood.

"You need sewing?" I asked.

Lee Sa and Kevin looked at me and then at each other. They giggled. Maybe that wasn't what they needed.

"Blue Dolphin needs sewing." Kevin pointed to his bottom. "Right here. In the butt."

Blue Dolphin. That was what Kevin called Guo Qiang. Had Guo Qiang hurt himself? But then certainly they wouldn't be giggling. Why did I always assume the worst? Kevin continued to dance around patting his rear end.

"Okay, okay, Kevin. Settle down," Lee Sa said. She turned and gestured down her own backside. "Guo Qiang got a huge rip in his swimsuit."

"Everyone saw his big, white butt." Kevin laughed some more.

Kevin enjoyed saying that word. I'd have to remember it. That was the last time I'd assume a talking Kevin meant I didn't have to pay attention. Where should I start? Had Guo Qiang ripped his pants? His bathing suit? Did he need me to bring him clothes? Had Lee Sa been coming to tell me this? Certainly not. She would have just called. I hoped she hadn't called and bothered Mother-In-Law.

"If Guo Qiang had listened to me," Lee Sa said, her hands on her hips. "He'd still have his suit. But you know Guo Qiang. He knows better about everything."

She spoke the truth. Guo Qiang always did breathe professorial air. But how forward of her to assume such a familiar tone. A sour taste filled my mouth.

"What happen?" I asked.

"Like Kevin just said." Lee Sa ran her hand through her short wet hair as she spoke slowly. "Guo Qiang stood at the edge of the pool watching Kevin swim. I told Guo Qiang that Kevin was a good swimmer. He could swim the width of the pool by himself. But Guo Qiang insisted on watching. And he was so worried about Kevin, he didn't look where he was going."

Lee Sa imitated Guo Qiang. She took several steps back, her hands up to her chin in concern, reaching out as if ready to grab a struggling Kevin. Certainly Guo Qiang must have felt the same concern I had yesterday when Kevin reached with his bare hands for the hot pan of brownies. We shared that common sense.

"Guo Qiang bumped into the lifeguard station and ripped his suit." She shook her head, giggling. "His suit must have caught on a nail or something. Then, again, maybe that suit's just old. He's had it forever. I remember when Zhu Dee—well, when he got it."

"Yeah," Kevin agreed. "When he ran into the lifeguard place, his suit exploded. Bwam!"

They both laughed. Lee Sa said something about Kevin's imagination, about television. I couldn't concentrate. There was that name again. Zhu Dee. Zhu Dee had given Guo Qiang a swimsuit. What kind of gift was that for a child to give? Or an old woman? Lee Sa fanned her hand over her mouth as much to try and capture a breeze as to shoo away the laughter which kept erupting from her mouth.

"Mom." Kevin pulled on the hem of Lee Sa's ancient bra. The cloth slid down. Any minute, one of those giant breasts would pop out. "I'm hungry."

"Let's go home then," Lee Sa said.

No, not yet. My heart beat fast, as if I'd just taken a sip of her mud-black coffee. I lifted my arm. I needed to find out about this Zhu Dee.

"Have some buns," I offered Kevin the bag of homemade buns I'd made for Guo Qiang. "Who is Zhu Dee?"

Lee Sa glanced at Kevin. Then she looked up with a smile too big for her face. A smile which didn't shine from her eyes.

"We'll just go home and eat," she said, grabbing onto Kevin and pulling his arm away from the buns. To go home. Away from me and my questions. "It's too hot out here."

"Zhu Dee?" Kevin asked. "Why, she's Mom's best friend."

How could I have thought otherwise? Perhaps Zhu Dee had just come for a visit and that was why I'd heard her name so often. Lee Sa let out an audible sigh. She patted Kevin on the head and pulled him forward. She must miss this friend.

"Miss Zhu Dee is from America?" I asked following them.

"Yes," Kevin said. "But, she lived here a long, long time. Mommy always called her a loco."

"Local." Lee Sa brushed the bangs back from Kevin's face. Smiled.

"She not live here anymore?" I asked.

"No more," Kevin said. "Mommy said—"

"Kevin, thank you. I can talk," Lee Sa said, putting her hand over his mouth.

We walked past the statue of the university founder. Birds chattered. A bee hummed as it flew past my ear. The rays of the sun beat down on me like sticks pounding a drum. But Lee Sa didn't talk. She stayed as silent as the statue. I was reminded of my good friend, Mei Ling. My days had become dull after she had left to go overseas. Until I met Madame Paper Cutter. And, of course, Chan Hai. Perhaps Lee Sa didn't have another good friend here.

"You must miss her," I said.

"Everyone does," Kevin said from beneath Lee Sa's hand.

Lee Sa took her hand away. I tousled his wet hair. What a sweet boy.

"Everyone," he said. "But your dear Mother-In-Law."

I laughed. He sounded so formal and respectful, just like a Chinese boy. I looked over at Lee Sa. But she frowned at him, making her face ugly.

"I'm sure dear Mother-In-Law miss this good friend, too," I said. "She just old fashioned. Not good with emotion." Not good with foreigners.

Kevin looked up at his mother. A yellow bird flew by. A machine turned on in the building nearby. Poor Lee Sa must be so lonely here. Like me.

"Don't be too sad," I said. "Is good Miss Zhu Dee go home. See her parents."

"Oh, she's not back in the U.S.," Lee Sa said, her blue eyes flashing at me. "She's in Malaysia—"

"Waiting for the end of a storm," Kevin said.

Lee Sa yanked on Kevin's arm as if to stop him from talking. But why wouldn't she want him to talk about the storm? Perhaps she didn't want him to talk about the end of the storm. Perhaps she had superstitions too.

"There is storm in Malaysia?" I asked. I hadn't read about that in the newspaper. "And she can't fly home?"

"No, no," Lee Sa said. "Kevin gets mixed up sometimes. She moved to Malaysia. She has another branch of her photography business there. Now." She pulled Kevin so fast, I thought he would topple over. "We better 'make a move,' as they say."

Why was she so eager to run away, to end this discussion? I thought of all the times I'd heard Zhu Dee's name. When Guo Qiang looked at that ancestral photo of Kevin and called it art. When Guo Qiang and I ate shrimp. And now when Guo Qiang's suit had been ripped. Zhu Dee seemed to be everywhere around Guo Qiang, like a bee buzzing nearby. An idea formed at the bottom of my heart that made my insides cold. Was I feeling anxiety over nothing? I caught up to Lee Sa who was already at the staircase.

"When did Miss Zhu Dee move?" I asked, touching her on the arm.

"I suggest you don't stay out here much longer," she said, hopping down the steps. "Those buns are shot."

"She's been gone forever," Kevin called over his shoulder. "She left after your dear Mother-In-Law came to town."

What did Mother-In-Law have to do with this? I watched them

go, my mind so full of noise I felt as if I'd been dropped in the middle of a rich man's funeral, including two sets of piercing bugles. Lee Sa's good friend moved to Malaysia. No, this was everyone's good friend. Even Guo Qiang's. How good a friend? Such a good friend that he cherished the photos she'd taken. Such a good friend that she had bought him swim trunks. Such a good friend that Mother-In-Law made a special visit to meet her. I remembered just last night asking Mother-In-Law when she had first come to Singapore. She had said she'd come when she sensed Guo Qiang's "heart was too lonely." Obviously "too lonely" meant that he had taken up with an American girl. Obviously Mother-In-Law had not been impressed with this Zhu Dee and had gotten rid of her in favor of a "proper wife."

Another machine turned on nearby. I jumped at the sound. I ached to be home, really home. I would go into our dark kitchen and help Mother start a fire under the wok. We'd sit out in the courtyard and shell greens while listening to ducks nearby. I would hold onto the strong arm of Chan Hai as we walked down the street together. I closed my eyes, wishing away these people, this fancy city, this security. I never wanted to see any of them again.

"See you tonight," Kevin called from midway down the staircase.

"Tonight?" I called back. What was he talking about?

"You probably haven't heard." Lee Sa stopped and turned. "I talked with Guo Qiang at lunch. We agreed six is best. Much later in the evening and Kevin gets cranky. Me, too."

"Good," I said, forcing my lips to curve into a smile as she and Kevin continued on down the steps.

I didn't bother to find Guo Qiang at the university. There was no need. He and Lee Sa had worked out the details for tonight. Besides, like she said, the buns were bad now. The humidity had turned them to mush. I headed down the steps toward the market, my chest burning as if I'd swallowed something too large to digest. An image came to me of the night Father had accepted the twenty thousand *yuan* from Mother-In-Law. Accepted their marriage proposal. Oh, how it had rained. How the cardboard over my head had turned to mush, as my half of the sky crumbled in my hands. I looked at the buns dangling from my wrist and felt the sky crumbling again. I couldn't let that happen.

Chapter Sixty-One
A Second Wife

My hand clutched at a packet of goatweed powder, an aphrodisiac I'd bought at the Chinese pharmacy on the way home. Perhaps this would cure Guo Qiang's disinterest in me. The Indian neighbor's cooling machine hummed, water from it drip-dripping on the cement below. Bamboo poles scraped against the window, as the Malay neighbor brought in her laundry, something she should have done hours ago. All her bright-colored clothing would fade with so much sun. How embarrassing that Guo Qiang needed such prompting. A special dress from Mother-In-Law, herbs from me. Did other women ever go through this? I couldn't imagine.

Footsteps sounded near the kitchen door. I'd finish adding the aphrodisiac to Guo Qiang's dumplings later. I stuffed the herbal packet in the chopsticks drawer, the cellophane crinkling as loud as thunder. No one need know the efforts I went to. I waited. Breathed. No one was there. Again.

I counted to ten. Then, from the chopsticks drawer, I removed the packet and continued filling dumplings. I would make two plates. One for Mother-In-Law and the guests, and one for Guo Qiang. The front gate scraped open. I put meat in the last of the dumplings and hid the leftover goatweed powder.

"You're back early," I said, meeting Guo Qiang at the gate. His face looked like that stone sculpture of the university founder. Rather than hand me his briefcase, he set it down next to the couch. "You've had a long day."

Here we were about to welcome friends into our home as a married couple. I had hoped he would have taken on a new attitude. But he seemed eager to remind me of his anger over yesterday's ignorance and punish me with his silence. Nothing about his mishap at the pool, nothing about his arrangements with Colleague to come over in an hour, nothing but angry silence. He seemed content to dig in the bull's ear, as Waipo would always say.

He slammed his way off to the bedroom to change his clothes. I did not follow. I had a dinner to finish. I returned to the kitchen and rinsed off the hatchet. Then I removed the fish from the plastic bag. I held onto the tail and cleaned off the shiny scales the fishmonger had missed. Guo Qiang appeared in the doorway. He hadn't changed out of his sweaty clothing. He held my suitcase in his hands. Good. He had found my gift.

"You better make a big meal," he said.

"I am."

I ran water over the body of the fish, letting the clear liquid clean away the blood and guts. He stepped into the heat of the kitchen and surveyed the countertop, every centimeter of which was covered with food. A cold appetizer, fish, meat, two vegetables, soup, and, for dessert, fruit.

"Colleague will be here in half an hour," he said, his nasal voice as official as if he were on the loudspeaker at home, telling me to pay my electricity bill on time.

"I know," I said, turning off the water.

"You know Lee Sa and Kevin are coming too?" His voice sounded incredulous. A smirk formed on his lips.

"I know many things." I looked up at him.

"Lee Sa must have called." He gave a nervous laugh.

"No." I placed the fish on the cutting board and slit criss-cross marks into the body with the knife.

"Don't tell me," he said, picking a piece of beef from the center of the cold appetizer dish. "She left a message and you actually listened to it?"

I turned the fish over and slit more marks. Our issues were deeper than answering machines. He knew that as well as I.

"I ran into her at the university, while I was out walking. We had a—" I made a slit from the tail of the fish to the mouth. "Long talk."

"It couldn't have been that long," he said forcing a laugh. "Or she would have told you about her aversion to fish."

"Oh?" I put the fish on a plate. "I'm making sweet and sour fish. It was a favorite of my English teacher in university."

"Lee Sa doesn't eat fish," he said, popping the beef into his mouth. Then he pinched his lips together and nodded as if the taste were not bad. "She says she can't stand having her food stare at her while she's trying to eat."

"That's strange," I said, sprinkling salt on the top of the fish. "I thought she would have been an adventurous eater. She told me that—"

"Yes," Guo Qiang interrupted. "The pre-brownie lecture about jumping off buildings and such. But it doesn't apply to her. She doesn't eat fish."

"No fish, then."

I put the plate aside. I took out a head of *gailan* vegetables and chopped. Not too small as to make waste. Not too big as to gag the eater. Guo Qiang watched. He was done. Almost. He rubbed his pudgy hand over a scuff mark on my suitcase.

"You left this on the bed," he said.

"Yes, I know." I rinsed the knife.

"You going somewhere?" he asked.

I looked straight at him, at those cold eyes which had been filled with venom, had laughed at me like an idiot, had stared right through me. He put his head down, unable to meet my gaze. Nervous. Confirming all I had heard and suspected.

"It's a present," I said, tossing a brown leaf into the sink. "I didn't have a proper box."

The saleslady had insisted I didn't need a bag. That she didn't have enough to be handing them out to customers who bought only one item. Guo Qiang unzipped the plastic suitcase and pulled out the tiny blue piece of cloth.

"I heard you've been too busy looking back," I said peeling the outside layer from a clove of garlic.

"You got this at the market?" He held up the small swimming suit.

"Yes," I said.

I had spent many minutes arguing with the bagless saleslady, telling her I wanted proper bathing attire, not underpants. Underpants that revealed every line and stick, that would be an embarrassment. But, just as she had no bags, she also had nothing but the small blue cloth which models on posters wore with happy grins oblivious to their nakedness. I had decided the message was more important than the actual suit.

"I needed a new one of these," he said, leaning against the counter. "But you and Mother shouldn't have been out in the sun all day. No wonder she's still napping."

I heard his criticism, that I wasn't taking good care of his Mother. But I wouldn't let him travel down that path.

"Actually," I said. "I was alone."

His eyebrows flickered up. He pulled away from the counter.

His lips pursed as if he wanted to say something.

"It's best I learn our neighborhood," I said. I didn't want to end up like Fourth Auntie with her bound lotus feet, living here forever and yet not knowing where she was. "I'm not a child. I don't want to be a country bumpkin forever."

I examined a shiny clove of garlic, free of the old outer skin. I'd made my position clear. Yes, he had had a lover. He had sacrificed much for this marriage. But we were now a family. That past gone. He nodded, putting his new blue bathing suit over his shoulder. He zipped up the suitcase, folded it to put away, then turned to leave.

"By the way." He stopped at the doorway. "Sweet and sour fish sounds good. I'm sure Colleague will like it."

Lee Sa appeared like New Year's firecrackers, her voice sounding loud in one place, laughing in another, as she clomped and heaved up the staircase at the end of the hall. She behaved as if this were her own island, as if she were the only one around. Surely the neighbors wouldn't appreciate all this noise. Mother-In-Law was right again.

I didn't go to the gate to greet them. Colleague would feel shame if I'd heard them from so many steps away. However, Mother-In-Law, who had awakened from her long nap, stood with the front gate wide open.

"I thought I heard you," she said taking a few steps into the hall.

"You did, indeed," Lee Sa called. "We don't go anywhere quietly."

Her shoes clomped near the door. She sighed so loud the windows shook. She must be right outside.

"You here," I said, going to the front gate.

If she hadn't been talking loud and walking next to Colleague, I wouldn't have recognized her. She wore an orange-flowered cotton dress that came down past her knees. It was the first time I'd seen her properly dressed. In her hands, she held a present wrapped in mountains of purple tissue paper. She had been kind enough not to bring brownies.

"Look at you," I said. "So lovely. Come inside."

"When Chao Ran lets me out," Lee Sa said, "I try to dress for the occasion."

She laughed a big horse laugh. Louder than the hum of air conditioners or the scraping of bamboo laundry poles. Colleague, who carried Kevin, plastered a smile of tolerance on his face. The fishhook scar near his eye trembled. Sweat rolled down his cheeks.

He and Mother-In-Law exchanged greetings, quiet greetings. I stepped away from the door and put my hand up for them to come in. If Colleague came inside, Lee Sa would follow.

"Wait." Lee Sa grabbed onto Colleague's arm and pulled him away from the door. "Will you get a load of that?"

She pointed out toward the playground. But I looked left and right, certain a neighbor's head would emerge. The back of my neck prickled.

"Isn't that beautiful?" Lee Sa grabbed onto my arm and directed my attention out over the playground, where reds and oranges splashed across the sky.

Certainly her voice carried to all twelve floors. Would someone call the police on us? And, if so, what race of officer would they send? A Chinese? A Caucasian? A Half?

"Oh, Mom," Kevin said. "You say that about every sunset."

"Well, they are all beautiful." Lee Sa swept her arm out wide. "They're all unique. And, besides, I match." She pointed to her orange dress and twirled around. "Too bad we didn't bring a camera."

"Too bad—" Kevin started.

"Why don't you give this to Leeway?" Lee Sa shoved the purple gift at Kevin, the mounds of wrapping burying his face, his words.

But I knew what Kevin had remembered. We all did. That their dear photographer friend Zhu Dee should be here. I looked to Guo Qiang. He didn't even glance toward the sunset. Instead he took my arm.

"Shall we go inside?" he said. "Have a drink?"

"Sounds good to me," Lee Sa said, barging in the door ahead of Colleague.

I went into the kitchen to fetch the men a beer and the rest of us cold Chrysanthemum Tea juice boxes. Lee Sa did not join me in the kitchen to offer her assistance, which was just as well. I enjoyed the moment of peace. I still felt Guo Qiang's firm grip on my arm. As if he were telling me, "We will move forward. We will."

When I returned to the living room, they had disappeared. Had they gone back outside in the hallway to make more noise? Down to the playground? Lee Sa's horse-laugh sounded. I followed the noise to the computer room. Colleague and Lee Sa stood huddled around the computer, Kevin seated on Guo Qiang's lap. Perhaps Mother-In-Law had gone back to her room for some peace, as well.

"Have you seen this?" Colleague looked up at me.

On the screen, a robot walked down a sidewalk, got into a car and drove off. Was this part of Guo Qiang's project with the Ministry of Transportation? I remembered his six-page letter which went into such detail about his work I had skipped most parts. Perhaps I should have paid closer attention. But, at the time, the words had seemed complicated, my heart had been so far away. I still felt distant. Now I realized that we both had sacrificed a great deal for this auspicious union. Now I wanted to learn. I needed to learn.

"Your husband is amazing," Colleague said.

"It is not just me." Guo Qiang turned crimson. He scooted Kevin further up on his lap and punched a key. "It is a joint effort, a blending of talents, a marriage of just the right abilities and artistry."

I took the tray over to offer them refreshment. My face felt as hot as Guo Qiang's looked. How could he reveal these thoughts, boasting of me as a member in his important project? Surely every day since our marriage I'd sacrificed while he worked in here every spare moment he wasn't drinking and swimming and shopping for frames. But how could he voice such thoughts?

"You're too modest," Lee Sa said.

Lee Sa ruffled Guo Qiang's hair. Colleague didn't even seem to notice. She grabbed a beer from the tray, surely to assuage him. But, rather than pass the drink to Colleague, she opened the can and took a loud gulp. Unbelievable. I handed Colleague the other beer. Then I kneeled down next to Guo Qiang, with the tray resting on my knees, and offered Kevin a box of Chrysanthemum Tea.

"Guo Qiang work very hard," I said. If this was the way we were supposed to talk, complimenting each other in public like this, I could do that.

"That's what I've heard," Lee Sa said. "Zhu Dee has only been working on the robot's eyepiece."

"Really?" I asked, picking up the tray and forcing a bright smile.

So she was still here. My heart thumped so strong and loud, as if the little boy with the stick were in there beating, beating, beating. My limbs moved toward the kitchen as if I were a robot. Lee Sa followed me. My skin vibrated so, the blood pumping through my veins. What had Mother-In-Law done? Pulling me away from my love to break up her son's love? This was a mess.

I reached into the refrigerator to get a beer for Guo Qiang. But my hand froze. I couldn't return to that room where everyone stood around and admired this "joint effort," this "marriage of talents" between my husband and his American lover. Had Lee Sa made up that story about Malaysia? Did Guo Qiang slip out each night to meet with her and work on his project? Their project?

"You like to cook?" she asked.

Lee Sa looked around at the dishes I'd prepared. Sliced beef and tea eggs as a cold dish, baby *gailan* vegetables, *baicai* vegetable with pork, sweet and sour fish, and the dumplings. Her gaze lingered on the fish.

"No, I not like cooking," I said. My insides burned. Normally I would never tell an esteemed guest that I hated preparing for their visit. But the words gushed forth. "But I do like eating good food."

"Well, what do you like to do?" she asked, leaning against the counter and putting the cold beer up to her cheeks.

My mind raced a million miles ahead. Did Mother-In-Law know that her son's love affair was not over? Did she care, as long as I was the formal wife who would provide a pure Chinese grandson? My brain clouded with hypothetical situations.

"Well?" Lee Sa asked, taking a sip of her beer.

How could Lee Sa ask me such a trivial question? Did she think I had no feelings? Or perhaps this was her attempt to steer my mind away from unpleasant thoughts. Waipo would have done the same.

"I like to teach children," I said. "And paper cuttings. I like paper cuttings."

She picked up a tea egg from the plate behind her and took a bite. So intimate. As if she were family.

"Paper cuttings, huh?" she asked. "Like those cute little shadow drawings of boys with peaches?"

"Yes," I said, rearranging the eggs to hide the empty spot she had created. "That."

"You must teach me how to do that," she said.

"Have you been wanting to learn?"

Whether her purpose had been to calm me with this inane discussion or not, it was working. My heart had stopped thumping so hard. My skin had stopped vibrating.

"Well, I wouldn't say that." She laughed. "But, hey, it'd be cool. I'd be the only one on my block back home able to do it."

"Oh, no," I corrected. "Lots of people in your block can do that. Many Chinese can."

"I meant back in the U.S.," she said.

So even Lee Sa, who'd lived here such a long time, still thought of home as a faraway place. Did she dream of home each night when she put her head on her pillow? What did Guo Qiang dream of? Or didn't he have to dream? My heart beat hard again. My neck prickled. I went to the sink and turned the faucet on to fill the steamer with water. The water sounded like a roar. Was Zhu Dee a good cook as well as an artistic photographer?

"Aren't all those tiny cuts hard—"

"You kind person," I said. "Tell me of Zhu Dee."

"Oh, that's right."

Lee Sa's eyes widened. She finished off her beer and put the empty on the counter. Then she headed for the dining room. Would she shout out her memories of Guo Qiang and his lover for all the neighbors to hear? Would she gather Guo Qiang and Colleague together so they could all contribute to the stories? I held onto the fabric of my white dress.

"You just reminded me of this," she said, returning to the kitchen with the purple gift. "A kind person who doesn't present her gifts properly."

"No, no," I said. I pulled my lips back as far as I could in what I hoped look like a smile. "You not need—"

"Let's not go through all that." Lee Sa waved her hand at me and set the gift on the counter. "I brought it because I wanted you to have it. End of story."

Why didn't she allow me to make a proper fuss? Perhaps she wanted to move on to the story of Zhu Dee. I accepted the gift.

"Well, aren't you going to open it?" she asked.

"Now?" I asked.

"Oh, don't be shy," Lee Sa said. "Let me help you."

She tore away the purple wrapping. I stifled the desire to grab her arms. How could she rip up something so lovely? Then bunch the thin wisps of paper into a hard ball of garbage? Was this a metaphor for what had happened to her good friend Zhu Dee and Guo Qiang? It's certainly what happened to Chan Hai and me.

She took out a small basket wrapped with see-through pink cellophane. The basket was filled with different-colored wood chips. Had she carved off a little bark from every tree in the neighborhood? Would she get in trouble for this? Why had she gone to such an effort?

"Well?" Lee Sa waited.

"This wood." I touched the pink cellophane. "You wrap so

nicely."

"Here." She tore the cellophane off the basket as roughly as she had ripped up the purple tissue paper. "You have to open it. Otherwise you can't smell it."

A smell filled the air, like the scents from the Indian stall near Lee Sa's. I put my hand to my nose, waiting for my stomach to dance, as it had the past couple of days. But nothing happened.

"You don't like it?" She put her hands on her hips.

"No." I put my hand down. "I like. Very much."

My stomach was okay. Had she put one of the Indian shopkeepers spices in the bottom of the basket? What was I to do with this? Perhaps it was a cooking additive. I sniffed. Perhaps it also had medicinal value.

"Chao Ran." She laughed. "Said you wouldn't know what it was."

"I know." I picked up a few of the pieces. Red, blue, green, yellow. Where did she find such trees? "Is bark chips with smell."

"It's potpourri." She laughed harder. "Or Pot Pour Ree, as Chao Ran says. It's for the bathroom. Or the living room. Or anywhere. My mother uses it all over the house."

"Potpourri?"

Chan Hai would be amused by these. I could just see him guessing, his dimples deep with laughter. I closed the door on those thoughts.

"I thought you said Miss Zhu Dee in Malaysia," I said, returning to the subject uppermost on my mind. Lovers.

"What? Zhu Dee? She is. Oh, she didn't have anything to do with this." Lee Sa looked around, as if fearful someone would overhear. "Although I felt as if I'd been to Malaysia and back by the time I got this stuff."

She paced the kitchen, her arms fluttering up and down. She looked like a cross between a blowfish and a giant bird. Surely she had something unpleasant to tell of Zhu Dee.

"The third place we went," she said. "The owner of the store said, 'Oh, yes, yes, we sell potpourri.' I searched through the entire hot, junky store, the whole time trying to keep Kevin from breaking this little figurine or throwing that bouncy ball. I couldn't find it. I asked the owner to please stop just sitting there and come show me the potpourri." Lee Sa stopped pacing and put her hands on her hips. "You know what he said? Can you guess?"

Her story was so hard to decipher. What message was she trying to convey? I shook my head.

"No stock now," she said, affecting the voice of an old Chinese man.

Lee Sa She lifted her hands up to the heavens. Did I get it? Perhaps she tried to tell me that I could look and look, but I would never find out about Zhu Dee.

"If he had no more stock," she asked, "why didn't he tell me that in the first place? Instead of making me look around half an hour on my own?"

I adjusted the flame under the pot. Her message was so convoluted. It would take many lifetimes to unravel the meaning. Or perhaps there was no meaning here at all.

"Why not just tell me right off?" She poked my arm. "Huh?"

"But," I said. "You not ask Mr. Owner if he have stock. You ask if he sell this potpourri."

"But why?" she said, putting her hands on her hips. "Why would I ask if he sold potpourri if I didn't want to buy some?"

"Maybe he not want to assume your business," I said.

"Funny." She picked up her empty beer can and shook it. "Chao Ran said the same thing."

Perhaps this was it. She used this story to tell me she didn't want to assume my business. I shook my head. All I could understand was how little she understood about this culture even though she'd been here so long. I looked to her feet. But they weren't tiny lotus feet like Fourth Auntie. They were long thin feet. She could do much traveling on feet like those. She had no excuse.

Kevin coughed his way into the kitchen. Had the tea been too cold for his body? Perhaps he needed a cup of hot water. I took a cup from the cupboard and moved to the hot water pot.

"Blue Dolphin says he's ready for a beer," Kevin coughed out. "Oh, and Mom –Zhu Dee says she's going to Taman Negara National Park this weekend. Can we go?"

My hand stopped pushing on the pot. I stared at the boy. I didn't want to miss a word he said.

"Kevin," Lee Sa shushed. "Now's not the time."

"No," I said, bending down and grabbing onto his hands. "Now good time. When you talk to Miss Zhu Dee?"

"I didn't," Kevin said, looking up at the food on the counter and scrunching his nose. "Blue Dolphin did. He got knee mail."

"A what?" I asked, looking up at Lee Sa.

She twisted at the ring on her beer can, as if it required the concentration of a dozen sages. I stared at her, pain stabbing at my chest. I inhaled as if the air in the room was ice cold instead of tropical.

"A what?" I repeated.

"He means an e-mail." The ring popped off, flipped from her fingers and landed at my feet.

"That's what I said." Kevin leaned down and picked up the ring top. Then he tapped the aluminum piece to his leg like a new toy. "A knee mail."

I'd heard about e-mail at university. The Administration advised us not to follow this trend, as it would take away from serious study. The only people who used the computer in such a frivolous manner were rebellious types. E-mail was a bad habit, like gambling. I had never thought of adultery. I opened the refrigerator and grabbed toward the beer, my mind spinning.

"They said they wanted beer." Lee Sa laughed a big horse laugh. "Not soy sauce and mustard." She took the bottles from my hand and put them back in the refrigerator. "Here, I'll do it."

All week I'd felt like a block of ice, not allowing any deep feelings to come in or go out. But now that I'd had a glimpse of Guo Qiang's heart, which was filled with a talented photographer who could not only understand his work but could help him, my insides shivered. I tried to breathe. I'd always be not just a new wife, but a second wife with no heart left at all. I might never produce a grandson.

Chapter Sixty-Two
Lee Sa Flips the Fish

Chopsticks hitting the various dishes sounded. Kevin coughed. Lee Sa laughed. I took my time in the kitchen cooking the last few dishes and cleaning up thoroughly after each course. What kinds of e-mails did Miss Zhu Dee send Guo Qiang? Were they technical memos or gushing letters about how she missed him, his colorful batik shirts, his doughy white skin?

"Ah-te-te-te-te-te." I dropped the top of the steamer in the sink and let cold water run over the two red marks which formed on my index finger. If Mother-In-Law had been next to me, she'd have had something to say about my foolishness. "Always going too fast. Never thinking." Poor Mother-In-Law was stuck out there listening to them all speaking in a foreign tongue. Was she as much a party to this love triangle? Advising me to tell my farmer I needed watering. What normal wife needed to tell her husband such a thing? Chan Hai would have needed no encouragement, no special dress.

Certainly Miss Zhu Dee's notes must have been full of technical babble. That's all. If there were more, why would Guo Qiang have agreed to marry me? Not only marry me, but spend his hard-earned money taking care of my parents through gambling defeats, sickness, and old age. I put the fry pan on the stove. This was the last dish, the fish Lee Sa wasn't going to like. I poured a thick coating of oil in the fry pan, watching it slicken the dark surface.

Of course, Guo Qiang had nothing to do with this marriage. That would explain why he had sent those long, thesis-like letters, hoping to bore me as much as I had tried to bore him. That would explain why he had whined to his mother in our Great Hall that I didn't know much English. That would explain why he had still not touched me. I understood now. He must have hoped his mother would call the whole thing off. Mother-In-Law, traditional Mother-In-Law, had greased this whole union.

I watched the oil heat up in the fry pan, little bubbles appearing here and there. I needed to get into the computer room and find some answers. Just see one note. If I could prove he still had love in his heart, perhaps I could pack my suitcase for real. Then again, what good would that do? I could never return to Chan Hai, not after having been a married woman. And our family would be back to financial insecurity. Well, at least I could threaten to leave him. I'd seen the fear in his eyes earlier.

I listened. Lee Sa spoke loudly. Was she repeating that potpourri story? I wished our guests would go home. That Guo Qiang and I could have a talk. I walked out into the dining room to retrieve empty dishes and make room for the fish.

"Oh, there you are," Lee Sa said. "Finally. Are you going to spend all night in the kitchen?"

"No, I just finish last dish."

"Sit down." She pulled me in a chair next to her. "We already have too much food, anyway. The dumplings are delicious."

"I make you some more," I said.

"Don't be silly. There's a whole other bowl over there." She reached over and picked up the dish full of goatweed-laced dumplings next to Guo Qiang's elbow. He hadn't even tasted one.

"Here," she said. "Kevin, try some. These are so good."

"No." I waved my hands. "No. He not want any."

"How do you know?" Lee Sa asked.

"New Wife Leeway's right," Kevin said to his mom between coughs. "I'm full."

Colleague looked over at Kevin's plate. It was empty. Still as clean as when I'd taken it from the cupboard.

"My son's on a special diet." He smiled. "His mother only feeds him brownies."

"Oh, be quiet." Lee Sa pointed her chopsticks at Colleague. "You try dealing with a hungry and cranky six-year-old. He wanted brownies."

Certainly Colleague felt shame that his son came to our house and ate nothing. Lee Sa at least was eating the dumplings. Then again, he should know we understood Lee Sa's strange behaviors.

"I sure he wait for last food," I said. "Last food always best. I make you special fish."

"Oh, but these dumplings are absolutely divine." Lee Sa scooped more on her plate. "You've got to try at least one."

She shoved one into Kevin's mouth. I hoped he'd spit it out. What effect would goatweed have on a child? I took the dish of dumplings from her and poured the rest onto Guo Qiang's plate before Lee Sa could take more.

"Hmm," Kevin said. "That is good. I want another."

"No, no." I jumped up. "I have special food just for you."

I went back to the kitchen to get the fish. The skin was a light crispy brown underneath an even lighter brown sauce. Surely Lee Sa and Kevin would enjoy this. That is, if they weren't offended by the way the eyes bulged out, all white and filmy. Perhaps I should chop off the head before presenting the fish. But Mother-In-Law would view that as a bad omen. I looked around for something to conceal the eyes. Next to the purple crumpled wrapping Lee Sa had brought, I found the perfect solution. A few pieces of the colored bark Lee Sa had brought.

I set the fish on the table, the head as far away from Lee Sa as possible. Any normal guest would be offended. But Lee Sa wasn't normal. And this way, she wouldn't be so close to the offensive eyes.

"Oh, no," she said, pointing to the eyes. "Normally, we use that as an air freshener, not a spice."

Kevin reached across the table with one of his chopsticks and pushed away one of the potpourri chips covering the fish eyes. He flipped the spice chip around with his chopstick as though playing a game of hockey. Mother-In-Law cleared her throat. Not pleased.

"Kevin, don't," Lee Sa said, giggling.

Mother-In-Law reached for the fish. Oh, no, this was not good.

"What a decorative idea," Lee Sa continued. "And I guess, since no one's going to eat that part anyway, it can't hurt."

Crunch. Crunch. Crunch. Mother-In-Law's jaw moved up and down, the round shape of the fish eye visible inside her cheek. Then she picked up the second eyeball with her chopsticks and sucked it into her mouth. Crunch. Crunch. Crunch.

"Some fish, Kevin?" I asked. "Is better than brownie."

"NO THANK YOU."

"Kevin." Colleague slammed his beer can down on the table.

"Behave." Lee Sa squeezed his leg.

"I am HAVE," he said scrunching his small hands into fists.

"Here." I filled a bowl of rice and put a bit of fish on top for him, anyway. "You like this."

He looked up from his plate. Shook his head. I wished I'd read that discipline book I'd given to Cheng Min on what to do when a child won't eat. I wished more that Cheng Min was right next door. Or even right across the table. I could do no wrong in her eyes.

"Auntie Leeway said she'd make you a paper cutting of an airplane if you eat some fish," Lee Sa said.

I looked at her, surprised. I'd never said that. I couldn't make airplanes. But, more than that, she'd never referred to me so dearly. Calling me "Auntie." Perhaps the goatweed had affected her.

"You will?" Kevin eyed the bowl of rice.

I only knew how to make traditional cuttings—birds and peaches and baby boys and dragons. But I enjoyed the sound of her voice calling me Auntie, the conspiratorial pressure of her toes on mine.

"I do my best," I said.

"You must eat first," Guo Qiang said. "Then she'll show you her magic."

Everyone was treating me so well. As if I were a treasured new wife rather than the intruder who pushed Zhu Dee aside. Perhaps Cheng Min was with us all in spirit. More likely, the goatweed had finally hit the target.

Colleague and Guo Qiang quickly ate off the top portion of the fish. After the eyes were gone, even Lee Sa tried, saying it was the most delicious fish she'd tasted. I watched as Guo Qiang tried to take the backbone out of the fish, so Colleague could get to the meat at the bottom. His chopsticks seemed too big for his chubby hands. Beer and goatweed powder had made him clumsy.

"Why don't you just turn the thing over?" Lee Sa took her chopsticks and joined the battle, poking at the fish as though it were a live snake.

"No, no," I said. "Is okay."

But she flipped the fish anyway, backbone down, brown crisp flesh up. Mother-In-Law stood up so quickly, she knocked her chair over. She went straight to her room, shutting her door so fast the hinges didn't have a chance to moan. I moaned instead.

"What's wrong?" Lee Sa asked.

"Nothing." Guo Qiang picked up Mother-In-Law's chair and reached for a chopstick full of *gailan*, as though his mother behaved like this every night.

She raised her eyebrows at him. Even the insensitive Lee Sa didn't quite believe him. She looked at me.

"Nothing wrong," I said. "We just . . . we not do that."

"Do what?" Lee Sa put both her hands up in the air.

"It is just silly superstition," Guo Qiang said.

How could he talk so? I had an urge to put my hand over his mouth or stuff purple wrapping in it. A shiver ran down my spine. Why was our culture dismissed as foolish around this woman? All her outrageous behavior pardoned? What spell did she hold over these men?

"Well, what is it?" Lee Sa laughed. "Chao Ran?"

"I've told you this before," he said, stirring the grains of rice around on his plate. "I'm sure I have. We don't flip fish."

"What?" Her eyes grew wide and uncomprehending.

"Like I said," Guo Qiang took another mouthful of vegetables. "It is silly superstition."

Yes, so silly that, while moments ago he had been devouring the fish, now he confined his chopsticks to the vegetable plate. So silly his mother had left the table without finishing. Why did he lie to this woman and let her behave with such ignorance? More importantly, why did her own husband not tell her these things?

"Chao Ran." Lee Sa pointed an accusing finger. "You never told me about some silly fish-flipping taboo."

I wished they'd all stop saying silly. I hoped the gods weren't listening. I hoped Mother-In-Law was in the bedroom saying prayers to get their attention.

"When have you ever cooked a whole fish?" Colleague asked. "You always get that stuff that's already chopped up and packaged."

"Yes, well," she said, putting her finger down, shifting in her seat. "What does it mean?"

"Mean your boat turn over," I said. My insides shuddered. "You sink."

"Ahhh." She poked at the fish with her chopstick. "Well, since none of us has a boat. Then I guess we're safe."

I nodded. I didn't add that the boat could be a symbol for other things—like a house, a marriage, a life. Sometimes, if you give voice to something, the gods make it happen. And, with Lee Sa here, the work of the gods was made too easy already.

"Besides," she said, shifting the attention from her error. "This might be a good omen for us. Look. Kevin's finished his food."

"Thank you." Colleague raised his can of beer toward me.

Heat rose to my cheeks. Lee Sa did as well as one could expect, considering she was a strange one and all alone, without any mother-in-law to help. Perhaps all she needed was for Colleague to reveal a bit more about the culture so she could be more sensitive to the needs and opinions of those around her—rather than just charging ahead like an angry bull.

"Let's make airplane," I said, feeling a need to move. To leave that ominous fish. My critical thoughts. "I need scissors."

I went to the kitchen, taking some dishes with me. Lee Sa seemed sluggish from all the beer and maybe the goatweed. She didn't offer to help clear. But again I was relieved. I was fascinated by her stories and behavior, but I appreciated some rest times.

Was there an antidote to flipping a fish? New Neighbor back home would know. That overzealous neighbor that I'd always thought a nutcase. I hankered for his advice. I had to laugh. Who could have predicted such a change in me?

I found scissors and carried the ball of purple wrapping paper to the living room couch. I unraveled the beautiful paper while Kevin sat close, his small hands on my knees. Lee Sa sat across from us. Guo Qiang and Colleague stayed at the table, drinking and eating everything except that bad omen of a fish.

"In old days," I explained. "This how girl judged to be good bride."

"Good ride?" Kevin asked.

"No." Lee Sa reached across and patted his head. "Good ba-ride—like wife, good wife."

"I guess Auntie Leeway not good ba-ride," Kevin said, pointing to the wrinkled paper cutting. "That doesn't look like an airplane. It looks more like that bird around your neck."

"Let's try again," I said, my fingers feeling the smooth yellow bird around my neck. Would I ever feel comfortable without Chan Hai's gift?

"Why do you fold the paper in half like that?" Kevin asked.

"Is way to do," I said. Too bad Madame Paper Cutter wasn't here to show us the way to make an airplane. To explain all the history. "I follow the way Master showed me."

"I'm sure you could cut it without folding it." Lee Sa leaned forward, as though ready to take the paper from my hands.

"Is not me who decide," I said. "This is art from many centuries. Started in Song Dynasty—"

Lee Sa got that wide-eyed, long look of confusion again. Like a horse who has lost her way. How strange to see that look over something we considered so basic, so simple. Common sense, Guo Qiang would have said.

"Long ago," I said. "Sixth century."

"And you're going to tell me everyone does it the same way?" Lee Sa laughed.

"Is tradition," I said, offended by her laughter. "One generation pass to next. Like your Halloween."

"Speaking of which," Lee Sa said, leaning back on the couch and turning toward the table. "Chao Ran, did you—"

"No," he said. "Not yet. The guard was still sleeping when I went downstairs this morning. I'll try to talk to him tomorrow." He shook his head at Guo Qiang. "All these holidays. You wonder why they keep getting perpetuated."

"I think it's so we don't feel all alone in this world," Guo Qiang said, pushing his chair back. "So we have a common bond with one another. A sameness."

Guo Qiang and Colleague began a big long debate on tradition, about which was most important in defining a race—traditional foods or traditional holidays or language. I listened, intrigued not only by the topic but by their ability to argue about anything from dust to culture, with the same intensity. Lee Sa, however, yawned loud enough to wake the dead and announced it was time to go home. Finally.

I stood in front of the sink, rinsing off the dishes. What a long day this had been. Guo Qiang and I had a common bond, a common culture, but still I felt all alone in this world. My whole being wilted with exhaustion.

"I'm going to bed," Guo Qiang said, coming into the kitchen with the folded newspaper.

Normally he didn't announce such an event. I wiped off the sink and countertop to keep away the hungry ants. A pit formed in my throat. Would Guo Qiang and I ever have a happy marriage with a bouncing baby boy? I finished cleaning up and went into our room, hoping to finally have a moment with my new husband. He was fast asleep on the bed. Again. Obviously the liquor had overwhelmed the goatweed powder.

I padded back out into the hallway, shutting the bedroom door behind me. My bare feet slapped across the tile floor. I wandered into his office. The computer screen was dark. I looked around his desk, decorated with neat stacks of files. The top file held drawings and calculations. The next file lots of letters. This must be it. The top note started, "Dear Professor Liang." Perhaps Miss Zhu Dee was not a first-name caller like Lee Sa. I continued to decipher the words. "Would you please advise us as to—" This was a memo from the university. I put it back.

The last file contained grainy black-and-white photographs. Had Miss Zhu Dee taken these? They certainly didn't look spectacular or talented or artistic or any of the other glowing terms Guo Qiang had used. There weren't any shots of him and his love laughing in front of the Singapore Merlion or toasting a beer together at the top of the Westin Hotel. They were merely pictures of a shipping container from different angles. I sighed. What had I expected? This was just an office with no hidden secrets about the direction our marriage was headed.

I was about to close the photo file, when I spotted a bit of white sticking out. A piece of paper among all these photos. I pulled the paper out. The dirty, crumpled paper had been folded and refolded many times. At the top of the paper were a bunch of numbers. Perhaps just more calculations about this stupid project.

I was exhausted. I started to fold the paper back together, when halfway down the page, I spotted the words, "Darling Guo Qiang." I sat down in Guo Qiang's chair with a loud creak. I held my breath. My heart beat against my chest.

"I know your mother thinks I'm nuts," the letter read. "That all foreigners are. And it's easy to convince myself that she's right. It's crazy, sometimes, how different our worlds operate. But, even if my head is crazy, my heart understands you."

A hand touched my shoulder. A warm large doughy hand. I jumped.

"Guo Qiang," I said, dropping the letter.

"What are you doing in here?" He rubbed his eyes. His gaze fell on the crumpled note on the floor.

"I was just," I said. "Making sure . . . just cleaning up a bit."

He picked up the note and tossed it in the garbage. Then he touched my arm.

"Don't worry about that nonsense," he said. "Whether you can make good airplanes or not, I think you'll make a good bride."

I heard the future tense in his words. The openness in his voice. At least there was some hope for us. I grabbed onto his arm.

Chapter Sixty-Three
The Boat Flips

An alarm sounded shrill and insistent. I moved the doughy arm off my stomach. A cool night breeze blew in through the windows. Surely it was too early to wake. The ringing continued. I reached out into the dark toward the clock on the bedside table, punching at buttons. The bright yellow dials read 4:30. Not the alarm. I sat up. The phone. I fumbled for my pajama top from the pile on the floor. The feel of Guo Qiang's clumsy paws still resonated on my breasts. He had called his relationship with Zhu Dee "nonsense." But his touch had been tentative, mechanical. So had mine. My insides felt cold and hollow.

I rushed out of the bedroom, tripping toward the insistent ringing. Light from the outside hallway spilled across the floor giving me direction. Just as I picked up the receiver and was about to push "talk," I sensed motion from the corner of my right eye. A figure sat up on the couch.

"Mother-In-Law?" I said, holding the ringing phone.

"The phone is ringing," she barked.

Why hadn't she come to answer it? Perhaps this was a pesky relative who called every month at this time. Then again, maybe she didn't feel confident enough to talk on the phone. I pushed the "Talk" button.

"*Wei*?" I said. "Hello?"

"Li Hui?" a woman's voice said. "I'm glad you answered first."

The voice was a comforting arm around my shoulder. Warmth rushed through my heart so fast, my eyes watered. I turned away from Mother-In-Law.

"Mother," I said.

She sounded near, as if I could scoot forward and our knees would touch. But it was early. Too early. At this hour, she would have just been rising. I imagined her standing in the booth outside of Zi Mei's. Had the weather turned cold? Why call me before making a fire beneath the wok to cook porridge?

"How are you?" she asked.

What would she say about Guo Qiang who wouldn't reach for me unless he was full of goatweed powder and, when he did, my limbs could only move like one of his robots? About Miss Zhu Dee who loved him? About Lee Sa whom Mother-In-Law thought was crazy but who was really just foreign? Surely Mother would rather hear of the lovely wet market and the big buildings and the stove that click-clicked on and the big cold refrigerators.

"Fine," I said. My voice caught. "I'm fine."

"Well, that's good." Her words sounded cold, as if she were a postal clerk just doing her job. "I know you're busy working and being a new wife, but—"

"I'm not working," I said. "Yet. Guo Qiang wants me to practice English first."

Tradition dictated that I was no longer a part of Mother and Father. When they died, I would be at the end of the line leading to their grave, just like any normal friend. I was part of the Liang family now. Still, how did Mother do that? Just cut off her feelings toward me and jump into this role of stranger? A chill ran down my spine. I leaned against the dining room chair. I wished I could see her face, her hands. Was she as confused as I? Silence filled the line. Perhaps, we'd lost our connection. I banged the receiver with my hand.

"Mother?"

"Your father's an unlucky man," she whispered.

Was this an apology? Surely not. Parents didn't make mistakes. Still Mother must know this was difficult. My cheeks felt hot. My brain muddled. Perspiration made my palm stick to the phone receiver.

"He—" she started. She sighed long and hard. "He never gave Chairman Huang the full twenty thousand. He only gave him half, saying he'd pay the other half later. He hoped to win big with that other half."

She took in a deep breath. More like a choked sob. Pain squeezed my heart. I knew what she would say.

"He lost instead."

"Mother," I said, trying to capture the full weight of her words.

Father had given my hand in marriage in exchange for twenty thousand *yuan*. The debt he owed Snakehead. But he hadn't paid the full amount? He'd gone and squandered half of it? The tile floor felt cold and unforgiving beneath my feet. My mouth went dry.

"Last night, a group of thugs came." She made a raspy sigh.

"They took off our front door."

"Oh, Mother." I imagined her sleeping in front of the door to keep out robbers. I imagined her shame. Why did Father always plow Mother through his dirt? And then me? "Is Father alright?"

"When you have time," she said. "Please send what you can. Those men promised they'd return."

"Return for what?" I asked.

But she was gone. I pressed the phone against my ear, hoping she'd come back. Come back and tell me this was all just a silly tradition. To wake the bride and scare her. A dial tone screamed in my ear. She wasn't coming back.

As I replaced the receiver to the holder, I wished for a brother. A brother to care for Mother. A brother to shoulder Father's burdens. A brother to allow me freedom to hold up just half the sky. For while Father had sent me on to another family, here he was already pulling me back into his troubles. He demanded that I hold up not just my half of the sky but his, as well. That was too much for me. A chill rippled through my body. Pressure built on my esophagus. Salt filled my mouth. I rushed to the kitchen sink and vomited.

My limbs felt drained. My mouth tasted of acid. What a violent reaction to Mother's news. At least my body was still sensitive. My mind was here, a thousand kilometers away. My mind was already focused on making breakfast and doing the laundry. I headed back toward the bedroom to brush my teeth and get dressed. Mother-In-Law still sat on the couch. Perhaps she meditated.

"Are you feeling uncomfortable?" she asked, reaching out and grabbing onto my arm as I passed.

"No."

Someday I'd be able to confide in her like a real mother. But not this morning. I patted her hand. Then I swallowed the bitterness that burned in my throat. Poor Mother. Why did Father always reach so high?

Mother-In-Law continued to hold onto me. She stared into my face, as though trying to read what was there. As soon as Guo Qiang woke up, I would get his advice. Where could I get a job today? Not next month. How could I help Father out of this latest bind? My stomach fluttered.

"I ate too much last night," I said, rubbing my stomach.

"I'm glad I'm not the only one." She leaned forward. "My stomach was so full, I couldn't sleep. I feel heaty. I think there was something wrong with that silly fish Li Zhi brought."

"Fish Li Zhi—Teacher Lee Sa brought?" I asked. Mother-In-Law was becoming foggy with age. Perhaps she hadn't answered the phone as she'd forgotten how.

"How could you forget already?" She yanked on my arm. "That fish with the colored decorations on the eyes. Such a silly woman."

The potpourri. Had there been some chemical which had made Mother-In-Law feel bad? Certainly Lee Sa would have said something. Then again she didn't even know what was in her brownies.

"Besides," Mother-In-Law continued. "The fish was too sweet for my taste. Sugar. Sugar. Sugar. That's all foreigners eat."

The fish. Of course. Li Zhi—Lee Sa hadn't brought it. But she had flipped the thing over on its backside. Now disaster had hit. Father had lost the front door to our house, and Mother-In-Law felt ill.

"Well, don't just stand there," Mother-In-Law said, pushing me away toward the bedroom. "Get busy. I predict the sun will be rising soon."

As I shuffled toward my room, I smiled. I might as well call Mother-In-Law a fortune teller for predicting the sun's appearance as assign Father's latest disaster to the flipping of the fish. Father brought disaster on us all by himself, without any help from fish.

I filled the steamer with a cup of rice and five cups of water. Why hadn't Mother-In-Law started the porridge? That was the first thing she did when she woke up. Then she washed yesterday's laundry. I looked to the window. The green bamboo poles stuck out, naked and alone. Not a strip of clothing on them. I click-clicked the stove on and put the porridge on to cook. Perhaps Mother-In-Law had just awakened, as well. But then, why did she lounge around like an Empress? Ah-ha. My training was over. The house was mine to take care of now. Hadn't she just said the other day that she was too old to be traveling?

I should have felt happy. I'd been in this new house only a week, and already Mother-In-Law felt comfortable leaving her son in my hands. Panic pushed against my throat. How would I get a job so I could send more money home if I had to care for the house, too? I went to the back of the kitchen, to the laundry area, and threw the dirty clothes on the floor—Guo Qiang's sweaty shirt from yesterday, his underwear, a pair of socks. I poured a few grains of soap powder on them and brush-brush-brushed. My arms soon ached.

The message Father had been given was clear. He had taken

away Chairman Huang's face by cheating him out of his winnings. Chairman Huang had returned the favor by taking off our front door, our "face." Had they left the door behind, so we could repair it? Our doors weren't like the small dog house openings here. They were grand and welcoming, and required lots of wood, expensive wood, to replace. Perhaps Father could dismantle the rice bin and use that wood for a new door. What did New Neighbor think of all this? Certainly this was proof certain that we were bad *feng shui*. Would New Neighbor put up another mirror?

I pushed Guo Qiang's shirt into a green plastic bucket of water. This batik cloth was difficult to get the soap out of. The bubbles sat in there, forcing me to rinse the shirt again and again. Had Miss Zhu Dee given him this shirt just as she'd given him a bathing suit? Would she be like one of these bubbles, constantly rising to the surface when I thought I'd rinsed her away? Finally, I wrung out that colorful shirt from Malaysia, turned it inside out, stuck the end of a bamboo pole through the sleeve openings, and hung the pole out the window to let the sun do the drying.

Then I stirred the porridge and scooped a large helping into a bowl. Mother-In-Law surely felt impatient, waiting for her breakfast so long. I took the steaming bowl and was rounding the corner into the living room, when I bumped into Guo Qiang coming toward the kitchen. A glop of the steaming rice porridge spilled over the side of the bowl onto my hand. Like hot glue. I reached over to wipe the porridge back in the bowl. Guo Qiang beat me to it, flicking the hot goop off onto the floor.

"What are you running for?" he asked.

"Mother called," I said.

He pulled me toward the kitchen sink, turned on the cold water tap, and held my hand under the gushing water. I looked at his pudgy face, his brows furrowed. An image of him begrudgingly removing his handkerchief to wipe Mother's long-life noodles from his shoes was replaced by this man who had just brushed burning porridge from my hand. He still had pudgy fingers and doughy skin. He still talked incessantly. But something had changed. My hand throbbed under the cold water.

"Mother mentioned you were acting strange," he said. His hair was damp from the shower. He had on a black shirt with large orchids, the collar twisted inside at the back. "That you ran to the phone. Ran to the bathroom. Now you're running with hot porridge."

"I got a call from home," I said again. I reached out and fixed his collar. "I need a job."

This wasn't exactly how I had planned to approach the subject. So fast. So direct.

"Mother-In-Law said you accused her of being wasteful." He pulled my hand out from the flow of water and inspected the redness before pushing it back under.

"I—"

"How could you say such a thing?" he asked.

We were like flies buzzing over two different grains of rice. He hadn't heard a word I meant, probably thinking only of the words which sounded like petulant noises to fill the air. I wanted to grab hold of him and ask him to listen. When could we wire money to Father? How could I find a job? Would I ever be able to hold up my half of the sky? But he was concerned more about his grain of rice, his mother. What could I say? If I said I'd never called Mother-In-Law wasteful, I'd be calling her a liar. If I agreed with what Mother-In-Law said, I'd be showing disrespect.

"Perhaps Mother-in-law was telling a joke," I suggested, forcing a laugh. "Mother-In-Law wasteful? That's too funny."

Guo Qiang looked at me. His mother didn't tell jokes. He must think me a country fool again.

"She must have seen me running around so much this morning, she thought I was trying to send some kind of message," I tried. "But I'm not like that. I'm honored to have such a wise Mother-In-Law."

"That's good." His face curved into a smile. "Slow down. I don't want Mother to get the wrong message."

My arm felt numb from the cold water. Like my insides. How could I sit here and worry about Mother-In-Law getting the wrong message when Mother and Father were in danger?

"—unharnessed energy is not a good thing." Guo Qiang was in lecture mode. "It's like a robot out of control. Did I ever show you that computer program? Of the robot gone mad?"

Had he? Or was he thinking of Miss Zhu Dee. The soap bubbles resurfaced.

"I probably didn't." His face turned red. He turned the water off, patted my arm dry with the dish towel, attempted to rinse the bubble away. "That's going to be red for awhile. Does it hurt?"

"It will eventually go away," I said looking into his eyes. "Neither of us will ever know it happened."

"You're right." He returned my gaze and brushed a stray hair from my face.

"Would you like some porridge?" I asked.

"I'll get it myself," he said. "You better clean up that mess in the dining room before Mother thinks she needs to do it."

I would fry up some garlic cabbage as a side dish. The vegetable would be good for Mother-In-Law's heaty stomach. Good for Guo Qiang. It was still early. We would eat and discuss this latest disaster. I might even joke to him about the fish.

I carried the fried cabbage out to the dining room. The hot bowl of vegetables made my burn sting. I quickly returned to the kitchen sink, the cold water. I let the water run until my hand felt numb again. Then I filled a bowl with porridge for Mother-In-Law. A half a bowl for myself. This morning my stomach felt coated with a layer of mosquito netting. But I felt the gurgle-gurgle of hunger. I needed to eat a little.

When I returned to the dining room with the bowls, Mother-In-Law was no longer on the couch. Nor had she come to the table. Perhaps she'd gone to the bathroom. I glanced at my watch. Only 6:53. Guo Qiang and I would have plenty of time to talk. I sat down across from him. He held his bowl up and shoveled the last of the porridge into his mouth.

"Is there any more?" He offered up his bowl.

I returned to the kitchen and scooped the remains of the porridge into his bowl, scraping the sides of the steamer to get every last grain. I had done this many times at home. I was good at getting every last grain. I would have to make more tomorrow. I could make more. I had to stop thinking like the poor farmer girl. Father certainly had. Surely Father was proud to now have a son-in-law, a successful son-in-law who made big money and lived overseas. Father was probably out each day buying foreign cigarettes and whiskey from Zi Mei to pass around among his friends. But why not pay up his debt first? Why make outrageous bets on the *mahjong* tiles, tiles which never showed him mercy? How could Father be so selfish? So stupid? That's what it was, if I was honest.

I returned to the dining room. Guo Qiang lifted a golden sliver of fried garlic to his thick lips. I put the heaping bowl of porridge before him.

"Did you and my mother have words," he asked, picking up the bowl and slurping the rice into his mouth.

I looked toward her closed door. She had been upset with me for making so much waste. For inviting loud Lee Sa and her misbehaved son over. She'd felt ill from the fish which she thought Lee Sa had brought. We hadn't had words. But surely Mother-In-Law was not pleased with me.

"No," I said. "Why?"

"Well, she's been spending a great deal of time in her room," he said, holding his chopsticks up and pointing in that direction. "She was there when I came home yesterday. You mentioned she was there in the afternoon. She's there now. Seems strange."

"She mentioned she feels heaty," I said.

"That would explain it," he said, nodding and shoveling more rice in his mouth.

"Mother called this morning," I said.

"How is everyone?" he asked, pushing his chair back. "Oranges should be in season now. The leaves turning. That crisp cold smell in the air."

"She didn't say," I said. "She was—"

"Some tea?" he asked.

I went to the kitchen and put some tea leaves in a cup, added some hot water. He was flying in another world, reminiscing about oranges and leaves. I needed to show him my world of broken-off doorways and bottomless debts. I brought the steaming cup of liquid to him, ignoring the stinging sensation on my hand, the burning in my heart.

"Guo Qiang," I said.

He blew on the top of the cup. Took a sip of tea. Stood.

"Chao Ran, Lee Sa and I are meeting for lunch and a swim," he said, his warm garlic breath just inches from my cheek. "Do you want to join us?"

"No," I said. The last thing I wanted to do was play in a swimming pool. I looked up at him. "I want to talk."

Guo Qiang took a step back, jingling his keys in his pocket. His eyes darted about the room. Perhaps he thought I wanted to bring up Miss Zhu Dee.

"Did you ever hear about Chairman Huang?" I asked.

"Oh," Guo Qiang said, heaving a garlicy sigh. "Before I forget, I want to bring my new bathing suit."

He turned away from me and padded off to the bedroom. How could I bring up Father's need for money while he was waiting to dash out the door? No matter what words I chose, Guo Qiang would not hear. The sounds from my lips would be as irritating as sticks scratching a cement wall.

"Now, what were you saying?" he asked when he returned, a swim bag over his shoulder.

"We can talk later." I kissed his fleshy cheek.

"That would be nice." He kissed me on the forehead. Then he stepped out the door. The slam of the gate vibrated in my heart.

I glanced at my watch again. 7:05. I wouldn't meet up with Guo Qiang until later, after he came home from work. I felt an urgency inside, as if my pulse beat double time. Surely Guo Qiang would agree to send them money. I would go to his office and talk to him formally. Then he wouldn't be so distracted with rice and tea and oranges and leaves.

I went into the bedroom to make up our bed. My first thought, as always, was of Chan Hai. Had his wound healed? Did he still work for Mr. Housewares or did he help at the tea shop now? Would I disappear from his heart like a burn to the skin? I fluffed up the pillows that said "Double Happiness" on them.

Last night had been awkward. Guo Qiang's hands were clumsy and cold. He talked the whole time, about the different zones of the body, how wouldn't it be interesting if you could transfer some of those actual senses to a robot? I was relieved when he was done, both feeling and talking.

I didn't feel my happiness double yet. But I respected Guo Qiang. Certainly Mother was right—the love—the happiness—would eventually come. The sun shone through the window on the back of my neck. It was time to get to market. Perhaps Mother-In-Law and I could see what was available. A store that needed a clerk. A restaurant that needed a waitress.

"Mother-In-Law?" I called, getting my purse.

She didn't respond. She couldn't still be in the bathroom. I knocked lightly on her bedroom door.

"Mother-In-Law?" I poked my head inside her bedroom. A lump lay on her bed. What was she doing back in bed? "Mother?"

"I was just taking a rest," she said. "You go on ahead."

Taking care of Guo Qiang and me in a strange land surely had taken its toll on her old body. She'd be glad to get back home to familiar surroundings, foods, and friends. I went in and pulled the cover up over her. The room was already warm, but it was best to have a cover if you were lying down. Still, if she went home, how would I handle everything? Lee Sa didn't act like she had trouble. And she had a child to care for, as well. Then again, her house was a disaster. Guo Qiang wouldn't be as forgiving as Colleague

"I made some garlic cabbage for you," I said. "That might help."

"There's no need to fuss." She pushed my hand away. "I just didn't sleep well last night. It was Li Zhi's fish. It kept me up all night. My stomach still feels funny."

Perhaps there was something on the potpourri that had reacted badly in her stomach. Perhaps she needed a good strong cup of tea to cut any bad oils lingering in her stomach. Yes, that might settle her a bit.

"I'm sorry," I said. "Can I get you some—"

"It's not your sorry," she said. "That foreigner, it is. Foreigners don't understand our ways. Never will."

The bubble surfaced again. Had Mother-In-Law said these same words to Miss Zhu Dee? I was tempted to join in and agree. But what she said—at least about the fish—wasn't true.

"What did I tell you?" she continued, slapping her hand on the top of the coverlet. "I told you not to invite that woman here."

"Mother-In-Law," I said. "I prepared that fish."

"What nonsense." Mother-In-Law sighed. She rolled away from me on her side into a fetal position. "What utter nonsense. Your food is salty but it never would make me feel this bad."

Funny how easily beliefs got started. I patted Mother-In-Law on the back. Mao Ze Dong had started the belief that women held up half the sky. So far, I felt as if I'd only held up a tiny cloud with all my might. For Mother's sake, for my own peace of mind, I hoped I could find some truth in that saying.

Chapter Sixty-Four
Only the Ghosts Would Believe

Customers pushed and pulled as they lined up at the various stalls at the hawker center directly behind the wet market. Humidity bathed my skin. A cockroach scuttled across the floor. The smells of marinated pork, fried rice, noodles, baby back ribs in herbal soup and warm fresh soy bean milk filled the air. This was as good a place to start looking for work as any.

I joined the line for the drinks stall. A healthy old Chinese man stood behind the counter stirring liquid in a vat. The vat looked small compared to his ample belly, the plastic cups like toys in his big hands as he filled each with the glutinous white liquid of soybean milk. Perspiration dripped from his several chins. Despite his bulk, he moved about as though hearing music rather than disgruntled shouts for *copi-o*, grass-jelly drink and soybean milk.

"You want what?" he asked when he danced by on his way to ladle out yet another order of the thick, steaming soybean milk from the large metal vat.

I'd always been protected by someone else—Counselor Zhang, Father, Father, Father. They had always said what I wanted. Now I had to voice what I wanted. I felt as small as one of those cups in the man's hands.

"You decide yet?" The big man handed three glasses of orange drink to a mother and her two children.

If I gave it some thought, I didn't really want to sweat all day selling drinks. I still had hopes to teach. Even tutor. But I kept seeing our house with no front door. I kept seeing a hand ready to bash in Father's face. Selling drinks was something I could easily do. Even in this foreign land. The healthy drinks stall man waltzed by again, and I put up my hand.

"I am the new daughter-in-law of Liang Yanzhu and Chen Jiagu."

"You want what?"

The man leaned forward across the shiny steel counter, grunting at the effort. Sweat dribbled down the side of his face. I cleared my throat.

"I'm now a member of the Liang family," I repeated in a louder voice.

"And you want what?"

He took out his dish towel and wiped the counter in front of me. Unlike in the village, he didn't throw down his towel, smile and shake my hand. He didn't offer me a celebratory glass of soybean milk. He was all business.

"I know you're busy, and that's why I'm here." My temples itched. "I'm a good worker. My last job was in a tea shop."

"You're from China, ah?" He looked at me. Had he heard of me or did my accent give me away?

"Yes." I smiled.

"Mainland or Taiwan?" he asked.

"Mainland." Had Guo Qiang attempted matchmaking in Taiwan, as well? Had Mother-In-Law been that desperate?

"You like Singapore?"

He threw the towel over his shoulder and glanced toward the customer next to me, not even waiting for my response. She held up two fingers in the air and pointed toward the grass-jelly dispenser. I waited for her to take the drinks and pay him two gold coins. Surely he'd turn his attention back to me when he had a chance. I waited through several more customers. The morning crowd thickened. A large delegation of men in business suits came streaming in. The drinks stall man seemed inundated. I went down to where he cleaned out the empty soybean vat in the sink.

"You seem awfully busy," I said.

He didn't respond. Perhaps he hadn't heard me. I waited for him to turn off the water.

"Morning's are always busy," he said, without looking up. "You want a drink, I'll get you a drink. There's no need to talk of other things."

I dropped away from the counter. My throat felt scratchy and dry. But I wanted more than a drink. Why, when he needed help, didn't he even show a flicker of interest in my offer? Why did he act as if he could dance through the day on his own? Perhaps he and the Liangs had a rivalry. Then again perhaps he was like College Boy—jealous of those with an education. I turned around and got in another line. The sign behind the glass window at the head of the line said *bakuteh*—pork ribs in herbal soup. The man dishing out the soup was also a Chinese. Maybe I'd have better luck here.

In front of me stood a short woman, her shoulder-length black hair bobbing up and down as she talked on her cell phone about stock prices. She wore a loose-fitting dress the color of bark. Pumps to match. Three children crowded next to her, the tallest of whom had her right arm in a sling. In her left, she held a thin green book. The second child, another girl, peered over the studious one's arm. The third child, a boy, held onto the woman's loose skirt. She nudged them forward each time the line moved.

Was she a teacher as well as a business woman? I wasn't good with numbers like Feng Gu or this woman, so I could never be a business woman. But then I had been good at teaching and I could come up with ideas for the tea shop. Finding a job wasn't just about talent, though. How did this woman get so lucky?

"Mother." The eldest turned. "Mother."

The woman, in a heated discussion over the price of some company's stock, waved away the girl as though shooing a fly.

"But, Mother," the girl pleaded. "I don't know this character."

Mother? Were these children all hers? I compared her to the three children. She had a round face like a moon and a nose that stuck high on her face. The children all had flat noses, high cheekbones. They didn't look like her. Perhaps she had adopted. But why would anyone adopt so many?

I peered over the eldest child's shoulder at her exercise book. Contentment. That was a tough one. The poor girl. Would her mother ever give her attention? This wasn't my business. Still I was reminded of Chan Hai helping the old lady and her peas. That hadn't been his business either. My lips itched to say something.

"You hurt your arm," I said.

The tall girl looked up sideways at me. Wary. What did I want? She chewed on the end of her pencil.

"Looks painful." I smiled.

"I fell out of a tree this morning at school," she said, looking toward her mother. "I broke it in three places."

"I liked climbing when I was your age," I said. "We had a peach tree in our backyard."

"Mother had to get off work to come get me," she said. She shook her head and sighed in disgust. "And now my marks will drop, since I can't write so well with my left hand. I surely won't have enough points to get into the higher stream. I'll be lucky if I get into university.

I'll never become a barrister or a doctor."

"So bad?" I asked.

"Mother said I should know better than to go climbing around like a monkey."

"That's it." I grinned at her.

She looked up at me. Her cheeks flushed. Her eyes widened.

"Know." I nodded and pointed to her thin green exercise book. "You just reminded me. To know." I pointed to the first character she'd asked her harried mother about. Then I moved my finger to the second character. "What's enough."

"What does it mean?" She cut her eyes toward her mother. The woman's eyes were narrowed, her lips pursed. But the object of her anger was at the other end of the phone.

"To know what's enough," I said. "Equals contentment."

"That's right." The girl smiled at me. "I always forget that one."

"It's easy to forget," I said, thinking of Father. "Too easy."

She copied the word down, her handwriting as illegible as Feng Gu's. I remembered being as concerned about my studies, as worried about pleasing my parents as this young one. We all start out so full of hope, so diligent. In the beginning.

The line moved forward. The mother paused in her telephone conversation to shout out her order. The man handed her three bowls of soup. She nodded for the eldest to grab them, as she returned to her phone. Then she looked at the girl's fresh cast.

"Why did you go and break your arm?" she scolded. "Now you can't even carry your baby brother's soup."

"Yes, I can," the girl insisted.

"No you don't." The woman snapped her phone shut. "I don't want you burning yourself on top of everything else."

A mother in the village would be just as angry. Still her words sounded funny. Blaming a child for an accident like that.

"They're all yours?" I asked.

She gave me a cold look, glancing at her phone, as if I were asking about her stock portfolio. I gestured to the children.

"How can you tell?" she asked. "They all look like my husband."

"And you didn't have to pay a fine?" I asked.

"Actually, I'm expecting my fourth." She looked at her stomach. "Four is the goal here in Singapore."

Four? Compared to our one-child limit, four seemed unbelievable. A miracle. Four? Oh, how life would be different if

Mother could have had four children. Surely Father would not have become such a gambler. And, even if he had, I would not be the one held responsible. No, held hostage. Perhaps Father would have even forgiven my union with Chan Hai.

I watched the two girls and little boy follow their mother like ducklings to the nearest table. I was reminded of Madame Butcher, who had always wanted a son and who had had her third child–a boy–taken from her body. Of my old school friend Cheng Min, burned when her house exploded. Did she still hear the voices of her girls calling to her? Now here I was, less than a day away from Madame Butcher and Cheng Min, and this mother said she could have four children. That it was the goal here to have four children. I felt as if I'd been kicked in the gut.

Then again, Singapore wasn't as crowded as China, despite the elbow-to-elbow crowd here at the hawker center. I couldn't imagine what the world would be like if our government let us have as many children as we wanted. Children would spill out onto the streets, into different countries, all over the place like grains of rice overflowing from a bin. I thought of Guo Qiang and Colleague and Lee Sa's ongoing debate. It wasn't just traditions and food and language that separated people. It was the rules, the belief of what constituted right and wrong.

"You want how many?" the pork ribs soup man asked me. And he wasn't asking about children.

I gave my introduction, in a loud voice this time, so he wouldn't have to strain to hear and lose patience with me.

"Perhaps you know my husband best," I finished, hoping he didn't have issues like the drinks stall man. "He works in the Computer Science Department at Nanyang University. Professor Liang."

"So there are four of you." The man nodded. His unkempt hair stuck out in all directions. His eyes darted around, fearful of moving too slow.

"Well, no," I said. "My father-in-law passed to the next world already. Two years ago in August."

He shook his head, probably thinking how life passes so fast, while he worries about the taste of his soup.

"That means three," he said, grabbing three bowls.

"I don't want soup," I said.

His eyes stopped darting about. He looked at me, his forehead furrowing. His lips turning downwards.

"I mean, your soup smells very fragrant," I added. "But that is not why I came to talk."

"That's not why you're standing in my soup line?" He looked at the man waiting behind me. "Next?"

My cheeks burned. I felt as if he'd tossed me in the Clean and Green bucket. I walked quickly to the farthest end of the hawker center, as if all the people nearby the soup stall could feel my shame. None of these food hawkers seemed in the slightest bit impressed with my family. Perhaps they didn't even know my family. At this rate, I would be here all day with nothing to show.

Rather than go for the familiar drinks or the stall which needed the most help, I picked one that didn't have a line. Where a young Chinese man about my age was dressed in a crisp, clean, yellow, button-down shirt as though he didn't really fit in here. He was busy reading a book. When I approached, he glanced up, ready to take my order.

"Can I help you?" he asked, turning the book over so as not to lose his place. Even his voice sounded different. Not the "Want what?" bark of the others.

"I used to work in a tea shop," I said, unable to look further than his long, bony fingers. I felt naked not mentioning my name or my family relations. But so far those hadn't been of any help. "I'm good with people, and I can sell anything—even dirty tea leaves. Can you use someone like me?"

"Wait a minute." He put both hands up. The palms were smooth and clean. "Let me ask Father."

He hurried into the back. Just as quickly, a rush of pleasure slid down my spine. The man hadn't turned me away. He was getting his father.

"Where's the soup guy?" A man pushed up against me, muttering to himself. He held two long sticks of fried *yutiao*, which he'd bought at the stall next door to dip in his soup. He tapped unhappy feet. I had an urge to take the ladle and start helping already.

"That's not a worker." We heard, rather than saw the soup guy. "That's a child. Look at her."

The customer behind me bored holes in my neck with his eyes. He knew the reason behind all this waiting. He knew the reason his fried *yutiao* was getting colder by the moment with no soup to dip it in.

"You promised, *Ba*," the young man replied to his father. "You promised if I could find a worker for you, I could take the job at the theater."

"I meant a good worker," the elder said. "That child won't last a day. She'll get married and have babies. You must find me a good male worker."

"In this day?" The young man's voice rang out throughout the hawker center over the sound of people chewing and slurping and talking and scolding. "Ha. You think any man wants to spend his life–"

A door slammed. The son had stepped out before condemning his father's business. My heart raced.

"*Tamade,*" the father swore.

"This is too troublesome." The man behind me shuffled away.

I felt dozens of eyes watching me, as they finished off their fried rice or slurped their noodles. Yes, this was troublesome. Very. And the rush of pleasure sank to the pit of my stomach. Then an old man emerged, wearing a ratty undershirt and grease-stained shorts. His thick, strong arms looked as if he'd been lifting pots all his life.

"You want how many?" he asked, pulling two long hairs on his chin.

"I want—"

"One bowl enough?" He looked around for the ladle.

"A job." The words came out like the high-pitched squeak of a rusting wheelbarrow.

"No need." He didn't look up. He stroked the two hairs on his chin. "This is a family business."

"But," I said. "Your son said you could use help. That your business is so prosperous, you need more than family for now."

"Never," he said looking me straight in the eye. "Never need more than family."

Why did I think I could handle this on my own? Why did I think just because the people were Chinese like me that they would welcome me? Help me? I walked out of the hawker center, back to the wet market. I still needed to deal with my new life, not just old problems. I still needed to buy a dish for lunch. I sidled up to the fish stand, relieved to be doing something familiar.

I checked under the gills of the fish on the top of the pile for fresh blood. What kind of fish would Mother-In-Law like for lunch? A pomfret? A sea bass? I would steam the fish with just a little salt—or no salt at all. The blandness would be gentle on Mother-In-Law's stomach. Perhaps she would recover.

"You want what?" The fish seller waved his arms at me, indicating that I was taking too long. Customers waited behind me.

He threw several fish on top of the pile. Several old fish—their gills rubbery and white with age. I dug deep in the pile, undeterred. I picked up a fish, the gills dripping with blood. But I wasn't thinking of fresh steamed fish anymore. I saw Father's face. He never knew what was enough. Most people would have been happy to be out of debt, to have a daughter living overseas and periodically sending home a modest income for him to live off of. Father always wanted more. Always gambled for more. He'd never be content. Still, I couldn't let my own flesh and blood fall prey to Snakehead Huang. Mother had said the ruthless man would return.

"You want to buy or not?" the fish seller asked, holding out his hatchet ready to clean and gut my selection.

"How much?" I asked.

"For you," the man said, wiping his bloody hand on his stained white undershirt. "Five dollars."

"Five dollars?" I exclaimed. The air around me suddenly smelled of cigarettes and aftershave. That smell. Where did I remember that smell from? "You sold the same fish to Mother-In-Law for three."

"Four then," the man said, already pulling out a plastic bag with which to hold the fresh fish.

"Too expensive," I said, looking past him toward another fishmonger.

Material brushed up against my shoulder as a hand shot out with four gold dollar coins for the fish seller. The fishmonger nodded and scraped the blade of his hatchet against the translucent scales of my silver round pomfret.

"Excuse me," I said, turning. "I was buying that."

The man behind me wore a tailored black suit like the delegation of customers I'd seen crowd around the drinks stall in the hawker center. He could have my fish. I'd go to another fish seller. Or we could just have a vegetable stir fry. His hands were laden with golden rings and bracelets. His jaw, a thick healthy jaw, set in a smirk. Those eyes. They shot up and down, as I'd remembered. Examining. I clenched my jaw. Bitterness filled my blood.

"I hear you're looking for a job," Snakehead Huang said.

Snakehead Huang had promised he'd get me someday. He had gotten me not once, but twice. What more could he want? My right arm coursed with blood. My fingers itched to slap his fleshy jowl. A scale hit Snakehead Huang on the cheek as the fishmonger scraped the sides of the fish. I breathed as if Waipo stood beside me throwing that bloody scale. He was the last man in this world I should show my anger toward.

"What happened to that rich husband your father found for you?" he asked.

I crossed my arms over my chest. His words made me feel dirty. So many things passed through my mind. That I had heard he had gone from closing quarries to taking poor old people's doors off. My, but he'd stepped down in the world, to that of just the neighborhood thug. I held my mouth together tight for fear even my breath would carry the words out of me.

"Waaah." He looked me up and down, the smirk on his lips widening. "Such venom in those lovely eyes."

Sweat ran down the inside of my arms. The cement beneath my feet felt strong. The bastard.

"You want what?" I said like one of the hawkers. I pulled my face into a smile.

"Just pleased to see a fellow villager in the crowd," he said, his hand sweeping across the market. He took the bag of fish from the hawker.

Fellow villager? Here we were speaking the same language, buying the same food, familiar with the same rituals. But this man was as strange to me as Lee Sa. Well, almost.

"How kind of you to concern yourself," I said. "I know a fellow villager waiting for his quarry to re-open. Another who is missing a door. Perhaps you'd want to help."

"You care," he said. "That's what I like about you."

Chan Hai had said the same words. From this man, though, it sounded like a threat. My scalp itched.

"And you?" I said.

"I'm busy here," he said.

"I see you have a new job." I indicated the other men in suits sitting at a table in the hawker center.

"Not new," he said. "I'm still Chairman of the Provincial Business Council."

Chairman. Such prestige. A position parents wished for their children. Yet he was such a turtle's egg.

"We're always looking for ways to improve the economy in our province." He extracted a gold name card holder from his suit jacket pocket, opening the thin carrier with his well-manicured fingers. "For ways to make better relations with our neighbors."

Only the ghosts would believe such charming words. Why did he insist on trying to impress me? I smiled so tight my cheeks hurt.

"For new people, like you, you must feel like Singapore is an awfully big place." He licked one finger and extracted a card. "That you've—you've tripped into this deep hole and you're not sure where to go." He waved the card like a priest waving incense. "But, really, it's just a small island, smaller than our village back home. There are only a few important people you really need to know." He winked. "Don't worry about some old man who doesn't want to give you a job scooping hot soup. That's not for you anyway."

He pushed the business information into my hand, giving my fingers a squeeze. I stepped back, knocking against the back of the fish stall.

"Careful." He took hold of my arm and pulled me close. His clunky hands felt greasy. His suit smelled ripe with sweat.

"I'm fine," I said, wiping his hands away.

"I know you are," he said, his eyes finding my chest. "And I have just the thing for you. None of this hawker stall nonsense where you sweat and sweat just to buy a sack of rice. One of my women makes so much, her parents just built a new home. Call me tonight," he said, handing me the five-dollar fish and pointing at the card in my hand. "I'll give you directions. The club doesn't get crowded until around midnight." He moved his eyes off of me and back to his colleagues. "I'll give the manager a call and let him know I found the perfect girl for the job."

The card felt dirty in my hands. Like manure. I dropped the information in the pocket of my dress. Here I'd spent all morning looking for a decent job so Guo Qiang wouldn't feel overburdened with Father's debts. I had instead been offered something far less virtuous. I needed to talk with Guo Qiang.

Chapter Sixty-Five
Not a Grain of Air Left

This time, when I went looking for Guo Qiang on campus, I didn't have to stop but once to find my way. The pool was outside behind a row of dorm buildings. Strange how having a purpose gave me so much direction.

A high metal gate surrounded a long, rectangular-shaped cement basin. This pool wasn't a murky reservoir, as I had expected. Or a small cement circle filled with green algae, like Millionaire Huang's pool. The basin held clear blue water, so clear you could see straight dark lines drawn on the bottom. The scantily clad figures of Guo Qiang, Chao Ran, Lee Sa and Kevin moved through the water. White plastic chairs were scattered around the sides of the pool. A strong chemical scent filled the air.

"Well, look who's here," Lee Sa called out from where she stood in the water near the edge of the pool, watching Kevin practice kicking.

I nodded a greeting and re-arranged the plastic bag of fish on my wrist. Why did her voice sound so loud? I reminded myself that she was crazy, and then that she wasn't. That was just what Mother-In-Law said. Perhaps her voice grated as my head was already filled with so much noise. I had spent the morning shutting off voices of doubt while I had searched for a job in the hawker center, voices of anger when I had run into Snakehead Huang. Now I just wanted to find Guo Qiang in a pool chair by himself, so we could sit and watch the palm trees swaying in the breeze. So we could talk about Father and no door on our house and Snakehead Chairman Huang's offer of a high level job that suited my talents. Instead here was noisy Lee Sa calling attention to herself despite the fact that she wore a bra that allowed half of her giant bosoms to fall out. Panties so small they slid up her backside.

Guo Qiang and Colleague swam toward the far end of the pool. When they reached the other side, they did funny flip-arounds and headed back toward the three of us. As though racing. Perhaps their race would end here. Perhaps I could ask Guo Qiang for some talking time.

Drops of water splashed against my cheek as Kevin held on tight to the side of the wall and kicked his little legs. I moved back to one of the white plastic chairs and sat down, the bag of fish on my lap. This would make a fine, bland lunch to soothe Mother-In-Law's irritated stomach. Would she feel better after her rest? Even if Guo Qiang agreed to send money to Father, what would Mother-In-Law say? Even a rested Mother-In-Law might prefer I take the job at the sleazy nightclub. For I knew that's what this was. I knew from the way Snakehead Huang's eyes had crawled up and down my body. His club was not like the smoke-filled room where Father used to play cards. It probably wasn't even like Mr. Farmer's Golden Dance Club where people sang songs and drank too much. Still, the mighty Chairman knew I didn't have to have this job. Could he be offering something which required a talent beyond the curves on my body?

Guo Qiang and Colleague splashed closer toward me. Guo Qiang wore his new, tiny suit. I could see the outline of his bottom so clearly. Colleague's suit was just as small. Their arms stroked smoothly through the water. No wonder Kevin called Guo Qiang "Blue Dolphin." He swam so easily. I thought of Chan Hai. I had been so impressed with his ability to swim. Yet, compared to these people, his swimming seemed so country style. "What's cute in the country doesn't necessarily translate to cute in the city," Guo Qiang had said that first night we had been introduced. I had thought him such a snob. But he had been right. This city was so different. I'd made some foolish blunders. Not knowing how to work the phone and not recognizing strange foods. But I would catch on. Surely. Perhaps a job at a real city club would be the perfect way for me to learn fast.

"Earth to Leeway," Lee Sa called.

"What?" I asked.

"Kevin wants to know what's in the bag."

She pointed to the plastic bag which held the fresh pomfret from the wet market. Why was this their concern? Why wouldn't they leave me to my thoughts? I held up the bag.

"Fish," I said.

"Ugh," he said, coughing and slapping the water with his fist. "I don't like fish."

"I know." I smiled. "I have talk for Guo Qiang. I came from market. Next time, I buy brownies."

"You should have brought your suit instead of that fish," Lee Sa said, following my gaze to Guo Qiang. "Once they start swimming, they don't break until they're done."

Guo Qiang was but an arm's length from the end of the pool. Surely he'd stop for a rest. Surely Lee Sa was teasing. I stood up, the sweaty plastic of the chair ripping away from my knees. I approached the side of the pool and leaned down to tap him on the head as his stubby fingers touched the side of the pool. But he flipped around. Off he went again.

"Today, they said they'd do 1.5k," Lee Sa informed. "That's about ninety laps. How many have they done so far, Kevin?"

I looked to Kevin. Let the boy tell me they were on lap eighty-nine. But he sank underwater. He was blowing bubbles.

"They're about halfway done," she said stretching her arms around and around.

I looked up at the blue sky and the few white clouds that danced nearby. Only five of us filled this area and we were all related. Spouses. Friends. Children. Yet, each of us seemed distant, spinning in our own worlds. Certainly my concerns were of little interest to them, so busy were they practicing swimming, exercising and enjoying. I felt like the man who had attended our wedding party, wanting us to sell his down jackets. How foolish of me to sit here wanting to intrude on the fun and ask my distinguished professor of a husband for more money for my idiot of a father. Or if that was too much, could I work for Snakehead Huang at a nightclub? After midnight? I was tempted to turn on my heels and return home. But the sounds of Mother's voice asking for help urged me to stay. I needed to at least ask my silly questions. I needed to know.

I returned to the sticky plastic seat. I followed Guo Qiang's progress back and forth. Back and forth. I felt tired. Dizzy. This relentless heat did strange things to my body. It would just take time to adjust to this weather. Just as it would take time to adjust to this marriage. Last night when Guo Qiang had led me to bed, I had felt so odd. I had closed my eyes, imagining that his doughy fingers on my breasts were thick, calloused ones. That his fleshy thighs against mine were strong golden ones. Surely, though I would grow to love Guo Qiang. Someday.

"Mom, come closer," Kevin screamed.

I looked over. Kevin held onto the wall with both hands. Lee Sa stood several meters away. When she inched closer, he pushed off the wall toward her.

Kevin didn't swim like Guo Qiang, but more like a water bug. And, like me, he wasn't very good at coming up for breath. He took small strokes, his little feet hardly making a dent in the water. My heart pounded, as if I were the one under that cold, engulfing water. Instead of Lee Sa, there was Chan Hai, and all I wanted was for him to pick me up with his big strong arms, to hold me close. I glanced over to where Guo Qiang swam, certain he'd heard me thinking of a love in my heart that didn't belong to him, a love that was still a faint but strong echo. But Guo Qiang kept on swimming. I needn't have worried.

"Good job, Kevin," Lee Sa called. "You're almost there."

Thank the gods. The poor boy had gone so far without any air. He put out his hand to grab onto Lee Sa. She backed up. How could she expect him to have so much air in his little body? Kevin swam further and reached for her. Again she backed up.

"Lee Sa," I called. "Stop."

She looked up at me and laughed so hard she fell backwards. Kevin grabbed onto her and lifted his head out of the water for air.

"Why did you do that?" He beat her on the shoulder, tears bulging at the corners of his eyes. "I almost couldn't breathe."

"But look how far you swam," Lee Sa said grabbing onto his small fists. "You thought you could only swim a little, and look what you did."

He wiped his eyes and looked. He had managed to swim almost half the width of the pool again. My heart thumped in my ears. He hugged his crazy mother.

"Did you see that?" Lee Sa called, holding Kevin up high. "Wasn't he great?"

"Great." I let the air out between my teeth. Then I added Lee Sa's favorite saying. "Good job, Kevin."

"Thanks," he said. "I had my power pack."

He stuck his hands into the front of his suit and pulled out a handful of purple.

"Oh, Kevin." Lee Sa grabbed at the floating purple pieces. "That's disgusting."

What was this? My stomach danced. Acid formed at the back of my throat.

"It's ruined," Kevin cried.

"Well," Lee Sa said, planting Kevin on the side of the pool. "That's what happens when you mix paper and water. You get mush."

Paper and water? Purple paper and water? Ah, the "bird plane" I had made for him last night. Why would I have thought any different? Mother-In-Law had gotten me to the point that I looked for craziness in these people when it wasn't there.

"Don't cry," I told him. "I will make another."

I took a tissue from my purse. Mei Ling and I had often complained about the harsh quality of the tissue paper we kept in our purses for the times when we needed to use the public outhouse. Finally I'd found a good use for this rough paper. Too bad I didn't have my scissors. Still I could try folding something.

"Are you going to stick around?" Lee Sa asked wading over to the side of the pool closest to where I sat.

"Stick round?" I asked.

"Are you staying?" She put her hands out palm down, as though telling a dog to heel. "Waiting?"

"I stay," I said. Guo Qiang had done thirty laps. If what Lee Sa had said was correct, he only had another fifteen.

"Aren't you worried about the fish?" She indicated the plastic bag on the ground next to me.

"You right." I looked around for a cooler spot. There was no shade here, though. Nothing but glaring sun. The pool. The pool? That would be a natural refrigerator.

"What are you doing?" Lee Sa said.

"Water cooler than air," I said, leaning down and dropping the bag of fish in this temporary refrigerator. "Stay fresher longer."

"That's disgusting." She reached over, grabbed the bag out of the water, and threw it back on the ground. "You'll get blood and fish parts in the water."

The sun was hot. Lee Sa was loud. An inner voice—was it Waipo?—beckoned for me to take my fish and wait for Guo Qiang at home. Instead, I retrieved the dripping bag from the ground, wondering why she had such a problem with fish. Seemed as challenging to her as my fear of the elevator. Why worry about a fish having eyes? She leaned over and picked at scales in the water, thrusting them off the tips of her fingers as though they had bitten her. Why worry about a fish making the water dirty when there were so many sweaty bodies swimming in the same water?

"Between you and Kevin," she said. "They'll probably have to do a special cleaning."

"Here," I said, hoping to get her mind off the dirtied water.

"Another plane for Kevin."

"Will you watch him a minute?" she said, heaving herself out of the water and pulling the small fabric out of the crevice between the thick cheeks of her bottom. "I have to go to the bathroom."

"I don't know." I said. "I can't—"

"Don't worry," she said, shooing my words and my concerns away with her hand. "He can swim. Just keep an eye on him."

"Eye on him," I said. "Okay."

Lee Sa disappeared inside a building at the far end of the pool. I took off my shoes and sat down at the pool's edge close to Kevin, letting my feet dangle in the water. He came up next to me and put the tissue airplane on my knee. Zoom. Zoom. Zoom. He was going to get it all wet again, all mushy. Mush. Like that cardboard umbrella I'd held the night Father handed me off to Madame Liang for twenty thousand *yuan*. Like my sky anytime Father made a move. When would he stop? Even my marriage had not been enough to numb the itch that made him want more, more, more.

"Here," I said, putting my hand out to Kevin. "I hold for you."

"Like that," he said, putting the plane in my hand and pushing my arm up. "Hold it right up, like that."

I did as was instructed. Such a funny child. Then he turned and pushed off the side and paddled around.

The water felt cool on my legs. But sweat beaded on my neck and forehead. I was reminded of the first time I'd gone to the reservoir with Chan Hai. How I'd sat on a rock and let my feet touch the water. How I'd felt cut in half then. Part of me wishing to be with Chan Hai. Part of me wishing to do right by my parents. My whole world had changed, but I still felt cut in half. I looked over.

Kevin no longer paddled near my feet. He swam further toward the middle of the pool. What was he doing? Surely, he wouldn't go far without Lee Sa there to catch him. I moved my feet up onto the side of the pool, standing and waiting for him to turn back. He didn't. Guo Qiang and Colleague had almost reached the far end of the pool. Would they realize Kevin was out there? Would they catch him if needed? I followed along the side of the pool. Why had I agreed to keeping an eye on Kevin? A ringing filled my ears.

"Breathe," I called. "Breathe like a water bug."

Kevin kicked hard, but he was headed for the far end of the pool. And he had yet to take a breath. I looked to the building into which Lee Sa had disappeared. When would she be back?

"Kevin." I knelt at the side of the pool and stretched out my arm toward him. If he turned and kicked toward me, he would be safe. "Come this way."

He lifted his face out of the water. Thank the gods. How could he scare me like that? He opened his mouth for air. He coughed instead.

"Kevin," I shrieked. "Over here."

Kevin splashed at the water, like a dog paddling. His back heaved up and down. Guo Qiang and Colleague did a flip turn at the far end of the pool.

"Help," I cried.

Guo Qiang and Colleague glided our way, still exercising, still enjoying. Couldn't they lift their heads and see we needed help? Now.

"Don't be afraid," I called to Kevin. "Good job. You can do it."

He didn't hear me. Surely his ears had already filled with panic, like the booming of thunder. I slipped into the water, my dress billowing up around me. My feet didn't touch bottom, but I held firmly to the edge of the pool. Kevin was only a heartbeat away. I could get him if I reached out as far as I could.

"Over here, Kevin."

I stretched out my arm. He grabbed onto me, pulling me away from the edge. I reached out for the side of the pool. But he climbed on top of me pushing me further away. He grabbed around my neck so tight, I couldn't breathe. How could he be so strong?

I fought to pull his arms away, sinking to the bottom of the pool. My lungs felt as if they would pop. My head felt light. My feet touched cement, and I pushed off hard. Like a miracle, we moved up and up and up. My head came to the surface of the water. I sucked a deep breath, but Kevin's arms were as tight around my neck as a string around one of those restaurant balloons.

We fell back underwater, this time not far enough down for me to push off the bottom. I kicked, not sure where we were going. Where was Lee Sa? Why didn't Guo Qiang and Colleague see us struggling? How did I end up in the middle of this pool? Oh, Chan Hai. My heart sucked up every grain of air in my body. My head exploded. Bang. Everything went black.

Chapter Sixty-Six
A Second Pulse

Darkness engulfed. So complete. As if I was walking through a muddy field on a moonless night in the village. All around I heard voices. I was headed for a grand celebration, like Chinese New Year.

"Why are you so wet?" Waipo scolded from one side. "You know better than that. You're a grown woman."

A baby cried as he jumped up and down on my chest. Up and down. Up and down. Who was this child? Why did he accost me so?

"Don't take my boy," Madame Butcher shrieked from behind me. "That's my boy. Please."

Warm breath on my cheeks sent shivers down my wet, cold body. Wet hair dripped on my face. Was this Feng Gu's *gege*, the friend Chan Hai had left alone in the reservoir? Did he have a secret to tell me? I put my hands up to touch Gege. How kind of him to find me. Did he know that Chan Hai thought about him everyday? Did he know that I thought of Chan Hai everyday?

"Li Hui," he called.

His voice was reedy, a boy still. Had he come to lead me to the next world? Madame Butcher's boy bounced on my chest again. So hard. Why didn't she control her child? Say no.

"Stop," I cried. My words came out in choking gasps.

"That's it." A hand patted my back. "That's it. Keep it coming."

"Li Hui?"

The voice sounded from a different world, but not the world of Waipo, Madame Butcher's baby boy and Feng Gu's *gege*. This world felt sharp, like cold water on my face in the morning.

I coughed, my insides exploding. I spat up buckets and buckets of water that filled that fancy pool that was bigger than Millionaire Huang's. I coughed until my stomach hurt, my throat burned. My neck felt slimy. I opened my eyes.

"Li Hui?" The voice of Guo Qiang.

The faces of the living filled my vision. Guo Qiang, Colleague and a young man I hadn't seen before. They kneeled around me, as though praying. The young man leaned back, emitting a sigh, ruffling his wet hair.

"You gave us a big scare," he said, his hand on my wrist as he listened to my pulse.

The ground felt warm beneath me. An ant crawled over my arm. A scare. My throat hurt. My dress was wet. The pool. Where was Kevin?

"Where's—" I started. My insides felt on fire. Acid covered my tongue. "Baby boy okay?"

"Take it easy." Guo Qiang eased me back down. "Kevin's right here."

I turned my head, cement scraping my cheek. Lee Sa sat on one of those white chairs, rocking a toweled bundle back and forth in her arms.

"Auntie Leeway." Kevin peaked out from the towel. "Next time you come to the pool—"

"I know," I said. "Next time I'll grab you faster."

"No." He sat up in his mother's arm, the towel falling down around him. "Next time you must hold my power pack higher."

Power pack? The toilet-tissue airplane. Is that why he swam so far? He thought he was protected by the power pack?

"I will," I said. And I would learn to swim better just in case.

A sob choked me. A few minutes ago, Kevin had called to me, telling me to watch how he could hold his breath. I had been curling my lips at Lee Sa's public display of flesh. I had been worrying about Father and how to ask Guo Qiang to wire money. I had been thinking of the reservoir and Chan Hai. The sky had been so blue. Now here we were all wet and sucking in the sweet air and feeling as if our lives were tethered to the earth with just a thin string.

"It's going to rain," Guo Qiang said, as if searching for some noise to fill the air.

Half of the sky had darkened, as if a curtain were being pulled across. But why should we care? Rain came and went everyday here.

"It's a good thing," the young man said. "That's why I took this shortcut back to my dorm. Otherwise—"

He dropped back into silence. I filled in the missing words. Otherwise I'd be meeting Waipo and Gege and Madame Butcher's son. Otherwise this would be more than just a big scare.

"I'm sorry," I said, pushing myself up. My head felt dizzy. I fell back again.

"Should I call an ambulance?" the young man asked Guo Qiang. "Maybe she should be seen by a real doctor. I'm just a student."

"That's a good idea." Guo Qiang looked at me, his eyes still filled with alarm.

"No need," I said. I had taken up enough of this student's time, gotten him all wet, made everyone worry. I was breathing. I would be fine. "I'm just feeling a bit heavy. Maybe I drank too much."

They all laughed with manufactured enthusiasm. I imagined I could see Lee Sa's fillings in her mouth. The wonderful sound echoed in my head.

"Well, then," the young man suggested. "At least you should lie down a while."

Guo Qiang picked me up off the ground, his fingers gripping around me tighter than they ever had. His hair was plastered against his head. His bare chest felt bumpy with gooseflesh. Cold. Scared. He put me on one of the long white plastic chairs. I had been sitting on one of these waiting for Guo Qiang to finish swimming his laps. Just a few minutes ago. Just a few minutes ago I'd been dry and thinking over how to ask Guo Qiang to help Father. It had all turned so quickly. The speed of the change shocked me as much as anything.

"Take it easy." Guo Qiang covered me with a towel, patted my arm, ran his hands through my damp hair. "Take it easy. I'm just going to talk to the student for a moment."

As Guo Qiang walked away, I closed my eyes to rest. But, as soon as I did so, my head spun. I couldn't breathe. I opened my eyes to make sure I was still part of this dry, solid world.

"We're going to get changed," Lee Sa said. "We'll just be a minute."

She and Colleague carried Kevin past. Despite her words, they moved slowly, as though wading through mud. They stopped every few paces and stared at the boy, ruffled his hair, squeezed his shoulders. Again my thoughts reeled. Lee Sa had just gone off for a minute. Just to the bathroom. How had so much happened in that short space of time? One minute, I was hanging onto the side, the next minute, I was trying to flap my legs. My lungs hurt. I had to stop thinking. Stop thinking.

"You guys can put me down now," Kevin said.

"I've got you," Lee Sa said.

"No, I've got him," Colleague said.

"You're squishing me," he said, wriggling out of their arms.

I had to smile. They were both probably so frightened, they didn't want to let him go. But he was young. He acted as if he'd just awakened from a nap and was ready to move on. Just like that young girl with the broken arm in the hawker center, Kevin was so full of hope. So fearless.

A strong wind blew, rippling the top of the water, toppling a chair next to me. Guo Qiang looked over, rubbing the cold from his arms. His face looked tired. Old. The student handed Guo Qiang a piece of paper—with his phone number? His dorm number? Guo Qiang surely would send a gift of thanks. A gift of money. We would be indebted to this young hero forever.

Mother's voice from this morning bounced off the walls of my head. "When are you going to get a job?" That's all I'd wanted to do. All I'd wanted to do today was send Mother and Father money. Salty water burned its way down my sore throat. I closed my eyes tight against the flood that was in my heart.

"I'm going to change." Guo Qiang's doughy fingers touched my arm. He held on. "This young man will stay with you a moment."

"I'm okay," I said. "Surely he has studies. He—"

The chair creaked next to me. The young man sat down, his shirt plastered to his chest like a coat of wet gray paint.

"Really," I said sitting up. "You don't need to trouble yourself further. I'm fine."

"No trouble," he said. "No trouble at all."

"Really—"

"Shhhh." He picked up my wrist again. "Quiet a moment."

He listened. Then he placed my wrist back on the chair. The wind churned, slapping us in the face. He had done all that was necessary. Why did he still feel the pulse in my wrist?

"It's going to rain," I said. "You best get back to your dorm. Besides, there's Lee Sa now. She'll stay with me. I've troubled you too much already. I'm sorry."

"My father practiced medicine all his life," he said. "I don't remember as much as he would have wished. But I do remember him telling me how, whenever someone got into an accident, the first thing they always did was apologize. As if they had done something wrong. As if they had control." He smiled at me. "Your lung meridian is still high. But you asked earlier about the baby."

Had Kevin been permanently damaged from being underwater

so long? Why had I let him swim on his own so long, certain that he'd be fine? That he'd do a good job, Kevin? I should have jumped in and grabbed him right away.

"What's this?" Lee Sa neared. She stood by me, her eyes focused on the men's changing room, as she waited for Colleague and Kevin to emerge.

"Surely, it's okay," I said, patting her arm. Kevin was young. He'd be fine.

"Yes," the young man said to me. "I'm not sure if it's a boy or not, but your baby should be okay."

"What?" Lee Sa stared at my stomach.

What? Why would he say this? Especially in front of loudmouth Lee Sa? My heart beat so hard my ears hurt. Surely he was wrong.

"How can you tell?" Lee Sa put her hands on her hips. "I thought you were a student here, which means an engineer of some sort."

"Well, yes." The young man blushed. "My father was a traditional Chinese doctor. He taught me some things."

"Like?" Lee Sa persisted.

She had a smirk on her lips. Her blue eyes danced with mirth. Oh, why did she have to be out here now?

"Her pulse—" He picked up my wrist again. "I felt an extra heartbeat earlier."

"That must be mistake," I said.

My veins coursed with blood. No. No. No. Not an extra heartbeat. Could Guo Qiang's seed have fertilized my fields so quickly? But I had felt strange for many weeks now. My monthly was late. I had felt tired and nauseous. This morning I'd vomited. I thought it had been the pressure and worry. No. I'd hoped it was the pressure and the worry. Now I knew. The farmer who had fertilized my field was not Guo Qiang. This farmer had to be Chan Hai.

"Uh-huh." Lee Sa nodded her head up and down like a horse who wanted to get rid of the reins. "Sure."

"Then," he said. "She cried out about a baby, wondering if he was okay."

"I ask about Kevin," I said. "He is baby boy."

Maybe it wouldn't matter who the farmer was. Mother-In-Law wanted a grandson. Perhaps she would never know the difference. My stomach contracted at the idea of that deception.

"She was asking about my son." Lee Sa took her hand from her hip and grabbed my wrist away from the man. Rather than the light touch of the young student, she held on as though pumping the heart herself. "I don't feel anything."

What a relief. Not that I expected her to feel an extra pulse. Still I was glad.

"Maybe," the young student said, looking to me to confirm or deny his diagnosis. "A woman always knows."

I remembered the faces of those children at the wet market. "All of them look like my husband," the woman had said. What if the child in my womb looked like Chan Hai? My hand flew to my mouth as sour bile filled the back of my throat. I shook my head. No, not this. Please.

"Surely." I looked up at them. "There could be another reason. My heart's had lots of excitement today."

"I could be wrong," he said, reaching for my wrist again.

"That's enough hand-holding," Lee Sa said. "I can take care of her now."

He got up to go. I had an urge to run after him and beg him to hold my wrist one more time and tell me there was nothing there. Nothing but anxiety and worry and water build up from so much heat. But I knew. His initial diagnosis was correct.

"How could he take advantage of such a situation?" Lee Sa paced back and forth. "This must be the Chinese version of the horny lifeguard who rescues women whether they're drowning or not. And I thought he was a nice man."

"He is nice man," I said, my voice quiet, quieter than I felt.

"Sure." Lee Sa stopped pacing and put her hands on her hips. "I guess some people will say anything to hold onto you."

What was she talking about? Had she already forgotten that the man had saved her son's life? Her loyalties shifted like the breeze in a storm. A strange woman not to be trusted.

"But he help us," I said. "He save me. He save Kevin."

"You're right," she said, staring at the changing rooms as though willing Colleague and Kevin to appear. "It just bothers me when people take advantage like that. That story about the baby. What a crock."

"Yes." I lay back against the chair and closed my eyes, for the first time relieved that Lee Sa was not a Chinese and understood so little about the culture. She didn't believe the young student. I would not have to worry about her passing on this information. "Silly story. Make him sound foolish. Like he try to be doctor."

Perhaps I could ask Mother to send me some red flowers from the herbalist in China. Perhaps they had such a medicine here. I hadn't even looked for such medicines, so concerned was I about finding a way to get Guo Qiang to my side of the bed.

"We'll have to hurry," she said.

My thoughts exactly. I tried to remember when was the last time my monthly had visited. But my mind was like the sky. Dark. Offering no history, no direction. A cool breeze made me shiver.

"What can I do?" The words escaped my mouth before I could stop them. Would Lee Sa help me? Would her loyalty shift to me for a moment?

"You're soaked already." She laughed looking at the sky. "It's the rest of us that are going to feel the difference.

She spoke of the weather. I spoke of my life. Of trying to hold up even a sliver of the sky.

"It's the rest of the us that are going to feel the difference," she said again.

She didn't realize how true those words were.

Chapter Sixty-Seven
The Yellow Bird

I stood up and grabbed onto Guo Qiang's arm. He and the rest of our group were dressed in clean, dry clothes. I pulled at the hem of my damp dress, feeling cold each time the wind reminded us of the impending shower.

"Are you feeling up to walking?" Guo Qiang asked. "I could try to get us a taxi."

"When it's about to rain?" Lee Sa asked, her long face scrunching into concern.

"You're right," Guo Qiang said. "We'll be waiting until next week before a taxi stops." He looked toward the direction of our apartment. "I could walk back and get our car."

"I can walk," I said.

Walking was the least of my problems. If I had to concentrate on keeping upright, perhaps my mind would stop thinking of other things. Like a baby boy with dimpled cheeks like Chan Hai. Guo Qiang stayed next to me, his palm under my forearm for support. The cotton of his shirt brushed against my arm. My insides prickled with fear. Not a baby. No.

Lee Sa and Colleague each held one of Kevin's hands. A thin, grateful aura surrounded them, like rice paper which covers New Year's candy. I wished to fall under that spell, but an extra pulse beat inside me. My stomach was in knots. I hoped that student was wrong. That my abnormal cycle and feelings were due to stress, this hot weather.

"The grass feels good," Lee Sa said, indicating where the warm grass tickled against her ankles. She patted Kevin's head, letting her hand linger.

The grass reminded me of the reservoir, of mosquitoes, of lime juice being rubbed on my legs by Chan Hai. Of his "big brother" rubbing inside of me. And now a baby.

"Look at the bird." Colleague pointed to a yellow bird which flitted across the dark sky.

The yellow was so bright. But, while I reached for the yellow bird around my neck that Chan Hai had given me, I recalled a different memory. Of that yellow dress of Madame Matchmaker's which looked like a caution light. She had warned me to stop my relationship with Chan Hai. She had told me that I would end up on a branch that bore no fruit. Here I had been given the juiciest peach available—an auspicious union that came at the right time for our family. Why then this? This that made our missing door and Father's new debt seem insignificant.

"Breathe," Lee Sa instructed us all, making me realize I'd been holding my breath. My lungs were constricted to the size of needles. And, try as I might, the air wouldn't fit in for long. "Doesn't that taste delicious?" she asked. "So cool. I love the air before the rain."

"I'm hungry," Kevin announced.

"I'll make you a super duper batch of brown—"

Lee Sa stopped. She caught Colleague's eyes. Confusion filled her face, as though perhaps the comfort food she grew up with was no longer appropriate. But then, what was?

"How about some rice porridge?" Colleague suggested. But his voice had lost the conviction with which he had spoken the night before. As if perhaps what he had grown up with wasn't necessarily appropriate either.

"I have good idea," I suggested, squeezing Guo Qiang's arm. "Come for lunch at our house."

Guo Qiang nodded his assent, although he tilted his head to the side and raised his eyebrows as if to ask was I sure. My stomach felt hollow. I didn't deserve such kindness.

"You probably want to rest," Colleague said, as if interpreting Guo Qiang's facial expressions.

"No," I said. "When I close eyes, I back in pool, trying to swim. I see darkness." And a baby who wouldn't look like Guo Qiang. "Is nice if you come. Keep me company."

"And Auntie Leeway can make me a better plane," Kevin added. "With her scissors."

"That sounds nice," Lee Sa said, turning to Colleague. "What do you think?"

I'd never heard her ask his opinion on anything. She was always so busy forcing her opinions on all of us. Perhaps something had drowned in that pool today.

"Yes, that would be nice," Colleague said, reaching across Kevin's head and rubbing Lee Sa's cheek. Then he turned to me. "That is, if you're sure you want company."

"Let's not go through this," I said, mimicking Lee Sa's voice. "We invite you because we want you to come. End of story."

Guo Qiang and Colleague laughed. Lee Sa smiled. Kevin looked up, furrowing his eyebrows.

"What's funny?" he asked.

Yes, what was funny? Here I was pregnant with a baby that didn't belong to my husband. Father was deep in debt again. This time my family was in danger. What was funny? Nothing. Nothing at all. A drop of rain splashed against my cheek. A giant teardrop. The rains were starting.

Chapter Sixty-Eight
Lee Sa's Good Story

Mother-In-Law stood at the gate in her polyester black skirt and flowered blouse. One side of the blouse hung higher than the other. She had fastened the buttons wrong. Surely she had heard us all coming and raced to the door. Then again, she held her parasol, as if planning to go out shopping at the market.

"Where have you been so long?" Her face looked pained. Lee Sa had that effect on her. But perhaps her stomach still bothered her. That would explain the lopsided blouse. "What's this? Is it raining already?"

"We were . . . swimming," Guo Qiang explained.

"Swimming?" Mother-In-Law looked at my damp clothing, my wet, straggly hair. "Looks as if you swam the longest."

She probably envisioned the village, where we girls swam in our clothes. She'd probably never seen the pool or Guo Qiang in his underwear-style bathing suit. And she'd have commentary to last several lifetimes, if she ever saw Lee Sa's revealing swim wear.

Guo Qiang had the hint of a smile on his face. He winked at me, filling my being with warmth, as if I were part of his team. But, just as quickly, I felt as if I'd taken a sip of Lee Sa's coffee. My limbs tingled. My heart felt lodged between my toes. Chan Hai's baby.

"Well, I hope in all your play, you didn't forget to stop at the market," Mother-In-Law was saying. "I've been standing here wondering if I should go. If you were going to go. That it was getting too late for anyone to go."

"I stopped there earlier this morning," I said. Hadn't I told her I was going to market?

"Well, that's good," she said. But again, she looked pained. She reluctantly stood back to let us in the house. "Well?" she asked as Lee Sa flopped on the couch and Kevin looked around for scissors to cut up an advertisement from the morning newspaper. Not the red advertisement of happiness. The white one. Of death. "Where are your groceries?"

I looked down. The plastic bag with the fish no longer dangled from my wrist. Had I left it rotting on the cement?

"I'm sorry," I said. "I guess I got so busy. I left the fish up at the pool."

"Unbelievable," Mother-In-Law said.

She shot a dark look at Lee Sa's exposed thighs, her bouncing bosom. She turned on her heel and swept off into the kitchen. I followed. I would change my damp dress later. Would Mother-In-Law have been happier if I'd reinvented my morning, telling her I'd neglected to shop as I was busy finding a high-level job? Father would. Father. What would we do now? My legs wobbled, as if I were still at the bottom of the pool, trying to find the surface. I grabbed onto the firmness of the counter.

"Looks like too much playing makes you a forgetful girl." Mother-In-Law turned on the faucet to wash the grains of rice in the pot. She let the water run so long that the pot overflowed, washing the few bad grains of rice over the side. She was probably so disappointed in me that she couldn't focus. "Perhaps next time, you best stay with—"

"I have a request for beer." Lee Sa came in the kitchen and opened the refrigerator like a family member. "To celebrate."

I could tell by the way Mother-In-Law banged the pot of rice on the stove, that she didn't appreciate the foreign woman digging around in our space. Lee Sa's behavior no longer bothered me though. Nothing could bother me now.

"This is nice idea," I said, hurrying over to the refrigerator to help.

"No, no." Lee Sa nudged me aside. "I know you have good intentions. But you tend to pick the wrong thing. We don't want to drink soy sauce."

I know she only meant to tease. I had reached for soy sauce and mustard last night instead of beer, my mind had been so far away. But her words felt like a pick hammering at my back. I'd always tried to do the right thing by Father and Mother. From insisting Administrator Zhang give our family a better job to helping Father's *mahjong* partner at the tea shop to marrying Guo Qiang. And now, as if I were back home standing in the aisles of a bus which had come to an abrupt halt, I felt myself pitching forward. The gods had pulled my feet out from under me. Lee Sa was right. So far I had picked the wrong thing. Always. What would I do now? I grabbed three beers for her, a juice box for Kevin.

"I get it right this time," I said. Would I?

"Good job, Leeway," she said, smiling and cuddling the cool drinks against her ample chest as she left.

Mother-In-Law emitted a deep sigh of disgust. She shook her curly head. She adjusted and re-adjusted the lid of the pot.

"Mother-In-Law." I reached in the cupboard for a package of nuts and a bowl. I poured the peanuts, their shells tan and hard, into the bowl. They plink-plinked against the sides. I wanted to mention about Kevin, explain about the desire to celebrate, then stopped. The pool incident would only add kindling to the fire she had built against Lee Sa. And hadn't she warned me the picture in the black frame was a bad omen? Hadn't she known something bad would happen when Lee Sa flipped the fish? Hadn't she told me Lee Sa was crazy? "It was a hectic morning."

"Don't make excuses for her," she whispered so fiercely, spittle landed on my arm. "She only knows how to play and celebrate and play some more. She brings over bad fish. Takes you out swimming all day. Turns your head around the wrong way. All you need from her is an English lesson, once a week. That's all."

She winced as she bent to turn the flame down on the stove. With one hand, she held onto her stomach. Was she still feeling heaty?

"Mother-In-Law?" I asked.

"It's nothing." She rubbed her stomach. "You all gave me such a fright, leaving and not saying where you were going. All the worries filled up my stomach until it's ready to burst."

"Your stomach has been bothering you for a long time," I said. "Maybe we should visit the clinic."

"For what purpose?" She played with the flame under the pot, making it just right. "To waste more? I'm fine. Really. Besides, there's too much work to do here. If you don't get busy, you'll soon have us living in a rat's nest, like Li Zhi's."

I didn't reply. Instead I took the bowl of peanuts to the living room. Mother-In-Law was haunted by Li Zhi, as if fearful that any acceptance of this foreigner would mean smashing every notion she held about her world. And, from everything I'd seen of Lee Sa, Mother-In-Law was right.

I locked myself in the bathroom. From the living room, I heard Lee Sa laughing, Kevin zooming about, Mother-In-Law putting dishes on the dining room table. I peeled off my damp dress and stepped into the shower, turning the water as hot as I could make it. Perhaps some hot water would make my monthly appear. For surely my monthly would come. It must. I stayed under the spray of water, watching as the clear liquid flowed down the drain. When had my monthly last appeared? I tried to count back, but the shelves in my head were empty. I couldn't remember.

There. I spotted something red. That was blood. I stepped out of the shower and, without even drying off, sat on the toilet. So there was a good reason to have the toilet so close to the shower. To be sure I'd seen blood. I held onto my stomach and pushed. Then I looked down between my legs. The white porcelain toilet bowl beneath the transparent water stared back at me. Laughing.

"Lunch is ready," Mother-In-Law called, her knuckles rapping on the bedroom door.

"Coming," I said.

But I wanted to stay a while longer. All I needed was to sit a while longer. I put my elbows on my knees and my head in my hands. Surely the blood would start to flow.

"Lunch is ready," Mother-In-Law called again. "Li Hui, where are you?"

"I'm here," I said, looking down at the bloodless toilet water.

I took the towel from the metal hook on the shower door and brushed at my wet skin. The cloth was rough, and I was reminded of Chan Hai's calloused fingers. The way he had brushed the reservoir water from my skin. I could almost hear him whispering, "How long do you want it to take?" as he led me the long way home, stopping at the deserted temple on the way. "Follow me." Was that when this had happened? If only I'd been allowed to continue following him, then I'd be laughing and full of joy at the happiness inside of me. Why hadn't I been allowed to do so? Damn Father.

But it was too simple just to blame Father. He was just a pebble in the ocean, as Chan Hai would have said, rolling this way or that, depending on the strength of the tide. He had only followed Madame Matchmaker's advice, a tradition that went back thousands of years. Before the Song Dynasty. But the rules of society had changed. Why hadn't our traditions? Again I heard Chan Hai's voice. He had teased me for turning to follow the same path home. "You don't have to walk up and back, up and back, always following the same trench. I know a different path. Follow me." Why hadn't I realized I was following the same trenches? Why hadn't I discovered a different path for us?

"Li Hui." Mother-In-Law knocked on the bathroom door, turning the knob back and forth as if to gain entry. "Are you alright?"

"I'm fine," I said, wiping away the tears in my eyes. I pulled my damp clothes back on and dragged a comb through my hair. I stared at my haunted eyes in the mirror, promising myself, "I'll be fine."

We all gathered at the dining table, all except for Kevin who was busy making another cutting. A large pot of porridge sat in the center of the table, a dish of tiny fried fish next to it. My stomach was full of worry and maybe more. I had no appetite for food. Outside, rain fell down in white sheets, the thunderous drops flooding the hallway. Guo Qiang had told me about this tropical deluge. How people ducked for cover, as their umbrellas couldn't protect them. How cars stopped on the road, unable to see to move forward. I longed to go outside and stand under that rain. Surely this sudden torrent was meant for me. But I would see a way to move forward. I would.

"Are you going to sit down?" Lee Sa asked.

I looked away from the window to the table. Guo Qiang had his hand on the back of my chair. Everyone looked up at me, waiting.

"I wouldn't want to sit either with this sorry lunch," Mother-In-Law said, her face pinched in pain. Was she still feeling uncomfortable or was she embarrassed by this sparse meal?

"I'm fine here with beer and peanuts," Lee Sa said.

"This is the best meal on a day like today," Colleague added, blowing on the top of his bowl as he stirred his porridge with a ceramic spoon.

"Auntie Leeway." Kevin ran over with his white airplane, which looked more like a poorly-cut triangle. He pushed me back further into my seat and climbed in my lap. "Will you give me some of that fish stuff like last night?"

I scooped several spoonfuls of porridge from the center of the pot. I didn't have that fish stuff like last night. On so many levels, I didn't have what I had yesterday. But he didn't need to know that. Perhaps no one needed know. Tap-tap. My toes tapped against the tile floor.

"You know." Lee Sa leaned over, as I spooned some rice in Kevin's mouth. She put her arm on mine. "I have to admit that after dinner last night, Kevin slept through the night for the first time since I can remember. I don't know if it was because of the food or all the paper cutting. Whatever it was, thanks go to you."

"This is good," I said.

Perhaps goatweed powder was a curative. I would have to give some to her. I needed to return to the herbalist right away anyway to see if they had red flowers. Tap-tap sounded again.

"She's not just saying kind words." Colleague slurped a mouthful of porridge. "Like I keep telling her—you put garbage in your body, your body act like garbage."

"Let's not start that." Lee Sa held up her hand. Gone was her earlier subdued attitude. Perhaps the beer had washed that away.

"Is like car." Colleague held up his spoon, as if it were a car. He started putt-putting the ceramic piece across the table. "You put sugar in the gas tank, it will eventually stop running."

"Please?" Lee Sa crossed her hands over her chest.

Thunder rumbled across the sky. I could see a long discussion emerging. I had been wrong to insist they come over. They didn't take my mind off my problems. The baby. And this lunch would take longer than plucking feathers from an old chicken. Kevin put his head down against my shoulder, his eyelashes fluttering closed. I wished to feel so relaxed.

"Why can't you see?" Colleague said, running his fingers along the outline of the car spoon. "Just because you grow up eating fish sticks and frozen dinners and endless supply of brownies doesn't mean our son needs to do same."

"I survived, didn't I?" Lee Sa leaned forward, putting her hand over his spoon.

Their bickering was as tedious as watching two amateurs play ping pong. I gritted my teeth and hoped the match would soon end. My shoes sounded, tap-tap.

"Kevin is better, isn't he?" Colleague responded.

"It could be from the rains," Lee Sa suggested without conviction. "Rain always clears the air."

"What's all this noise?" Mother-In-Law whispered to me in Mandarin.

"They're just saying that Kevin is feeling better," I translated.

"Did he get sick from the fish, as well?"

Mother-In-Law looked at the boy, who had fallen asleep in my arms. She held onto her stomach, as if it might bulge out and fall over. She had barely touched her porridge. Tap-tap. Lee Sa picked up another peanut and popped it in her mouth. She leaned over and nodded toward Mother-In-Law. Then she raised her eyes at me for understanding. Maybe admitting for once how little she understood.

"I just telling Mother-In-Law that Kevin feel better," I explained.

"He—I mean she—want to know if anyone have sore stomach. She have sore stomach."

"You should take her to the clinic," Lee Sa said.

"No need," Guo Qiang said. He took a last slurp of his porridge, then looked over at Lee Sa. "Li Hui is just new wife. She is not accustomed to Mother's diet. Is not strange Mother feels bad."

Lee Sa's eyes grew wide. Her mouth dropped open, showing her gold fillings. She grabbed onto her beer can.

"I have heavy hand in cooking," I explained. "Too much salt."

"Oh, give me a break." Lee Sa pushed her chair back. "This is all starting to hurt my stomach."

"You not like salt either?" I looked at her pile of peanuts. Why did she eat them if she knew they were bad for her?

"No, I just can't stand listening to so much criticism of the new wife," she said. "I'd be happy if someone made me meals and did my laundry and cleaned my house. You seem to get nothing but grief. No wonder you're a nervous wreck."

She pointed to my legs. To the tap-tapping of my white sandals on the floor. She was right. I was nervous. If only my nerves were from salt. I wanted that small problem.

"Lee Sa." Colleague put his arm on Lee Sa. His eyes were filled with alarm.

"No, seriously." She yanked away. "This is ridiculous. How can you blame a sore stomach on too much salt?"

"I happy," I said, shifting Kevin on my lap. His weight, a pleasure at any other time, now felt like a twenty-kilo sack of rice. I needed to get up.

"Well, I hope so," Lee Sa said. "Otherwise, someone more appreciative will come along and scoop you right up. I hope Guo Qiang and your dear Mother-In-Law realize that."

"Lee Sa." Colleague stood and went to the window, as if willing the sky to stop spitting on us, so he could take his noisy wife home.

"You do know what the young guy did to her at the pool, don't you?"

Lee Sa dangled her empty beer can in her hand. Smiling. She wasn't going to tell this story.

"Does anyone want tea?" I stood up and lay Kevin on the couch. She wasn't going to tell this story. I couldn't let her tell this story. "I have Jasmine or Oolong."

"You won't believe it," Lee Sa said. Like a dog who had sniffed a juicy bone, she wasn't going to let go. She didn't realize the bone was that bad fish bone from last night. And she was about to flip our boat, our marriage, our lives.

"He feel for my lung meridian," I told them. I reminded her. I cleared the dishes like a robot, even pulling away Colleague's bowl just as he was about to take another mouthful. Now he had to leave, didn't he? And take his loud wife with him.

"Listen to your lung whatchamahicky, and?" Lee Sa stabbed my arm with her fingers.

"Nothing." My voice sounded like a clap of thunder.

Like that thief Waipo always told me about, the one who had tried to steal the silver clapper from the temple bell, I was too nervous. Kevin stirred on the couch. Mother-In-Law looked up from her porridge. Guo Qiang raised his eyebrows. My hands had just knocked the clapper up against the bell. The bell rang for all to hear.

"Oh, come on." Lee Sa bounced up and down in her seat. "It's such a good story."

"You want to help me in kitchen?" I said, picking up an armload of dishes.

What did she know of good stories? She hadn't known about the blind men and the elephant until Colleague had told her. Even now, she didn't seem to understand that story. She only saw things from her point of view. I needed her to be sensitive. Just this once. I nodded my head for her to join me.

"She's going to help you?" Mother-In-Law pushed her chair back. "I have to see this."

Lee Sa turned to Mother-In-Law and pulled her mouth into a big smile. She obviously enjoyed the attention her story-telling had elicited. I stood in front of Lee Sa with the armful of dishes, as though waving a white flag in front of a bull. I didn't really want to be trapped in the kitchen with Mother-In-Law and Lee Sa. But that would be safer than Lee Sa throwing stories around out here.

"That man held onto your wife's wrist like he was taking her to a dance." Lee Sa scraped her chair back as she stood. She twirled as if at a dance, then gave a loud horse-laugh.

"Be quiet, mommy." Kevin turned in his sleep. "You're hurting my ears."

She hurt my ears too. I smiled, but my heart had drained of all its fluid. My chest hurt, as if I were still struggling underwater for a breath of air. A thin glaze of sweat covered my body, but I shivered.

With my loaded arms, I nudged her. I would lead her to the kitchen. Heat burned my face.

"Then he made up some cock-and-bull story about her being pregnant." Lee Sa laughed again, pointing to me and making a balloon shape over my stomach. "That he could feel two pulses."

"She's nuts," I said in Mandarin.

"Two pulses?" Mother-In-Law said. "So soon?"

A clap of thunder shook the apartment. Lightening blazed across the sky. My hands at the end of my long arms opened up. As if reaching for Chan Hai. An enormous crash reverberated throughout the apartment.

"Shall we take a walk," I said. "Or something?"

"It's raining," Guo Qiang said.

Colleague stared. Mother-In-Law stared. Our rice bowls lay shattered at my feet.

Chapter Sixty-Nine
The Computer Knows

A light drizzle had replaced the violent deluge. I held an umbrella over Mother-In-Law's head. A taxi passed, spraying muddy water on my legs. Mother-In-Law held on to my wrist. Her short, stubby fingers moved up and down as though trying to find that second heartbeat as she pulled me forward toward the clinic. Guo Qiang followed several meters behind, certain that this was a woman's issue.

"Mother-In-Law," I said. "We need not do this now."

"Oh, yes," Mother-In-Law said, her face grim. "That temple priest said your pregnancy would be difficult. He promised a grandson." She tapped my wrist with her pudgy forefinger. "If your pregnancy is this easy, then perhaps he got the sex of the child wrong too."

I looked toward the street as another taxi passed and was reminded of when Little Wu Lu had forced me into Snakehead's van. He had had his arms locked around me. No matter how I had squirmed, I couldn't loosen that hold. Mother-In-Law's fingers around my wrist were not tight. But I felt as trapped.

As we stepped up to the reception area of the clinic, a woman opened the window, eager to see a customer. She had short dark hair. She was already pulling a queue number down from the wall for us, although no one else waited.

"We need a pregnancy check." Mother-In-Law rapped her knuckles on the counter.

No. I needed time to think. I wished Mei Ling were near. Or Madame Paper Cutter. Or even Feng Gu. I couldn't let my auspicious marriage crumble like a soggy piece of cardboard over my head.

"Actually," I said stepping up to the window. "My mother-in-law needs the check. Not me."

Guo Qiang came up behind us. I latched onto his arm, rubbing my stomach and pointing to Mother-In-Law. Perhaps Lee Sa wasn't such a horrible person. That potpourri, which no Chinese person would ever bring as a gift and which obviously had made Mother-In-Law feel ill, might just be like that old man on his bike who had pulled in front of Snakehead's van. My chance to escape.

"Yes," Guo Qiang agreed, nodding. "My mother has not been feeling well."

"I didn't come here to be bullied by the two of you." Mother-In-Law elbowed her way between us so that she could stick her nose through the window. "I came to find out how much of that priest's prediction was true."

"Mother, please," I said. "Lee Sa's crazy. You know that. Why would you waste time and money to see if one her silly stories is true?"

"I have a gut intuition," she said, rubbing her belly. "Perhaps that's why my stomach's been feeling so strange."

"That was Lee Sa's silly fish," I said.

"The doctor has time to see you both," the receptionist offered.

"There," Guo Qiang said, patting Mother-In-Law's back. "You see?"

"See what?" Mother-In-Law winced and held onto her stomach. "See that the receptionist is good at talking you into spending twice as much?"

"Not expensive." The receptionist came out from behind her booth. She held onto Mother-In-Law's other arm, leading us into the waiting area.

"I don't need a doctor." Mother-In-Law shook her arm loose from the receptionist. "I never have."

"Of course, you haven't," the receptionist cooed. "I'll tell the doctor that you're here."

Mother-In-Law leaned against the wall of the waiting room. I breathed a sigh of relief. Perhaps there was still a chance for me to jump out the van door, to escape examination.

Guo Qiang and I sat in plastic green chairs waiting for Mother-In-Law. My skin itched. Guo Qiang rifled through the only reading material available in the sitting room, a parenting magazine. Each page showed a baby. A baby being held by a proud father while the mother looked on. A baby being fed formula by her mother. A baby and her mother smiling at one another. None of the women in the pictures looked like me.

"Perhaps you want to go back to the apartment and get some work done," I offered, handing him his umbrella. "I can take care of Mother-in-law."

Guo Qiang swatted a mosquito off his arm. He glanced up at the doctor's closed office door. He flipped another page.

"You've already spent more time than you should dealing with emergencies today," I said. "Really, we'll be fine."

Guo Qiang tossed the magazine on the table. Then he looked over at me. He shook his head.

"I'll wait," he said.

He picked at a piece of lint on his trousers. My insides burned. I didn't want him to wait. Alone I could convince Mother-In-Law of the waste of doing a pregnancy check. Alone I could think of how to handle this new disaster.

"Mother called this morning," I said, feeling like the child who had walked by our apartment the other day trailing a stick against the walls. Hoping to irritate. "She said Chairman Huang is after Father for a gambling debt."

I waited for that look of disdain. For him to stand and tell me he was returning home. My pulse beat in my temples.

"I'll take care of it," he said, picking up the magazine and opening it again.

He focused on a picture of a baby sitting in front of a stack of blocks. A life insurance ad. Why was he so agreeable? So reluctant to leave? Did he sense that my parents and their debts were now not important at all? My mouth tasted sour, as if I were sucking on old garbage.

The door to the examining room opened, and the doctor emerged. He was short, making his lab coat look like a dress. A stethoscope hung around his collar like a necklace. He wore small glasses with wire frames. Mother did not follow. He looked over toward us. Then he moved one slow step at a time in our direction. Guo Qiang and I stood.

"She wants to go home," the doctor said, his eyes on the floor. His long thin fingers twisted a gold pen opened and closed.

"Of course," I agreed. "It's a miserable day. I don't know why she insisted on coming out—"

"Home to China." The doctor adjusted his wire glasses and peered up at us.

"Home to China?" Guo Qiang repeated, like one of the robots on his computer screen.

"She knows it's time," the doctor said, nodding his head.

I swallowed. So Mother-In-Law wasn't just tired of my cooking and my lazy intellectual ways. She wasn't just eager to put me in charge and get back to her friends in the village. She knew something was wrong with her and wanted to be home.

"What's your opinion?" Guo Qiang asked, his eyes studying the doctor's face.

"There are always things we can try," the doctor said twisting the pen open. Guo Qiang nodded, as though ready to test any solution. The doctor cleared his throat and glanced up. "But, it's about time."

Aiya. The gods were too cruel. Yes, I had hoped for some escape from my impending baby examination. But this was too much. I reached for Guo Qiang's arm.

"There must be something." Guo Qiang patted my hand away.

"I see this all the time in elderly Chinese." He put the pen in his lab coat pocket.

"But, there's never been anything wrong with her," Guo Qiang said.

The poor man. Questioning the words of the doctor even. My heart felt squeezed.

"You could take her to Mt. Elizabeth for another diagnosis," the doctor nodded. "But let me just show you."

He led us into the examining room, where Mother-In-Law lay on a table, resting with her eyes closed. She looked fragile and small beneath the paper sheet that covered half her body. Why wouldn't she sit up and bark about waste? Why didn't she even open her eyes to see us here?

"Your son is here now." The doctor spoke in gentle tones. "And your daughter-in-law."

Mother-In-Law grasped at the paper sheet. A clock ticked the time away on the doctor's metal desk. A machine near the examining table held a screen that fuzzed black and white. How could all these sterile sights and sounds possibly predict a life's end?

"Here," the doctor said. "Let's get this warmed up again."

He picked up a round flat instrument attached to the machine. He rubbed the tool on Mother-In-Law's stomach, moving up and down and back and forth. What was this?

"See," he whispered, pushing down on the instrument. "There."

The screen on the machine showed a mass of gray tones. Some dark, some not so dark. What did this mean? I looked to Guo Qiang whose eyes were intent on the screen.

"And, there." The doctor took his free hand and pointed on the screen to an area which was darker than the rest of the gray.

"I don't see anything." Guo Qiang ran his hand through his

hair.

"I look at people's insides dozens of times a day." The doctor looked down at Mother-In-Law, then lowered his voice even further. "Believe me, those dark patches don't belong."

"We did have bad fish last night," I offered.

"We did?" Guo Qiang asked, his voice rising above a whisper.

"Mother-In-Law said it made her feel bad," I said. And surely that's what had made me throw up. No, surely that wasn't. But I couldn't think about that now.

The doctor nodded, guiding us away from Mother-In-Law. We stood in a small circle next to his metal desk. Too much whispering over Mother-In-Law would make her nervous.

"Did anyone else feel sick," he asked. "Did she throw up? Was she sweating?" He didn't wait for a response. "Did she complain of pain?"

"Pain, yes." I jumped in, before he could throw out another question. Guo Qiang squeezed my hand. "Pain and, well, she's been saying she feels full, even when she hasn't really eaten much at all."

The doctor nodded. But his eyes didn't fill with relief that I'd provided an explanation for the strange dark tones on the screen. Instead he pulled out his gold pen and twisted it back and forth, back and forth.

"Food poisoning doesn't make your stomach feel full," he said, leading Guo Qiang and me back to the screen. He used the tip of his gold pen to point to the black areas. "This does."

"Doctor," Guo Qiang whispered. "I'm not questioning your ability, but I work with computers for a living. I just don't see what you're seeing."

"Doctor?" Mother-In-Law opened her eyes. "Am I done?"

"Yes, yes." He moved over and helped her sit up. "Now I've told your son that all you need is the comfort of your own home. That he's working you ragged here." Mother-In-Law shook her head, raised her hand to protest. But the doctor continued. "So, he's going to make sure that happens."

Guo Qiang forced a smile. A lump formed in my throat. I was grateful that the attention was diverted from me. But this was too sad.

The doctor led us toward the door, while Mother-In-Law stood behind the examining table and put her skirt back on. He patted Guo Qiang on the arm as though comforting an accident victim. How could this be?

"Mt. Elizabeth has a good oncology department," the doctor said. "But, remember, home to China is where she needs to go. And soon."

The doctor opened the door for us all to go and Mother-In-Law shrieked. We all turned to see her face twisted in anguish. Her eyes small as dots. A chill ran down my spine.

"Mother?" Guo Qiang ran to one side. The doctor supported her on the other. "What is it?"

"Why are you so eager to send me away?" she barked.

This wasn't pain. This was anger. Guo Qiang's face relaxed. He stood back.

"But, Mother-In-Law," I said. "The doctor said—"

"That receptionist said you had time to see us both." Mother-In-Law glared at the doctor. "But you spend many minutes with me and you don't even look at Daughter-in-Law."

"I spend as much time with each patient as is necessary." The doctor pushed his glasses up on his nose. "Your daughter-in-law looks fine today."

"Of course she looks fine," Mother-In-Law said. She lowered her voice to a whisper. "Who wouldn't look fine when the temple priest promised them a son?" She resumed her forceful tone. "She may have happiness. In fact, that's the only reason we came to see you today."

"Mother-In-Law." I patted her back. "We can come another—"

"Instead," she said. "You put some fancy machine on me that does nothing but make my stomach all sticky. And you tell me nothing about Daughter-in-Law. What a racket."

"Our clinic." The doctor nodded, his eyes sympathetic. "Is monitored by the Ministry of Health."

"Obviously not close enough," Mother-In-Law said, moving away toward his desk.

What was she going to do? Look for a certificate? While the doctor had spoken in hushed tones, she must have guessed that his diagnosis was not good. And she had wished for something simple. Something curable. I had too. My nose burned as my eyes filled.

"Let's take you home," I said. "You should rest."

"I'm not going anywhere." Mother-In-Law planted herself in the chair in front of the doctor's desk. "I'm not going anywhere until the doctor tells me what I want to know."

What had happened to her barking about this not being a good clinic? My mouth went dry. Certainly a clinic monitored by the Ministry of Health would be able to identify a pregnancy. I shook my head. No.

"Mother," I said. "Surely you're not going to waste your time on one of Lee Sa's foolish tales."

"You're right. That foreigner is full of silly stories. And terrible food." Mother-In-Law rapped her knuckles on the metal desk. "But you have been acting funny. Not able to eat in the morning. Rushing off to the bathroom. Dropping an armload of dishes. There's always the chance."

"Let' just have a look-see." The doctor shrugged his shoulders, patted the table. "That way everyone will be satisfied."

No. The doctor's ticking clock banged in my ears. I couldn't think of one person who would be satisfied.

"This is not necessary," I said, backing toward the examining table. I looked to Guo Qiang for help. "Really."

Guo Qiang stared in my direction, but he didn't seem to hear me. He looked over my shoulder, his eyes wide and spacey. As if he were somewhere else. Perhaps he was still wondering how one minute life was fine with his mother complaining about salt and the size of the chopped meat, and, the next minute, her life was coming to a quick end.

"Guo Qiang?" I called.

His eyes shifted to my face, then the examining table. He looked at the doctor who had pulled out the same tool he'd used on Mother-In-Law. Then he tilted his head to the side, nodding.

"Great idea, doctor," Guo Qiang said, stepping forward and helping me up on the table. "A control subject."

What? Was this all this was? I took a deep breath. Thank the gods.

"Madame Liang says you may have happiness," the doctor said, squeezing some jelly onto the end of the tool.

"No. no." I held my wrists tight around my stomach.

"When was your last menses?" he asked, nodding for me to lift my dress. "Have you been feeling different?"

"No," I said. I'd felt different every single day. Exhausted, lonely, dizzy, hot, scared, devastated. "No," I repeated.

The words echoed loud in my head. No. No. No. I could hear Chan Hai telling me, "You're full of no." He hadn't believed all my no's. But this doctor seemed to. So far, he hadn't listened to my heart with his stethoscope. He hadn't reached for my wrist to check for a second pulse.

"I was sure she vomited this morning," Mother-In-Law reported from her chair. "The children have only been married for a week, and they haven't been as . . . well, as active as I'd hoped. But, the Temple Priest did say—"

"The heat bothers me," I interrupted.

"It usually takes about six months to adjust to the weather," the doctor said.

He rubbed the cold tool around my stomach. Like Mother-In-Law said the tool felt sticky. Like gum from an aloe plant. Oh, Chan Hai. Let me just get out of this doctor's office, and I'll quit calling your memory back. I'll leave you alone. I'll move forward.

"This time next year," the doctor continued, "Your body will react to the slightest temperature changes. So, on a day like today, you'll feel cold."

I smiled and nodded, my lips quivering. I didn't trust myself to make conversation. My throat ached.

"Looks pretty much the same to me," Guo Qiang said staring at the screen. His features relaxed into a smile. He saw hope, hope that Mother-In-Law wasn't really ill, that the doctor had misdiagnosed what he'd seen.

"Yes, all the pictures are grayish," the doctor said. "You have to get used to that."

"See, there." Guo Qiang pointed to a small dark spot. "That's not gray. That's just like Mother's."

"Very good." The doctor nodded at Guo Qiang. "You spotted it." The doctor moved the tool around, pushing in. Then he hit a button on the machine. "This is better than expected." The doctor turned to Mother-In-Law. "You mentioned a week, but I'd say at least two. Maybe three weeks."

"What?" I said, pushing the doctor's tool away and pulling my dress down. So the doctor wasn't just comparing my stomach to Mother-In-Law's. This machine he had did everything. Identified unexpected growths of every kind. Sweat prickled under my armpits. "What nonsense."

"That can't be." Mother-In-Law shook her head. "According to my calculations, the first time they made rain was three days ago."

Guo Qiang looked from me to Mother-In-Law, then back to me.

What was she talking about? Who made rain three days ago? And what was this new prediction of the doctor's?

"Young people are difficult to figure out, aren't they?" The doctor looked up and winked at Guo Qiang. Then he fiddled with some buttons on the machine. "Sometimes we just don't know what to expect. Do we?"

"Oh, I know," Mother-In-Law said, patting her hair and standing.

Thank the gods. I slipped down off the examining table and reached for her arm, just as the doctor pushed a button on the machine. Out came a piece of paper displaying a replica of what we saw on the screen. He brought his lips into a big smile, handing me the grainy image.

"There's the heart," he pointed with the tip of his gold pen.

Mother-In-Law grabbed for the photo. She turned the paper this way and that. The black and white image reminded me of an ancestral photo.

"Let's go home," I said.

"Is that the male member?" Mother-In-Law asked.

"Oh." The doctor chuckled. "You won't be able to identify the sex for many months. Right now." He tilted his head to look at some numbers on the edge of the paper Mother-In-Law held. "This baby is only twenty-four days old."

"That can't be," Mother-In-Law said, holding the paper far away from her, as if it had a stench.

"Let's go home," I repeated.

"This is the latest in imaging technology." The doctor's eyes crinkled into a smile. "It's accurate almost to the day."

"A computer does these calculations?" Guo Qiang moved closer to the machine. He bent and examined the manufacturer's label. Then he focused on the image on the screen.

"This particular model is from Germany." The doctor nodded and tapped the screen with his pen, as though eager to show off his machine to an appreciative audience. "It hasn't failed me yet."

"Computers are so silly," Mother-In-Law said, clasping the grainy image to her bosom as she headed toward the door. "We know the real dates."

"Yes, we know the real dates," I insisted. "Let's go home. Now."

How would we get past this situation? Guo Qiang was a modern man, I reminded myself. He programmed robots to act like humans. He spoke of traditions in philosophical terms, the same way he did about dust in the air. He had even seen past the ancestral-looking black and white photo of Kevin, calling it art. Rather than shrink from the taboo the photo represented, Guo Qiang had found a way to reframe this piece of art. Still my legs shook as I walked toward the door. My heart beat in my ears.

"Let's go home," I said. "Now."

Guo Qiang cocked his head, his eyes darting left and right as if he were reading a computer printout in his brain. My voice had been too loud. Like that thief College Boy. So desperate. Would he sympathize? Would he reframe this situation for us? Besides, I wasn't the only one guilty of holding another love in my heart. He had also had a lover before me. An American at that. Surely he would consider these things. We would work this out as a team.

"Wait," he called.

I stopped, my hand on the doorknob. The round steel knob sweating beneath my fingers. I turned and looked into his eyes. Those eyes looked so cold. As cold as that first night at our house in the village when he had pulled a long life noodle from his shoe in disgust. As cold as a stranger. As cold as someone who could not see a red border to frame this unhappy situation. Surely he wouldn't confront me in public? In front of his dying mother? His dying mother who had only wanted a "proper wife" for her son. A pure Chinese grandson to continue the family's cycle of life.

The image of that fat young man in the park in the village crossed my mind. The Little Emperor Madame Paper Cutter had called him. He had turned on his father because he hadn't been allowed to study the way he had wanted. Guo Qiang, with his thick cheeks, his angry stare, his petulant lower lip, seemed no more mature. Was he so angry with his mother for not being allowed to marry his American lover? Was he so disappointed in her choice? I closed my eyes and shook my head, begging him not to do this.

"It's not mine," Guo Qiang whined, his voice thin and reedy. He may as well have been whining about my inability to speak English, about too much fat on his meat. "It's not mine."

"What?" Mother-In-Law dropped the picture of the twenty-four-day-old fetus as if it were on fire. She stumbled out of the doctor's office, howling as though the fiery pits of hell had opened up to claim us.

Guo Qiang supported Mother-In-Law as her agitated frame shook like a leaf in the wind. He led her along the sidewalk back toward the apartment, both of them oblivious to the rain which still fell from the sky. I ran up next to them, fumbling to open my umbrella. I reached out to hold the opened vinyl covering over Mother-In-Law. Guo Qiang's narrowed eyes stopped me. It was them against me now. Waipo had always said you must fight to be friends. But had she even meant this kind of fight?

"Mother-In-Law," I said, letting my arm retreat, letting the umbrella fall to my side. "This is all a misunderstanding."

"Don't." Mother-In-Law lifted her head from Guo Qiang and shouted. "Madame Matchmaker mentioned you were a wild one."

Two little girls came up behind us, and I waited for them to pass. They skipped by, one after the other, pointing to the sky where the sun tried to shine through, the rays turning the sprinkling raindrops to gold. They opened their mouths and put out their hands to catch this gold. I was not like that. Trying to catch gold wherever I could. I had worked hard all my life. To get a good job. To take care of my parents. To be a good daughter.

"No, Mother-In-Law," I said in a low voice. "I am not. I've never been wild."

"Eating out in restaurants where you had no business," she continued, her voice so loud, she sounded like the village loudspeaker.

The two little girls stopped ahead and turned to stare. So did several shoppers. My skin burned with shame.

"Mother-In-Law," I said, wanting to reach out and stop her words, her anger.

"Yes, Madame Matchmaker told me all about you," she said. She stopped shaking. Her back was now rigid. Her eyes as small as black pebbles. She pointed her stubby forefinger toward my chest, stopping herself before she touched me, as if I were now a foul person. "How you were never mindful of consequences."

She was right. I hadn't planned for this consequence. But neither had Chan Hai. We hadn't been given time to make such plans, so busy was I trying to help Father. Father who never thought of consequences when he stared at the *mahjong* tiles and made bets he could not pay. Why was his behavior excused and mine a crime?

"How you went off to study," Mother-In-Law continued, her voice shrill. "Without thinking of who would marry you afterwards."

A young boy rode past on his bike, staring at us, pedaling so slow that he teetered like an old man. How could Mother-In-Law make my studying sound so frivolous? As if it was a party I wanted to attend. A game I wanted to play. My heart beat hard with disbelief.

"The words you speak are not right," I said.

"How you ruined all your chances of getting a good job at university," she shouted.

A teenager picked up a stray wrapper on the sidewalk and carried the garbage to the Clean and Green container on the corner ahead of us, just so he could watch our drama. But it was not I who had ruined our chances. I had done my best to get a good job, to make a good life for our family. It was Father who never knew what was enough. Who was never content. Blood coursed through my temples.

"You are not right," I said.

"How you had trouble keeping a simple tea seller's job." She laughed with disdain.

A woman stopped on the sidewalk, pretending to fuss with the grocery bags on her wrist, her head cocked to the side, listening. I had not even wanted the tea seller's job. I had studied to be a teacher. I was only trying to help Father. Then Feng Gu. How had my good intentions been so twisted? My lungs felt empty as if the wind had been knocked out of me.

"No," I said.

"And now this." She indicated my stomach with her hand.

Two boys walked by arm-in-arm, their eyes on my stomach. Yes, I had made a mistake. Not in loving Chan Hai, but in not being careful. Like that young girl in the market who had fallen out of a tree and broken her arm. But I would always make mistakes. That didn't make me wild. That didn't make me evil.

Guo Qiang and Mother-In-Law stared at me. So did the faces of this gathering crowd. I thought of Madame Tsui Ping and how she had drawn such attention at our tea shop when she had had an anxiety attack. She had been accused of being a spy for reading English novels. Had she felt such anger, as if the stone engraver held his chisel to her temples? Had she felt such disbelief her heart felt cracked open like a chicken's egg? Had she felt as if she'd been grabbed about the legs and dragged thumpety-thump on her back to a new place? What had made her go crazy? Where would I end up?

"Mother-In-Law, please," I said.

"You little whore."

She spat in my face. Spit was no worse than a taxi spraying mud on my legs. Yes, it was. But I wouldn't think about it. I wiped my cheeks with the back of my hand. I looked to Guo Qiang. I didn't expect him to defend me. But this was ridiculous. Surely his eyes would tell me as much. He looked ahead down the road, as if he hadn't heard a thing.

"Mother—" I said.

"Don't call me that," she said, shaking her closed fist at me. "Don't ever call me that again. You are no longer part of this family."

I looked to Guo Qiang again. Would he say anything? He looked over and nodded with his mother in agreement. Just like that. The two of them picked up their pace, leaving me behind. I watched them go, their heads held high, their backs straight. So righteous. They knocked past the Clean and Green bucket. I stared at that silly green garbage can. Clean and Green. Madame Liang had wanted someone clean and green for her son. I had been green, and, oh so naive. But I wasn't clean. So she was throwing me away. They both were.

I should have felt great sorrow. The heavy burden of Father and his debts back on my shoulders. The shame of failing yet again. Instead, the heavy thumping against my temples had ceased. A warmth filled my chest. I felt as safe as if the shimmering gold raindrops falling from the sky were real pieces of gold which would feed our family for many years to come. In the back of my mind I heard Lee Sa saying my name. Lee Way. Freedom. Space. Mother-In-Law and Guo Qiang had put me back on my two feet. They'd given me the freedom to return to my love. I smiled and turned my head to the sky, letting the drops of gold fall down on me.

Chapter Seventy
A Village Passed Through

Waipo had a saying: "Once you pass this village, you'll never see this shop again." She had said this when I wasn't moved by the story of the Farmer and his Horse. She had said this to remind me to look for the beauty in whatever situation I found myself. I'd never pass through this time in my life—this shop in the village—again. As I packed my toothbrush and toothpaste in the bottom of my plastic suitcase, I heard her voice reminding me of this. But what would she hope I learned from this situation? How would she want me to behave? Would she approve if I called Chan Hai? I missed him so.

Out in the living room, Madame Liang spoke on the phone. She didn't sound like an ill woman who had just been diagnosed with stomach cancer. She had been given a burst of energy. In fact, she hadn't been off the phone since we'd come home hours ago. She had made several calls, including one to Madame Matchmaker. I had heard that conversation. Oh, what a disappointment I had been. She would be sending me home as soon as possible. She needed another wife for her son. And she didn't have much time. I'd caught snatches of conversations with relatives. Not to discuss her illness, her sudden return home. No, to discuss the potential marriage candidates Madame Matchmaker had put forth for Guo Qiang. As I went to the dressing table to collect my face cream and lipstick, I paused by the bedroom door to listen. Now she was on the phone with the airlines.

I wanted so much to speak to Chan Hai my blood itched. Too bad there wasn't another phone. Too bad I wasn't the folk hero Ma Lian with a magic paintbrush, able to draw a phone and make it real. I felt as impatient as the day I had waited at the post office in Xiamen to call the village. It had only been but a few months since I had done so, having received the happy news of a teaching assignment. I'd had to wait in line then. I'd been so sure Orange-Haired Aunty in front of me was an auspicious sign. I'd been so irritated by the construction worker behind me. The construction worker who had then fallen and been crushed by overhead beams. Surely Father would look on my failed marriage as a disaster worse than beams falling on all our heads. Why then did I feel so giddy?

I opened the closet door. I had hung but a few items of clothing next to Guo Qiang's immense supply of shirts and pants. My belongings were easy to spot. Easy to remove. From the first hanger, I pulled down the pants Chan Hai had given me and my thin, white blouse. Those simple, comfortable clothes. The soft fabric in my arms felt like an old friend. I couldn't wait to feel Chan Hai's strong arms around me again.

I reached in the pockets of my pretty white dress and removed the pool-wrinkled name cards, those of Snakehead Huang and Lee Sa. I tucked them into the pocket of my pants. I put my hands back to untie the bow. Yes, the pretty dress had been a present from Madame Liang. But she had intended this special outfit for someone else. The wife of her son. I was no longer that person. I didn't want to be reminded that I had ever tried to be.

"Li Hui?" Madame Liang didn't even knock before opening the bedroom door.

She glanced around the room, as if checking to see that I hadn't taken anything that wasn't mine. Her eyes focused on my white dress, her lips curling in disgust. I was no longer a woman who needed to dress up to beckon her farmer to the fields. I was a temptress, a whore.

"I have reservations for us," Madame Liang said. "On the first flight tomorrow morning at ten. We'll stop in Hong Kong on the way home. Stay for a day."

She put great emphasis on the name of that country, like a threat. What was she telling me? Why would we stop off and stay anywhere together for a day?□

"Fine," I said. Again I wished I was Ma Lian with a magic paintbrush able to draw a plane and make it real. I was ready to leave now.

"Your father knows." She handed me the phone. "He agreed this is best. You're welcome to check."

Agreed what was best? Check what? I felt a strange prickling sensation around my brain. She stood by the door, her lips pursed together in a thin line. Certainly I needed to call Father. But this time Chan Hai came first.

"Thank you," I said. "I'll make that call."

She leaned against the doorway waiting, one hand on her stomach.

She gave a nod of her head, as if to say, "Go on, now. Dial." She had always been intrusive, but now I wanted my privacy. I deserved my privacy.

"You really should take a rest," I said, reaching out to guide her to the sofa. She flinched at my touch and backed away. □

"Don't you go talking long on my phone and running up a bill," she said shuffling over to the couch. "I'll be waiting here. I'm watching the time."

"Don't worry," I said.

I closed the bedroom door, went to my purse and dug through the contents until I found the corner of the cigarette pack Chan Hai had handed me after our dinner at the Fat and Happy Pork Soup Shop. The wrinkled stub of paper still held his neighbor Chicken Lady's number. I sat at the dressing table and dialed the number. The phone rang long and hollow. I hoped I wasn't interrupting the Chicken Lady's chores. I hoped she would get Chan Hai for me. This phone system was so inconvenient. Chan Hai and I would have to get our own phone. So I could reach him anytime of day or night. So I could call from our house to our flower shop and be the first to tell him that he was the father of a beautiful boy. Or girl.

I shook my head. I was jumping way too far ahead. How foolish.

The phone rang and rang. Why wouldn't anyone pick up? I was reminded of the story of the fisherman who had dropped his knife off the side of his boat. How he had marked the side of his boat where the knife had fallen. Then he had rowed to shore, jumped out of his boat, and searched the waters near the mark, expecting to find his knife. Surely I was as foolish as that fisherman. While my heart had remained frozen in time, life in the village had moved on. Surely the Chan Hai of two weeks ago had long since passed. Surely our love was lost somewhere in the deep, dark waters. I dropped the phone to my chest.

"*Wei*? Hello."

The voice of Chicken Lady barked from my chest. I lifted the phone back to my ear. Chickens squawked in the background. Foolish or no, I would search these waters.

"Is Chan Hai there?" I asked.

"Who is this?" The woman had always been suspicious. This time I found her suspicions irritating. I needed to speak to Chan Hai before Madame Liang retrieved her phone.

"I'm his friend," I said with great enthusiasm.

"Ah, I remember you," Chicken Lady said. "You're that girl that often called. Just a minute."

She dropped the receiver so it clank-clanked on the ground. She had never before offered to get Chan Hai for me. Perhaps he had spoken of me. Perhaps Chicken Lady had just become more accommodating. The boat had moved on. That, or he was right nearby. Someone fumbled with the phone at the other end.

"*Wei*? Hello."

That deep voice. My heart stopped. How I'd missed that voice every second of every minute.

"Chan Hai?" I whispered.

Chan Hai breathed hard into the receiver as though warming my ears on a cold day. I could almost see him standing there, his long eyelashes blinking at me in surprise. As if I were a ghost.

"What can I do for you?" His voice sounded wary.

"Oh, Chan Hai," I said.

There was so much I wanted to tell him. How I'd loved him even when I'd tried not to. How I was really a water bug now, after the episode with Kevin in the pool. How we had happiness now. I didn't know where to start.

"I'm sorry," I said.

I heard his steady breathing. What would he say? What could he say?

"Where are you?" he asked.

"Singapore." I swallowed the word. The country no longer was a source of pride, one that would be followed with the distribution of foreign cigarettes. I gripped the receiver in my trembling hands. "But I'm coming home."

Tears burned down my cheeks, dropping on the gray dressing table, making splotches like rain drops. I hadn't been wise like he was. I had followed in the trenches, back and forth, back and forth without even realizing that was what I was doing. Would he forgive me? Would he take me in his arms and forget I'd married another man? Ask the village to forget?

"I told you," he barked.

I cringed as I waited to hear him scold me for not following him. As I waited to hear him tell me that he had moved on.

"I told you that country was too hot for anything but cockroaches."

His voice was gentle. Soothing. I could see him smiling, making dents in his cheeks.

"It's probably going to get hot over there, as well," I said.

I could already hear Zi Mei's jaws working, as she stopped every customer, laying her hand on their arm. This would be the scandal of the year. Perhaps of our lifetime. My throat burned.

"Water Bug," he said. "You know I'm used to heat."

I thought about his best friend, Feng Gu's *gege*, drowning. For years Chan Hai had dealt with people telling him how terrible he was. He would forgive me. Protect me. Love me. Water Bug he'd called me. I wiped the tears from my eyes. I swallowed.

"Are you finished with the phone yet?" Madame Liang called out from the living room. The legs of the couch scraped across the floor as she got up. She would be at the door soon, demanding the phone back.

"I'll come over when I get home," I said.

"I'll be waiting," Chan Hai said.

I clicked off the phone, cradling the toy-like plastic to my chest. I wasn't a foolish fisherman. I hadn't dropped my love over the boat into murky waters. Chan Hai and I rode the boat together. We moved forward together. Now we just needed Father to join us. Life was good. We would be fine. Maybe.

I pushed the numbers for Zi Mei's place. I gripped the receiver so tight my fingers hurt as I prepared to listen to Zi Mei's cheery voice at the other end, prattling away about this unfortunate incident while she sent slow-moving Don Don up to get Father.

"Are you finished with the phone yet?" Madame Liang was at the door. She held out her hand to take the phone.

"I'm still trying to get through," I said. A half-truth.

"I thought I heard you talking," Madame Liang said stepping into the room. She sat on Guo Qiang's side of the bed and peered into my suitcase examining the contents. "I'll just wait here."

The air in the room felt tense. Each scratch of my face, each breathe that I took examined. I pulled my face into a tight smile, now eager to hear the gossipy voice of Zi Mei. I didn't even fear Father's anger and disappointment exploding across the wire like a firecracker. I longed for anyone to pick up the phone. The phone rang and rang at the other end.

"*Wei*?" Zi Mei answered. "Hello?"

"It's me," I said. "Li Hui."

"Oh, Li Hui," Zi Mei said with great exaggeration. "I imagine you want to talk to your father."

Her voice sounded loud. Too loud. Was she shouting for the benefit of Madame Liang? Certainly not. Perhaps she already had an audience of listeners, eager to hear of Li Hui's unfortunate marriage.

"Don Don," she said. "Go get Li Hui's father."

She muffled the mouthpiece. Then the phone clank-clanked against something. The side of her shop? Had she let the receiver drop? Perhaps Don Don had refused to go.

In the background, I heard voices. Lots of voices. I imagined a whole crowd of villagers seated on the benches outside Zi Mei's shop, bouncing their legitimate babies, knitting, and sorting greens as they traded news. Had the village heated up so fast over my failed marriage? Or were people still worried about the removal of our front door? No matter. Chan Hai and I would ride the boat together.

"*Wei*? Hello?" Father's voice sounded strong. Almost proud.

"Father?" I said. "My plane comes in day after tomorrow. Madame Liang," I nodded to her sitting on the edge of the bed, "asked that I check with you."

"Yes, " he said. "You just follow her directions."

Follow her directions? I had expected anger from Father. Criticism over this botched union. This simple and kind request felt too strange.

"What do you mean?" I asked.

Madame Liang shifted on the bed. She ran her hand over the bedspread, as if she weren't listening. I took the phone and walked to my side of the bed, the dressing table. As far away as possible without appearing rude. I sat down.

"She's paying us a very reasonable sum to—" He cleared his throat. The sound of a match igniting filled the receiver. "Yes, a very reasonable sum to, uh, keep her family name. Clean. Much money. Much money." He inhaled deeply on his cigarette. "Don't you mess it up."

"Oh, Father."

Now I understood. The side trip to Hong Kong. Madame Liang didn't want me returning to the village carrying another man's child. What a slap in the face that would be for her family. Perhaps Father didn't realize Chan Hai still loved me. Would take me back.

No one need ever know that this happiness was inside me while I was a member of the Liang family. Besides this would be Father's happiness too. A grandchild.

"Trust me," Father said, inhaling hard on his cigarette. "This is best for everyone. You just be a good daughter and listen to Madame Liang."

"No, Father," I said, turning away from Madame Liang. "Chan Hai and I will find a way. To get the front door back. To get out of debt. This is not the way."

"Who?" Father spat.

"Chan Hai and—"

"Did the sun burn a hole in your brain, Li Hui?" Father's voice was a low grumble. "I don't want you anywhere near that donkey's ass. He's already messed this up enough."

Here I thought Father would be relieved that Chan Hai was willing to take me back. That he would have a grandchild soon. Instead he was pulling me in a different direction. Again. Planning my life with no Chan Hai, no Chan Hai's baby. With only a big payoff from Madame Liang.

"Do you hear me?" he said.

He inhaled again and again on his cigarette as if daring me to challenge him. I felt as if I'd been punched. My heart burned. My breath was caught inside.

"Father, no," I said. "No."

"You don't know how high the sky is," he whispered. "How deep the earth is."

Maybe I didn't have all that knowledge. Maybe I shouldn't speak out to some one elder and thus wiser than me. Maybe I should remember that he was my father. But I'd learned something these past few months. These past few days. Something that not even Waipo had told me. I wasn't just Father's daughter. I was his son too. The son who needed to take care of his parents forever, giving them money each time they fell down the well of debt, leading their casket to the other side of the River of Sleep, visiting their gravesites twice a year with spirit money, good foods and love. As the one and only child, I was responsible for holding up our entire sky.

And, if Father insisted on leading the way, as traditionally a father should, we'd end up with cardboard mush in our hands. With his drinking, his debts, his recklessness. With all due respect, I couldn't let him do that to us. To me.

"Like I said." I held my tone firm. "I'm coming home to be with Chan Hai."

With that I pushed "End." A long sigh shuddered through my body.

"You're a crazy child." Madame Liang's voice made me jump. I'd forgotten she was there. I looked at her reflection in the mirror. Those small dagger-like eyes. "A crazy one to speak to your father that way."

She stood, straightening the folds of her skirt. Crazy? I was crazy? Why? Because I wanted to go home to the man I loved, just as Zhu Dee had wanted to be with Guo Qiang? Just as Lee Sa was with Colleague? What was so crazy about that? I thought of Lee Sa. She was insensitive to our ways. Certainly. What would Lee Sa think if she knew her repetition of the story of the man at the pool had created this misery? What would she suggest I do about Father? I had a strange urge to pick up the phone and call her. I still had her name card. I looked at the phone. What would a crazy woman do?

"I'll take the phone now," she said, putting her hand out, erasing my foolish notions.

She shuffled out, closing the door behind her. I turned and stared in the mirror. My eyes looked tired. Tired and old. Like Madame Paper Cutter's. I glanced up at the paper cutting of the phoenix taped to the top of the mirror. I would be home with her soon. I would be home with Chan Hai. We would be fine. No, perhaps we wouldn't be. Not if Father had his say. Certainly Chan Hai and I could have another child. But only if Father allowed us to do so. And betting on that would be as foolish as Father who bet all of our lives away with his poor *mahjong* tiles.

I sighed. Too bad Chan Hai wasn't next door in Malaysia, like Guo Qiang's American lover, ready to meet me at a National Park and run away together. Here we could have four children. We would be far from Father's pull. From his disasters. I lay down on the bed. So many dreams I had. So many dreams.

I woke with a start. A cool breeze blew in through the window. The sky was light. Was it morning already? Was it time to go to the airport? I had only laid down for a moment on top of the bed covers, so exhausted from my conversations. I sat up in a daze. A sheen of sweat covered my body. I had had a fitful sleep. Dreams about Chan Hai. About the happiness inside of me. About the future. About

Chan Hai struggling to swim in the reservoir. I felt lost.

"Li Hui." Madame Liang's voice was sharp. "Hurry up."

I glanced at my watch. The hands under the small glass face read eight o'clock. I had slept too long. Dreamed too much. What if, after our initial meeting, every word from Chan Hai's mouth was covered in thorns? I stood up. I didn't have time to shower. What if the baby was a girl? We couldn't have four children in China. Would Chan Hai be as happy as I? Mother had swaddled me so that Father wouldn't know I was a girl. Would I have to do as she? Would I become like her? I grabbed my suitcase and hurried out into the living room. What if we had no money to eat, no money for clothes, no money for school? And Father continued to gamble.

Madame Liang and Guo Qiang sat at the dining room table. They wore the same clothes they had had on yesterday. How strange. A bowl of porridge sat in the center of the table. Such a late breakfast?

I looked out the living room window. The sky was filled with colors, reds, oranges, blues, pinks as it had been the night when Lee Sa had come for dinner. It was night time. I set my suitcase down and pulled out a seat. I sat down and helped myself to some porridge. Madame Liang's bowl was half full. Had she only taken a little? Guo Qiang's bowl had been scraped clean. Surely they had already eaten.

"I thought it was morning already," I said. What a strange sensation. What a panicky feeling.

Madame Liang pushed her bowl toward the center of the table. Guo Qiang sniffed as if words from my mouth were a bad scent in the air, like that dust from the factory. Would his small eyes, his scrunched up nose be the face of disgust I'd see on every relative in the village? For how long? Months? Years? Forever?

The sound of children shouting filtered inside. Other people's children. Not ours. The air around us felt thick and difficult to breathe. How was it that this morning we had been a family and now we were three strangers? How was it that this morning Guo Qiang couldn't stop talking about robots and policies and foods, and now he couldn't manage a word? How was it that our life had flip-flopped so quickly? I thought of myself in the pool. One minute I had been on dry land, the next minute I was gasping for air. I held onto the table.

Guo Qiang helped Madame Liang up and led her to her room. For all his spoiled ways, he was loyal to his mother. Never mind that she wouldn't accept his American lover. Never mind that she had gotten him into this failure of a marriage. Never mind that she was already planning Wedding Number Two. He remained respectful. I felt a twinge of guilt. I had spoken so harshly to Father. Perhaps I was crazy.

I turned to finish my cold porridge. More of my dreams surfaced. What if our daughter grew up and left us, spitting in our faces with disrespect. Saying no, no, no, as I had just told Father. And I hadn't even bothered to ask about Mother. Or the door. My scalp itched. I couldn't get home fast enough. At the same time, my stomach felt queasy at the idea.

The gate clanged shut. The sound of Guo Qiang's heels echoed down the hall. Of course he would go out. After today when his mother was pronounced a dying woman, and he had lost his wife not in the pool but as the result of a computer print out. Surely he needed many drinks.

I got up from the table and retrieved the phone from its base. I would call Zi Mei. Just like Kevin, Zi Mei always told me what I needed to know. She would tell me if Father had been so upset he had shouted at her for two packs of cigarettes and a bottle of liquor. If Mother was fretting. If I had any hope of marrying Chan Hai. Zi Mei answered on the third ring.

"It's me," I said. "Li Hui."

"Oh, Li Hui," she said, her voice no longer for show. "Your father was just here. Let me go get him."

"No, no," I said. "That's okay. I don't want to trouble you." Perhaps he had been hoping I would call back. Had been waiting for me to apologize for being so disrespectful. I felt pinpricks of shame. "Was he? How was he?"

"I guess it's not easy getting a divorce. All the talk. All the sadness," she prattled. "You poor child."

So she knew. The whole village knew. What stories had Father told her?

"How is Mother doing?" I asked.

"Oh, you know your mother," Zi Mei said. "She muddles through any storm."

"Yes," I said.

A storm. That's what I was. I thought of Madame Tsui Ping. The storm she had created at the tea shop. This was worse.

"But she's much happier now that the door is back on the house,"

Zi Mei said. "That was a scare not having that door, I tell you. A real scare."

"When did this happen?" The base of my spine tingled.

"Oh, earlier today," Zi Mei said. "After lunch sometime. Those thugs came back saying Chairman Huang had had a change of heart. Can you imagine?"

After lunch? That would have been after I had met Chairman Huang in the wet market. What had given him a change of heart? Would his change of heart last? Would it extend to the rock quarry? Or was he just trying to show the hold he had over Father and then me?

"Well, I better go," I said. "I'll be seeing you day after tomorrow."

"Yes, I know," Zi Mei said. "Your father just arranged a car to take him to the airport to meet you."

A car to meet me? As if I were an important dignitary? Or an errant child who needed to be led home before I visited Chan Hai? Father. How could he? I thought of Little Wu Lu who had forced me into the van to realize his own dream. Father's plan seemed no more dignified.

I stared at the phone in my hands. So light. Like a toy. I had an image of myself several months earlier riding home in the pouring rain to stop Father from arguing with New Neighbor. Outside a couple had walked by arm in arm. When a motorcycle went by, splashing the pair with water, the boy had taken out his toy slingshot. So protective. So sweet. So useless. I thought of that now. Would the love Chan Hai and I held be as useless against Father as that plastic slingshot?

Nothing had changed in the village. Nothing. I thought of how Chan Hai had warned Little Wu Lu about traveling to Singapore illegally in a boat. Little Wu Lu would be trapped, he had said, like a grasshopper in a box with too few air holes. I looked out the window at the magnificent sky which looked like a painting now. If only I were the folk hero Ma Lian and could paint a town for just Chan Hai and me, we would have peace. But would we ever find peace in the village? With Father? Or would I be like a grasshopper in a box unable to breathe?

I sat at the dressing table and ran my hand over the prongs of the comb. Then I set the comb down and rubbed dust from the corner of the small table. I reached for my sore neck. Ever since I'd spoken with Zi Mei, I'd been restless. As if she were the village priest announcing that I was to be sacrificed to the miserable dragon this year. And I didn't have any firecrackers. And, when I was forced outside the village walls, I looked up at the dragon to see he had the face of my father. What was I going to do?

I looked in the mirror. I was no longer the young girl who had graduated in the warm light of summer four months ago. That girl had been naive, trusting, and ready to achieve anything. Just like that young girl with the broken arm in the hawker center who had called out her dreams of being a barrister or a doctor as if it were as simple as studying, as simple as ordering a bowl of herbal soup. Again I heard Waipo's voice telling me, "Once you pass this village, you'll never see this shop again."

Argh. I went to my purse for my scissors. I needed something mindless. I would make a handful of cuttings for Kevin. Despite his lack of humility, his stubbornness, I would miss the talkative little boy. In fact, despite her insensitivity, her cultural arrogance, I would miss his crazy mother too. She made me think about things I'd taken for granted. Like the food we put in our mouths. The traditions we kept in our hearts. I took the rest of the purple potpourri wrapping paper from the living room table and returned to the dressing table in my room. As soon as I put my scissors to the delicate paper, I felt the stiffness in my neck disappearing. A sigh escaped my being.

I started off with a simple cutting—the bird Madame Paper Cutter had shown me to make in three simple steps. I remembered her words: "A true teacher needs a true challenge." She had said it in response to my poor job at the tea shop. Now it seemed like a prophecy. I had a true challenge. Chan Hai waited for me. But so did Father. I knew who was more reckless, who would stop at nothing. The same man who had insisted I throw away my education when I didn't get the top job offer. The same man who had insisted I marry to save him from debt. The same man who had insisted I get rid of happiness in exchange for a reasonable sum. Father. I didn't want to be part of this battle. I didn't want Chan Hai to have to endure such a fight. What would I do? I lay the cutting on the table.

I picked up another piece of paper. The scissors in my hands moved automatically, cutting the purple paper into flowing robes. The Moon Goddess. I smiled as I remembered the different versions Madame Paper Cutter and I had of the story. In mine, the goddess had been shot to the moon for stealing something that wasn't hers. In Madame Paper Cutter's version, the archer loved his wife so much he didn't want her to be hurt. He could easily have shot her back down to earth, but his arrow would have killed her as well. So he let her fly away to immortality. True love. Was my love with Chan Hai true? If so, how could I bear to hurt him? How could I bear to drag him through the mud with Father?

From the living room, I heard Guo Qiang stumble in. He clanged the gate shut. The table legs scraped against the floor. The cushions of the couch wheezed. The sounds of a drunk man. I closed my eyes. My head hurt as if I too had had too much to drink. I was tired of cuttings. Tired of trying not to think.

I put my hand against the back of my neck and let my head roll back and around. Up on the mirror I spotted the cutting Madame Paper Cutter had given me. Of the phoenix. I stood and peeled off the pieces of tape which held the delicate cutting to the glass. I turned the cutting over in my hands. Carved into the wings was the character, "Fly." Fly, she had told me. Fly. Oh, how I wanted to fly like the magical phoenix and sprinkle gold dust like rain from the skies. I wanted Chan Hai to fly next to me. Why was that so much to ask? How could we fly?

Out in the living room, Guo Qiang lay passed out on the couch, his face red from too much drink. His forehead beaded with sweat. I leaned down and put my hand in his back pocket and extracted his wallet. I pulled out all the bills. So many. I knew this was not right. But, as Madame Paper Cutter would have said, I was desperate. I wasn't sure what I would do with all these bills. But I knew that, to deal with Father, I needed money.

My heart beat against my chest. The scenery went by in a blur of green. What was it Guo Qiang had said? For every 500 meters of road, they employed one caretaker. He stared at the road ahead, every once in a while reaching over and patting his mother's arm. Strains of sad love songs played. But my mind was too busy to hear music. The sound of people talking bounced off the walls of my brain, like ping pong balls on a table. "Stay away from that donkey's ass." "Water Bug, come home." "Once you pass this village, you'll never see this shop again." "You're a crazy child." "Fly." I rubbed my sweaty palms over my comfortable black pants. Chan Hai's pants. I reached up to move my hair off my shoulder. Still I felt as if Kevin's arms were around my neck, strangling me, pushing me down under the dark water. China was my home. Chan Hai was my home. What was so scary?

"*Dao le. Dao le,*" Madame Liang announced. "We're here."

Here we were. I took a deep breath. My throat burned. Here I was at the airport about to board a plane with the venomous Madame Liang. A plane that would take us to Hong Kong where we'd spend a day. Then back to the village. And Father. I no longer felt giddy.

The control tower looked down on us like a beacon. The terminal felt cold, a frozen breath. I looked around. Ticket counters lined the aisles, their billboards announcing planes that went everywhere. Paris. Tokyo. Los Angeles. And Hong Kong. That was our counter.

To the right of the ticket counters, a young Malay woman with dark skin and a long dress stood next to a flower stall. She sold an orchid to a hurried foreigner with a big nose. Would Chan Hai ever get a chance to sell flowers? If so, when? Where?

Further down, a couple held hands in front of a ceiling-high round fish tank. Fish of all shapes and colors swam through red and purple corals. I wished to go over and watch. To be holding Chan Hai's hand in front of that tank.

Down at the end of the hall, there were restrooms. Next to them an elevator with a large green sign that said, "Parking Lot. Taxis." Taxis. I felt in my pocket. My fingers touched the folded wad of bills I had taken from Guo Qiang. I now had lots of money for taxis. Unlike the time I had escaped from Little Wu Lu, had taken a taxi home, and then had had nothing to give him. But where would I go? My other hand fingered the wrinkled name cards—that of Lee Sa and Snakehead. Taxis. Snakehead had offered me a job. But he was interested in only one thing. In getting money out of me anyway he could. Like Father. The thought made me shudder.

The speaker crackled as a woman announced a flight boarding for Los Angeles. Lee Sa had offered to help me find a job. But would she have? Would she now? What difference did it make? I too would soon be going home.

I followed Madame Liang and Guo Qiang over to the ticket counter where he battled with the ticket agent over seats, the English words flying like pebbles in my face. I would soon be home where all was familiar again. This trial would be over. So why did I feel as though I were trapped in that ceiling-high fish tank? And Father was standing with his nose pressed to the glass? Why couldn't I catch my breath? I put my arm on Madame Liang. If I could just put some cold water on my face perhaps I'd feel better.

"I need to use the bathroom," I said.

"You'll have plenty of time for that when we get to the plane." She flicked me off as though shooing away a fly.

I saw a businessman talking on his cell phone, several young men wearing backpacks and very little clothing, an old woman standing alone checking her boarding pass, and a policeman strolling up the hall. Again my gaze strayed to the bathrooms, the elevator, the sign that said, "Parking Lot. Taxis." Taxis. A shiver ran down my back.

"Passengers of Southern China Air Flight 0297 bound for Hong Kong may begin boarding at Gate 2," a voice crackled through the loudspeakers.

"That's your flight," Guo Qiang said putting his arm around his mother, then guiding her toward the glass doors that would take us through passport control. She grasped onto his shirt, her eyes widening. This would be the last time that they would see one another. I looked down the hall toward the elevator. The sign. Taxis. I turned my gaze away to the fish tank.

Although the water inside the tank was clear, the image of the muddy reservoir came to me. The memory of last night's dream. The reservoir had looked cool and tempting, but in the center Chan Hai had struggled to stay afloat. He had been tired. Tired of swimming so many years against the current. Against Father. The air around us had been too hot, too unforgiving. I shook my head. No, I would not get on this plane.

"I just have to go to the bathroom," I said while they exchanged words.

"No." Madame Liang looked over. "I told you to wait."

"I can't," I said, continuing down the hallway. "I can't wait anymore."

I hurried down the hall, begging Madame Paper Cutter's phoenix to give me energy. To let me fly. Voices surrounded me. "Come home." "Your father will meet you at the airport." "I'll be waiting." "Come home." But I couldn't return to the clutches of Father. I couldn't return to the village. I saw that clearly now. No life existed for me back there. No job. No baby. No lover. Nothing. Chairman Mao Ze Dong had said women hold up half the sky. But, with all respect, he was wrong. I couldn't hold up any of the sky in my village. With my family.

When I got to the elevator door, I looked back. Guo Qiang eyed me. I smiled and held up one finger, as if to say, "Just a minute." When he turned his head back to his mother, my skin prickled. My mouth went dry. I pushed the elevator button located above a small Clean and Green garbage container. I pushed the up arrow again and again as I'd seen Lee Sa do to hers. I wouldn't think about this moving box. About Kevin saying you could get stuck in one forever. About my trembling knees. I would survive such a short ride up to the taxi stand. I had to.

The elevator bell rang loud and clear. Like the silver clapper that the thief had tried to steal. I wanted to put my hands over my ears.

"Li Hui?" Madame Liang called out. "Where are you going?"

Her voice thundered out so loudly certainly everyone in the terminal heard. I saw Guo Qiang drop her arm and hurry toward me. I looked back at the heavy metal doors of the elevator. Open. Doors open. I had to get on this moving box. I took in a deep breath. And another. And another. I closed my eyes, breathing in the smell of Mother's porridge cooking, the warm arms of Chan Hai around my waist, the sound of a baby laughing. The doors to the elevator opened. I breathed in my simple dreams. Then I rolled my heart and dreams into a tiny ball. A rock, not a pebble. I felt for the name cards in my pocket. I stepped inside that moving box.

"Miss."

A stern male voice stopped me. A police officer in a dark blue uniform with shiny silver buttons stood in front of the elevator, one hand touching the nightstick at his side. With his other hand, he kept the elevator doors from closing. Guo Qiang paused many meters behind, a cruel smile in his eyes. I swallowed. I was so close. If I could escape them, I would find a way to live. Just as I had figured out my way in the tea shop.

"Yes," I said, my voice confident, strong. Not that of a turtle hiding her head.

"You dropped something." He tilted his nightstick, pointing the end to the floor.

"What?" I looked to where he pointed. There lay the pool-wrinkled name card of Snakehead. I stepped off the elevator, reached down and grabbed the worn paper. The name card felt dirty in my hands. Like a used tissue. I turned to the Clean and Green bucket under the elevator button and tossed that dirty tissue away. I still had Lee Sa's name card. I would keep hers.

"Sorry," I said.

"Next time you'll be fined," he warned, letting his hand drop from the elevator doors. "Be careful."

I nodded my appreciation, jumping inside just before the doors closed. I thanked the gods that the officer's biggest concern was a piece of trash on the floor. Or was he the omen that Orange-Haired Aunty had never been? I pushed the TAXIS button, thanking the gods for giving me one more chance to show my love for Chan Hai, to move forward rather than follow Father back and forth in the same old trenches, to save face for all of us. I would dive in this reservoir, and this time I would swim like a water bug. I would. I stared at the light moving upwards with each floor, thanking Waipo for reminding me not to pass too quickly through this village. This time I would find a way to hold up my half of the sky.

Acknowledgements—

This book has long been a dream of mine. I wish to thank the many people, who helped turn that dream into something tangible. Especially:

My mother, Georgianna McBurney, who once said to me, "You can't climb that rock." Then she not only stopped herself and said, "Yes, you can," but she's been pushing me to climb rocks ever since.

My father, George McBurney, who insisted so many years ago that, if I travel anywhere, I should go to China. And who believed my writings belonged in something besides a magazine article.

My in-laws, Meizhu and Yizhu Lin, who, with their generous spirit and captivating stories, showed me—and continue to show me—a different side of the elephant.

My sisters- and brother-in-law, Qinying, Huizhen and Huiqun, who shared childhood memories, stories, and experiences.

My brother- and sister-in-law, Huiguan and Pinhua, who built a six-story house so we would always have a place to come home.

My nephew, Ji Hua, who shared his culture shock when coming to the US, especially his absolute horror that teachers told students Taiwan wasn't part of China.

My brother, John, and sister, Holly, who gave their unreserved support and encouragement (and actually offered to read first drafts during vacations).

Teresa Leyung Ryan, who reached out when I had just moved to the US and was searching for a writing club. She led me to the California Writers Club and made sure I got involved.

Edie Matthews, who invited me to join her critique group. The other critique group members (especially Ro Davis, Steve Lawlor, Jackie Mutz and Helen Vandenberg), who patiently gave their advice through several rewrites.

All my supportive friends at the California Writers Club, including Martha Alderson, Barbara Drotar, Lian Gouw, Martha Clark Scala, Barb Truax, Carol Wood, and especially Bob Davis, who believed in my work and insisted I just needed a good editor.

Debbie Fordyce, Sherry Fryhling, and Melissa West-Kevan, the best kind of friends one can have, who offered support and encouragement until the last sentence was written (even after having read through early drafts).

Frank Baldwin, my first good editor, who encouraged me to keep going.

Charlotte Cook, for being not only a phenomenal editor, but a great friend.

Cliff Garstang for his thoughtful translation of legal-ese.

The Komenar Publishing team, especially Sioban Bowyer, Jasmine Nakagawa, Carly West, Julie Smith, Laura Davis, Elisabeth Tuck, Erika Staiti, Marc Kaplan, Charlotte Cook and Bette Kaplan for believing in me and Li Hui's story.

—Jana McBurney-Lin

May 2006